Praise for

FORTRESS DRACONIS

"What a splendid story; it grabbed me and wrenched me full force into a gripping adventure. And the wonderful thing is, there are two more books to come."
—Dennis L. McKiernan

"I think that Michael A. Stackpole is incapable of writing a book that isn't imaginative, intelligent, and sympathetic. On top of that, *Fortress Draconis* is ambitious, even for him. It can hardly help being exciting and satisfying. When future readers name the writers who followed the Asimov-Clarke generation, and the Zelazny-Silverberg generation, they'll have to mention Michael A. Stackpole."
—Stephen R. Donaldson

"A compelling and engaging escape."
—*Publishers Weekly*

"With a deliciously evil antagonist and some truly remarkable supporting characters, this is a terrific read."
—*Booklist*

"A powerful epic fantasy that is wholly grounded in the gritty realism of battlefields and sacrifices."
—*Romantic Times*

THE
GRAND
CRUSADE

Book Three of the DragonCrown War Cycle

Michael A. Stackpole

BANTAM BOOKS

THE GRAND CRUSADE
A Bantam Spectra Book

PUBLISHING HISTORY
Bantam trade paperback edition published December 2003
Bantam mass market edition / September 2004

Published by
Bantam Dell
A Division of Random House, Inc.
New York, New York

Library of Congress Catalog Card Number: 2003062790

ISBN: 0-553-57851-0
Manufactured in the United States of America
Published simultaneously in Canada

OPM   10   9   8   7   6   5   4   3   2

TO STEPHEN KING

Writers learn to write while reading, and his work is
the mother lode of characterization, drama, and dialogue.
And he writes books about writing that have stood me in
good stead since before I was published. Thank you.

ACKNOWLEDGMENTS

As always, the errors in this book belong solely to the author. That there are so few is because of the efforts of friends. First and foremost, Anne Lesley Groell has been more patient than a whole pantheon of saints waiting for this book, which was incredibly overdue. Her gentle and firm insistence that I would have it done, as well as her willingness to take it in pieces, allowed me to pull it all together. T. A. Trainor and Kassie Klaybourne offered invaluable advice concerning the logistics and problems of lots of people, wagons, and horses moving off to war. Thanks to Rachel Stanley for suggesting a word. And Robert M. Wolanim (*www.nuada-music.com*) who sent me a beautiful piece of music inspired by *The Dark Glory War*—reminding me that there can be a lot of magick in these words.

Most of all, however, I have to thank all the readers who have so patiently waited for this book. There are times when the trials of my personal life made me think that Will and the others had it easy. Your kind reminders that you were waiting really kept me going. I write stories I like to read—the fact that you like them, too, never ceases to amaze and inspire me.

THE NORRINGTON PROPHECY

A Norrington to lead them,
Immortal, washed in fire
Victorious, from sea to ice.

Power of the north he will shatter,
A scourge he will kill,
Then Vorquellyn will redeem.

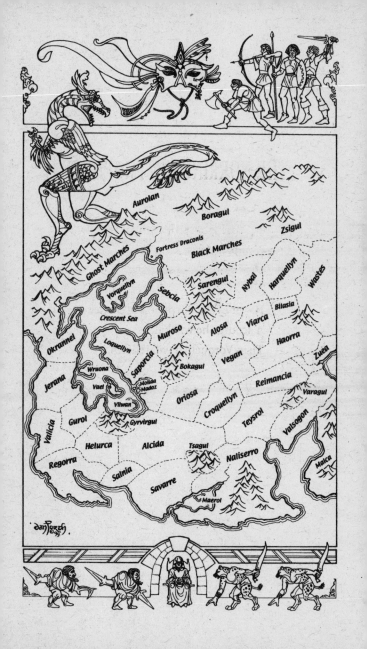

THE GRAND CRUSADE

PROLOGUE

The crisp winter cold penetrated the walls of the villa that King Scrainwood of Oriosa had taken in Narriz. A chill radiated through the varied stones used in the building's construction. But he felt no draft and, indeed, no winter winds howled outside. Darkness had come with preternatural silence, and Scrainwood could feel portent and power gathering.

Something had happened out there, something at once terrible and yet wonderful. The possibilities raced through his mind, each to be sorted, weighed, then used as a lever to move other bits and pieces of what was the world. All would be to his advantage. Eventually. Although, he ruefully admitted to himself, he and his nation were in a difficult position.

The leaders of the world's key nations had been summoned to Narriz, the capital of Saporicia, to deal with the threat of conquest by Chytrine's Aurolani hordes. While the Northern Empress' troops had been thoroughly routed in far Okrannel, their assault south through Sebcia and Muroso had been relentless and powerful. Sebcia had fallen quickly, Muroso was in the process of falling. Sarengul, the urZrethi stronghold north of Oriosa, had likewise been invaded.

His nation looked to be the next in line for conquest, and King Augustus of Alcida had threatened to invade Oriosa from the south, so any battle against Chytrine would be fought well away from his own lands. He'd done that to force Scrainwood's hand, and Oriosa's king hated it.

But he had acquiesced for two reasons. The first was that he had long danced on the edge of a knife. Oriosa had been covertly neutral, providing a haven to Aurolani troops to stage raids in the south. Scrainwood could justify his actions a dozen different ways and never let himself think about the underlying one: he was terrified that Chytrine would have him murdered as she did his mother.

As bad as some might find me on the throne, my death would be worse. Scrainwood reached up and adjusted the green leather half mask he wore. At one time he'd had high hopes for his eldest son, Erlestoke. He'd been strong—far stronger than his father, Scrainwood openly acknowledged—and a brilliant military tactician. If he were going to allow Oriosan troops to oppose Chytrine, he would have wanted Erlestoke to lead them.

Erlestoke, however, had long since had a falling-out with his father and had instead traveled north to Fortress Draconis. There he had risen to be the second-in-command. Fortress Draconis, unfortunately, had been the first victim of Chytrine's renewed assault on the south, and Erlestoke had been slain in the fortress' defense.

That left Scrainwood with his other son, Linchmere. His younger heir had been fat, soft, weak-willed, and infantile when it came to dealing with the realities of the world. Linchmere wanted to lead Oriosa's troops against Chytrine—his first and last display of spine. When his father had denied that request, the prince had run off. Rumors abounded as to his whereabouts. Scrainwood hoped the most common was true: that his son had run off to fight in Muroso. *There he will die and another problem will be solved.*

His cold-blooded dismissal of his son surprised him, but only for a moment. He toyed with the signet ring on his right hand and with the merest of whispers invoked the magick on it. After his mother's death he'd had it made to warn him of hostile intent in anyone near him, and in Yslin some of the sorcerers from Vilwan had refined and strengthened the magick.

He felt something akin to the prick of a pin as the spell sparked to life. He braced himself for the first hint of anger, for he had felt it often, especially in the councils of his peers. They hated him because they knew his nation would be the last to fall to Chytrine and yet, if they gave vent to their hatred, he would go over to Chytrine fully. And if he did that, then the might of Oriosa would just make their nations fall the faster.

But this time no warning of animosity came, and its absence pleased him. He knew his peers saw him as crafty and treacherous—they fully expected him to betray them to Chytrine because they did not think he could possibly oppose her. He was not strong enough to do so. They were not aware, however, that he could defy her and she could do nothing about it.

The second reason he had given in to King Augustus in the matter of Tarrant Hawkins—an ancient enemy now calling himself Kedyn's Crow—was that Augustus had ceded to him the possession of a fragment of the DragonCrown. He'd quickly secreted it away, then had those who had done the hiding killed, so only he knew where it could be found. Without that portion of the Crown, Chytrine could never complete its reconstruction, denying her ultimate power.

His ring began to burn. Scrainwood's gaze flicked left and right, then settled on the room's far corner. Shadows had thickened there, and something moved within them. The movement frightened him more than the mild hostility he sensed through the ring because it was wholly unnatural.

"Who are you?" Scrainwood kept his voice even and tried to infuse it with a commanding tone. But he failed and knew it. The only thing that pleased him was that he and his visitor were the sole witnesses to that failure. "Show yourself."

A smallish humanoid shambled from the shadow, and that it could move at all surprised Scrainwood. The amount of damage that had been done to it fascinated him. Despite the cold, the man wore no shirt, allowing an easy study of the ghastly wounds on chest and hip, as if something had stabbed clean through him. The left arm hung limply and the shoulder, which had been mangled, showed signs of a hideous bite wound. Lastly the creature's head lolled as if its neck had been broken.

But there should be no way it could move with those wounds.

Fire ignited in dark eye sockets and revealed to Scrainwood a face he'd known from decades before. That face grinned, then the voice—the unmistakable voice—filled the room with scorn. "Scrainwood, Scrainwood, king on high, Oriosa's liege, yet afraid to die."

Gelid tendrils squeezed the king's bowels, but he did not allow himself to double over. "Bosleigh Norrington."

"Once, but now no more." The *sullanciri* sketched a bow. His head flopped forward with a wet click of bone fragments. " 'Tis now Nefrai-laysh at your door."

Scrainwood let his nostrils flare. "Is your mistress so bold that she sends her herald here to the Council of Kings?"

Nefrai-laysh grabbed a handful of his own blond hair and pulled his head up so he could look at Scrainwood. "Bolder is she, as you shall see." He whirled and his limp left hand swept past the corner from where he had appeared. "She desires to be presented to thee."

A golden light started as a spark in that dark corner,

then expanded into an oval that grew as if fire had been applied to a parchment sheet. Scrainwood raised a hand to shade his eyes from the brightness, but a heartbeat later the light had died.

Striding from the corner came a striking woman, tall and strong, with a cascade of golden hair that fell in ringlets well past her shoulders. She wore white clothes and furred boots—very much the sort of attire Scrainwood would have supposed to be utilitarian in her realm, up to and including the cloak, furred hat, and soft white scarf covering the lower half of her face.

It occurred to Scrainwood that Chytrine was powerful enough, and possessed of such charisma, that she might be what Princess Alexia of Okrannel would become in her later years. But he knew, almost instantly, that this judgment was wrong because the swirls of blue-green color in Chytrine's eyes bespoke a malevolence that he did not think Alexia could contain.

Alexia could hate hotly, but never coldly and inhumanly like this.

Chytrine paused a half-dozen paces before him and the ring spiked pain up his arm. Scrainwood staggered at the sensation. His knees buckled and a quick kick in the ass by Nefrai-laysh drove him onto the floor. Scrainwood snarled, but refused to cry out.

Chytrine glanced past him at her herald. "Do not treat so valuable an ally thus." She gestured casually and something behind Scrainwood crashed to the floor. Given the clatter that followed, he assumed the *sullanciri* had been cast into the small side table that held a silver platter with bread and cheese—a late repast Scrainwood had not touched.

The Northern Empress smiled down at him as she drew off kid gloves as white as the delicate flesh they had sheathed. "Finally we meet, King Scrainwood. You have been a valuable ally, though your continued worth is in question."

Her words came coolly, but with an edge, and Scrainwood would have been moved to terror, save that his ring did not convey a corresponding sense of hostility. "I do not know what I have done to anger you."

A rustle and clatter behind him suggested that Nefrai-laysh had crawled to his feet. "I have come from Vael, on a mission I did fail. But there, I did hear, a Crown fragment you have near."

"Lies."

Before his denial echoed from the walls, Chytrine lashed him with her gloves. The blow stung a bit, but not as much as it could have, for his mask took the brunt of it. "There is no need for you to lie, King Scrainwood. I am not a stupid woman. You sought the stone, you have it safe, and I am grateful you managed to wrest it from the thieves who removed it from Fortress Draconis. You have saved me much time in this endeavor. Moreover, you can and will claim that you had no way to let me know you had it, since I have always communicated with you and have never given you a means to reach me. You would hold yourself blameless, and I cannot easily refute that claim."

Scrainwood's left hand rose to his cheek. "Why did you strike me?"

She peeled the scarf back to grace him with a frigid smile. "Because I can. Because you are powerless to stop me, and because you need to acknowledge the hopelessness of your situation. Though my aide is broken, it would be nothing for him to pop your head from your body as if it were a grape from a stem."

The king started to protest, but Nefrai-laysh's right hand grabbed him by the back of the neck and squeezed. Not too hard, but none too gently, either—and it was enough to choke Scrainwood's words into a squawk. He began to shake and his bladder let loose, flooding warmth down his thighs.

Chytrine watched him for a moment, then wrinkled her nose. "Despite your treachery, Scrainwood, I have chosen not to punish you. I shall instead reward you beyond your wildest dreams."

He glanced up at her. "And how will you do that?"

"Very simply, Highness. I shall make you one of my *sullanciri*."

The shiver that shook him almost let him slip from Nefrai-laysh's grasp. "You would do that in exchange for the fragment?"

"No, no, you mistake me. I said I am going to reward you. I *am* going to make you into a *sullanciri*. If you desire the change, you will be rewarded handsomely. If you do not, the process and results will be more painful."

"You can change me against my will?"

She laughed, and he did not find the sound completely without warmth. "I am able to control dragons against their will. The Vilwanese and other mages may make much of needing a person's consent to perform magick, but this is a matter of convenience. Overcoming the will is not simple, but less complex than reanimating and motivating something which is dead. I could deal with you that way as well, but you would not be nearly as useful."

Chytrine's smile grew as she returned to his side and squatted. "Besides, you have known all along I want only one thing: domination. And since you did not oppose me, I have been able to get this far. In my world, you shall be even greater than you are now. Indeed, the king of my *sullanciri* is from your nation. I am grateful to you, so the power I give you will be incredible."

Something rang false to Scrainwood. "The Norrington of prophecy is also of my nation. He who will be your doom."

Chytrine snorted a laugh, then stood again. "The vaunted Norrington is no longer a problem. Now, you do wish to be on the winning side, don't you? You wish to see those who hold you in contempt brought low? As my agent, you will be crucial in making that happen, King Scrainwood. The power I will give you—the information I will give you—will turn them all on each other and shatter their alliance. My victory will be your victory."

The Oriosan monarch thought for a heartbeat, then another. He had no heirs. He had a realm that would always be hated whether Chytrine won or lost. Without the Norrington, she would not lose, and power would flow to him, power that would allow him to punish all those who hated him.

Scrainwood shifted his shoulders, slipping his neck from Nefrai-laysh's grip. He sat upright. "I am, as always I have been, your creature, Most High Empress. Work your will on me, so I may best serve our cause."

"Very well, Scrainwood of Oriosa." The Aurolani Empress nodded solemnly and reached out to caress his cheek with cold fingers. "It shall be done."

At the touch of her flesh to his, Scrainwood knew again every agony he had forgotten and those he would suffer in the future. He burned and froze, felt the devouring nibbles of maggots, the razored stabs of swords and withering glances, and the soul-wrenching torsion of knowing that, in the end, he would be betrayed and everything would be for naught.

But even as all that swirled through him, he did feel a pleasure. The fear that had balanced him, that had kept him playing Chytrine off against the rest of the world—the fear of the fate that had taken his mother—slipped through his fingers as fluidly as her blood had. And, in its absence, he was reborn a Dark Lancer.

Sephi, a dark-haired, slender woman—more than a child, though barely seeming so in form—hid in the shadowed doorway of the room housing the king and his visitors. She was part of the royal household and had been elevated to that position as a reward for her help in identifying Crow as Tarrant Hawkins. It was a reward the king had approved of, though it had come at the suggestion of his aide, Cabot

Marsham. The odious sycophant wanted Sephi as his bed-mate, and having her assigned to the household brought them in closer proximity than Sephi had any desire to be.

She had accepted that role, however, because of her devotion to Will Norrington—the Norrington of prophecy who would destroy Chytrine. After she had betrayed Crow to Oriosan authorities, she took the skills at espionage that she used to employ for Oriosa and used them in the service to the Norrington. She did it in part to make amends for having caused trouble for Crow, but more so because she believed Will *was* the only means by which Chytrine would be defeated.

In Will's service she watched the king and learned secrets she could send to him in letters. She had no idea how many of her missives had actually reached him in Muroso, but she had faithfully sent them with riders and soldiers bound for the war. And she continued to spy, remaining in the royal household despite the chances of discovery.

This, however, was too important a bit of news to be entrusted to a letter. Sephi hunched forward, with her hands flat on the cold stone floor. What she had seen through the keyhole had kept her riveted, for a *sullanciri* appeared, and then Chytrine herself. Already Sephi began to berate herself for not running off and alerting the Saporician authorities.

Part of her knew that was foolishness, since they would never believe such a wild tale. *King Augustus would, however, and he is here in Narriz.* She knew she had to get to him so he could act, but she needed a moment more to collect herself because Chytrine had said one thing that left her breathless.

The vaunted Norrington is no longer a problem. The words echoed through Sephi's skull. She thought of Will's smiling face. She could hear his voice and could not imagine him, like his father and grandfather, ever having gone over to Chytrine's service. *And she said it with such finality, he must be dead.*

She screwed her eyes shut against that possibility, because his death meant the end of the world. Tears gathered in her eyes and splashed down, spattering coldly against her hands. She pressed her body into a small ball and fought to gain control. Finally, she reached up and wiped the tears away.

He's not dead, she just thinks he is. Wouldn't be the first time she was wrong.

That thought brought a smile to her face. Her tears stopped, but then her smile froze as she continued to hear a *drip drip* sound. She knew it wasn't tears, but had no idea what it was.

Then she opened her eyes.

A man stood towering over her. Dark in mien and cold, he looked down at her through a bestial mask she almost thought she recognized. The eyes regarding her had no warmth or kindness, but instead were filled with an elemental curiosity. The blue orbs had white moving through them, much as slender ribbons of cloud move through a summer's sky. The movement gained in speed and, for a moment, was the figure's only motion.

Then came another *drip*.

The mask was more than just a mask, flowing up into a cowl that ran down into a cloak. It had been fastened to the figure's neck by the knotted arms of the creature that had once worn the skin. In the dim light Sephi saw enough bony plates to know it was the flesh of a Panqui.

From there it was but a shudder for her to realize it was Lombo's skin. *And if they have killed Lombo, then the Norrington could be dead as well.*

She straightened up and met the *sullanciri*'s cool gaze. "Your grandson, Will, is dead?"

Nefrai-kesh nodded solemnly. "He died more of a hero than any of us will ever be."

Sephi hung her head and raised her hands to cover her face. She let herself sob once, then darted into the corridor and would have gotten free, save that Nefrai-kesh flicked his cloak, and the flaccid flesh that had covered Lombo's tail swept her legs from beneath her. She crashed down hard, striking her forehead on the ground, then rolled to the far wall.

Nefrai-kesh crossed to her and dropped to one knee. His hand caressed her cheek, then tucked an errant lock of dark hair behind her ear. "You, too, shall die well. Had you not been so curious, you might have lived."

Sephi narrowed her eyes. "I was spying for your grandson."

The *sullanciri* smiled. "He commanded loyalty. He was a Norrington truly."

"He still is. The greatest of them."

Nefrai-kesh paused for a moment, then said solemnly, "You are a fool if you believe that, child." His hand slipped into her hair and closed on her neck right below her skull. His fingers tightened and her neck snapped. "And yet there are parts of me that hope you were right."

CHAPTER 1

Princess Alexia of Okrannel raised a gloved hand to shade her eyes as the green dragon upon which she rode dipped his right wing and began a lazy circle. Below lay Narriz, dusted in snow and spread out in several concentric semicircles emanating from the crescent harbor to the west. King Fidelius' castle stood on the highest hill, with a clutch of cylindrical white towers that soared toward the sky. The brightly colored flags and pennants flapping away added an element of reality that banished any hope that she was dreaming.

Beneath her the dragon's flesh undulated as powerful muscles drove its wings. Though the air so high was quite frigid, the heat from the green dragon's body made the space beneath a long red cloak quite warm, and she gladly shared that warmth with Crow. She pressed herself against his side, then turned and kissed his scarred right cheek.

He smiled and his brown eyes sparkled. "What was that for?"

"To make sure you don't forget that I love you. And that I support you, no matter what happens below."

He tightened his arm around her shoulder. "Thank you."

The dragon turned his head back toward them. "Perrine is circling the castle's courtyard. We are welcome."

Resolute, a Vorquelf with sharpened elven features, pointed ears, and eyes of pure silver, curled his lip in a sneer. "Hardly welcome, Dravothrak. We will be tolerated until we deliver our news, then we will be reviled. We bring them word that hope has died, and few will have the heart to continue on past that."

Prince Erlestoke of Oriosa adjusted the black mask he wore. "They know they cannot stop you from landing, Dravothrak, so they accept with feigned grace what they cannot prevent."

The prince's words came in grim tones that nearly matched those Alyx had gotten accustomed to hearing from Resolute. The Vorquelf had been fighting over a century and a quarter to free his homeland from Chytrine, with no success. Will Norrington had been the key to her defeat and his death at Vael seemed to seal the fate of the Southlands' free nations. Arriving at the gathering of world leaders to tell them hope was indeed dead was something she had never anticipated.

She looked again at Crow. "I do wish you would let me be the one to address the council."

Erlestoke nodded in agreement. "Or me. They will accept it better from either of us."

Crow shook his head and his beard brushed against Alyx's cheek. "First and foremost, Will was my charge. I should have kept him safe. And while I agree with everyone that he chose his time of passing, and chose nobly and well, the burden of his death bears most heavily on me. Second, and you all know this is true, King Scrainwood would blame me even if Will's ghost appeared, absolved me of responsibility, and cursed Scrainwood for an idiot. Short of you throttling your father and replacing him, there is nothing that can be done to prevent the blame from falling on me."

The prince's hazel eyes blazed. "Who says throttling him is not an option?"

Crow's chin came up. "I do. The third reason I have to deliver the message is simply that we know that whoever delivers it will be reviled and never trusted again. None of the rest of you can afford to be moved out of the way given the discussions that must take place. Alexia and you, Highness, have the military expertise that will stop Chytrine's troops."

Resolute's sneer melted into a mirthless smile. "You make no case as to why I should not address their august majesties, my friend."

"You mean, aside from the fact that you openly hold them and their councils in contempt?" Crow laughed quickly. "This is a council of humans, Resolute, and they will not take well to being lectured to by one old enough to have known their great-grandparents. Moreover, you will need their help if you are to retake Vorquellyn. For you to speak to them would be to jeopardize that goal. This will need to be handled diplomatically."

Dravothrak opened his mouth in a serpentine grin. "I will not lecture, but you will permit me to emphasize the gravity of the situation, yes?"

Alyx nodded. "As we discussed."

The dragon bobbed his head twice, then folded his wings and they plummeted from the sky. Their cloaks, scarves, and blankets snapped in the rush of air. Frost nibbled at Alexia's cheeks and her eyes watered. She held on tightly to the leather riding harness and watched the tear-blurred castle grow ever larger.

Then, suddenly, Dravothrak spread his wings again and beat hard with them. His head came up, his tail went down, and his mighty legs absorbed the impact of his landing. Snow billowed up around them, as if they were caught in the heart of a blizzard, then Dravothrak breathed a fiery plume that reduced the snow to steam.

Alyx and the others slid from the dragon's back in the fog, to the accompaniment of screams and harsh curses. Then, Perrine descended down through the mist. The female Gyrkyme, who had been Alexia's lifelong companion, landed lightly, furling her raptor's wings. Tall and slender like an elf, but covered with down and feathers after the pattern of a falcon, she smiled and hugged her sister.

"King Augustus called the crowns together when I told him you were coming. They were grumbling, but this display silenced the lot of them. Well done, Dranae."

Dravothrak, now having assumed the form of a tall, powerfully built man with dark hair and a full thick beard, bowed his head. "I am glad it was effective." He fastened the red cloak at his throat and gathered it about him to cover his nudity.

Alexia peered into the thinning fog, seeing dim forms moving through it. "Which way?"

Before Peri could answer, a small, green, humanoid creature, with four arms, four glassy wings, two legs, and two antennae above compound eyes, buzzed in through the fog and circled the group. "This way. Qwc knows. Come, come, hurry, hurry." In the blink of an eye he was off again with a ghostly vapor vortex curling in his wake.

Alyx slipped her right hand through the crook of Crow's elbow and followed the Spritha. Dranae and Erlestoke came next, with Resolute and Peri bringing up the rear. Dressed for winter—and most armed for war—the company struck a sharp contrast with those assembled for the council. The guards stationed on the walls and along the passages were outfitted for combat, but Saporicia had clearly sent its best troops northeast to the Murosan border. These soldiers were old or very young—and some were still pale from having seen a dragon land in the courtyard, then vanish in flame and fog.

The royal retainers for the various leaders wore finery that mocked the state of the world. Alyx suppressed a shiver as she imagined whole households planning how they could array their wardrobes to best advantage. While the kings and queens would deliberate, their staffs would battle each other, pressing advantages and wresting concessions. Politics necessitated they look ahead, past Chytrine, to position themselves to take best advantage—even if that positioning might be exactly what allowed Chytrine to take over the world.

Ahead, Qwc hung in the air at each intersection, making the courtiers sent to escort them shrink back. Some did so at a buzzed word, but at least one clawed at his face. The Spritha had spat a smothering wad of webbing at that man, and Alyx's horror was transformed into wicked delight as she recognized the purple face as that of Cabot Marsham, King Scrainwood's aide.

Marsham, his face still sticky with white tendrils, started to snarl, but Erlestoke cut him off with a sharp command. "Back away, dog. You should feel blessed he deigned to notice someone as insignificant as you."

Marsham's chubby face drained immediately of color. He gagged, then turned and darted away, heading up the stairs to which Qwc pointed. The chamberlain slipped twice in his haste, crying out as he barked his shins once, but scrambled on quickly.

Erlestoke laughed. "He looked as if he'd seen a ghost."

Alyx graced him with a raised eyebrow. "You *are* believed dead, you know."

"Indeed. Shouldn't he have been happier to see me?"

Resolute just growled.

They mounted the broad stone stairs and ascended to the second landing. The short corridor leading east opened into a large room with vaulted ceilings and fanciful murals depicting spring revels. Three large windows at the room's far end admitted a flood of morning light that silhouetted many of the functionaries in the back rows of benches. Toward the front, however, where rulers and their most important advisors gathered behind tables and banners proclaiming their nations, Alexia had no difficulty recognizing faces.

She likewise recognized the expressions which, at first, as they caught sight of Erlestoke, went from shock to guarded delight. Then some, rather quickly, darkened. Others followed, heads turning to confer with companions. Necks craned, heads bobbed, then whispers began to filter back and forth, filling the chamber.

King Fidelius, a small man of middle years with thin grey hair and a withered left arm, opened his strong hand in greeting. "Princess Alexia, it is good to see you. Had we known you were coming sooner, we would have prepared a proper welcome. Your friends I recall from Yslin, save the man in the cloak and this one, who, if my eyes do not deceive me, is Prince Erlestoke of Oriosa."

Alyx nodded, drawing off her cloak and scarf. "Your welcome is appreciated, Highness, as is the speed with which you all assembled. We bring you news of great import. This is Kedyn's Crow, and he has accepted the responsibility to make our report."

Crow stepped forward. He'd spent a quarter century traveling with Resolute and waging a private war against Chytrine. Scars crisscrossed his body and old injuries made him ache, but even though the pain of Will's death weighed heavily on him, his shoulders did not slump and his head did not sag wearily. He moved with the strength of a younger man—strength born of a conviction that Chytrine had to be stopped no matter the cost—and seeing that strength brought a smile to Alexia's face.

He made her proud, and that made her love him even more.

Crow slowly drew the mittens from his hands and unbuttoned the sheepskin coat he wore. "My lords and ladies, I bear grave news. In Yslin you were presented with a lad, Will Norrington. He was the fulfillment of the Norrington Prophecy. He was in my care and under my protection. With me and my companions, Will did much good, from

Vilwan and Port Gold to Fortress Draconis, Meredo, and Muroso. His courage and spirit can be attested to by thousands.

"Yesterday Will spoke for humanity at the Congress of Dragons on Vael. He spoke eloquently, arguing that the dragons alone should be custodians of the DragonCrown fragments. He argued one of Chytrine's *sullanciri* to a standstill and when the dragons agreed with him, the *sullanciri* attempted to murder one of them. Will prevented that murder, but could only do so at the cost of his own life."

Crow's words tightened into a croak as his hands balled. Alexia reached out, closing her hand on his shoulder. She felt the tremor running through him and squeezed.

King Scrainwood slowly rose from behind Oriosa's table. He unfolded himself and straightened in a manner that somehow struck Alexia as wrong, but she could not place why. He moved as a man might, but there was something else there. Something evil, which came through in the venom saturating his words.

"*The* Norrington is *dead*? What further proof is needed that you are indeed the traitor, that you are Chytrine's agent? You betrayed heroes an age ago, and you betrayed Will Norrington now." Scrainwood pointed a quivering finger at Alexia. "Come away from him, Princess. To be near him is to be in jeopardy, and to call him friend is to hold a viper to your breast."

Alexia started to mouth a protest, but Crow unballed a scarred fist and laid it on her hand. He gave her a glance full of love and confidence, then hardened his expression and turned to face the crowned heads.

"This ends *now*, King Scrainwood."

Scrainwood's eyes widened as he opened his arms. "You dare threaten me, here and now? You *are* evil's agent."

Crow snorted. "And how do I threaten you, King Scrainwood? I have no sword. Is it that you still feel the sting of my slaps on your cheeks? Is it your shame that wounds you, and your memory of it that makes you fear me? Fear rules you, and it infects all of you here. I have never liked you, nor have you ever liked me, and that is the way of the thing. It cannot be allowed, however, to doom the world."

He looked past and around Scrainwood. "For a quarter century there have been two strategies for dealing with Chytrine and her threat to the Southlands. One has been defensive, as exemplified by Fortress Draconis, and perverted by Oriosa's covert acquiescence to Aurolani pressure. Do not be smug. All of you have adopted this strategy to a greater or lesser extent. The fact that you are here, not at the head of armies pushing into Muroso, is further proof that you think this strategy can win.

"Resolute and I, on the other hand, have waged a war against her. We have cost her troops and leaders. We have thwarted plans. We have slowed her advances. We may not have stopped her, but we are only two. As part of our war we sought the Norrington. We plucked him from the slums of Yslin, trained him for his role, watched him assume it and acquit himself well."

Crow's voice tightened a bit, but deepened as well. "One of you dismissed him as gutterkin and a whoreget, yet he won his place in history. While still a youth, he inspired men with a willingness to fight and even die for him, and many did—all in opposition to Chytrine. His death won for us a neutrality among dragons. As a nation they will not fight for Chytrine."

Scrainwood sniffed. "A better man would have won them to our side."

"Silence!" Crow's shout produced astonished expressions on faces long unaccustomed to taking orders. "You are all playing at games. You need to make serious decisions, and you can't do it with posturing, nor with a lack of information, and it is information I bring."

He turned and pointed to Dranae. "This companion of ours is Dravothrak, a dragon in manform. He is our ally, as

Chytrine has allies. In the mountains of Sarengul he slew one of her dragons. There are others among dragonkind willing to help us."

King Fidelius stroked his chin. "What do they desire for their help?"

Dranae nodded slowly. "What you do. The destruction of the DragonCrown."

A woman in a black robe stood at the Vilwanese table. "What of Adept Reese? Was he slain, too?"

Crow shook his head. "No, he has remained on Vael to receive instruction in the ways of dracomagick."

Her eyes widened. "On whose authority?"

"His. Mine. Does it matter?" Crow's hands again became fists. "Have none of you been listening? You ask after authority, after allies, assuming that you can look past to the time after Chytrine. But the job before you is to deal with Chytrine. You failed twenty-five years ago to end this threat, and for all that time I accepted the burden of your blame. Well, no more. If the world is to survive, you will have to do something other than plot and scheme."

He stabbed a finger off to the northeast. "You have a horde pouring in this direction. It has devoured Sebcia. It is consuming Muroso. It has invaded Sarengul and struck at Bokagul. Oriosa will not stop it. *You* must."

Crow's shoulders slumped a little. "Will Norrington accepted the responsibility for saving the world. The actions he took have hurt Chytrine and made her vulnerable. If you give her time to recover, you will have betrayed him, your people, and yourselves. Because every second you fail to act is a second in which she grows stronger, and a second in which the chance to stop her slips further away."

He straightened his shoulders and raised his head, then turned and strode from the room. The guards at the door made no attempt to stop him, despite Scrainwood's hissed orders. Alyx fell in behind him, and Resolute beside her. Beyond the door, in the small corridor, Crow hammered a fist against a stone wall.

Resolute smiled and rested a hand on the back of Crow's neck. "I thought you said this needed to be handled diplomatically?"

Crow growled, then pressed his forehead to the cold stone and smiled. "Well, that was my intention, but I assumed that if they were going to hate me, they might as well have plenty of reason. After the last war against Chytrine I told them this would happen. It was gratifying to remind them of it. But I don't know that it will do any good."

Alyx stroked his arm. "I watched them. Augustus smiled and my great-grandaunt did not, so I consider those both solid points. Queen Carus of Jerana and King Fidelius listened, and they are key players. You reminded them all that Scrainwood could not be trusted, and he did little to reassure them on that point. They liked seeing Erlestoke there."

Crow turned and slumped back against the wall. "There is hope, then, slender though it might be. This is good." He raised a hand and caressed her cheek. "You and Erlestoke will have to carry on the political battle, since I am useless."

Alexia frowned. "You're never useless, and I will be needing your help."

"Oh, I'll help as much as I can." The corner of Crow's mouth twitched in a grin. "I'll distract Scrainwood. While you are rallying the crowned heads, I'll write my memoirs, with all the details of the last campaign against Chytrine. Trying to get at the manuscript will keep him preoccupied, I hope."

Resolute nodded and the upright stripe of white hair shifted as if kissed by a breeze. "No matter what they think of you, Crow, the assembled leaders know that to do nothing is to die. It is a spur that will drive them to action. With luck, the princess and Erlestoke can unite them, and we will put an end to this scourge for once and all time."

CHAPTER 2

Kerrigan Reese sat cross-legged on the stone floor and studied the seamless silver globe in his hands. He could see himself easily in its polished surface, his face all piled up around a fat nose and diminishing until his ears became little more than buds. He looked singularly unappealing, but though possessed of a normal amount of vanity, concerns about his looks shrank to insignificance. He was less worried about the globe's visual distortion because another aspect of its nature held his full attention.

As the globe distorted reflected light, so it seemed to distort magick. The first spell the portly mage had cast on the globe had confirmed that it was enchanted, but the energy he had put into a simple diagnostic spell was quickly drawn and shredded. It seemed to him as if it had been a thin cloud stretched and dissipated by an unfelt wind.

His mind raced, both in puzzling out the globe and because of other recent events. Will Norrington's death still hurt. Not only had Kerrigan lost a friend—the only friend he'd had his own age—but he should have been able to prevent Will's death. He had failed to act and while he acknowledged that Will knew what he was doing when he sacrificed himself, Kerrigan's failure gnawed at him.

Will's dying act, however, had saved the life of Kerrigan's new master, a dragon named Rymramoch. Rymramoch's physical body lay in the Congress Chamber, deep in the fastness of Vael, though the dragon traveled and observed through means of an elaborate wooden manikin. Until a confrontation with a *sullanciri* in the chamber, Kerrigan had no inkling that Rymramoch was anything but a powerful mage.

The dragon had traveled with the help of Bok, a hirsute urZrethi male with malachite flesh. He had turned out to be quite a surprise. As with all of his race, Bok could shift shape, but Kerrigan had labored under the impression that he was little more than a beast. Part of that mistake had been because of common legend that said male urZrethi driven from the mountains slowly went insane without the company of their own kind. The urZrethi matriarchy portrayed males as feebleminded, and during his time in Bokagul, Kerrigan had seen little to contradict this depiction.

Bok, or more correctly Loktu-bok Jex, turned out to be centuries old, very well educated and traveled, and quite capable of working formidable magick. His spells had animated the puppet in which Rymramoch's consciousness had resided and Kerrigan had never detected a thing. And as if Bok's going from beast to civilized savant was not enough of a shock, Bok had told Kerrigan that he was Chytrine's father.

"Your mind is wandering, Adept Reese." Rymramoch, resplendent in a crimson robe embroidered in golden serpentine designs, nodded. The puppet pointed a gloved hand at the globe. "Focus on the globe. Divine its secrets."

Kerrigan nodded and cleared his mind of everything but the globe. He cast his diagnostic spell again, with much the same results. He had confirmed that the globe was magickal in some manner, but got nothing else useful in that regard. What he did notice, however, was that his spell was shredded differently this time, the energy swirling away in another pattern.

It flowed, much as urZrethi magick flows. He shifted his approach and, instead of casting a human diagnostic spell, went for one he had learned from an urZrethi instructor. It flowed from his hands and covered the globe with a dark coat. Occasionally little lines of silver, like lightning, would flash here and there, then the spell evaporated.

The results of the urZrethi magick did not tell Kerrigan much, other than that Bok had cast a spell on it. That spell seemed suited to little more than masking other magick. He knew that to peel that spell away would take a lot of hard work and many hours, and he did not feel he had time to waste.

Moreover, he had an idea.

Kerrigan began to shape a spell in the urZrethi style, imagining it to be smoke rising from an extinguished candle. He poured energy into it, giving the wisp of the spell life, then sank the slender thread of it into the shield spell. Kerrigan's new spell flowed with Bok's magick—at first on the surface, then down through the protective layer. The trickle of energy he expended on the spell was insufficient to trigger a reaction by Bok's spell, so little by slowly his thread drifted on and in and finally reached the globe itself.

The flowing sensation of his spell had pleased Kerrigan, and had tickled the palm of his right hand. When the spell touched the globe, however, that tickle became a stab of agony that felt as if the ball had sprouted a spike and driven it straight through Kerrigan's hand. A wave of fatigue washed over him and the world dimmed for a moment. Kerrigan wavered and slumped to his right as the globe rolled from his hand and onto the floor.

Kerrigan watched the ball jump and twist, then flatten into a thick disk, stretch into a tall cylinder, and finally gather itself into a roiling thundercloud. All motion froze for a second and a keening wail sounded, then the silver ball expanded and resolved itself into the shape of a warrior. Though only a foot high, the model had been worked with exquisite detail, right down to the way the man's long hair moved against his shoulders.

It shouldn't be moving. Kerrigan shook his head to clear it, and the figure's details faded for a moment, then became sharp again as Kerrigan concentrated. The figure actually looked familiar and after a moment's reflection Kerrigan realized it was modeled on a statue of Prince Kirill of Okrannel, Alexia's father, that Kerrigan had seen at Fortress Draconis.

The little figure bowed to him, then melted back into the silver sphere.

Kerrigan levered himself up into a sitting position again. "What is that?"

Rymramoch's head canted to the side, then the puppet gestured and the globe floated to his outstretched hand. "It is little more than a toy we use to train ourselves in magick. Bok did layer it with a protective spell, but you worked through that quickly enough. The device may have seemed greedy to you, but dragons use it and barely notice the demands."

The puppet's fingers curled up and inward, sinking into the ball. Kerrigan caught a hint of magick, then the hand opened again. "There, I think that should work. As a device, it allows one to concentrate. The figure you created is something you remember?"

"Based on a statue I saw at Fortress Draconis, yes." Kerrigan shifted his shoulders. "What am I supposed to do with the thing, just make models?"

"No, no, quite a bit more." The puppet tossed the sphere to him again. "When you penetrated Bok's spell, you made a connection with the ball. The magick in the ball drew strength from you to allow itself to function. You found that taxing, yes?"

Kerrigan nodded. "All spells require energy to make

them work. You have to be careful in case you exhaust yourself and collapse."

"Because your body produces the energy you use to cast spells?"

"Exactly." Kerrigan answered quickly, but realized that he'd given the rote Vilwanese answer. Though he had learned to parrot such things to his tutors, he had secretly questioned the source of magick. The difficulty was that on Vilwan no one believed magick functioned any other way.

The puppet folded his arms over its chest. "You realize there is a flaw in your description, don't you?"

The young man's brows furrowed. "You think it is obvious. Not to me."

"Permit me to show you. If you were to go out and run up and down the mountain here, you would expend a lot of energy, wouldn't you? You'd feel exhausted."

"Of course."

"And what else would happen?"

Kerrigan thought for a second, then patted his stomach with his left hand. "I'd lose some of this."

"Exactly, and yet, you, the most powerful magician humanity has known in ages, waged a near-constant thaumaturgical battle at Navval and lost not an ounce. How is that?"

Kerrigan started to answer, then frowned. "The energy doesn't come from me?"

The puppet shifted its hands to the small of its back. "It is possible for you to produce energy to work spells, though it should not be used directly to cast them. This is the grand error taught on Vilwan, and you were well instructed on your limitations there because of this presentation. What your masters did not tell you is that while they have studied how much energy a body produces, the simple fact is that even human magickers can use more energy than that."

The young man frowned. Rymramoch had informed him that in the days after the time of Kirûn, the creator of the DragonCrown, the teaching on Vilwan had changed.

Kirûn had been from Vilwan and, in order that the nations of the world would not destroy the Vilwanese sorcerers, they chose to hobble their disciples. Because of the threat posed by Chytrine, Kerrigan had been taught forbidden knowledge and spells, progressing well past anyone else on the island. But even *his* education was flawed.

"If what you are saying is true, there is another source of energy."

"No, it is the source of magick." The puppet gestured and the silver sphere flowed like water through Kerrigan's fingers, then pooled on the floor. "Magick is most easily seen as a river, though it is far more vast and varied. It has currents and eddies, cool flows and hot, fresh, brackish, and stagnant aspects to it. It pervades reality—all realities—in some places being weak and in others very strong. Here it is moderately strong, and just being here one soaks it up, much as cloth will drink in humidity. It is this ethereal moisture that is the extra energy humans wield."

"Then why do we become tired, if it is all around?"

"Why does the man who lives near a river feel thirst?" The puppet laughed easily. "The energy you expend is the energy you use to divert magick into your spells. There are times, Kerrigan, when you have drawn magick into you without thinking, and the energy came effortlessly. It is easier and more likely to happen with Elder magicks, but that you can do it at all marks your intuitive talent for magick."

Kerrigan shook his head. "You mean there is no limit to the spells I can cast because I can draw on this river of magick?"

"I did not say that, and that belief is one that has doomed many a foolish sorcerer." Rymramoch shook his head. "You have seen rivers. What happens to the stones in them?"

"They are worn smooth."

"They are worn *away*." With a flick of a finger the puppet commanded the pooled silver to re-form the sphere. "A dragon may be granite to magick, but you would be sandstone. Plunge yourself in without caution and you shall melt away to mud. Mind you, what you *will* be able to do will be beyond the ken of humanity, and perhaps even the elves and urZrethi. It would even amaze the Oromise, but not me, not dragons."

"Oromise?" Kerrigan shook his head. "What is an Oromise?"

"Not a what, but who." The puppet pressed gloved fingers one to the other, then flatted palms together. "Back in forever ago there was magick, and in that flow resided creatures. Dragons were one such, though in a form we would hardly recognize. When we reached awareness, however, we sought a place to stop within the flow of magick. We tried to create havens, but met with little success for we are creatures of air and fire, and two elements do not a universe make.

"The Oromise are creatures of earth and water. They, too, wished to create a haven, and where their magicks and ours overlapped, we succeeded. Dragons and the Oromise formed an alliance and shaped this universe and this world. Elves came later, for their element is wood and vital for holding the others together. Dragons and the Oromise welcomed them through benign neglect and did not dispute their making our world fertile."

Kerrigan glanced at the ball. "Can you make it look like an Oromise?"

"Not I, for I was many years yet unhatched when the Oromise last felt the sun on their faces—if, indeed, they had faces." The puppet shrugged. "What I tell you now is legend. I only have it fourth or fifth wing."

"How old are you?"

"*Very* old. I remember the war to wrest Vareshagul from the urZrethi. I fought in it—sinking most of the island and leaving Vael as the only remnant—and I have resided here since. Even so, the Oromise are but legend to me. They are the nightmares that haunt our dreams, and that a dragon can be haunted should signify much."

Kerrigan shivered. "But I have never heard of them."

"That is because there was a war of Dragons and Oromise for dominion over the world. The Oromise were builders and tinkerers. They created machines and creatures. The *kryalniri* you saw in Bokagul and Muroso, these are very like the things they set upon the elves to keep them occupied as we fought. Many other creatures are theirs as well, with a few quite mundane and even beloved, like cats. They created much before the war, and adapted much more for war."

"But what about the gods making the world?"

Rymramoch shook his head. "Humanity, rising in times well past that of the Oromise, needed to explain things. Gods are convenient when no other explanation presents itself."

"But Resolute has said that our gods are but dim shadows of the elder gods he knows about."

"Resolute's knowledge of things is not without error, and even the elves do not remember the Oromise precisely. They know there was something there, and their facility for the invention of gods is no less potent than that of men."

"So the gods don't exist?"

The puppet laughed. "Oh, that is a topic of heated debate among dragons. Does the act of believing and worshipping create an entity that becomes a god? Are there yet other interlopers who have come to our world and assumed that role? We do not know and know of no way to find out. The simple fact is, however, that if there *are* gods, they played no part in the Oromise war. Dragons drove the Oromise from the face of the earth and deep into its heart. They have been entombed there forever through dracomagicks, but they anticipated us.

"One of their last acts was to create the urZrethi. The urZrethi, led by powerful chieftains, fashioned their own empires and dug deep into the earth. They raised mountains as they went, seeking to free their masters. Dragons went to war with them as well, the last great battle being the one for Vareshagul."

The puppet plucked an errant thread from the left sleeve of its robe. "Until that time the urZrethi were a patriarchy, with strong males having harems. In order to save their race, the urZrethi shifted the entire social structure. The reason strong males like Bok are exiles is for fear they will again invite the wrath of the dragons upon the urZrethi."

Kerrigan shook his head. "But if Bok is that kind of threat, why is he here? Why is he your friend?"

"Because Bok is not stupid, nor a servant of the Oromise." The puppet's voice took on an edge. "Centuries ago, when I first met him, I knew he would be crucial to setting things to rights again. With your help, I am hopeful we can truly accomplish it this time."

CHAPTER 3

Alexia accepted the folded note from the Vilwanese signal-mage and nodded in thanks before closing the door of her chamber behind him. Unbidden came the image of the last time she held a letter in her hands. Will Norrington had brought it to her in Caledo, asking her to read it for him. *He had been anxious and so very grown-up.*

She looked at the unsealed side of the folded parchment. Her name had been written on it in a clear hand, and equally clearly had been written the name Markus Adrogans. It surprised her that Adrogans had written to her here in Narriz, and so quickly after her arrival. That meant her appearance had been so shocking that Jeranese officials had communicated it to Adrogans, or that Adrogans had a superior spy network already in place. She actually doubted neither, but suspected the latter was truly the case.

The note was clearly the transcription of a message sent by *arcanslata,* and his use of that form of communication indicated an urgency. She had heard, in whispers, that Adrogans had taken Svarskya and liberated Okrannel. She doubted it was a gloating message, but she couldn't rule that out entirely, for Adrogans had nothing if not a massive ego.

One that matches his genius at the art of war, however.

She flipped the paper over and broke the seal, then unfolded it. The penmanship of the message's transcriber did not match the note's content, nor the sender. The crabbed hand added to the unreality of the message, leaving her uneasy and sad.

> Dear Princess Alexia,
>
> It is my sad duty to inform you of the death of your cousin, Count Mikhail. In the campaign to liberate Okrannel he served with distinction and unquestioned courage. Were it not for his efforts, I would be writing not from Svarskya, but before the gates of the Three Brothers.
>
> The taking of the Three Brothers was entirely due to him and his work. Not only was he critical in planning the operation, but he chose to lead troops in the most dangerous assault of all. He took Varalorsk, slaying the Aurolani commander and receiving a mortal wound in return.
>
> He has been buried there, at the site of his greatest triumph.
>
> As he lay dying, he asked me to tell you that dreams can come true. He said you should believe in your dreams.
>
> I would also have you know that as we entered Svarskya and overcame the Aurolani forces, we did so with your cousin's name on our lips. In his name your homeland was freed.
>
> With sorrow and respect,
> General Markus Adrogans
> 9 Thaw
> Svarskya, Okrannel

Alexia slowly refolded the paper after the second reading. She remembered Misha very well. She had been raised in Gyrvirgul as Preyknosery Ironwing's daughter. Not until she was seventeen had she traveled to Okrannel and met her cousin there. As had been determined by the Crown Circle—the Okrans nobles who dictated the details of life in exile—every noble child was to spend a night on their native soil and the dream they'd had that night was believed to be prophetic.

She smiled. Misha had awakened and told her of his dream. He was incredibly proud of it, for in it he was older, strong of limb, and the victor at a battle that liberated the Three Brother citadels from the Aurolani. He knew that he should not have told her about the dream, and she had not betrayed his confidence to anyone.

And, at his insistence, she shared her dream with him. Later they both recounted their dreams before the Crown Circle. The dreams were recorded and studied, to be woven into some grand gospel that would prove beyond any shadow of a doubt that Okrannel would again be free. The Book of Dreams had become something of incredible force, with people confirming the veracity of fact and rumor by saying, "You'll find it in the Book of Dreams."

She shook her head. "But your death wasn't written there, Misha."

Alexia crossed the tower room and, impulsively, almost threw the letter into the small fire burning in the hearth. She would have, but just the feel of the parchment was a tangible link to her cousin. She'd last seen him on the plains outside Svoin, right before she and the others in her small company had sailed to Port Gold to liberate a portion of the DragonCrown from the Wruonin pirates. He had been in great spirits and confident of victory. It was not hard to imagine men willingly following him into battle.

Part of her wondered if, had she been there, Misha would yet live, but she dismissed that thought as unworthy. Adrogans, though he approached things differently from her, had never been a man to spend troops needlessly or carelessly. To wonder if she could have saved Mikhail devalued his skills and his sacrifice. He was an able warrior and leader, and to have liberated Varalorsk was no mean feat. It had never fallen before and somehow, with his spirit there to guard it, Alyx thought it never would again.

Rubbing her thumb over the broken red wax seal, Alexia seated herself beside the fire and closed her eyes. It took her a moment to become comfortable, then she projected herself away to the Communion of Dragons. When she had done this before, she always appeared on a mountaintop and had to make her way through a cavern and down to a subterranean lake. This time, however, she appeared on the quay, beside the dark boat that would bear her to the island where the Communion members gathered.

Though she had projected herself much closer to her goal, she smiled as golden letters appeared in the dark water. *The secrets within remain secrets without, for the good of all the world.* That warning appeared on the arch over the mouth of the cave, and was repeated here so she could not forget. Those things learned in the Communion could not be shared back in the physical world, though she would remember them and be able to act upon them.

The boat onto which she stepped had been styled after a dragon, with a proud head above the bow. At the helm stood a mechanical dragonman. She nodded in his direction. "Maroth, take me forth."

The boat slowly began to drift away onto the black lake. That the water appeared to be a starless sky she took as a fitting omen to mark her cousin's death. But she refused to see it as an ill omen, even though Chytrine's forces had moved south with the power of a world-devouring storm. The Northern Empress would gobble up the stars themselves if she had the chance, of that Alyx was sure. With deliberations just beginning in Narriz, Alyx was uncertain if the world could assemble the forces needed to stop Chytrine.

Out of the darkness loomed an island. When last she

had been at the Communion, it had reminded her of a citadel akin to Fortress Draconis, but gradually its form had changed. It had become more primitive, with tall trees dominating broken towers, and menhirs mocking tumbled stone fortresses. Snow swirled over the grounds, teased by winds she did not feel or hear. Alyx wondered if the island had taken this shape because another member's will had imposed itself, or if other constructs had been stripped away to reveal something more primal.

The boat slipped up to a small dock and she mounted a set of crude stone stairs. She climbed to the gap in a low wall, then walked down into a snow-laden bowl. A hundred yards on she came to a circle of standing stones with two more individuals at its heart. One, the Black Dragon, she had seen there before. The other she recognized instantly, despite his being only rendered in shadow.

She smiled broadly. "Father Ironwing!" Alyx threw her arms around the Gyrkyme and hoped the Communion would allow her to feel him in her embrace. It did, and allowed her to feel his returned hug.

The Gyrkyme keened a laugh. "It is very good to see you here, my daughter. You are well after your many adventures?"

"Yes, and Peri is, too. We are in Narriz, hoping the crowns will remain united to fight Chytrine." She released him, then turned and bowed to the Black Dragon. "And you, sir, I hope you are well."

The man who wore a dragon's head bowed it in return. "Better now than I had been. I was speaking with Preyknosery here about things he has learned that might have a bearing on your future. While you have been fighting, he and other Gyrkyme have been out gathering information."

Alyx smiled at her adoptive father. "What have you learned?"

The elder Gyrkyme smiled easily. "Of the world, much. Do you recall, daughter, how I taught you to read the seasons? Specifically, do you recall how I taught you to know if a drought would come and the summer would blaze?"

She nodded. "The animals that leave the mountain heights for the winter are slow to return. They remain near water. Birds migrate earlier, other creatures change their range. You're seeing this?"

"This far north the winter has not loosened its grasp, but by the new year, it will."

"That's month's end."

"It is, indeed. Further south animals are preparing for a hot summer of little water."

Alyx nodded slowly and the Black Dragon smiled. "You were right, Preyknosery, she catches the significance. As Chytrine's troops were at an advantage in the winter, having been born in a boreal realm, so they will be discomfited by a hot summer. That will give you an edge."

"I am thankful for it. Now we will have to strike; all that remains is choosing where and deciding with what. That latter point will be the more difficult, since we do not know what the crowns will decide."

Preyknosery scratched at his throat with a talon. "Our eyes have seen much of men as well. While the winter and snows make traveling difficult, troops are on the move. Alcida is moving the most, but other places are as well."

"Companies? Battalions? Regiments?"

"All of them, but not all are directed toward Chytrine's troops." The Gyrkyme frowned. "Many borders and passes are being reinforced, especially in the east. Alosa, Vegan, Reimancia, and Teysrol see themselves as bastions to stop the spread eastward. They are also posting more troops on their own eastern frontiers to discourage adventurism."

Alyx sighed. "And in the west?"

"Those nations that helped Adrogans win Okrannel are buoyed by success and are sending troops east, but the roads are long."

"Ships would bring them quickly to Saporicia."

The Black Dragon shook his head. "It is as you imagine,

daughter. The western nations have fought and won, and while they would love more victories, the liberation of Okrannel makes them feel safe. If Chytrine takes Saporicia before they get there, they can oppose her in Alcida. As King Augustus threatened to fight in Oriosa, so they can fight in his realm. If, on the other hand, there are concessions that will reward them for speed, they will move with speed."

She closed her eyes. "It is as Crow said. They will play politics and let any chance they have at victory slip away." Alyx opened her eyes again and looked up at Preyknosery. "What of the urZrethi and elves?"

"Of the elves we know nothing. We are not welcome in their realms, so we do not study them. The urZrethi, however, are friends to the Gyrkyme. There is fighting in Sarengul and armies are being raised. Varagul is supposed to be sending a regiment across Reimancia and Vegan to help in the liberation of Sarengul. Bokagul is likewise raising an army."

Her violet eyes sharpened. "Did you hear anything of the Oriosan and Murosan troops fighting in Sarengul?"

The Gyrkyme shook his head. "All is in chaos there and a number of our scouts never returned. I believe they died over Muroso."

"And Muroso is falling?"

"I am afraid that it is. Caledo was not gone when last seen, but I would assume it has fallen by now. There were many refugees fleeing into Bokagul and Saporicia. The Aurolani have killed many, and the winter has killed its share, too."

The Gyrkyme frowned deeply. "Most disturbing of all is that Chytrine's armies seem robust despite their losses. The Ghost March and Okrannel had good harvests, so her troops have food. The stores from Fortress Draconis are sustaining many as well. Sebcia and Muroso tried to destroy supplies, but the onslaught's speed took so many by surprise that the Aurolani did manage to capture a lot of what they needed."

Alyx glanced at the Black Dragon. "No word from Communicants from Sebcia or Muroso?"

"No, and that is most grim."

She nodded. One Communicant had been Princess Dayley of Muroso. Alexia had last seen her in the Murosan capital, Caledo. While she supposed it was possible Dayley had not had time to come to the Communion, Alyx feared she was dead. *And if she is dead, her blood kin likely share the same fate.*

Alyx sighed. "No less grim is the situation outside Muroso. Will Norrington died on Vael. He sacrificed himself to save a dragon from death, but all we got from that is a ragged neutrality among the dragons. They will not come out for or against Chytrine as a group, but individuals can and have chosen sides. We have several powerful ones in our camp, but Chytrine has more."

The Black Dragon hugged his arms around his belly. "The Norrington dead." His voice came in a hushed whisper that sent a chill up Alexia's spine.

She chewed her lower lip for a moment. "We don't know if Will was *the* Norrington, or if that mantle will transfer to another. A Murosan princess is carrying Will's child, and one of his half brothers is fighting in Sarengul with the Oriosan Freemen. That's why I asked after them."

"I shall see what else I can learn, daughter."

"Thank you, Father Ironwing." Alyx shook her head. "We half expect everyone to trot out their own Norrington heir, and the worst part is that King Scrainwood already has one available. If these heirs cause factions to form and then are actually expected to lead troops into the field, Chytrine will eat the Southlands up bit by bit."

The Black shook his head. "That would be a complete disaster. Is there any chance the Norrington isn't dead?"

She shivered. "No. I saw him die with my own eyes. And with him died the hope of the world."

The Black laid a hand on her shoulder. "That's not true. Chytrine cannot yet complete the DragonCrown, so she is still thwarted. Once she has all the pieces and can refashion the Crown, she will have no more need of armies. You must remember that. While her armies have to be stopped, as long as the Crown is safe from her, there is always hope."

"I understand what you are saying. I just wish I felt it more in my heart." Alyx's eyes narrowed. "Politics will deny us the tools we need to stop her."

"There are others who will deal with the politics, daughter." The Black Dragon smiled at her. "You were trained by Preyknosery here to be able to lead armies. This you do very well. The hope of the world now rests upon your shoulders. As long as you are prepared to do what you were trained to do, as long as you make the most of whatever opportunity you are given, you will succeed beyond your wildest dreams."

CHAPTER 4

S o, I see you are alive."

It surprised Prince Erlestoke to hear his father's voice, but that did not stop him from sliding the whetstone along his sword's blade. He stroked the metal twice more, then raised the blade and let lamplight play over the edge. It wasn't sharp enough, so he laid it on the leather protecting his thighs and bent to his task again.

"Damn you, Erlestoke. Look at me! I thought you were dead."

This time the prince did turn his head and looked up. There his father stood. The day before, in the Council Chamber, was the first time Erlestoke had seen his father in over five years. The man looked older, with the streaks of white in his hair and beard. The green mask he wore hid wrinkles, but the decorations on it made his father look poxed. Age had shrunk him slightly, and his voice had an edge just this side of hysterical. Bony fingers clutched the doorjamb.

Calmly, Erlestoke replied, "You may have thought I was dead, but did you care?"

Hazel eyes blazed from within that mask. "I am your father. How can you even ask such a question?"

"Simple, Father." Erlestoke leveled the blade at him, pointing at his face. "You cut no notches for having lost a son on your mask."

Scrainwood's jaw slackened for a moment, but his eyes narrowed quickly enough. "I must subordinate my personal feelings to the needs of the state. If I were to cut those notches, everyone would know I believed you dead and hope would be lost. I could not display my private grief."

"No? Then how about your personal *joy* at seeing me alive again?" The prince rasped the whetstone over the edge. "Marsham looked as if I'd reached from the grave and clutched his throat. You looked stricken as well. You had no greeting, no wave, nothing. All you cared for was seeing that your enemy, Crow, had entered the chamber and that I was apparently in league with him. Had you any concern for me, you would have been there, in that doorway, last night."

The king's head came up and nostrils flared. "I am your father. I expected you to come to me."

"I'm sure you did." Erlestoke laid the broadsword down and stood slowly. Though not much taller than his father, he had the build of a warrior in his prime, which made Scrainwood appear to be a figure made of rags and broomsticks. He slid his chair in against the table, laid the leather over the sword, then opened his arms wide. "Did you wish an embrace, Father? Or did you just want me coming to you, telling you I had been wrong to support the Draconis Baron, and that your way of things is clearly the wisest course?"

The offer of an embrace tightened the king's grip on the doorjamb, but the following question loosened it. The king straightened up and even let a bit of a smile twist over his lips. "No, I want no embrace. While I would have hoped your experience would have benefited you and blessed you with wisdom, when I saw you in Crow's company, I knew it had not."

The prince crossed the small palace room and poured red wine from an earthenware pitcher into a roughly thrown mug. He did not offer his father any, but pointed to the pitcher as he drank. The wine cut the scent of oil from the sharpening, but did little to cover the taste of disgust. "Just so you can have more justification to hate Crow, were it not for him, I would not be alive. I guess saving the life of the crown prince could hardly be considered treason."

His father snorted and while he entered the room, he did not join his son in drinking. "The survival of Oriosa is of paramount importance. If that act had to be classed as treason, a way would have been found."

"Marsham would have delighted in it, I am certain."

Scrainwood shook his head as he walked past the small table with the wine and stood before the fireplace. He held his hands out and rubbed them together. "You are, without a doubt, a brilliant military leader. Dothan Cavarre taught you well—in a futile cause, you will agree, but he taught you well. Your trek from Fortress Draconis speaks to your ingenuity and courage. Alas, your martial skills are useless in the political arena, and keeping a nation together is a purely political job."

For a heartbeat Erlestoke wanted to hurl his mug at his father. He could see it hitting him, shattering. Blood and wine would splash against the wall and slowly drip down. Erlestoke saw it all with crystal clarity and the only thing that stayed his hand was his knowledge that the mug would shatter before his father's skull did.

Instead, he swallowed, lowered the mug, and smiled. "It is well for you that courage is not needed to govern."

Another snort from his father. "Oh, I know intimately your opinion of me, Erlestoke. Princess Alexia delivered your message from Fortress Draconis. You urged me not to live my life as a coward. Anything you do not understand, whatever does not fit within your military paradigms, you label cowardice. The fact remains that while Sebcia and Muroso are gone, my nation lives."

"But for how long?"

"Every heartbeat is a gift. It is an opportunity."

Erlestoke blinked. "An opportunity for what, Father? What do you think will happen here? Chytrine is going to sue for peace and you will broker some treaty that will raise Oriosa to glory? Do you think you will ride back into Meredo, raise an army, and crush her?"

"Me? Don't be foolish. I know my limitations." Scrainwood shot him a sidelong glance. "You don't know yours, when it comes to politics at least. And your brother, wherever he is, knows nothing of his—which are considerable."

The prince allowed himself a smile. "I've seen him, you know."

"Your brother?"

"Yes."

"Where? *Where?*"

In the face of his father's near apoplexy, Erlestoke sipped more wine. "In Sarengul. He'd come from Meredo with the Norrington. He's one of the Oriosa Freemen."

Scrainwood poured himself a swallow of wine and tossed it off quickly. "He always was lucky, though his runs always ended badly. As will this one."

Erlestoke shook his head and set his cup down on the table. "I don't think so. He was more himself—his *old* self, before our mother died—than I have seen in a long time. He'd lost weight, gained scars, but, more importantly, he has gained respect."

"Fah. Sycophants mewing over him because they thought his buttocks would be filling the throne." The king wiped his mouth with his sleeve. "Once they saw you were around, they doubtless abandoned him."

"You are wrong." Erlestoke almost added the word *Father* to his comment, but the man standing before him didn't seem fatherly or even sympathetic. Concern for

Linchmere, or pride or amazement Erlestoke could have understood, but dismissive contempt was not the sort of thing a father should have for a child who, however late in life, had found his place.

"You spoke to me, Highness, of not knowing my limitations. Politics you may understand well, but not the politics of a military company in the field. Men rise and fall on merit because all the titles and money back home mean nothing on the battlefield. Though Linchmere is traveling under an assumed name, the men know who he is. Because of you there was no love for him, and he'd not helped his cause while still in Oriosa by being a useless fop. And Linchmere may be naive enough to believe the men do not know who he is, but the simple fact is that they like him and respect him for things he has done. He's not a great warrior, but he has heart and determination."

"Determination?" Scrainwood broke the word into each of its syllables, stretching it, layering increasing disbelief on each successive one. "That boy never stuck with anything in his entire life."

Erlestoke's head came up. "He stuck with you, didn't he?"

The king gaped at him for a moment, then turned back to the fire. "Well, then, fighting in Sarengul may be Linchmere's opportunity. I suppose that half-wit of a Norrington was with him?"

"Will's half brother? Yes, Linchmere pointed him out to me. They are fast friends."

"That's good. It builds more loyalty to the throne. It is a complication, though, having a Norrington in Sarengul." The king shrugged. "I foresaw it, though, and have summoned his little brother here from Meredo. It will be important to have *our* Norrington here."

"Will is dead. There is no other Norrington."

"Now you are the one who is wrong, my son." Scrainwood waved an off hand in the general direction of the Council Chamber. "Virtually every king, queen, and lordling with pretensions will have a Norrington or claim to be one. If only I could claim that your mother slept with Kenwick Norrington. I could, I suppose, and point to your survival on the journey south as evidence of your being the Norrington."

Erlestoke stared at him speechless.

The king shook his head. "No, that would be too transparent a stratagem. Much better to go with the real Norrington."

"I don't understand you." Erlestoke raked fingers back through long brown hair. "A horde of Aurolani troops are rolling over Muroso, on their way here, and you are contemplating games of power and influence? They will not stop her army."

"No, my son, they won't, but they will give us the troops necessary to do it. You don't seem to understand how stupid some of these people are. They were willing to commit troops and pledge support because the Norrington prophecy guaranteed them a victory. Now they don't know. They are prepared to panic. They will be out of control, and you know precisely where they will fall. Oriosa, which they never would have thought of attacking for fear of angering the Norrington, now is the nation that lost the Norrington. You did not save him, and you are an Oriosan. Crow, gods rot him, is an Oriosan and he did not save him. I did nothing to protect him. They will pour into our nation unless distracted by some other bait. Fighting over who the true Norrington is will occupy them, and support for their candidates can be bought by regiments."

As much as he hated it, Erlestoke had to admit that his father had a point. The nations that were not on the front lines needed to exact a price for the use of their troops and supplies. They would have to be coaxed into giving until the security of their own nations could be threatened, and if the people felt insecure, revolts could topple dynasties. With gold and offers of power, strikes by *sullanciri,* Chytrine could wreak havoc on the alliance raised against her.

"Will there be enough troops to stop Chytrine?"

The king snorted. "I would not know. As you have pointed out, my knowledge of armies is deficient. I am mostly concerned for preserving Oriosa. Either Chytrine will assault our nation, or others will pull it apart. One solution, of course, is for you to lead an army to crush Chytrine."

That stopped the prince short. "What did you just say?"

The king held his hands out to the fire, then rubbed them together. "I believe you heard me. You could raise Oriosa against Chytrine. We would be invincible, with your skill and the determination of our people. You purge our nation of Aurolani forces—I know where all of them are—then you proceed against her. Would you want that command?"

Erlestoke stopped and considered for a moment. An army of Oriosans would be a formidable force indeed. He assumed the nation could provide three regiments of well-trained soldiers, and twice that of irregulars. That would give him nearly ten thousand troops, which would be more than enough to deal Chytrine a crushing blow, especially when delivered to her flank and trapping her army in Muroso and Saporicia.

In his mind's eye he could see the force, see it arrayed in battalion after battalion. Stout infantry in the center of his formation, with heavy and light cavalry on the flanks. At a word, trumpets would blare and the troops would advance. They would join in combat in some summer field, driving the Aurolani troops before them.

He found the image appealing enough that he almost agreed to his father's offer. Something in the older man's smile, however, and the slow ease with which he warmed his hands, warned Erlestoke from being so accepting. He blinked a couple of times, then smiled and remembered something from the Congress of Dragons.

"I would agree, Father, but you would find my price very costly. Still, if you meet it . . ."

The king turned his head and studied his son for a

moment. "And your price is what? My abdication? You wish to possess the crown?"

"No, Highness, just part of it." Erlestoke smiled. "I wish to possess the fragment of the DragonCrown you have under your control."

He expected his request to trigger another flash of fury, but Scrainwood actually appeared to be considering it seriously. While others might have taken heart in this, the prince did not. He suspected it was a sign he'd blundered into a trap his father had long since laid out for him.

"I would do anything for my nation, Erlestoke. Many will contend I have done too much. If you wanted to be king, that I could accept, because I know you would use every means at your disposal to guarantee the safety of Oriosa. I believe you would do this now. My possession of that fragment—which only King Augustus knows of—is my last guarantee for our nation's safety. If a plan is presented to invade Oriosa, I will threaten to deliver that fragment to Chytrine."

"You couldn't."

"If it were the only way to save my nation, I would." The king turned to face his son. "Fortunately, it is *not* the only way. In fact, you have it within your means to guarantee our safety forever, and in exchange, the ruby fragment will be yours."

"Name your bargain."

Scrainwood's voice dropped to a hoarse whisper. "Give me the secret of firedirt and dragonels."

"*What?*"

"Come now, you have spent years at Fortress Draconis. You have commanded dragonel batteries. You use a draconnette. If we had those tools and firedirt, no nation would dare attack us."

"I can't."

"Of course you can. You were loyal to the Draconis Baron, I understand that. He was of the opinion that the secret of firedirt would be used irresponsibly, but these are dire times." The king's voice dropped even lower. "Rumors have it that in Svarskya, Jeranese General Markus Adrogans captured dragonels and a factory for making firedirt. The secret is already in the hands of one nation, a nation that is imperially minded and has a grand leader. If you do not give me the secret, once we defeat Chytrine, we will face a new and even more dangerous menace."

The news about Adrogans was disturbing, but Erlestoke shunted it away. "I cannot give you the secret because I do not know it."

"What? Did the Draconis Baron not trust you? He was jealous of you, wasn't he? He kept the secret to himself because he knew, someday, you would supplant him."

"No, Father, he did not mistrust me. He trusted me further than you ever have." Erlestoke shrugged. "He wanted me to learn, but I put it off for a variety of reasons. The order to teach me was never given, and none of those who know the secret will reveal it unless so ordered by the Draconis Baron."

The king's hands clenched down into tiny balls of bone. "You are a fool. The greatest secret in the world, and you put off learning it."

"As you put off preparing to oppose Chytrine?"

The hands opened slowly as a little laugh rolled from his father's throat. "If that was a mistake, you are compounding it. Your nation will die because of it."

"I'll do my best to see that doesn't happen. One thing, however, Father."

"Yes?"

"I want that fragment of the DragonCrown. We cannot chance Chytrine getting it."

His father's nostrils flared in a sneer. "It is safe. She will not have it." He paused. "Unless you think I would give it to her."

"It doesn't matter what I think, Father. I just know I won't give it to her."

Scrainwood shook his head. "It is safe. I will not be giving it to you."

"And if I feel the need to come get it?"

The king's eyes tightened. "You would rise against me? You would raise an army against me?"

"It would not take much, as those loyal to you are not great in number. Most are like Marsham, and a stern look will mortally wound him."

"I should have seen it. Yes, of course." Scrainwood pointed a quivering finger at him. "Take arms against me and you will rue the day you were born. I will not be done out of my nation. You think I cannot fight, but you are wrong."

The king turned and stormed from the room, leaving the door open behind him. Erlestoke stared after him, then sat back down at the table. He picked up the sword and the stone and shook his head.

"Not nearly sharp enough."

CHAPTER 5

Ultimately, Erlestoke found sharpening his weapons to be unsatisfying in the wake of his father's visit. The visit left him unsettled because of the variety of pictures it painted for him. While he liked the idea of leading an Oriosan army to smash Chytrine, his father left no question that it would have to be a rebel army. No matter how often Erlestoke would deny wanting the throne, his father would always see him as desiring it.

The vices of the father become the frame through which he views his children. Erlestoke shook his head. Even if he *had* known the secret of firedirt, he'd never have entrusted it to his father. *Oriosa would be better off a memory than to give my father that sort of power. His bargaining was a sham to see if I had the secret—he never could bring himself to trust me.*

Like it or not, when leading troops into Oriosa he would have two enemies. Not only would he be fighting Chytrine's forces, but loyalists supporting his father as well. The thought of shedding Oriosan blood in a civil war was not one he wanted to entertain.

His rejection of it led him to darker thoughts, however. If his father could use a fragment of the DragonCrown as a bargaining chip to gain knowledge of firedirt from his son, how would he use it with Chytrine? She might agree to the deal Erlestoke had rejected. In fact, in terms of strategy, it would make perfect sense for Chytrine to arm Oriosa with dragonels and firedirt. The weapons would be useless if the supply of firedirt were cut off, which she could do at any time. Until that point, however, any army marching into Oriosa would get mauled, which was to her benefit.

Just how far his father had gone into the enemy camp Erlestoke could not tell. He'd always had the impression that the king's alliance with Chytrine was informal and quite passive. His father had gathered a great deal of information about the Aurolani troops in his realm and, in an effort to placate old friends like King Augustus of Alcida, had even made some of that information available. Indeed, he had offered to let Erlestoke know where to strike to rid Oriosa of Chytrine's troops.

This indicated he had not gone over to the Aurolani side completely. And his bargaining for firedirt further suggested that the king was uneasy with Chytrine and did not trust her. He could also be playing both ends against the middle, and doubtless was. *And it is being played for* his *benefit, not that of Oriosa, I am certain.*

Erlestoke harbored few illusions about his father and what he was capable of doing, but he also knew the man tended toward passive, subtle manipulations instead of outright action. He actually had subjected Crow to a trial instead of having him murdered outright. While part of that might have been a desire to see Crow humiliated and broken, the simple fact was that his father was not the sort to resort to murder. While he knew that many people detested him, he did not want to give them proof of perfidy.

Many people openly assumed that he'd had his wife, Queen Morandus, murdered. Erlestoke had been sixteen when Nefrai-kesh slew his grandmother and two years later was sent off to Fortress Draconis for the first time, to live with his aunt and the Draconis Baron. His mother would come visit and there, with Ryhope, seemed to find peace. She greatly enjoyed sailing in a small boat and often would spend hours on end laughing, with the wind in her hair and the spray bright on her face.

Erlestoke was not with her on the day she vanished, but he had accompanied her many times before, manning the tiller himself, so the story of how she died rang true. She had been sitting in the bow as the boat sailed along under a light breeze and trailed her left hand in the warm water. Queen Morandus had been singing and while the tillerman did not recognize the song, he said she sounded happy.

One moment she was there, and then the next she flew from the boat, as if yanked out by her hand. There had been no time for a scream, just the abrupt ending of the song. The tillerman brought the boat about immediately and furled the sail. He searched the area, using an oar to keep circling where she went down, but he saw no bubbles, no body, neither cloth nor blood. Those who knew the Crescent Sea said it was possible an emperor shark had taken her, perhaps attracted by the gold glint of her wedding ring, but many common folk assumed the tillerman had blood on his hands and the ring in his pocket.

Her death had hurt Erlestoke greatly, but more so had been his father's indifference to her fate. The prince had wanted to return to Oriosa with an urn of ocean water to memorialize her, but his father refused to allow him to do so. Scrainwood had said he wanted to stay as far away from the sea as possible, and certainly wasn't going to allow a bit of it in his realm, no matter the reason.

The prince also knew that his brother had been deeply affected by their mother's death. Though he was twenty years of age at the time she died, Linchmere didn't pay a visit to Fortress Draconis for five years. When he did come, he spent much of his time morbidly staring out to sea, but refused to see the boat his mother had loved, much less chance a ride in it. Erlestoke understood the latter fear, but not the former. Each year, on the anniversary of his mother's death, he made an offering to Tagothcha, the *weirun* of the sea, to induce him to take good care of his mother's mortal remains. The boat was something she loved, so he made certain it was kept in good repair and found himself idly wondering what had become of it now that Fortress Draconis had fallen.

These thoughts and more cluttered Erlestoke's mind as he donned cold-weather gear, wrapped a scarf around his face, and left the palace. Any Oriosan would have recognized him as a countryman, but likely would not have made him out to be the prince, since his mask was black and relatively unadorned. He wore it in honor of the Freemen fighting in Sarengul and it felt better on his face than his life mask ever had.

Into the snowy streets of Narriz he wandered, intent on losing himself. It was not a difficult task, as the city had grown up organically and haphazardly. Cow paths and goat tracks became meandering roads with buildings hulking on each side. Snow covered everything, but had been churned into brown mush by wagon wheels and hooves, with more dung than dirt to it. He did his best to avoid the big puddles, though the oilskin cloak he wore warded him well against the wet and filth.

He knew enough not to wander down to the docks, for they were a land unto themselves. Erlestoke feared no man in a fair fight, but in the realm of seamen, a landsman like him would never be in a fair fight. He laughed at the idea that some drunken sailor and his crew mates might accomplish what Chytrine's gibberers, dracomorphs, *kryalniri*, and dragons had not, but also knew that such things would amuse the gods, so they might just happen.

He kept to the middle city, back away from the docks, newer than the coastal portion of the town, but older than the estates of merchantmen who had grown wealthy from trade. Though he was a prince, he'd spent much of his adult life among soldiers; therefore, he felt at home among those who were not nobility.

His wandering took him to a large tavern that advertised itself as the Galloping Stallion—and he noted that the signs at the north and west entrances chose different ways to spell that name, neither of them correct. Traffic appeared brisk, and smoke rose from two chimneys, so he entered and took three steps down to the main floor, ducking his head so as not to bump a rafter as he went.

Across the crowded room was a second set of stairs that switched-back to a second floor. People coming in through the north entrance headed for that and up. They looked to be family groups, or slightly better dressed and moneyed than the harder bitten crowd down below. Erlestoke chose to remain on the lower floor, which had shadows enough to grant him the anonymity he craved.

He headed off along the left wall, bearing for the huge hearth in the north wall. To his right, past a tangle of tables, lay the bar, which filled the center of the floor. Benches lined much of the walls, and decorations, such as they were, featured bits of tack, odd animal skins, odder bones, and at least one vylaen head. At least, in the half-light, that's what he made it out to be, but it could have been the head of a bear cub, albeit a strange one, with sharpened ears and a bone spur piercing the right one.

Before he got too far, he felt an iron grip banding his left arm above the elbow. His right hand jerked toward the floor, and the hilt of a dagger he had sheathed on his forearm filled it. He turned to face the person who had grabbed him, using his body to shield the dagger from sight, should its sudden employment be needed.

Resolute's eyes half lidded. "The way you got the knife is good, but had I desired one in your kidney, you'd be thrashing on the floor right now."

"Following me, Resolute?"

The Vorquelf shook his head, then waved his left hand at a small round table in a corner. Though the tavern was crowded, with men standing and crouching here and there, the round table had four stools available, and one halfdrunk ale in a wooden tankard at the spot nearest the corner itself. "I have been here a while, but if you are going to be so careless, perhaps I *should* be following you."

"May I join you?"

"Please."

Erlestoke waited for Resolute to take his place again, then took the seat to the Vorquelf's right, which let him rest his back against a wall. He kept his voice low. "Why am I careless?"

"Multiple reasons. Your blood makes you a target for those who thought you were dead and had planned accordingly."

The prince smiled and waved at a barmaid. He pointed to Resolute's ale and she nodded. "You must be joking. Cabot Marsham is the only person who could dream of succeeding my father were my brother and I dead, and my father would never leave the kingdom in his hands. Moreover, the man would not dare strike at me."

"No, but those who back him might. You know he is weak and can be manipulated. If he were not, your father would not keep him on. While here, Marsham has met with representatives of various noble houses. Those who covet power might have been planning your father's downfall, and your presence means their puppet would no longer be center stage."

The Vorquelf frowned at him. "Why are you looking at me strangely?"

Erlestoke sat back and cleared his throat as the barmaid set his ale down. He tossed her a silver coin and she snatched it up quickly. He sipped the ale, then understood why so little of Resolute's had been drunk.

"I guess what surprises me, Resolute, is your interest in Oriosan politics. Your history being what it is, I'd not thought you interested in much more than your homeland's liberation."

Resolute's face sank into a grimace and he drank some ale. That did nothing to lighten his expression. He glanced at the prince and nodded. "There was a time, Highness, when this was true, but the sword I wear has changed that. Will gave it to me. It is an ancient elven blade named Syverce. It comes from a homeland that no longer exists and is a blade of great consequence. Because it accepts me I know I have a greater duty than just the liberation of my homeland. The scourge that is Chytrine must be ended, and having you writhing in a pool of blood with an assassin's knife in your back will be a great comfort to the enemy."

The Oriosan marveled that Resolute's broad shoulders remained square despite the obvious pressure he felt himself under. "It's not really Oriosan assassins you are worried about, is it? Do you think Chytrine has agents here?"

"I *know* she has agents here. So does everyone else." Resolute laughed wryly and swung his head to survey the crowd. "There are men here who would sell their children for the coppers off a dead man's eyes, so taking foreign gold in exchange for information is nothing. They do not worry me as much, though, as the ordinary folks."

Erlestoke looked around. He saw nothing unusual in the tavern's clientele. They might be a bit rough around the edges—though the man who vomited in a bucket that had been used to bring him beer did wipe his mouth on his sleeve with élan. To the prince's eye they seemed quite normal, with men predominant, a few Vorquelves like Resolute, and two urZrethi women huddled nearest the fire. They had shifted the shape of their faces to make themselves purely hideous, which stopped advances by anyone on the upright side of blind drunkenness.

"I don't see the threat here."

"You will, once word is out. It will ooze from the confidential councils." Resolute's voice remained low. "The first news will be almost happenstance, reporting our arrival and the lack of our friend's presence. I have little doubt the crowns will decide to say he's remained on Vael. Soon enough, though, a chance remark will be overheard, or someone will decide his path to power benefits from the revelation of the death. When word gets out, hope will die for these people. Some will rally to fight, some will lose all heart, and others will be angry. Their fury will be directed against you and Crow, even Princess Alexia and me."

Erlestoke started to deny that vision, then looked at the various faces around the room again. Many were happy, laughing and almost carefree, but others were wary and watchful. Some were even nervous. The same nervousness could spark a fight because of a chance remark, or an innocent bump. The death of the Norrington could be the sort of provocation that might motivate a crowd to act with violent intent.

"Again, I bow to your wisdom." Erlestoke sipped ale to wash the sour taste from his mouth. "So, you've come here to watch men and gauge their temperament?"

"No, that is merely a pastime." The Vorquelf looked up and his eyes brightened. "I came for quarry and here it is."

Before he'd finished speaking, Resolute was up and out of his chair. He slipped behind another figure, one almost as tall as he, wearing a dark cloak. Though Resolute crowded in tight behind the person, Erlestoke did catch the flash of a dagger pressed to the back of the cloak. *Right over where the kidney would be on a man.*

The cloaked figure bowed his head, then turned and joined them at the table. Resolute snapped something in Elvish and the other Vorquelf male, with long black hair and bright blue eyes, took a chair that left his back open to the rest of the common room.

Resolute sat again and smiled coldly. "You recall I said everyone had agents here?"

"I do."

"Well, this one belongs to General Markus Adrogans." The Vorquelf's silver eyes sharpened. "I've been waiting for him, because we need to have a good long chat."

CHAPTER 6

King Scrainwood had found the conversation with his son utterly dissatisfactory. He realized that the chances of his son's turning the secret of firedirt over to him had been slender, but to learn that he did not even possess it had been a vast disappointment. Scrainwood could not discount the idea that Chytrine would eventually betray him, despite her having made him a *sullanciri*. He would have done the same thing in her place, so he had to plan against that eventuality. His possessing the secret of firedirt would have given her pause and would have also given him the power to hold Erlestoke at bay. Now those chances for survival had been squandered by a son who had better things to do than to learn the greatest military secret in the world.

As he wandered in the suite of rooms on the estate he had borrowed from the Oriosan merchant Playfair, Scrainwood entertained no illusions about Chytrine's treachery. He'd seen for himself what she had caused to be done to the Azure Spider. The man who had once been a legendary thief, and had actually stolen a fragment of the DragonCrown from

Jerana, had been transformed into an arachnomorph. She'd done it to punish him for losing that same fragment to Princess Alexia and her coterie. The Azure Spider had been made into a *sullanciri* and had died a parody of what he had once been.

Scrainwood, too, had been made into a *sullanciri*, though she had not told him what his powers were, and he felt not the least bit different as a result of the transformation. Chytrine had hinted at his being her secret weapon, and had urged him to continue doing what he had done for decades since she'd had his mother slain. The implication was clear: if he failed, he would be slain, and his being a *sullanciri* would not matter one way or another in that regard.

He stopped to ponder the irony of his seeking a way ultimately to render Chytrine powerless when all the crowned heads in the city would have thought such a bold plan was quite beyond his grasp. They saw the Northern Empress as a threat to their nations, but he knew her as a far more personal one. They would not have put his doing anything to save his nation past him, yet they underestimated what he would do to save himself.

Either I find a way to stop her, or I make myself so useful to her that she will not discard me. He laughed sharply at that last idea. *She* will *discard me, but if she hesitates, I gain more time to find a way to destroy her.*

As the echoes of his laugh died, a tiny rap came on the door. Before he could call out, it cracked and Cabot Marsham poked his head into the room. "Highness, you have a visitor."

Scrainwood's nostrils flared. "Do I look as if I wish to receive a visitor?"

"No, Highness, but . . ."

The king gave him a stare that by all rights should have caused his skull to explode. That the man did not immediately retreat suggested the visitor was of some import. *There can be only two people who warrant such attention.*

Scrainwood hesitated for only a moment, then nodded. "Send the witch in."

Marsham just opened the door more widely and Grand Duchess Tatyana of Okrannel entered. Swathed in winter clothing, the ancient crone appeared to be an oversize doll of careless manufacture. He would have expected her to collapse at any moment beneath the weight of her costume, but the fire burning in her ice-blue eyes hinted at boundless energy.

Scrainwood forced a smile. "A pleasure as always, Grand Duchess."

"Not even your odious aide lies that well, Highness." Tatyana turned, looked at Marsham, and the man vanished. The door clicked shut behind him. "He is a toad, that one, and ambitious."

"I know. Like a toad, he will get all puffed up, attract attention to himself, and be slain." Curling his fingers in toward his palm, Scrainwood inspected the nails on his right hand. "It must be something of consequence that brings you here on such a night."

"Indeed, Highness." Tatyana moved to one of two chairs positioned before the fireplace. The golden highlights washing over her face did nothing to soften its aspect. "Have you more of that wine you offered me in Yslin?"

"I do. You truly think our discussion merits it?"

"I hope you will think so, Highness."

"I am dubious." Scrainwood crossed to a sideboard and poured two crystal goblets of wine, then brought one to her. "I half expect to have you say that now your nation is liberated, you will sever all ties with me and that our business of the past is concluded."

Tatyana took the wine and shook her head. "No, Highness, now is the time when our alliance needs to be strengthened. While it is true that my nation has been freed from Aurolani oppression, there is no guarantee that Chytrine will not bring more troops to bear on it and drive

Marcus Adrogans away. What we have won so quickly, we can lose just as quickly."

Scrainwood frowned as he sipped his wine, but the vintage was good enough to ease his expression. "I will admit to being confused, Duchess. Perhaps you would enlighten me as to how you see the current situation."

The crone sat back and sipped her wine contentedly, then gave him a smile that contained too much superiority to make him feel confident. "The situation is simple, Highness. My agents have been in Okrannel for years, scouting, noting things, and more of them have traveled the country in the wake of Adrogans' army. What I have learned is disturbing. It would appear that, over the last quarter century, Chytrine has been using Okrannel as a breadbasket. There have been good harvests and the bulk of the foodstuffs have been heading into Aurolan to allow her to build up her army. It is also supposed that much of it has gone to Vorquellyn and has enabled her to create these new creatures, the *kryalniri*. They are supplanting the vylaens and are quite formidable."

"So I have heard."

"In my councils we have supposed she may well have more creatures, more horrible creatures, just waiting to be unleashed. And she is likely to have the same in such numbers that she can push back into Okrannel at will."

Scrainwood swirled the wine in his goblet. "If that is true, we are all doomed."

"Not if we play things as carefully as you have in the past." She sat forward again. "Sebcia and Muroso have fallen, or will, shortly. The latter has cost her much in resources, primarily because of the intervention of a dragon. Saporicia, we can suppose, will further bleed her of troops and supplies, but we both know the Saporicians have never truly had the belly for fighting."

The king nodded. "They sent no troops to help liberate Okrannel."

Tatyana's eyes blazed. "Exactly."

Scrainwood snorted. "Neither did Oriosa."

The Okrans noble half bowed her head, but her smile did not diminish in the least. "But you sent the Norrington, Highness. He was worth more than all the regiments you could have mustered."

"Neatly said, Duchess." Scrainwood sipped more wine, then moved closer to the fire. He'd not felt cold until she entered the room. "So, your supposition is that Chytrine's army will pour through Saporicia, too?"

"Yes, and that will bring her to Alcida. Augustus is the key here, and you are his friend. He knows and trusts my niece, Alexia, and will let her lead the armies that he will gather." She set her goblet down on the spindly table at her left hand. "Among those assembled here, only Augustus and Queen Carus are capable of bringing together the nations that will be needed to destroy Chytrine. Moreover, Saporicia is a trap. With Oriosa and Bokagul to the east and Loquellyn to the northwest, Chytrine's troops will be limited in their ability to move. Her supply lines will be stretched. Her troops will be vulnerable."

He nodded. "She will be bled and keep funneling troops into Saporicia, which means she will not be bringing them to bear on Okrannel. You have a chance to fortify your nation against her return."

"You anticipate me."

"But what of the Adrogans question, Duchess?"

Tatyana's head came up, and she appeared puzzled, which was the first time Scrainwood had seen that expression on her face. "He has taken Okrannel. He liberated it. He shall be rewarded and glorified."

"Ah, but adding Okrannel to a Jeranese empire would bring him more glory, would it not?" The king smiled as her face darkened. "Have you not heard the rumor that Adrogans now possesses the secret of the dragonel? With it he can carve an empire. Valicia and Gurol will have to defend against that possibility, meaning Alcida and our alliance can abandon all hope of aid from the west."

He watched her struggle to regain her composure. So focused had she been on the freeing of her nation that she never paused to imagine that the liberator might not want to give it up. "If such rumors prove true, it would be most dire indeed. It could well and truly mean the end of the alliance. It would be the end of everything."

"Only if Adrogans were to turn the weapons against us and not Chytrine."

Tatyana snorted. "You have met him. He is vain and has a sense of himself that would elevate him above all others. Can you imagine he will not use those weapons against us?"

The king returned to the sideboard and refilled his goblet. "I can imagine many things, Duchess. I imagine you came here to ask me to aid you in developing a strategy that will draw Chytrine's troops further south. As you are one of those who think I am Chytrine's creature, you were also prepared to offer me something of import in exchange for my cooperation. You have no troops to coerce me into doing what you wish. What do you have to offer?"

She smiled in a way that made his flesh crawl. "I offer Oriosa a chance at redemption."

Her words surprised Scrainwood. "If you can do that, those who have judged you a witch have sorely underestimated you. Your powers would rival those of Chytrine herself."

"I make no such claims, but I can offer you redemption, you and your nation." She took up her goblet again and studied it as firelight flickered through the ruby depths of the wine. "It is part of the prophecy, all woven together. You see, in the time before my grandnephew died at Fortress Draconis, you and he had many discussions of things of great import. You both were aware that the war would not be won then, which is why you chose not to accompany Lord Norrington to the north. It is why you sought to rescue the sword Temmer from Bosleigh Norrington. My nephew Kirill, you see, was possessed of much the same skills at prophecy that I am, and he knew you were the key to Chytrine's defeat. After all, Norrington is just a location patronymic, and as the King of Oriosa you have every right to claim it. You are the Norrington, sire, or your son is."

She held up a finger to forestall comment. "So, at the risk of your own safety, to prepare the trap that would destroy Chytrine, you endured decades of abuse and doubt. You confided in no one, but you did your part. You let Chytrine scout from your nation, but you told others of her strength. It was the hardest thing you have ever done, being true to the word you gave Kirill before his death. You were true, however, and because of it Chytrine will be defeated. Your role will be revealed. As a sign of the veracity of this alliance, the document that betrothed the infant Alexia to your son Erlestoke shall be revealed and our dynasties shall be united. The two nations that saved the world shall be as one, and the glory of both shall be restored."

The sheer audacity of her plan astounded him, and yet he saw it could easily work. As a lie it was grand, and with a minor amount of document fabrication, the evidence to support it would be irrefutable. The traitor Hawkins had been destroyed by songs, and the hero Crow had been made by them, so buying bards and having them deliver the tale to the common folk would sway them. In the world's relief at Chytrine's destruction, many a hero would be exalted, and Scrainwood could easily be among them as the one who did what had to be done to save the world.

"It is a bold plan, Duchess, and brilliant, I must say that." Scrainwood nodded slowly, then brought the decanter over to her and topped off her wine. "As presented, there really is little for me to lose. Letting Saporicia become a battleground saves my nation from the same. If, by some mischance, your vision of a victorious future is in error, where the battles are fought will matter little. There is no reason I should not agree."

She sipped and closed her eyes as she savored. Her face

did not become pleasant, but just a bit less forbidding. "Then we have a pact?"

"With a condition."

"That being?"

"You will have to be the one to raise the question of Adrogans' possession of dragonels. You will have to push to have the secret shared. I cannot. I think if you were to suggest that the rumor has been heard, and the sharing will let us meet Chytrine as equals, the message will be heard best. If the rumor is not true, no harm done, for the disappointment will be folded into determination to fight harder. And if it is true, then we bargain such that dragonels shall be given to those troops who come to fight."

She nodded slowly and sipped again. "Done and done. I do find that rumor disturbing. Your method of handling it will bring the truth to light. If you were to bring it up, duplicity would be suspected and the damage would be done."

"We are agreed." Scrainwood slowly smiled. "And do not think I have missed your ulterior motive."

Tatyana's head came up. "What do you mean, Highness?"

"The sealing of our dynasties. You expect Oriosan gold to be invested in the rebuilding of Okrannel."

"It would be a hope, yes."

"Good, then as we liberate pieces of Saporicia from the Aurolani, perhaps we need an international zone in the south, including the port city of Sanges. It would facilitate trade between our nations if I had an ocean port."

"That would require the death of the Saporician royal house since they would never agree to it."

"Certainly whoever the liberators raised to lead the nation in the aftermath of that tragedy would happily grant such a boon to his allies."

The old woman nodded. "If Chytrine does not manage it, there are ways it can be handled."

"I shall check the lineage and perhaps find a suitable

family branch with a daughter to marry to Linchmere. It would make things tidy."

"Indeed, it would." Tatyana tossed her wine off with the gusto of a gutter-whore in a dockside tavern. "Your hospitality and time are always appreciated, Highness."

"Pity you have to leave so soon, Duchess."

She stood and laughed at his remark. "Such sincerity cloaking a lie. Will they never realize you are far more dangerous than Chytrine could ever be?"

He smiled. "No, they will not. It is just as well. It allows them to sleep."

"Then, while they sleep, I shall be about my work." Tatyana bowed her head to him. "Fare well, King Scrainwood. Together we shall guarantee a future for the world that will suit us perfectly."

CHAPTER 7

Prince Erlestoke regarded the Vorquelf sitting across from him. Smaller than Resolute and slight of build, he still had the sharp features of an elf, including the pointed tips of ears rising through a curtain of fine black hair. His intensely blue eyes had no pupils, which made his glance a bit unnerving, though less so than Resolute's. Erlestoke saw no tattoos, but the Vorquelf wore long sleeves and had his tunic laced up tight beneath a thick sheepskin coat. He even wore gloves, so the prince couldn't see if he sported rings or other jewelry.

Resolute hissed at him in Elvish, and Erlestoke knew enough to catch some words. The tone in Resolute's voice filled in more, leaving Erlestoke with the impression that Resolute was full of both fury and contempt for his companion. The other elf kept his face composed, betraying no emotion, then slowly shook his head and spoke carefully enough that Erlestoke could understand him clearly.

"I've not sought to hide from you, Resolute. Upon my arrival in Narriz, which was only yesterday, I immediately joined our brethren here. I asked after you, but was told

·you had no congress with them. I did not seek you out, but I do not shrink from you either."

Resolute snorted, then slowed his Elvish speech. "Do you still call yourself Banausic?"

"It seems fitting, still, for I am ever practical."

"You served Chytrine once. I have not forgotten."

"Nor have I, but I have a better master now." The Vorquelf lifted his chin. "I have served Adrogans well. I liaised between the Nalisk Rangers and the Blackfeathers. I was with them, ahead of the army, from the Highlands to Svarskya. I gave them no cause for complaint."

Resolute's eyes narrowed, but he said nothing.

Erlestoke took the opportunity to ask a question. "I've heard a rumor that Adrogans has the secret of firedirt. Is it true?"

Banausic regarded him coldly. "That would be no business of yours."

Resolute's hand immediately closed on Banausic's right forearm and squeezed. "It is business of ours, so you will answer the question."

The other Vorquelf tried to keep his face impassive, but pain tightened his eyes. "Very well. We sailed, the lot of us, on the night Svarskya fell. We sailed past the hulk of a ship and saw that dragonels were being recovered from it. I believe it was a workshop where firedirt was made. I would know more, but we were sent forth quickly, and Tagothcha sped us here with uncommon alacrity."

Erlestoke nodded to Resolute, and his companion relaxed his grip, but did not remove his hand from Banausic's arm. "How deadly was the battle? In what condition are Adrogans' troops?"

"Not nearly as torn up as they should be. Adrogans planned and executed the campaign brilliantly, but the Aurolani forces barely opposed him. At every turn when we should have paid mightily, we won through without much trouble. At first we thought this was due to Nefrai-kesh's absence, but he was there at the defense of Svarskya. It is thought many of his troops and dragonels were called off to the battle for Sebcia, since we were not expected to be at Svarskya so quickly. But even firedirt was poorly employed. Adrogans' troops are in very good shape and fully capable of launching a new campaign."

Erlestoke nodded and glanced at Resolute. "With dragonels he could create an empire for himself. We know this will be suggested in the councils, splitting them. Do you think this is why Chytrine let him have Svarskya so easily?"

Before Resolute could answer, Banausic tapped a finger against the tabletop. "Fear of that is why Adrogans swore those of us he sent here to secrecy. He said that he did not know if it was a trick by Chytrine, but we were to listen for such rumors. He will not admit to having firedirt or dragonels for he does not want the alliance shattered."

Resolute nodded slowly. "A wise man, though wise in which way, I wonder? An army will let him build an empire, or will let him take Chytrine's gift and wreak havoc with it against her. Which way will he go?"

Banausic shrugged. "I am no witch to know his mind, but I would bet on the latter case. He is a proud man, and the very idea that Chytrine gave him Svarskya rankles. He has liberated Okrannel, true, but I think he would like to be known as the one who destroyed Chytrine."

The prince drank some more ale and let the bitter, woody fluid sour his mouth before swallowing. He shivered, then looked at Resolute. "Why do I get the feeling that this war is going to come down to people choosing to do whatever they want while the crowns dither?"

"Because you think clearly." The silver-eyed Vorquelf's nostrils flared. "You have an *arcanslata* to communicate with Adrogans?"

"Yes."

"Good. You will allow me to use it when I request."

Banausic hesitated for a moment, then shrugged. "As you desire. Anything else?"

"Aside from telling me what you tell him?" Contempt

seeped back into Resolute's words. "When I spared your life in Okrannel, you promised to share with me what you saw on Vorquellyn."

"Svoin had not yet fallen, then you were called away."

"So you shall make good on your promise. Now."

"Here?" Banausic lowered his voice and hunched forward. "What I have to say is not meant for other ears."

Resolute gave him a bone-chilling stare. "The prince has already been brought into our circle. Look about. Who will hear you? Do you think these people understand what we are saying?"

The black-haired Vorquelf slowly nodded. "In the last quarter century I have been brought to Vorquellyn three times. It is a horrible place now—not the place we lost, but a harsh land, as if the entire island had been swept by fire, then seeded with weeds. Foul bracken overgrows everything, save where debris-choked rivers have backed up into stagnant fens. There are wildlands where creatures of unspeakable aspects roam. Their voices shatter the night and their blood stains the few streets that can be passed. Where beauty and serenity once reigned, now the flash of claw, the rending of fang, and shrieks of pain are the norm."

While the words Banausic spoke were terrible enough, the tone of his voice stained them with agony. Erlestoke felt a lump rising in his own throat as the Vorquelf's voice shrank. In his words the prince caught flashes of Oriosa's future if Chytrine were not stopped.

Resolute remained unmoved. "Your sentimentality is touching, but of little use to me. What was it you felt important about your sojourns home?"

"It is not my home. It is not any of our homes." Banausic's voice deepened angrily. "My first trip came after the last war, after Svoin fell. Many of us were taken to Vorquellyn, though family were left behind so we would be compliant. On that journey many of us were roughly used. Before the retreat, many places were sealed with great wards, including the *coriiesci*. Do you know what one is?"

Erlestoke shook his head. "I've never heard the term before."

Banausic tapped a finger beneath his own right eye. "Vorquelves have eyes all of a color because we have not been bound to our homeland. We have the eyes of children, despite our age. At some point during our adolescence—which starts as young as yours, but might continue until we have seen fifty winters—we are brought to a *coriiesci* and there bound to the homeland in a ritual. It is possible that the land will reject us, but such rejection is the stuff of legend."

"You waste words, Banausic." Resolute shook his head. "The *coriiesci* are spiritual centers. You would consider them temples, but they are more—and, perhaps, less. The rituals that bind us take place in the courtyard before the main building. Once one is bound, the building is open to him. Therein we learn the consequences of our binding, what our role will be."

"Yes, it is as Resolute says." The blue-eyed Vorquelf frowned. "On that first trip, Chytrine was present and there, in the courtyard of Saslynnae's largest *coriiesci*, I watched her make the Croquelf Winfellis into the *sullanciri* Quiarsca. She also sought to bind her to Vorquellyn, but that ritual failed. I do not know why, save that Winfellis had been bound to Croquellyn."

Erlestoke nodded. "She rules the island?"

"To the best of my knowledge, as Chytrine's puppet, yes. She also oversees a variety of programs for the Aurolani—for, you see, witnessing her transformation was not the only reason we were taken there. Many of us were charged with the duty of seeking the DragonCrown fragment that had been hidden there, though our inability to penetrate the sealed *coriiesci* hampered us. Others, those with white hair, were taken off to duties more foul."

The Vorquelf hesitated. "You have seen the *kryalniri*?"

The two of them nodded.

"I was told of matings between Vorquelves and vylaens. Those children gotten on our females by vylaens did not thrive, though the opposite was not true. Some were compelled to couple through sorcery, others did not care, and yet others did so willingly. As I said, I was exempted, perhaps because of my hair color, or some other factor. After a year or so, I was returned to Svoin, but my snow-maned companions never did return."

"Stallions to cover enemy mares."

Banausic shot Resolute a venomous glance. "You cannot judge them. Were you there, you would have been drained to produce whole armies."

"And I would have found a way to slay them all."

"Perhaps you would, Resolute, but few have your focus." Banausic shrugged and looked down at his hands. "It mattered not, for the second time I was taken to Vorquellyn came a decade and a half later. Saslynnae had changed a bit—I saw a certain amount of destruction around the harbor. Whole blocks had been leveled, save for a *coriiesci*. There clearly had been fighting, but whether an internal struggle or invasion, I do not know."

Resolute frowned. "What kind of damage? Dragonels? Dragons? Magick?"

"Not dragonels. Magick, yes, but its nature I do not know."

Erlestoke shrugged. "I never heard of anything or anyone going to Vorquellyn."

"Nor I. A mutiny, perhaps, brutally repressed. Go on with your tale."

"Of course. The weather was bitter. Fitting, perhaps, for what Chytrine attempted failed bitterly. At the central *coriiesci*, where she had made Quiarsca, she attempted to bind one of the *kryalniri* to Vorquellyn. Neskartu took the position of father and Quiarsca of mother. They stood proudly on their plinths. The cold wind tugged at Quiarsca's red gown, and her golden hair streamed back like flames. Even Neskartu let his form waver as if the breeze could touch him. Those of us who had been brought there were placed around the depression in which the *kryalniri* waited.

Usually, Prince Erlestoke, the witnesses who participate are limited to parents and four friends or family members—with substitutions allowed if family or parents are not available. Chytrine used a full dozen of us, according her creature great honor.

"The ritual went as expected, with the balances of energies maintained, the right words spoken, and the offerings made correctly. As happens, a shell of blue energy flooded the bowl as if the seep from a cool spring. It rose to a dome, which became opaque, then dissolved as might a mist."

Banausic's eyes narrowed. "I expected to see the *kryalniri* with adult's eyes, but Vorquellyn had rejected her. As the mist evaporated, she shrank, crippled, with limbs twisted and knotted, much as that man in the corner there."

Erlestoke turned and looked over by the fireplace. An old man huddled near the fire. Arthritis had so swollen his finger joints and twisted his hands that his fingers could not curl in to touch his palms, but shot off at a sharp angle. When he went to take a taste of his ale, he had to grab the tankard with both hands, and clearly could only lift it so far, because of pain in his elbows and shoulders. A staff rested against the wall behind him and Erlestoke did not want to watch him struggle to rise or walk.

"As you can imagine, Chytrine's rage towered above the storms rolling in. She tried the binding twice more, with similar results, so that project was abandoned."

The prince nodded. "She wanted them bound so she could open the *coriiesci*?"

"That, yes, as well as to complete her domination of Vorquellyn."

Resolute smiled slowly. "Vorquellyn resists her. Good."

"I don't know whether it is Vorquellyn or the prophecy."

"What do you mean?"

Banausic sighed. "The last time I was there was seven years ago. We were taken to Saslynnae and the main *coriiesci* again. The city had been cleaned up quite a bit.

Banners had been hung, fountains repaired, and flowering plants again overflowed from public garden plots and window boxes. There was the air of a festival about things, and we were even given fine clothes to wear.

"Two dozen of us ringed the bowl, with Nefrai-kesh and Myrall'mara on the parental plinths. Chytrine herself led a young female with eyes of silver like yours, Resolute, into the bowl. The empress kissed her on both cheeks, then announced to all of us that Isaura was the daughter who had been born to her on Vorquellyn."

The black-haired Vorquelf grabbed Resolute's forearm. "That time the ritual worked. I think the participation of a Norrington defeated the prophecy, for the girl emerged with adult eyes. Even though my stomach twisted in on itself at this victory, I could not help but smile because she was so proud."

Resolute's left hand tightened into a fist. "Describe the woman."

"Slender and tall, with white hair and your eyes. Obviously a Vorquelf, but different as well. She was bound to the land, though. I saw it."

The Oriosan prince frowned. "White hair, slender . . , she could be the one described by Alexia as being borne away from Navval on a dragon."

"Yes, the one who saved Will's life." Resolute ran a hand over his jaw. "So did the presence of a Norrington allow her to be bound to Vorquellyn, or did her future role as the savior of the one who would redeem Vorquellyn cause the land to accept her? Or, is it some combination of both, with Nefrai-kesh playing his own game?"

Erlestoke shivered as an icy snake slithered down his spine. "I don't know which of those I dislike the most."

"Hate them all or none, it doesn't matter." Resolute looked at Banausic. "Was she able to open the *coriiesci*?"

"Not that I saw. I suspect her mother of not wanting to risk her in case the magicks sealing it could hurt her. That was the impression I gained, in any event. The land resists

Chytrine yet." Banausic smiled. "Is it not as I promised you? I told you I had important information."

Resolute opened his mouth to say something, but closed it and simply nodded. Then he added, "What you have said is indeed of value. You will tell no one else what you have told me. No one, do you understand?"

"I shall not say a word, but there are others who know. Others who were there might speak."

"And admit they were in Chytrine's service? I doubt they would be so foolish. If you hear any such idiots, mark them and tell me."

Banausic's head came up and a defiant expression slid onto his face. "You are now the master of Vorquelves?"

Faster than a snake could have struck, Resolute grabbed Banausic's throat. "No, I am just *your* master. What you have told me is of value, and you shall be of value again. Your words confirm that our homeland *can* be redeemed. In the future, you and I will see that it is. Defy me and jeopardize that future, and you doom yourself."

CHAPTER 8

Kerrigan rubbed his hands together. While there were countless spells he could have used to warm them, he opted for mere friction. Though he had been on Vael for barely half a week, in those five days he had learned much that caused him to reevaluate his life and the way he saw magick. It shifted his view of everything, at the same time both unsettling and pleasing him.

First and foremost he saw how Vilwan had hobbled itself and its practitioners. Kirûn had been such a threat that the wizards had to reassure the lords of the world they would cut their power back, or be destroyed. And it was no coincidence that the Murosan Academy's magicians learned early how to duel. They likely had begun training as a force to counter what had been seen as a Vilwanese threat.

Kerrigan imagined that the Grand Master who had followed the first DragonCrown War had fully intended for the most responsible of human mages to be able to realize their full power, if only in secret. The difficulty was that if spells and methods were not taught early, the ability to pick them up later might not be successful. Kerrigan and the others he had trained with had clearly been schooled under other methods, but even out of a group of thirty or so—at best it seemed there were thirty of them—only he managed to excel.

He did wonder if Rymramoch's description of how the energy to cast magick worked was something the people of Vilwan had ever known. Instead of tapping the river, they drew on their own personal strength to catalyze the ambient magickal energy they absorbed. Under Rym's instruction, Kerrigan learned to use his personal energy to open a link to the grand flow of magick. It took so little energy to do it that he rarely felt tired even after long hours of working spell after spell.

But using such energy required care. It would be simple for him to tap the flow to refresh himself or even warm his hands. The difficulty was that flesh was frail, but the human capacity for feeling the power infinite. A moment's flagging of attention while warming his hands would burn them off. That was the reason spells had been shaped, to define and limit the energy flows, as well as give the magician something on which to concentrate.

Spells were a means of mental discipline, and Kerrigan had been subjected to mental discipline all his life. He finally saw what Orla had been trying to teach him before she died. On Vilwan Kerrigan had been a brilliant *arcanorium* wizard. In the peace and solitude of his study, given the right materials and enough time, he could work miracles. Even before he had set out on his adventures, he likely had been the most powerful human mage on the face of the earth.

But that power counted for nothing because I could not apply it where it was needed. A war was the antithesis of an *arcanorium.* While laboring in Orla's shadow he had done little to fight the enemy effectively. Even after her death, his efforts had been meager. He used simple spells to great effect, but until the siege of Navval, he still had been more scholar than warrior. *And, even there, I experimented more than I fought.*

Kerrigan looked up around the circular chamber. It appeared to have been formed naturally, but there was enough of a taint of dracomagick present that he could not be certain it hadn't been shaped specifically for its current purpose. The floor had been finished with concentric circles of white and black marble, and he stood at the centermost circle. The significance of his being on the bull's-eye was not lost upon him.

Four thralls stood in the room along the walls. The scaled dracomorphs topped eight feet in height and rippled with muscle. In their next stage of life they would grow thicker armor, with spikes sprouting, their muzzles jutting, and intelligence brightening their eyes. While capable of speech, they were not capable of much thought, and performed all manner of menial services for their elder brethren.

Rymramoch, in a scarlet robe, stood beside the one at the east side of the room. Bok, malachite-fleshed and still quite hirsute, crouched beside him. The urZrethi no longer acted like the animal he had appeared to be when Kerrigan first met him. He did, however, remain taciturn and often squatted, adopting a posture he had come to find comfortable in his years as Rym's aide.

Kerrigan had intended to nod to indicate his readiness, but before he could, the first thrall raised a hand and threw a melon-sized stone at Kerrigan's head. Because of magicks worked on him by the Vilwanese, the young mage knew the stone wouldn't hurt him. The purpose of the exercise, however, was not to test the strength of the dragonbone armor that would rise through his skin to protect him, but to see if he could prevent that spell's invocation through other means.

The young mage cast quickly. His first spell surrounded him in a sphere of energy that tinged his vision blue. That first stone, and two more that had been thrown right after, blazed like gold in his vision. A little trail of sparks followed them even as a duller gold image preceded them, allowing Kerrigan to see where they would travel. He became instantly aware that one would miss, while the others were on target.

He drew on the river of magick and cast another spell—one he knew intimately. With barely a thought he reached out and deflected the stones heading for him, so that they would travel wide. He did the same with two more, then bent his mind to linking with all the stones. He grabbed them but did not stop them. Instead he tethered them to himself and drew them into an orbit around him.

Another trio of stones came in, and he spun them into orbit as well. Some he sped up, others he slowed down, nudging them all until they lined up together. Another spell surrounded them, compressing them and heating them until the stone melted. He tightened the spell, using more energy to do so, and could feel the heat coming off the rock. Tighter he drew the spell, until the molten stone had been shaped into a large black ball.

Kerrigan would have smiled and been satisfied with himself, for what he had done was impressive, but he had absorbed the harsh lessons of his adventures. As he began to slow the sphere's orbit, another smaller stone sped in at him. In its wake came a nasty combat spell. If the stone hit him, the dragonbone armor would manifest, preventing him from casting any spell to deflect the combat spell. If he somehow stopped the armor, the hurt done by the stone would probably be enough to destroy the concentration needed for the defensive spell.

In a split second he could feel panic rise, but he shoved it away and acted, for failure to act guaranteed failure. With a moment's concentration he flicked a last thought at the spell surrounding the sphere, then quickened the orbit to interpose the ball between him and the incoming spell. The rock passed beneath it, heading straight for his middle. Another thought, a momentary search for a spell, then a quick smile.

Kerrigan twisted his body and the stone passed harmlessly by.

The spell that had been coming at him hit the sphere with full force. Little blue tendrils of lightninglike energy played over it, igniting little pinpricks of fire here and there. Had it hit Kerrigan, it would not have sprouted flames, but instead inflamed his nerves to a degree that he would have felt as if on fire. The spell vented itself on the sphere, then dissipated.

The manikin that was Rymramoch applauded politely. "Very well done, Kerrigan."

The young mage shrugged. "It wasn't that hard to trick your spell into believing the ball was me. I just added some things that made it share the most likely elements that you used for picking me out as a target."

Rym nodded, then gestured, and the ball came floating to his hand. "I know what you did, and that was quick thinking. Better yet, however, was the way you turned aside from the stone. Magick is not always the answer."

"So I have learned, Master."

"How are you feeling?"

Kerrigan considered for a moment, then nodded. "Good. I am not nearly as tired as I would have been had I attempted any of this back on Vilwan. Controlling the flow is more difficult than tapping it. Orla said there was a fast route to power, and that Neskartu was teaching that path to his students. Would I be wrong if I thought that meant they had no discipline?"

"They clearly have some, Kerrigan, but Neskartu was not concerned about their survival. He made them into living weapons—much as I think the Vilwanese intended you to be. The difference is that Neskartu's disciples embraced the idea willingly. Perhaps they did not understand the full consequences of their action." The puppet hesitated. "Did I say something wrong?"

Kerrigan shivered. "Orla said I had been *forged,* that my

destiny had been forged. You think they wanted to make me into a weapon to use against Chytrine?"

The puppet canted its head. "Look at your age; think about the special group of children you were part of. I think they wanted many weapons, but you were the best. You were even better than they could have hoped, and in you perhaps they saw a return to their former glory. Perhaps they saw a chance to have a Kirûn they could control. I do not know."

"A Kirûn they could control?" Kerrigan looked down at his hands and shifted his shoulders as another shiver ran the length of him. "They saw me as a thing, not a living being."

"I am certain that is the right of it." Rym tucked the ball under his right arm, then waved Kerrigan forward with his left. "Walk with me and I shall explain some things to you."

The youth looked up. "I'm not sure walking is going to make me feel better about people who thought they could shape me the way I shaped that stone."

Rym's laughter did little to ease the tightness around Kerrigan's heart. "Not my intention. Your masters were fools, clearly, but they provided you to me. I will not thank them for that, but instead be grateful for the opportunity we now have to undo things that should have been undone centuries ago."

Kerrigan fell in beside the puppet as they left the chamber. Bok followed a step behind, and after him came the thralls. The company walked down a narrow corridor leading to a grand gallery. Rym dismissed the thralls with a wave, then began the trek back to Kerrigan's quarters at a leisurely pace.

"What is it you know of Yrulph Kirûn, Kerrigan?"

"He was evil. He created the DragonCrown and died before he could take over the world."

Bok gave throat to a gravelly chuckle. "It would not have pleased him to be reduced so."

The puppet nodded. "I shall trust your judgment in

that matter, Bok. His easy dismissal is more an indictment than the words used to describe him. I did not know him, Kerrigan. I was not an intimate of his as Bok was, but I did hear him speak. I know of the situation that surrounded the creation of the DragonCrown."

Rym gestured with his red-leather-sheathed left hand toward the open side of the gallery. "Vael was once Vareshagul. You know dragons destroyed it because it was home to the urZrethi and they were working to free the Oromise from the depths of the earth where we entombed them. The place contained the deepest delvings of the urZrethi and down there, in the darkest bowels of the planet, we yet patrol against the return of the Oromise.

"You know little of the lives of dragons, but you have seen thralls and dracomorphs. They are the midlife stages of our being. Before that we are animals—fearsome animals and keen hunters. During our life cycle we enter and pass through every stage we have known since the dawn of everything. From eggs we hatch into fat serpents all tooth and muscle, then we grow legs and become lizard-dogs that would snack on drearbeasts. Most of the thralls remain in the depths, under the command of dracomorphs. They patrol, and were there any real threat, dragons—full dragons, ancient dragons—would be summoned to destroy the Oromise."

Kerrigan craned his neck to look down into the deep crevasse that disappeared into shadows. "If there is still fighting going on down there, why don't you know what an Oromise looks like?"

"Down there we fight feral urZrethi and other creatures the Oromise created. We do not know if there are passages into the Oromise prisons from which these things emerge, or if there are just pockets and colonies so deep we never rooted them out. We have to assume they are still trying to reach their masters, and they have to defend against our doing that, too."

Kerrigan turned toward Rym. "You said dragons

trapped the Oromise down there, but I could take what you've said as meaning that they've fortified themselves down there and you're just making sure they don't get out again."

The puppet shrugged. "As is the way with ancient tales, the truth is hard to discern. Suffice it to say, our young live down there, fight and die down there. Those smart and strong enough to survive to later stages of life grow in power and size."

"How many thralls are down there? Hundreds? Thousands?"

"Thousands of legions. It is a bloody war yet, but has not always been so." Rym pulled him away from the edge and continued their journey. "There was a time when the war seemed over and a rift developed among dragons over whether or not vigilance needed to be maintained. It took centuries for things to come to a head, and no decision could be made. It was agreed that we needed an arbiter to help us decide, and we chose Yrulph Kirûn to be that arbiter. He proposed the creation of the DragonCrown, into which would be worked the Truestones of our best and brightest. Through it he would know their thoughts and gain all he needed to craft a solution to the problem."

Kerrigan held a hand up. "What is a Truestone? I mean, I gather that the stone that rests in your chest is Rymramoch's Truestone. For it to be destroyed would cost you your life. How is that?"

"Dragons of sufficient learning and power are able to create a Truestone. The easiest way for you to understand it is to say that it is a physical manifestation of our soul. We can remove it for safekeeping, then venture forth on dangerous missions, for as long as it is not destroyed, we will not die."

"But, in the Congress Chamber, I saw your body, or what I thought was your body, all stiff and stonelike."

The puppet nodded. "So our bodies become when our Truestones are removed for a prolonged period of time.

Those who gave theirs to their DragonCrown are well hidden and quite petrified. They assumed that the Crown would facilitate communication, and it did, but in ways unintended."

"How so?"

"Any dragon of a Crown lineage could be controlled by the Crown. The degree of control depended on how strong the blood link was. Dravothrak, for example, is a grand-nephew of a Crown dragon. That is why he was linked to the fragment we have here."

Kerrigan rubbed a hand over his mouth. "No one expected Kirûn could control dragons. Did he know?"

Rym looked at Bok. "You've given it much thought through the centuries."

The urZrethi shifted his shoulders uneasily. "He never gave any such indication to me, but he must have suspected, else those abilities would not have been in the Crown."

Kerrigan nodded. "How many Crown lineages are there?"

"Six."

"But there are seven Crown fragments."

Rym nodded. "There are, and therein is the mystery. Who or what gave the Truestone for the key fragment, the controlling fragment?"

"Do you think it could have been an Oromise Truestone?"

"That possibility has made restless the sleep of countless dragons." Rym slowly shook his head. "If the Crown is re-created and Chytrine's greed is what fuels it, things will be bad enough. If it is the Oromise, we are not looking at the fall of civilization as a consequence, but the end of all life. You can see, therefore, why alacrity is called for in this matter."

Kerrigan nodded. "I'll do my best."

"You'll have to do better." Rym passed his left hand over the stone sphere and triggered a spell. The little blue tendrils of lightning played over the sphere for a heartbeat.

Kerrigan screamed and collapsed as the bolts skittered beneath his flesh. His body shook and muscles twitched involuntarily. He tasted blood from where he had bitten his tongue. His back bowed once, then his muscles went flaccid.

The puppet stood over him. "When you made the ball into your magickal image to intercept your spell, you made it a conduit to yourself. That was a grave error. I know you will be doing your best. Just make it better. The fate of the entire world rests on your ability to do just that."

CHAPTER 9

I saura sat in her chambers in far Aurolan and shivered. Though the air was cold enough to condense her breath into a white mist, the chill was not what made her shiver. She felt very alone, and that surprised her, because she had been alone before. Still, it had never been quite in this way because, somehow, she had always felt another presence out there that kept her company.

She should have been happy—quite overjoyed, in fact. Her mother's enemy, the Norrington, was dead. He had died on Vael. Nefrai-laysh had taken much delight in describing how the young hero had leaped through a magickal wall to save the life of an old, foolish dragon. Rymramoch had long opposed her mother, and the death of a lesser enemy was traded for that of a greater. The news had been the cause of much rejoicing in the frigid north.

It had not warmed her, however. In the *sullanciri*'s description of Will Norrington, Isaura recognized the young man whose life she had saved in Meredo. Whims, the flow of magick, and pure chance had led her to the bed where he lay. She'd known instantly that one of her mother's creations had wounded him, so she undid the wound and he lived.

Until the report of his death, however, she'd not known who he was. Fear took her then because her mother had told Isaura that she would be betrayed. Isaura had hoped she would not be the one to betray her mother, then she discovered she had. She had saved the Norrington of prophecy. She had saved the person who would kill her mother.

Worse yet, his death saddened her. From the moment she heard, and perhaps before, she had felt alone. She wondered if it had not been chance that took her to him, but some sort of fate. Perhaps she was somehow bound up in the Norrington Prophecy. The prophecy might use her against her mother, making her betray Chytrine. She wanted to hate that idea, but she couldn't. The sadness she felt at Will Norrington's death made her feel as if she would have traded her mother's life for his, and that mere thought was treason of the highest order.

Wind howled at the window of her tower, then ice hissed as a gust pushed crystals in past the magick warding the chamber from the outside. She turned from the small bookstand and the thick, leather-bound volume she had been fingering and let a weak smile tug at the corners of her mouth. "Drolda, you never desert me."

The ice crystals swirled, then resolved themselves into the image of an older man. Water congealed into a beard and long hair, both of which flowed down into the furred cloak that covered him. Glassine hands emerged from beneath the cloak. The icy figure wove his finger through a complex series of signs in a language only they understood.

Isaura nodded slowly. "Yes, you have been listening to rumors that are true. The Norrington is dead. He sacrificed himself for another." She opened her hands and wanted to give voice to her sadness, but could not find the words.

Concern etched crevasses on Drolda's frozen face. He signed, but not what she expected.

"What do you mean he is not dead? Did his sacrifice transfer the burden of his fate to another?"

The ice man shook his head, then stiffened.

A voice, deep, bestial, and growling, echoed through her room from the doorway. "Will no have death."

Isaura turned, bringing her head up and moving to eclipse Drolda. The ice man had never before lingered in the vicinity of a *sullanciri,* and certainly never in one's sight. It disturbed her that this one, Hlucri, could move so silently she did not hear his approach, and that he dared enter her chamber unbidden. *Has my mother set this newest of her creatures to spy on me?*

As her silver-eyed gaze met his jet eyes, the hulking *sullanciri* dropped to one knee and rested his knuckles on the ground. He had been created from the Panqui that had so ruined Nefrai-laysh. Isaura had seen the massive wounds on the other *sullanciri.* She offered to repair the damage, but making the Panqui over had taken precedence. Nefrai-kesh had demanded her help in doing that.

The Panqui's vitality had impressed her, for Nefrai-kesh had pulled him off Nefrai-laysh and literally stripped the flesh from him. The huge creature had lain in a slowly spreading pool of blood, tissue hanging in ragged tatters, his claws still clenching, his teeth gnashing as they set about doing their work. Hlucri had been the first *sullanciri* Nefrai-kesh had created without her mother, but he knew the magick well, and the result had been even more impressive than the original.

Hlucri, when standing on his thick hind legs, topped her by two feet, and ran twelve from the tip of his tail to his crown. Their magick had covered him with a new flesh of jet and jade. Stripes, from deep green to a softer, milkier tone marked his skin, with the darkest green forming a mask around his black eyes and up to his tall ears. While the skin felt and moved like supple leather, it could be hardened like armor with a thought. Spikes could sprout wherever needed, though fang and claw would serve the *sullanciri* best.

Hlucri lowered his head and gazed at the ground. "Forgive Hlucri intrusion, Lady Snowflake."

Isaura blinked. "Lady Snowflake?"

"Your Will-name."

She stiffened, then Drolda flowed into view at her side. She read what he signed, then nodded.

"The Norrington saw me? He knew who I was?"

"No. True-you known not." The *sullanciri*'s nostrils flared. "Safe with Hlucri."

Isaura closed her eyes and passed a hand over her face, wishing her mind and emotions would quiet. For the brief moment she believed Will Norrington had known who she was, her spirit had soared. It was as if that loneliness had vanished, as if whatever she had been linked to had reestablished contact. Hlucri's denial again demolished that link, leaving her alone and confirming that it had been Will Norrington with whom she had shared a bond.

Will Norrington, whom I saved and who was later slain.

A shiver started at the base of her spine and she let it banish her confusion. "What can I do for you, Hlucri?"

The creature opened his arms wide. "Hlucri newspawn know-nothing."

Isaura nodded. His transformation had taken place only three days previous and he had slept most of the time since. *Grichothka* had been caring for his needs. She had looked in on him occasionally but had not found him awake until now.

"How did you find your way here?"

The *sullanciri* tapped his nose by way of answer.

Drolda signed quickly and Isaura laughed. "Very true, Drolda, he will have much interesting to smell here."

The *sullanciri* shifted around until he sat on his haunches. His head came up and he grinned with a mouthful of sharp teeth. "Know many smells."

"You will know more, but first . . ." Isaura pointed to Drolda. "You will forget you saw my friend here."

Hlucri breathed in, then tapped his nose again. "No smell, not there."

She wasn't certain if the *sullanciri* was telling her Drolda really didn't exist for him, or if her secret was safe, but she decided the latter sufficed. "Thank you. Please, follow me." She turned to invite Drolda along, too, but he had already dissolved into snowflakes that teased her hair before slipping back out the window.

Isaura descended the tower stairs and began thinking about how she could best describe life in Aurolan. She loved her home and knew of its beauty. The wonder of new snow over old, and the artistry of wind-carved sculptures. She wanted to share the subtle nature of the seasons, which were more than variations in temperature, and the songs of the wind and ice in the darkest of nights.

But all that seemed to demand too much of her. She felt exhausted even though she could have roused herself to explain it all were she guiding the Norrington. He would see the things she described, he would understand the beauty. He would see that Aurolan was not evil, that it did not deserve destruction.

She glanced back at the hulking beast moving through the shadows behind her. She had to look, for she could not hear him and could barely see him. She didn't feel as if she were being stalked, but instead protected. It gave her cause to wonder what sort of things Nefrai-kesh had worked into the magicks used to create Hlucri.

"My mother's citadel stands above one of the many cavern complexes throughout Aurolan. Snow and ice cover the surface, but the caves run deep and rents in the earth run deeper. Molten stone flows red and gold through the depths. Water heated below rises to bubbling pools. It keeps the caverns warm enough for life, and life does thrive here."

Hlucri sniffed and bobbed his head.

As they reached the ground floor, Isaura guided him to

a door and opened it. The stairs there wound tighter and descended in a sharp spiral. Warm, moist air from below gradually enfolded them, and where the colder air met the wet, a thin layer of fog hung suspended. At the base, the stairs opened onto a wide balcony that provided a clear view of a large central cavern with small tunnel mouths dotting the walls much as stars blot the sky.

Sidestepping a small clutch of young frostclaws, Isaura reached the edge of the balcony. "Down there, on those terraces, various fungi are raised to feed upon."

A squawk and a crunch sounded from behind her. She turned and found a headless frostclaw in Hlucri's right hand and a dribble of blood flowing along his lip as he chewed. Isaura frowned for a moment. She was less concerned that he'd killed a frostclaw than with his apparent ease in doing so. As a *sullanciri* he needed to be a formidable fighter, but young frostclaws were notoriously elusive. *Speed and hunting instincts will stand him in good stead.*

She politely refused the offer of a red raw haunch, waved him forward, then pointed to the level below the mushroom terraces. "The water drains there and goes down into a vast series of ponds and lakes. Fish are farmed in them and the muck from the bottom of the ponds is brought back up to fertilize the terraces. The fish are fed with refuse and even our dead. Nothing is wasted here."

Hlucri brought his right arm back and hurled the half-eaten carcass out into the cavern. Feathers trailed in its wake and floated softly down as the body plummeted into the depths. It missed one of the runoff streams by several yards, but another clutch of frostclaws fell on the body and tore it to pieces in seconds.

Isaura turned to face the *sullanciri*. She rested her fists on her hips. "Doing that sort of thing is not going to make you very popular around here. I can understand your being hungry, but you can't just kill things and eat them whenever you wish."

"Hlucri asks, someone else kills?" He shrugged his shoulders. "Time wasted."

"What did Nefrai-kesh do to you?"

The *sullanciri* smiled. "Made Hlucri *your* servant."

That struck her as odd. Nefrai-kesh had always been the *sullanciri* who cared the most about her. He brought her gifts and told her of the world, but even so, he had been distant. He hid behind his masks. *And now the mask he wears is the skin of this Panqui.*

"Well, if you are *my* servant, then please, no more needless killing. Some things are raised for food, and some for other work." She pointed off deeper into the cavern. "That tunnel leads off to mines and foundries. Our smiths might not turn out the fine work of urZrethi or elven metalworkers, but their steel is a match for anything a man has done. If we had silver and gold, I have no doubt our smiths would excel at working it, too."

Hlucri nodded. "South-riches come soon."

"Yes, they will." Isaura again felt she should have been pleased by that prospect, but she was not. The south had yielded crops in abundance before the war, and the new year should bring even more as the conquered lands were farmed. It did strike her as odd that her mother had not yet organized groups to go out and colonize those areas, since the human population would have fled before the armies. It could have been that she intended the armies themselves to turn farmer, but doing that would make them vulnerable to attack.

Hlucri's suggestion that plunder would be flowing north seemed right, but she was unaware of anything coming back from the south. In fact, the only plunder she knew of were the fragments of the DragonCrown her mother had liberated from Fortress Draconis. Her mother needed them to destroy the Crown and free the dragons, but wouldn't bringing other things back make sense, too?

Then it struck her: her mother feared the corruption of the south. In Aurolan, where everyone had a purpose and those things they needed, baubles would be nothing but trouble. The glint of gold, the glow of a gem could cause strife as those who coveted such items sought to possess them. The delicate balance that made life in the north possible would be destroyed by the southern wealth.

That explanation made perfect sense to her. Up above, across the valley from the fortress, stood the Conservatory. Neskartu, before his death at Navval, had taught students from the south how to wield great magicks. They had all been housed in the Conservatory and Isaura though it was so they could concentrate on magick, but the truth of it dawned on her now. They had been isolated so the southern influence could not bleed into the Aurolani population.

Then she looked back into the cavern and realized how hollow that reasoning was. *Grichothka* and vylaens were her mother's subjects. The latter were not stupid at all, but the former were simple creatures who required vylaens to lead them. While a shiny bit of metal might attract a gibberkin's eye, it would not be more valued if it were gold than silver or just bright copper. The vylaens might see more value in things, but their minds ran to magicks, and their pleasures were derived from them.

What is my mother doing? Isaura knew the history of the south's trying to destroy her a generation previous. The Norrington Prophecy certainly posed a threat, but how much of one? Would the southern kings have risen against her if she had not sent troops into their lands? And now, with the Norrington dead, why would she continue a war that the south could not win?

Isaura staggered back a step, then suddenly found herself scooped up in Hlucri's arms. She wanted to command him to set her down and never touch her again, but the gentleness with which he held her helped counter the empty feeling she had inside.

I thought I knew my mother, but it seems I do not. Does that mean I am the one who will betray her? She shivered. *Or has she betrayed herself?*

Isaura laid a hand on Hlucri's shoulder. "You may put me down. Thank you."

"Your servant." The *sullanciri* set her on her feet, but did not remove his hands until she was steady. "No harm to you."

She caressed his green-and-black cheek. "I believe you, but there is no one who can stand against she who could do me the most hurt."

CHAPTER 10

Had she desired to do so, Alexia could have been seated with the Okrans delegation to the Council of Kings. She knew her place was there, and dearly wished to support her grandfather. She would have done exactly that save that the old man appeared even more diminished in the wake of his nation's liberation. She could not imagine how he clung to life, but while he did, Grand Duchess Tatyana served as his voice in the Council.

Tatyana would not have tolerated Alexia's joining the Okrans delegation because Alexia insisted that Crow be given a place by her side. Alexia really didn't think Crow would come to listen, but she had made it known that a seat for him was the condition of her joining her family. Regrets that she and her companions could not be afforded seating were advanced, so Alexia instead sat with the Alcidese faction and no one seemed to attach any import to that shift.

As ministers rose to make preliminary remarks thanking King Fidelius one more time for hosting them, Alyx wished she could have been with Crow and well away from the large chamber. Crow had very much taken to writing his memoirs. While it seemed tiring work, and left his fingers stained with ink, he was happier in doing it than she'd seen in ages. His pleasure brought her pleasure, which made the councils endurable.

Many others in the room looked miserable, with long expressions mocking the bright smiles pictured in the murals. She glanced quickly at Prince Erlestoke. He still wore his black mask, but sat at his father's right hand. He did not look overjoyed to be there, but listened intently to all that was being said. After the sessions they would meet to brief Resolute and Crow, and Alexia had found Erlestoke's insights to be sharp and incisive.

The last minister seated himself, and King Fidelius stood at the table strung with Saporicia's blue-and-red banner. He hugged his right arm across his chest, clutching at the elbow of his ruined arm. "I have had grave news from the north which I am sorry to have to share with you all. Caledo has fallen. King Bowmar is dead. There is no word from his son, Bowmar, no word of other members of the royal house."

Alexia's skin tightened with gooseflesh. Princess Sayce had been left behind at Navval less than a week before. The army besieging it had been destroyed by a dragon, but the larger army attacking the nation's capital, Caledo, had its own dragon. The city's fall was inevitable, but she hoped some of the royal family had survived. *Without their leadership . . .*

The Saporician monarch's brown eyes tightened. "Refugees are already streaming over the border. We are organizing the fleeing troops to strengthen my fortresses, but dragonels will sweep them away. The peasantry is being brought along as quickly as possible, but I have neither the space nor the resources to deal with the disaster. They are coming south with nothing but the clothes on their backs. A greater catastrophe than the fall of their nation will occur if we cannot deal with this problem."

A buzz ran through the council chamber as ministers

and their masters bent heads in discussion. Alyx felt certain more people were discussing the portents of Muroso's collapse than plans to deal with the refugees. As much as she hated that fact, she knew it was natural. Their primary concern would be stopping their own nation's fall, and putting food in the mouths of Murosan peasants wasn't going to accomplish much in that regard.

King Augustus rose slowly. "Within the hour orders will be communicated to Yslin to send supply ships here. They will arrive by afternoon tomorrow, good wind and Tagothcha willing. I will send more relief by land, but it will take longer to get here."

King Scrainwood smiled. "Ships already laden with supplies? Are you prescient, brother, or would this have been enough to feed an army?"

Augustus' expression darkened. "Is there anyone here who did not anticipate this turn of events? King Fidelius has said he expects his border fortresses to be destroyed. No single nation has been able to stand against the might of Chytrine and, indeed, only in Okrannel, where a coalition force fought, were we successful in opposing her."

"I meant nothing by that, Augustus, other than a clever play on words." Scrainwood rose and adjusted his green mask. "I know these are tense times, and I regret that any attempt at levity is met with suspicion. I, too, shall give orders to have supplies sent overland. In two days we should have relief coming from Meredo. Those refugees that enter my nation shall be welcomed, as will any you wish to divert to Oriosa, Fidelius."

The Saporician king nodded. "You are both gracious. I know, Augustus, you did not intend to impugn the reputation of Saporician warriors. Your kind offer of help in fighting Chytrine has been noted, and I will call upon you as needed."

Augustus would have protested, but Tatyana rose to her feet. She made a pretense of bending down and lending an ear to whatever King Stefin might be saying, then nodded.

"My nephew wishes to applaud his brothers from Oriosa and Alcida, but would offer cautions and a plan that will best serve us all."

"Please, Grand Duchess, explain." Augustus inclined his head in her direction before seating himself. He glanced back at Alyx, but she could only shrug.

"My nephew would not want you to take this in a wrong way, King Fidelius, but to refuse entry to Alcidese troops is folly. Were it not for the valiant effort of King Augustus—then but a prince—Okrannel would have lost as much or more than Muroso. Because of his efforts we were preserved and able to liberate our homeland. You should accept help from Alcida and any other nation that offers it, especially Jerana."

Queen Carus of Jerana kept her face impassive, but turned to look at Tatyana. "Did your nephew believe we would refuse to aid our Saporician brethren?"

Tatyana let shock tighten flesh over sharp cheekbones. "By no means, Highness. He knows you can offer the greatest of help. In liberating Svarskya, your general Markus Adrogans captured dragonels. He has the secret of firedirt. Certainly you mean to share that secret with all of us so we can fight Chytrine openly and with equal power."

Alyx found it impossible to get a true read on Queen Carus' reaction to her great-grandaunt's words. It was obvious that the queen had been shaken, but Alyx could not tell if that was because Carus did not know about Adrogans' possessing dragonels, or if she thought the secret had been well hidden and was surprised at its discovery. Resolute and Erlestoke had told Alyx of Adrogans' discovery, but the news had not leaked from their circle.

Queen Carus fingered her throat before replying. "Your intelligence sources are either better than mine, Grand Duchess, or you trade in rumors. I tell you all now that I have no communication from General Adrogans that indicates he has dragonels or firedirt. I shall, if you deem it necessary, ask him that question directly. I will order him to reveal the truth to your representatives in Svarskya and they may speak with you directly."

"That would be appreciated, Highness." Tatyana thinned her lips in a tight smile. "I do believe you can understand the worry some of us might have until this matter is resolved. All of Okrannel praises General Adrogans for doing what was deemed impossible, but we know how men are with conquest. They become possessive. One could look at his burning Svoin to the ground as a callous act. He has secured Okrannel, but has he impetus to return it to my nephew? What if he, misguided and against your wishes, were to make Okrannel a province of Jerana? With his having dragonels and firedirt, none of us could wrest it away from him, nor stop him if he sought to expand Jerana into an empire."

The room fell silent as Queen Carus rose to her feet. Though small in stature, she possessed a presence that commanded respect. Her brown eyes narrowed and her voice did not waver despite her hands having tightened into white-knuckled fists. "It would not be right of me to remind you, Grand Duchess, that while your nation existed in exile in Yslin, courtesy of King Augustus, it was my nation that dealt with the Aurolani troops infesting Okrannel. It would not be right of me to mention that more Jeranese blood has been spilled in fighting the Aurolani in the last quarter century than any other nation, save for those now so cruelly subjected to Chytrine's predation. And it would be wrong for me to imply that your suspicions about Markus Adrogans in light of all he has done to liberate your nation are petty, bitter, ungrateful, and unworthy. I shall not communicate them to him.

"Let me make one thing abundantly clear: Jerana has no desire to be an empire. And I have no desire to be Chytrine. I have seen in those who have escaped Okrannel the toll exacted on those who are conquered. I know the hatred felt for the conqueror. I have no desire to be the author of one, nor the recipient of another. I know the same is true of Markus Adrogans, and the possible possession of a dragonel would not change him."

She took her time, looking about the room carefully, meeting all eyes. "If General Adrogans does indeed possess dragonels, he will bring them into play against the Aurolani. While we may be political creatures, he is a warrior, and he understands that the greatest threat to the world is Chytrine. To lose sight of that is to lose everything.

"Now, King Fidelius, I, too, would offer the aid of my nation for yours. I will have supplies sent, and with them will come troops to fight for you. If you are foolish enough to refuse them, I pray King Augustus will grant them safe harbor in Yslin until such time as reason prevails."

Augustus nodded and Scrainwood extended a hand in the queen's direction. "Your troops will be welcome in Oriosa as well, Highness."

"You are most kind, King Scrainwood."

"Thank you." Scrainwood idly stroked his goatee for a moment. "It strikes me, Highness, that you could take one more step to ease the fears of a Jeranese empire springing up."

Carus regarded him warily. "And that would be?"

"Simple, Highness. Instruct General Adrogans to come here and report to us himself on the Okrans situation. The nuances of speech and posture are so lost in *arcanslata* messages. I am certain that would soothe many a worry."

Alyx frowned. Ordering Adrogans' appearance in Narriz likely would do what Scrainwood suggested, but would leave his army without its head. While she knew the other leaders with the army, none had Adrogans' skill at motivating people and outthinking his opposition. As his ship headed south, an Aurolani fleet could head west from Muroso and the fight for Okrannel would be on again.

She smiled in spite of herself. *Adrogans does not travel by ship.* The overland route to Narriz would take nearly a month. By that time Narriz could easily have been overrun and Okrannel could be facing a major assault.

Queen Carus nodded. "I shall order General Adrogans to appear before us to report on the Okrans situation."

Scrainwood clapped his hands. "Splendid. Now, Grand Duchess, does this ease your nephew's concerns?"

The old woman nodded. "It pleases him, yes."

"And you, King Fidelius, will you let Jeranese and Alcidese troops enter your nation to defend it? Would that invitation be extended to the troops of any other nation that wished to aid you?"

The incongruity of Scrainwood's crafting a compromise left Alexia cold, but not as cold as Fidelius' reaction to those questions. The Saporician king had never been a big man, but he seemed to shrink a little. To allow foreign troops into his nation was to admit his own troops could not stop Chytrine. That was a reality and everyone in the room knew it, but to concede the point was to admit that his nation was helpless. Just as it could be imagined that Adrogans might never give up Okrannel, it could be imagined that the southern half of Saporicia could fall to Alcida and never be ruled by the Saporician royal house again.

A greater reality impinged as well. By allowing troops to enter Saporicia, Fidelius was letting his nation be chosen as the battleground where Chytrine would be stopped. Whether she was or not, the damage done to Saporicia would be incalculable. Armies on the prowl seldom respected rights or laws, so his allies could do as much damage as Chytrine's troops. Just the demand for firewood would lay waste to forests that supplied the world's best shipyards. Villages and towns would cease to exist, and if Chytrine had other, more terrible weapons to deploy, whole swaths of the countryside could be despoiled and remain so for centuries.

Against the threat of certain annihilation those considerations might have paled, but Fidelius would always be haunted by the question of *what if* his troops had held? Could his nation have been saved? Could it have saved itself? Was there a way to avoid the misery the war would bring to his people?

Conflicting emotions played over the king's face. His lower lip quivered, and he seemed on the verge of giving an answer when Scrainwood's voice, soft and serpentine, slithered into the chamber.

"You must agree, my brother, for the Norrington is no more."

That whisper shook Fidelius as if he'd been slammed in the chest with a dragonel ball. "Yes. You are all welcome. Come. Save us all." His words, delivered quietly—seeming more a prayer than an answer—drifted through the hall like mist.

Even Scrainwood respected the silence that followed. The Oriosan king sat slowly and his face betrayed no feeling. Alexia felt a hollow pang herself as the despair in Fidelius' voice sank into the hopeless void opened by Scrainwood's comment. That void closed quickly, however, as sound crept slowly back. Around the chamber crowned heads spoke with military advisors. Heads nodded and shook. Ministers made notes.

One by one, the leaders of the world's nations rose and pledged troops. Some, from faraway places like Valicia, Malca, and Regorra likely would never make it in time to be of use. Other units, from closer nations that had to worry about Chytrine, were not much storied or tested. Even taking those things into account, however, the forces gathering would be considerable and, properly led, might be enough to stop Chytrine.

Augustus rose. "I thank all of you, my brothers and sisters, for your willingness to send your warriors to shed blood here. Twenty-five years ago we faced this same threat and failed to deal with it bravely or directly. Chytrine's evil has festered in the world for too long. We must not lose heart this time. She must be stopped. She *will* be stopped."

Even Alyx felt her pulse quicken at Augustus' words. Cheers and applause rang out from all the delegations.

Even her grandfather seemed to rouse himself from his stupor to clap twisted hands. That brought a smile to her face, and it would have remained there save for a glance toward King Fidelius.

As all the others celebrated, he scrubbed his good hand over a very pale face. Others might see the tears smeared over his cheeks as being born of relief or joy, but she knew better. He was already mourning those who would die and Alexia bowed her head to join him, silent within the jubilant din.

CHAPTER 11

With the sky cloudless and bright blue, and the sun shining ferociously, it might have been possible for Markus Adrogans to imagine spring had arrived early in Svarskya. The carpet of snow covering the landscape and the frosty air that steamed his breath argued against this, but he had a feeling the winter would lose its grip sooner rather than later. He had made contingency plans to deal with an early spring and would be happy to employ them.

What a few weeks might bring, however, did not concern him. He stood on a hilltop outside Svarskya. With him was Alcidese General Turpus Caro, and propped up in a litter was a wounded Okrans warrior named Beal mot Tsuvo. Adrogans would have wished, with her injuries, that she'd remained in the older part of the city, but she refused to be left behind.

And she has earned the right to be here.

Beal mot Tsuvo had led a contingent of her clans folk in an assault on Svarskya. The fighting had been fierce and initial reports had listed her among the slain. Teams removing the dead had found her, cold, wounded but somehow clinging to life. Her right leg and right arm had been crushed and were beyond redemption. But Vilwanese warmages and a magicker from the Loquelven Blackfeathers had begun the process of making her into a *meckanshii*. They would shape and graft onto her stumps new limbs of metal.

Two others stood beside her. Mistress Gilthalarwin of the Blackfeathers seemed untouched by the cold. Her long black hair hung in a thick braid and her cloak had been thrown back, revealing studded leather armor and the hilt of a curved sword. Her dark eyes focused distantly and Adrogans refused to even hazard a guess at what she was thinking, for the minds of elder races were well beyond his ken.

A small human clad in a threadbare cloak and breechcloth, with no hat or gloves, wore a sour expression. Ragged cloth swathed his feet. The Zhusk shaman shook his head, dislodging a wisp of grey hair to dangle in front of his eyes, then glared over at Adrogans. "You hardly need this."

Adrogans smiled. "Be still, Uncle. We must know it before we decide if we need it."

Below the quintet the hillside facing the city had been dug out and framed up. Stout wooden posts had been squared and used to reinforce the redoubt's walls and floor, and a dragonel had been wheeled up into it. There, ropes and pulleys had been used to move it into place and secure it. A second, smaller hole had been dug a quarter of the way south to house a cask of firedirt.

A young man of Alcidese origin approached and saluted. "If you are ready, General, we can proceed with the demonstration."

Adrogans nodded, then held up a hand. "You have no doubt you know how this works, Captain Agitare?"

The man smiled. "Yes, sir. Before I served under Princess Alexia and even General Caro, I spent three years at Fortress Draconis. Parsus was at Draconis for eight. We know how this works."

The little Zhusk sneered. "Only the ironmen know the secret of dragonels."

Agitare shook his head. "Begging your pardon, Master Phfas, but the *meckanshii* know the secret of making firedirt. They crewed the dragonels at Fortress Draconis, but the Draconis Baron had teams of us learn how to use them. If Chytrine could make the *meckanshii* magick fail, the dragonels would be useless, so he had backup crews ready."

"Proceed, Captain."

The Alcidese officer waved a hand and the quartet of men in the pit began to work. "Parsus has that bag of firedirt there. It's enough for one charge. We use a bag and fill it with a wooden scoop because metal might spark, and we don't want sparks. He pours it in, then Nerus compacts it with that ram. Ebrius, he's got the iron ball there, and Cassus is wrapping it in cloth to make sure the fit is good and tight. Nerus rams it home and the dragonel has a full belly."

Adrogans watched the men work and saw no traces of fear. He'd seen the destruction firedirt could cause when the Aurolani forces had used boombags against his troops. The bag was little more than a lot of firedirt and metal shrapnel. It literally shredded men and horses, with the force of the blast enough to knock people down even if they were unhurt. Had the Aurolani employed them to keep him out of the city, they would have ripped his army to pieces.

They had not, however, and Adrogans was fairly certain why. A quarter century earlier, Chytrine had introduced dragonels at the siege of Fortress Draconis. The Draconis Baron had taken possession of the only existing weapon and a meager supply of firedirt. He had managed to duplicate the dragonel and firedirt, as well as innovate a number of other weapons. He then manufactured them and used them to make Fortress Draconis unassailable.

At least, unassailable until Chytrine returned with more dragonels and other weapons that shattered it.

The Draconis Baron had steadfastly refused to share the secrets of dragonels and firedirt with the nations of the south. Adrogans had even heard rumors that he had sent assassins out to deal with those inventors who had succeeded in duplicating firedirt. While Adrogans assumed those rumors to be false, he did not doubt the Draconis Baron would have gone to such lengths to keep the weapon secret. While dragonels might have stopped Chytrine in Sebcia or Muroso, had the secret been freely known, the south would have dissolved into a series of wars that would have been even more ruinous than Chytrine's campaign.

Agitare pointed to the pit again. "The firedirt used in the dragonel's belly is of a fairly large grain, but the firedirt Parsus is using now to prime the touchhole is much more fine. It will burn more quickly and ignite the larger grains. They will burn slowly and build up great power, which is what will hurl the ball to the target."

"Very good." Adrogans looked left to a soldier carrying a big red flag. "Signalman, give the sign to the city."

The man waved the flag briskly, and down in the city, atop one of many snow-covered hovels, another red flag waved back. The man waving it stopped quickly enough, then slid down the roof and got well away from where he had been standing.

The Jeranese general smiled. "It seems, Captain, that your target is clear. Please, continue the demonstration."

Agitare again saluted, then entered the pit and plucked a small torch from a hole in one of the posts. He bent over, sighted down the length of the dragonel's thick brass barrel, then brought the flame to the touchhole. In an instant a plume of thick grey-white smoke shot up into the air, and for a heartbeat Adrogans did not think a dragonel was very impressive at all.

Then the weapon roared and spat out a huge gout of flame that illuminated the heart of a jet of smoke. The very ground shook, and the thunder started his ears ringing. A swirl of smoke drifted back to sting his eyes, but even nascent tears couldn't prevent him from seeing a black speck as it flew through the sky. It arced down and smashed into a roof, billowing snow into a cloud and sending up a spray of broken red tiles. A heartbeat later the roof sagged, then collapsed inward and part of the building's outer walls crumbled.

He tugged at his ears in a vain attempt to stop them from ringing as smoke dissipated and snow drifted back down over the ruined building. Brilliant tactician though he was, he knew anyone who had seen what one small ball had accomplished could calculate the destructive force now at his command. Ten or twenty of the dragonels would be enough to batter down any wall. While the balls would not be the most effective against massed troops, filling a dragonel with smaller shot or stones or jagged metal would rip them to pieces as the boombags had.

So, this is what the Draconis Baron saw.

Turpus Caro's normally florid face had lost some of its color. "It is smaller than a siege engine, easier to move, and far more powerful. As long as there is firedirt and shot, it is formidable. And the effort to employ it . . ."

"Yes, a few men, quickly trained, can do a lot of damage."

The Loquelf closed her eyes. "Even after we slay Chytrine, this will be her legacy. It will destroy the world."

Adrogans frowned. "There are many ways the world could be destroyed, and this is but one of them. Chytrine is still the greatest threat, and we must concentrate on her. Besides, we know how the dragonel works, but as General Caro implied, without firedirt, it is useless. Captain Agitare, what is the supply of firedirt?"

The young man stopped several steps below the hilltop and looked up. "There is not much in the storehouse where we got this lot, but there is brimstone, charcoal, and saltpeter stored there. You could smell the brimstone in the smoke, couldn't you? We know it is a mixture of all three, but we are working on the proportions. After that it needs to be moistened, then dried, and we are working on that, too."

"Good. How much shot and how much firedirt will you have when you get the formulation correct?"

"For shot, as much as we want. You can feed them almost anything and it will work, though round iron balls still work best. There are not that many left behind, but the molds were recovered from the ship. We have twenty dragonels. At current supply levels, we could have enough firedirt for fifty shots each, though that will take a lot of transporting."

"Thank you, Captain. Round up everyone who has had experience at Fortress Draconis and form them into a dragonel corps. Keep me informed on the production of firedirt."

"Yes, General." Agitare hesitated. "If I might make a suggestion, sir?"

"Yes, Captain?"

Agitare pointed to the crew on the dragonel. "They're all part of the Wolves, sir. I would like to make the Wolves over into your dragonel corps. They're all trained and smart and sworn to Princess Alexia. You can *trust* them, sir."

Trust them. Adrogans ran a hand over his chin. It pleased him to see that Agitare recognized the great responsibility he was being given. Letting an Alcidese unit sworn to the service of Princess Alexia hold the secret of firedirt would go a long way to quell anxieties about what he might do with those dragonels.

"Very good, Captain. The Wolves will be my dragonel corps. Carry on." He saluted and dismissed Agitare, then turned to the others. "Shall we inspect the damage?"

Four men advanced to take up Beal mot Tsuvo's litter. Snow crunched beneath boots as the small procession worked its way into the outskirts of the city and along narrow streets to the place where the ball had landed. Adrogans found himself between the elf and Phfas. He felt uncomfortable and that surprised him.

He glanced sidelong at Phfas. "Share your mind with me, Uncle. Does Mistress Gilthalarwin's dark outlook trouble you, or have you some new concern?"

The little man cackled. "She is right. Dragonels will doom everyone. And you are right. Chytrine is the immediate threat. Your possessing dragonels will eclipse that threat. And yet Chytrine will have her victory since you will not be trusted."

"I know that is a possibility, but I cannot just take the dragonels out into the sea and dump them." He glanced back over his shoulder at Beal mot Tsuvo. "Had I but a handful of dragonels, I could have cleared the breach she sought to enter. I could have saved her the pain of her injuries, and saved many of her kinsmen from death. To throw away something that would let me save lives like that is evil."

"So you are trapped."

"I am trapped." He sighed. "If I use them, I will become the enemy. If I do not, the enemy will win."

Phfas spat. "You will never even get the chance to use them. The trap will close too fast."

Further conversation ended as they rounded a corner and came upon the house that had been hit. It had been a modest building of mortar and stone, broader than it was deep, with a red tile roof. The force of the roof's collapse had blown open the shutters, letting them look inside. The ball had clearly snapped the central beam, bringing the roof down and parts of the walls with it. While that exact a hit might have been lucky, almost any building would seem fragile against the power of a dragonel.

Phfas began to scramble in through a window, but Adrogans held him back. "It may settle more, Uncle."

The little man grumbled, then nodded. "Make the Wolves look."

"I will." Adrogans turned from the building and found a signal-mage wearing a purple robe puffing his way along the street. He bore a sheaf of papers and relief spread across his features as he spotted Adrogans. "You have something for me?"

"For you, General, and for General Caro." He glanced at the Loquelf. "Nothing yet for you, Mistress, but when a message does come through, I will find you instantly."

"You are very kind."

Adrogans thought her voice distant and her response wooden, but the message he was handed aborted any consideration of the Loquelf's mood. He read it quickly once, then more slowly before looking up. "Who did the transcription from the *arcanslata*?"

The mage, whose bald pate was steaming with exertion, nodded. "I did, General."

"So, there was no mistake on this end of the exchange."

The man frowned. "Mistake? The message seemed very unambiguous, General."

"To you, perhaps, yes." Adrogans started to read aloud. " 'General Adrogans, I write to ask if you have possession of dragonels and firedirt. If so, please reply with numbers of same and any other relevant details. You are also hereby ordered to report immediately to Narriz to speak before the Council of Kings about Okrannel. Signed Queen Carus.' "

Phfas snorted. "The trap has closed."

"What is ambiguous in that message, General?"

Adrogans met the signal-mage's stare openly. "I should think it is clear. I am ordered to report to Narriz immediately, but we know that is impossible. By ship the journey would take four days, but Queen Carus knows I do not travel by ship. By land it will take a month, and only if there is no snow or anything else to hinder me. I cannot report immediately. This leads me to believe, then, that while you have transcribed the message correctly, the person who inscribed the message heard it incorrectly."

The mage started to protest, but clearly thought better of it. "So, then, General, it would be your desire for me to reply that the message needs to be sent again so it can be verified. Do you wish me to ask specifically about the use of 'immediately'?"

"No. We will save that inquiry for the next message. Take your time, be exact. Draft your message, bring it to me, then send it. These messages are clearly too important to hurry them."

"Yes, General." The signal-mage bowed and withdrew, but at a much more leisurely pace than he had employed earlier.

Caro extended the message he'd been given toward Adrogans. "I have been ordered to report on whether or not you have dragonels. I am allowed to stay here, however."

"Then you can reply truthfully, my friend. I do not have dragonels. The Wolves do."

Caro laughed. "You're shaving the truth thin enough to read through."

"We have no choice." He glanced back at the building they'd demolished with one shot. "Unless we want all of our homes to look like this, before or after Chytrine is dealt with, we cannot give dragonels away. One hint that we have them, and the alliance that brought us here will evaporate. If it goes, so goes any chance of stopping Chytrine."

CHAPTER 12

Alexia had an abiding hatred for politics, but had to concede that it proved useful at times. As predicted, Alcidese supply ships arrived a day after they'd been sent for. Alcidese troops also arrived at the same time: the Alcidese Throne Guards, the Queen's Light Horse, and the Alcidese Iron Horse. As they disembarked, trumpets sounded and blue banners unfurled, making for a display that swelled hearts and even rekindled lost hope.

The grandeur of the troops arriving was not lost on anyone, especially since the two thousand were being supplemented by another three thousand marching up the coast road. Kings and queens were quick to make sure their contributions to the fight would seem no shabbier, either in numbers or appearance. Jerana's contribution came first, with two infantry regiments and two battalions of light horse. Other leaders scrambled to get their troops moving, or hired mercenaries and formed ersatz Foreign Legions right there in Narriz.

The scramble to produce troops and supplies became one of three sports that kept the politicians occupied. The second was the hunt for the truth concerning Adrogans and dragonels. The Jeranese general's request for clarification of the message sent had been seen as a ruse at the start, but then General Caro sent a message stating unequivocally that Adrogans did not have dragonels. Alyx knew he *did*, and could hardly imagine Caro lying to his king, or being induced to lie, so there clearly was some trickery involved. Everyone else in the town either thought Adrogans was lying or telling the truth. As a result, a lot of words were wasted in heated arguments backed by no information at all.

The third game had all but been eclipsed by the first two, and that was the production of new Norringtons. While there was still some effort being made to promote new candidates to fulfill the prophecy, the latter part of Will's legacy fit so well with the need to create military units that things got melded together. Just as Will had led the Freemen, new Norrington candidates became the core of companies and legions.

Curiously, only Scrainwood held his Norrington back. He'd sent for Bosleigh Norrington's second son by Nolda Disper. Whereas her first son, Kenleigh, did appear to be a Norrington, the second, Redgrave, did not. One look at him left no question that he was his mother's son, with her blue eyes, white-blonde hair, and willowy form. His face, however, had a pinched quality to it, and the light of intelligence burned dully in his eyes. She'd only seen him once and found the youth apparently in awe of how a button fit through a buttonhole.

That Scrainwood didn't advance his candidate loudly caused Alexia some anxiety. That show of restraint, as well as his behavior in the Council, made her very uneasy. He was planning something, and she knew she'd not like it, but exactly what he was planning she could not imagine.

That it would make trouble for Crow and the world, however, she was certain. Therefore, she was determined whatever he was scheming would not come to pass.

She looked up from the pages of Crow's memoirs and

over at the man scribbling away at a desk near the window. "Do you really think describing Scrainwood's eyes as being 'tight set together' is wise?"

Crow set his quill down and smiled at her. "I would omit him if I could, but I cannot, so the truth will have to suffice."

Alyx set the pages down on the bed, then slid off it and crossed to where he sat. She stroked his white mane. "Leigh really was like your brother, wasn't he?"

The man nodded heavily. "He was. I had a responsibility to him and wasn't able to acquit it. You'll see, as I write, how brave he was."

"I'm certain. Resolute has not changed at all."

"He's just gotten deadlier." Crow looked up and smiled at her. "All this was so long ago, and yet setting it down brings it all back. I've not thought on some of these things or these people in a long time. Far too long."

"Or, in the case of Scrainwood, far too *often*." Alyx leaned over and kissed him. "Sometime, when this is all over, will you dance with me as you danced the night you all went off on your first adventure?"

"Gladly, my love." Crow slid his chair back and gathered her in his arms as he stood. "In fact, if I remember how the tune goes, I could hum it and we could practice."

She smiled, resting her hands on the soft doeskin of his tunic, but before she could answer there came a knocking at the door. Alexia gave him a quick kiss, then strode to the door and threw it open. "Yes?"

"This is where we'd find Crow?"

The man who spoke was the largest of the trio gathered at the door, and seemed larger still for being swathed in a heavy coat and a furred cape of rough manufacture. A furred hat he'd already removed, letting her see thick auburn hair shot with grey, and the evergreen hue of the woolen scarf wound round his neck matched his eyes.

Behind him stood a slightly smaller man, and one who was younger, too, but had red hair and shared enough facial features with the giant for her to imagine they were father and son. The third man, by far the smallest both in height and breadth of frame, wore clothes far more fashionable and decorated with bits of ribbon. He leaned on a stout walking stick.

All three of them wore masks and the markings proclaimed them to be Oriosans. Alyx feared for a second that Scrainwood might have sent them to kill Crow or steal his manuscript. Yet none of the men wore swords, and the long, thick, canvas-wrapped bundle slung over the youngest man's back hardly seemed a threat. Still, she'd have swung the door shut in their faces and gone for her sword, save for the gasp from Crow.

"Kedyn be praised." Crow's voice shrank as thickness in his throat choked off his words.

The large man nodded, then looked down, almost embarrassed. "Been a long time, Hawkins."

"Yes, a long time." Crow left the table and thrust his hand at the giant. "I never thought I'd see you again, Naysmith Carver! Welcome; come in."

Nay took Crow's hand and shook it heartily, then the two men embraced, Crow almost disappearing in the other man's grasp. Alyx took a step back, still surprised, for the Naysmith Carver she knew came only from stories Crow had told and the pages of his memoirs. To her Nay was still a youth, not a man of years with a son.

Looking past the Carvers, she smiled at the third man. "Shall I assume you are Rounce Playfair?"

Rounce, whose brown hair had retained its color save for white side locks, limped forward and took her hand in his. "And you would be Princess Alexia of Okrannel." He kissed her hand. "An honor."

She bowed her head. "The honor is mine. I understand that over the last quarter century, you have provided Crow with a great deal of aid, no matter the threat to you."

The merchant shrugged as the younger Carver closed the door. "Fooling Scrainwood's agents was not difficult.

Those who were not stupid were smart enough to understand the value of a bribe."

Nay released Crow and both men covertly swiped at tears. The larger man stepped aside, then grasped his son by the back of his neck and drew him forward. "This is Borell, the youngest. He's been a big help."

Crow shook hands with Borell, then introduced Alexia. Both of the Carvers mumbled greetings and started to genuflect, but she stopped them. It seemed to make them more uncomfortable when she began to gather chairs for them to sit; but she bled the tension off by sitting first, then bidding them to join her.

Crow smiled as he looked at Nay and Rounce. "How are you come here? What have you been doing? Tell me everything."

Rounce laughed and unbuttoned his jacket. His left leg remained straight, and he leaned his cane against it. "I've given Resolute messages to pass along from time to time. Hasn't he . . . ?"

Nay snorted. "Would have been quicker to shout it into the wind than tell Resolute."

Crow laughed. "I'm sure Resolute intended to pass all your messages on to me, but was waiting for an appropriate moment. A moment of ease or peace, when home news would be welcome."

Alyx shot him a wry glance. "Is there *ever* a time with Resolute that would fit that description?"

"No, and apparently that is the problem." He smiled at her, then again looked at Nay. "Last I knew, you returned to Valsina with Leigh."

"Yes. He never got right in the head. He knew you saved him, and he loved you for it. But the loss of his father, your betraying the lot of them—that let him hate you. Scrainwood helped. Leigh took Nolda as his wife but wasn't home much. Wasn't 'til the queen's murder that he went full mad, though."

Nay glanced left toward his son. "Maud Lamburn, you

remember her, she married me. Five children, four lived. Her sister May lives with us too. She married about the same time as Maud. Her husband ran off after a year. Left her with a child. Smithing was good enough to support us all. Borell has worked with metal since being a child and is very good."

Crow smiled. "I can see you have your mother's eyes."

"Thank you, sir." The man's voice came softly and clipped the *you*.

The big man's bushy brows arrowed together. "Where's Tsamoc?"

"Your promise to him has been fulfilled. He kept me alive all these years and just a week past, he saved all of us at Vael. Leigh tried to bring a mountain down on us and the mightiest of the dragons. Tsamoc formed a great arch, holding the roof of their chamber up. He is more magnificent now than he was at the bridge, my friend."

The smith thought for a moment, then nodded. "You're without a sword again, are you, Hawkins?"

Crow laughed. "I am."

Nay looked at his son and nodded. Borell picked up the parcel he'd carried, and with a murmured "Beg pardon," hefted it onto the bed. As he began to undo the ties that bound it up tight, Nay began to speak.

"Before leaving Fortress Draconis, all the pieces of Temmer were gathered. The hilt came from you. No one wanted the other pieces, so they came back to Valsina. They got tucked away and there was no thinking on them for a while. Then the dreams started. Working away at the forge, someone would come up and say, 'It's time.' He'd pick a piece of the sword out and we'd set to working."

Nay's green eyes glittered as they focused distantly. "Just like that they'd come. Odd lot, all, not sure why they were there. They'd just come, say it was time. There was no reforging Temmer. Failed more times than worth remembering. When they came, when they made their pick, they made a new blade around it. That worked."

Borell threw back the last tie, then unrolled the parcel. It contained four swords, with two hilts toward the head of the bed and two toward the foot. Each had a scabbard and the hilts differed, with one looking much older than the others. As Alyx looked at them, she felt a desire to draw one. Her hand started forward, but she stopped and caught Nay looking at her.

"Forgive me, Master smith."

"None needed. They're fated blades. Borell can explain best."

The young man glanced at his father and swallowed hard. His voice started small, but grew more confident as he hefted the first sword. "This was the first one. I weren't but five years old when the wizard from Muroso comes to find my father. Hull, his name was. They made this sword. Its name is Heart."

He set Heart down and picked up another, the one with the oldest hilt. "This one came next. It's got Temmer's hilt. It was an elf helped make this one, an old elf who called himself Magarric. He said its name is *Alarien,* which I guess means 'hand' in Elfspeak."

Crow nodded. "It means strong hand and protector. It's a grand title among elves."

"And this is a grand blade." Borell smiled as he set it back down. "I watched as they made it, with all the sparks and magick. I got to help on the next one, when the urZrethi came to do his dream-bidding. He was called Bok."

Alexia stiffened. "Bok? He's green and furry?"

Nay nodded. "Very gentle and a mage of the first order."

"Bok?" She glanced at Crow, then at Nay. "He didn't have a red-robed mage with him, did he?"

"He came all alone."

Borell nodded in agreement. "He didn't say too much, but spoke proper. I had to gather special wood to burn for the forging, and other for making the hilt. I carved the pieces myself. He called this one Crown."

The next sword he lifted differed from the others in that

it was a bit longer and decidedly thinner. "This one is Eye. I had the same dream my father did five years ago. A woman mage named Arimtara came that time." Borell fell silent and blushed.

"The boy was sweet on her." Nay's voice carried with it the indulgence of a father for a son's youthful crush. "Something odd about her, though. Strong as she was beautiful. Could have done the forging with her magick alone save that she said Borell had to help. He did. They made Eye."

Borell laid that blade down, then flipped open a small pocket that had been sewn into the canvas parcel. From it he drew a small, dagger-shaped amulet on a silver chain. "After the swords there was only one little piece left. Another woman came, an old woman, must have been three years past. She was from Vilwan and helped shape this. She called it Spirit and said it wasn't much of a sword, but she wasn't much of a mage, so it would have to do."

Rounce shifted in his chair. "Orla was the only one of these mages I happened to meet. I liked her, and was saddened to hear of her death."

Crow nodded. "She was very special, and underestimated herself if she didn't think she was much of a mage."

The merchant sat forward and massaged his left knee. "Just over a month ago I learned you were in Meredo. I tried to convince Nay that we needed to go and help you, bring you these swords, but he refused."

Nay shrugged. "Wasn't time. Three weeks ago a dream came. You said about Tsamoc and the arch. That was the dream. Time to go was then. Rounce figured you would be here, so we set out.

"First time around Temmer was enough to cause Chytrine all sorts of hurting. Four times that and some, now." His green eyes slitted. "They're swords for heroes. Choose."

Alexia drew back as he pointed at her. "These are your

swords to give, Master Carver. You must have intended them for specific people."

He smiled. "One was for Hawkins. Knew that all along. Thought one was for Resolute. That idea has faded. Thought one was for the Norrington, but not anymore."

She started to tell him Will was dead, but the big man shook his head. "The dream."

Alexia nodded, then looked at Crow. "Which is yours?"

The white-haired man smiled and reached for Alarien. As his hand closed on the hilt, what she had taken for old brass glowed golden. Crow stood and unsheathed the gleaming silver blade. Elvish writing, washed in gold, writhed its length, and seemed to shift and sway as if golden grass teased by spring breezes.

He turned to look at Nay, with tears running down his cheeks. "Temmer was autumn, and its breaking was winter. This is spring, with promises of summer."

"Might have felt something like that in the forging." Nay nodded solemnly. "Now you, Highness."

She wanted to protest that she already had a sword, a very nice one, given to her by the urZrethi of Bokagul, but one of these blades called to her. It wasn't the way a *sullanciri* blade had called to her. She'd wielded the blade once used by Malarkex, and it was a foul thing. That sword had wanted her to be an agent of chaos and destruction. It wanted to use her, not be used by her.

She reached for the first sword, Heart, and the moment her hand closed over the leather-wrapped hilt, she knew it had been meant for her from the moment of its forging. Three and a half feet long, with a slight curve at the tip, Heart was both stout and light. Blood grooves ran the length from crossguard to six inches from the tip. There, both sides of the blade had been sharpened, allowing her to thrust as well as stab.

As swords went, Heart had been made by a master who knew both his craft and what would be demanded of the sword. Moreover, the magick in it bound the blade to her. It felt like a natural extension of her arm. She had no fear of its failing her. For as long as she lived, no other sword would she draw. That came to her in a flash, and the truth of it made her tremble.

She bowed her head to Nay. "Thank you."

"The swords choose their own. It's what is meant to be." Nay stood and waved a hand at his son. "The others will find their masters."

Crow rested a hand on Nay's shoulder. "Prince Erlestoke should see the blades. He's a hero."

"Arrange it. Got the others all arranged, Borell?"

The young man slung the parcel over his back again. "All set."

"Wait, you can't go yet."

Nay looked at Crow. "You're an important man, though many don't know. Won't be taking up your time."

"You're not." Crow frowned. "Nay, a week and a half ago—even though it seems like months now—I spoke with my brother, Sallitt, for the first time since Fortress Draconis. The fact that I let everyone think I was dead, and that I didn't try to talk to my family, had hurt him. He thought I didn't trust him. When my father took my mask, I did stop trusting my family, and that was wrong.

"Rounce knew who I was because I needed his help to search for the Norrington, and to make war on Chytrine. I trusted him with that secret and I would have trusted you, but I was afraid what would happen if Scrainwood found out."

Nay shrugged. "You had your reasons."

"But I was *wrong*. I am sorry if you hurt when you heard I was dead. I'm sorry if you hurt now, thinking I thought so little of you that I didn't believe I could trust you."

The large swordsmith shook his head and landed a hand on Crow's shoulder that staggered him. "No tears were shed for you. Never believed suicide. When Crow tales started being sung, of Crow with Resolute, the truth was there. Fact is, you *are* important."

"But what's more important is spending time with friends." Crow smiled. "You must stay here, for dinner at least. Scrainwood has Rounce's estate, so you can't go there."

Rounce smiled. "He does have a point, Nay."

"You always were the smart one, Hawkins." Nay squeezed Crow's shoulder and smiled. "We'll stay. The wife would skin me for impolite if not."

"Good, very good." Crow smiled broadly. "We'll all get caught up. It'll be a long night, but with friends, it won't be nearly long enough."

CHAPTER 13

Kerrigan remained wary of Rymramoch's magick, but over the next three days he never found himself ambushed again. He'd not liked being tricked, and that he had been tricked so easily hurt his pride. He struggled with putting all that aside. He accomplished it when he drew two lessons from his disappointment.

The first thing he realized was that as much as Rym seemed to like him, and as much as he appeared to be human—even though he was but a puppet—he was *not* human. Rymramoch and all of dragonkind had a focus in the matter of the DragonCrown that differed sharply from that of humanity. They wanted the Crown destroyed and their ancestors alive again when their Truestones were returned to them. Kerrigan could understand their goal and even applauded it, but knew its accomplishment was not the same as the defeat of Chytrine. Dragons would take the Crown from whoever offered it to them first.

The second perception that came to him seemed modest in comparison. Rym, the dragons, and even Bok had lived for centuries and had understanding of magick, the world, and perhaps even fate that he did not possess. Kerrigan was talented in the ways of magick. Everyone said so, and he knew it as well. In the short time Rym had directed him, he had grown incredibly, both in his ability to shape spells and his ability to fuel them.

But his talents with magick, no matter how they grew, could not confer upon him the wisdom that centuries of life and experience would provide. Kerrigan knew he needed that wisdom, and to avail himself of it he had to trust others. Until he made that realization, he had no inkling of how little he had trusted in the past.

Granted, his upbringing had not really been conducive to trust. As he looked back, he knew Rym's take on his role at Vilwan was correct. He had been shaped as a weapon, but never had he been told that was his purpose. He certainly wouldn't have understood the full import of such a thing, but there were ways he could have been informed and prepared to accept that role. As it was, his life had been a continuous cycle of tutors and testing, with praise stinted and criticism in abundance. Despite his performance in any trials his masters could devise, there was always a lack of belief in what he could do.

His only recourse had been to manipulate his teachers, and he'd learned to do that well. Manipulation, however, breeds contempt for others. The only tutor he'd really respected—at least of those who taught him after he was of an age to think for himself—was Orla. He'd not been able to manipulate her. She had a clear goal for him, to prepare him for the war, and while she brooked no foolishness, she also praised him appropriately for his efforts.

Her, he trusted. Orla, as she lay dying, had told him to trust Crow and Resolute. Likewise, she'd told him he could not trust Vilwan. She clearly knew their plans for him. She helped further those plans, but also tried to make him more than some magick sword to be thrust into Chytrine's belly.

Rym's little ambush might not have inspired trust in

anyone else, but it did in Kerrigan. Rym could have remonstrated all day and all night about the need to be careful, but that simple demonstration brought the lesson home in painful relief. It also started Kerrigan thinking about the links between various things, and how spells have effects on people and items.

Kerrigan rolled up the sleeves on the brown robe he wore and looked at Bok. The urZrethi squatted in the corner of the antechamber they used as a workshop, piecing together some odd device full of springs and gears. The urZrethi shifted his hands and fingers into the tools needed to make things fit, and when that was insufficient, a small burst of magick would light the project. Kerrigan had no idea what he was doing, but assumed that the device would be used later in some sort of test.

"Bok, I need information."

The urZrethi smiled and did not turn his head. "I'm certain of that, Adept Reese."

Kerrigan snorted, then wandered over and sat on the floor facing Bok's right side. "When I was at Fortress Draconis, I placed a spell on one fragment of the DragonCrown. I modeled the spell on something Neskartu had created. That spell killed my mentor, but the spell I created was intended to make Chytrine paranoid. I didn't want her thinking clearly."

Bok nodded. "You've explained this before. It was a good plan. Anything more overt and she might have noticed. Do you want to know how much it is likely to be affecting her judgment?"

"I'd like to know that, yes, but that's not the main question I have."

The urZrethi set the assembly of gears and springs on a small workbench, but did not shift his limbs back into their normal form. "Chytrine is unique in many ways. Your spell would have exploited a natural weakness in her nature. I doubt it is having an overall effect, but it nudges and pushes from time to time. It is not as if you have blinded her completely, but as if the blues or greens she sees are off."

Kerrigan thought for a moment, then nodded. "You do think it is having an effect on her, though."

"You weave magick well, Adept Reese. I am certain it is effective." He picked the assembly up again and began to attach curved silver plates to it, shaping it into a sphere. "Is there something more?"

"Yes, but I don't know how much you will tell me."

The urZrethi's smile grew, splitting his thick, dark beard. "I have told you I am her father."

"Yes, and that you knew Kirûn."

"And it has only taken you eight days to decide you wanted to know about that?" Bok laughed, then spoke to the air. "You thought he would be more impulsive, Master, but I told you he was patient."

Kerrigan frowned. "I'm not playing a game here."

Bok gestured with a hand that shifted from wrench to hammer. "Don't imagine that I think you are, Adept Reese. Rymramoch and I merely discussed how soon you would ask after my past. That you have delayed this long is taken as a good thing. I would vouchsafe that if you'd not had an idea that could be helped by knowing my history, you'd have refrained from asking even longer."

"Probably." Kerrigan shrugged weakly. The most personal discussions he'd had were with Will, Lombo, and Orla, and all three of them were gone. He didn't think sharing confidences with them was what doomed them, but losing someone he'd gotten to know still hurt deeply.

"I shall tell you the story as I work, Adept Reese. If there are details I leave out, ask. When I hit upon what you need to know, tell me, and I can save the rest of it for another time."

"I will."

Bok smiled. "Rymramoch has told you that after the destruction of Vareshagul, all of urZrethi society changed. Many males had been killed, so the survivors were in a minority. Women reshaped our society, deciding who would breed with whom. You saw, in Bokagul, that many urZrethi males are feeble of mind though strong of limb, and the *coraxoc* often choose them for these traits. Males are not challenged or trained for much of anything beyond hard labor but, on occasion, there is a throwback to the old times. I was one such, born almost eight centuries ago. In me was not only intelligence, but the ability to work magicks.

"I came from a family of sorceresses and, being a quiet child as well as precocious, I watched spells being worked. I learned much quickly, but what I learned best of all was to hide my abilities. You may have thought my choosing to act the simpleton beast was difficult, but it is the earliest role I ever adopted."

Kerrigan nodded. "Watching magick being performed is not learning the intricacies of it. I can't imagine how you mastered spells . . ."

"I was fortunate. I had a sister who was very intelligent, but her magick abilities were weak. She practiced her lessons hard, and found that if she could reduce things to the point where I would understand them, she could grasp them. Daily she imparted to me the finer points of thaumasophy. By the time two decades had passed and I was to be severed from the maternal community, banished to a life in the mines, I knew enough magick that I could have challenged my grandmother in a duel."

"And that's why you are a Bok? Why you were exiled?"

The green sorcerer shook his head. "I was not so foolish. I was quiet little Loktu, a dreamer. One day I wandered off into the mountains of Bokagul and vanished. I made my way west and stowed away on a ship bound for Vilwan. I hid out there, watching and studying, going unnoticed for the longest time. I wanted instruction, but there are urZrethi Magisters there and I knew they would object to a male of their race being trained in magick.

"Fortune smiled, however, when I encountered a young Magister named Yrulph Kirûn." Bok's dark eyes glittered as he fitted another plate onto his construction. "He was much like you in some ways—young and skilled, though he was whipcord lean, with white hair and cobalt eyes. To look at him you'd think a stiff breeze could knock him over, but he had the power to control hurricanes. He had an insatiable curiosity about everything, and saw that magick could make so many lives better. When he found me he didn't see an urZrethi vagabond, but someone whose potential would be wasted if I were not trained.

"He hit upon an artifice by which I could prove my worthiness to be trained. He instructed me in some simple combat magicks and I mastered them quickly. Kirûn then set about spreading a rumor of a ghostly figure, tall and cloaked and hooded, haunting the south end of the island. He said he would find this creature and bring it to bay. We played a game, he and I, where I let myself be seen from time to time, building excitement, then he issued me a challenge. We met for a duel."

Bok set the construct down again and shook his head. "In those days, Kerrigan, the wizards of Vilwan dueled famously. The battle we fought lasted for over an hour, with spell being met by counterspell. A huge audience gathered and were awed. I'd shifted my shape, of course, to be tall and gaunt, and I remained hidden in a hooded cloak and old robe. We unleashed lightning and hellfire, created phantasms that shredded each other, summoned creatures not seen before and banished them to pits from which they had been drawn.

"And, finally, as we had agreed, we asked each other to hold. I said to him, 'You are the best of Vilwan and my master. I would be your apprentice.' And he opened his arms to take in all the Magisters who had taught him, and said, 'I am but an apprentice here, myself, but if my masters give me leave, I would happily instruct you.' "

Kerrigan clapped his hands. "The Magisters fell all over themselves to welcome you."

"They did. There was protest when my true nature was

revealed, but none could deny my abilities. Kirûn put it simply: I could be trained and thereby made useful, or could be released to whatever mayhem I could commit. Since the urZrethi Magisters already knew any unsupervised male was a problem, they were forced to adopt the plan. Even so, word was sent back to Bokagul and I was made Bok."

"So you and Kirûn were friends."

"Very much so, and for a long while—or long as reckoned in human terms. We were friends until the end, or close to it." Bok's face closed. "This next part I will tell because you will ask. It is not the whole cause of the rift, but a large part of it. Kirûn changed in little ways and became obsessed with things. His curiosity had led him to uncover knowledge about the Oromise. At least, I think that is the truth of it because he became interested in the creation of new life. At first it was simple. He used magick to do more quickly what herdsmen had done for centuries and bred stronger, more desirable animals. To me, being urZrethi, that seemed the way of things and right. But Kirûn took things a step further."

The human mage nodded. "I know he caused matings between elves and *araftii* that produced the Gyrkyme."

"Yes, and that experiment turned out well, all things considered. I did not know, until later, that the elves were compelled through magick to couple with the birdbeasts. As I had seen males of my kind all but forced into stud service, I am not certain I would have objected had I known. It didn't really matter, though, because Kirûn had worked magick on me, too."

Bok looked away and his eyes dulled. "You know dragons can assume human form. The Gyrkyme tell you that cross-species matings can be viable and even fertile. Kirûn knew that dragons and urZrethi were mortal enemies and I think he made himself believe that we could find peace if there were someone to bridge the gap between us. Among his friends was a dragon, a female, who assumed human form. She and I . . . Chytrine is our daughter."

Kerrigan's mouth dropped open. "A dragon and an urZrethi? But she appears elven . . ."

Bok closed his eyes, then shook his head. Slowly his body shifted its shape. He became taller and more angular, supple of limb. Ears sharpened and rose through dark hair. Even his eyes grew larger and more elven. If not for the malachite cast of his skin, Kerrigan would have taken him to be an elf.

"Chytrine could appear to be anyone. She can even assume dragon form. There was a dragon at Porasena, in Alcida. I believe that was her."

"But if she is a dragon, why does she need other dragons?"

Bok smiled, but still maintained his elf shape. "You saw Vriisuroel at Navval. She is not nearly as powerful as he is. He helped raise her and would destroy her if needs be."

"Why doesn't he?"

The urZrethi shrugged. "His mind is his own. Let it suffice that he opposes her now, even if it is for his own reasons."

"Chytrine became Kirûn's apprentice, didn't she?"

"She learned much from him, and from me, and Vriisuroel and others. She helped shape the DragonCrown. She knows more about its power and its abilities than anyone else."

Kerrigan frowned. "You said that you didn't think Kirûn knew the Crown would let him control dragons, but that he must have or else those abilities would not have been part of it. Could she have worked them into it without his knowing?"

"As you worked the spell you did on that fragment?" Bok's face tightened as he thought, then he nodded. "Yes, that could be one explanation."

Kerrigan chewed his lower lip for a moment. "All that you told me fits with an idea I have. I created a search spell that can find fragments of the DragonCrown, but that's because I know their nature. More important than finding them, however, is finding her. From the fragment here, perhaps I can pick up a hint of her. And I can perhaps use a trace of the spell that's affecting her."

Bok held up his right hand. The thumb grew into a sharp thorn that he pressed to his own palm. "A drop of my blood would give you half her nature."

"That would be enough, I think."

"Perhaps, but why take chances?" Bok pointed deeper into the fastness of Vael. "Let us get something of her mother, too, and make certain your spell will not fail."

CHAPTER 14

High up in the tallest tower Svarskya had to offer, General Markus Adrogans studied a map of the world. One of his aides had retinted the nation of Okrannel red, as it had been represented on maps before Chytrine's forces had destroyed it. The aide had also taken the liberty to recolor the whole of the nation even though the army had not ventured into the northeast and had little intelligence about the situation there.

The possibility of an Aurolani force lurking on the Crozt peninsula was but one of many things weighing on his mind. Foremost among them was the political situation brewing in Narriz. Adrogans smiled, recalling Phfas' saying that politics was not brewing but festering. He couldn't disagree, but the methods he had for lancing that boil were limited.

His game of asking for clarifications had only bought him a couple of days. His denial of possessing dragonels had not been accepted by the crowns. His allied commanders all brought to him messages from their leaders requesting clarification of his denials. Like General Caro, they replied that Adrogans did not have them; but politicians are naturally suspicious, so requests kept coming.

At least the way they are worded becomes more inventive and entertaining.

The crowns clearly feared his taking the dragonels and building an empire. It fueled renewed requests that he leave immediately for Narriz. That would remove him as the head of his army and lessen the threat he represented. As a result he was under a direct command to quit Svarskya within a day to begin his journey.

He turned from the map and looked at his advisors. "In Narriz the situation as they see it is simple: the Aurolani have quit Okrannel, we have dragonels and are about to take over the world. This makes us a bigger threat to them than Chytrine, even though she's far closer to Narriz than we are."

Turpus Caro clutched scarred hands around a tankard of steaming mulled wine. "King Augustus does not feel that way. I would guess none of the leaders who are facing her assaults directly see us that way, either. It's the western nations who fear us. Their efforts in the east are minimal, but if their fear makes them turn on Jerana, you would have no choice but to move south and create the empire they think you intend to create."

"A self-fulfilling prophecy, yes." Adrogans nodded slowly, then looked at the raven-haired elf. "Mistress Gilthalarwin, what do your leaders say in this matter?"

She shook her head. "We have no one in Narriz. I have sent discreet reports back to Loquellyn, but I have received no reply. My leaders know we will not assist you in empire building, so the matter is a distraction they deem beneath their notice."

Adrogans accepted her words for their meaning, but the tightness in her voice suggested something was wrong. He'd not been privy to her messages back to Loquellyn in the past, nor had he known the frequency of her communication with her home. The fact that she'd mentioned not hearing back he took as significant, but had no idea what it might indicate.

Beal mot Tsuvo had been seated in a tall, thronelike chair. "You have liberated Svarskya. The Guranin Highlanders will follow you and do what you bid. We do not fear your building an empire because the first two nations you would have to subdue would be Gurol and Valicia. Both of them contributed to Okrannel's liberation and you would not dishonor them that way."

She motioned with the stump of her right arm. "A thousand more Highlanders have entered Svarskya, so our forces swell."

"I know. Thank you." The forces he had been given to win Okrannel's freedom had numbered six thousand. The fighting had not been nearly as hard as it should have been, but casualties and weather had cost him a quarter of his force. The influx of Guranin volunteers and a thousand refugees from the lost city of Svoin had more than reinforced his army.

This influx of people did augment his army nicely, but did not represent the whole of his reinforcements. More Zhusk came to the city, and while they appeared, like Phfas, to be feral creatures, they possessed great power. The Zhusk allied themselves with elemental spirits called *yrûn*. Phfas' union with air allowed him to perform miracles such as stopping an arrow in flight, or triggering an avalanche. Phfas' spiritual power mocked his tiny physical form, but he and the other Zhusk were invaluable to the army in too many ways to enumerate.

Adrogans himself knew the *yrûn* well, for he was half Zhusk. Before the battle for Svoin he had undergone the rituals that bound him to the *yrûn* and vice versa. He had some command of air, earth, water, fire, and wood, but his mistress was the *yrûn* of Pain. Even as he stood there, he could feel her clutching him loverlike from behind, her talons sinking into his shoulders and her razor teeth gnawing at his neck.

But that was a small price to pay for what she gave him. Pain luxuriated in the misery of others, and through her he could feel it as well. When he pushed his awareness through her and into Crozt, he sought the sort of discomfort armies know on the march and felt nothing. It heartened him, but did not make him believe the Aurolani had abandoned Okrannel.

"As you all know, I have been ordered to leave Svarskya for Narriz at this time tomorrow. The only caveat to the order is that, in my judgment, the situation here has to be stable."

Caro shook his head. "Under no circumstances is it stable."

The Jeranese general smiled, but held up a hand. "I appreciate your enthusiasm, and I agree with your assessment, though I think you are defining instability a bit more broadly than our masters are."

The white-haired man shook his head. "To combat foolishness, I would declare the situation unstable were there nothing more sinister than snow drifting in the streets, but that is not what prompts me to make my declaration. Captain Agitare has reported that they have hit upon a good formulation for firedirt. He wants to refine it, but he is getting power equivalent to that of the Aurolani firedirt."

Beal glanced over at him. "Why refine?"

"The firedirt the Aurolani left behind does not appear, according to what he and others can recollect, to have the power of the firedirt used at Fortress Draconis."

"Of course!" Adrogans clapped his hands. "She did leave us the dragonels, but gave us inferior firedirt. It wouldn't matter when we chose to use the weapons against others who didn't have them, but matched up against her dragonels, we would deploy too close and be smashed. That's why she felt safe in doing that."

The Alcidese leader nodded. "And the dragonels she

would recover after a battle, thanking us for dragging them along. She thought this out."

Phfas hissed. "Nefrai-kesh did this."

"True, Uncle, very true." Pain clawed down Adrogans' chest, then raked her talons across his belly. Even if the goal of the Okrannel campaign for Chytrine had been to give him underpowered dragonels, inflicting more damage on the army that won them would not make them any less effective. In fact, had his army been more chewed up, his reliance on them would have been far greater in anything he did in the future. Nefrai-kesh, however, had refrained from doing maximum damage to the army, for reasons Adrogans felt would never be made clear.

Caro set his tankard down. "Because we have uncovered her deception in this area, we have to assume it was meant to lull us into a false sense of security. We have to guard against immediate attack. For all we know there is a fleet departing the Ghost March right now, or leaving Vorquellyn or even Muroso, headed in this direction. Moreover, if Chytrine has agents in Narriz, she could already be aware of the orders that summon you there. She could target you for assassination or, worse yet, capture and convert you into one of her *sullanciri*. For you to follow the orders you have been given would seriously jeopardize the war against Chytrine."

Adrogans nodded in agreement. "All of us here—not just in this room, but in this city—realize we have a duty. Our mission was to take Okrannel from Chytrine, but that was because it would hurt her efforts at making war in the east. We still need to press her and cause her more problems. In a grand sense, the situation here *is* stable, and it is up to us to make it unstable.

"Our options here are very limited. Regardless of my refusal to travel by water, we have not enough ships to move a significant portion of our forces anywhere. If we are to do anything, it will be by land. Logically, we should go into the Crozt region and secure it, which effectively wastes my

army since the terrain there would allow small Aurolani
units to keep us tied up for a long time. Those same units
would be too small to lay siege to a reinforced Svarskya, especially if we have dragonels to discourage them."

Beal nodded. "If we reinforce the old city's walls, a garrison of a thousand should be enough to hold it against five
times that number."

"Agreed, and that is the project I want you to devote
yourself to. Until your arm and leg are prepared, you're not
going anywhere, and the best of the new troops we have are
your clansmen, so the repair and defense of Svarskya are
now your responsibility."

"Thank you, General."

"Don't. It will be a thankless task. At the worst Chytrine
will send a dragon to melt the city and you'll all die. At best,
you'll die of boredom. The fact is, however, I need someone
I can trust to do this. You'll also have Svoin volunteers and
the Okrans Kingsmen to help you. Any other refugees
flooding in will be trained and you can release better units
to join us."

Caro sipped his wine, then smiled. "Join us where?"

Adrogans sighed. "The war in the east consists of a
strong push south and now southwest. Saporicia is going to
become the battleground because King Augustus cannot
afford to wait for Chytrine to get south. If you look at the
Narriz harbor and draw a line east to Bokagul, you have the
line Augustus must defend. The mountains and the ocean
secure his flanks."

The elf frowned. "This suggests you think Oriosa will
hold against her and not just let her troops wander
through."

"Augustus has to think that, too. We know that because
he's not yet invaded Oriosa. He'll have forces on the border
to screen against that possibility, and Oriosa has to hold or
become a battleground itself. King Scrainwood may be a
cowardly snake, but he does have a sense of self-pres-
ervation."

Adrogans turned to the map again and the others gathered around, with the elf supporting Beal mot Tsuvo. "So, we have to guess at what Chytrine and Nefrai-kesh will do. Something you said, Turpus, about a fleet gathering in the Ghost March or on Vorquellyn makes me wonder. The conquest of Vorquellyn was the greatest seaborne invasion the world has known and was wildly successful. Chytrine attempted to duplicate that feat with the invasion of Vilwan. Its failure has undoubtedly led people to believe she is not going to use the sea anymore. Many would point to the fact that we shipped troops here for this campaign without opposition as proof that she *cannot* rule the sea."

The Zhusk shaman snorted. "She wanted us here."

"Exactly, so there was no reason she would harass us at sea. This is not to say she could not have done so, but that she chose not to do so. And remember that Nefrai-kesh, when he was Lord Norrington, led a waterborne invasion of Okrannel and did win a victory on the sea. He's not afraid of shipping troops."

Turpus set his tankard down on Valicia. "A fleet in the Ghost March could land anywhere. Once the forces are locked in battle in Saporicia, the fleet could place troops behind the lines."

Beal's blue eyes became slits. "You're thinking tactically. Think politically." She tapped her index finger on a spot further south. "The Aurolani will sail down and take Yslin."

Her words came in a hoarse whisper that filled Adrogans' belly with ice, and Pain delighted in it. A strike at Yslin would cut allied forces off from their reinforcements by land. Oriosa would no longer be threatened by Augustus, so it could go fully over to the Aurolani camp. Alcida would fall and other nations would follow. Chytrine would conquer them, or they would bargain with her as Scrainwood had.

Blood had drained from Caro's face. "Do you honestly think she has a fleet gathering in the Ghost March?"

"It's immaterial. She did not lose all of her ships in the

Vilwan invasion, and she is using ships to supply troops in Muroso. We can and should assume they are shipping from the Ghost March. What I suggest we have to do is to move the bulk of our forces up and around into the Ghost March. We disrupt whatever she is doing there. If she is preparing an invasion of Yslin, we do our best to stop it. If all she is doing is running supplies, we stop them."

Caro nodded slowly. "We really can't tell the crowns of our suspicions about the Yslin invasion, can we?"

"No." Adrogans shook his head. "It's like the dragonels: it's a problem they cannot deal with. If they plan against it, Chytrine punches down through weakened lines and it doesn't matter. Some nations will assume that Yslin isn't the target, but that their own nation is, and they will stop giving troops and supplies, so the effort against her fails."

Gilthalarwin raised an eyebrow. "Don't you fear the fleet might sail up the river to Lakaslin and destroy Jerana?"

"As much as you fear it might land at Rellaence and destroy your home." Adrogans sighed. "Being there to stop Chytrine from attacking Jerana or Loquellyn or Yslin will not defeat Chytrine. Only one thing will. Just as she can strike at our homes and make us fear, we can do the same. With every mile we stab into the Ghost March, she has to worry about our turning north and bringing war to Aurolan. The leaders down south won't see it that way, so we must see it for them. We have to do what they will fail to command us to do."

Caro's lips tightened into a grim smile. "There are those who would consider this mutiny."

"Yes, but they are the ones who wear the crowns." Adrogans forced a brave smile on his face. "We're the ones who shed blood for the crowns and, at least this time, that makes for all the difference in the world."

CHAPTER 15

Alexia looked up from her place in the chair beside the fire as Crow entered their chambers. "Snowing again, is it?"

He nodded, shrugged off a heavy cloak, the shoulders of which had been dappled by snow. "Not very much, but it's coming from the north, just like Chytrine's forces will." Crow glanced at the small table beside her and the sheaf of paper stacked there. "You read what I wrote today?"

"I hope you don't mind."

"No, not at all." He frowned. "There were things I'd not thought on for a long time. That's why I went for a walk, and I guess I was out longer than I thought."

The hesitation in his voice rasped against her heart. "I didn't realize that you and Seethe . . ."

Crow hung the cloak on a peg on the back of the door, then stood there, tall and strong-limbed, in fawn leathers and brown boots. His white mane half hooded his face and weariness lined it. His hands gathered at his belt, his fingers interlaced. He did not look at her as he spoke.

"Seethe and I were lovers. She was beautiful, in the way that elves are all beautiful, and she had a vitality to her that was beyond human. We were all embarked on a heroic quest, and she seemed very heroic. Even so, she needed someone, much as I did. It would have been more remarkable that we did *not* fall in love with each other."

Alyx nodded slowly and kept her voice barely above a whisper. "She was the one Chytrine made into Myrall'mara?"

"Yes."

Alyx recalled the first time she'd seen that *sullanciri*. It had been in Yslin, when Chytrine's creature had organized a network of urchins to search for Will Norrington. When confronted by the heroes who stormed her headquarters, she had made a grab for Will, but Crow stopped her. *She bared her breasts and told him he could never stab her.*

"In Yslin, you would have killed her, wouldn't you?"

Crow nodded slowly, but no words came for a moment or two. Then he looked up at her, his brown eyes glistening. "She was not Seethe. She was as twisted as the children she had warped. I would have killed her. I should have."

Alyx gave him a small smile. "That was the first you had seen her?"

"Since leaving Chytrine's sight, yes."

"It must have been a surprise, and reopened a wound."

He raked fingers back through his hair. "A surprise, yes. And a reopened wound, too."

"Twenty-five years is a long time to carry that sort of burden."

He shrugged uneasily. "There were other things that made it secondary. After I was disgraced, my life was over. When Resolute found me, he rebuilt me in his image. He made me Crow. Seethe rested with Hawkins, so was not much revisited. There were times it was a great comfort to imagine that Hawkins had never been, and that I was always just Crow."

Alyx straightened her legs, untucking them from

beneath her bottom, then leaned forward with forearms on her knees. "Was there no one for Crow?"

"What are you asking, Alexia?"

"If during the time you were Crow you were without love and companionship."

Crow folded his arms over his chest. "Why are you asking?"

She nodded toward the papers, giving herself a moment for the lump in her throat to go away. "I read there a lot of longing, about the joy of loving and being loved, and touching and being touched. I know you, Crow. I love you, and I know the passions that run in you. That you could have gone so long without intimacy hurts me."

He closed his eyes. "Resolute and I were at war with Chytrine and that was not an easy course. Our paths did run parallel with others, here and there. There were women who offered comfort, seeking the same, but we knew there was no future. Weeks, months, years off and on, here and there, I wasn't always alone. Things would end because they had to. No regrets, but some tears."

He reopened his eyes and looked at her. "Until you, Alexia, I never wanted a future. I never thought one was possible. And now, here I am, in the twilight of my life, seeing what I missed."

Alyx stood and walked to him. "But it was something you were not destined to have, Crow."

"I guess not."

"Until now." She reached out and took his hands in hers. Wordlessly she led him to the bed and made him sit on the edge of it. "I am glad you were not denied companionship, my love. If I could, I would thank them for giving you what no person should be denied."

"Alexia, I . . ."

She pressed a finger to his lips. "You need say nothing, lover." She grasped the hem of his tunic and drew it up over his head and off. Bending over, with hands to either side of his hips, she kissed the trio of scars running from right hip to collarbone. She kissed them gently, lingering for a heartbeat or two, her eyes closed. Up and up she moved, the hair on his chest brushing softly over her nose and chin. When she reached his nipple, she kissed that more than once and felt him slide fingers into her hair.

His fingers tightened as he drew her head back and up. "You don't have to do this, Alexia."

"Silly man. I *want* to do this." Her right hand came up to hold his head, and she kissed him quickly and fiercely. Her lips pressed to his, then parted. Her tongue darted out, flicking against his lips and teeth. Her grip tightened on his head, as his did, and she pressed him down onto the bed as their kiss deepened.

Alexia pulled her head up and smiled as she looked down at him. That he was handsome she would not deny, despite the scars and white hair, the age lines at the corners of his eyes. To others that might have been all that mattered, but to her it was an added benefit, for what she desired lay within. It shone through his brown eyes, and in his smile. She could feel it in how he touched her, his hand in her hair, the other at the small of her back.

She kissed him again, quickly, then buried her face against his neck. Her teeth grazed his flesh, then her lips closed on it. She could feel life pumping through the arteries there and feel muscles stretch as he tilted his head to give her clear access. Even a whispered sigh thrummed against her lips. She sucked a bit harder, then pulled her head up sharply.

He gasped and she smiled before ducking her head to lick over the mark she'd left. As she brought her head up again, she smiled. "I love you, and I want *our* future. And I want you, very much, my husband."

Crow smiled. "Our future, yes."

Alyx slid back off him until her feet were on the floor again. A hand pressed to Crow's chest prevented him from rising. She tugged off his boots and stockings, then loosened his belt. She took her time sliding his trousers off, and kissed him over the hipbone where the trio of scars descended and a more recent scar crossed them. Freeing him of the trousers, she bid him get under the covers, then she quickly disrobed and joined him, lying side by side.

She let him gather her into his arms, pulling them tight together, belly to belly. His hair felt soft against her stomach and chest and his arms strong around her. She sighed, closing her eyes, and nuzzled his neck again. "Make love with me, Crow."

"Yes, Alexia, yes." Crow's left hand came up as he pulled his head back. He tipped her face up and kissed her deeply and passionately. His breath came softly on her cheek. As they kissed, she clung to him and, at her urging, he came up and over her as she rolled onto her back. She tightened her embrace with a hand at his neck, the other at the small of his back, then locked her ankles behind his knees.

As he entered her they began to move together in a fluid dance. Sensations flowed over her in rising waves, the same as the heat built between them. Her hips thrust to meet his, her hands stroked his back, then clutched and squeezed, holding him tighter. He rose on his hands, arching his back as urgency increased. Kisses quickened, multiplied, their bodies shifted and though each became inarticulate, they understood each other completely. Their ascent to their mutual goal steepened as exertion coated their bodies with a moist sheen.

Then their passion exploded, the heat spiking, hearts racing, breath coming short and fast, even ragged. She slid her arms up around his back, tugging him down onto her. He resisted for a second, then his elbows bent and he covered her. She tightened her embrace, determined to keep him there. She licked at his neck, at that mark, tasting the sweat their pleasures had produced.

Alyx wanted to tell him how much she loved him, but words were still too far away. Love burned in her, making her hold him even more tightly. She licked again at his throat and could feel his heart beating as hard as hers. His breathing made her smile, his scent filled her head, and for her not only did the world end outside their bed, she had no need for it.

Crow came up on his elbows and tried to slide to the side, but she held him firmly. "I don't want to crush you."

She shook her head. "You are not, and I want you right there. For now."

"For now?"

Alexia nodded slowly. "There are other ways I want you, too. Most of all, though, I want you to know you are loved and desired. That there were others to love you through the years makes me happy, but none of them knew you as I do. None of them value you as I do."

Crow smiled. "You think so?"

"I *know* so." She raised her head and kissed him quickly. "If they had, they'd never have let you go."

"Just as long as you never let me go, that is all I care about." Crow stroked her hair with a hand, letting his thumb brush over her cheek. "Many have suggested I've been very lucky to have survived this long. That luck is nothing compared to the luck of my finding you."

"Not luck, Crow, fate. You're fated to see Vorquellyn liberated. You have given your life to that task, and the world is going to give you something back." Alexia licked playfully at his neck again, then squeezed him with her arms and legs. "As for your luck, lover, you might try pressing it just this once."

"Yes, Princess?"

"Yes, husband. I have you. You are mine, and I do not mean to let you go." She smiled. "Tonight is our night, the portal to the future. Come. Together we pass through it, and we shall never look back again."

CHAPTER 16

Two things made sitting in the Oriosan delegation tolerable for Prince Erlestoke, but only just. The first was seeing Cabot Marsham's reactions to him. Over and over the prince caught the odious little man watching him. When he did, he would smile sweetly, but always let a hand curl into a fist or drop to where the hilt of his sword should have been. Such things would always make Marsham blanch or fidget. Erlestoke realized this was the rough equivalent of teasing a child, but he took some pleasure in it nonetheless because the frustration of naked, grasping greed is always a joy.

The other thing was the new sword he'd been given. Crow and Alexia had sent him a message and he'd gone to their rooms as soon as he was able. There he met a man and his son, a smith from Valsina. Erlestoke had never before heard of Naysmith Carver, but his father had never spoken much of the first expedition against Chytrine.

The prince had found the smith to be a man of few words, but fewest among them the word *I*. That made him a welcome relief from every minister and lordling infesting the capital. Nay's direct manner reminded Erlestoke well of the soldiers he'd commanded at Fortress Draconis, especially a *meckanshii* weapons-master who had been left behind in Sarengul. The prince hoped Verum still lived.

Nay's son had laid out two swords and the prince immediately found himself attracted to one of them. The longsword had a thick forte to the blade, but tapered quickly to a sharp point for thrusting. The pommel cap had a crown shape to it, and leather wrapped the wooden grip. The crossguard was unremarkable save for two inch-long spikes at each end running parallel to the blade.

Nay had explained how an urZrethi sorcerer named Bok had come and helped him work the blade with a fragment of Temmer in it. That news had given Erlestoke pause on two counts. He'd met Bok at Vael and thought him little more than an animal. The prince didn't like deception and found himself inherently not trusting the work done on the sword.

On top of that was the portion of Temmer that had been worked into it. The jagged fragment bridged both the forte and more slender part of the blade for a foot and a half. UrZrethi runes had been worked around it and washed in gold, making them match the crossguard and pommel. Temmer had been a powerful blade with baleful magick, but he feared that less than he did his father's reaction to learning he possessed a sword with a piece of Temmer in it. His father had remained convinced through the decades that, had Temmer been his, he would have been a great hero.

In many ways Erlestoke thought Temmer had worked its terrible magick on his father. Even without touching the sword, his father had been broken by it. The sword made him realize how much of a coward he truly was, and he never fought against that aspect of himself. His father would likely see the blade called Crown as meant for him, and a way to redeem himself.

But despite his misgivings, Erlestoke had accepted and

drawn the silvery blade. From the moment it slid free of the
scabbard, he knew it had indeed been meant for him. It fit
his hand perfectly and he was able to whip it about with the
flick of a wrist. The stout forte would permit him to parry
much heavier weapons. The ease with which the blade
moved would wend it through guards, picking out weak-
nesses in armor, spilling blood, and ending the lives of
those who threatened the world.

The prince wished he could have worn the sword to the
Council. Courtesy and custom allowed only King Fidelius
to wear a sword, for they were in his capital. Decorum
would permit him a single knife as a sign of his rank.
Erlestoke had chosen a long and utilitarian one, which he
had brought with him from Fortress Draconis. It comforted him to have it tucked into a boot, and time after time
he resisted the temptation to draw it and stab it into the
table in frustration.

Yet another minister rose, this one from Helurca. He
wore brightly colored silks of green and blue that mocked
the winter's howling. Erlestoke could understand the desire
to dress gaily in the depth of winter, but in councils where
the fate of the world was being decided, it seemed quite inappropriate.

Then again, the prince reminded himself, *the fate is not
being decided here, just endlessly debated.*

The Helurcan cleared his voice. "The people of Helurca
would also express their alarm at the flouting of this council's directive by General Markus Adrogans. His blatant dis-
regard for the command to appear here casts his previous
tactics in their true light. We cannot trust what he has told
us about the Aurolani threat to Okrannel. We cannot trust
what he has told us about dragonels. Yes, we acknowledge
that other nations have had their agents report back a lack
of dragonels in his possession, but how do we know he has
not fooled them into believing he does not have them?"

Erlestoke shook his head. The Helurcan minister had at
least avoided the eruption of anger created when his

Reqorese counterpart had suggested the soldiers in Adrogans' army had allied themselves with him and his fledgling empire. King Augustus' response had been the most acerbic when he suggested that it was Reqorra's own weak sense of self that made it possible for them to imagine others would not hold their nation above personal concerns. True to the internecine squabbles that infested Reqorra and spawned such suspicions, the delegation dissolved into a hissing squabble that ended the minister's speech.

The Helurcan continued. "For all we know, General Adrogans has his troops on the march south. He could have told those under his command that they would be coming to succor Saporicia. They would accept that explanation with selflessness and good hearts, hastening on while he plotted to use them to further his own ends."

With his nostrils flaring in disgust, Erlestoke rose. He felt Marsham clutching at his sleeve. He looked down at the grasping little man and Marsham recoiled as if stabbed through the heart. "I beg the minister's pardon, but this is patent nonsense and born out of an utter lack of understanding of troops."

The minister sniffed. "I know well your reputation, Prince Erlestoke, and meant to cast no aspersions on it . . ."

"Perhaps not, but you misunderstand the sort of men I have led. You misunderstand those Princess Alexia has led, that King Augustus commanded in Okrannel, and indeed those we are going to ask to fight for us here in Saporicia. No soldier accepts selflessly the orders to march halfway across the world. They will grumble and cavil, almost as much as you are."

The bald Helurcan minister raised himself to his full height and let his jowls quiver. "I hardly think . . ."

"No, you don't think. At least, not like a soldier. They'll follow Adrogans, but that's because they trust him. He's earned that trust. In taking Svoin and Svarskya he did what no other leader has done, and with fewer casualties than could ever have been imagined. When last you met in Yslin and gave him that duty, none of you imagined he would have gotten this far, this fast. He tells you he is moving his troops to continue the fight against Chytrine, and yet with no evidence to the contrary and all evidence to support his claim, you find reason to doubt it. You are being foolish."

"So say you now, Prince Erlestoke, but your nation is not one facing invasion."

Erlestoke rubbed his forehead with his left hand. "Do you not see the map, Minister? My nation is on the forefront of the invasion. Chytrine is closer to Oriosa than Adrogans would be to Helurca for a month yet, *if* he were heading south."

The Helurcan's eyes hardened. "You know your nation is in no jeopardy."

The Prince's spine stiffened. "Meaning exactly what, Minister?"

The Helurcan began to answer, but another voice, strident and furious, drowned him out. "Meaning he is a fool, as is everyone in this room, with an exception or two."

Resolute strode into the middle of the chamber, shrouded in a ragged cloak made of mottled gibberer scalps. Their irregular shapes and bare patches reminded Erlestoke of charnel mounds strewn over the plains around Fortress Draconis. Resolute's cloak had been fashioned from dozens of scalps, each one harvested after horrible fights. Erlestoke felt certain they represented but a fraction of those he had killed in his long war against Chytrine.

King Fidelius roused himself from his seat in objection. "The Vorquelves have no standing here. You will not be heard. You are out of order and shall remove yourself."

"No, I will not leave, and I *must* be heard." The Vorquelf's voice rasped roughly. "For over a *century* I have listened to men debate about Chytrine and how she would be dealt with. My interest is obvious. Men saved me from the fate that overtook my homeland. My kinsmen in the other homelands would not move against Chytrine to save Vorquellyn."

He glanced around the room, his argent gaze sending a tingle through Erlestoke as their eyes met. "The other elves think Vorquelves like me impatient, and I am. I will admit to wanting my home back, very much. But my desires are greater now. They have to be."

King Scrainwood snorted. "Had you been with us a quarter century ago, we would not be in this predicament."

"And had you a spine then, King Scrainwood, the same might be said. The future that would have come from either one of those things is unknowable. The lessons drawn from that failure are inescapable. Without courage, without determination, it will be a smaller council that meets in a year or a decade. So it will go until there is no one else to meet."

Resolute swept his cloak back, giving everyone full view of his powerful arms, decorated as they were with arcane tattoos. "I have listened for ages, but no more. You debate issues that do not matter. Even you, Prince Erlestoke, quibble over a point that is immaterial. If Adrogans is marching this way, for empire or succor, what does it matter? Neither will stop Chytrine, and stopping Chytrine is what must be done. To think about anything else is futile. Or, worse, it is completely irresponsible—more so than your predecessors were when they made Crow a scapegoat and hid behind him from their worst nightmares."

The silver-eyed Vorquelf pointed at Princess Alexia. "At least they had some foresight. They had the wisdom to train this woman in the ways of war. They envisioned her leading an army to defeat Chytrine. You know of her battles. You know of her feats. She has not failed at anything you have given her to do, yet what do you do now? You sit here and argue over trivial matters when you should be arguing over who will give the most to her army."

Ministers and rulers rose to object, and Resolute snarled. His right hand snapped into a fist, then opened again. One of the tattoos on his forearm flashed, then a gout of flame shot from his palm. The golden jet singed an overhead arch, and the heat of it drove people back. Even Erlestoke raised a hand to shield his face.

"You are *not* listening!" Smoke rose from Resolute's closed fist. "There has been time for talking. Now is a time for action. Every time you have acted in concert against Chytrine, she fails. If you lose sight of that, it is the ultimate failure."

Grand Duchess Tatyana struggled to her feet and began speaking in a low voice that demanded attention. "These councils have too long been without such cold reality. We, brothers and sisters, are given too often to deliberation of no consequence. The reasons do not matter, and to discuss them would be to continue in that vein."

"As you do now, witch."

Tatyana glared at Resolute, but the Vorquelf did not quail.

"Resolute is right. Alexia has been trained for a lifetime to lead the army we will assemble. Our ministers can discuss anything they desire, and likely will, but to us must fall the task of planning a war. A war that will destroy Chytrine. A war that will liberate Muroso and Sebcia and even Vorquellyn. As my nation has been saved, so should all nations be saved."

Tatyana's declaration ended and silence descended in the chamber. Resolute's words had brought a blush to Erlestoke's cheeks, and he was not alone in feeling embarrassed. Tatyana, in turn, offered those assembled the chance to abandon, at least for the moment, the petty squabbles that had defined their discussions thus far and move toward the grand goal of their common salvation.

King Fidelius, who had retreated to his seat with Resolute's incendiary display, again rose. "There is much wisdom in what has been said here. With due deliberation . . ."

Resolute spun, his mangy cloak swirling out. "With *due*

deliberation there will be no more Saporicia. You must act *now*. Plans must be made and the army must move. By the new year, the expeditionary force must be headed north."

"But that is only a week hence!"

Resolute nodded. "Yes, Highness. Ten days. They could be the final ten days your nation knows. Is that what you desire?"

"No, of course not."

"Good, then do what must be done." The elf opened his arms wide. "*Lead!* Demand plans be drawn, *now*! Give us all a reason to celebrate the new year. If you don't, we'll just remember it as the *last* year."

CHAPTER 17

Alexia found herself rising with the others to applaud Resolute. Sour disdain twisted his features, but Alexia shook her head when he looked at her. His expression lightened just a little, but the set of his shoulders and the tightness of his jaw betrayed his true feelings. Resolute shrugged, letting the gibberer cloak cover him again.

She moved from the Alcidese delegation and reached him first. "You were very eloquent."

His silver eyes remained cold. "I was less so in Yslin when Crow was a youth. Look what happened."

"Do you fear the same thing will happen now?"

The Vorquelf shook his head. "No. You will not let that happen. I saddled you with the responsibility."

Alyx nodded. As he'd spoken, he'd defined her as a weapon that had been shaped to oppose Chytrine, and she could see how that message would resonate with those gathered. That had been the goal of those who agreed to let her remain with the Gyrkyme. They provided her tutors and training. King Augustus had then provided her with troops and had seen to her gaining practical experience as a leader.

Resolute's words had reduced her to an object, but she knew the Vorquelf knew better than that. At one time she would have agreed with his characterization and even thought there could be no higher praise, but she had grown beyond that now. A mere weapon couldn't accept the responsibility he'd directed toward her.

A hand gripped her left wrist tightly. "It is as this one has said, Alexia. You will lead the world to victory."

Alyx looked down at her great-grandaunt. "Thank you for supporting him, Aunt Tatyana."

The old woman looked up at Resolute. "I have waited a long time to hear another refugee speak the truth."

Resolute's eyes hardened. "My truth is different than yours. Your nation is free."

"Not as long as the Nor'witch exists. She can threaten it at any time." Tatyana squeezed Alyx's wrist again. "In your planning, this must be taken into account. Adrogans must be made to hold Okrannel free. You see the wisdom there."

The vehemence hissing through the old woman's words sent a shiver up Alyx's spine. That Tatyana wanted Okrannel to remain free was not in doubt. Alyx suspected, however, that her great-grandaunt wanted to make certain that Adrogans' dragonels would remain in Svarskya. *Suspicious as she is she assumes he has them, therefore she wants them.* Alexia sighed, knowing the old woman was not alone in her desires, and that many would bring similar considerations to Alyx as campaigns were planned.

"I do, Aunt Tatyana, and will bear it in mind." With a twist of her wrist, she freed her arm. "There is a lot of work to do, and I should be about it."

"Of course." The old woman clutched her hands together. "You will have my full support. This is the outcome long *dreamed.*"

Alyx had to smile. None of the interpretations she'd ever heard bore any resemblance to the reality of how her nation had been freed. She was fairly certain that Tatyana had worked diligently to find portents in the book, and probably had circulated rumors through the exile community.

And now she is counting heavily on my dreams. Alyx had told the Crown Circle of a vivid series of battles in Saporicia and Muroso that shattered the Aurolani forces and sent them scurrying home. She didn't recall mentioning a coalition force or other leaders or any of the details that were likely to emerge from the meetings in Narriz, but she was certain confirmation of all of it would be found in the Book of Dreams.

Gasps sounded from behind Alyx and she turned quickly, only to see Peri land in a flutter of wings in front of her. "You must come now, sister."

Alyx looked at the Gyrkyme warrior. "I can't. There is so much I have to do now. Could Resolute . . . ?"

Peri shook her head. "Crow sent me."

"Did something happen? Is he hurt?"

"He's fine, but you have to go to your chambers now." Peri grabbed her by the hand and led her through the crowd. Resolute followed in their wake. Those military advisors who had been headed for her instead redirected themselves to King Augustus or Prince Erlestoke. Alyx wasn't sure if it was Resolute brooding behind her, or Peri's raised talons that cleared the way, but she was grateful for either.

The trio hurried through the castle and reached the tower. Ascending swiftly they entered the chambers and Alyx's heart caught in her throat. Crow sat in one chair beside a roaring fire. Opposite him, still huddled in a thick cloak over begrimed red riding leathers, sat a fiery redhead wearing a purple mask. Her hands were wrapped around the barrel of a steaming tankard.

"Sayce, when did you get here?"

The young woman looked up, then rose. Crow took the tankard from her before it could fall from her hands. Alyx advanced, meeting the smaller woman halfway and embraced her tightly. Sayce's hands tightened on Alyx's tunic and tremors shook her.

The Murosan Princess pulled back a bit, chewing her lower lip. "No one will tell me where Will is. They just say he didn't come here with you. Where is he?"

Alyx looked at Crow, but he shook his head. "She was frantic when she got here. I calmed her down as I sent for you."

"I understand, love." Alyx hugged Sayce tightly again. "Will isn't here, Sayce." As much as Alyx knew the young woman had to hear that Will was dead, Alyx couldn't force the words out. Sayce was carrying Will's child and loved him deeply. *To tell her would be cruel ... but not to tell her ...*

Resolute rested a hand on Alyx's shoulder, then pried the two women apart.

"Resolute, no."

The Vorquelf looked at Alyx and shook his head. "The sword Will gave me carries with it grave responsibilities. This is one I accept."

Sayce looked surprised, then a bit afraid, but she let Resolute steer her back to the chair by the fire. "What is it, Resolute?"

The Vorquelf dropped to a knee and took her hands in his. "You are carrying Will's child, aren't you?"

"How did you know?"

Resolute's expression remained tight, but not grim. "Princess Alexia knew. She brought us the happy news at Vael."

"Does Will know?"

"Do you think we could have kept it from him? He was overjoyed when he heard." Resolute swallowed hard, his voice remaining full with only a hint of strain. "That news completed a process in Will Norrington. When Crow and I found him, he was a lawless boy. He looked at responsibility the way he looked at the law. He sought to avoid both.

Gradually he came to accept that he was the Norrington. He accepted that he was part of something larger than himself. You saw him take responsibility for the Freemen in Meredo. Had you seen him with our raiding force, and the way he defied a dragon in Sarengul, you would have seen that process almost complete."

"Will defied a dragon?"

"Yes, and in the same way he saved your life in Bokagul, he saved all of us from dragonfire. He saved a portion of the DragonCrown. He went to Vael to argue against his father for dragonkind to join us in opposing Chytrine." Resolute squeezed her hands, holding on tight to them. "Until he learned you carried his child, he was accepting the responsibility he'd been given for others. Your child made him complete. Your child gave him a future. His purpose always was to defeat Chytrine, and he was bent on it because of the prophecy, but at last he could see beyond the prophecy and that completed him."

Sayce listened carefully and nodded solemnly. "So, where is he? Did the dragons require he remain on Vael?"

"His duty required that." The Vorquelf hesitated for a moment. "Nefrai-laysh attempted to murder a dragon. Will prevented that murder. It cost him dearly. It cost him his life."

The snap of the fire filled the silence. Sayce's mouth opened soundlessly, then she slumped back in the chair. She tugged her hands free of Resolute's and covered her face. Her whole body shook and tears rolled from beneath her mask to fall from her jaw and spatter her leathers.

Alyx started forward, but Resolute held up a hand and stopped her. She glared at him, angry that he would not let her comfort Sayce. She was almost as angry that he had so effortlessly lied to her. Alexia had not shared the news of Sayce's condition with Will. Resolute was probably correct, that Will would have been happy with the news, but a conversation he'd had with Alexia indicated that the opposite was just as likely. Resolute had not lied about Will's maturity, though, and she hoped that it would have made things turn out as Resolute described them.

The Vorquelf rested his hands on Sayce's knees. "Listen to me, Princess. You and your child *are* Will Norrington's future. He was willing to sacrifice himself to thwart Chytrine so that you and his child would thrive in a world without fear of her. All of us are determined to see that future become true. We need you to be part of our effort. When Will saved you—when he loved you, when he made a child with you—he bound you to us. And us to you. What seems an end now is a continuation. If you are with us, we cannot fail."

Sayce lowered her hands. Red rimmed her blue eyes and tear tracks still glistened on her cheeks. "I love Will Norrington. I would follow him anywhere. Whatever must be done, will be."

Resolute nodded once, then stood. Alexia stepped in and dragged Sayce up into a hug. Peri moved behind the Murosan Princess and likewise embraced her. Alyx and her sister hung on tightly as Sayce began to cry again. They pressed in close, holding her until the tremors had subsided into quivers. They eased her onto the bed and, mercifully, sleep claimed her.

Alexia pulled Resolute out of the room. "Why did you lie to her?"

"Not for the reason you think, Princess."

"What reason would that be?"

Resolute lifted his chin. "You think I manipulated her with a lie so I would have my own Norrington to use. You know I'd told Will that if he did not suit my purposes, I'd have him getting children on women so there would be one that would suffice. You've been steeped in a room of politicians. They lie, so you assume any lie is political."

His assessment tightened her stomach. "Why did you do it, then?"

"For her. For Will." The Vorquelf folded his arms over his chest. "In her grief she would have been a pawn. Now she has focus. She knows Will died to save her and her child. She is bound to us, now, as a group. She will seek counsel from us. Will you lead her wrong? No. Nor will Crow nor I. We will shield her from those who seek to manipulate her."

"We can't let anyone know. That is the first line of defense."

"I agree, Princess, but I also know secrets have their own power. This one will not remain hidden."

Alyx nodded. "What did you mean when you said you lied for Will?"

Resolute smiled ever so slightly. "Will had nothing but contempt for those who would use him. He would not want his child used. I do not believe she will be."

"She?" The Okrans Princess gave him a hard violet stare. "What do you know, Resolute?"

He thought for a moment. "Prophecies, Princess, are always open to interpretation. Your aunt does it freely. Nuances of the Norrington Prophecy in the original Elvish are indefinite about the gender of the Norrington. Since Will was male, that left other possibilities to be explored."

"You expected he would father a child?"

"You already know I did not rule that out."

She frowned. "Did you know of his liaison with Sayce?"

"From the moment he stopped talking about her, yes." The Vorquelf tilted his head to the side. "This surprises you?"

"That you didn't do anything to stop it. With the creation of a child, Will might have been stripped of whatever he had in being *the* Norrington. You should have guarded against that."

"I am an *agent* of that prophecy, not its master. I can only react, not control." He pointed to the closed door. "As I reacted there, in speaking with Sayce. It was a duty demanded of me."

* * *

Sayce slept until early evening, at which time she supped on soup and bread. As she ate, she told them of her last days in Muroso. As she was preparing to lead the troops in Navval south in a flanking attack on the army besieging Caledo, she received an urgent message from her father, King Bowmar. There was no holding the capital, so he had ordered an evacuation. Her brother, Crown Prince Bowmar, was to lead the retreat southwest to Zamsina and make a stand there. She was to race along the coast road, gathering up all the people she could and bring them to Saporicia.

"I did the best I could to fulfill my command. I sent heralds ahead to prepare the people, but they were not ready. Overburdened carts, the sick, the old." She shook her head ruefully. "The road is littered with the dead, all staring barefaced. There was no cart, no family, not bearing at least one life mask of someone who died in the evacuation."

Alyx, sitting on the edge of the bed, patted her knee. "What news of your brother? Your family?"

"My father died in Caledo. So did many others. My father engaged in magick duels with many of the *kryalniri* and slew all but one. Taking Caledo was not without cost for Chytrine, but survivors we met on the Zamsina road told of waves and waves of gibberers pouring over walls that dragonels had shattered. The white city of the plain is now the color of blood. Where it once was proud, it is now like a mouth full of broken teeth.

"My brother did make a stand at Zamsina, but all messages from him ceased two days ago. I am left to assume he is dead as well." She touched her mask. "I will have to be notching this mask. As nearly as I know, I am the last member of the royal house still alive."

Alexia smiled. "Then there is hope for Muroso yet."

Sayce's head came up. "Do you think they sent me out because they knew I was pregnant?"

"I don't know, Sayce." Alexia shrugged. "Will had confided in me concerning his feelings for you. In Navval you were sick in the mornings, and I drew a conclusion."

"On that, you told Will I was carrying his child?"

Alyx nodded. "It never occurred to me that there might be a mistake."

Sayce smiled and patted the hand on her knee. "I'm glad he knew. I'm not sure I believed it from Resolute, but I know I can trust you, Alexia."

"It is always my hope that you can, Sayce."

"I do and will." The Murosan Princess smiled. "Unless someone else comes to claim the throne, I will exercise my right and place all my troops under your control. You will find no more determined fighters in the world."

"I know. Thank you." Alyx sighed. "With them, we have a very good start. We'll free Muroso."

"And avenge Will."

"Yes, Sayce, and avenge Will."

CHAPTER 18

Kerrigan's eyes burned, less from fatigue than the vapors deep in Vael. After Bok had made his suggestion that they locate Chytrine's mother and draw a magickal sample from her, they set about getting permission to do just that. Rymramoch agreed with the request, but Sarealnya's family did not. At least, not immediately—and without their agreement, locating her would be all but impossible.

Sarealnya, as it turned out, had donated her Truestone for the DragonCrown. Some inquiry informed Kerrigan that she had produced the yellow stone, which made it all the more important for him to have access to her. He'd cast a spell on the yellow stone that, he hoped, had been triggered by Chytrine. He was counting on using traces of that spell as part of the spell that would locate her.

Prior to getting permission, Kerrigan worked on refining the spells he would need to cast in his hunt for Chytrine. The actual searching spell would check everyone it met against a list of criteria to determine if any of them was Chytrine. He ordered the criteria, starting with the traces of his spell, since that would be the easiest to reject and since he could easily define it. After that he would check for impressions of Bok and Sarealnya—provided he could get the information he needed about her.

He had to make other adjustments to the spell, and realized, as he worked, that he had been very lucky in the past since he had not been cautious. When his spell found a match, it triggered a pair of "heralds." Those spells shot out north and south of the target, then angled home to Kerrigan and informed him of their success. Through simple triangulation he could determine where the target had been at the moment of discovery.

The problem with that set of spells was that, as with the sphere, they were linked directly to him. A sorceress of Chytrine's abilities could easily analyze one of his heralds and trace it back to him. The little demonstration Rymramoch had given him would be nothing compared to what Chytrine would exact in retribution. He needed to insulate himself from her revenge. He also needed to make sure she could not react quickly and kill the heralds.

His first refinement to the spell was to increase the number of heralds to a full dozen. They would shoot off in all directions, including up and down, before turning to report their success. Some he made very powerful, and very likely to attract her notice, while others he kept humble, so they might escape to report. If she figured out what the spell was and managed to kill some of the heralds, she might just think she got them all.

Then, instead of having them return to him, he designated fixed targets for them to head toward. There they would trigger other heralds who would then head directly for him. He could have continued linking spell to spell to spell to distance himself yet further, but he didn't like the delay in reporting that would result. Some risk was unavoidable, and he accepted that.

When Sarealnya's family agreed to show him where she lay, they sent a great-granddaughter of hers, Arimtara, to lead him. Arimtara had shifted her shape to appear human, but her attempt fell shy of perfection. Kerrigan could not tell if it was deliberate or not. She towered over him and was hairless, with ears closer to the sharp shape of an elf's than a human's. The sulfuric color of her irises was quite remarkable, but the way golden highlights swirled through them had a hypnotic quality. Broad-shouldered and thickly muscled, she wore a loincloth, sandals, and a studded leather jerkin that covered her upper arms and breasts, but not much more—and Kerrigan could not tell what creature had produced the leather.

At the head of a small company of thralls, Arimtara brought them down deep into Vael, through narrow passages with rough walls. Noxious gases made Kerrigan lightheaded a time or two, but she and Bok carried him out of danger. The dragons and Rymramoch suffered no ill effects from the gases. If Bok even noticed them, Kerrigan couldn't tell.

Finally, they reached a small hole Kerrigan could barely squeeze through. He did manage it, however, then straightened up in a tall, humid cavern. Puddles dotted the floor, and in the center of it lay a huge dragon with her wings furled and her tail curled around to cover her foreclaws, looking very feline.

Well, feline until you look at the head. Sarealnya boasted three pairs of horns, the last and largest of which spiraled back from her crown. A bit of fang showed at the edge of her mouth. Any single scale of her muzzle, delicately patterned and arranged as they were, could have served as a warrior's shield and covered him from ankle to throat.

Bok perched himself on a stalagmite, shifting his hands and feet for a good grip. His form rippled for a moment with a shiver. "It makes sense she chose this place."

"Yes, she loved it."

Kerrigan almost asked why, then invoked a simple dracomagick spell Rymramoch had taught him. Dragons had an ability to read the impressions and resonances created by items through the passage of time. Looking through a dragon's eyes, the cavern came alive with stone flowing from stalactites to stalagmites, dancing in the pools. Stalagmites, in a rainbow of hues, reached upward and glistened with the mineral wetness that made them grow.

"This is a very beautiful place."

Arimtara looked at him as if he were watching the dawn and telling her what the sun was. "Get what you have come for."

Blushing, Kerrigan made his way to where the dragon lay and approached the tip of the tail. Ideally he'd have liked a fragment of scale, but he'd agreed not to disturb her. It was believed that the dust that had gathered on her would have been connected to her for long enough that, according to the Law of Contagion, there would be traces of her essence that he could use.

He quickly gathered dust into a small pot, then cast a preliminary diagnostic spell on it. It would determine the strength of the essence and let him know if he needed to gather more dust. The results came back instantly and he frowned. "This isn't going to work."

The puppet wandered over. "What is the problem?"

"The Truestone is an embodiment of the dragon's soul. It is the source of its essence. Without it being present in the body, those things close to the body don't pick up an impression. While the wood of your body would be strong for your essence, Master, I doubt I would gain much of anything from the dust on your dragon form."

"This is not good."

Kerrigan shook his head. "No, but there could be another way."

Arimtara strode over quickly. "The agreement was that her form would be left undisturbed."

"I know, I know." Kerrigan set the pot down carefully. "You said she loved this place. Seeing what little I did, I did gain some impressions of her. I think I could use them. I'd have to cast the spell here to make it work."

Rym's face oriented toward Arimtara. "Would that be acceptable?"

"Yes, but be quick about it." Her expression darkened. "There have been incidents nearby and I do not want to linger here."

"I'll work as fast as I can." Kerrigan lowered himself to his knees, then sat. He slowed his breathing and did what he could to order his mind. He let the plink of water into a puddle become his focus, then he used the dracomagick to push into the room and peel time back. Layers evaporated as he went, the centuries eroding, until he found himself watching the day the magnificent yellow-gold dragon entered the cave. The entrance had been much larger then, but with the flick of a talon she cast a spell that shrank it to its present tight dimensions. She settled herself. Her scaled flesh rippled with muscular tremors, then she laid her head down and appeared, for all intents and purposes, to go to sleep.

Kerrigan latched on to the sense of peace she exuded and began his weaving. He used knowledge of the spell he'd cast on the DragonCrown fragment to embroider that peace. The intent of the spell certainly contrasted with it, but the two elements still wound round each other with an almost playful ease.

Then he turned his attention to Bok and cast a diagnostic spell. In the blink of an eye he got all the information about Bok he could possibly use. Some he discarded as extraneous, like age, but other bits he selected and twined around his previous work. He used Bok's threads to tighten everything down into a roiling ball of blue, with gold and black counterpoints pulsing through it.

That ball was his model for Chytrine, and with it in hand, he prepared to cast his search spell in a wide arc. He heard a pounding in his head, but banished what he assumed would be a terrible headache. He pushed past it and dipped into the grand river of magick. He teased a trickle into his spell matrix and quickly the spell took on a life of its own.

Locating Chytrine would be no easy task. Kerrigan supposed she would be in Aurolan, but Bok had mentioned her appearing in Alcida to destroy a town called Porasena. Facing northeast, Kerrigan swung his open palms as wide as he could, releasing the spell over an angled line running west-northwest from Vael, and again south-southeast. If she were anywhere from Yslin to Okrannel, the spell would betray her presence.

The spell expanded out and away, leaving his flesh tingling. He shook his head and heard the pounding renewed. "What's happening?"

Arimtara snarled at him. "Cast more quickly, manling. They know we're here."

"Who does?" Kerrigan rocked and tried to get to his feet. "I'm done with the casting."

The female dragon pointed them back toward the entrance. "Then *move!*"

Rymramoch came on in a clatter of wooden limbs, then Bok grabbed the puppet and slung it onto his back. Kerrigan started to move after the urZrethi, and Arimtara shoved him roughly in the back. "Hurry."

The thralls had already headed toward the entrance. The one nearest it screamed and reeled back. To Kerrigan it looked as if he had suddenly grown a grey beard. The thrall tore at the thing biting at his throat, ripping it free, and smashing it against a stalagmite. Blood ran down his chest, but already two more of the small creatures had attached themselves to his thigh and belly.

More poured through the entrance in a grey flood. They looked nothing like any beast Kerrigan had ever seen. They hopped like rabbits, but had a bristling mane over their shoulders and skull. Needle-sharp teeth filled their jutting muzzles and the forearms, which appeared spindly, sprouted talons. The tail reminded him of a rat's tail, save

that it had a whip's suppleness and ended in a round brush
of fur with the same sort of stiff quills in it as the mane.

"Gvakra!" Arimtara pointed past Kerrigan. "They'll
make a meal of your soft flesh in seconds, and these are the
small ones."

Thralls pulled back, their hands full of quills, their flesh
scratched and torn. The gvakra snarled and yipped as they
came on, darting and leaping. Some made grazing attacks,
opening little wounds, while others went for the kill. The
thralls ripped them free, crushed them, and pitched them
aside; but always more came, and they began to get larger.
The smallest had been sent through to open the hole, and
the bigger ones—the size of a large dog or small pony—
squeezed through.

Arimtara growled deeply enough that a thrum sent icy
echoes through Kerrigan as he watched the thralls begin to
fall. "I have to kill their lead—"

Her comment ended abruptly. Kerrigan whirled. A giant gvakra, ghost white, had entered the cavern from some
entrance lost beyond Sarealnya's body. Twenty feet tall if an
inch, it had wrapped one hand over Arimtara's head and
lifted her bodily in the air. Her hands clawed at its wrists,
tearing out bloody clots of fur, but even as she hurt it, the
gvakra's forearm muscles bunched.

It'll crush her skull!

Panic flashed through Kerrigan, jolting him and puck-
ering his flesh. Thralls screaming and the high-pitched yips
of dying gvakra pounded at him. Off to his left the wave of
small creatures had reached Bok. Several had already torn
Rymramoch off him while the urZrethi shifted his skin
into spiked armor and his hands into short chopping
blades.

Kerrigan wanted to wail, "Not again!" but the words
never left his mouth. His fear was for his friends and allies,
not himself. That core of courage rose through the anxious
ocean roiling inside him and became an island of strength.
Not again, if I act!

His right hand came up in a gesture, casting a spell he knew very well. The spell hit the titan in the right shoulder and elbow, twisting its body around. Kerrigan smashed the monster's elbow against the stone dragon's snout. The joint shattered and, better yet, bone shards severed nerves, numbing the arm and robbing it of power.

Then the first of the gvakra reached him and chomped hard on his left arm. The dragonbone armor rose and protected him, then remained in place as the creature kept worrying him. Another bit his right knee and another tried to take a mouthful of the roll of fat beneath his right shoulder blade. They shredded his robe as they attacked. Their snarls rose in a buzzing cacophony and the sheer weight of them staggered him back against a stalagmite.

He could feel the bites, but they were no more than the pins and needles of a sleeping limb returning to wakefulness. Realizing the creatures couldn't hurt him, Kerrigan shoved away from the stone and began to run to the cave entrance. As he moved, more and more of the beasts came after him. They tried to get a piece of him, but often bit another of their own kind. The pair or a trio would drop away in a cannibalistic ball.

Kerrigan reached the entrance and spun as best he could, then wedged himself into the opening. Crushed gvakra squealed, and larger ones seeking entrance clawed at him, but to no avail. The magicker reached up to pull one creature off his face, and cried out as quills punctured his hand. For a heartbeat he thought the magick might have failed, but it would only protect him from the evil intent of others. His pulling on the gvakra was not protected.

It occurred to him, as the writhing carpet of gvakra covered him like windblown snow on a tree trunk, that he might exhaust himself with the magick and become vulnerable. He reached out and began to draw power from the river. He knew that if he wanted to, he could fill himself with it and modify the dragonbone armor. Little needles would sprout from his skin and inject poison into the gvakra. They would swell and die of asphyxiation, twitching and hoarsely gasping at his feet.

Other things came to him, wonderful and wicked things. He could use the power to heat the very air around him to the point the beasts would combust. Or he could draw away all heat, so they would freeze so completely that to touch one would be to shatter it. The possibilities that came to him were infinite, as would be the power he could use to wield them.

Kerrigan almost embraced that idea, and imagined the river flooding into him, but he recalled Rymramoch's warning. To do that, to let the river rush into him, would wear him down and destroy him. He shivered and refused to do it, but he did draw a little more energy and cast a diagnostic spell.

Gvakra, as far as magick was concerned, were not very complex creatures—and closer to rabbits in anatomy than Kerrigan would have ever guessed. Once he had their measure, he triggered yet another spell. Starting with those gvakra around him, and slowly spreading out in a sphere, the feral creatures went to sleep. They dropped off his body with soft plops, save for a couple whose jaws would not loosen.

The larger, wolfish ones did not fall asleep instantly, but became sluggish. Their attacks slowed enough that the beleaguered thralls had time to react. One thrall's clawed swipe ripped a gvakra head off, while another left its tormentor in thrashing pieces. Bok stabbed both bladed hands through the chest of the one nearest him, then shook and flung off those that had been impaled on his spikes.

Kerrigan looked to see what had become of Arimtara. He hoped his spell had had enough effect to slow the monster she fought. In the dimness he saw her rising and gasped.

He gasped because she rose from a basin that had been the giant's belly. A thick rope of bloody intestine slid off her left shoulder, but caught on a spike sprouting from her elbow. Her shoulders remained hunched forward and more powerful than before. She'd grown a long tail and her fingers ended in hooked talons.

She turned with the beast's blood pouring off her in rivulets. Beyond her, in ever-decreasing spurts, blood fountained up from a rent heart. Arimtara looked around at the handful of surviving thralls, Kerrigan, Bok, and the puppet. "My thanks for your efforts, Kerrigan Reese. Effective, but why didn't you slay them?"

He shrugged uneasily. "I just didn't." He didn't want to admit that it never occurred to him to kill the things, save in the power fantasies he entertained. "I think we can go now."

She shifted her shape back to the more slender one she'd worn when leading them there, though now naked since her clothes had not survived transformation and combat. "You don't have to be here when your spell finds her?"

"No." Kerrigan fingered his shredded robes. "I'd like to be somewhere else, really. With fresh clothes and hot food."

She spat. "Yes, something to get this taste out. I will take you back." She waved Bok toward the entrance, then lifted the puppet and tossed it to the urZrethi. Arimtara turned to the thralls and hissed a command to them.

In response, they stooped, found stones, and began to dash out the brains of the sleeping gvakra.

She glanced at Kerrigan. "You may not see the need to kill them, but I do. There will be more. There always are. And, alas, this will always be so."

CHAPTER 19

In the two days since Resolute's address to the Council, things had progressed with a bit more speed, but not nearly enough to satisfy Alexia. It had been agreed that senior military advisors and staff would form a planning group to address the needs of the Saporician war. They were to have political oversight which, thankfully, did not include King Scrainwood. Erlestoke took his place.

Alexia had hoped she would be enough to occupy the place of the Okrans delegation, but Tatyana pointed out that since Alexia would be the supreme commander, she rose above her national status, so someone had to be there to represent the Okrans' point of view. The crowns had agreed, and Alexia suspected it was more to get Tatyana away from them than it was to help plan the invasion.

The political element rendered nothing simple. It was agreed, for example, that accurate maps and suitable tables would be vital for planning. Wrangling then started over whose cartographers would do the best work, and who should have access to whose charts. Some minor Saporician lords seemed to be of the opinion that if their holdings were listed as "impassable wastelands" on a map, the war would just pass them by.

There was similar confusion and obfuscation in the lists concerning personnel and equipment. On parchment, every unit in Saporicia or on its way was stuffed full of elite fighters who, bearing only a knife and an evil glint in their eyes, could win the war single-handedly. Alexia knew this was patent nonsense, but it was a matter of pride that each nation's contribution be seen as the equal of any other nation's, and politicians lobbied hard for their soldiers to be the first into battle. They expected that would mean they would be the first to glory. When Alexia pointed out that it would mean they would likely be the first to *die,* her words did not change the politicians' opinions at all.

Alexia dispatched Peri, Crow, and Dranae to make covert inspections of the troops gathering. They assessed the units based on morale, experience, training, equipment, and leadership. Those units that had noble leaders of little experience were considered far less reliable than, say, the Alcidese units whose leaders were career soldiers. At Crow's suggestion, they also kept track of supplies and the prices of commodities in the markets, since shortages of staples would kill an army more quickly than any enemy force.

Alexia also wanted Sayce to help, but news of Will's death had crushed her. Alyx felt torn between needing to plan and wanting to care for Sayce. She despaired of being able to help her friend. Then, at Crow's suggestion, Nay came and visited Sayce. He presented her with the amulet that contained the last bit of Temmer. He hung it around her neck on a stout bit of silver chain and almost immediately Sayce's melancholy lifted.

She came to Alyx and fingered the tiny dagger. "He told me that this was meant for me and for my child. He said it was part of the Norrington legacy." Alarmed that Nay knew of her condition, Alyx questioned Crow, but he denied telling Nay anything. Alyx reluctantly accepted the idea that the fragments of Temmer communicated a lot of information to the man who had shaped them anew, and Sayce's revival told her that was a very good thing.

Sayce pitched in immediately and became Alexia's stalwart aide. Her support proved vital for a number of reasons. The Murosan troops were well aware of the spirited defense of Navval that Alexia had led, and with Sayce at her side, their allegiance transferred over easily. Sayce also had a tolerance for the politicians and a skill at extorting from them just a little bit more of whatever was needed. For reasons unknown to Alyx, Tatyana took a liking to Sayce, and even Sayce had described her great-grandaunt as "not as bad as you might think if you get past that crusty exterior."

Alyx refrained from saying she'd like to get past it with the sword Heart. As it was, Sayce managed to mollify Tatyana, and use her to bring other politicians to heel. The Murosan Princess' effort did speed things along. As a result, only two days later, they had a room, they had maps, they had troop estimates, and they could begin to go over the basics of the campaign.

The meetings had been moved out of the castle to the main garrison in Narriz. The big, blocky building had four stories, the topmost being made of two large rooms and the rooftop of the third floor. Wide windows and doors to the exterior let people wander out and talk. The planners occupied the northernmost room, so the vistas kept them focused on the problem at hand—the invaders coming from that direction.

Alexia waited for all the doors to be closed, interior and exterior, before she began speaking. The military folk, and even the politicians, with Sayce being the exception, were all older than she. In some of their eyes she could see respect and a willingness to listen. Others kept their gaze hooded as they waited to evaluate what she was saying. Still others watched her with flat expressions that meant they would be promoting their own agendas and would disagree with her just because it would give them a position from which they could negotiate.

She hated that latter group with a passion. She knew she was right, and while she did not mind having her conclusions questioned, she expected those who asked the questions not only to see the wisdom of her answers, but to abide by those conclusions. The connivers would simply choose to ignore her wisdom, even though they knew they would acquiesce in the end, for their own advantage. They would be a stumbling block she did not need.

Alyx began speaking quietly, forcing them to listen closely. "Saporicia is a nation rich in military history. The northernmost region is referred to as the highlands, and consists of mountains and valleys that can make fighting treacherous. We are fortunate in that the highlands will slow the enemy and perhaps allow us to trap and kill any Aurolani force coming along the coast road from Muroso. It will certainly make any resupply from that direction difficult."

She turned to the map on the wall and traced a line with her finger diagonally from the Loquellyn border to where the borders of Muroso, Oriosa, and Saporicia met. "Down here, at this juncture, we have the fortress city of Fronosa. In the past it has proven very useful in stopping invaders, but how long it will stand against dragonels, we cannot guess. Its advantage is that to reach it the troops must come up a road of switchbacks, leaving them very exposed."

A Helurcan cavalry general shook his head. "A dragon could just melt Fronosa and the way would be clear."

Alexia's eyes became violet slits. "That possibility holds for anything in this war. Chytrine has, so far, been sparing in the use of her dragons, for reasons we cannot comprehend. It is foolish to assume she will continue to do so, but there must have been reasons why she has just not unleashed them so far."

Others began to offer opinions on that subject, but stopped abruptly as Alexia slapped the map with her open

palm. "Enough. I am not satisfied that any of you understand the strategic and tactical concerns we face. We can
speculate idly about why our enemy does what she does,
and we will still be doing that when she's standing right
here with her troops surrounding us. It is pointless. If you
do not understand that you have to know the battlefields
better than you know your own homes, you will be killing
yourselves, your people, and the rest of us, needlessly.
There will be time for debate later, but, for now, listen."

A Savarese nobleman sniffed. "I thought we were here
to plan a fight, not be lectured on geography. Find me the
enemy, and I will slay her. It is as simple as that."

Alexia's nostrils flared, but before she could say anything, Tatyana turned on the man who had spoken. "Words
have power, my lord, even foolish words. Those you have
just now uttered have fallen from the lips of many a warrior. Many a *dead* warrior. If you do not listen, you will,
most assuredly, *die.*"

The old woman's words ended in a hoarse whisper, but
the nobleman did not protest. He turned almost as white as
the lace frill collar he wore. He bowed his head to Alexia
and shrank back a step or two.

Alexia resumed her lecture. "Here, south of Loquellyn
and north of the Saporician Sea, we have plains split by two
large rivers flowing down from the highlands. Those rivers
have few fords and are freely navigable. The cities at
the fords are fortified, but not well. If the army were to win
through at Fronosa and strike northwest, they could take
the northern plains. That would deprive Saporicia of much
grain come next harvest, prevent Loquellyn from easily
coming to our aid, and let them resupply from shipping
along the coast or in the Saporician Sea itself.

"Here in Narriz we are only seventy-five miles from
Fronosa, as the Gyrkyme fly, but the Bokagul foothills
make the trip here difficult. As was done in Muroso, a series
of hit-and-runs and delaying attacks will slow the Aurolani
host and keep them away from the capital."

She moved her hand south of Narriz. "Here we have more plains that are very suitable to battles and have seen many. The plains rise a bit toward Alcida, and the whole area around the southern seaport of Sanges is thickly forested and would make for a savage place to fight."

Alexia placed a hand over Bokagul. "Bokagul was attacked by Aurolani forces, but repulsed them. I do not expect much help from the Bokas, but I do believe that flank will hold. Any army coming through Bokagul would do so slowly and, with Gyrkyme scouts and other troops ranging out there, we should be informed of any impending attack.

"Loquellyn, on the other hand, is an unknown. There is no Loquelf representative here. The Loquelves did send troops to Fortress Draconis, and their Blackfeathers are still with Adrogans in Okrannel. One of the things we must do as quickly as possible is find out what their disposition is. Assuming Loquellyn is a secure flank would be foolish and leave us open to disaster."

She turned from the map and pressed her hands together. "The fighting will be in the northern plains. There are key sites, like the ford cities and a few others, where battles have been fought for ages. We will benefit from the experience of other commanders and not make the mistakes they made."

A Salnian captain raised a hand. "You've not mentioned the Oriosan flank."

"Meaning?"

The meaty man smiled. "I should think it's fairly obvious. Prince Erlestoke might be representing the Oriosans here, but he's not really in charge, is he? Regardless of what his father might do, what if Chytrine attacks there and the nation just collapses? Her hordes would be pouring through the southern plains in a heartbeat, and be here in Narriz a heartbeat later."

"You have a valid point, Captain Venes. That potential *is* a problem. We need to find a solution for it. Have you a useful suggestion, or were you merely attempting to embarrass Prince Erlestoke with pointless gibes about how his father rules the country?"

The comment surprised the soldier. "I wasn't . . ."

"Because," Alexia continued, "if the prince were to take offense and demand satisfaction of you right now, out on the rooftop, I would gladly act as his second. You don't seem to understand what is going on here, despite everything that has happened. Let me explain it very carefully for everyone."

She pointed to Sayce. "Princess Sayce has seen her nation shattered, her family slaughtered, cities razed, and the countryside despoiled by an invader that is relentless. Chytrine is bent on nothing shy of the conquest of the whole of the world. Why? It doesn't matter. There will be no bargaining with her—no matter what you think King Scrainwood has done. If she succeeds, petty jealousies and rivalries will not only be forgotten, they will have been the *cause* of her victory.

"Chytrine's troops are relentless and savage and brutal, but they are *not* invincible. We can stop them. We will stop them. We will drive them back through Muroso. We will drive them back through Sebcia. We will destroy them and their leader."

She shook her head. "This is not a gallant battle, this is a *war*. She has fought without quarter asked or given. She made war on the children of Vilwan—*your* children. The butchery in Sebcia and Muroso defies description. She has broken the mightiest fortress in the north, and none other has been able to stand against her. If you look upon this as a chance to win glory for yourself, you will die stupidly. Your children will die screaming. Is that what you want? Is that what any of you want?"

Venes shook his head. "No, of course not. The point about Oriosa remains, though."

"It does. So what would you suggest?"

"Scouts. A screening force."

"Each is possible. It will be your responsibility to offer a plan or two." Alexia posted fists on her hips and looked around the room. "Other immediate problems?"

King Augustus stepped forward. "We will have a multinational force gathered. Each nation uses different signaling methods, different terminology for war. We will need to set up liaisons between units in any one force to make sure orders are understood, signals are read correctly, and the like."

"Agreed."

Her mentor smiled. "I would be honored to work on organizing that sort of thing, Princess."

She nodded. "Thank you."

The Helurcan general spoke up. "Along those same lines we need to agree on a chain of command, equality of ranks, and guarantee that one nation's troops will follow orders from another commander if their own leaders are struck down."

"Agreed, in principle, but how do we determine who should lead and take precedence? Will any lordling want to surrender his command to a commoner with more battle experience? Would you like to see someone who knows nothing directing your men in battle?"

"No, of course not."

"Good, I agree. Give me a solution."

A smile slowly grew on the man's face. "It would be my pleasure to do so, Highness. It will take some thinking."

"You have until this afternoon."

More problems were raised, and Alexia shared out the hunt for solutions. Some people got to work on the problem they themselves raised. Others were paired because their problems were similar or Alexia had a sense that even though they were from different nations, they would get along well. Moreover, since she knew everyone in the room by reputation and history, she brought together those commanders she knew she needed to work well together.

What she hadn't shared with them were two big things. The first was her overall strategy for opposing Chytrine.

She'd hinted at some of it, but what she wanted to do was bold, and while some of it had been tried before, never had all the elements been combined. Nefrai-kesh and Anarus and other *sullanciri* might have military experience, but she wanted to hit them with so much, so fast, that their chances of coping with it were minimal.

The second big thing was who she would have in command of the armies. A force as large as the one she was dealing with had to have commanders who were close to the battle. There were going to be leaders from one nation who would be subject to orders from someone of another nation. What would be most important for the force to work, however, was if the leaders of the units themselves had confidence in each other, then in the leaders giving the orders. As long as the warriors gathered could solve problems together, orders just became more problems to solve. She would bind them together, brother to brother, before telling them how they would be linked to higher command.

The questions were beginning to taper off, and people became anxious to break away to work on solutions. Things had gone better in that regard than she expected, and she had to credit Tatyana with a part of that. The crone kept the politicians cowed, and that proved very useful.

Suddenly the door from the stairs burst open and Kerrigan dashed into the room. "Get away from her, now!"

Alexia frowned. "What's going on, Kerrigan? What are you doing here?"

"Get away from her. She's not who you think she is." The young mage advanced, pointing a quivering finger. "That's not your aunt, Princess. That's Chytrine!"

CHAPTER 20

Prince Erlestoke gasped and dropped a hand to his waist, prepared to draw a sword that wasn't there. The absurdity of being in Chytrine's presence with nothing more than a dagger shook him, as well as did the certainty of their mortal peril. Kerrigan's voice didn't contain a note of panic, just confidence and excitement. That he could be wrong seemed to have occurred to no one in the room.

Save Tatyana herself. She pressed her left hand to her flat chest and staggered. She reached out with her right hand and Sayce took it, helping to support her. The old woman bowed her head for a moment, then raised it, weakly. Her voice, however, had lost none of its edge.

"How can you accuse me of being Chytrine?" She swallowed hard and tried to straighten up, but it seemed the weight of the world had landed on her shoulders. "Everyone here knows me. They may fear me, but not as much as the Nor'witch. You have been addled, boy."

Kerrigan drew himself up, lowering his accusing finger. "But you are. My magick found you." A note of indignation tinged his words. "You have to be!"

"Do I? I know little of magick, but I know enough to assume our enemy could cast a spell that would make me appear to be her. Who knows how long ago she did so?"
Tatyana's icy blue gaze swept the room, sending a shiver
through Erlestoke. "Have you found her, or just another of
her little traps, boy?"

Alexia strode to Kerrigan's side. "Is that possible?"

"Well, yes, but . . ."

"Of course it is possible." Tatyana smiled slowly as she
clutched at Sayce's left shoulder. "You have been fooled,
boy, simply fooled."

"But . . ." Kerrigan's brows arrowed together. "The thing
of it is—" In mid-sentence he flicked his right hand at the
crone. A blue spark shot from his fingertips straight at her
face.

Tatyana's left hand came up with the ease of someone
brushing a gnat away, though her hand glowed gold and
the blue spark popped out of existence. After a moment's
hesitation, Tatyana's hand slipped to Sayce's slender neck,
took hold of the chain, and jerked it tight.

The old woman's eyes blazed. "I don't play at tricks, boy.
Now you can die."

Tatyana's hand came down with a slash, as if she were a
sword duelist saluting her foe. A scarlet sphere congealed
out of the rent in the air. Silver sparks and blue darted over
the surface. It shot in at Kerrigan, but all he could do was
shove Alexia away before it hit him. The resulting blast was
enough to scatter everyone. Erlestoke spun to the floor and
found someone else on top of him.

He shoved off the floorboards and regained his feet
quickly. Kerrigan had been knocked back twenty feet, almost all the way to the door, where his robe smoked and his
body twitched at the feet of Rymramoch. Augustus and
Alexia had likewise managed to regain their feet.
Chytrine—for she had proven herself to be the Nor'witch
with that bit of magick—dragged Sayce with her as she
stalked toward the doors to the roof.

The old woman looked back over her shoulder with a gold fire now roiling in her eyes. "Do not be foolish. It is her life if you follow me."

Bok vaulted the prostrate Kerrigan and bounded toward Chytrine. "This has to stop now, Chytrine."

As the malachite urZrethi leaped at her, Chytrine swept her left hand around. Invisible force smashed the urZrethi into the wall and he slid to the floor in a broken heap. "You had centuries to stop me and you failed. Again."

With another gesture she blasted open the doors for which she was heading. Out on the rooftop a fiery horse landed and a small dark form tumbled free. As he came to his feet, his cloak brushed the horse's tail and burst into flames. Above him, astride the horse, sat Nefrai-kesh, the King of the *sullanciri. And the hooded cloak he is wearing is Lombo's flesh!*

The smaller figure Erlestoke knew to be Nefrai-laysh. "My father's made me clean of limb and, Mistress, so full of vim, it's gladly your enemies I'll cut and trim."

Though the lesser *sullanciri* drew a sword, the Oriosan prince advanced. "Chytrine, you're not taking her."

"No? You should listen as well as your father does." The old woman turned and lifted her right hand high. Sayce clawed at the chain, her face purple and her feet barely scraping the rooftop. "I'll leave her corpse then."

"No!"

The shout surprised both Erlestoke and Chytrine. The Aurolani Empress looked up at Nefrai-kesh. "You dare order me?"

"Only to prevent an error, Mistress. Bring her."

"This worthless thing?" Chytrine gave Sayce a shake. "She is nothing."

The *sullanciri*'s voice strengthened. "Seek, Mistress. She carries my great-grandchild. From her springs the new Norrington."

Tatyana's face blossomed with an obscene smile. "Oh, perfect. How stupid they are." She tossed the princess to

Nefrai-kesh, who caught her and laid her athwart the saddlebow. As Nefrai-laysh moved to eclipse Chytrine, his father reached down, took the empress' hand, and swung her up behind him.

"I will return for you."

Nefrai-laysh laughed. "Concern yourself not, for where I am got. I have here work to do. Slashing and cutting, stabbing and gutting. I'll find my way home before you."

The flaming horse sprouted dragon wings and with a powerful beat that singed Erlestoke's hair, it leaped into the air beneath its burden. Though terrible, it was also beautiful. Its tail lengthened, the red-gold flames cooling into blues and greens. As it rose a wingtip touched a pendant, instantly converting it to flame.

Nefrai-laysh tapped his black sword against the roof's stone. "Attend me, Prince, it's long since I've slain one of royal blood."

The *sullanciri* lunged. Erlestoke filled his left hand with his dagger and parried the stroke. His dagger screeched as the *sullanciri*'s sword pared a curl of metal from it, but the prince had known the dagger would be of little use. As he parried the blade wide, he pivoted on his left foot and smashed his right fist square in Nefrai-laysh's face. Bones cracked, and while the prince felt something go in his hand, he knew more had gone in the enemy's nose.

The *sullanciri* reeled back, raising a hand to his flattened nose. He pinched it with fingers and drew it up with a startling number of pops. Nefrai-laysh snorted, blowing black blood and mucus down to the stone where it bubbled and smoked. He brought his hand away, flicked more fluid from his fingers, and studied Erlestoke with eyes that were balefires.

Nefrai-laysh doubtless intended to say something, but never got the chance. Alexia flew into him. Having come at a run, she leaped and smashed both feet into his chest. The blow hit the *sullanciri* as hard as Chytrine's spell had hit Kerrigan, lifting him from his feet and knocking him back against the crenellated wall that ringed the roof. His shoulder caught one of the merlons, twisting him, then, in an eyeblink, he somersaulted backward and disappeared.

Erlestoke leaped over Alexia and ran to the wall. Shouts and screams came from the street below. People scurried in panic. Nefrai-laysh cut at some, lunged at others, killing no one but wounding several and speeding the rest away. All the rest save two.

A large man held a thick staff ready for combat. "Is this all you're about now, Leigh?"

The *sullanciri* stopped. "Nay?"

"You've changed little."

"Nay, Nay, what a day. I'm glad it's you I spy. Pray, prey, then we'll play, because now, my friend, you'll die." Nefrai-laysh darted forward with blinding speed, sweeping his blade down in a cut that would take Nay's legs off at the knee. Though the man swung the staff down to block, the *sullanciri*'s blade would have sheared right through it.

The intervention of another blade prevented that from happening. Borell cast aside the scabbard that had encased the sword Eye and caught Nefrai-laysh's blade before it bit into his father's staff. The *sullanciri* pulled back, surprised, then whipped the blade up and around in a cut that should have cloven Borell's skull right above the line of his mask.

The youth ducked, then lunged, stabbing Nefrai-laysh through the stomach. The *sullanciri* gasped and leaped back, pulling himself off the blade. Borell bore in, blocking another cut, then twisted his sword up over Nefrai-laysh's guard and drove the point into one of those balefires.

The *sullanciri*'s body jerked back, ripping the sword from Borell's grasp. Nefrai-laysh's back bowed and he screamed fire to the heavens. His feet came off the ground and he seemed to hover there for a heartbeat or two, then the fire in his eyes went out and a flaccid body fell like an empty glove to the cobblestones.

Alexia shouted down to Nay. "Take his sword and come up here, the both of you."

Erlestoke turned and headed back into the room. He found King Augustus crouched near Bok. Over by the door Rymramoch had sunk to one knee beside Kerrigan. The prince moved to the urZrethi. "How is he?"

Augustus shook his head. "Not dead, but hurt badly and probably dying. I've sent someone for healers."

Erlestoke looked up at the wall. Plaster had cracked where Bok had hit it, and dark blood stained the wall where he slid down. He did seem to be breathing, but the rattle coming from his chest was not a good sign.

The prince rose and crossed to where Alexia stood with Rymramoch. Kerrigan's limbs had been straightened and, save for muscle twitches, he would have appeared dead. "What did she do to him?"

The puppet shook its head with a jerky motion. "Magick of her own devising. It was very powerful. Even being in the proximity of him makes my ability to control this shell difficult."

Alexia knelt and took one of the young mage's hands in hers. "He's cold. Is he dying?"

"Most likely."

Alexia sat back on her heels and looked up. "What happened? Why are you here?"

"Why didn't I keep him safe, you want to ask?" The puppet started to gesture, but his right arm froze awkwardly. "On Vael Kerrigan progressed swiftly. He learned things and was able to devise a spell that pinpointed Chytrine's location. He cast his spell to find her and learned she was in Narriz. With the help of another dragon, we arrived last night, stealthfully. Here in Narriz he cast his spell again, but very gently, so she would not notice. Apparently she did not notice. He came here directly and you saw the rest."

Erlestoke shook his head. "He cast another spell at her. What was that?"

"A little annoyance spell. It's something most mages learn very early and casting a counter to it is almost reflexive." Rymramoch canted his head. "In her case it was, and she was exposed."

Alexia sighed heavily. "She's been here in our councils the whole time. She knew everything we would do. She urged us to do things that would waste time and misdirect forces. Because of her half the army that could have been at Fortress Draconis was off freeing Okrannel. She raised the point about Adrogans having dragonels, and who better to know the truth of that situation than she?"

"Easy, Alexia, this is in no way your fault." Erlestoke crouched beside her. "She was able to stir up trouble, yes, but her exposure will unite everyone."

The princess blinked at him. "Unite them? Have you lost your senses? They'll be slaughtering each other out of fear. They'll think every other lordling is an Aurolani agent. They'll accuse your father of being a *sullanciri*. It will be madness. And that madness will be compounded when they learn that Sayce is carrying Will's child, and is now in the hands of Chytrine."

Erlestoke smiled. "At least you know you'll have the Murosan troops with you."

"Sure, *if* I decide to go haring off to Aurolan to save Sayce, which is not the object of our exercise."

"No, you're right. The object is to destroy Chytrine." Erlestoke rose as Nay and Borell came through the door. He nodded to them, then turned to face the assembled nobles and soldiers. "I expect you will all want to go report to your superiors what has happened here. Let's make certain you are all aware of what *did* happen."

He looked around the room, meeting the gazes of all assembled openly and coolly. "Chytrine's imposture was exposed before any strategic or tactical planning could be discussed. The basic material we had covered should have been obvious to all of you. More importantly, she will now be operating off what she thinks we are thinking. All of those problems we faced before will now require even harder work, but we have an advantage that we did not have before.

"Second, and of vital import, this young man, Borell Carver, slew a *sullanciri*. Chytrine has been deprived of one of her prime lieutenants. Throughout this war she has lost *sullanciri* at an alarming rate. Without them, her ability to control her troops is sorely impeded."

Venes shook his head. "What about her getting the new Norrington?"

Erlestoke shrugged mightily to cover the shiver running down his spine. "Princess Sayce may indeed be carrying Will Norrington's child. The fact is, however, that the child will not be born until the autumn. Lest you forget, the Norrington Prophecy is not a good one for Chytrine. By taking the child, she is just clasping a snake to her breast. That, however, is immaterial as far as we are concerned. Our job is to smash her armies and chase her back home. We'll get there in time to save Sayce and let her child be born in a civilized land."

He waved them to the doors. "Go, report. We shall resume tomorrow."

The soldiers and nobles filed from the room, leaving only Augustus, Bok, Alexia, Kerrigan, Rymramoch, and the trio of Oriosans. "Is there anything you can do for Bok?"

The puppet looked toward the urZrethi. "If someone could convey me over there, I do believe I might help."

Nay and Borell grabbed him at the elbows and carried him toward Bok. When the puppet was a dozen feet from Kerrigan, he regained use of his limbs. He completed the journey on his own and knelt to attend to the urZrethi.

Alexia laid a hand on Erlestoke's shoulder. "Thank you for what you said."

He shrugged. "I know how you must be feeling."

"How's that?"

"People think my father is Chytrine's plaything. At least you had a bit more generational insulation on that count."

Alexia laughed. "Okay, you do know." She shook her head, then laughed again.

"What?"

"I was just thinking, remembering. I don't know how long Chytrine has assumed Tatyana's identity, but I hope it's been at least ten years." The Okrans Princess smiled. "The first time I met her, I bit her."

Erlestoke smiled. "You did, did you? I never bit my father."

"Try it."

"No thanks. We have too much work to do." He gave her a wink. "We're going to figure out a way you'll get to bite her again, and this time we'll make it really hurt."

CHAPTER 21

Alexia hesitated for a moment at the top of the steps and looked down into the semicircular amphitheater that normally housed Saporicia's Congress of Guild Masters. The stairs she stood poised to descend split the various tiers and led directly to the open half circle in which Guild Masters would stand to debate various points of law and policy. Against the back wall, beneath gorgeous murals of Saporician history, a dais had been built. Upon it sat one large throne, which King Fidelius occupied as he would in normal times. To his right and left sat smaller thrones for King Scrainwood and King Augustus, respectively.

Others had gathered below in various factions, but Alexia's attention was drawn to the low table that had been placed before the throne. On it lay Kerrigan, shrouded from throat to toes in a white sheet. His body still twitched and shivered, but the damage done by Chytrine's magick could not remain hidden. Her spell had wasted his body. Had he not been so fat to begin with, Alexia was certain, he'd have long since been wholly consumed.

She slowly descended and heard the scrape of Crow's boots as he followed her. On that main floor three groups were prepared to argue. Centermost was a knot of sorcerers from Vilwan. Off to the left waited Peri and Resolute. To the right, Dranae, Rymramoch, and a powerfully built female, who apparently was another dragon in human form, had gathered.

The leader of the Vilwanese contingent turned, saw Alexia, and smiled. "Very good. Now that they are here, we can proceed."

Alexia recalled the woman's name and rank from the general councils. "I have only just been summoned, Magister Tadurienne; I do not know what this is about. Has there been some change in Kerrigan?"

The woman folded her hands into the sleeves of her grey robe, which had black striping at cuffs, collar, and hem. The color matched her hair and proclaimed her to be skilled in the arts of conjuration. "No change in his condition, but there is a change in his status."

Alexia frowned as she joined her sister and Resolute. Crow stood behind her. The princess looked toward King Fidelius. "Please, Highness, enlighten me."

He gestured with his good hand toward the Vilwanese. "Because Kerrigan is a minor citizen of Vilwan, they are petitioning to take custody of him and return to Vilwan with him."

Alyx frowned. "They wish to extradite him like a criminal? On what charge?"

"No charge, Princess." Tadurienne kept her voice respectful. "This is not extradition. It is a compassionate repatriation."

" 'Compassionate'? How can that be, Magister? Unless I am misinformed, you've not been able to figure out what is happening with him."

"True, but we have hopes." She waved a hand toward the dragons. "Even they have been unable to unlock the magick Chytrine used, but on Vilwan we have the greatest minds assembled, who will be able to do what they cannot."

Crow cleared his throat. "How is it that Kerrigan is a citizen of Vilwan? I understood that all students on Vilwan were subject to the nation of their birth until they reached the age of consent, at which time they may renounce their old citizenship and become citizens of Vilwan. Heslin never did that, and remained an Oriosan until Chytrine took him."

Tadurienne smiled. "It is simple. Kerrigan was born on Vilwan."

"That is a lie." The puppet Rymramoch clapped gloved hands together. "Had he been born on Vilwan, the taint would have been there. I studied him. He did spend virtually his entire life on Vilwan, and he may have been born on an island, but it was not Vilwan."

The Vilwanese Magister held a hand up and conferred with her compatriots. "I have no information about the place of his birth. His parents are full Vilwanese citizens. He has no other home. He is ours."

Resolute glanced over at Rymramoch. "Why do you say he was born on an island?"

"It's obvious."

Dranae smiled easily. "Resolute, for us, reading the traces and taints on a person is as easy as reading gibberkin sign is for you. I never read Kerrigan, but with you the mark of Vorquellyn is strong, no matter that you've spent ten times as many years away from there."

Tadurienne opened her hands. "As fascinating as this discussion about taints and traces is, it really has no bearing on the case at hand. Kerrigan Reese came from Vilwan, was trained on Vilwan, and is of Vilwanese extraction. No one here has the capability of helping him, and we do. If you want what is best for him, you will give him to us now. Time, you can all plainly see, is of the essence."

Crow again spoke. "With all due respect, Magister, but Kerrigan's last tutor, Orla, gave him deathbed instructions.

She told him he was to stay away from Vilwan. In Meredo he defied your attempts to lure him back."

"He is but a child, subject to childish fancies."

"But Orla was not. She was your equal in rank. He sought to obey her orders, and she gave the responsibility for him to Resolute and me."

"Did she?" Tadurienne pointed to the twitching body. "And you chose to leave him on Vael for instructions in magicks no human has ever mastered, and *this* is the result! I would submit, King Fidelius, that Crow has proven himself unsuitable as a guardian. Regardless, Orla had no authority to turn her charge over to either of these adventurers. Before she left Vilwan she had a discussion with her superior which, I have been led to believe, resulted in a difference of opinion. That doubtless prompted her giving Kerrigan the orders she did, not any true concern for the boy."

Scrainwood toyed with his goatee. "Magister Tadurienne's objection to Crow's stewardship of Kerrigan Reese does bear weight. By his own admission, he who lost the Norrington now has lost Adept Reese."

King Fidelius nodded in accord, but King Augustus waved that notion away. "By all accounts, Adept Reese was powerful and wise beyond his years, and certainly more skilled at magick than the Vilwanese assembled here. He had the trust of the Draconis Baron, which we all know was not easily earned. Kerrigan Reese, could he speak for himself, would undoubtedly hold all but himself blameless for his current condition."

Fidelius nodded. "Your point is well-taken, Augustus, but the legal problem still exists. Orla did not have the authority to transfer custody to anyone. While she might have suggested he stay with Crow and Resolute, she could not give him over to them. Their claims in this matter must be rejected. As to why or if she told Kerrigan to stay away from Vilwan is likewise immaterial."

"Thank you, Highness." Tadurienne smiled cautiously. "If there are no other objections."

"I have one." Rymramoch raised a hand. "You referred to this as a compassionate repatriation, and you cited having the greatest magickal minds present on Vilwan to help deal with this problem. I would submit that is not true."

The grey-robed woman bowed her head. "I will agree we do not have dragons with us, but were you wishing to come, we would welcome your assistance."

"You mistake me, but I do not think deliberately so. I will be going nowhere until my compatriot, Bok, is ready to travel." The puppet clasped its hands together. "My point was simply this: all the minds you have gathered there will be unable to plumb the depths of this spell."

Tadurienne's voice dripped with sarcasm. "I can appreciate that *you* have had difficulty in that matter, Rymramoch . . ."

The dragon's puppet cut her off. "And you've had less than I?"

"No, but . . ."

"Permit me a question. Do you know *why* you have had difficulty learning anything about the magick on him?"

The Vilwanese woman grew cautious. She spoke in low tones with the other two sorcerers, then shook her head. "No."

"It is because that is the nature of the spell she cast. It is meant to frustrate magick cast upon it." The puppet looked up at the three kings. "Even I have heard the story of Chytrine's first assault on Fortress Draconis. She cast a spell that undid the healings that had been performed. This spell functions much along the same lines. If it were a swordsman, it would be adept at parrying every attack thrown at it. The pitifully simple fact of the matter is that there are a limited number of diagnostic spells available to any race. I have tried all I know and they have failed. Even the magick I use to move this shell around is affected by the one she cast."

Fidelius sat back and rubbed his right hand over his

face. "So you are saying there is nothing the Vilwanese can do to save his life?"

"There is no way they can determine what her spell is doing to him. They are afraid of something, however." Rymramoch nodded toward the body. "They're afraid the spell she cast will change Kerrigan Reese into one of her *sullanciri.*"

Alexia gasped and pressed back against Crow. That possibility had never occurred to her. "Could that be happening?"

Tadurienne held her hands up. "It cannot be discounted. If he were to become a *sullanciri,* he would be most powerful and dangerous. On Vilwan he could be contained and destroyed."

Crow laughed. "I am unaware of any *sullanciri* who have been slain by Vilwanese agents—save Neskartu, whom Kerrigan slew after he distanced himself from Vilwan."

The King of Oriosa shook his head. "Please, Hawkins, no petty displays of temper and jealousy."

Alexia felt Crow shiver at the accusation coming out of Scrainwood's mouth. She reached back, found his right hand, and squeezed it. "More games, lover." She kept her voice a whisper and felt her hand squeezed in return.

Fidelius frowned. "It is likely true that he could be best contained on Vilwan. It seems the only course is to grant their petition."

"Wait, Highness." Resolute held up a hand. "There is a question that has yet to be answered. Magister Tadurienne, you said you have no information about where Kerrigan Reese was born. Did I hear you correctly?"

"Yes."

"I would like you to tell us, then, the purpose of the Vilwanese expedition that went to Vorquellyn at the time of his birth. There your people engaged Aurolani forces in fierce fighting, then withdrew again."

Alexia had no idea what Resolute was talking about, but

the blood drained from Tadurienne's face. "I believe you are mistaken, Resolute."

Rymramoch waved a hand and, just for a heartbeat, Resolute's magickal tattoos glowed blue. "Of course, yes, the island. Kerrigan Reese has the same taint as you, Resolute. He was born on Vorquellyn."

Resolute's voice gained an edge. "How many were there, Magister? How many were born on Vorquellyn? Were you thinking the children born there would be able to forge a link to the homeland as we do? Had you heard of Chytrine's breeding experiments and the dismal results, then decided you could do it better than she could?"

Tadurienne lifted her chin and clasped her hands at the small of her back. "I am aware there was an expedition sent to Vorquellyn. I do not know its purpose. I do know there was great loss of life. It could be as suggested that the purpose was for children to be born there. I do not know, nor do I know if Kerrigan Reese was one, or if any others yet live. That is all I can tell you on this matter."

Resolute snorted. "You have told us enough. Kerrigan Reese was born on Vorquellyn. Orla knew that, which is why she turned him over to me. My claim to him would supersede any Vilwanese claim."

Tadurienne shook her head. "You are not lord of Vorquellyn, Resolute. If you shape your case that way, then Chytrine has the best claim to him."

"Then I will act as her agent in the matter, unless there is anyone else here who wishes to do that." Resolute looked around the room and Scrainwood seemed to shiver when the Vorquelf's gaze landed on him. "No? Good, it is settled."

The Magister took a step forward. "It is not settled at all."

Resolute's hand dropped to the hilt of his sword. "It can be very settled, if you so . . ."

"Resolute, stay your hand." The words came in a new voice and Alexia turned to face the speaker. Up at the head of the stairs she saw another elf with a flowing mane of white hair and skin fair enough to match. Her eyes seemed at first to be solid copper, but as she descended the step, Alexia saw they had white dots in the center. She wasn't certain if the elf was a Vorquelf, but she clearly was blind.

Resolute immediately crossed to the stairs and mounted them, then took her hand in his and guided her down. His attention and devotion to her surprised Alexia, for Resolute had only ever been stern, stiff, implacable in combat and ill-humored even when apparently happy. Given that her hair matched his, the princess wondered if they were brother and sister.

Her attention remained on them for only a moment. Another figure appeared at the head of the stairs, tall and strong, with his wings furled. Peri cut a joyous squeal short and her father winked one big amber eye at her. Then he nodded at Alexia and she returned the nod. *He must have brought the elf, but how and why?*

Resolute led her to the center of the floor, but she began to shake as they neared Kerrigan's body. The silver-eyed Vorquelf steadied her and moved her back away, interposing his body between her and the twitching mage.

"My lords, this is Oracle. She is the one who uttered the Norrington Prophecy." He turned to her. "What are you doing here?"

"Seeing, Resolute. Doing what I always do." She smiled beautifully and had a playful tone in her voice that broadened Alexia's smile and even seemed to lighten Scrainwood's expression. "There are things I have seen, messages I have been given. One of them is for you. The Norrington is waiting."

Resolute stared at her, opened his mouth, then closed it again. "But Will is dead."

She reached up and traced fingers over his furrowed brow. "The Norrington is waiting. He awaits you within the Saslynnae *coriiesci* on Vorquellyn."

"What? How?" Resolute staggered back a step, then shook his head. "That can't be. It's impossible. Why would he be there?"

"To redeem Vorquellyn, he must be born of it, Resolute."

Oracle's voice remained soothing. "The Norrington is reborn there so he can fulfill the prophecy."

"Just like Will to get himself stuck in the heart of enemy territory." Resolute closed his eyes. "Not only do we have to defeat her troops, to get in there we need a Vorquelf who is bound to the homeland."

Confusion contorted King Fidelius' face, so Crow explained. "When the Aurolani despoiled Vorquellyn, the Vorquelves who had been bound to it felt intolerable pain. They have passed from this world and away from their pain."

"Could not someone like Resolute be bound to the land?"

"Yes, Highness, he could, or Oracle, but the prophecy says the Norrington will redeem Vorquellyn. To get to him, however, we have to get into a sealed site on Vorquellyn, and we can't do that without a Vorquelf who has been bound to the homeland."

The king closed his eyes for a moment, then nodded. "A snake swallowing itself, yes. Is there no other way in?"

Resolute shook his head. "Even Chytrine has tried to get in and has been unsuccessful. The *coriiesci* wards are powerful enough that I don't think dracomagick will break them."

Rymramoch canted his head. "It could, but there would be nothing left of the place you wish to use."

Fidelius sighed. "Without the Norrington, Chytrine goes unvanquished. Is there nothing that can be done? Isn't there any other way?"

"I think there is, Highness." Kerrigan Reese clutched the sheet around him as he sat up. "I think the lesson Chytrine just taught me will be very useful in that regard."

CHAPTER 22

Kerrigan looked around at those in the room. The expressions of surprise on their faces—save for that of the masked puppet of course—baffled him. He realized some time had passed since Chytrine had hit him with her spell, but he didn't know how much. He stroked fingers over his jaw to see how much beard had grown, but he found more remarkable the loose flesh there and the hard press of cheekbones than he did some stubble.

A grey-robed Magister clapped her hands. "This is a miracle."

Kerrigan snorted. "Not a miracle by any means. It was difficult, but I just unlocked her spell."

The woman nodded. "As any true son of Vilwan would have done."

The young mage shook his head and drew the sheet more tightly around him. It was a surprise to him that there seemed to be more sheet than he would have expected. He'd anticipated some of the effect of his work, but not quite this much. He smiled in spite of himself, very pleased to be free.

King Fidelius looked down at him from his throne. "You must understand, Adept Reese, we were given little hope for your survival by anyone here. The mages of your homeland were puzzled by the spell, as was Rymramoch."

Kerrigan shrugged. "It was a difficult one to deal with." He glanced up at the king. "I hope you don't mind me asking, but who is she and why is she here?"

The woman preempted the king's reply. "I am Magister Tadurienne. I have been sent to bring you home."

"Home. You mean Vilwan?" The young man frowned. "I have no home, save where my friends are. Where the fight against Chytrine is."

"You are yet young . . ."

Resolute barked a quick laugh. "You say that, yet everyone here was baffled by the spell from which he found a way out."

Tadurienne sniffed. "I did not say he is not talented. He is. With more seasoning, he would have been able to avoid it or counter it faster."

"That might be true, Magister, but I won't get that training on Vilwan."

The Magister blinked. "You are still addled by your experience. You need rest. The magick has wasted you. You need to recover. On Vilwan."

"No, see, you don't understand at all." Kerrigan swung his legs around and faced her. "Her spell didn't waste me, *I* wasted me. The spell would have killed anyone from Vilwan and left a corpse without a mark on it. If people hadn't seen it cast, and if she'd taken just a bit more time, I would have seemed to die in my sleep."

Tadurienne nodded confidently. "And you wasted yourself to change yourself, so the spell would no longer recognize you as the target. A scapegoat transference of magickal identity. You learned that on Vilwan."

Kerrigan groaned. "No. How stupid do you think she is? That's an ancient idea, and she made sure it would not work."

Rymramoch clattered forward a step. "Perhaps, Kerrigan, you can elucidate on the nature of the spell and your method for dealing with it. I think even the Magister should be able to grasp your explanation."

"Okay, it is really pretty simple." As he made that comment he noticed Princess Alexia smile indulgently, and Crow rest his hands on her shoulders. "No, it really is simple, I promise."

"I believe you, Kerrigan, and will listen intently."

"Thank you, Highness." He sighed and continued. "Chytrine's spell has two main components. Think of it as a nut with a shell. The shell is very complex and works to disrupt magick. It also had a part that would frustrate scapegoat transferences, with terrible results for the people trying it. Talk about wasting, oh it would have been awful, with parts withering and dropping off, and suppurating boils and . . ."

"I believe you said this would be simple, Kerrigan."

"Yes, Magister." Kerrigan gave the puppet a quick smile. "That shell is why your spells didn't tell you anything. The meat of the spell, though, was the really tough thing. It's like a blanket that cuts a mage off from the source of magick."

Magister Tadurienne shook her head. "That is impossible. We are the source of magick."

"No. If that were true, I would be dead. There are things I have learned about magick that Vilwan might once have taught, but not for centuries now. Not since the time of Kirûn." Kerrigan rubbed at his throat and found a lot of spare skin there, too. "Someone from Vilwan would have found himself wrapped in a smothering blanket. Magick would be but a memory, and any spell used to break out of that blanket would fail. No Vilwanese mage has sufficient power to break out."

She glared at him. "But you managed it."

"I did because I know more than you, both of magick

and Chytrine. You know I fashioned a spell that found Chytrine. I was able to do that because I had her essence. She is half-dragon and half-urZrethi. Her strengths lie in those areas when it comes to magick. Human magick she knows mostly through Neskartu, and he was Vilwan-trained, but not in the ways of elven magick. There I detected a weakness. I knew I had been cut off from the source of the power I needed to undo her spells, and I had to make that connection again.

"I decided to modify an elven spell because the way they are formed is simple. They grow, and I imagined a seedling just pushing its way up through the ground, through rocks and all, to reach the sun. Until it could reach the sun, however, it needed energy. So, I cast another spell on myself, a modified healing spell that sped up my metabolism. It ate up my fat and gnawed at muscles and bones. I could have starved to death, literally, but the first spell grew and pushed out through both meat and shell. It reached the source of magick, flooded energy into me, and I was able to take her spell apart."

He opened his hands. "So, here I am, no thanks to Vilwan."

"You know not of what you speak, Kerrigan Reese." Tadurienne advanced and took his chin in hand, raising his face. "I have known of you since you were but a babe. You were special, even from the start, better than your brethren. All of you were bred for one purpose—to be able to oppose Chytrine. While others did nothing to prepare for her return, we did. We prepared you. *Everything* you are is because of Vilwan. We chose your parents, we saw to it they mated, we saw to your birth and raising."

"I thought you told us, Magister, you knew nothing of Kerrigan's birth."

"Forgive me, King Fidelius, I had forgotten." She released Kerrigan's chin, then patted him on a cheek. "Our case stands. He is yet a minor and he is ours. He will come with us."

Her imperious tone sparked anger in Kerrigan, but he tamped it down. Keeping his voice even, he looked her squarely in the eye. "I'm not going with you."

"Of course you are. No one here can stop us from taking you."

He looked at her frankly. "You don't want to test that statement, Magister. The fact is, if you meant what you said about Vilwan having created me to oppose Chytrine, then taking me back to Vilwan is stupid, isn't it? If you were sent here to get me back, you have to see why that is wrong. You forged me, just to resheath me when I am best prepared to strike at her? You know Vilwan created me and others to oppose Chytrine so the world would see Vilwan as the savior of civilization and, in that role, you could expand your power back to what it was when Kirûn existed. To withdraw me now makes no sense unless you have entered an agreement with Chytrine."

"How dare you, you insolent whelp?" Tadurienne's slap snapped his head around. "She is Kirûn's legacy and we want it expunged from history."

He raised his left hand to cover his cheek. The sting slowly faded, as did the venom in her words, leaving only the fear behind. "That's it, then? You fear I am Kirûn come again? You think you forged too well and now you need to control me? Orla *was* right."

"Orla was a fool. I said I knew you as a babe. I have always opposed your training. You have proven yourself a danger and you must be reined in." She took a step back and lowered her hands to her sides. "You will be coming with me."

Kerrigan glanced left and right. Resolute, Dranae, Peri, and Crow had moved into positions where they could physically intervene and prevent his removal. He slowly raised his hands out at shoulder level, showing his friends open palms. The flesh beneath his upper arms quivered as he spoke. "Let her do what she wishes."

Tadurienne's nostrils flared. "I command you to come with me."

"No." Kerrigan slowly shook his head. "You've struck me, Magister. You touched me. I now know you. I have your essence just as I had Chytrine's essence. You can do nothing to compel me to go with you."

Power began to gather around her. Red sparks swirled between her hands as they came up to waist level. The red light intensified, then the woman snapped her fingers back, shoving the heels of her hands in his direction. The scarlet energy boiled out at him.

Kerrigan didn't even bother to gesture. He knew the spell before she cast it and picked one tiny piece of it that was tied to her nature to undo it. That component was all he needed to block it, which he did with minimal effort. As if he had pulled the linchpin from an axle, the rest of the spell just fell apart. By the time the energy stream reached him, it was already evaporating.

Tadurienne stared down at her hands as if they had betrayed her. She set her shoulders and began another spell.

Kerrigan held his right hand out, then closed it, snuffing the spell as effectively as if it had been a candle flame. "No, Magister. If that spell goes wrong, you will suffer. Don't make me prove again there is nothing you can do."

Tadurienne looked past him at the kings. "My lords, you have just seen what he has done. He has disobeyed a direct order of a superior. He is out of control. Give him to me or you will have another Kirûn to deal with."

King Augustus stood and descended to the foot of Kerrigan's table. "It strikes me, Magister, that Adept Reese has exhibited incredible control, especially for one of his youth. Had you struck me as you did him at his age, you'd have had a foot of steel pinning your heart to your spine. With the power you say he has, he could have done much worse."

"Moreover, you could not control him." Even though Scrainwood spoke for him, Kerrigan still found his voice irritating. "He has bested Chytrine. You, having recovered your memory, will now agree he was born on Vorquellyn, which would strengthen Resolute's case for guardianship."

Tadurienne's voice seethed with fury. "You will find, my lords, that Vilwan has done much for you in the past. You jeopardize our future dealings. This is something I suggest you consider long and hard. I will wait a day for your decision, King Fidelius, then I will be forced to communicate to you the Grand Magister's thoughts on the future of our relations."

She turned on her heel, and with her aides trailing behind a step, stalked up the stairs and out of the Guild Master Hall.

Kerrigan slipped from the table and staggered when his feet hit the ground. He found himself caught from behind by strong hands beneath his armpits. "Thank you, Resolute."

"My pleasure, brother."

That sent an odd thrill through Kerrigan. He looked over at Rymramoch. "Where is Bok?"

"Resting. Heavier than a truncheon blow is the wrath of a spiteful child."

"Is there anything I can to do to help him?"

The puppet nodded. "Just seeing you are well will be a tonic to him."

Kerrigan looked down, saw his toes, smiled, then gathered the sheet up between his legs. "Let's go. Clothes, then Bok, then *food.* I'm *starving.*"

Alexia accompanied Kerrigan as far as the palace, then excused herself and returned to her rooms while people scurried about to find him suitable clothing. Once back in her chambers, she seated herself beside the fireplace and closed her eyes. Taking a deep breath, she calmed herself, then projected herself into the Communion.

She found herself on the quay, with the dragonship ready and Maroth at the helm. She also found she had been anticipated, for the Black Dragon waited for her there on the quay itself. "Greetings. I *was* coming to see you."

"I thought you might. Preyknosery reported to me his success in bringing Oracle to Narriz." The dragon's ears twitched. "Are you feeling manipulated?"

"Not per se, but I do feel you are orchestrating events to what seems to be my advantage. Chytrine is revealed to have been disguised for years as Tatyana, shattering morale. In the wake of that, and the more disturbing news of the Norrington's death, hope is resurrected because Oracle comes and says the Norrington is waiting. I know you were part of having her brought to Narriz."

"What is your difficulty with this?"

Alexia lifted her chin and, clasping her hands at the small of her back, she met the Black Dragon's stare openly. "I don't know who you are, so I don't know why you are doing this. All you have done has been to my benefit, and has hurt Chytrine, but I am uncertain how you benefit by it all."

The Black Dragon nodded. "There are many ways I benefit, daughter, but not the least of them is in the furtherance of the Communion's mission. We seek a united and peaceful world. Chytrine opposes it; therefore I do what I can to discomfit her."

"But, with a mind like yours, outside of this place, you must be doing more."

He laughed. "You, Alexia, and Markus Adrogans, even your Prince Erlestoke, are far more competent to lead troops than I. You do that well. I do this well. My efforts elsewhere would be wasted."

The princess frowned. "How long have you known that Tatyana was really Chytrine?"

The Black Dragon canted his head. "Very good. I've known for over twenty years."

"How did you know?"

"Tatyana was a member of the Communion. Chytrine took her on one of her trips into Okrannel—on a precursor to your dream raids. Chytrine did not know she was of the Communion, and Tatyana was able to communicate for a time before she perished in Aurolan."

"And you didn't say anything?"

"How could I? I learned the information here. I could not speak of it in the world."

"You didn't tell me."

"There was no need, was there? You already disliked her and did not trust her. She thought her secret safe and her efforts effective. Had she not been exposed, I would have told you that anything she heard would go to Chytrine's ears, and you would have been cautious. That would have been enough."

"It might have been, but now things are in jeopardy. The crowns are in an uproar over the betrayal."

"That's not what concerns you, is it, truly?" Warmth threaded through his words. "You're concerned because she has always promoted you as the leader who would destroy Chytrine. You wonder if she has been laying some sort of a trap."

Alexia bowed her head. "Again, I wonder if you can read my mind."

"Your question, Alexia, is normal."

"This is more than a commander wondering if she has the ability to lead troops into battle."

His jaw dropped open in a dragonish smile. "That I understand. You are young and though trained well, this is a war unlike any fought in centuries. Lord Norrington, the last man who led troops against her, failed and became her creature. You wonder about that. You also wonder what she saw in you that made her so certain you were not a threat— for if you *were* a threat, she would not have urged you on others."

"You're right, she doesn't think I'm a threat."

"Perhaps she is wrong."

Alexia laughed. "I would have to be an idiot to lead an army into battle, counting on the fact that my enemy is that stupid."

"I agree, but I think you fail to look at a basic truth. She underestimates you. She underestimates everyone, but most especially you because she sees you as a tool of her own making. The fact that you have been hostile and closed to her, the fact that you have taken up with Crow, all of these things lead her to believe you have no depth. The fact that you love is something she cannot understand: your love for Crow, for Perrine, for your friends, this is incomprehensible to her. She doesn't understand that you are doing things for others, not just for yourself.

"She sees you as someone bent on military glory, and she expects you to act like it. Markus Adrogans has been raised to be your rival to spur you to excesses. Those excesses will be punished. But you know better than all that."

Alexia nodded and could see the wisdom in the Black Dragon's words. Alyx always had been stiff in dealing with Tatyana, from the first when she bit her, on up through her taunting her with the possibility of carrying Crow's child. She even knew from talking with Crow that Chytrine had offered him the chance to be her consort and he had refused her. Alexia had won a prize Chytrine had sought for herself, which could have further clouded her thinking.

The princess swallowed. "She knows what I feel is the wise course for the conduct of the war. She knows what I will do."

The Black Dragon shrugged. "So you will do things differently. The advantage you have, my dear, is that when the best battle plan falls apart, you are able to think, to order, and to *lead*. Chytrine's minions do not have that freedom, nor are the stakes as high for them. You fight to guarantee for others what they have long since surrendered. All other things being equal, that will win the day."

Alyx gave him a wry smile. "But will all other things be equal?"

"Not if you do the job you are capable of." The Black Dragon smiled broadly. "They will be very uneven, and in your favor. And Chytrine will pay dearly for her arrogance."

CHAPTER 23

Alexia waited until Crow had finished spreading the map of the eastern half of the world out on their bed before she began to speak. It showed Saporicia in great detail, the same for Oriosa, Muroso, and Bokagul. Loquellyn, Sarengul, Sebcia, and the north were rendered less exactly. She would have preferred things to be far more precise, but to have asked for more work on the map might have tipped people off as to what she was thinking.

"I wanted to share with the six of you what I am proposing for our battle plan. I trust you both to be able to execute what I plan, and to keep this a secret until we reveal it to the crowns. There will be many objections for a whole host of reasons, but our people, the military people, will accept it, so their leaders have little choice but to agree. Still, the moment we make it public, Chytrine will know and will plan accordingly."

The others in the room nodded solemnly. Augustus, Peri, and Crow faced her from across the bed, Dranae and Resolute from the foot, and Erlestoke stood at her right hand. The Oriosan Prince nodded slowly. "I'm sure whatever you are thinking will come as a surprise."

"I hope so, but I also want you to tell me where I'm wrong." She began by pointing at Narriz. "Our troops are gathering here. I will need to split our forces into three groups. The main group is the one I shall lead. It will comprise over seventy percent of the personnel we have and will head north, up the Delasena River valley. We will be aiming for Bacirro, which is the city the Aurolani will threaten after they bypass Fronosa. After we break part of the army there, we will press them back toward Fronosa. There is a weakness there I want to exploit. We will retake Fronosa and move into Muroso . . . Yes, Highness, what?"

King Augustus folded his arms across his chest. "You know I have the utmost confidence in you, Alexia. But what makes you so certain that you will retake Fronosa so quickly?"

"Sire, I know I will take Fronosa because the taking of that city—and all the other cities I shall mention—was the substance of the raid dream I told to the Crown Circle and Tatyana."

"But Tatyana was Chytrine."

"Yes, she was." Alyx gathered her hands at the small of her back. "Chytrine seemed to believe strongly in the power of prophecy, especially as realized in those dreams. Look at my cousin, Mikhail, taking the Three Brothers. That was what he dreamed, and it came true. That strengthened belief in those prophecies. Mine is one that she has always told me I must fulfill."

Erlestoke frowned. "Why would Chytrine believe these dreams would come true?"

Alexia shook her head. "I don't know if she does or not. If she does, it could be because she sees them as elements working toward the fulfillment of some dream or prophecy she knows about. Her belief or not is immaterial, however. What is important is that she believes that *I* believe. Her assumptions about me are not realistic. She sees me as a younger, less experienced Markus Adrogans. Once she sees me moving in the pattern she is expecting, she will believe she has me right where she wants me. She will lay her trap and snap the jaws shut on me."

Augustus scratched at his chin. "That is a dangerous assumption to make."

"But we'll know if it is a valid one by her first move after Fronosa. If she goes after Bacirro with a weak force, one I can crush, we'll know she is offering me bait."

"Sister, when would she strike?"

Alexia rolled her shoulders uncomfortably. "The exact moment I can't be certain, but I would have to win several victories. Morale would have to be high, and word of the prophecy would have to spread before she was going to make an attempt. In my dream, the grand battle took place in Sebcia, at Lurrii. The closer we get to there, the more she will assume I am looking past a small battle toward the final one. It would be a fatal mistake for me to do so."

Resolute let a low growl rumble in his throat for a moment. "You do not accept your dream as prophecy, even though your cousin's dream did come true."

"No, I don't, Resolute, for one simple reason: I never dreamed that night. I never had the chance." She smiled. "My cousin, against all protocols, confided his dream to me. He was happy and I was a bit jealous. He asked me about my dream, and I lied. I made things up. I had been schooled in history, so I recounted a series of battles I knew had taken place historically, and I kept them away from Okrannel because he might know our history. Then, when I went before the Crown Circle, well, they already knew what I had dreamed. Whether it was my cousin or someone else listening, I don't know. So I told the same lie again, in more detail. Fronosa got tossed in just because it was a link between Bacirro and Paloso on the Murosan coast."

The Alcidese King shook his head. "I see the logic in your assumptions. But if she thinks too much about it, she may well see the truth."

"That's why I don't intend to give her that chance." Alexia pointed to the hills district northeast of Narriz. "I want to put a small force in here, one that is highly mobile, to harass the troops she will have in the area. It, ultimately, will be the force that takes Fronosa. Primarily what I want from it is to hit and run, disrupting supplies. It's something we have done before, and her commanders are likely to see it as a nuisance force as it was in Muroso. When we need it to hit hard, however, it will. That's not all, though."

Alexia looked at Erlestoke. "Captain Venes raised a valid point about Oriosa. That flank has to be secured. Right now, with Oriosa neutral, we both have the same measure of security, though Chytrine does have troops in your nation."

"In my father's nation."

"Erlestoke, *you* may see Oriosa as his, but the people of Oriosa see it as yours." Alexia rested a hand on his shoulder. "What I want you to do is to take a force and march right up through Oriosa. Chytrine will recognize the threat you pose and have to devote troops to oppose you."

"Her troops will oppose me, certainly, but they will be second in line. My father does have his supporters among the nobility. They will also oppose us with troops." Erlestoke pressed his black mask tighter against his face. "You're asking me to initiate a civil war."

"No. I'm asking you to assume your rightful place at the head of an Oriosan army. You're not going to be there to make war on your father, and the people will know that since you will not lay siege to Meredo. You will bypass it and keep going. You'll pick up troops from those lords who oppose your father and when Chytrine attacks, she will be attacking Oriosans. That will cause the countryside to rise up to support you."

"You understimate Oriosans if you think I won't be shedding their blood."

"No, I don't think I am, Erlestoke. I know what you've done. I know what Crow did. I know your brother joined the Freemen. I've had a good chance to look into the hearts of brave Oriosans. I know they will fight, and will even fight for you." She gave his shoulder a squeeze. "What I want from you is to find a way to bring them to us. You didn't like what your father was doing and you chose to leave. Your people didn't like it any better, but they didn't have that choice. Now you can give them a choice, if you are willing."

Erlestoke sighed heavily. "I don't know. This is something I must think hard about. I know this needs to be done, I just don't know if I can do it. When do you require an answer?"

"You have a day."

The prince jerked back, then nodded. "A day. Okay."

Alexia glanced at Resolute. "I want you to lead the hill force."

"No."

"What?"

Crow smiled. "I told you."

"I can't lead it, Alexia. You're expecting me to say it is because I have no standing. Save your breath. I cannot lead it because I am not going to be available."

Alexia frowned. "What are you talking about?"

The tall Vorquelf looked down at her with argent eyes. "Have you forgotten what Oracle said? Will's waiting for us on Vorquellyn. That's where I'm going. I'm taking Oracle with me."

Alexia felt her guts begin to knot up. "That's insane, Resolute. You'll be slaughtered once you hit Vorquellyn. You yourself said you need a full-blooded Vorquelf to get where Will is waiting, and none exists."

"It doesn't matter, Princess. It has to be done. In all your thinking about what Chytrine may or may not take as prophecy you neglected one thing: it was the Norrington Prophecy that started all this. You might not want to believe in it, but I do."

"Resolute, I *do* believe. I believe Will was the embodiment of it, and that what he did has set things in motion so we can destroy Chytrine."

"I like that interpretation, Princess. I wish I could afford to believe it the way you do. Oracle says Will is waiting. The prophecy says Will will vanquish Chytrine and redeem Vorquellyn. For all I know my death, Oracle's death, there, on Vorquellyn, may be required." He shrugged. "Besides, you need someone going to Loquellyn to convince the Loquelves to come through the highlands and help you out. Might as well be me."

Alexia looked at Crow. "Can you talk sense to him?"

"It would be the first time in our long association. Besides, I know how stubborn he is. He's going to do what he said he's going to do. I assume you're going to need someone to watch your back."

Resolute nodded. "I will, but it won't be you, my friend. You're going to be leading the hill force that takes Fronosa."

"But . . ."

The Vorquelf shook his head. "Who better?"

Crow laughed. "I could name a dozen. Prince Erlestoke, for one. Adrogans for another."

Erlestoke smiled. "I'll trade assignments with you."

"Your father would love that. No."

Augustus frowned. "What are you going to do about Adrogans, Alexia?"

She shook her head. "I will keep him aware of what we are doing, but there is not much more I can do. His people are too far away. His cavalry could be here in a month and a half, perhaps, and be another two weeks trying to find us in Muroso. The trek would ruin them. His infantry couldn't be here until late summer."

The king leaned forward and traced a line from Svarskya around through the Ghost March. "He could take the shorter route."

"He'll fight every step of the way." She smiled. "It will give Chytrine something to think about. Do you think he would do it?"

"If he was of a mind to have created an empire, he'd already have declared Okrannel to be part of it. You'd never get approval to order him to do that."

"So I just keep him aware of what we are doing and hope he takes the hint?"

Augustus chuckled. "I think you have no other course. In fact, I'm certain you will be told to give Adrogans orders to stay in Svarskya. I might suggest you entrust them to Resolute for delivery."

The princess smiled. "I'll do that. Dranae, what do you think?"

The dragon in manform folded powerful arms over his chest. "In my time with you I have learned to trust your judgment, all of you. Your strategy seems sound. I will fight alongside you. I believe Arimtara will also. It will give you some counters to any dragons Chytrine might use."

"Good, thank you." Finally, she looked at Perrine. "What about you, sister?"

"There is one thing I don't like about this plan."

"What?"

"I cannot be with all the groups at the same time." Peri flashed talons. "The Nor'witch has had her way too long. She thinks you a fool at her peril, sister. We will make her pay dearly for her mistake."

CHAPTER 24

Isaura had never seen her mother in such a state. Chytrine had the slender young woman fast by the wrist, dragging her along through the caverns beneath her citadel. She'd returned to Aurolan barely hours before with Nefrai-kesh and a prisoner. Isaura didn't want to think of the woman that way, but her fear and the manner in which Chytrine had her bundled off by *kryalniri* really left her no choice in the matter.

Isaura's white hair flew behind her as they sped on. Her mother, slightly shorter and thicker, with gold-blonde hair, made her way through twists and turns effortlessly. She entered tunnels Isaura had never known existed despite living her entire life in Aurolan. Traces of magick around some entrances led her to believe what were now open had recently been shut away.

The gibberers following them, dragging another prisoner, did not have trouble negotiating the course. She was uncertain if that was because they had ventured this way before, or if their devotion to Chytrine kept them in dogged pursuit.

Chytrine looked back over her right shoulder at Isaura. "Daughter, it is imperative that I share with you some information. Though you are not blood of my blood, nor flesh of my flesh, you are truly my daughter. What I have withheld from you until this point was only so you would be ready to know it. I was easily twice your age before this truth was made manifest to me, but you are far more mature than I was."

"Thank you, Mother."

Their pace slackened a little as their surroundings grew a bit warmer on the downward path. "I need to tell you of the world and its origins. There was once a time when all that existed was a swirling chaotic ball. Imagine every blizzard you have ever seen, combine them and lace them with the elements, and even that will not be close to what existed. From within that chaos came a people, wise and powerful. They are the Oromise, and they shaped this world out of the chaos. They made it their home."

Chytrine's voice had sunk into husky soft tones, taking Isaura back to the nights when the empress had told her soothing tales of Aurolani heroes and their grand exploits, or milder tales of boreal creatures who were alive with magick. The story her mother was telling her now would have had that same fantastic character to it, save for the tight grip on her wrist and their relentless progress deeper and deeper into the folds of the earth.

"The dragons came to this world, and the Oromise welcomed them. They were not the dragons we know now, but mere worms, barely capable of thought. The Oromise protected them and nurtured them, developing them into the grand creatures they are. That is why dragons have no native culture. They are true beasts of the chaos, and live to destroy. It is their nature and, foolishly, the Oromise thought they had carried the dragons past it.

"Elves then entered the world and the Oromise were kind to them. At that time forests covered the face of the earth, and the elves spread far and wide. They did not disturb the dragons, and the dragons barely noticed them. All would have been at peace, but the elves are creative creatures and they paid homage to the Oromise. They fashioned things of wood and metal, beautiful things, creating in imitation of the Oromise, who created so much. The elves offered them worship and sacrifices. That pleased the Oromise. It also made the dragons jealous."

Indignation filled her mother's voice. "The dragons attacked the elves, burning and killing, stealing the treasures they fashioned for the Oromise. The Oromise reacted and struck the dragons down. They demanded the return of the stolen things, and the dragons—yet treacherous worms—agreed but plotted. Jealous servants that they were, they revolted against the Oromise and a great war ensued."

"That's horrible, Mother."

"It was. Most horrible. The Oromise created many manner of creatures to aid them in their battle. The urZrethi yet exist, as do some others, in pockets, here and there. *Grichothka* and vylaens are descendants of some, and the *kryalniri* I have made in the image of others. The war ravaged the lands, splitting the forests, poisoning rivers and oceans, and doing more damage than we could possibly imagine. The dragons tried to create their own allies, but the best they could do were the Panqui. Despite that lack of success, the dragons were most terrible in war, as they yet are.

"The Oromise realized that by engaging in the war they were letting dragons inject chaos into the world. The very act of war was destroying the place they sought to preserve, so the Oromise withdrew, inward, into the earth, and walled themselves away. There they have waited, quiet and peaceful, knowing a time would come to reclaim what is rightfully their creation."

They came around a corner and the nature of the passage changed. Up to that point the walls had been little worked and bore all signs of being natural formations. The path had been smooth, something Isaura knew was not likely to occur without help, but she accepted it without thinking. Now, however, a broad staircase opened down to a large semispherical room. It had no floor, but descended into a dark well, the bottom of which Isaura could not discern. A narrow causeway extended halfway into the room.

Her mother paused at the top of the stairs. "I did not know of this place until the time of Kirûn. When those who came to kill him arrived here, I fled deep into the tunnels. You know I can assume many forms, including the dragon you have ridden in high summer. This is because I am of a dual nature: both urZrethi and dragon. Loyal servant to the Oromise and rebel. I unite these two aspects and seek to undo the injustice perpetrated by the one half. Down here, safe, I heard the Oromise whisper to me. I learned the truth, and it made me free to do all that needed to be done."

Chytrine gave her wrist a tug. "Come, you'll see."

Wordlessly, Isaura drifted after her. She stopped on the bottom step and allowed two *grichothka* to bring the prisoner to the causeway. She had been bound hand and foot and was forced to kneel toward the end of it.

Chytrine dismissed the gibberkin with a wave. The furred creatures scampered up the stairs and out of sight. Isaura fought the urge to race after them and instead watched her mother move onto the causeway.

The Aurolani Empress grabbed the prisoner by her brown hair and hauled her head back, extending her throat. The woman, Vionna, had once been the queen of the Wruonin pirates and servant to the empress. She had obtained a fragment of the DragonCrown for her, but lost it again to the Norrington and his companions. She had become a grave disappointment to Chytrine and through the whimpers and trembling of bluish lips, Isaura assumed the woman knew that.

Chytrine's voice filled the room's bowl. "Hear me, ancient Masters and Mistresses. In Your purpose I have been engaged. Another of Your servants has been destroyed. I offer You this sacrifice in hopes You will find something of worth to enable this unworthy servant to continue her service to You."

Vionna's eyes grew wider. "Sacrifice? Don't do this."

The empress' gold eyes half lidded. "You are scrap from which They will make a masterwork." She took a step back, then kicked Vionna full between the shoulder blades. The pirate grunted and skidded toward the edge, then slipped off. She made a desperate grab for the causeway lip with her knees, but failed and fell screaming into the darkness.

Isaura shivered. She had never liked Vionna, so would not miss her. She did not know what her fate was to be, but that did not concern her. Yet her mother's coldness, the sharpness of the kick, that was something she had never seen before. Though she loved her mother dearly, this was an aspect that unsettled her.

A weak wave of magick pulsed up through the well and gathered in the room's bowl as smoke gathers beneath a roof. Isaura could almost see it as smoke, drifting and boiling, then it all contracted and flowed toward one spot on the wall opposite the stairs. The stone there began to glow red and shift. The redness flowed into an oval shape. A dark line formed across the middle, from edge to edge, then it opened as might an eyelid. Beyond it Isaura could only see blackness, but a blackness with depth, as if the sky robbed of stars.

Chytrine dropped to her knees and by reflex Isaura did as well. A voice, neither male nor female, and somehow plural, filled Isaura's head. "Your gift, our pet, pleases. Joy will be had from its working. Who behind you stands?"

"This is my daughter and heir, to be learned in the ways of Your service. She is Isaura."

Isaura felt an intensity of attention paid to her, as if a hard stare, but one capable of penetrating her flesh and bones and even her soul. She kept her head bowed and her body rigid. Somehow she choked back a scream.

The presence withdrew. "Also pleasing. Your choice we approve."

Chytrine bowed far enough forward to touch her head to the stone. "Your service is what I live for. Your pleasure is my only pleasure."

"Tell us how your endeavors have our cause advanced."

"All is prepared for the grand victory that shall sweep opposition away. Discord has been sown in the enemy. Your great gift of firedirt has been passed to the most rapacious and ambitious among them. Already they fear his advances and this blunts their efforts in the east. There, they are putting the trust of their armies in a young woman. She believes in the power of prophetic dreams—dreams that will lead her in a series of victories. With Your other gifts, we will break her cycle of dreams and shatter her forces."

"And of the Norrington?"

"He is gone, and with him their hope. They move from clinging to that prophecy to this one about Alexia."

"The worms nothing suspect?"

"No. They are aware that I alone can reassemble then destroy the DragonCrown. They will give it to me and I will re-create it. Instead of destroying it, however, I will use it to force the greatest of the dracomages to unmake the magicks that hold you prisoner. You will be free once more."

The eye widened slightly. "Magick stains you."

"Yes." Chytrine hissed, sat back on her heels, crossed her arms, then drew them back. Her hands ran across her collarbones to her shoulders, then down over her breasts, belly, hips, and thighs. In their wake glowed a blue mist with a golden lattice playing through it.

That lattice dissolved and Isaura caught a sense of residual magick. She could not discern the nature of the spell, but she knew who had cast it. She had seen him at Navval in Muroso. He had slain a *sullanciri* and thwarted the efforts of the Aurolani sorcerers to bring the city's siege to a quick conclusion.

"Cunning spell, pet. You noticed it not?"

"No, Masters and Mistresses, but he who cast it has been dealt with."

"You should have given him to us."

Chytrine again prostrated herself. "Forgive this unworthy one."

"We shall, for reasons that defy logic. Of the crown, three pieces remain."

"Two we are close to getting. The last, however, is elusive. It will be found. Your will shall be done. I have made arrangements that even if I fall, I shall not fail."

Isaura shivered. She had no idea what her mother meant by that, for she had been given no instructions. If her mother trusted her, she would tell her. *And if she does not, then how can I truly be her heir?*

"See to it you do not fail."

"Never."

The voice ceased and the eye closed, but the magickal intensity in the room did not slacken. Suddenly the hole snapped open again and something flew from it, spat forth wetly. It hit high up on the stairs, and began to slide down, but claws extended through the thick mucus coating it and scrabbled against rock.

The creature got its feet beneath it, then sliced apart the membrane encapsulating it. The turgid coating sloughed off and flowed down the stairs, leaving a lithe female form covered in closely cropped black fur, save for the tip of the tail and a thick midnight mane covering neck and powerful shoulders. The tail lashed once, then the tufted ears rose.

The creature turned to look at Isaura, revealing a whiskered muzzle and bright blue eyes. Lips peeled back to flash ivory fangs. Still weak of limb, the thing could not stand, but did manage to drag her legs up and twist. "What have you done to me, witch?"

Chytrine glanced over her shoulder. "You have had the honor known to few of my *sullanciri*, to be transformed by my Masters and Mistresses into a tool of their will. You were once Vionna and would have been a queen. They have made you a god. You are now Nekaamii and shall be second only to Nefrai-kesh. You will be his consort, doing his will and mine."

Nekaamii hissed, then stretched her muscles. She pulled her right hand before her face and watched, fascinated, as her claws retracted and extended. She licked at her yet wet fur, then her eyes narrowed. "At least I am no longer cold."

The Oromise voice resumed. "Our reward pleases you, pet?"

"It is more than this one could have ever hoped."

"As is your service to us. You will free us again, and our pleasure shall know no limits. Our gratitude will similarly be unbound." The opening again closed and the magick fled as if drawn into the void beyond it. Isaura shivered again and slowly climbed to her feet.

Chytrine remained on her knees for a moment, whispering in a tongue Isaura did not understand, then bowed deeply before rising. The empress smiled at her daughter. "There is much for you to learn. The first is to be able to find your way here. The Oromise will always protect you. You need not fear them, daughter. With them as your allies, there is nothing for you to fear."

"I know that, Mother." Isaura smiled as sweetly as she could.

"Good, this pleases me. Come." Chytrine mounted the steps, avoiding the remains of Nekaamii's afterbirth, climbing in the wake of the *sullanciri* bounding up the stairs. "With what you have learned today, you need never fear anything again."

Isaura glanced back at the bowl and felt her skin crawl. "No, Mother, I know that as well." *After today, I fear you. And that is more than enough fear for a lifetime.*

CHAPTER 25

It struck King Scrainwood as odd that while he had quite a few clandestine meetings with women, none of the meetings were the sort of assignation that would please him. Granted, none of the women were the sort with whom he sought that sort of assignation. Certainly not Tatyana, and not the woman before him now.

He shivered slightly, remembering the times he had spent with Tatyana and never having had a clue as to her true identity. Chytrine had played him well, using Tatyana to measure his loyalty. It amused him ever so slightly to have been the one to pass on to Tatyana the news that Adrogans had dragonels, when Chytrine had told him this in the first place. *She must have been laughing mightily inside—if she ever laughed.*

The woman bowed before him. "Thank you for granting me this audience, King Scrainwood."

"Your request was unexpected, Magister Tadurienne." Scrainwood smiled slyly. "The day you granted in your ultimatum has passed, and another. King Fidelius has not given you custody of Kerrigan Reese. Indeed, the boy is treated as if emancipated."

Tadurienne's right hand strayed to the lacy courtesy mask she wore and stroked it over her temple. "We find this yet to be a problem, but we do not see an immediate solution for it."

The king stood, opening his hands. "I have none either. If this is the reason you have come here, your time is wasted, as is mine."

"If you will indulge me, Highness . . ."

"See to it you don't bore me." He crossed from his throne to a small side table and poured himself a goblet of wine. Another one waited there to be filled, but he refrained. Raising it and sipping, he turned and nodded to her. "You may speak."

"Thank you, Highness." Though he heard tightness in her voice, the ring he wore did not even hint at hostility. "To us it appears as if Vilwan and Oriosa are facing some similar problems. We have Kerrigan Reese, a son of ours, who shows no loyalty. While he could well be successful, without preparation, our role in his victory will go unrecognized. Our place will be diminished."

"Indeed, and I can imagine why you would not like that." Scrainwood sipped again, then lowered his goblet. "You would liken Erlestoke to Kerrigan Reese?"

"I knew you would catch the allusion, Highness. It applies to Erlestoke more than Linchmere, but you suffer the difficulty of a possible compounding of the situation. If both your sons emerged heroes, their popularity would eclipse yours and perhaps end your reign."

Scrainwood nodded slowly. "You've perhaps missed the fact that my reign may be ended in a matter of months. Chytrine or my allies will invade Oriosa. My chances of surviving that sort of onslaught are negligible. You seem to be suggesting something needs to be done to position ourselves to benefit from the aftermath of the war. But unless I see a way to survive, this is a pointless exercise."

The corner of Tadurienne's mouth tugged up in a bit of a smile. "We believe there is a way this can be done. Your survival for ours, Highness."

"If you can guarantee my survival, you are greater magicians than even I could have imagined."

The Magister nodded. "I have been speaking with many leaders, Highness, and there are certain anxieties that the leaders of smaller nations share. Adrogans' likely possession of dragonels threatens everyone. Likewise, Alcida's strong presence is seen as a threat. Why would they withdraw from Saporicia? They will need recompense of some sort for their efforts, and will hold on to key cities until their price had been paid. As they build an empire, the collision between them and the Jeranese empire is inescapable. The nations between them do not feel secure."

"Fascinating scenario, but I fail to see what it has to do with my situation."

"A strong Oriosa is seen as the only deterrent to an Alcidese empire. If Oriosa is strong, then it is poised like a dagger that can strike at Yslin and split the Saporician provinces from Alcida proper. The western nations are prepared to vote in council to support the war in Saporicia, provided there is an agreement that no foreign force invades Oriosa. Your eastern neighbors are not going to invade unless they are threatened by Chytrine, and the war in Saporicia should keep her involved."

The Oriosan king set his goblet on the table and clapped politely. "Spoken as someone who has no understanding of warfare whatsoever. The fact of it is simple. As Alexia presses in the north, Chytrine simply must engage in another attack. She will go through Oriosa to strike at Narriz and cut off all supply from the south. Alosan and Vegan troops will pour into the north—we can but hope they slaughter each other, since there is little love lost there."

"We do not disagree with your analysis, Highness, but we would point out that if the battle moves quickly enough to Muroso, Oriosa is no longer a viable option for Chytrine." Tadurienne pressed her hands together flatly. "We have organized a legion of our finest war-mages and will make them available to Princess Alexia. They will be under her orders, of course, but will be in a position to turn the tide in key battles. Others of our people will be available to facilitate transport of personnel and materiel, such that the move into Muroso should be swift."

"Provided Chytrine does nothing unusual."

"Oh, Chytrine will, certainly." Tadurienne shrugged. "We will be there to oppose her. We will also give you, quite in secret, another legion of mages versed in a variety of arts, for you to use as you need to maintain order. If you need them to destroy infestations of Aurolani troops, they will. If you need them to extract information from suspected collaborators, they will."

"If I need Aurolani sympathizers killed?"

Tadurienne nodded. "They are yours to command."

"So, you will actively guarantee my place on the throne by providing me secret marshals to rid me of my enemies. The price for this will not be small."

"No, but hardly beyond that which you can pay." The grey-robed Magister folded her arms, slipping her hands into the opposite sleeves. "As Kerrigan Reese indicated, after the days of Kirûn, Vilwan diluted the power of its students. That clearly was an error, but it was done in a time when many feared a sorcerer of great power. Kerrigan Reese himself has such power, and we cannot discount the idea that something he may do will result in a regeneration of that fear. If our role in the defeat of Chytrine is seen as minor, then it might be possible to suggest we are done away with.

"What we would want of you is simple: your support in demanding Vilwan again become strong. You will point out and promote our activities against Chytrine. Your support, and your invitation for us to set up a satellite school in

Oriosa, will prompt other nations to do likewise. We all benefit."

"Indeed, we do." Scrainwood turned and filled the second goblet, then extended it in Tadurienne's direction. "Please, enjoy my hospitality."

The Magister gestured and the goblet floated to her outstretched hand. "You are most kind, Highness."

"No, in fact, I am not, but you knew that. If you did not, you would not be here." He raised his cup to her. "May what we plan come to fruition in the best way."

Alexia sat back in the chair and groaned as Crow's strong fingers began to knead the muscles of her neck and shoulders. "Oh, do not stop."

"As you command, Highness." His thumbs worked up along the back of her neck, forcing her head forward. They pressed in hard there, releasing tensed muscles, then she felt a light kiss. The kiss fell over a mark he'd left there during their lovemaking the previous night, and it made her smile. "It is almost time for you to come to bed, you know."

She groaned again. "I want to, Crow, very much, but there are so many reports to read through. All these units, and I have to compare what officials say about them, then what you, Peri, and Dranae say about them. And then we have all the supply reports . . ."

"All of which will wait. You will benefit from a good night's sleep, and I mean to see you have it."

She turned her head and glanced back at him. "You'll be sleeping elsewhere, then?"

He laughed. "I would prefer to hold you, my love." His voice dropped. "And I think you would sleep better if you did not harbor the secret you have been carrying for the last two days."

Alyx stiffened. "What do you mean?"

Crow's hands left her neck, as he shifted to her left and dropped to a knee. "I know you. When we were discussing the strategies for the war, you told Resolute you never dreamed during your dream raid. You lied to him. You did dream, and that dream has come back to you these last couple of nights. You need to let it out. You can tell me what it was."

"No, I can't, Crow."

"Why not?"

She turned in the chair and took his hands in hers. "Because if it comes true . . ." Alyx pressed her lips together in an effort to forestall tears, but one leaked down her right cheek regardless.

He squeezed her fingers. "Shhhh, it can't be that bad."

"Yes, it can."

"Tell me, Alexia. If it has something to do with me, you have to let me share the burden."

"No, because if I don't believe it, it can't be true."

Crow smiled up at her. "Darling, if it disturbs your sleep, you already believe it. Tell me."

She drew in a deep breath, held it, then exhaled quickly. "I was seventeen at the time, so there was much of it I didn't understand. It was confusing, just like a dream is supposed to be. I was lying on my back, in bed, with my lover sleeping beside me. We held hands."

She smiled at him, then caressed his cheek. "I didn't know who it was then, and never thought about who until the last couple of nights. He had white hair and a beard, just like you. He was you; *is* you. I was happy. Then there appeared a figure and I was paralyzed. I could do nothing. She took the pillow from beneath your head and placed it over your face. You could do nothing either, you did not struggle. She was smothering you."

Crow's eyes widened. "Okay, now there's two of us hoping your dream does not come true."

"But it doesn't end there." Alyx swallowed hard again. "Like I said, it was a dream. My father appeared and he destroyed the person smothering you. That's impossible, I know that, but that is what I dreamed."

"Anything after that? Did we survive?"

She shook her head. "No, nothing after that. Other events intervened and I never had another chance to sleep that night. When Mischa told me his dream, I couldn't tell him mine. I didn't lie when I said I made my dream up. I did."

Crow rubbed a hand over his jaw and tugged on his beard. "I don't like the dream but, as with the Norrington Prophecy, things have to be right for that stuff to come true. Perhaps we take steps to make sure the circumstances are not right."

"So you *are* sleeping elsewhere tonight?"

"Let's not be insane, shall we?" He slipped his fingers into her hair and drew her down into a kiss. Their lips met, parted. He licked softly, she reciprocated and gave in fully to the kiss. When finally they broke it, they both smiled.

"Oh, Crow, I much prefer this feeling to one of dread."

"I quite agree." He stood and pulled her up into his arms. He hugged her around the small of her back, bringing their hips and bellies together tightly. "Do you recall, in that dream, feeling as if you had made love before you fell asleep?"

"At the time, Crow, I had no idea what that felt like, so, no."

"Good, so having that feeling is not part of the dream." He kissed her throat and murmured against it. "Which means . . ."

". . . that instead of sleeping apart, we have to sleep very much together?"

"My thinking exactly."

Alexia smiled. "I can see now how you've survived a quarter century of war with Chytrine."

"Animal cunning, really." He glanced toward their bed. "Well, my dear, shall we be on the safe side?"

"As everyone is counting on me to save the world, prudence would be best." She smiled and kissed him on the ear. "Thank you, lover, I shall sleep very well in your arms."

CHAPTER 26

K errigan listened to the instructions Princess Alexia gave the gathered soldiery, but with only half an ear. Though seven days had passed since his victory over Chytrine's spell, he still did not feel comfortable in his skin. Seeing his toes was still a novelty, and there was a lot more loose skin than he could have imagined. He just sagged everywhere and that took a lot of getting used to.

There was also a lot more muscle to him than he would have thought—though, in an odd way, it made perfect sense. He'd built up a lot of muscle just hauling his own bulk around. He no longer massed as much as Dranae, and his ordeal had just drained him of fat and hadn't given him anything to replace it. It was true that he felt better and could move more quickly, but he found that distracting at a time when distracted was the last thing he needed to be.

The undertaking Princess Alexia described was fascinating, but he'd heard the briefing before, and had even helped her work out the numbers. Under her command she would have thirteen thousand troops. Three thousand would go with Erlestoke on his mission, though she did not mention what his command would be doing to the assembled officers. A second subcommand under the Salnian General Pandiculia would draw off three thousand troops as well and move considerably west to the Varasena River and head north along it. Crow's two battalions would operate in the hills and had been supplemented by a legion of Vilwanese warmages, making them more effective than just elite cavalry alone.

The bulk of the force, under Alexia's direct command, would head up the Delasena River valley. There they would wait for Pandiculia's force to sweep east, then they would push toward Fronosa. If everything went perfectly, Alexia's force would reach Bacirro five days after leaving Narriz, and fourteen days later Pandiculia's troops would arrive after their long trek. Another five days' march would bring them to Fronosa, approximately a month after quitting Narriz.

The problem was that there were all manner of things that could go wrong. Leaving Narriz, the army would consist of roughly three thousand cavalry, including replacement mounts and supply wagons. The cavalry column would stretch for twelve miles, so the last unit in line would move out four hours after the first had started on the road. Moving at that pace the cavalry would far outstrip its supply wagons, but arrangements had been made to ship fodder up along the river and cache it.

The infantry would not race away from its supply wagons, since they would move at the same pace; but while the cavalry would reach Bacirro in two days, the infantry would take five. The infantry column would stretch for two miles and have the joy of marching along a road churned to mud by thousands of horses.

Getting the people assembled and moving was a titanic task, and keeping them supplied made that seem insignificant. A cavalry regiment required nearly eighteen tons of fodder for all its horses per day. While the snow would be retreating, the plains would offer little in the way of good fodder this early in the season so all of it would have to be shipped upriver. The army would consume five tons of food in a single day and keeping them supplied would require constant traffic between a key city like Bacirro and wherever the troops were. Just as Resolute and Crow had done in Muroso, cutting supply lines would slow the army and leave it weakened.

In her briefing Alexia left the impression that Resolute would be working with Crow in the hills, but Kerrigan knew that wasn't true. Resolute was bound for Vorquellyn with Oracle, and would travel with Pandiculia's troops as far as Sanurval. When she turned east, he'd push on north into Loquellyn. From there he'd get a ship and go to Vorquellyn and find Will.

The news that Will was waiting in Vorquellyn had shaken Kerrigan. He'd seen Will die at Vael and keenly felt that death. Not only had he failed to prevent it by his inaction, but Will had become a friend. It wasn't until Will's death that Kerrigan figured out he'd been his first friend—or first human friend, since Lombo had been a friend, too. Alexia and Crow and the others had become friends, but it was not the same bond he shared with Will.

When they find him, I wonder if he'll be mad at me? The question seemed a bit absurd, since Will would have been through death, so little things like being angry at a friend might well seem trivial. By the same token, Kerrigan's failure to prevent that death gnawed at him.

Right there, in the room where Alexia briefed her troops, Kerrigan had confronted Chytrine. He'd known, despite her denials, that Tatyana was the Nor'witch. He should have hauled off and blasted her with the nastiest spell he could imagine. That would have rid the world of her menace once and for all.

Maybe. He'd not blasted her for two good reasons, and one pretty bad one. The overarching reason he'd not hit her with some terrible spell was that he didn't have one he was comfortable using under stress. His tutors had taught him some basic combat magicks, but they'd never really encouraged him to practice. Given the power levels at which he operated, an accident could seriously hurt someone, so their caution was probably wise.

Second, he'd had an odd feeling about Chytrine. It took him a while to piece it together, but given her dragon nature, he concluded that her Truestone had been left elsewhere, probably back in Aurolan. Its lack meant that she'd survive, no matter what he did to her physical shell. It would have been a disaster if everyone believed he'd killed her, only to have her rise up again a month, year or decade later after her body reconstituted itself.

The last reason, the bad one, was that he'd felt the need to expose her as truly being Chytrine to those who thought she was just another sour old witch. Moreover, using the spell that she batted aside so easily seemed clever. He wanted to ambush her to show how smart he was. It worked, but she struck back and struck back hard.

Up in the front of the room, Alexia clapped her hands together. "That's it. Those are your assignments. I know you will want to communicate what you've been told to your superiors, but I ask you to refrain. Tomorrow I am presenting our full plan to the Council. I know there will be objections, but I would prefer it if they were spontaneous instead of studied. This plan has been created by all of us. We know it will work, and we know it has to work. Political considerations are going to have to be secondary to our needs if we are to defeat the Nor'witch."

Captain Venes gave her a nod. "Given as how the crowns harbored Chytrine among them, revealing too much is likely to make my life shorter. I'm saying nothing."

"Good, thank you." She smiled. "In two days we have the New Year celebration. We will move out after that. Tell your people they'll be here to celebrate, then they'll get the chance to make the new year one of true joy. You're dismissed. Enjoy yourselves, as it will be a long slog before we do that again."

Applause rose from within the military folk and Kerrigan joined in. Alexia blushed, then laughed as Qwc fluttered in tight circles around her, clapping all four of his hands. Various and sundry leaders filed past her, shaking her hand, tossing her a salute, or nodding respectfully. She returned their gestures, calling to them all by name, wishing them luck and telling them she looked forward to their service.

Soon enough the room emptied save for the princess' longtime companions and a couple of new ones. Resolute closed the door behind the last of the soldiers as the rest of them gathered around the table upon which a large map had been laid. When Resolute joined them, she began speaking in muted tones.

"This is the most difficult part of the whole operation. We have four different missions, and we cannot all be together—as much as that would be my preference. Some of you I know well, some not nearly so well, but I value you all for your courage and intelligence. Unfortunately, we must split this august company so we can best accomplish our goals."

Resolute reached out and tapped Vorquellyn's image. "I'll take Oracle with me. We'll travel fast, get in, get Will, then go north to Aurolan. We'll kill Chytrine and rescue Sayce."

Alexia's head came up. "You're not going alone."

"I said I'm taking Oracle. We'll get Will."

"Don't misunderstand me on purpose, Resolute. I know you want to travel fast, but you'll be going with a blind woman and riding into the most dangerous territory possible. I don't doubt your abilities, but I'm also going to be realistic here. I want Bok, Rym, and Kerrigan to go with you."

The Vorquelf folded his arms over his chest. "An urZrethi, a puppet, and Kerrigan? Why not just hitch me to a plow and have me carve you a furrow all the way there? Bok is not here because he's still recovering from injuries.

Rym, with all due respect, is a doll. Kerrigan is likewise not healthy."

Alexia looked at Kerrigan. "You have anything to say?"

Kerrigan frowned, then swallowed hard against the lump choking him. "Yeah." The word came out hoarsely, so he swallowed again, biting back tears, then looked up at Resolute. "You're going to go get Will. I need to be there. I need to see he's okay. And . . . and you can't tell me that what I can do won't help. Maybe my being born on Vorquellyn is important to all of this."

Resolute's face closed so tightly it all but clicked shut. He turned his head fluidly toward Alexia. "I do not like it."

"But you will acquiesce?"

"Only because I must."

Crow smiled at his friend. "Oracle told you that you would have help, didn't she?"

The Vorquelf's nostril's flared. " 'Help' is a term open to interpretation."

"Accept the help, Resolute." Alexia sighed, then looked at Erlestoke. "Yours is the most delicate mission. I would like Nay and Borell to join you. You'll also have Preyknosery and a wing of Gyrkyme scouts."

The prince nodded. "That will work well. If you expect me to hook up with Bokas, having the Gyrkyme there will help enormously."

Dranae, who was standing next to Arimtara, extended a hand. "Highness, I was wondering if I, too, could be attached to the Oriosan mission. We have been supposing that when Chytrine learns of it, she will attack. Her most efficient strike will be to send a dragon to immolate the prince's troops. I believe I can provide a bit of a surprise for her pet."

Erlestoke smiled. "That's fine with me. I like how you handle a draconette as well, so I would be happy to have you with me."

Nay and his son, who stood between Resolute and

Dranae, both nodded. "Was planning to go home anyway. Be thankful for the escort."

Alexia smiled. "You'll be more than a traveler, Nay. Borell has killed a *sullanciri*. He's a hero and someone to make Oriosa yet more proud."

Borell just blushed and said nothing.

The prince nodded at him. "I'm happy you're coming along."

Crow hooked his thumbs behind his belt buckle. "Perrine will go with you, Alexia. You should also keep Arimtara with you, if she wishes to join the fight. You know you will face dragons, so having one on your side will be very useful."

"But that leaves no one to accompany you."

"There's always Qwc."

The Spritha swooped low, then landed on Crow's right shoulder and hugged his head. "Thank you, but no. Qwc cannot."

Alexia frowned. "What do you mean?"

Qwc hopped off Crow's shoulder, then walked across the map to Resolute. "Help. Qwc helps Resolute."

The grave tone of the Spritha's voice surprised Kerrigan, for usually Qwc's voice was light and full of fun. The Spritha were known to have the odd ability to know when and where they were required to be at times of importance. If Spritha precognition was the reason Qwc had to be with Resolute, there would be no dissuading him, so no one tried.

Crow shrugged. "I have the Vilwanese to join me. I met Adept Jarmy on Vilwan, and he was at Svoin. For the Vilwanese to have recalled him from Svarskya and put him in charge of this company of war-mages is a great honor. I'll be fine, though I will miss you all."

Peri smiled. "You'll see us at Fronosa in no time."

"I will indeed."

Alexia looked at the female dragon. "Arimtara, will you join us?"

The dragon glanced at Peri, then Alexia, and nodded. "The three of us, sisters of havoc. This pleases me."

Kerrigan shivered as cold cut at his spine. He looked around the table and knew he'd not see some of them again. He didn't fear for his own survival—and that did not come out of any overconfidence on his part. He assumed no matter what happened, Resolute would survive it all and would drag him clear of disaster. Crow, Alexia, Peri, Erlestoke; as much as he wanted to believe they would all emerge from the war alive, he could not shake the feeling that they would not. *Will, Orla, and Lombo have died. They were as special as any of us.*

He almost laughed as it hit him. Vilwan had created him as a weapon. They'd bred him. They'd taken care with the incidence of his birth. They had trained him, never imagining that he would be more than that weapon. He'd had no friends, no connections with the world, and they thought that would make him just that much easier to control.

What they had not counted upon was that he *was* more than a weapon. What they wanted from him was to selflessly devote himself to Chytrine's destruction. He never would have, or, rather, he never would have succeeded, for he had no stake in her defeat.

Now, however, the deaths of one or more of his friends could be prevented by his actions. The deaths of thousands could be prevented. Out of Vilwan's control he had become bound to the world. Orla had been right: he needed to stay away from Vilwan. He needed to remain with people who liked and respected him for who he was. It was because of them and his connection to them that he would fight harder.

He would stop Chytrine not because those who created him demanded it, but because those people he loved needed him to stop her.

Alexia pressed her palms to the map and looked around at them all. "Tomorrow the crowns will object to this plan.

We will hold firm, then we will go out and preserve their realms for them. I fully expect, if we succeed, that politics will undo the best of what we have done. That won't matter, however. We will have ended Chytrine's campaign to rule the world. May the gods bless us one and all. Or, barring that, take no notice of us and just let us do what we must."

CHAPTER 27

Atable had been added to the central circle of tables in the Council for the expeditionary force. Erlestoke sat there, with an empty chair to his left. Beyond it, at the third place, sat General Pandiculia, looking very military in the uniform of the Salnian Heavy Horse Guards. The crimson surcoat added a bit of color to her tanned face and contrasted well with the black of her hair.

The empty seat had been Alexia's place, but she was on her feet in the middle of the room, a large map tacked to a display board. She carefully explained the composition of her forces, reciting in exact detail the names and histories of officers, as well as the number and nature of the personnel in each unit. She then undertook to discuss all the aspects of the supply needs for the army. An hour into her recital, she had already caused a number of ministers to fall asleep, and not a few of the crowns dipped as their wearers began to slip away.

Her shift to a description of the campaign itself did little to rouse them, for she omitted any hyperbolic or stirring descriptions of what she expected to happen. Even though the crowns had been lulled and even stupefied by her presentation so far, as she closed on his role in the adventure, Erlestoke braced for reactions.

"It is, of course, vital for us to secure our eastern flank. If we cannot do that we stand to lose Narriz and sever our line of supply. If that happens, our force will wither and die." Alexia pointed to the Oriosan border with her right hand. "Under the leadership of Prince Erlestoke, a modest force will enter Oriosa and move northward."

"What?" King Scrainwood leaned forward at his table, squinting at the map. "Troops will enter my nation? Impossible. We all agreed that there would be no troops moving into Oriosa."

Alexia straightened up. "Highness, a reading of that resolution indicates no *foreign* unit will enter Oriosa. The troops we are sending in will be under your son's command. Everyone here knows he has no desire to depose you, merely to render his service to the world at large."

Scrainwood shot Erlestoke a venomous glance. "Everyone here knows he has repudiated Oriosa. He *is* foreign."

Augustus raised an eyebrow. "But you had him at your side in our previous discussions, Scrainwood."

"Did you put him up to this, false friend?" Scrainwood shot to his feet. "This is exactly what we feared. The frostclaw's muzzle is in the tent, and the rest will be there soon enough. The resolution we passed was to guarantee the sovereignty of the weaker nations, and already they have found a way to undo it. That cannot be tolerated!"

Erlestoke rose calmly. "Father, this is not what you think."

"No? Did I hear incorrectly? Is my son going to lead an army of foreign troops onto my soil? Are you going to march them through Oriosa and engage Aurolani troops? Those troops will only come in to oppose you when they fear your flanking maneuver. The idea that you are to prevent the same by Chytrine is a blind."

"You may have the utmost confidence that she will not invade Oriosa, Father, but as the princess has pointed out, we cannot operate under that supposition. If I do not march through my home, we will be inviting Chytrine to do it, to strike here at Narriz. And, lest you forget, Meredo is on the road they will travel to get here."

"Your *home*?" Scrainwood pounded a fist against the table. "You've not been there in five years, and have barely spent half your life there. You do not know the people, the proud people, who have no desire to be invaded. I will not let this happen. *We* will not let this happen. It has already been decided."

The leaders of smaller nations nodded and their newly roused ministers aped the head-bobbing and took on grave expressions. Their fears were obvious, for if a nation's borders were not to be respected, the prelude to the building of empires was sounding. They had to wonder if Alexia could be as greedy as Adrogans. They wondered if their nation would be the place where the burgeoning empires would collide.

Princess Alexia moved to the center of the tables and stared intently at his father. "Highness, with all due respect . . ."

"Faugh, you have no respect for me. You hate me; don't bother to conceal it. Your contempt is palpable."

"I was speaking to you as the King of Oriosa, not the man who lurks beneath that crown." She opened her arms. "I speak now to all of you. You have given troops to a vast army with which we will destroy Chytrine. Once you gave troops, they ceased to be yours because the people you have given to this cause are warriors. They understand and accept dangers few of you have known and *none* of you have volunteered to endure. They are going out to fight not only for the glory of their nation, but to preserve the future of *all* nations. In doing so, they have passed from your control and into mine.

"I am aware of what you voted and what you intended.

I know what you fear. The question you need to ask your-selves—the question you should have asked a generation ago—was this. Which is more of a threat to your nation: the people of the south, or the Aurolani Empress? A quarter century ago you came up with the wrong answer. This time your soldiers and I have come up with the right one. We will deal with it."

Her violet eyes hardened. "You have sent good people to fight, to bleed, to die. They are willing to do so not because you bid them to, but because they know it has to be done. They are not fighting for their own immortality, but for the lives of their children and grandchildren. They are fighting for your subjects, not you. And they will fight *in spite* of you, because they know Chytrine is more of a threat than any petty political squabbles."

Venebulius, the King of Salnia stood. "General Pandiculia, I order you to withdraw our troops from this alliance."

The Salnian officer didn't even bother to stand. She just shook her head. "No, sire."

"You are pledged to me, General."

Pandiculia straightened up in her chair. "I pledge to be loyal to you, sire, but to serve the nation of Salnia."

The king pounded a fist against his barrel chest. "I *am* Salnia."

"No, sire. The nation existed before you, and it will exist after you. Forced to choose between you and the state, I choose the state. My people will stay with me." She shrugged easily. "So it is with all the troops in the army. As the princess said, we're willing to shed our blood for our homes, and we'll do it whether or not you think it is a good thing."

Venebulius' brown eyes flared. "Die on the battlefield, then, for you shall never be welcomed home."

"If that is your order, sire, as long as you are on the throne, I have no home."

King Augustus shook his head. "I shall speak for myself,

though I suspect King Fidelius will agree, that brave people such as you will find a home in many grateful nations."

Scrainwood snarled. "This is *mutiny* and you abet it, Augustus. I thought you a friend, but you encourage my son to depose me. You will welcome the vipers who are his confederates."

"It is not mutiny, Father, it is realism." Erlestoke pressed his hands flat to the top of the table and leaned forward. "Muroso does not exist. Sebcia does not exist. Fortress Draconis is gone. Vorquellyn, Okrannel, the Ghost March, all these places were once independent and free. Bit by bit Chytrine has nibbled away at everything. Yes, we have gotten Okrannel back, but at great cost. Now Saporicia is threatened.

"You are all political. If Nefrai-kesh came riding right into this hall and said that Chytrine wishes peace, you would listen. If she said that she wishes Muroso to become a buffer state to keep our realms distinct, and promised you generations of peace, would you accept it? Any of you shaking your heads are lying. You *would* take it, and why? Because you could tell yourself you did the best for your nation in ending the scourge of war."

He straightened up. "You are sheep listening to wolves who say that the last of your brothers they took would be the final one. And, as sheep, you can't fight the wolves. You listen to their lies because you have no choice. But we, the warriors, are your wolfhounds. We can and will destroy the wolves. You may choose to deny us leave, but we will do it anyway. We have seen the flock dwindle and we will not stand by to watch it anymore."

Erlestoke looked directly at his father. "I am bringing troops through Oriosa, Father. Do not oppose me."

"You will find the borders closed and hearts hardened against you, Erlestoke. You propose a civil war."

"No, Father, I propose an end to fear. I don't want your throne. Do not force me to take it from you."

Scrainwood again slammed a fist onto his table, then

looked around at the other crowns. "Take a good look at me, brothers and sisters, for soon you will be in the same state as I. You will be dispossessed, not by Chytrine, but by those who would use her as an excuse to do as they will. If you do not stop him, you are complicit in the crime he commits, and my retribution will be to your detriment."

The King of Oriosa stalked from the room, with Cabot Marsham scurrying in his wake.

Once they had departed the chamber, Alexia began speaking again in low tones. "The decision as to how, when, and where Chytrine will be engaged has passed from your hands. The question before you all now is this: will you support your countrymen with more troops, more supplies, and more money, or will you put victory against Chytrine in jeopardy out of your own vanity and fear? King Scrainwood has made his choice. Will you be as foolish as he is, or will you find the spine necessary to save the world at risk of your own life—just as your warriors are willing to do?"

Queen Carus cleared her throat as low murmurs rose. "How certain are you of achieving victory?"

Alexia shook her head. "We have planned as best we can, using all the knowledge we possess of the enemy. Chytrine may have new things to show us, and we will change our plans accordingly. I cannot guarantee victory, but if all I could do was prophesy doom, I'd still be back planning a course that would succeed."

The Jeranese Queen smiled. "I am not a military strategist, but I see no flaws in your plan. You have my *full* support."

Erlestoke was uncertain why she emphasized the word "full," but the leaders of nations close to Jerana read a particular significance into it. Gurol and Valicia pledged support for the plan. Slowly, and with much posturing, most of the nations present fell in line. The Salnian leader refused but since the best thing he could have supplied them with was General Pandiculia, his support was moot.

With the plan agreed to, King Fidelius adjourned the Council and invited everyone present to spend the two days of the New Year's festival celebrating there in his court. He promised feasting and entertainment unmatched. Since few were the leaders who could return home even with a good tide and favorable wind, his invitation was greeted with applause.

Erlestoke smiled down at Pandiculia. "They're more excited about the festival than our plan."

"At this point, so am I." She shrugged. "I don't envy you your part in this."

"You'll have the worst of it, I think." Before he could continue, a masked mage appeared at his side. "Highness, if I could have a word?"

"Certainly." From the mask and accent he knew the man was from Muroso, and given the markings on the mask he suspected he knew what the man wanted. "I have to warn you, however, that there is no way I can convince the princess to let you and your Addermages range to Aurolan to free Princess Sayce."

The man, in his mid-thirties, with thinning brown hair and dark eyes, smiled. "Glad to know you've heard of us, Highness, but that's not what I am here for. I'm Rumbellow, by the way."

"Pleased to meet you, Rumbellow." The Murosan mage, if stories could be believed, had single-handedly slain an Aurolani slaving party, then led the former captives south. He'd gathered around himself thirty Murosan mages of various skill levels. They'd pledged themselves to Sayce's service, and after she had been taken, they'd agitated to go after her. "What is it I can do for you and the Adders?"

"We want to come with you to Oriosa."

"What?"

"We want to be part of your force, sire."

Erlestoke winced beneath his mask. "You're not going to find Sayce in Oriosa."

"We know that." Rumbellow lowered his voice. "We had

gathered last night to strike out on our own for Aurolan, when a Vorquelf came to us. Copper eyes, but she's blind. She said she saw two paths for us. One was the one upon which our toes had already trodden. She said it would lead to Sayce's death, our transformation into *sullanciri*, and the destruction of everything. The other, she said, was to join you. If we did, there was a *chance* Sayce would be saved."

"Oracle. You talked to Oracle."

"Yes, sire." The mage nodded. "The Adders are not quite as fearsome as our name, but we are the ones who have survived our nation's being overrun. That's got to count for something."

Erlestoke smiled. "I've spent much too much time running from the Aurolani. I know precisely what it takes to elude them. That you have done so counts more than you can imagine. I will be pleased to have you and your Adders in my command."

"You won't regret it, Prince Erlestoke."

"I believe you."

The mage started to turn away, but Erlestoke laid a hand on his shoulder. "Rumbellow, tell your Adders that if Sayce can be saved, she will be. She's smart and resourceful, and so are the rest of us."

The man smiled. "Yes, sire, thank you. Happy New Year to you."

"And to you, Rumbellow."

Alexia came over as the Murosan departed. "The answer is no."

"It's a different question. The Adders have joined my command."

The princess smiled. "I don't envy you the headache, but it's one less for me. I also don't envy you . . ."

"Don't say it, Alexia. We knew how he would react."

"Yes, but I hoped . . ."

Erlestoke shook his head. "I learned a long time ago not to pin my hopes on my father. He's hoping I will balk at killing Oriosans. That's the only way he wins, because he can't fight a civil war."

"Will you?"

"It is my preference not to." He shrugged wearily. "If they stand between me and Chytrine, I'll have no choice. If they are not helping me, they are helping her, and there's a heavy price they'll pay for that mistake."

CHAPTER 28

A lexia stood on the stone balcony outside what had once served King Scrainwood as a receiving room. With the king's hasty departure, Rounce Playfair had once again taken possession of the estate and invited all of Crow's friends to spend the two-day New Year's festival there. As was the custom, the previous night they had all gone to the gala hosted by King Fidelius at the palace. The second night was meant for more intimate gatherings of true friends.

Alexia wore a gown that was not as fashionable as the one she'd had on the previous night, nor was her long hair bound up to expose her neck. She felt comfortable—perhaps not as at ease as she might in leathers or mail—but such clothes were not meant for greeting the new year. Besides, she would be wearing them soon enough and for quite a long time.

She looked out over the city of Narriz and saw lights blazing, both in buildings and in small processions as people wandered the streets, singing gay songs of good fortune. Not only were the songs their gifts to others, but they were meant to be omens of the new year. Alexia certainly hoped they would be and that people would sing for joy throughout, but she was too realistic to imagine that would be true. Even if her forces were victorious, there would be families who would lose loved ones, and their songs would be anything but joyous.

Also out there, distantly, she caught the huskier songs sung by warriors. Valiant tales voiced lustily, unit histories and ballads of great heroes also filled the night. The warriors had a much better idea of what their year would be like, and their omen-songs invited courage and gallantry to visit them. Some were wishing they would not falter, others were laughing in the face of doom; but whichever, the singing bound them closer—and in that closeness they would come nearer victory than without it.

She wondered for a moment if someone out there was singing a song of Crow or Will. She hoped so. Word had fast circulated that Will was dead, but just as quickly Oracle's statement that he was waiting on Vorquellyn raced through the city. The warriors all knew Will was waiting, and each seemed to think the Norrington was waiting for him. "You just get us started, General," she heard often enough, "and we'll be helping the Norrington finish the Nor'witch."

Alexia sipped her wine. The red was dry, with just a hint of bitterness. It tasted like the winter, but had enough body to promise a full spring. Preyknosery had predicted the weather would turn quickly enough, meaning the roads would likewise turn to mud and slow everyone down. And as hard as that would be, she still preferred it to having soldiers with frostbite.

She shivered and imagined what it would have been like had Kerrigan not exposed Tatyana. Chytrine herself would have helped shape the south's strategy. She'd have moved troops into Oriosa prematurely and ambushed Erlestoke's command. With that wing of her army crushed, Alexia would have been forced to withdraw and wait for Chytrine to press the war into Saporicia. And at that point, had

Chytrine offered a political settlement, the crowns would have taken it and the Aurolani problem would have passed to another generation.

She heard the scrape of a boot on stone behind her and smiled, knowing that step anywhere. "I wondered if you'd notice me gone."

"Instantly, beloved." Crow leaned on the balustrade beside her. "Rounce asked me to recount the story of his wounding, which, given his embellishments, he remembers a bit differently than I do. He's made it into a comedy."

"I noticed you were laughing."

A smile bared Crow's teeth. "I was indeed. You know that I've not seen him since the first campaign. Resolute always spoke with him. I would have thought him bitter, but he's not. He dealt with his wounding much as my brother did. Neither let what happened keep him from being a whole person. They scored a victory over their tragedies."

She turned and lifted a hand to caress his scarred cheek. "Not unlike *you*."

He kissed her fingers, then glanced down at his hands. "I wasn't whole until I met you. The second time I met you. I had run from being Hawkins. I'd utterly abandoned who I had been and become Kedyn's Crow. Until I saw you, I never felt I wanted anyone to know that Hawkins had done more than kill himself."

Alexia smiled. "The night you saw me was in the town of Stellin. You saved my life with a long bowshot."

"That shot was inspired. I was outraged that a vylaen would think of ambushing you. Then you saved my life at Svoin and again at Tolsin."

"I, too, was inspired." Alexia untied a small leather pouch from her gown's belt and extended it to him. "This is for you, beloved. For the new year."

Crow set his wine goblet on the balustrade and opened the pouch. He poured the contents into his left palm. "This is your anklet."

She nodded. Like many noblewomen, she had an elven

charm that prevented her from conceiving while she wore it. "That is how much I want you and our future together, Crow."

"I have nothing to give you, Alexia."

She raised an eyebrow at him. "Given what you have in your hand, how can you say that?"

"Ah, well, yes." Color flushed his cheeks. "I meant that the gift I have for you is back in our room. I meant to give it to you privately."

"You realize you're just digging yourself in deeper here, don't you?"

Crow laughed. "I guess I am." He straightened up, turned, and gathered her into his arms. "I will give you all you desire, Alexia. I will give you all that I am, my future—everything. I will love you always and in all ways."

She leaned forward and kissed him, much preferring the taste of his lips to her wine. "I know, Crow. It is the same for me."

He hugged her tightly. "Cold, lover? Shall we go back in?"

"On your arm, it would be a pleasure." She linked her hand through his elbow and let him guide her into the main room. Off to the left were tables laden with food. Kerrigan hovered near them, with Oracle, Rym, and Bok. Nay and his son were speaking with Dranae, Arimtara, and Prince Erlestoke. Rounce and several other Oriosans of his acquaintance were gathered around Perrine in the center of the room, while Resolute brooded in a distant corner. A group of four musicians played in the corner opposite the Vorquelf, filling the room with gentle songs and cheer. Qwc darted through the air as if a hummingbird moving between flowers, listening in to each conversation, then moving on before making a diving raid on the food table.

The two of them crossed to where Resolute stood. "The happiest of new years to you, Resolute."

"And you, Princess."

The gravity in his voice concerned her. "Are you incapable of enjoying yourself, Resolute, or does some immediate problem keep you from celebrating?"

"Forgive me if my behavior dampens the atmosphere, Highness."

"That's not what I meant, Resolute. I do want to know what you are thinking. Of all the undertakings this year, yours is the most arduous."

The Vorquelf remained silent for a moment, then nodded slowly. "I have many unknowns to deal with, and Oracle's visions keep changing. Today she informed Banausic that he would be joining me. He's a logical choice since he has been on Vorquellyn, but he did not want to go. The company I will be leading is blind, sick, weak, reluctant, or made of wood. At least Rymramoch is useful because his limbs can be made into kindling."

Crow shook his head. "With Kerrigan along, you'll have no trouble starting fires."

"I wish that were true, Crow, but it isn't." The Vorquelf looked across the room. "He's very powerful, yes, but he is not a war-mage. Princess, you saw him kill Neskartu. He didn't use a combat spell. The way he did it was quite novel, I admit, but given what we will be facing, I could use someone who put his sort of power into more offensive spells."

Resolute shrugged. "Then again, I'm not sure I want to see Kerrigan have to make that change. He's not a killer. And for him to have to kill might change him, and I don't know what he would do if he did."

Crow rested a hand on Resolute's shoulder. "It's not that you are anxious about what you have to do, it's that you're anxious about having to lead that party. You'd do it by yourself gladly, but having the responsibility for the others . . ."

"Yes, my friend, that is most of it." Resolute managed a small smile. "Will gave me the sword that demands I accept such responsibility. On Vorquellyn, I can thank him yet again."

Alexia smiled, but it quickly faded. "You'll need to tell him about Sayce and his child."

"I know." Resolute's eyes glittered. "They will be saved, both of them, mother and child. This I vow."

"Be careful of such vows, Resolute." Crow laughed lightly. "I vowed to see Vorquellyn free in my lifetime. See where it's gotten me."

"I say it with that in mind, my friend."

Laughter from near the food table brought Alexia around. A blue winterberry skittered across the floor as Qwc, wielding a fork half as tall as he was, repeatedly dove and stabbed at it. The Spritha came up and around in a loop, then twisted around and made a low run at the elusive morsel. The fork scraped the floor, but only batted the berry away. It rolled toward Kerrigan instead.

The mage stopped it with his foot, then plucked another fork from the table. He held it suspended between his fingertips, then magick shimmered around his hands. He drew them apart, and as he did so the metal lengthened and thinned. Almost effortlessly, he transformed the fork and lofted it to the Spritha. "Here, Qwc, catch."

Qwc dropped his fork with a clatter and plucked the foot-and-a-half-long silver spear from the air. With a high-pitched giggle, the Spritha flew upward, then threw his head back and flipped over, allowing himself to fall into a dive. As he neared his target, his wings flashed out. He leaned left, then right, and stabbed the barbed tip straight through the winterberry with a pop of purple juice.

Qwc laughed triumphantly, then licked at the juice running down the shaft of the spear.

Everyone in the room applauded, though whether for Kerrigan or Qwc, Alexia could not be certain. The mage looked at Rounce. "Please forgive me ruining that fork, Master Playfair."

Rounce waved the apology away easily. "Do not be worried, Adept Reese. I'll have the rest melted down and shaped into winterberry skewers. And you, Qwc, will keep that one as my gift to you. May you find it useful in the coming year."

Qwc nodded emphatically.

Resolute frowned. "If Qwc uses that on aught but winterberries, we'll be in serious trouble indeed."

"Leave the voicing of omens to me, Resolute." As everyone watched Qwc's antics, Oracle had found her way to his side. "Things are not as dire as you fear."

"Right now, you mean. You are the one who has told me that the future constantly shifts. Just the creation of that spear could change things."

"So it could. So it has." Oracle turned her sightless eyes on Alexia. "Fear not, Princess, I shall make no cryptic remark as concerns your expedition. When it comes to battles, things shift so quickly that there is no predicting outcomes."

"It's my task to make sure the possible outcomes are limited."

"It is a formidable task you set yourself." Oracle's lids closed for a moment. "When a life is ended, all its potential is released. All its possibilities are released. That is why war is so chaotic."

The princess nodded, then realized Oracle couldn't see her. "I know."

The Vorquelf's copper eyes snapped open. "Chytrine revels in chaos. Even in losing she can be victorious."

Alexia smiled. "I thought you said you weren't going to be cryptic."

"I didn't think I was. Conduct your war carefully, Princess, but do not shy from using the chaos. Chytrine might enjoy it, but she cannot control it. Do what you know best and you will emerge the victor."

Oracle then turned to Crow and moved close to him, kissing him on his scarred cheek. "And you, brother Crow, you are close to fulfilling your vow. Sleep lightly, ride hard, and trust those who earn it."

Crow kissed her back. "Be safe on your journey, Oracle. All luck to you in the new year, and peace."

"If I have the one, I shall have the other." She turned to Resolute and took his right hand in her left. "And now, cousin, I have a vision of you dancing with me."

Resolute's face tightened. "I have not danced since we were children."

"Unless your eyes have changed, Resolute, we yet are."

"You know what I mean."

"And you know my vision is never wrong." Oracle tugged at his hand. "Come, dance with me. The others will join in. As we all dance together now, we shall dance a year hence."

Resolute looked at her. "Is that, too, a vision?"

"A hope, Resolute, a hope." Oracle smiled warmly. "And a hope is best to start the new year."

CHAPTER 29

The first day of the new year dawned bright and cold, but Resolute had seen enough years to know this was winter's last gasp. Soon, the sun would blaze high and hot, coaxing the plants to grow. Hard winters always brought flooding, but flooding always brought warm springs and early harvests.

But this year, the first harvest would be of blood—though he had seen plenty of fields flourish when fertilized with blood. *Blood, manure, and carrion.* The plants would grow, but he wondered if there would be people enough around to benefit.

The line of General Pandiculia's troops stretched out from the gates of Narriz along the coast road, heading north and eventually west. They would travel on the west side of the Delasena, while Alexia's troops would use the river road to the east. To avoid confusion, Pandiculia's troops were sent out first, and those who would travel later cheered them on their way.

Resolute and his companions traveled with them as a convenience. He would have much preferred just to head off on his own at a fast clip, but Bok was not yet suited to it, and he had reservations about Oracle's ability to deal with a hard ride. Banausic had dutifully assigned himself to her care, and that annoyed Resolute. Still, it gave the raven-haired Vorquelf something to do, which meant he wouldn't be too much of a nuisance. Rymramoch traveled in a big box strapped to a pack animal, so he was likewise no trouble.

The Vorquelf cast a glance back at Kerrigan and noticed him shifting awkwardly in the saddle after only an hour on the road. Since his bones were no longer thoroughly insulated with fat, the saddle rubbed more roughly. Curiously enough, Kerrigan bore his discomfort silently, nor did he cast a spell to ease his suffering.

Resolute would have expected either complaints or magick. Back when they first met, the portly mage had made a very bad first impression on Resolute. But now the transformation in Kerrigan had surprised the Vorquelf, surpassing even that of Will Norrington. Will had been a feral thief in Yslin. And while he knew little of the world, he was a born risk-taker who did not shy from adventure. He might have fled from responsibility, but when he eventually grew into it, his penchant for action made accepting responsibility and succeeding possible.

Kerrigan had been very much the opposite. He had been responsible and deliberate to the point of fussiness. He made mistakes that had cost them dearly, and he had succumbed to melancholy on countless occasions. Unlike others, however, he did not let his failures consume him. As Will had grown into accepting responsibility, so Kerrigan had grown in an understanding of his own power and potential. He acknowledged his mistakes so he could avoid repeating them. In one so young, who had been coddled and insulated from reality, that desire was both rare and vital.

Kerrigan looked up and caught Resolute's eye for a moment. The youth's face opened questioningly and Resolute frowned by reflex. Kerrigan looked down again immediately and slouched so abruptly that Qwc almost lost his seat on the mage's shoulder.

Resolute cleared his throat. "Kerrigan, come here."

The youth's head came up again, then he urged his horse forward and drew abreast with Resolute. "Yes?"

"Something concerns you."

"It's just . . . I don't want to bother you with it."

Resolute controlled his frown. "What have you been thinking about?"

"Well, since no one is going to let me cast any of my searching spells for now, I was trying to think about how we will find Will and get him out of the *coriiesci*. You have a plan, don't you?"

"No."

"No?" Kerrigan's face knotted. "You have to have a plan."

"Please, Kerrigan, we seek Will. I don't need to hear you admonishing me the way he would."

"Sorry."

The Vorquelf turned to look at Kerrigan and while he wouldn't let himself smile, he did his best to erase a grimace. "Oracle has said Will is waiting for us. She has no specific vision that tells us how we will find him, but the Norrington Prophecy itself suggests there must be a way, else it would not exist. It may be something as simple as Will being hidden and waiting to escape until we arrive. It may be that we have to do something more drastic. We have a lot of time to get there."

"Okay, right. I have been thinking, though . . ."

"Would you like to share your thoughts?"

Kerrigan nodded, then looked down as he spoke. "Banausic has described much of what he saw there. The rituals that bind someone to Vorquellyn sound very powerful."

"They can destroy people if they go wrong."

"I remember. Two key things, though: elves didn't have to officiate at the ceremonies that worked."

Resolute nodded. "It is Vorquellyn which accepts or rejects. That's one thing. What's the other?"

"I think that to go through the ritual, one only has to have been born there. I mean, I think Vorquellyn might accept me."

A prickling feeling ran up Resolute's spine. "Are you suggesting we perform the ritual on you so you can enter the *coriiesci*?"

"Well, yes. I was born there after Chytrine took the island, so I have a more recent connection than you do."

"That was also true of the *kryalniri* Banausic said was rejected."

"I know." Kerrigan looked up at him, his green eyes wet. "But if . . . no, *because* Will is waiting there, I'm willing to take the risk to free him."

"To atone for his death?"

"You say that like you think it's stupid."

Resolute shook his head and glanced up along the line of soldiers. "On one level it is stupid, Kerrigan. There is nothing to atone for."

"How can you say that?" Kerrigan's voice rose and tightened. "I could have prevented his death."

"No, you could not have. Isn't that true, Qwc?"

The Spritha huddled close against the sheepskin collar of the mage's coat. "True, true."

"What?"

"Kerrigan, the Spritha know where they are supposed to be at times of importance. You came late to the Council Chamber. Qwc flew immediately to the place where he caught Rymramoch's Truestone. He knew where he had to be, and when the time was right, he was there again. Your job was to make certain that he would not fail to hold on to that Truestone."

"But I should have caught the stone first."

"No, and that is why there is nothing to atone for. Will knew what he was doing when he went for the stone. He was showing the dragons that we are willing to sacrifice ourselves for others. He saved a life where Nefrai-laysh only wanted to take one. That lesson was a vital one. Given that the dragons want to reassemble the Crown and that we had pledged to leave our piece of it there, they should have immediately joined with Chytrine. She has the most pieces. It only makes sense for them to do that, but they did not because of Will's sacrifice."

"How can they trust Chytrine?"

"They may feel forced to. She was Kirûn's apprentice. They might think she is the only one who can destroy it. Their reasons, however, are as immaterial as they are misplaced. The prophecy is the key to all events and must be our guide."

The Vorquelf glanced at him again. "There's another thing to consider, and Oracle's news confirms it. When the prophecy was uttered, we thought it applied to Lord Norrington, or to Leigh. Perhaps it did. Each of them underwent a transformation. We know Will is waiting for us, and death will have been quite a transformation. Perhaps he had to grow into being the Norrington of the prophecy, and his willingness to make that sacrifice was the last threshold he had to pass."

Kerrigan looked over, searching his face. "Do you really think that is true?"

"I've spent a long time, Kerrigan, believing in only a few truths. One is that the more Aurolani I kill, the fewer will stand between me and getting my homeland back. Another is that I'll succeed within Crow's lifetime. Lastly, I accept that Will Norrington is going to be a part of getting my homeland back. The details around all that don't matter."

The mage shrugged his shoulders. "I guess not. You were really tough on him, you know."

"I'm tough on everyone, Kerrigan."

"Why?"

Resolute slowly felt a smile spread over his face. "Probably out of habit."

"Not that I'm trying to pry, but it just seems . . . you're being talkative today."

The Vorquelf nodded slowly, even as a little laugh from Oracle reached his ears. The previous night, dancing with her, he'd felt things he'd not allowed himself to feel for over a century. For an evening he swam up through the lake of blood and flesh and vengeance that had been his life and drew in a clean breath. It had been intoxicating and dangerous—for his guard slipped. And while he didn't actually abandon the burdens he'd shouldered, he had leaned them against a wall for a moment. And he had enjoyed it.

"I have lived a long time, Kerrigan. I saw the pain of the adults who survived the rape of Vorquellyn. I watched them leave. I have also seen many well-meaning people head out to deal with Chytrine or her creatures, and I have watched them die. When I am tough on people, either they get good, or they get hurt."

Kerrigan nodded. "And they don't get close to you until they are good, so they're less likely to die."

"Not always. I'm used to them dying. I just wish, for once, it would be of old age."

The youth shook his head. "You choose not to have friends, and I was never allowed to have them. Will was really my first friend. I didn't think he would be. I didn't like him at first."

"Will was like that."

"But he grew on me, probably as he matured." Kerrigan's eyes flashed. "Do you think he'll be angry?"

"Angry?"

"You know, for his dying?"

Resolute closed his eyes for a moment, then shook his head. "No. He made his choice and was content with it. I think he'll be happy to be back. And, knowing him, he'll come back with a fistful of treasure from Turic's realm and stories to tell about his time there."

Kerrigan laughed. "That's true."

"And I would not worry about his being angry with you. He likely won't even recognize you."

"I don't care about his recognizing me. I just hope Chytrine won't."

Resolute's lips peeled back in a predatory grin. "Oh, by the time we get to her, she'll know us all."

Kerrigan glanced back. "Seven against an empire."

"Eight, counting Will."

"Right." Kerrigan's voice shrank. "It will be eight, won't it?"

The Vorquelf reached out and slapped a hand against Kerrigan's shoulder. "That's the only command I'll give my little company: no dying."

"Disobey that order and you'll kill us?"

"Worse, I'll bring you back."

Kerrigan frowned. "If you go back to being quiet, will your sense of humor go away, too?"

"I wasn't joking."

"Okay, well, I think I'm all talked out now."

Resolute laughed, and discovered he didn't mind the sound, as alien as it felt rolling from his throat. "We will do what we must, Kerrigan. We may be the smallest force in this war, but our mission is the most vital. We can't fail, so we won't. Anyone who gets between us and our goal will discover I can be distinctly unfunny, and I won't mind making that quite obvious to them."

CHAPTER 30

General Markus Adrogans found Pain's quiescence mildly disturbing. It had been nearly a week since his troops had quitted Svarskya and begun the arduous trek into the mountains that separated Okrannel from the Ghost March. The Okrans in his command were able to spin out nightly stories of the battles fought in those fastnesses, both against the Aurolani and, before them, the Norivese. They made no attempt to disguise their contempt for those who had lost their nation at the same time Vorquellyn had fallen—though the stories of their battles left no question that the Norivese had once been formidable foes.

Being from Jerana, Adrogans knew little of the Norivese. In times past they used to sail down the coast and do some raiding, but they seldom hit anything beyond rich Okrans ports. Their galleys had sported black sails with a big red ball in the middle and they had been savage enough raiders that the Jeranese had not mourned their conquest. Feelings toward them had been much hotter in Okrannel, since it was much more frequently a target of their raids.

Though it did boggle his mind that the Aurolani could have been seen as an improvement by the Okrans, there was logic to it.

After all, the Aurolani had been content to let the Okrans occupy these mountains. Prior to that, the mountains had been something of a no-man's-land. Both nations claimed it, and regularly fought over it, but seldom in anything more than a bloody skirmish or raid. The Norivese preferred to attack by the sea and the Okrans could call up enough troops quickly to fend off landward raids. When Noriva fell to the Aurolani, the Okrans occupied the mountains. Unfortunately for them, they arrayed themselves to defend against raids and when Chytrine came for Okrannel, she brought armies.

Standing in his stirrups, he studied the long line of men, horses, and equipment working its way through the mountain valley. He had scouts and outriders throughout the mountains, and Gyrkyme overhead to guard against surprises, but even knowing the path was clear did not allow him speed. Though winter would be retreating soon enough, in the mountains that far north it would be a slow process. So his troops still struggled through deep drifts and consumed a lot of food to keep up their strength.

And, ultimately, they could travel no faster than their supplies and equipment, and those moved along at the torpid pace of eight miles a day. The travel day was long as well, starting before dawn and ending after sunset, with the bonfires created by the forward scouts luring the men into camp.

The twenty dragonels were difficult to move because both they and their supplies were heavy. Soldiers grumbled because none of that stuff could be eaten, and they'd not seen the dragonels in use enough to realize their power. In fact, his troops tended to discount that power since they'd already defeated an enemy who had dragonels, conveniently forgetting that the weapons actually had not been used against them.

Despite the grumbling—*and when was there ever an army that did not grumble about something*—morale was high among the troops. But there was no reason it shouldn't be, since these were the men and women who had fought a winter war and won against an enemy better used to winter than they were. One and all were ready to shed their heavy clothes and fight "in proper weather." They very much liked the fact that they were violating nebulous orders from far Narriz. None of them were fighting for their countries; they were fighting for him and their comrades.

Phfas rode up beside him, letting a yellow-toothed grin split his leathery face. "The progress is good."

"You are not worried about how quiet the *yrûn* are?"

The Zhusk shaman shook his head. "This far from home they grow sleepy."

Adrogans frowned. "I did not think they were tied to place as *weirun* are."

"They are tied, as are you, to the place you were bound to them." The skinny little man shrugged. "If you listen carefully, you will hear them."

The Jeranese general passed a hand over his eyes. "They will not be as useful to me as they have been, then?"

Phfas shook his head curtly. "The Zhusk may venture far from home, but the *yrûn* do not."

A bubble of annoyance rose from the pit of his stomach. Pain had been terribly useful in pinpointing enemy formations based on the misery of the troops waiting for him. While he had not enjoyed her riding him as she glutted herself on the pain of a battlefield, the times she had let him project agony into creatures had been very useful and had saved countless lives.

He thought for a moment, rather surprised at his reaction. The loss of battlefield information was the most critical to his situation, for with that information he became a better general. Knowledgeable about his enemy, the condition of the troops, the possibility of hidden reserves, all of those things let him issue orders that made his force more effective.

The ability to project pain, on the other hand, made him a better warrior—a superior warrior. On the surface that might seem a very good thing. It certainly had boded well for his people when faced with boombags at the Svar Bridge. Without that ability, serious damage would have been done to his troops and might have even prevented him from taking Svarskya.

What made him a superior warrior, however, would make him less of a good general. He had no fear of combat, and had seen more than his share of it in his long career. Even on the winter campaign, he had fought and been in personal jeopardy. Despite that, his true role was to rise above the skirling chaos of battle and issue orders that would win victories. Empowered by Pain or any other *yrûn,* he would forget what he was best at and forget what his people could do.

He glanced down at Phfas. "Why didn't you tell me about this?"

Another shrug, then a little grin. "I have never been so far from Zhusk."

Adrogans laughed. "How does it feel to be mortal again?"

"I have been linked with *yrûn* for longer than I have not. I feel naked and old."

"If that's going to be a problem for you and your other people, I can arrange for you to head back to Okrannel."

The little man rubbed a bony hand over his nose. "No. Some stories tell that the Zhusk came from the north. We hunted these lands before the Okrans. I want to see where we came from."

"Do you think you will find another place to reconnect with the *yrûn?*"

Phfas shrugged. "It matters not. This is no longer the *yrûn's* war. It is no longer a Zhusk war."

"Then why do you come?"

The shaman threw his head back and brayed out a sharp laugh. "Are you like the others, nephew?"

Adrogans growled. "Don't speak in riddles."

"Think clearly. It is no puzzle."

Adrogans scraped a hand over the stubble on his jaw. The Zhusk were an aboriginal people who existed on the Zhusk Plateau, near the Okrans border with Jerana. They acknowledged no masters, paid no tribute, and in their homeland could be very nasty fighters. Adrogans had assumed that because he was half-Zhusk and had fought so long against the Aurolani that Phfas and the others had joined the fight out of a sense of personal loyalty. With their homeland no longer threatened, he wondered if they would return home.

"It is still a puzzle."

Phfas shook his head, then laid a hand on Adrogans' knee. "Even you stop thinking of the Zhusk as *men*. This war is a man war. The Zhusk do not *like* any other men. We see them as foes, but they are still *men*. If we abandon our kindred to the Aurolani, we are not men."

Adrogans dropped his right hand to Phfas' left. "I beg your pardon, Uncle. You are right. I had stopped thinking of you as men."

"It is a common affliction . . . among men." The shaman traced a finger along the long line of people struggling through the valley. "All of them are far from home. None of them have *yrûn*. If they go on, so do we."

The scouts located a good place to camp before the eight-mile mark, and Adrogans called for an early halt to let men and beasts rest. He wondered if his association with Pain had blinded him to the hardships his people were feeling, so the early rest and some extra rations buoyed spirits.

Duranlaun, a Gyrkyme warhawk, reported to Adrogans just after the sun had gone down. "My scouts have ranged far ahead of the column. By footfall you have four more days before you leave the mountains."

Adrogans nodded and rolled out a map on which he had been tracking the army's advance. "We'll be coming out into foothills that have some drainage heading east, but nothing navigable. What have you seen beyond the mountains?"

The Gyrkyme tapped a talon about an inch from the mountains at a point near a delta that indicated a river that originated in the Boreal mountains of Aurolan. "There is a large settlement here. It is built over the ruins of a city. It does not seem that old, but has some fortifications built up. Log palisades, some earthworks; nothing substantial."

"Do you think we can take it without dragonels?"

"Possible. I will send more people out there and we will bring back plans as best as we can draw them."

"How far away are the Nalisk Mountain Rangers?"

"A day."

"Good. I'll have orders ready for you in the morning to take to them. I will want them to reconnoiter." Adrogans scratched at his beard stubble. "Anything remarkable?"

The Gyrkyme blinked large amber eyes. "A road to the east. It is a muddy track, but sufficiently well traveled to be free of snow. There are barges at the encampment, but they are iced in the river."

"So, whatever is being shipped is desired so much to the east that they're hauling in the winter, not willing to wait for the barges to get free. Have your people search the delta for a place where the barge cargo can be loaded on ships." The general thought for a moment. "It has to be lumber. If they were mining ore, they would refine it there and ship it out. We'd see the smoke from the foundry and forges."

Duranlaun nodded. "The forests are being harvested. For the palisades, certainly, and fuel, but more."

Adrogans nodded. If they were harvesting lumber, it was probably going for shipbuilding. That idea sent a thrill through him. "Also track what they're bringing back in. They have to be doing something to feed the people."

"As you wish, General."

The Gyrkyme saluted. Adrogans returned it, then the winged warrior departed the tent.

Adrogans stared at the map. Seven hundred and twenty miles separated him from Sebcia, if he marched all the way through the Ghost March, past Fortress Draconis and down along the route Princess Alexia had taken to Oriosa. At his present rate of travel it would take him three months to complete the journey—and that only if there was no fighting to slow him down. Realistically, he'd be contested every inch of the way, and Chytrine might hit him with a force so powerful that his entire army would be wiped out.

That had always been part of the calculation. While locating and destroying an invasion fleet was his immediate mission, doing all he could to force Chytrine to devote troops to deal with him came in a very strong second. It would be all but impossible for his troops to reach Sebcia and play any part in the war against Chytrine there unless they used ships, sailing past Vorquellyn to Sebcia.

Unfortunately, that bit of strategy was out of the question, but the sea might have its uses. As it stood, his supply line was hideously stretched through the mountains. Any supplies coming for him in Svarskya could be diverted to the Ghost March. Taking this first town and using it as a supply base would be vital. Once he did that, the push east would be a bit easier. He'd also have a haven to retreat to— and, from there, withdrawing into the mountains was also possible.

Adrogans tapped his own finger to the map where the Gyrkyme had placed the town. "I don't know what your name is, but you will be famous. You will be the first victory in the Ghost March campaign, and your fame will live on long after I am dead."

CHAPTER 31

Though she had not been invited to the meeting, nor was Isaura barred from it. Her mother's *sullanciri* assembled in the fortress' Grand Hall. Morning light slanted in through frosted windows, lengthening and thinning the shadows of the creatures her mother had created to serve her. Isaura knew those of the south feared her mother's generals, and some did make her uneasy, but she never had seen them as the nightmare beasts others did.

Isaura had not come to the meeting to see them, however, but to see her mother. In the week since she had been introduced to the Oromise, Isaura had seen virtually nothing of her mother. The lack of contact concerned her primarily because her mother had not quite been herself. Having a spell cast on her via one of the DragonCrown fragments clearly surprised and angered her, and Isaura had feared that her further reaction would carry her deeper into the paranoia the spell had inspired.

Watching her mother sweep into the room quickly dispelled that notion. Chytrine had chosen to shape herself with the same proportions as an elf, though she did overtop Quiarsca by an inch or two. Moreover, the empress had layered thick muscle on that slender frame, much as some Vorquelves did, and a gentle blue tracery of arcane symbols decorated the pale flesh of her arms.

Her arms and face were the only skin that showed. Chytrine wore a gown of drearbeast leather, tan and supple save where fur trimmed it around the waist, collar, and hem. The garment had to be heavy, but she moved effortlessly in it. Her golden hair remained loose, falling to cover her bare shoulders, for the gown had no sleeves. She wore no weaponry, but there was no hint of vulnerability about her either.

The empress took her place at the curve of a horseshoe-shaped table. "You have all pleased me with your efforts. Anarus, despite some setbacks, the conquest of Muroso has been splendid. I expect your performance will continue to shine under the direction of Nefrai-kesh, for he will now command my army of the east."

The lupine *sullanciri* nodded, then snarled in Nefrai-kesh's direction. Part of the snarl came from his being subordinated to the other *sullanciri*, especially since Nefrai-kesh had lost Okrannel. Still, Nefrai-kesh had been the first of Chytrine's new *sullanciri* and her most faithful, so his being elevated could have surprised no one.

Isaura suspected more of the snarl was for Nekaamii, who hung on Nefrai-kesh like a cat-skin cloak, purring and caressing. The king of the *sullanciri* somehow ignored her, but he couldn't have found her antics unpleasant. With the flick of a hand he could have tossed her off. That her actions were annoying Anarus was apparent, and for some reason Nefrai-kesh wanted him distracted, but Isaura could not imagine why.

Her mother continued. "Our war with the south progresses very well—so well that our resources can be shifted and our drive focused. Nekaamii, you will proceed south to where preparations have been laid on to launch an amphibious assault. The fleet is massing in the Ghost March, larger than you have ever commanded before. Nefrai-kesh will direct your assault to where it shall do the most good, but you must be prepared to move inside two months."

The feline pirate *sullanciri* licked at Nefrai-kesh's right cheek. "I will do anything you bid me, my lord."

Nefrai-kesh raised his hand, scratched behind her ear, then let his hand slip down to take hold of her throat. "Of course you will, and you will succeed, or die trying."

The *sullanciri* tried to mew, but it came out broken before he relaxed his grip.

Chytrine slowly smiled and Isaura felt herself smiling, too. Her mother's serenity had returned, and with it a clarity that made Isaura feel secure. She still recalled that her mother thought someone would betray her, but now she hoped that was just because of the spell. *I don't want to be the one who betrays her.*

The empress nodded toward Ferxigo, the urZrethi *sullanciri* at the end of the table opposite Myrall'mara. "You have dealt with your assignment splendidly, so I am entrusting to you the defense of Aurolan. To aid you will be Hlucri and my daughter, Isaura."

Isaura gasped and Chytrine looked up at her. "What is it, daughter? Did you think I would send you into the field with my troops?"

"No, Mother, I had not thought that far. What surprises me is that you think we are in jeopardy."

Nefrai-kesh nodded solemnly. "Aurolan is not an easy place to threaten, but to assume we are invulnerable is to leave us open. It is doubtful that the south can muster a force sufficient to attack and destroy our homeland while holding off our armies. Still, they are clever, and could well try to repeat the folly of the past. We must guard against that."

Myrall'mara—luminous, tall, and slender—hissed almost silently. "It will be Resolute."

The sulfur-colored *sullanciri* shrugged her shoulders and shifted her shape enough that she sprouted a brush of short white hair on her skull. "He has failed to destroy Aurolan for over a century. He will fail again."

Nefrai-kesh shook his head. "As formidable as Resolute may be, he is not the true threat. Markus Adrogans is."

Anarus growled loudly. "You should have smashed him at Svarskya."

Chytrine slapped a hand flat on the table, with a crack like ice snapping. "The Okrannel campaign was conducted as per my directive. Adrogans will bear watching, but his own people will watch him, too. He will be leashed. But Adrogans is not your concern. You, Anarus, will consolidate Muroso, then you will wait. Tythsai will be responsible for operations in Saporicia, and you will perform as Nefrai-kesh directs."

The wolf-man bared his fangs. "For what shall I wait, Mistress?"

Chytrine smiled easily. "Prince Erlestoke will be leading an army into Oriosa, to come behind our lines to attack us. It is my intention to destroy that army. You will be the instrument of its destruction, then you will press on back through Oriosa and strike at Narriz."

Anarus let a growl rumble from his throat. "Forgive me, Empress, but that strategy is obvious. They will be prepared for us. If Princess Alexia pushes into Muroso, my supply lines will be cut."

"There are many things which are obvious, Anarus, and so we intend them to be." The Aurolani Empress pressed her hands together in an attitude of prayer. "The southerners are given to believe a certain set of dreams will come true, and they will not. Their beliefs will lead them into a trap, which will break the back of their army. Saporicia will be lost; they will panic. And they will lose sight of the obvious.

"At Vael it was pointed out that my armies march forth and take nations even though those nations have nothing to do with the recovery of the DragonCrown. They see me as being bent on domination while the true quest *is* to recover all the pieces of the DragonCrown. They think I wish to do this in order to command dragons to destroy them, and it will be useful for that, yes. But it is useful for so much more."

She looked around the room, stopping briefly to survey Isaura, where she sat back away from the table. "It is not to conquer the world for the sake of its possession that I wage this war, but to restore the world to the peace it once knew. Such peace cannot exist in the face of grave injustice, and re-creating the Crown will allow me to provide justice. Then all will be well with the world.

"As you know, where our troops go, we search for the DragonCrown fragments. Our magick in that regard has been inefficient, but a spell used to locate me has showed me a new way to search for things. As you are out acquitting your duties, so I shall be here, shaping that spell into another that will show us all of the fragments, including the key fragment, wherever or *whenever* it is. As long as the south is fighting for its life, it will be distracted enough not to oppose us in any serious sense, so we shall succeed."

The empress glanced to her left at the elven *sullanciri* seated there. Of all her mother's servants, Quiarsca looked the most unchanged. Golden hair cascaded down to her waist, and the gown she wore tucked tight at her slender waist. Even the bit of color to her skin did not look out of the ordinary, but the same could not be said of her eyes. They looked to be hollow holes in her skull, not as if they had been torn out, but as if they were invisible orbs.

"Your work, Quiarsca, has progressed very well. The *kryalniri* have been a valued addition to our forces. Your new project has proven even more successful. You found it satisfactory, Ferxigo?"

"Yes, Mistress, as I have reported, most satisfactory."

"Excellent. Please continue."

The elf nodded, then raised her face in Chytrine's direction. "In light of the news from the south, do you wish more work to be done on opening the *coriiesci* at Saslynnae?"

"No. You will guard it, of course, but waste no more energy there. It has defied us for a long time, and will continue to do so."

Isaura raised a hand. "Mother, I am certain I could open it."

"Are you, child?"

She nodded. Though several years had passed since the ritual that bound her to Vorquellyn, Isaura could still feel the connection to the island. When the binding had been successful, she had immediately been drawn toward the *coriiesci*. She'd had a sense of sanctuary, and that surprised her, since the place had long been described as a place of enemy power.

"It would yield to me, Mother."

"I am pleased to hear that, Isaura, and I do believe you, but I shall not risk you there. You are now truly the heir to my realm and my secrets, so to you falls the unenviable task of waiting here to fulfill my destiny, should the worst happen." Chytrine smiled. "Besides, child, our enemies are coming to open it for us. I should not deprive them of that honor."

Nefrai-kesh's frown registered on the Panqui-flesh mask. "Do you not treat the information too lightly, Mistress?"

"I think not. Oracle has said the Norrington waits in the *coriiesci*. They will have to get into the *coriiesci* to liberate him. That is the point at which they will be most vulnerable." As she spoke, Chytrine held her right hand out, palm up. As her fingers curled inward, they shifted into the scaled talons of a dragon. "They will be dealt with brilliantly, I have no doubt, won't they, Quiarsca?"

The *sullanciri* nodded. "You need fear nothing, Empress."

"I fear nothing at all." The empress turned her head and looked finally past the undead warrior-woman Tythsai to Myrall'mara. "And you, my deadly beauty, to you goes the greatest honor."

The Vorquellyn *sullanciri*'s head came up. "Yes, Mistress? I am given my release now?"

"You are." Chytrine's voice shrank. "How well I remember what you asked of me when I made you into one of my Dark Lancers. You desired only one thing, to avenge the slight done to me by Tarrant Hawkins, when he refused me. I told you then I would not release you to avenge me until the time was right. I deem that time now."

Myrall'mara's smile broadened and, for a heartbeat, Isaura caught a glimpse of pure beauty. It faded quickly enough, as a darkness hooded the *sullanciri*'s face, but Isaura forced herself to remember it. Myrall'mara, who had always been cold and distant, just for that moment had seemed warm.

"It shall be done, Mistress. You will be proud."

"I already am, pet." Chytrine surveyed her generals. "They have gathered their courage and will strike. We will lure them onward, then destroy them. Those who survive will know the glory of our true purpose. Those who do not will languish, quite rightly, in the obscurity of the deluded and foolish. Go forth and conquer. Be swift and ruthless, for in the pursuit of victory, there is no vice."

CHAPTER 32

I would prefer it if Kerrigan would attend me."

The mage's head came up as Oracle spoke. Banausic stood beside her horse, his arms raised, ready to help the blind Vorquelf from the saddle. He'd been her faithful servant throughout the journey, so why the change here at Otedo, Kerrigan couldn't imagine.

Kerrigan smiled. "I would be happy to help."

Oracle graced Banausic with a smile and waited patiently. The other Vorquelf glared at Kerrigan for a moment, then Resolute snapped at him, "Petulant glaring is not *practical*. Go do some real work."

Kerrigan dismounted from his horse and grasped Oracle around her slender waist. He felt her hands on his shoulders as she slid from the saddle. She was much lighter than he would have imagined—which made him realize he'd really not thought much about her at all. He'd actually been a bit afraid of her and, while being cordial, had pretty much left her alone on the trip.

Aside from Qwc and Bok, he'd pretty much left everyone alone. Resolute had slowly sunk back into his usual sullenness. That was less than pleasant, but somehow more comforting than his smiles and laughter. Kerrigan admired Resolute's ability to focus on the problem at hand, but to have done that day after day for over a century certainly boggled the mind.

The journey to Otedo had been largely uneventful. In a few places flooding had washed out the road, so the whole column had to pause while holes were filled in or bridges created. Kerrigan could have helped out with magick, but Resolute had expressly forbidden him from doing so. Bok concurred, so Kerrigan remained relatively idle—except when he took his turn digging or hauling like the others.

Resolute's reasoning had been sound. Chytrine knew Kerrigan was a powerful mage. She had hoped her spell had killed him, but eventually she would learn that it had not. By restricting his use of magick, it would make it more difficult for other spies to recognize him and report his location. While Kerrigan didn't like the thought that Chytrine still had agents in the south, he accepted it as true and did as he was bid.

After ten days on the road, the column finally reached Otedo—though they had been able to smell it well before. The Varasena River flowed into a vast, swampy delta that encompassed several navigable channels. Otedo was located where the river flowed into the delta, and while the river might have pushed the city's effluent toward the sea, it did so slowly. The locals claimed the swamps yielded lovely fish and crustaceans because of the fertilization, but Kerrigan wasn't sure he was going to find anything that had been swimming in nightsoil appetizing.

The city itself had once been Saporicia's capital, but the centuries had not been overly kind to Otedo. Mildew covered cracked paint and plaster, and even the newest buildings suffered from severe weathering. Though it was still the district capital, the officials who had greeted them at the gate seemed more weary than proud, and accepted them into their city as a duty, not a privilege.

Troops were to be billeted in houses, apparently not a popular thing. Resolute's company, along with General Pandiculia, accepted an invitation to be housed in the Lord Mayor's palace. The building would have been big for a tavern, but was not much more impressive than one in terms of accommodations. Still, it did come with servants to care for the horses and any other needs they had, which was welcome after a week on the road.

Oracle squeezed Kerrigan's shoulders with her hands. "Give me your arm, Kerrigan, and lead me within, please."

He complied, letting her grasp the inside of his right elbow. He moved carefully forward, letting her know about the steps up to the doorway, and ready to catch her if she stumbled.

The Vorquelf laughed. "I will not break, Kerrigan. I may be old by your reckoning, but I am no crone."

"No, of course not. I beg your pardon." Kerrigan was glad she couldn't see him blush. For a moment or two he wondered why he felt embarrassed, then he realized it was because he had made a mistake. Granted, he was being presented with a new situation, so he had a lot to learn, but he should have asked her what she desired instead of assuming.

"Please, Mistress Oracle, where shall we go? Tell me how best I can serve you."

"My room will be up the stairs to the right, and down the hall, next to the last on the left."

"Let's get you there, then." Kerrigan nodded, then bunched the muscles in his forearm to let her know he was ready, and they forged on into the palace. To the left a short set of steps went down into a half-sunken room, and on the right stout wooden stairs led upward. They mounted the steps and ascended, then he took her down a narrow corridor to the room she had mentioned. Though small, it faced south and caught sunlight. It also had a view of a dense garden with a throng of spring green plants.

Oracle freed her hand from his arm and found the bed

by feel. She turned and sat on it; the straw in the mattress scrunched loudly. "This will do for a night or two."

Kerrigan nodded, then blushed. "Yes, Mistress, it will."

She glanced at him with her sightless eyes. "You fear me, Kerrigan. Why is that?"

Her question surprised him, but he answered almost without thinking. "You see more than you tell."

Oracle nodded. "It is the nature of my gift to see many things. You have studied the clairvoyant arts on Vilwan. Did you not see many things?"

"Some, yes, but they did not want me delving into the future."

"Or were they afraid you might look into the past?"

A shiver ran down his spine. "It probably was that, yes. They wanted to hide my origins and my purpose from me."

She laughed lightly, almost a birdsong sound. "They did that, and in doing so did themselves a disservice. Had they defined for you what your duty was, and told you of the glory you would win in acquitting it, you would still be under their control. They were afraid that if you were a weapon and knew it, you might develop the ability to think for yourself and rebel. Instead, they let you think for yourself, and you reject being a weapon."

Kerrigan sagged into a wooden chair beside the wall, and was a bit surprised when it did not creak as much as he expected. "I'm not a weapon. I'm not a killer. I mean, people and things have died because of what I have done, but . . ."

". . . but you are not like Resolute."

"No." Kerrigan hunched forward, his hands clasped, his elbows on his knees. "Resolute is so . . . intense, but around you . . . I think that's another reason I fear you. Because Resolute fears you."

She laughed again, and clapped her hands. "Resolute, afraid of me? Oh, you are an innocent delight. My dear Kerrigan, Resolute is no more afraid of me than you are of Qwc."

"But the way he acts around you is different . . ."

"Of course it is. A long time ago, when Vorquellyn fell, the three of us escaped together. I was the eldest, by a handful of years, then my sister and Resolute, both of the same age. He is my cousin, and he was young and even less well prepared for life off our island than you were when you first left Vilwan."

"That's not possible."

"Oh, but it is. Resolute was a dreamy youth. He loved reading tales of legend. He used to write poetry. He won prizes for it, and had even composed a poem as a gift for me, since it was coming time for me to be bound to Vorquellyn. He worked very hard on it, but would not read it to me before it was time."

"Resolute? *Poetry?*"

"Resolute was thought by many to be a most frivolous youth. He would spend days and days out in the hills pretending he was Raisasel or some other great elven hero, slaying dragons or rescuing maidens. At times he even talked my sister and me into playing along, which we did happily."

"Your sister? Where is she?"

Oracle lowered her head. "She is now the *sullanciri* known as Myrall'mara."

"Oh, I'm sorry."

"As am I." She looked up again and a tear rolled down her cheek. "There are times I see things I cannot speak of. Where we are now was one of those things. I saw it many years ago, and knew that for it to come true, she would be turned. If I warned her, I would kill this future, and thereby destroy the world's salvation."

Kerrigan shivered. Oracle's gift had demanded great responsibility. He'd failed to save others from death, but she'd had the harder task. She had to hold back, letting them die—*or worse*—so the best possible future could unfold. *If it can be done.*

"Do you see similar ruin for me?"

"I've seen you asking me that question, all the while knowing I could not reply to it whether I had the answer or not." She shifted on the bed, drawing her right knee up and wrapping her arms around herself. "What I can tell you, Kerrigan, is that your journey is far from over. You have changed much, physically and mentally. You have learned much, but you are still young."

She tapped her own chest with a hand. "In here, Kerrigan, in your heart, you are still a child. And that is a wonderful thing in so many ways. Your innocence shields you. Resolute was that innocent once and, deep down inside, the child he once was still lurks."

"I've seen bad things, but he must have seen worse."

"Sometimes it is not what you see, but the vantage point from which you see it." A rueful smile twisted her lips. "Resolute dreamed of heroes. He accepted the mythic tales as truth, but you can imagine how they differ in the telling from the reality. Your own adventures will one day be the same, of course, but you already know the reality. For Resolute, what was all glory, duty, and honor became fire, blood, horror, and pain. That which he had held to be true and beautiful was turned into a falsehood that mocked him."

Kerrigan frowned heavily. "So he has gone all the way in the other direction?"

"Not entirely. He still hopes. The part of him that revered the romance of the past was what allowed him to look for the Norrington. It tells him we will find the Norrington on Vorquellyn, and that we will free him. If he was hard on Will—and hard on you or Banausic—it is because he wants and *needs* to have his original vision proven true."

"And that's why he's hard on the Aurolani, too?"

Oracle smiled. "No. He just likes killing them." Then she looked at him openly, almost as if her eyes were sighted. "He has done much to put you and the Norrington in a position to destroy Chytrine and redeem Vorquellyn, but you will not be required to go as far as he did. I know it scares you, to imagine yourself slaying as he does."

"Is that something you see?"

Oracle shook her head. "No, just something I feel. But true, for all that."

The youth looked down at his hands. "I won't let myself do that, you know. I can't."

"It would be a dark course that led you to that place, Kerrigan. It is not a broad path, and the entrance to it is distant."

His head came up. "But it still looms in the future?"

"It does."

"Well, I guess I'll have to watch my step." He set his shoulders and exhaled sharply. "Vilwan is afraid I might be another Kirûn, but no one is nearly as afraid of it as I am."

"Be careful, Kerrigan. It will be fear that leads you to that path." She slowly smiled at him. "But your heart, though young, is strong and good. Use its strength to overcome your fear, and you will never need to know that darkest of futures."

CHAPTER 33

Raindrops pattered over the hood of Erlestoke's oilskin cloak like distant, arrhythmic drumbeats. His horse shook its head, flicking water off, and glanced back, as if wondering why his master would choose to pause there. The rain wasn't heavy but the day was cool, and heat leeched away as they stood there.

The prince ran his hand over his face. After Alexia left the capital, his force had departed Narriz and traveled slowly toward Oriosa. He hadn't known what to expect, so he didn't push his people hard. He wanted them rested and, that morning, had ordered them to see to their weapons and armor, just in case the border was closed.

Because he didn't know how his father would react, he had sent scouts ahead, and most had returned with benign reports. They'd penetrated to the outskirts of Meredo, reconnoitered the nearby villages, and two had chosen to go into the capital itself. Those were the two who had not returned.

Those were also the two now dangling from a leafless oak at the border. A man and a woman, they'd been bound hand and foot, then hanged. White lace courtesy masks had been tied around their eyes, providing a sharp contrast with the grey of their flesh.

Erlestoke turned in the saddle and looked at Dranae. "There are those who say Oriosans always look for too much symbolism in things, but I think there is no mistaking the message here. They were executed as spies, with the masks granted to honor their courage. We are not wanted; we are invaders."

The big man smiled. "You knew this is how we would be seen. Did you really have hopes your father would change in the week we've taken to get here?"

"Not hope. I just wished it would be so." He pointed at two scouts and then at the corpses. "Cut them down. Organize a burial detail."

The scouts advanced as ordered. Further along the road, where the meadow through which they had passed began to shift into hills forested with evergreens, a small group of riders was coming toward them. The party consisted of a half-dozen of the Meredo Guards and two others—one a youth, and the other a man Erlestoke recognized.

Holding up his hand to restrain his troops, Erlestoke rode forward. Dranae, Rounce, Nay, Borell, and Rumbellow advanced behind him, but kept a respectful distance from those approaching. The Gyrkyme, Preyknosery, circled lazily overhead. Erlestoke did note, with pleasure, that two squads of scouts moved out to either side of the hanging tree, ostensibly to honor the dead, but also within a range where they could cut down those approaching with a flight of arrows.

There is, after all, no flag of truce showing.

The Oriosan party reined up short of the border. Their horses stamped, and some lowered their heads to nibble at the bold tendrils of grass poking up through the thin snow. The guards, with green pennants hanging from their lances, remained watchful, but made no threatening motions. The older man spurred his horse forward, then glanced back and, with a curt nod, beckoned the youth to accompany him.

Erlestoke flipped back his hood. "Cabot Marsham, how unexpected to find you out in weather like this. Then again, wet and cold so suits a worm like you."

His father's aide curled his lips in a sneer. "Denigrate me all you wish, Erlestoke, for a true Oriosan will take your insults as high praise."

"Erlestoke?" The prince's eyes hardened. "You are becoming far too familiar for your own good. Have you forgotten who I am?"

"A freebooter, no more. And no more a true Oriosan." Marsham reached beneath his own cloak and produced a packet wrapped in oilskin and tossed it on the ground. "There, your father has issued an edict that disinherits you and your worthless brother. He has taken Lady Norrington for a wife and has proclaimed her sons to be his rightful heirs. Bow before Prince Redgrave."

Erlestoke laughed aloud and, to the boy's credit, a scarlet flush spread over his face. The prince looked from him to Marsham. "It infuriates you that you were not considered worthy for anything more than delivering messages in the rain. Now, give me the packet."

Marsham snarled. "I am not yours to command, Erlestoke Noland. In there is an order to strip you, and any who travel with you, of your masks. It is all legal, and shall go into effect the moment you step onto Oriosan soil."

Nay had slipped from his saddle and picked up the thick bundle of papers. "In here?"

"Have someone read it to you, Carver. You'll find your home has been seized. And you, Master Playfair, are now master of nothing."

Nay glanced back at Erlestoke. The prince had no doubt that at a word, at the flick of a finger, Naysmith Carver would smash in Cabot Marsham's face. Erlestoke fought the temptation to let him do it.

"Master Carver, if you please. The papers to me."

Nay nodded, then pointed the packet at Marsham. "Remember something. Masks are earned. Being born to one isn't earning it." The smith straightened up and looked at the guards again. "Duty to Oriosa is how it started, how it still goes. You've done nothing."

The little man tugged his mask back into proper position. "I have served my king faithfully."

The prince extended his hand and took the packet. "You'll find that serving my father is not the same as serving Oriosa. Thank you, Master Carver."

Nay nodded once. "Don't need anyone to read them."

"I know, but reading them would be a waste of time." Erlestoke flipped it over and saw it had been sealed with his father's ring. He tossed the whole thing to Rumbellow. "If you don't mind, incinerate it."

The Addermage smiled and deftly caught the packet in one hand. His lips barely moved, but in an instant the papers were burning furiously. Rumbellow then threw it back onto the Oriosan side of the border.

Marsham, pale and sodden, trembled in his saddle. "You have been warned. If you enter Oriosa, you will be outlaws. Your passage shall be contested, every step of the way, and your bodies shall be left where they fall."

"I doubt that." The prince pointed to two of the Guards. "From the marks on your masks, I see you are from East Country. Taloso?"

The gangling blond looked startled. "Me, Highness? Er, sir . . ."

"You'll ride there today. You'll tell Count Storton I have returned to Oriosa, that I have come to protect the nation. You will tell him that I don't come to wage war, but to prevent it."

Marsham wheeled his horse around and grabbed the guardsman's reins. "He's lying. You'll deliver no such message. It will be treason if you do. You and your family will be stripped of your masks."

Erlestoke nodded. "You will. Right after Count Marsham strips me of *my* mask."

Marsham scowled furiously as Erlestoke's companions circled more closely around him. "You will not get away with this, Erlestoke."

"I'd not be so confident if I were you, Count Marsham. Think about it. Under my father's orders, these two were hanged here. You were sent to confront me and my army at a time when, justifiably, we would be enraged. You did not even ride out beneath a flag of truce. My father intended I should slay you, and likely this pretender, too."

All color drained from Marsham's face.

"My father knows you are a schemer. He can't trust you, wanted you dead, and assumed I'd kill you as soon as look at you. The story probably circulating through Meredo is that you came to offer me your fealty. Because I killed you, none of your allies would trust me, thus isolating me from those who would fight against my father. You are a small price to pay to prevent our countrymen from joining me."

Erlestoke again looked at the guards. "Which of you was to see to it that Count Marsham did not survive to report back?"

Two of the guards smiled and raised their hands.

"Thank you." Erlestoke nodded to the captain of his scouts. "Kill them."

In an instant, two dozen arrows hissed through the air and thudded into their chests. Both men sagged in their saddles, then fell to the ground in a clatter of plate and mail. Redgrave reeled from his saddle and vomited.

Erlestoke's hazel eyes hardened. "Oriosans are not assassins; I will not tolerate that behavior. The two of you from the East Country, you will ride out now and bear my message. Go."

The two of them reined their horses around and galloped back the way they had come. The two remaining guardsmen looked very nervous, though not half so nervous as Marsham. He couldn't seem to tear his eyes away from the riddled bodies of the assassins.

"Count Marsham."

The little man gave no sign of hearing.

"Attend me, Count Marsham!" Erlestoke put an edge in his voice, and the little man quivered. But he did force his gaze to the prince. "You are a treasonous dog—and I apologize to dogs for saying that. I know I cannot trust you out of my sight. By rights I could kill you for the insults you have offered me here, but I shall not. I will give you a chance to live, which is more than my father was willing to do. Will you prove yourself useful to me?"

"I am yours to command."

"Not quite the answer I sought, but it will have to do." The prince rubbed a hand over his jaw. "I know you have plotted against my father. You will go to your supporters and enlist them to my cause. They are all guilty of treason, but I can be forgiving and even understanding. You will tell them this for me. You will return with their answers, and I will measure their loyalty in the lances and swords they send to aid me, do you understand?"

"Yes, Highness, completely. I am your creature, heart and soul."

"A pledge of cowardice and corruption; how comforting."

Redgrave slowly stood with Borell supporting him. "What of me, Highness?"

"You, my brother, are a long way from your home in Valsina. Would you like an escort back there?"

The skinny young man nodded. "Please, yes. Thank you."

The prince did raise an eyebrow. "You can, if you wish, return to Meredo."

Redgrave shook his head. "I don't expect your father intended me to return either."

"Probably not, since he knows I don't believe you are the Norrington." Erlestoke smiled. "But you are *a* Norrington, and we would be pleased to have you with us.

By the time we get to Valsina, you can decide how much further you wish to go."

"Thank you, Highness." Redgrave accepted a boost from Borell and climbed back into his saddle. "I'll go as far as you need."

"Good." He looked at Marsham. "Now, go about your duty. Hurry, before I change my mind."

Marsham set off at a hasty trot.

One of the two remaining guards ducked his head nervously. "And what of us, Highness? What are we to do?"

"You have the simplest job of all." Erlestoke smiled. "Do your duty. Welcome us to Oriosa, and wish us well in all we do."

CHAPTER 34

The moment Alexia had dreaded since leaving Narriz had arrived. She tried to steel herself for it, but it was not an easy task. Pain and fear she could defeat, and would defeat yet again. This, however—this sense of loss— just opened a hollow in her belly that would not close.

She knew, in part, it was because of how wonderful the latter half of the week had been. Her troops had made the journey to Bacirro quickly. The Delasena had not yet flooded and the drainage was sufficient that the roads were not washed out. So while plenty of snow and dirt was ground into cold mud that froze each night, it never got boggy enough to slow the carts or the soldiers. It took them only six days to reach the city. And the citizenry, who had already learned about Muroso from the refugees encamped in tents to the south and west, welcomed the troops into their homes.

Alexia had given strict orders about conduct and made very clear the dire nature of punishment if her troops behaved like the enemy. The vast majority of the army comported themselves as guests might, but a few people did get out of hand. Unit leaders made swift examples of those who violated the rules, and the whole of the unit worked to repair any damage done. By and large, order reigned, allowing most troops to work preparing defenses for both the city and the refugee encampments.

Alexia did send scouts out, but not Crow's formation. She kept them close, but scattered so no spies would discern that they were working as a unit. Her intention was to send Crow and his people back south, as if they were to gather more troops and lead them north. When they got halfway back to Narriz, they would head east, into the hills, and disappear.

The scouts she chose did manage to range east and had a number of skirmishes with Aurolani troops. Gyrkyme reported smoke rising from the area around Fronosa, but not the city itself. Bodies were being burned, and the presence of Aurolani scouts to the west of the pass indicated the city had fallen.

A bit more disturbing than that was news that the scouts she sent west had not linked up with General Pandiculia's forces. In less than a week, those troops were supposed to reach Bacirro, putting them in position to oppose whatever army came in from Fronosa. If they did not arrive in time, Alexia would have to hold off the enemy alone. And any siege of Bacirro would begin with the wholesale slaughter of refugees, or their fleeing into the city and swelling it to the point where the supplies would evaporate.

All of those concerns did occupy her, but still there was Crow. They had been given rooms in the home of a prominent merchant whose brother led the Bacirro Horse Guards. While not the most opulent of the rooms they had shared, the accommodations somehow suited them best. The bed was big and warm, and a fireplace nearby produced more than enough heat to hold the cold at bay. The room even had a bathing alcove with a huge wooden tub, and after six days on the road Alexia had very much wanted to scrub herself clean.

While she attended to business that first night, Crow had heated the water and scented it for her with sandalwood. Then he sought her out and conducted her back to the room while steam still rose off it. He removed her boots, then slowly stripped her of her clothes. She made to slip his tunic off him, but he gently put her hands aside.

"Be patient, my love."

She watched him closely and bit back a smile as he freed her from the last scrap of clothing, then slowly circled her. He kissed her shoulders, front and back, again gently pressing her hands back to her sides. Standing behind her, he moved her thick braid aside and kissed the back of her neck. She felt the heat of his breath against her skin and pressed back against him. Just feeling him there, his chest pressed against her shoulder blades, made her shiver.

He whispered in her ear, "Princess Alexia, you are everything I desire, I need, and I love in this world. Allow me to care for you." He kissed her again on the back of the neck, letting his teeth graze her flesh. Then, with his hands on her hips, he slowly walked her to the bath and held her hand as she stepped into the water.

She groaned aloud as the warmth washed over her. Leaning back, she closed her eyes and smiled. While she had accepted that long marches, hard saddles, harder ground, and an all-pervading sense of cold was likely to be her lot in life, the luxurious heat of the bath and a scent that was not sweat, blood, or manure pleased her enormously. She relaxed her shoulders and arched her back, letting her spine pop.

Then Crow's strong hands drew her right foot up out of the water. The cool air hit it instantly, but Crow's hands compressed her foot, rubbing, smoothing and soothing, caressing and kneading.

Alexia gasped and opened her eyes. "Oh, how did you know?"

"Lucky guess. You don't mind?"

"Mind? My other foot is jealous."

He winked at her. "It will have its turn."

He was as good as his word, massaging the other foot, then her calves. His strong fingers found knotted muscle and bled away the tightness. Then he produced soap and a soft cloth, washing her feet and lower legs. He shifted forward and repeated the massage with her hands and arms, then washed them as well.

As his ministrations continued, Alexia began to lose herself in the sensations. The heat and the firm pressure of his touch, the weight and softness of the wet cloth as it slid over her body, felt sublime. She lifted her chin as he washed her throat, then sank down a little to let the water lap at her collarbones.

He moved behind her and drew her wet braid from the water. He unplaited it, then began to soap her hair. He lifted the mass to the top of her head, rubbing and massaging. One hand or the other constantly started at the nape of her neck, working up and over into her hair. Warm suds dripped down over her face and shoulders. With her eyes closed she could feel it move inch by inch over her skin.

Then equally gently he used a small bowl to scoop up water and rinse her hair. He gathered it up and twisted it to wring out most of the water, then let it hang over the back of the tub, resting it on a towel that absorbed much of the remaining moisture.

Crow leaned close and kissed her on the cheek. "I should likely get you out of there before the water cools off."

She opened one eye and smiled. "You know, there are ways we could heat it up. There's plenty of room for you."

His smile blossomed against her cheek. "For another night, my love. Now I think it is our bed that needs warming."

As she stood, he wrapped her in a thick bath sheet. He gathered her hair in another and dried it, then dried her body, sinking to his knees to get her legs. As he rubbed, he brought a rosy glow to her flesh, pausing every so often to shower her with soft kisses that made her breath come more quickly.

Unable to stand it any longer, she sank long fingers into his hair. "Take me to bed immediately, Crow, or I shall not be responsible for what I do."

He grinned up at her, his beard brushing her thigh. "As you command, Princess."

That night, they had not needed a fire to stay warm. On the other nights they'd had fires, but more for the warm glow of the light, and the way the flickering flames danced shadows over their bodies. Though their daily duties might have necessitated their separation, each night they were together. In the morning, when they would awake holding each other, separation seemed only possible because of that evening's promised reunion.

But now had come the time for Crow to leave for good. They had both tried to ignore that fact in the morning, treating it as any other. They almost accomplished it, save for one point when he could no longer speak and just held her closely; and a time when she pressed her face to his neck and stained it with tears.

She had gotten up, dressed, and gone out to attend to her duties. She acquitted them well, though Peri and Arimtara noted her distraction and covered for her. Most of what had to be done was clerical work, as supplies kept flowing into the city and had to be allocated. Though no bard's song ever layered glory on a quartermaster, without warehouses bulging and the means to get supplies to the troops, a war could be lost before even the first soldier fell.

By noon, when Crow and his people were set to depart, she finished and returned to their room. His saddlebags waited on the bed along with Alarien. Crow sat on the edge of the empty tub, knotting some of the sandalwood shavings into a small scrap of silk.

He smiled as she entered. "This will smell better than anything on the road."

"I hope it will remind you of me."

"It will." He stood and came to her, enfolding her in his arms. "I love you, Alexia. I don't want to leave, but if your plan is to succeed, if *our* future is to be assured, I must."

She frowned. "When I formulated this plan, it was supposed to be Resolute leading this group. You were supposed to be with me."

"And I will be. In Fronosa, and soon enough." He tightened his hands at the small of her back, pressing her to him.

She smoothed her hands down over the soft doeskin of his tunic. "I know you know the plan, and are confident you can accomplish it, but you are to take no unnecessary chances."

Crow smiled. "I know that is a directive you give all your commanders, although I'd like to think it holds special meaning for me."

"It does, Crow, I love you. But, more than that, I trust you. Do what is needed, and we will be together in Fronosa. Not soon enough, but soon."

He nodded, then kissed her deeply and held her for a long time. Not nearly long enough, but sufficient that his scent and that of the sandalwood became linked. Reluctantly she let him go and watched from the window as he and his five legions rode south.

He turned in the saddle at the gate and waved, then again at the crest of a far hill. She returned his wave both times, then nodded as he vanished from sight. *In Fronosa, my husband. There I shall bathe you.*

CHAPTER 35

"Y ou'll die for luring me into this trap," Resolute hissed at Banausic, as multiple individuals moved from the shadows in the warehouse district in Otedo.

The black-haired Vorquelf held a hand up. "It's not a trap, Resolute."

"No?" Resolute raised his head and hooked his thumbs in his sword belt. "There are a dozen of them, and you make thirteen. Why do you yet work for her when she will lose?"

One of the shadows stepped forward, allowing the weak yellow light from a guttering streetlamp to illuminate his face. As with all Vorquelves, his eyes had no pupil. In the dim light, only a hint of sapphire showed in them, and likewise the darkness made his brown hair seem almost black. Resolute didn't need the colors to recognize him, and he determined that this one would die first. *Not because he is more of a threat than any other, but because I should have killed him long ago.*

Predator held his hands up, open and empty. "It is no trap, Resolute. We have come a long way to find you."

Resolute's silver eyes narrowed. "Go back to the Yslin slums. Otedo has nothing for you. Nor do I, so your trip is wasted."

"Wait."

"Why?" Resolute's nostrils flared. "Why should I wait for you to say anything? What have you been since our homeland fell? You have been a canker on society. Alcida welcomes us, yet what do you do but prey on the people of Yslin. Worse yet, when a call was made for all keepsakes of Vorquellyn, you withheld something vital. You have done nothing to help redeem our home, so I owe you nothing."

Resolute had expected Predator to take umbrage at his words. He expected the thief to launch himself at Resolute, along with the other members of the Grey Mist. He had intended his words to enflame Predator's passions, but instead each one seemed to shame him. With each sentence the thief's head bowed and his shoulders slumped a bit more.

"You are right, Resolute. You owe us nothing. We have caused trouble. Our work could have convinced men that we were not worth saving, that our homeland was not worth redeeming. While we did save the Norrington in Yslin, that might well have been too little, too late."

Resolute nodded slowly. "Your point?"

"My point is this." Predator looked at the figures lurking in darkness. "It's time we did something right. We're going to Vorquellyn with you."

"You're what?" Resolute couldn't cover his surprise. He wasn't certain what was worse: having a pack of thieves join him, or the fact that his destination was common enough knowledge that the worst of the slum-dwellers in Yslin had heard of it—and with enough time to travel to Otedo. "I want explanations, and I want them now."

"Ships have been plying the waters from Narriz to Yslin, and they've seen other ships. We all know the fight is going to be in Saporicia." Predator's features sharpened. "Amends is still getting up a militia of sorts, all fancy dressed to fight the war. The lot of us realized that if things are going to happen, you'll be in the thick of it. We remembered the Norrington Prophecy, about Vorquellyn being redeemed. We know you'll be part of it, so we came to join you."

"The Norrington is dead."

That revelation staggered Predator. "He is? Will? That little roof-runner?"

Resolute nodded solemnly. "He died preventing his father from killing a dragon."

Predator shook his head. "That can't be. If he's dead . . ."

"Then your trip is wasted," Resolute concluded.

Banausic held his hands up. "Listen to them, Resolute."

"Unlike you, Banausic, I do not have time to waste with gutter scum that can be distracted by shiny leaves and sour ale." He glared at Predator. "Go home."

Predator's head came up. "No."

The silver-eyed Vorquelf folded his arms across his chest. "There is nothing here for you. Go home."

The thief looked puzzled. "Oracle said . . ."

"She said what? She told you that you had to come here?" Oracle was the reason for his journey, and she'd already saddled him with Banausic. Now it seemed her meddling had brought him a dozen city-dwelling elves. For a moment, all the aggravation he'd known trying to teach Will Norrington how to survive in the countryside came back to him. In its wake came a wave of melancholy that broke his anger.

Predator replied in a small voice. "She didn't tell us anything, Resolute. I just remember the prophecy. She said Vorquellyn would be redeemed. You've said that for a long time, too. You know, you're not the only one who wants to see that."

He turned and opened his arms, taking the others in. "You think we don't care because we just stayed in Yslin's slums and paid no attention to anything but ourselves and our concerns. You judge us all by yourself, but we aren't as strong as you. You think we didn't care, but we did and do. It just hurt to think of it being so far away."

"You could have done something, Predator."

"What, Resolute?" The thief laughed. "Amends and his ilk have worked on generations of men, trying to ingratiate themselves. It did no good, and they never convinced either the humans or our other brethren to launch an attack. What other course was left to us? To do what you did?"

Resolute nodded solemnly. "Exactly."

"Oh, Resolute, you've forgotten, haven't you? The brothers Right and Might, Victory—you knew her— Seethe even, and dozens of others. All of them walked the same path you do, but you now walk it alone. They're all dead, and Vorquellyn is no closer to being free."

"This is not a path for the weak."

"I know." Predator held out a hand. "So show us how to be strong."

Resolute snarled and balled his fists. "There isn't time to show you."

"We're not helpless, you know."

Resolute shook his head. "This will take more than stowing away aboard some Alcidese supply ship."

Light laughter sounded from the shadows.

Predator smiled. "We didn't stow away."

"Then how did you get here?"

"Loquellyn once gifted one of their galleys to the Kings of Alcida." Predator shrugged. "They didn't know how to use it, so we borrowed it."

"How did you . . . ?"

Predator's chin came up. "You were very young when our homeland was lost. I might not yet have been bound, but I had served on a galley my uncle commanded."

Resolute frowned. "I saw no silverwood shark in the harbor here."

"Of course not. We have it hidden in the swamps. Most of the crew is still with it."

"How many?"

"A legion or so, including some healers who wanted to come."

Resolute's eyes narrowed. "How did you know to come here?"

More light laughter sounded from the shadows and color came to Predator's cheeks. "We got here by accident. I know how to make the ship work. Navigation, on the other hand . . . We were trying for Narriz and ended up here. Oracle said . . ."

"Oracle said you were meant to be here."

"Yes. Look, Resolute, I didn't find Narriz but I know I can get us to Vorquellyn."

"No, we'll go up the Varasena."

"But that will only get us to the headwaters, then it's overland through Loquellyn. We'll have to get another ship. Let's just strike out from here."

Resolute cocked his head. "You said you wanted to come with me, correct?"

"Yes, but . . ."

"Then you will go where I go. I have my orders." He thought for a moment, then nodded. "Bring your ship into the harbor. We'll leave in a day or two, once we get provisions. Is there a problem with that?"

"No, no, we can do that." Predator gave him a dark stare. "The Norrington's really dead?"

"The Norrington *died*. Oracle says he's waiting for us on Vorquellyn."

"All the more reason we should get there by the quickest route."

"We will." Resolute smiled. "You'll just have to row fast, then walk faster."

General Pandiculia gave them whatever provisions they needed. She stood at the river quay as the Vorquelves brought the silverwood ship up the Varasena, docked, and began to load it. She shook her head as she watched them work, then smiled at Resolute. "Interesting crew you have there."

"Utterly lacking in discipline, scruples, and combat experience." He sighed. "I'll keep them out of the city so you don't have to deal with the aftermath of their thieving ways."

"Actually, I was thinking I'd trade you crack troops for them. They are actually working well. My troops, as you saw on the road, are just going to be slow. We'll never make the rendezvous with Alexia on time."

"You have my sympathy."

"And you, mine." She stared distantly toward the north-east. "I don't expect our paths to cross again. I wish you luck."

"I extend to you the same. I'll send reports if I can."

She shrugged. "Save the reports. Just kill things."

Resolute laughed. "As you desire, General."

She headed out to get her own troops moving, so Resolute helped with the loading and expedited matters. By midday the ship was ready to go. The Grey Misters took to the oars and began to propel the ship up the river. While quarters were cramped, ample room was found for everyone in the party, with Rym's box being lashed to the deck between the mast and aftcastle.

In the forecastle, Resolute could look down into the rowers' galleys and watch them pulling hard on long oar-like levers that connected to the gears and belts that drove a paddle wheel at the ship's aft. The ship, which rode far lower in the water than any human ship, still moved up the river with fair speed—even though they sailed against the current.

Predator's numbering of the crew was not off by much, but calling them a legion was a sore misapplication of that word. At least a quarter of them he'd press-ganged from the wastrels. Vorquelves who had been bound to the island found themselves in such intense pain as it was despoiled that they left the world. Other, younger Vorquelves so felt the pain of abandonment that they resorted to drink and other vices to distract themselves or propel themselves into oblivion. Fresh air and a distance from their vices of choice seemed to have benefited some, but a score of them would be useless when it came to making the overland trek.

Of the rest, about a dozen were pure civilians who either were healers, or disaffected members of Amends' appeasement clique. Resolute fully expected they would whine. Or, worse yet, try to exert control over the expedition.

The remaining crew had potential, but not much of it. While the Grey Misters were a formidable street gang, that didn't make them warriors. All of them had a dagger or two, but few had swords, and there wasn't a bow among them. A few had gotten enchanted with tattoos such as he had, but he saw nothing that would help them in combat. Even their uniform of leathers would be of little use. He had to hope that they ran into very little resistance—or that he and the others could just outdistance the Grey Misters if forced to run from trouble.

The political refugees, rather predictably, sought audiences with Oracle. Resolute wasn't sure if she saw things concerning them, but every one of them approached him later and pledged fealty. He harbored no illusions about their obedience in the future, but at least the problem was deferred for a bit.

The journey upriver went swiftly enough, with the eight hours of light allowing them to cover two dozen miles a day. They found simple anchorage along the river and camped away from settlements. Resolute would have liked to stop at Sanurval, but they reached it in the middle of the day, so they took the western fork of the river and bypassed it. He didn't mind having spies report to Chytrine that an elven ship was moving up the river, but he didn't want her to be alerted as to who was on it.

After five days they reached the headwaters of the Varasena: a small lake in the foothills of the range that separated Loquellyn and Saporicia. They made their last camp there and left the worst of the crew and a couple of the politicos behind to ship back down to Otedo. Resolute wrote out a message to be delivered to King Fidelius in Narriz, but he assumed it would never get to him. It really didn't matter, since it contained all sorts of incorrect information about where his group was and where they were heading.

The following morning the Grey Misters bid their compatriots a fond farewell, then shouldered the packs they'd all been issued from the ship's stores. People joked about what they should call their group. Half of them were in favor of Resolute's Legion.

The other popular name was the Forlorn Legion.

Resolute preferred that name, but rejected it. He looked at the haphazardly organized gang of brigands, cutthroats, politicos, and innocents and shook his head. "What we are is the *First* Legion. The first to fight Chytrine, the first to return home. Let us go forth and do all we can, so we will also not be the *Last* Legion."

CHAPTER 36

T he westernmost town in Noriva went by the name of Nowhere. As Duranlaun reported, it had a palisade and a number of buildings, but not much else. Muddy streets were flanked with longhouses to shelter the foresters, while smaller buildings functioned as taverns, dining halls, and whorehouses. A flag flew from the highest rooftop, but Marcus Adrogans could not recognize the blue-and-white banner as belonging to any nation or unit.

If the entire population of the place amounted to more than a thousand, Adrogans would have been surprised. For his army to sweep over the town and destroy it would have been simple. One volley from the dragonels would have shattered the wooden walls and left the place defenseless. What passed for a militia there was a half legion of men who seemed more intent on stealing money from drunks than providing any sort of security. But they wore livery matching the flag, which hinted that they belonged to a greater authority. And the fact that they were men and not gibberers did give him heart.

Adrogans watched the village from within the trees on a

nearby hilltop. His army had approached and camped close by, but managed to remain undiscovered—mainly because Nowhere's guards did not venture beyond the palisade.

Adrogans had seriously considered using the dragonels to obliterate Nowhere, as such an attack would give his fireteams practice with sighting and reloading quickly. It would also let his other troops get an idea of just how powerful the dragonels were. While all of them knew Fortress Draconis had been laid low by the weapons, even those who had once visited the northern stronghold had trouble conceiving of how much power it would take to accomplish that end.

But while that plan of attack would have doubtless been successful, it posed several problems. First and foremost, he didn't want to squander his supply of firedirt. Second, if anyone did escape, then Chytrine's forces would have warning that he was coming—with the dragonels. He also could not imagine the Aurolani Empress' having failed to dream up defenses against her weapon, and he didn't want his people running into such defenses, since the slaughter would no doubt be hideous.

Third, and most important, destroying the town would eliminate it as a source of intelligence and would further alarm people. Adrogans sought for a way to win the people over and have them work for him. Of course, he also didn't want Chytrine to know they were working for him, so in consultation with General Caro and others, he came up with a working plan.

He looked down toward where Caro sat at the head of a ragtag mounted column and nodded. Caro raised a hand, then let it fall, and his Alcidese Horse Guards began their descent from the hills. Behind the three hundred of them came four hundred men and women on foot, all armed, comprising the Svoin and Okrans volunteers.

While the numbers were impressive, their appearance wasn't. Their uniforms had been removed and replaced with the motliest collection of garments that could be found. They looked every bit a group of refugees or, worse, soldiers turned to banditry. Caro would ride down with his troops, demand the town throw open its gates and proclaim him their leader. "After all," he would note, "if that bastard Adrogans can have an empire, I might as well, too."

By the time Caro's cavalry reached the town, the gates had been closed and the closest thing the town had to a mayor mounted the wall and spoke with him. While Adrogans could hear nothing of what was being said, he recognized gestures. After one particular one, a Warhawk swooped and exploded a firecock over a small portion of the wall. That caused the mayor to see his situation in a new light.

The gates were thrown open, Caro was welcomed, the flag came down, and a new one went up. The town of Nowhere now owed fealty to King Caro the First. The celebration of his coronation went on well into the night.

During that night the bulk of Adrogans' army moved around Nowhere behind a line of hills to the south. They pushed on for several hours and set up camp in a huge meadow the Rangers had located before. A stream of scouts kept Adrogans updated about the events in Nowhere on an hourly basis, but it wasn't until midmorning that Turpus Caro reached the camp and was able to explain everything to him.

Caro's normally red cheeks had yet more color—half from drink and the rest from cold, Adrogans suspected—and he was smiling broadly. "The initial resistance was halfhearted. Dalanous, the governor of the Nowhere District, was a minor courtier who was given the assignment when Noriva's crown princess began to take a proprietary interest in where he slept and with whom."

Adrogans raised an eyebrow as he broke a small loaf of bread in two, then tore off a smaller piece and dipped it in broth to soften it. "Noriva has a government, then, and royalty?"

"A queen, not a king. As near as I can make out, Chytrine doesn't really care who is doing what in Noriva as long as grain is harvested, ore is dug, cattle tended, and anything else she needs is taken care of. There are various small political subsets in the countryside, but the queen is at Logbal. The women have reorganized the society around sisterhoods, since Chytrine seems content to harvest only males when a slaving run is made. Half the men sent to Nowhere ended up there to prevent their being taken."

"And the rest?"

Caro shrugged. "They're out harvesting trees. No one knows for certain what all the wood is for, since it travels east of Logbal into an area that the Aurolani patrol themselves, but everyone assumes it's for a fleet. All the shipwrights and sailors have been scooped up, so the conclusion seems inescapable."

Adrogans nodded. "Wood harvested now would have to be seasoned before it could be used. If she is taking it now, the fleet couldn't be ready for a year."

The Alcidese general shook his head. "If she wants the fleet now, she has magickers to season the wood. It might not be as good as if it were given time and unenchanting the wood would ruin the fleet, but if she is looking for a quick strike somewhere, a hastily assembled fleet would suffice."

"I'd not thought about magick being used on that scale, but that does make me mindful of something else. I'll want a slice or core from each log. Then we can have our magickers use those to keep track of where the wood ends up. They might even be able to tell how it is used."

"Good idea." Caro raised the bowl of soup before him and drank, then wiped his mouth on his sleeve. "Dalanous was willing to accept me as his master primarily because I said I'd be paying a visit to Logbal. He's happy to have me gone, and if I can take over, he'll be my best backer. If not, he just puts the old flag back up."

"How far away is Logbal?"

"We can make the capital in a week and a half." Caro tucked a small crust of bread into his left cheek to soften. "There are other settlements along the way. This little ruse would likely function on most of them. Dalanous says virtually none of them have defenses, since the Aurolani don't like it, and there are no other threats."

"We will bypass a few. We have to assume word will get out about you, and we don't want people to know exactly where you will be." Adrogans posted his elbows on the table. "We have two possibilities to deal with. The first is that the queen . . ."

"Winalia is her name."

Adrogans thought for a moment. "So Queen Winalia decides to send some troops out to oppose you. Given that the Norivese apparently have no defenses, I assume what would pass for a militia would be easy to overcome."

"I would agree."

"Then the second case is likely to be the one that comes to pass. Someone in her court passes word to the Aurolani and they send troops. In that first encounter we will have a chance to maul them. After that, we're fighting every step of the way to the shipyards, up the Boreal Pass, and on into Aurolan."

"We'll want to have that encounter well past Logbal, then, so we can use the city as a place to fall back to."

The Jeranese general shook his head. "I'd rather not. It will be a town without defenses, so falling back would just mean the slaughter of innocents. Once the Aurolani know we have dragonels, they will bring their own."

"If they have any in Noriva."

"Good point, but one we can hardly count on. If they had to, they could ship them in from Muroso or Saporicia."

"At least that would relieve some of the pressure on the troops in the south."

Adrogans nodded in agreement. "True, it would, but so will pressing forward, hitting hard, moving quickly. We were able to take Svarskya because we did nothing that conventional military wisdom would have dictated. We fought a winter war using guile and trickery. We have to continue to do that, because if they don't know where we are, they have to waste time and energy finding us. All of that wears their troops down, stretches their lines, and makes it easier for us to find a weak spot to exploit."

"I agree with all that." Caro laid his hands on the table and leaned forward, lowering his voice a little. "I know our troops are good, and the dragonels will make them better, but we don't even number six thousand. What would you guess she will have opposing us? Bear in mind we assume she is massing to launch a fleet south, so she will have to be staging troops to board the ships."

Adrogans rose from the table and stalked over to the back of the pavilion, where a map of the world had been pinned to a board. He studied it for a moment, then shook his head. "I have no idea, my friend. We can count on Alexia having as many as fifteen thousand under her command. I would put the Aurolani force at that number or more—up to twice that many. And, just as we faced the *kryalniri* in Okrannel, I am even willing to bet there are other unexpected things that will augment her force.

"As for the troops gathered to ship out, let us take a guess. How many people would you want to take Narriz or Yslin?"

Caro shook his head. "Narriz I do not know well. Yslin, however, I would want ten thousand."

"And if the assault came in from the sea, with ships bearing dragonels that battered the waterfront into rubble? What if you could land troops there, unopposed? How many would it take, then? All they have to do is bottle up troops up in their towers, then bring the dragonels along to crash those towers down."

The Alcidese horseman paled slightly. "Maybe five thousand."

"You're more conservative than I am. I would put it at three, and only because I think the citizenry would fight as well. Narriz would require two."

"Two thousand?"

"I was actually thinking only two. Blasting the city from the sea would lead the people to surrender. You might need a garrison force of several hundred, but it would fall quickly, especially if the fighting in the north was fierce."

Caro thought for a moment, then nodded. "These dragonels really can be devastating, can't they?"

"Yes, quite. The Draconis Baron was right in refusing to share knowledge of them." Adrogans tapped the map where the Boreal Pass led from Aurolan down into Noriva. "We'll use your number. Five thousand. That's what we will face."

"An even fight. It will be horrible."

"If we leave it an even fight." Adrogans smiled slowly. "Your exploits, King Caro, are just the beginning of making sure Chytrine underestimates us. If she feeds us her troops one mouthful at a time, we'll chew them all up and make it to her home in time to spit out the bones."

CHAPTER 37

Erlestoke's army made swift progress through Oriosa for a variety of reasons, and that both pleased and worried the prince. The primary reason was the good condition of the roads. The King's Highway curved up and around from Meredo, past Bokagul, to the Muroso border at Tolsin. Good roads meant the troops and supply train could move quickly. Speed was going to be of the essence if he was going to be able to rendezvous with Princess Alexia's forces—which he desperately wanted to do.

Their progress also made him happy because the deeper they got into the country, the closer he was to being on the battlefield dealing with the Aurolani. Between the Midlands and Norweshire, the tiny region known as Dales provided an excellent battleground. The hilly countryside had only a few sites where an organized battle could be waged. Because he fully expected a dragon to be deployed to destroy his force, and because he could meet it with Dranae, he wanted to be able to lure the Aurolani into one of those fields. He would be able to deploy his reserves as flanking forces that could pour onto the battlefield as needed and chase the fleeing Aurolani when their forces broke.

Erlestoke did realize his intentions were optimistic, but he still wanted to get to Dales. Even if he didn't meet the enemy, the wooded hillsides would be wonderful for hitting and running, something he would be forced to do if faced with a superior force. Having Bokagul at his back would be good as well. He wasn't certain what to expect from his kinsmen. He hoped for support, but would settle for neutrality and guard against treachery.

But the fact that there had been no opposition so far surprised and worried him. His father had let him pass unopposed around Meredo. The lords of the Midlands and Midmarch had always been closer to Meredo than Norweshire, Hawkride, and the East Country, so he was marching right toward his father's strength. Sythara, the county with the longest border with Alcida, tended toward neutrality in internal politics, and had strong family ties with Alcida.

On the sixth day they approached the junction of three roads. The Sythara Road went south to Alcida. The Toloso Road headed east-southeast to the capital of the East Country, passing through the county of Hawkride, a place best known for containing the ruins of a city called Atval. It had been destroyed by dragons in days long past, but had once been a place of glory. While the current rulers could claim no line back to the rulers of Atval, they all had married cadet branches of their families into those of the Hawkriders. But, instead of loyalty, they merely got contempt.

So it really did not surprise Erlestoke when scouts reported that an army of a thousand or so warriors from Hawkride stood astride the road. It did strike Erlestoke that they were barring the northern King's Highway, and not the Toloso Road, but such was their pride. *They could not abide the idea that I might just ignore them and ride past.* The scouts further reported a score of nobles and warriors were waiting at the crossroads beneath a pavilion and a flag of truce.

Erlestoke called his military leaders together and got them to deploy their troops on a broad front. As he and a small group rode forward to parley, he intended that his troops crest the hills that surrounded the crossroads. His troops numbered roughly three times those of the Hawkriders. Having that display of strength backing him would likely make his adversaries slightly less bold— though there was nothing in Hawkrider character to suggest they would be cowed into submission.

He chose his companions carefully and rode forth with only six in his entourage. Nay, Borell, Dranae, Rumbellow, and Redgrave joined General Quantusa of the Jeranese Crown Horse. She was his most senior military leader. The command of the troops behind them was left to General Percurs of the Alcidese Throne Guards. If there looked to be trouble, Percurs would deal with it.

Erlestoke's party reached the pavilion, but he did not dismount. He remained instead in the saddle and leaned forward, resting his hands on the stock of his quadnel where it rode in a saddle scabbard by his right knee. The prince looked down at the two nobles lounging in chairs, sipping wine from crudely thrown goblets. He thought he recognized one of them, but both were rather young so he could not be certain.

"I believe, my lords, you have an army astride the road I wish to take."

One of the two—the more cadaverous, with a sallow complexion and hair thinner than his newly grown beard—slowly stood. He wore a tabard over a coat of mail; both hung to his knees. The center of the tabard was Oriosan green, though closer to spring colors than evergreen, with white side panels and sleeves. A sword belt secured it at his waist and on his breast was a hawk in flight. His mask, likewise green with a white stripe outlining it, bore marks that suggested his father was dead and that he had attained the rank of count. Even more curious was a mark beneath his right eye—a crown that indicated he was in line for the Oriosan throne. As with Hawkriders in general, he had a hawk's feather dangling from the mask at the left side.

Erlestoke almost raised a hand to his own mask to feel that same mark, but he refrained. That mark was on his life mask, which he had abandoned in the last days of Fortress Draconis. His mistress had taken it and their son south— *and likely are somewhere in Meredo even as I sit here.* The mask he currently wore was simply black, and matched the one sewn on a field of green that had become his force's banner.

The Count of Hawkride lifted his chin and affected to peer down a slender nose at Erlestoke. "My troops are here to defend my nation. You are an outlaw. You will leave my nation now."

Erlestoke was not sure what surprised him the most. Hawkriders seldom wanted to admit they were part of Oriosa, much less claim it as their nation. The count's open defiance of Erlestoke hinted at a trap, but that could just have been the count believing lies the King had told about support nearby. While he suspected the count was not going to believe King Scrainwood actually intended him to sit on the throne, having that mark might win him some support from other lords who wanted at least the appearance of legitimacy from any new ruler who replaced the king.

Erlestoke kept his voice even. "I have no desire to kill Oriosans." He refrained from saying, "Or Hawkriders." He took a deep breath, then let it out slowly. "I have urgent business to the north, in Muroso and beyond. Do not hamper me."

"A veiled threat, Erlestoke?" The skinny man laughed, and in that laughter Erlestoke caught enough that he was able to recognize the man. "If you have no desire to kill Oriosans, I suggest you turn around and march back to Saporicia."

"I can't do that, Count Wightman."

"Then it seems there is little we can do."

Erlestoke sat back in the saddle. "We could find a way past this impasse. Instead of our armies fighting, we could settle this matter ourselves, man versus man."

Wightman's face went grey. "You would demand satisfaction of me?"

"Of course not, my lord, for you have not offended me. If each of us was to choose a champion, and their combat were to decide things, your duty and honor would be acquitted. When my man defeats yours, we will pass unmolested."

"And when he fails?"

Erlestoke opened his hands. "It seems I would have to return to Saporicia."

"Very well." Wightman turned and pointed to a very large man in mail and Hawkride livery. "Trusher, you will be my champion. Byard, you will be his second." He came about full circle and looked at Erlestoke. "An exchange of strokes?"

"Until one man cannot rise? Yes." Erlestoke turned and nodded to Dranae. "Would you mind?"

The large man smiled. "My pleasure to serve."

Dranae slid from his saddle and the men of Hawkride craned their necks back to look up at him. A few of them laughed, but most just got a bit ashen-faced. Erlestoke liked their reactions, but noticed their leader did not seem to make much of Dranae's size.

Borell also dismounted. "Highness, he will need a second."

Erlestoke nodded. "Of course."

The Hawkride champion moved from the pavilion onto a patch of meadow where green tendrils were just beginning to grow up through the winter-bowed gold grass from the season before. He eyed Dranae up and down, then sneered dismissively. Trusher accepted a full helm with only a narrow eye slit, then pulled on gloves. He drew a broadsword that seemed serviceable enough, but had some arcane runes etched the length of the blade.

Wightman smiled. "I trust you do not mind that he wields a magickal blade."

Ah, that explains the lack of fear. "Does he?"

"Yes, this is Temmer reforged. Its pieces were recovered from Fortress Draconis and it was re-created. He is invincible with it."

"I'm certain he is." Given the man's size, which was huge, the prince was pretty certain he'd have triumphed over all of the warriors he'd faced in Hawkride. "Dranae, will that sword be a problem?"

"None, Highness." Dranae pulled on a helmet with a steel cage. "He'll get the first blow since we are the invaders?"

"Yes."

"Understood." Dranae stalked toward his enemy. Grass crunched beneath his feet and slowly rose to hide the evidence of his passing. The only weapon he bore was a stout club, iron bound at the end, which was as thick as Erlestoke's upper arm.

The Hawkride warrior brought his sword up in a salute, then spoke in a loud voice. "I am Sir Fawke Trusher, Champion of Count Wightman, as was my father before me, and his before him. You are an invader, and I vow you shall step no further into my nation."

Dranae bowed toward his foe. "I am Dranae. I have fought at Vilwan, Wruona, Fortress Draconis, and even in Sarengul. I have no grand lineage, and I am not invading Oriosa, but coming to its salvation. You, sir, have the first blow."

Trusher looked about him, from Count Wightman, to the semicircle of Hawkriders backing him. He raised his sword over his head, and said, "May Turic receive you happily."

The sword flashed down in a heavy blow that caught Dranae on the left shoulder. Mail popped and bent, then the sword bit through it. Blood splashed on the blade and began to drip through the mail. The heavy blow had not gone deep enough to shatter bone, but it had carved flesh and muscle, doubtlessly driving rings deep into the wound. More important, it staggered Dranae, making him drop his maul, and drove him to one knee.

But that was as far as it drove him. He gasped and hunched that shoulder forward, but did not fall. While their masks hid much of their expressions, the open-mouthed gaping of the Hawkriders clearly expressed their surprise at Dranae's survival.

Trusher backed off, letting blood drip from the blade to the ground. Dranae got up, then wavered for a moment or two before regaining his balance. Borell appeared and pressed the haft of the maul into his right hand, but didn't steady him. Dranae nodded, then shifted his shoulders gingerly, and croaked, "My turn."

Trusher nodded.

Dranae brought the club back in one hand, then whipped it forward in a cross-body blow that caught the Hawkrider square in the chest. Mail pinged as it broke, and Trusher *oof*ed as the strike lifted him from the ground and dropped him back into the line of his supporters. Several staggered from their feet, and Trusher's helmet popped off. Temmer lay in the grasses at his side, and those who scrambled from beneath him could not revive him.

Byard, a blond man of medium build, scooped Temmer up and drove toward Dranae, who had again returned to his knees. Before he could reach him, however, Borell drew Eye and shielded Dranae. The Hawkrider cut low at his unarmored foe, but Borell turned the stroke with ease. Again Byard attacked, but Borell parried. And when he did riposte, he let the blade skitter off mail, holing the man's tabard, but nothing else.

Erlestoke frowned. "Call your man off."

"No, to the first blood, these two, to decide things."

"That was not our agreement."

"It is now."

"First blood, Borell." Erlestoke saw Nay ride forward. "Your boy's good."

"He is. Others did the heavy work in the forge. Getting him learned in how to use what we made seemed wise."

Oh, and how well he learned.

Byard clearly did not like being thwarted, especially by someone whose mask showed no sign of either nobility or military training. He feinted high, then switched his slash low, but Borell nimbly leaped above the attack. He ducked the return cut, then lunged and pinked Byard in the right knee.

Borell pulled back, having drawn first blood, but Byard lunged and slammed his right fist into Borell's jaw. The youth's head snapped around and his body followed, flopping all loose-jointed to the ground. Byard raised the sword, prepared to finish what Trusher had started.

Thunder clapped.

Byard pitched back and thrashed on the ground as blood fountained from his chest. Temmer spun in a lazy circle and plunged point first into the ground.

Wightman looked at Erlestoke and shrank back. "What did you do?"

"Your man cheated." Erlestoke worked the cocking mechanism on the quadnel. The barrels rotated and a fresh one seated itself, ready to be triggered. "By the way, that's not Temmer. Dranae, do you want to take care of it?"

The man nodded and slowly stood. He plucked the sword from the ground and grabbed it hilt and point. His muscles bunched and more mail pinged as rings parted and flew. As Dranae began to bend the blade, his body shifted and grew larger. While his face and head remained the same, his hands scaled over into talons.

The blade bent, then snapped.

Nay snorted. "Not even tempered well."

Dranae tossed down the pieces of the blade, then knelt by Borell. "He'll be fine, save for the bruise on his jaw."

Wightman's nostrils flared. "This was unfair from the start. I don't know what he is, but he is not a *man*."

"No, but he *is* my champion." Erlestoke rested the quadnel across his thighs. "Now, I could have him change into his true form and your little army would be scattered. I don't think you want that. Nor do you want me marching my army off to Hawkride."

"No, I don't want that."

The prince pointed toward Wightman's mask. "I don't know what my father promised when he gave you the crown, but you don't trust him, and you have no reason to. Regardless, you've lost whatever you thought you were going to get by not being able to stop me. So I have a choice for you."

The count looked up. "What's that?"

"You can return home now, and I will let everyone know that I consider anyone treating with you in any way to be guilty of treason. I will deal with them after I deal with you, and your best hope is that Chytrine kills me, because that's the only thing that will stop me from returning to destroy you."

The slender man shivered. "Or?"

"Or you and your people join my force. You know the Aurolani are here, most in the Midlands and Dales. If I'm defeated, your army isn't going to be enough to stop them. But together we might, and I clearly will have time to revise my opinion of you."

"You'd really let me leave?"

Erlestoke nodded. "You, yes. Your people, no. I need them too much. I suspect that showing them we have a dragon on our side, as well as appealing to their sense of obligation to a nation where we all wear masks because of our shared history, would bring them over to me pretty easily. What do you think?"

Wightman swallowed hard, then drew his sword, knelt, and offered it in Erlestoke's direction. "I think, Highness, I pledge myself to your noble cause, for the sake of Hawkride, Oriosa, and the world."

"The ordering of your priorities needs some work, but we have time for that." Erlestoke raised his voice so it might even carry to some of the sharper ears in the Hawkrider formation. "I accept your fealty, Count Wightman. Your forces married to mine will guarantee victory. To the north and our destiny."

Wightman's close advisors likewise took a knee, and seeing that prompted cheers from both armies. Wightman looked up as the soldiers' voices filled the valley. "What are the chances we survive this?"

Erlestoke shrugged. "Doesn't really matter, does it? We are off to acquit our duty to the world. If we fail, there will be no reason to survive."

CHAPTER 38

Night had fallen and the sense of unease Kerrigan had felt entering Loquellyn had built to where he could not sleep. The trek to that point had been full of paradoxes and false starts, and had proceeded far more slowly than pleased Resolute. He'd wanted to crest the mountains quickly, then move down into the Assariennia River valley and follow it to Rellaence. He assumed they would find transport to the capital there, which would speed their trek along.

But from the start it was apparent even to Kerrigan that any plans Resolute had formulated would not survive contact with the Grey Misters. And Kerrigan had found himself in the unusual position of being far more prepared for a long trek through forest and mountain and marsh than most of the people with him. The trip began with a day's march through fetid swamps, where the party had broken up into smaller groups to camp. Kerrigan had been charged with the duty of moving from place to place, using magick to start fires since the Grey Misters had no inkling of how to do it. He also showed them how to pack moss into boots to ease blisters and a half-dozen other things he'd learned from Lombo and Resolute.

It struck him as paradoxical having these Vorquelves looking at him with astonishment, much as the younger apprentices on Vilwan might regard him. Here they were, all older than he by well over a century, but they were completely out of their element in the countryside. More than one grumbled about the trip. Muscles that ached from rowing had gotten no respite dragging boots free of sucking mud, and the closeness of the mountains did nothing to hint that further travel might get at all easier.

Qwc acted, as he had before, as morale officer for the expedition. He took to finding little things in the forest, from flowers to bones, teeth, claws, and feathers, and bestowed each on a Grey Mister. With great solemnity, he gave each one of them a warrior name like Bite or Scratch or Stab. His vocabulary kept him mainly to short words, packed with as much violence as he could muster, which pleased the Vorquelves no end. But also it focused them on what was coming and they did their best to find extravagant boasts about how they would earn their names.

At night the Spritha shared a tent with Kerrigan. The little creature would stab his spear into the ground, then flop down too exhausted to flutter a wing. "Finding words harder than finding things."

Kerrigan always laughed. "You've not found me my war name, Qwc."

The Spritha would look at him and smile as his eyes slowly closed. "Your name will find you."

As difficult as it had been to get out of Saporicia, things changed for the worse once they entered Loquellyn. Something about the place felt wrong. While the sun would shine during the day, the colors appeared muted. It almost seemed to Kerrigan that spring had not yet come. He saw no buds on trees, no flowers struggling to raise their heads. What new growth he did see were poison ivies that wrapped around trees, or the sort of quickly flowering plants that, in a summer, could come to take over a whole meadow. None of it felt right, and evidence of that kind of invasion increased as they moved deeper into the mountains.

The Grey Misters also continued to be a problem. They lacked discipline and did not take well to Resolute's instructions on how they should comport themselves in camp. Had he had his way, they would have had cold camps, with no fire, and round-the-clock-guards. They would have been silent and blended into the surrounding area, but the Grey Misters had no better chance of doing that than Kerrigan did of breathing at the bottom of the Crescent Sea.

So Resolute took to making a second smaller camp away from the main one. Everyone in his original group took shelter there, with Resolute, Banausic, Bok, and Kerrigan sharing the watches. Kerrigan usually got the dawn watch, letting him sleep uninterrupted—Bok usually got the first watch for the same reason—so the company's two magickers would be well rested if their abilities were ever needed.

But now something brought Kerrigan to full consciousness. He'd not fully fallen asleep, but had just begun to drift into dreams that had grown darker by the minute. He felt as if he were wandering in a cavern so vast and lightless that he could see nothing. When he finally made a light, he discovered he had wandered into the throat of some mighty beast that began to chew him up and swallow.

He sat up and threw off his blankets, then shivered as the cooler night air hit his sweaty flesh. He quickly pulled on some clothes and left Qwc sleeping soundly. Slipping from the tent, he drifted toward the guard station and found Resolute sitting there, his eyes focused into the darkness.

The Vorquelf held a hand up and Kerrigan halted. He looked in the direction Resolute was looking, but he could see nothing. It would have been simple for him to invoke a spell to allow him to see in the dark, but if there was something out there—something working for Chytrine—the chances that it could detect his magick were good.

Kerrigan moved to a small boulder and pressed his stomach to it. He still stared in the direction Resolute had been watching, but nothing registered. Their camp had been built on a small wooded rise, which gave him a view of roughly half the slope. When there was still light he could see a small stream, and at night he could hear it gurgling, but he caught no splashes to indicate anything approaching now.

Then he heard it, off to his right. He raised his left hand to catch Resolute's attention as he pointed with his right toward the sound. Then he heard a second sound and turned to sight down the line of his arm. It had sounded so close, he was certain he could see it.

And see it he did as it leaped onto the rock and lunged, engulfing his right arm to the elbow. Its jaws shut hard, triple rows of needlelike teeth piercing his sleeve, then clacking hard on the dragonbone armor. The creature's dark eyes widened, then it shook its head, trying to shear his arm off. When that failed, hindquarters bunched and the creature jumped back off the rock, yanking Kerrigan from his feet and dragging him off into the woods.

The dragonbone armor saved the mage's stomach from being sliced open by the rock, but did nothing to stop brambles and branches from whipping his face as the creature bore him away. Thorny vines lashed his face and hands, tearing at his clothes. The creature whipped its head again side to side, and Kerrigan's shoulder ground in the socket. His left knee smashed into a tree. He rolled onto his back, increasing the pressure on his shoulder, then rolled back in time for another bramble to slash him above the left eye.

Kerrigan panicked for a second, utterly lost until an absurd awareness somehow broke through. As he was being hauled behind this creature, his belt buckle gouged the earth and scraped it up, filling his trousers. It was undignified. And for Kerrigan, who had always been fastidious and precise on Vilwan, this was an outrage and that eclipsed the pain long enough for him to kill the panic and act.

At one time Kerrigan's spell of choice—his reflexive choice—would have been the telekinesis spell that had served him so very well. Of late, however, there was another spell he had been using so often it had become second nature. Within the wet confines of the creature's maw, his right hand tightened into a fist. His hand opened again, his fingertips tickling the beast's soft palate, and he cast his spell.

With enthusiasm.

For several days he had been doing little but making fires. The gout that erupted from his hand shot straight down the creature's gullet, ejecting a golden flare from its cloaca that burned off its thick tail. The beast's entire body spasmed, giving his arm one last strong jerk, then detached. The creature's mouth remained open, flames guttering from between its teeth.

Kerrigan gathered his feet beneath him and stood, despite the pain in his knee. He jumped up and down twice, letting the dirt fall from his pant legs, then swiped his left sleeve over his forehead. It came away stained with blood. That surprised him, but didn't make his knees quiver as it might once have done.

That was the old Kerrigan. The old, fat, slow, terrified Kerrigan. He worked his right arm up and around in a circle, feeling the rising stiffness, but certain nothing was broken or torn. Back the way he'd come, he heard shouts, screams, and the sounds of fighting from the Grey Mister camp. *No, no more dying. Not if I can help it.*

Since the Aurolani forces had already found his party, Kerrigan knew his use of magick could give nothing away. *And if it could, the roasted beast would have long since done it.* His right hand came up over his face and he invoked a night vision spell. Looking about, he could see shapes and shadows moving. Up at his camp something misshapen and spiky leaped out into a knot of shadows, scattering them. Resolute's silhouette appeared atop the rock, with his hands flicking forward as his urZrethi bladestars spun into the night.

Kerrigan darted left, around the base of the hill, and drove directly toward the Grey Mist camp. The sounds of battle filled the night, killing any chance that the enemy would hear him coming. As he approached he found another of the things that had attacked him. It reminded him somewhat of a gvakra, though the body was more squat, with a thick hide and tail somewhat akin to a reptile. Instead of a mane, it did have a fleshy frill that sprang up around the neck.

The creature spun to face him, but its thick tail smashed into a tree, halting its progress. Kerrigan flicked a finger in the beast's direction, using his telekinesis spell to crush its shallow skull. Its body shook once, savagely, right down to the tip of the tail, then it just lay still. He moved on.

As he went, he thought hard. When he was on Vilwan he'd had virtually no training as a combat mage. His masters, quite rightly, has assumed that he could innocently injure someone just because he was so strong in magick. *And that was before I knew how to tap the true source.* But despite their misgivings, he was not without some combat spells. He further assumed some of the things attacking would also have spells, so he planned accordingly and smiled as he moved.

Approaching the camp, he triggered a spell once used by Neskartu against the mages in Navval. While really little more than a nuisance spell, for magickers it was the rough equivalent of scraping claws over slate, and very loudly. Those few magickers amid the attackers reacted instantly, casting their own counterspells to fend it off. Their efforts instantly identified them, so before he even broke into the circle of battle, he triggered a quick combat spell that sent blue sparks out, each leaping from a splayed fingertip. They traveled before him as if a cloud of ensorcelled midges, then, as he entered the Grey Mist camp at the north end, they shot forward toward their targets.

Chytrine's *kryalniri* had been elegant and sylvan, but these creatures more closely resembled Resolute than they did the slender elves of Loquellyn. These wore fur, as did gibberers, but not the disorganized motley of those Aurolani fighters. These creatures had large dark splotches defined by a crisp webwork of tawny fur that rippled over thick muscles. They did have bestial heads, more canine than anything else, with huge fangs that flashed yellow in dying firelight. Some wore mail, others pieces of plate armor—but more as decoration than protection. They used curved blades, longer than the gibberer longknife, and slashed bloody wounds that spun elves to the ground.

The magick-users among them appeared little different than their brethren, save that they wore no metal and wielded staves and wands. One turned and swatted at the blue spark headed for him, but it burned through his hand and sank into his chest. Another of them snorted the spark. Fire shot from his eyes and ears as his body jerked and he flopped to the ground. The sparks reduced two others to torches, while the last cast a defensive spell. The spark moved about its perimeter, seeking a weakness it could exploit.

The screams and deaths of the mages did not go unnoticed. The Aurolani warriors turned and came at Kerrigan instead. They hurled knives or whatever else was convenient. Many missed him, but those that hit bounced off his armor. For a heartbeat Kerrigan imagined himself just standing there, letting them hew in vain at him, but he knew that if his strength failed, he would be cut down, so he acted.

He thrust his left fist into the air and triggered a spell that created a burst of searingly brilliant light. Creatures and elves alike shrieked and covered their eyes. All the combatants stopped, blinded, which broke the momentum of the enemy attack and gave the Grey Misters a moment to recover.

Kerrigan made good use of the break as well. As he had done at Vael, he cast a diagnostic spell, immediately getting a sense of the creature nearest him. While he had hoped he would understand enough of them as a result to make them all go to sleep, the necessary information eluded him. Instead he learned enough to pinpoint the nerves that registered pain in their bodies. He made a quick reversal on an elven healing spell and cast it.

The first creature hit shrieked. Its back bowed as every muscle clenched, then released. It crashed to the ground and thrashed, while others just fainted in agony. The spell passed through the enemy, convulsing some, rendering others limp, and caused the remaining magicker to lose control of its defensive spell. The spark darted in and punctured its chest, and it fell with smoke trailing from its nostrils.

The Grey Misters pounced on their enemies and began to slaughter them. Kerrigan cast a spell and scattered them from the one closest to him. "I want this one alive. The rest, I don't care."

The Grey Misters slunk away from Kerrigan's prize, then began ripping other creatures apart. Kerrigan would have turned from the bloodbath, but he forced himself to watch. He understood the anger and fury of those who had been attacked. He let himself imagine they were relieving all the feeling that had been pent up for as long as they had been away from Vorquellyn, but that illusion soon faded.

Watching them descend to bestiality, he shivered. *As they are now, I could be, if I let myself go. And with my power, this would be as nothing.*

He shivered again, then gestured and lifted his prisoner away from the carnage.

CHAPTER 39

The look of fury on the prisoner's face surprised Isaura. Pure venom flashed in her blue eyes, and her fingers curled into claws. She did not rise from the wooden bench, even though the chains hanging from her manacles would have allowed it. Scuff marks on the ground gave clear evidence of how far she could get, and Isaura hung back from that line.

She placed the tray of food on a small stone shelf, then raised both her hands to calm the prisoner. "I've brought you food, more than they have been giving you. I know the guards have been stealing from you."

The woman's blue eyes narrowed. "Some sort of game, is this? You starve me, then feed me, and out of gratitude I tell you what I know?"

"No, nothing like that."

The woman's gaze darted toward the doorway as Hlucri shambled in. "Lombo? Oh, by the gods, what have they done to you?"

The *sullanciri* squatted in the doorway and sniffed. "Princess Sayce. Lombo dead."

The woman looked stricken. Her hands slackened and she slumped back against the rough-carved wall of the subterranean prison. "Lombo dead. Will dead. Muroso dead." Then she raised her hands to her face with a rattle of chains, and her body shook with sobs.

Isaura felt her stomach tighten. Never in all her days had she seen another person cry. She had cried, but no one else—neither her mother nor any of the *sullanciri*—had cried in her presence. *And never have I heard such despair in a voice.*

Isaura reached out a hand and would have gone to her, but Hlucri held her back. Sayce's head came up, her eyes sharp, then she snorted. "Why did you stop her?"

The *sullanciri* shrugged. "Hlucri keeps her safe."

"You once did that for me. You were a friend. A friend who would have helped me escape from here."

Isaura stepped back. "Escape? You can't escape from here. You would never make it south again."

"Better to freeze to death than starve here." Sayce rubbed a hand over the soiled stomach of her dress. "I'm pregnant. I need food."

"I know you need food. I know the guards have been stealing it." Isaura turned and got the tray again. "Hlucri told me, so I made sure I was bringing you your food. I didn't know you were pregnant."

Sayce stood, but slowly. "I am. Almost three months. I am carrying Will Norrington's child."

"I see." Isaura extended the tray in her direction. "Will you take this? I promise there is nothing here to harm you. Or the child. The crock has soup. The bread and cheese are good."

The red-haired prisoner took a step forward. Isaura couldn't tell if she intended to lunge for her or not, but Hlucri made the question moot when he took the tray in one paw and extended it to Sayce. The princess took it and set it on her bench, then sat herself.

"There, you've done your good deed. Now you may go."

Isaura looked back at the door. "I wanted to talk to you. Besides, you know I can't leave you that tray and the crock."

Sayce frowned, then took the lid off the crock. A little steam rose from it. She sniffed, then raised the crock in both hands and drank. She half gagged for a moment, then chewed and swallowed. She wiped her chin off on her sleeve and snorted.

"I wasn't expecting meat. Do I want to know what it was?"

"Frostclaw. We eat them sometimes."

"Better than being eaten by them." Sayce broke off a small crust of the bread and started to chew. "What did you want to talk about?"

Isaura clasped her hands together at her waist. "The Norrington."

The princess stiffened. "I don't know that I want to talk about him. That's very private."

"I met him once. I saved his life."

Sayce stared hard at her. "How?"

Hlucri grunted. "Lady Snowflake."

"But how?" Sayce toyed with the pendant at her throat. "Who are you? I saw you waiting for the Nor'witch when I was brought here. Why would you save Will?"

Isaura lifted her chin. "In Aurolan my rank is equal to yours. I am Chytrine's daughter—not by blood, but by choice. I am her heir. I am Isaura."

Sayce raised an eyebrow. "Ah, so you save Will so he can kill your mother and you inherit this frozen wasteland?"

"No, it was nothing like that at all." Isaura tried to sound casual, but knew the shock had to have registered on her face. "I saved Will because he had been attacked by one of my mother's creatures. I know she did not intend that to happen—at least, I believed so at the time. Now, I don't know, but it doesn't matter because I saved him."

"So you were cleaning up after your mother's monster?" Sayce tore another hunk off the crust of bread and folded it around a piece of cheese. "I don't believe that. There had to have been another reason."

Isaura hesitated. The prisoner was right. She had cast herself and her path onto the flow of magick and had gone wherever it drew her. She found herself looking at a dying youth, and she would have cured him regardless. The fact that a *sullanciri* had hurt him did spark in her a desire to correct that error, but it hadn't been the only reason she had done it.

"I do not know *why* I did what I did." She faltered for a moment, then forged ahead more quietly. "I would do it again."

"Why?"

"It was the right thing to do."

Sayce laughed, then nibbled at the bread and cheese. "Saving your mother's mortal enemy was the right thing to do? Your mother was my family's mortal enemy, and I would have killed her in an eyeblink. I would have let her die the way Will was dying and been happy to have it happen."

"No, you don't know her. She's not evil."

"No?" The Murosan princess drank more soup, then chewed more meat. "Your mother has plunged the world into war. She has dragons that are burning cities to the ground. Her troops slaughter thousands as they pour into cities."

Isaura's eyes widened. "I was at Porjal. I saw what the people of the city did to attack *grichothka*. They set traps that would maim and cause pain. They did that so the screams of the wounded would cause fear, and because a wounded person requires care. They were cruel by intent!"

"Because Aurolani troops invaded their homes, killed their families, and took away everything, including their hopes and dreams." Sayce's eyes blazed from within her lavender mask. "You have to ask yourself why they did that. Did we have a piece of the DragonCrown in Muroso? Did your mother ask if we did, if we would turn it over to her? No, her ravening hordes came with the worst winter ever, blowing through Sebcia and plunging straight into Muroso. For no reason at all."

The woman's vehemence shocked Isaura. "The south is a threat to Aurolan. The south invaded a quarter century ago."

"Yes, after your mother laid siege to Fortress Draconis. But Aurolani forces invaded Noriva and Vorquellyn without any provocation."

"The south is corrupt." Isaura spoke quickly, but even before Sayce's laughter could reach her, those words sounded hollow. Her mother had told her how the south was corrupt, and she had seen it. The waste, the filth of their cities, those things disgusted her when compared to the austere purity of Aurolan. The south was just a rotting cesspit by comparison.

But I did hear laughter there. Rich laughter, from a variety of people. She'd heard it in the tavern where she healed Will, heard it in the streets, heard it in shadows and in the light. It sounded full and warm, much as Sayce's laughter did. That Sayce could laugh while so far from home, in such dire straits, surprised Isaura.

Sayce swiped at a tear that dripped from beneath her mask. "That was funny, the south being corrupt, especially coming from Chytrine's heir. I don't mean to laugh *at* you, but, if you believe that . . . you've led a very sheltered life, haven't you?"

Isaura frowned. "You are making fun of me."

"I am, but don't go. I'm sorry." Sayce returned to her food and finished the soup quickly. "I just want you to understand that, because of your mother, my nation no longer exists. My father and mother, my brothers and sisters, nephews, nieces, and cousins are all dead. I have no family at all, save the child I am carrying, because of your mother or her agents. Your mother has taken from me everything but the will to live, and she'd take that if she knew how."

"That's not true."

Sayce looked up at her. "Does your mother know you are here?"

"No, but this is something with which she should not be bothered. She has more important things to do."

Sayce looked at Hlucri. "You only told Isaura about how my food was being stolen?"

The *sullanciri* shrugged. "Best done that way."

The Murosan looked back at Isaura. "Why did you want to talk to me? Really?"

Isaura looked down at her hands. "I saw many things in the south. Things that made me feel odd. I love my mother, but things being done in her name were horrible. I don't know. I am confused. I know she is good. She loves me and her people, but I don't understand any of this."

Even as she uttered those words, the place her mother had taken her to came back. The Oromise were pushing her mother to do what she was doing. Her mother had told her of the dragons and how they betrayed the Oromise, but her mother had told her many other things that her time in the south seemed to contradict. None of it made sense.

Sayce's lips pressed into a grim line. "You're not the only one who doesn't understand. Have you lost friends in the war?"

Isaura remembered the *kryalniri* Tribulation. "One. I do not have many friends here. They hate me, like you do, or fear me."

Sayce smiled. "I know fear and hatred. My father was king, so people sought me out to win favor or power, or they slunk away from me, afraid. I was not a person to them, but an object. I was a means to power or a way to direct it. At least, I was until Will. He didn't see me that way. He just saw me as a regular person, and he even risked his life to save me."

The Murosan nodded. "And you saved him before that, so if not for you, I'd not be here. My child would not be here. I guess I owe you for more than the soup."

Isaura shook her head. "I did not save Will for you or your child."

"But the food."

"Well, yes." Isaura smiled as she saw genuine gratitude blossom in Sayce's eyes. "I will make sure your food is good. For you. For the baby."

"You will come, too." Sayce's shoulders slumped a little. "I've used up all my curses on the gibberers that brought me food. They're not much for conversation anyway."

Isaura nodded. "I know. I will return. Often, if I can."

"Will you bring me news of the war?"

"I seldom know any."

"If you do learn anything, I want to know." Sayce removed the bread and cheese from the tray and set it on her bench. She handed the tray to Hlucri. "This is for later."

"Of course."

"Isaura."

"Yes?"

"You know I will try to escape. I would use you as a hostage if I had to." Sayce kept her voice even. "It is nothing against you, but I cannot have my child born here. I won't let that happen."

Chytrine's daughter nodded. "You know I won't help you escape."

"But will you stop me?"

Isaura hesitated again. "Only to save your life."

"Not the answer I wanted, but it will have to do." The Murosan princess leaned back against the wall again. "I would like a bath and clean clothes. Can we do that?"

"Will you give me your word you won't try to escape during the bath if I arrange it?"

Sayce thought for a moment, then nodded. "You have my word of honor."

"I believe you." Isaura accepted the tray from Hlucri, then turned toward the door. "Fare well, Sayce. I look forward to talking to you again."

"You know where to find me."

"I do, and I shall."

CHAPTER 40

As the fog lifted on the battlefield, Alexia decided she did not like what she saw. She'd already known that the Aurolani forces would have the high ground, as they had reached the battlefield a day before Alexia's troops. The broad plain on which they would fight sloped gently up toward the northeast, and was split by the road running from Bacirro to Fronosa. The ground at the base of the slope was marshy, which would mean her troops would be slow to move forward and that all the Aurolani had to do was wait until they were just reaching steadier footing, then launch a devastating charge.

She would have cursed the delay that hadn't let her get further away from Bacirro to choose the battlefield she would have preferred, but it would have been to no avail. General Pandiculia had been scheduled to arrive in Bacirro by the nineteenth of the month, and it was already the twenty-second when Alexia realized she could wait no longer. She'd had the Alcidese Queen's Light Horse unit out scouting and harassing the Aurolani horde, but all they could really do was kill scouting units. When Tythsai's troops reached the plains, they stopped their advance and the Light Horse reported back their number and disposition.

But there were things they could not have known. The scouts said the Aurolani forces were the usual mix of gibberers, vylaens, hoargoun, with a scattering of renegade men and *kryalniri*. They didn't see any dragonels, but there were plenty of supply wagons filled with firedirt, so she had to assume the weapons themselves were on their way. The Aurolani forces numbered roughly six thousand, with one quarter being cavalry. Their numbers gave her forces a two-to-one advantage, which would have all but guaranteed victory save for two factors.

One was the terrain. The other was the presence of two battalions of draconetteers. They used small dragonels that shot a grape-sized ball. At close range it could penetrate armor, and even if it couldn't, the force might be enough to knock a warrior down. While draconetteers could not shoot as fast or as accurately as an archer, neither did they take a lot of training to produce.

Alexia further suspected that the presence of draconetteers was not sufficient to explain the need for so much firedirt. She believed that somewhere just beyond the crest of the hill, the Aurolani had set up several batteries of skycasters—short, squat weapons that used a charge of firedirt to loft a missile in a high arc. The missile was itself packed with more firedirt and fused, so it would explode in the air above the battlefield. The resulting spray of iron shrapnel could shred flesh and destroy many a unit.

The Aurolani had arrayed themselves simply. A pair of cavalry battalions formed each wing, with one battalion drawn back in reserve. Similarly three battalions of infantry were held back. A regiment of heavy infantry, including one battalion of draconetteers, occupied the center, while the other two lighter regiments overlapped the center and the two wings. The lighter regiments had a gap between them, which is where Alexia assumed the skycasters would be located. Once the fog had burned off, she would have a Gyrkyme scout confirm her suspicions.

She carefully arrayed her troops. Two regiments, one behind the other, made up her center. On each wing she placed one regiment of heavy infantry. Behind the heavy infantry each side got two battalions of heavy cavalry. Then, on the extreme right, she stacked three battalions of light cavalry. In reserve she kept some heavy cavalry, and roughly half of her infantry. That infantry was largely made up of mercenaries and untested volunteers, whom she did not want to rely on until she had seen how they would fight.

She tried to project herself into the mind of her enemy, but that enemy was an undead *sullanciri*, which made the task very difficult. But while the Aurolani had the superior tactical position, the sheer press of numbers should be enough to drive them back and break them. It would be a victory won with a lot of blood, but it would be a victory nonetheless.

Losing is less of a problem for the Aurolani, since all they really need do is bleed us. The Aurolani hordes seemed able to withstand incredible losses. Alyx supposed it could be all bluff on Chytrine's part to demoralize the south, but to keep coming after having an army wiped out in Muroso was something the south never would have done. The Aurolani just kept pushing, and Alexia could not shake the idea that she was being trapped.

The battle also wasn't arrayed exactly as she had said it would be in her supposed dream, but it was close enough to cause her to wonder what Chytrine was thinking. Getting into her head, however, was even more difficult than understanding Tythsai. From Alexia's perspective, however, the proposition was simple. If she thrust her forces forward, both skycaster assaults and draconetteers would weaken her formation enough that Aurolani cavalry would punch through, and her infantry would then slaughter whoever was left.

That meant her strategy was pretty clear: she could not advance her troops the way the Aurolani hoped she would.

Alexia, wearing golden mail girded at the waist with her sword belt and bearing the sword Heart, mounted her horse. She rode toward the east and the rising sun, to the point where the light cavalry waited. She reined up at the rear of that formation, then nodded to a signalman. He blew an alert, then the battalion designators, followed by an advance. He repeated the series of notes, and other buglers in the force relayed them throughout.

Because she could not send her infantry forward, she had to entice the Aurolani to come to her. The only real advantage she had over the Nor'witch's troops was that her troops had discipline. They would not break, run, or act without orders. Everyone had been told what the plan was, so they knew their part and were willing to play it. That was especially true if it would keep them out of range of the skycasters.

The light cavalry, led by the Alcidese Queen's Light Horse, raced out and around on an arc from east to north. They splashed through the wet turf quickly enough, then headed up the incline toward the Aurolani left wing. The young sun shone brightly from polished helms. Tabards and pennants of red, green, and white flapped and snapped, and the three battalions raced forward in good order.

The Aurolani cavalry unit toward which they headed had only six hundred members. It began to shift so the warriors could countercharge. The riders—gibberers mostly, with a few *kryalniri* and more human renegades—kept their frostclaw mounts under control with difficulty. The feathered beasts snapped tooth-filled jaws at the oncoming horsemen, and their huge, sickle-shaped claws twitched in anticipation of rending flesh.

Alexia's troops knew the effective range of a frostclaw charge was not much more than a hundred yards. While the creatures could cross that distance in an amazingly short time, their nature as pack hunters didn't give them a lot of endurance. Normally another frostclaw would pick up the chase where the last abandoned it and, if allowed to lope, any one of them could chase prey forever. At the end of the charge, however, their strength would begin to flag, and they would begin to look for easier prey.

The Alcidese horsemen reached that range and began to wheel northeast, presenting their flank to the Aurolani troops. The soldiers loosed a flight of arrows from their short horse bows. The arrows flew in a high arc and landed mostly on target. The shots were not aimed, but many found flesh or bounced off armor. A few Aurolani fell, and more than one frostclaw bit at an arrow in its side, but the volley had done little more than harass.

Then the Jeranese Royal Cavalry executed the same maneuver and hit more of the cavalry with arrows. Behind the enemy lines drums boomed and banners shifted. Alexia found it easy to imagine the skycasters getting adjusted to cover the left flank. As the Jeranese horsemen completed the curl and headed back around to their lines, the Aurolani cavalry broke into a charge, but without organization. Some frostclaws started, others followed, with six hundred of them coming in waves.

The third light cavalry unit in her charge slowed as the Aurolani charged. Unlike the other two units, the Murosan First Vengeance were not armed with horse bows. They possessed crossbows and released a volley that flew in virtually a flat arc, well aimed. It scythed through the first wave of Aurolani cavalry.

Frostclaws shrieked furiously as the steel-headed quarrels slammed into them or pitched their riders from the saddle. Some warriors found themselves dragged behind their mounts, while others, less fortunate, had their mounts turn on them, gnawing themselves free of their burden. Those frostclaws that went down spilled their riders to the ground. Other frostclaws leaped over the dead and dying and kept coming, but more common were collisions between a charging beast and one thrashing in the throes of agony.

A bugle blew near Alexia, which brought the Alcidese and Jeranese units around to the east again, reversing their retreat. They moved a bit wider, so the Aurolani charge would pass between them and their own lines. They raked the Aurolani with another volley, then each archer began to pick targets. Again the shots killed few but pricked many, and drove the near flank to turn toward the center of the battlefield, causing more confusion.

The Aurolani lead element did hit the Murosan light cavalry and blasted into it hard. Horses reared and toppled, entrails spraying out from slashed bellies. Swords flashed silver one moment, then rose red. Blood sprayed from severed limbs, and men clutched at cloven faces or at the lances that had pierced their bellies. Frostclaws bit horses across the muzzle, crushing their skulls, though occasionally a steel-shod hoof dented a temeryx pate.

The bugle that had signaled the light cavalry to turn also triggered other activity on Alexia's line. Both light infantry regiments that formed her center began to withdraw, with the front ranks turning and running away, back through their own lines. From her vantage point she could see them reach the back of their own formation and regroup, but to Aurolani eyes—and especially those of the frostclaws—her troops were running.

The frostclaws that had turned toward the center read nothing but prey behavior in the retreat, so they sprinted toward the opening. Mud and tufts of grass splashed up, soiling their white feathers. The soft ground slowed their charge, but it mattered little. The riders could not control their mounts, and their mounts wanted prey.

The infantry retreat, however, opened a gap that allowed a pair of heavy cavalry battalions—the Alcidese Iron Horse—to charge into the center. As the frostclaws left the swampy part of the battlefield, the heavy cavalry, with armored knights hunched behind stout lances and thick shields, slammed into their line straight on.

Frostclaws flew, with bloody feathers drifting down to mark their flights. Lances transfixed the creatures and were abandoned. Swords came to hand, hewing and chopping. One valiant Aurolani warrior raised his unit's standard to rally his comrades, but two Alcidese Iron Horse cut him down and brought the nine-skull banner back with them to great shouts from the rest of her army.

The Iron Horse continued their charge and screened the Murosans, letting them retreat. Some of the draconetteers in the Aurolani center shot, but at that range their attacks were little more effective than the long bowshots by the light cavalry. Alexia's light infantry surged forward in the wake of the charge, finishing off what was left of the Aurolani cavalry. Off to the right, the light cavalry reformed forward of the swamp line, ready to play the harassment game once more, while the Iron Horse trotted back around to take their position again.

After less than an hour of battle, the Aurolani had lost one cavalry wing, she'd lost less than five percent of her cavalry, and the skycasters had not been used at all. Because of their lack of discipline, the Aurolani troops had literally been decimated.

Alyx nodded to the bugler, who blew a holding order. The waiting began. Tythsai could clearly see that Alexia was not going to advance and fall into her trap. The skycasters would have been effective against slow-moving troops, but not cavalry—not unless the battlefield was arranged such that a charge had to be channeled into a killing zone where the skycasters could be preaimed and ready to go. Alexia's study of Saporicia indicated there were only a couple of places where that sort of thing was possible—the closest one being the pass at Fronosa.

If Tythsai advanced, she risked having her troops mauled by Alexia's. The southern force had more people, and they were better disciplined. Alexia had enough troops that she could entirely envelop the Aurolani formation. Such an overwhelming victory would be expensive in terms of casualties, since no quarter would be asked or given. It would also risk the capture of the skycasters and regardless of what happened with dragonels in Okrannel, Alexia was pretty certain the *sullanciri* did not want to lose those weapons.

The sound of drums on the other side shifted and the light infantry divisions began to move back. Alexia looked at her bugler. "Call our cavalry back, please."

He did as she bid him, and her light cavalry retreated through the marshes. The Murosans quitted the field last and the army cheered them mightily. The battle might be being fought in Saporicia, but everyone in the force felt the Murosans deserved to draw blood, and were happy they had.

They'd also left people on the battlefield. Those bodies would be recovered, life masks would be carefully borne away, friends would be mourned, then the warriors would prepare to march out to the next battlefield.

Alexia rode back toward the center and her pavilion. Arimtara took the reins of her horse as she dismounted. The dragon studied her for a moment, then half lidded her eyes.

"You could have let me become my true self and incinerate great chunks of that force."

"I could have, but I didn't."

"Why not?"

Alexia pointed to the troops arrayed in the field. "Two reasons. The first is that I want to use you to the best advantage, and that will come later. I don't know when, but you have the ability to turn the tide of a battle. Moreover, you can oppose a dragon, and I don't want Chytrine to send one against us too early. I want you to surprise her.

"The primary reason, however, is because the army needs to feel unified. This was not much of a battle, but everyone did what they were supposed to do. They all felt the fear, they all feel the exaltation of victory, and they all have lost friends. If you had destroyed that host, it would not have been *their* victory, it would have been yours, and they'd not be coming together the way I will need them to if we are to win in the final battle."

Arimtara nodded, then cocked her head to the side. "You were clever enough to plan a battle that cost them cavalry. Could you not have planned further and cost them more?"

"Possibly, but it would have cost me heavily." The princess looked across the battlefield toward where Tythsai's banner was shrinking away. "Right now she is thinking that I am tricky and a coward, since nothing I did here had the scent of boldness. I could have had the light cavalry go after her flanks again and again, but I was content to let her retreat. She will always expect that I will let her disengage, which is good, because the one time I don't, the one time I press forward, this army will be through her force faster than grass through a goose. If I'm going to destroy that army, I need its leader thinking I'll never do anything of the kind. Once she is convinced of that, we'll kill her again."

CHAPTER 41

Resolute raised a hand to stop the others behind him. He slowly crouched on the woodland trail and peered through the woods. The Grey Misters who had joined him might well have been quiet enough to sneak around Yslin, but in the forests of Loquellyn they made as much noise as a herd of cattle—complete, in some cases, with lowing complaints about thirst or blisters. A few even sported wounds from the engagement with Aurolani troops several nights back, but those Vorquelves tended toward stoicism and remained quieter than their brethren.

Resolute turned his head slightly to the left and saw Qwc perched on his shoulder, his spear at the ready. The argent-eyed warrior pointed off north-northeast, then nodded, and the Spritha took flight. He darted between trees with the angular precision of a dragonfly in flight.

He returned quickly and flashed enough fingers to communicate the fact that nearly a score of individuals waited in the brush. Resolute nodded his understanding, but the Spritha did not stop. With his spear held in his lower two hands, the upper pair pantomimed settling a

crown on his head. Resolute raised an eyebrow, Qwc nodded enthusiastically, and the Vorquelf actually managed a
smile.

He stood and cupped his hands around his mouth.
"Trawyn, Princess of Loquellyn, you need hide no more.
Those who were hunting you are dead."

His call got no response, but he'd not expected one. "We
have met, Highness, when you welcomed a Gyrkyme into
the palace at Rellaence, not yet a year past." Resolute tried
to use his best Elvish to speak to her, but among the
Vorquelves eloquence had eroded. He dimly recalled a time
when he liked weaving words into patterns and formal se-
quences, but much blood had run between that time and
this.

Resolute started down through the trees in the direction Qwc had flown. "I am coming to you. You will see me
before I see you, and you may decide what to do then."

As he moved down the needle-and-leaf-strewn slope,
he sought signs of the elves' passage. He thought he would
see wet leaves showing from beneath a layer of dry, or a
plant stem crushed underfoot. He even watched for threads
caught on thorns, but until she stepped from the brush before him, and two archers with nocked and drawn arrows
flanked him, he'd seen nothing.

"You're Resolute, but you could be one of *her* creatures."

Trawyn was not as he remembered her. Her auburn hair
had been long and flowing free, but now it was hacked off
to less than a finger length. Her left eye was still a pure blue,
but a bloody rag hid the other socket. In Rellaence she had
worn gowns, but here her clothes were more the castoffs
peasants would give to beggars. Dirt and blood smudged
her cheeks and hands, and her one eye had a dark circle beneath it.

Resolute instantly dropped to a knee. "I am Resolute,
and I would never in life become one of her creatures."

Trawyn raised a hand, then lowered it, and the archers

relaxed their pull on the arrows but did not take their hands from the bowstrings. "You said the things chasing us are dead?"

"Oversize gibberers and some lizard-dogs?" Resolute shifted to Mantongue as Qwc lighted on his shoulder. "They ambushed us several nights ago. They got more than they bargained for."

The elven princess shook her head. "Are you arrogant, Vorquelf, or do you seek to scourge me with the fact that you, a child, have fared better than we have?"

The pain in her voice, along with the wearied accusation, indicated how close to the breaking point she was. Another time he might have risen to the bait, but he refrained. "I referred to Kerrigan, not myself. Bring your group, join with us, and tell me what has happened. We've been sent here to Loquellyn to see if you will help oppose Chytrine. I'll assume you'll decline, and I would like to know why."

Trawyn's party numbered seventeen. All of them were wounded, and two very seriously. In their flight from the capital, they had trekked up the Assariennia River. Pursuit was relentless, and intensified when they got into the mountains. Her people had been days without anything beyond winterberries picked in haste and water drunk by the handful, whether fresh or stagnant.

Resolute led the group back to the Grey Mist camp, where the healers, including Kerrigan, set about doing what they could. The human mage took a look at Trawyn's right eye and cast some spells, but could do nothing more than shake his head. "I would heal it if I could, Princess, but there is nothing there to heal."

She nodded. "One of the *turekadine* gouged it out, and I was obliged to slice the eye off the stalk because its hanging on my cheek distracted me."

Resolute authorized the building of fires, which the

surviving Grey Misters took to gladly. Water was hauled and set to boiling, first for tea, then to turn roots, berries, and dried meat in a soup the refugees could consume without gagging. The Vorquelf set out pickets in pairs, and the Grey Misters took that duty very seriously. Those who did not have immediate watch spoke with the princess's party and learned all they could about the events in Loquellyn.

Trawyn huddled beneath a blanket as night began to fall. The fire crackling before her danced shadows over her face. She cupped a bowl of broth in her hands, but stared past it into the flames. "They came without warning, Resolute. It wasn't the way they'd come for Vorquellyn. They didn't have that number of ships, and our fleet stood ready to oppose them. No, they came stealthily, and were among us before we really had any chance of opposing them."

A shiver ran down Resolute's spine as she spoke. Part of it was from the returning memories of when his home was overrun by the Aurolani. Snatches of mayhem backlit by fires, bloody faces, pieces of limbs, screams that ended abruptly—all of those came to him. They tried to overwhelm him, but could not, because for every Vorquelven scream, he had torn dozens from the throats of gibberers. For every hacked limb, he had harvested legions. What the Aurolani had done to Vorquelves in a handful of nights, he had avenged over a century.

What truly wormed its way into him was the despair in her voice. She was far older than he, and bound to a homeland, but she sounded so lost and distant. He'd heard such tones in the voices of men, but never in one of his elders. He'd come to think such hopelessness was the province of the short-lived. Hearing it in her voice unsettled him, disrupting what he had thought was a fundamental truth. That an immortal could despair made him question whether or not he would prevail in his quest to free his homeland.

Trawyn's eye half shut and her shoulders hunched forward. "They took our ships first. I did not see it, but one of our number had been a sailor. He survived the destruction of his ship only to die on the run. He said a great hole in the ocean opened up, and his ship was drawn into a maw studded with teeth. The beast crushed the ship, and he would have been swallowed but somehow he was expelled through the gill slits and made it to the surface.

"Those same beasts, or some just like them, then came into harbors throughout Loquellyn. They beached themselves, smashing quays and ships. They opened their mouths and from them rushed *nyressanii*—in Mantongue you'd likely call them demon-frogs or fright-toads. They had slick, leathery flesh, mostly black but decorated with stripes of brilliant red, green, and yellow. The slime on them burned if you touched them. Their webbed hands and feet had claws, and they were capable of prodigious leaps. For all that, though, they were able to move quietly and quickly into the cities, slaying guards."

She slowly shook her head. "After that came torpid old ships—creaky barges, nothing more, loaded with *turekadine* and their little hunting beasts, the *slurriki*. They brought the slaughter you saw on Vorquellyn. You've fought them; you know they are bigger and stronger than gibberers. We fought back as valiantly as we could, but the *nyressanii* had slain many warriors."

Kerrigan sank to his knees near the fire and held his hands out toward it to warm them. "So Loquellyn has fallen as Vorquellyn did?"

"No." Trawyn blinked and looked at the human mage. "I remember the adults from Vorquellyn and the pain they were in when their nation was conquered. We did all we could for them, even giving them tinctures of dreamwing, but it did nothing. The Aurolani did not come to conquer Loquellyn. Their troops have already withdrawn in some cases—into Muroso by the coast roads."

Resolute nodded. "They came for the DragonCrown fragment we left with you. Did they get it?"

Trawyn shook her head. "No."

"Where is it?"

"I don't know."

"I don't believe you. Highness."

She snorted. "Good of you to add my title. It softens the fact that you say I am lying."

"Tell me what you know. It is still in Loquellyn?"

Trawyn shrugged—which clearly had taken much effort. "We had stored the sapphire fragment in the palace vaults. It was as secure a place as we could find."

Resolute arched an eyebrow. "The Rellaence *coriiesci* would have kept all away from it."

"All but those bound to Loquellyn." She bared her teeth in a feral manner. "We could not have been certain that someone might not have been compelled or induced to enter the *coriiesci*. Aside from that, having a fragment stored there would have been disruptive. The *coriiesci* is a place for peaceful reflection and isolation from the outside world. Ensconcing the fragment there would have destroyed the peace, so we put it in the palace vault."

The princess' voice softened. "They had captured my mother and my sister. I watched the Aurolani begin to torture them. I listened to their screams and I could stand it no longer. I led the Aurolani to the vaults and opened them. I saw the fragment was no longer there. This is when they began to assault me, out of fury and anger. I passed out, and when I recovered, I was alone, with dead *turekadine* surrounding me. I made my way from the palace, found others and fled, only to find ourselves hunted."

Kerrigan frowned. "So the fragment is still out there?"

"I do not know."

The Vilwanese mage looked at Resolute. "If the Aurolani are hunting it, we need to get it first."

Resolute shook his head. "No, we don't. Our mission is clear. We're heading north, to the coast, and from there we ship to Vorquellyn."

"But we can't let Chytrine get another fragment of the crown."

"The Norrington Prophecy says nothing about the Crown, Kerrigan. We have to get Will, go north, and kill the Nor'witch."

Kerrigan glanced back toward another fire. "Um, might you want to consult Oracle on this?"

"No."

"No?"

Resolute sighed. "You know that if this is something we need to address, she will tell us. We needn't ask her."

"At least let me cast my search spell for it." Kerrigan began to smile, which was something Resolute had not seen since the night their camp had been attacked. "I have worked on the spell. It's faster, more subtle, and can't be detected without a lot of work. At least we'll know where it is. If they're hunting it, we might want to skirt that area."

Kerrigan's logic was inescapable, but clearly the youth realized that Resolute didn't want Chytrine to get another fragment. *If I know where it is, we will have to rescue it.* He wanted to refuse Kerrigan's request, but he also didn't want to be stumbling into a knot of *turekadine* either. A little voice inside his head even asked if perhaps the fragment would be a key to freeing Will. While he tried to dismiss that idea, the possibility started another shiver down his spine.

"Yes, Kerrigan, cast your spell, but be careful. You don't want Chytrine's creations tracking us here because of it."

Kerrigan's smile shrank. "I *am* careful, you know. I wouldn't let that happen."

"I know that, Kerrigan. I beg your pardon. Please, employ your spell." Resolute looked at Trawyn as Kerrigan began his casting. "You'd best eat, Highness. In the morning I'll detach some of my people to take your party south to Saporicia. You can tell Princess Alexia what happened here. She'll need to know this flank is not secure, and that more

Aurolani troops—different troops—will be joining the battles."

Trawyn set the soup bowl down. "Some of my people will carry that message, but I'm not going back. I will be going with you."

"You can't. You're wounded."

She fixed him with a single blue-eyed stare that he could almost feel lance through him. "What if someone did manage to hide the fragment in the *coriiesci?* You'll need me, if not for that, to lead you north."

Resolute sighed. He'd hoped to be paring his numbers down, easing the burden of finding food, for quick movement, and just for the sake of cutting down on chaos. As with Kerrigan's point, however, her arguments could not be dismissed.

He scrubbed a hand over his face. "Your noncombatants go."

"Along with your worst wounded?" She gave him a half smile. "If there are more than fifty of us, it will be difficult to pass unnoticed."

Resolute smiled, as her thoughts clearly paralleled his own. The Aurolani had killed and wounded a third of his Grey Misters. He could easily send almost half his group back, including both his and Trawyn's worst wounded, and get down to half a legion. Those who remained would be the ones who were best suited to the sort of dangers they would face.

"Fifty is good. Send away seven of yours."

"It shall be done."

"Got it!" Kerrigan smiled broadly. "That worked better than I imagined." He started to point northwest, roughly in Rellaence's direction. "Wait, that's odd."

Resolute frowned. "What is, Kerrigan?"

Confusion clouded the young man's face. "What do you know about a DragonCrown fragment that has a diamond in it?"

Oracle laid a hand on Resolute's shoulder and knelt by

the fire. "That is the fragment we had in Vorquellyn. I saw it long ago, before the conquest."

"That is interesting." Kerrigan shook his head. "You know the one we took from Vionna? The one that came from Lakaslin?"

"I remember it very well, Kerrigan."

"Good. It's off in that direction, the one I pointed to."

"What does the Vorquellyn fragment have to do with it?"

"Well, that's the thing." Kerrigan shrugged. "The two of them, they're traveling together. Whoever took the Lakaslin fragment from the palace already had the Vorquellyn one. If Chytrine finds one, she finds them both. They're not exactly on our line of march, Resolute, but . . ."

The Vorquelf nodded. "Don't worry, Kerrigan. They are now."

CHAPTER 42

The week-and-a-half journey to the Noriva capital of Logbal went far better than Adrogans would have expected. The original strategy of skipping some towns while taking over others, as they had done in Nowhere, underwent a certain amount of modification as the troops moved forward. Adrogans used his cavalry to range faster and deeper and let it secure small towns and crossroads settlements in Caro's name. The infantry, which moved more slowly, consolidated the gains and accepted the surrender of the larger towns—none of which was very big at all.

And the toing-and-froing of his troops meant that the supply train with the dragonels could pass unnoticed through the countryside. The conquests were accomplished with very little violence, and not much alarm had been raised. Some individuals, like bards and tradesmen, were allowed into towns further along the line of march, both to spread Caro's story and news of how benign the raiders were. Moreover, the story they told—if it got to Aurolani ears—would be pleasant news indeed.

Caro's story was a welcome one in Noriva. He let people

know that Adrogans had, in fact, captured dragonels in Svarskya and decided to create his own empire. Caro had escaped with some loyal followers and headed north into Noriva because Adrogans was bound south to go after Valicia and Gurol. The people of Noriva did not want dragonels blasting their towns and, better yet, the absence of Adrogans meant that the Aurolani were not likely to head west to fight with them in their domain.

Adrogans did not concern himself with what might happen if those rumors made it out of the Ghost March and back to the crowns. Most would assume it was Aurolani disinformation designed to cause a panic and would ignore it. Those who did believe would raise more troops, which would be a good thing in case Chytrine did prove victorious. For the most part he expected the south would never hear the rumors, and that worked very well for him.

When the troops reached Logbal, Caro rode at the head of a thousand horsemen made up of the Alcidese Horse Guards, Matrave's Horse, the Jeranese Queen's Guards, and the Savarese Knights. All were very well disguised, with not a scrap of original uniform to be seen—though most buried some part of it beneath layers of other clothes. They looked very much like a horde of freebooters, and while they maintained a certain amount of discipline concerning maneuvers, their manners and comportment of speech had lost all traces of civilized company.

Adrogans, with a patch over one eye, his head shaved, a beard newly grown, and in the attire of a Zhusk shaman, trailed Caro with Phfas beside him. A squad of horsemen had approached Logbal under a flag of truce and presented demands to speak with Queen Winalia: "For the price of an audience, he shall return to her what is hers and offer her what she does not possess."

It took a while for that message to get communicated, giving Adrogans time to study the city close up. Logbal—as its name implied—consisted mostly of log construction, though there were some of the larger buildings and a few defensive towers that had been built of stone and mortar. Most of the people lived in longhouses that lay on terraces over the five hills that resided within the ribbon of wooden walls surrounding the capital. Trenching and revetments had been dug and built such that getting siege machinery like a ram close enough would be a slow and deadly process. While the main road came in from the west, the gate it led to faced south. A ram would have to snake around south, west, and then north to hammer it, all the while subjected to raking shots from trebuchets and cadres of archers.

Dragonels would not have been so hampered. They could have just pounded the walls themselves until they disintegrated into a pile of splinters. Because Caro's horde had no siege machinery, the citizens of Logbal had to feel secure, but having had the western towns taken, and the loss of tax revenue that resulted from their conquest, meant their city could not sustain itself.

After an hour, an envoy from the queen appeared at the gate. Caro and his senior advisors were welcomed into the city, and a party of citizens was sent out to act as hostages while the talks took place. Crown Princess Tisdessa was among the hostages, so Adrogans assumed the queen was not planning any treachery.

Phfas studied the princess as they rode past, then snorted. "A fine woman. The Nowhere man should have welcomed her."

Adrogans smiled in spite of himself. "Dalanous was not much bigger than you, Uncle. Legs like hers, she would have snapped his spine in the throes of passion."

Phfas looked again, then shrugged. "The warriors she would breed are worth the risk."

Logbal's main road had long since been churned into a thick mud, and was distinguished from the other roads only by the amount of gravel in the mud. People lined the streets, peered out from doorways, or stood on roofs to watch them ride past. Many did wear clothing made of skins, but none had the quiet dignity of the Zhusk. The general lack of color amid the people's clothes and their homes combined with the ubiquitous streaking of mud over buildings, animals, and especially children. It reminded Adrogans of the most squalid of slums in Yslin or Lakaslin, yet the people here seemed more bovine than their feral urban cousins.

Similarly, the building that passed for a palace in Logbal mocked its counterpart in other capitals. It possessed a delightful stone façade that even extended back a dozen feet on each side. From that point on, however, it was a log longhouse with a thickly thatched roof. They dismounted and entered through a pair of tall wooden doors that admitted them to a cold stone foyer. The rest of the building's floor had been paved with stone, but they were not joined with mortar as they were at the entrance. Straw had been strewn over the stones, though thinly enough that Adrogans could not tell if the distribution was by accident or just stingy.

At the far end of the longhouse—all but hidden in the smoky gloom, Queen Winalia sat in a throne that dwarfed her. Adrogans reflected, as they approached, that the chair had to be huge, for the queen herself was not a small woman. Rumors of her being a tall, obese person had not been inaccurate, save that she and the skins she wore appeared to be clean, and her smile had more teeth in it than fewer.

Caro stopped a dozen feet from the throne and bowed low to her. "Greetings, Queen Winalia. I come to tell you that the western portion of your domain is secure."

The queen shifted, sagging slightly to the left. "Secure in your fist, Caro. You are a long way from Alcida. Do you secure it for me, or for Augustus?"

"Had my lord wished to possess the Ghost March, he would have kept it when he rode through a generation ago."

"Perhaps he has changed his mind." Her brown eyes

moved sluggishly, studying Phfas, Adrogans, and the three other soldiers that had accompanied them. "I saw him then. He slew my grandfather."

"My condolences, Highness."

"None needed. He was a grasping weasel of a man—my grandfather, not Augustus. He needed killing in the worst way." She sighed. "Alas, Augustus was kind and just slew him quickly."

Caro's white brows knitted together. "You seem somewhat dispassionate about your kin."

Winalia smiled slowly and sat up, shedding the bovine image she'd earlier projected. "And this makes you think that even having my daughter among the hostages might not guarantee your safety?"

"That thought did occur to me, yes."

She laughed aloud, though her mirth quickly broke into a hacking cough. She spat to the side, then wiped her mouth with the back of her hand. "Good one, that was. Worth a bit more than my daughter."

Phfas shot Adrogans a glance that betrayed just a hint of concern.

But Caro remained composed. "If you kill us, we kill them, and you lose the west."

She shook her head. "I lose the west, and the Aurolani lose their source of lumber and other things. They'll take the west back for me."

"They'll take the west back, but they won't return it to you. Which is why I have allowed trade to continue. I did not want them alarmed."

Winalia considered for a moment, then nodded slowly. "What did you want?"

The Alcidese general exhaled slowly. "I am assuming the Aurolani are building a fleet to the east. While I have been forced to become a reiver while fleeing Adrogans, I am still a loyal son of Alcida. I would like to destroy the Aurolani fleet before they can launch it. Barring that, I want ships to carry me south so we can continue the fight."

"Goals as honorable as they are impossible." She lazily flicked a hand toward the east. "I've traveled to their shipyards to have it impressed upon me how important their effort is. Your men may be brave, but you have not even a regiment. You'd be slaughtered wholesale."

"Perhaps, Queen Winalia, you would raise troops from among your people to help us."

She laughed again, slapping a thick thigh that quivered fluidly. "I am not pleased that the Aurolani know I exist. I will not send my troops against them and remind them of that fact. Besides, I could raise perhaps another regiment, but you would still be vastly understrength, and their defenses make what I have here look as nothing."

Caro folded his arms across his chest. "So the alternative is for us to spend the duration here?"

She snorted. "I would offer you sanctuary, but that might anger the Aurolani. It might also anger Adrogans."

The Alcidese leader frowned. "Why would Adrogans concern you?"

"You have fled from him, which means he is formidable. You have also let it be known that he is not following you, but you continue to flee. I think it is possible that in a month I could awake to find him and his dragonels at my gates if I help you."

"No, Highness, you have no need to fear that, I assure you."

"Ah, Caro, you sound so sincere." She shook her head. "But you give me assurances you cannot back up."

Adrogans took a step forward. "Forgive me, Highness, but General Caro speaks the truth. Help him, and Adrogans will not appear in a month and destroy your city. I guarantee you that with a solemn pledge."

Her dark eyes sharpened. "And who are you that I would believe you?"

He stripped the eye patch from his face. "Markus Adrogans, at your service. Help us, and you never need fear us. Fail, and those dragonels will raze your city by dusk."

"Oh," she said. "This is a bit of a complication."

Adrogans shook his head. "I thought it was quite simple."

"No, not at all. Now I have to figure out where I am going to put all of your people."

"Ah, that I understand, Highness. Do not let it concern you overmuch, however." Adrogans smiled and heard Phfas chuckle beside him. "After all, we'll only be here a very short time."

CHAPTER 43

The smoke from his first quadnel shot blew back into Erlestoke's face. His eyes teared and he couldn't see, but it didn't matter. He knew the shot had missed the on-rushing temeryx. Not only had the beast shifted in the last second, but he'd heard no screech following the weapon's discharge.

Blind though he was, Erlestoke worked the charging lever, spinning the barrels. He locked the new one in place, then primed it for another shot. The smoke cleared enough that he saw the beast, and found it far closer than he expected—*save in a nightmare*. Making matters worse, his horse saw it and began to leap away. Not only did that make the frostclaw even more intent on attacking, but it robbed Erlestoke of any chance of shooting accurately.

This is it!

The frostclaw leaped for him. Its little foreclaws rent the air. Its head came up and its mouth gaped, revealing rows of sharp, serrated teeth. The rear muscles bunched and released as the creature became airborne. Its lozenge-shaped pupils dilated and a hiss rose in its feathered throat as one leg came up. The sickle-shaped claw cocked back, ready to carve through man and mount.

As it reached the apex of its leap, a brown blur streaked through the air and swooped up in a whispered rush of air. For a heartbeat brown wings eclipsed the snowy beast, then Erlestoke could see it again. The frostclaw's muscles had already begun to soften, and white feathers drifted down. A red crescent had been slashed across its throat, all but severing the head.

The body twisted in the air and did hit the horse at the shoulder, but hit it broadside. The claw did snap down by reflex, but caught in the mail skirt of Erlestoke's coat. Rings popped, but the claw tore only metal and leather, not the flesh beneath it. The dead beast hit the ground and thrashed, but the horse's renewed leap carried it out of danger.

The prince thrust his quadnel into the muzzle of a gibberer and pulled the trigger. The muzzle blast singed fur and the lead ball blew through its skull. It pitched back, its body flaccid, and other charging gibberers folded around arrows piercing them belly and chest.

Erlestoke raised the quadnel in a salute to Preyknosery Ironwing, and the Gyrkyme warrior shrieked again in acknowledgment before folding his wings to swoop on another target. While other Gyrkyme used light spears and lances, Preyknosery preferred long curved knives with which he could carve up his foes. Mastering such weapons took a long time, according to the Gyrkyme in his company, and few warriors had lived long enough to attain his level of expertise.

Dranae's draconette barked and a *kryalniri* abdomen started to leak crimson. The prince cocked the quadnel again, but before he could prime, aim, and shoot, three arrows crossed in the *kryalniri's* breast. Its last words rode a red tide, then it collapsed.

Erlestoke had taken the Oriosan Prince's Guards, a heavy cavalry unit made of expatriates who swore fealty to

him, and driven them into a vale while positioning his infantry units in the hills east and west. Locals had indicated
this heavily wooded area had been home to Aurolani
forces, though their reports had grossly underestimated the
enemy strength. Fortunately, the prince always applied
the "Cavarre" rule when planning an operation: calculate
the number of people needed to do the job, then double it.
He'd learned that from the late Draconis Baron, and so far
in the campaign it had worked well.

He'd wanted to press on to the Midlands and begin
rooting Aurolani forces out immediately after the
Hawkriders joined him, but political considerations delayed his plan. In Count Wightman's company, he took the
whole of his army into Hawkride, then north. That added
six days to his campaign, and while he hardly desired to
strengthen Wightman's position in any way, the fact that he
could now draw on Hawkride for supplies did help enormously. In addition, they picked up a number of huntsmen
who knew the countryside to augment his scouts.

It struck him as an ill omen that the first day in the
month of Toil had him seeking out and slaughtering formations of Aurolani troops in his homeland, but that was
how the month of Seed had ended. He'd not realized just
how many enemy troops had found Oriosa to be a safe
haven. Moreover, Nay and Count Wightman both seemed
to be surprised by the numbers themselves.

Erlestoke had to assume that the Aurolani were pushing
more troops into Oriosa. He based that conclusion on the
unanticipated numbers *and* the presence of *kryalniri*. Their
addition to Aurolani forces had been relatively recent and
rather thick in the combat troops sweeping down through
Sebcia and Muroso. It made perfect sense for Chytrine to
use part of that army to enter Oriosa and prevent his advance.

The prince had long since concluded his approach was
not a secret. He hated to admit it, but his father was the
prime candidate for the person who would have betrayed

him to the Nor'witch, but he certainly wasn't alone. He could only hope that enough reports came in to confuse matters. Chytrine would have to overcommit troops to slow him down, which would make Alexia's task much easier.

It will get us killed all that much faster, however.

A Gyrkyme spear transfixed a frostclaw, though the beast's momentum ripped the weapon's barbed head from the ground. It kept coming, but an Addermage cast a quick spell that ignited the spear. The frostclaw's breath came as a dragon's might, then it curled up and died, with smoke rising from its muzzle. Elsewhere a rider charged his horse into a small knot of Aurolani, knocking gibberers flying, while a slash opened a vylaen's skull.

Steadily and onward the cavalry advanced. They moved mostly at a trot, but burst into a gallop as clear ground and the need for a charge presented itself. The Aurolani gave way and their magickers did damage for as long as they lasted. Temeryces proved the most difficult foes because of their speed and hideous weaponry, but arrows, spears, and lances wounded them before they could get close enough to face steel, evening the odds. While they did kill and maim men and horses in equal numbers, they also died in droves.

Erlestoke's men took to the grim business before them with great heart and passion. In many ways this was the easy bit of warfare, for the enemy was easily identifiable and hopelessly outnumbered. The operation more resembled a drive to find some rogue catamount that had been taking sheep than actual warfare. The Aurolani troops were not men, they were beasts, which somehow made it easier to accept the merciless way his troops slaughtered them.

The ease of victory brought with it a worry that he would have to address later. When they faced whatever army Chytrine sent against him, he couldn't have his men assuming it would be as easy as this. The Aurolani they were chasing from hills and hollows had no opportunity to show discipline and training. In fact, it could have very easily been half-trained troops who were sent south to scout out his army. The Aurolani leader likely had other, more experienced, troops out there as well, watching and reporting back. Just fighting against the green troops slowed Erlestoke and gave the enemy his measure, while the enemy was able to amass reinforcements and build a force that could overwhelm him.

He dreaded the idea that he would be facing Nefrai-kesh. Others in his command didn't because Nefrai-kesh had lost Okrannel to Markus Adrogans. While Erlestoke liked hearing that he was the equal of the Aurolani leader, he knew better than to believe it. Not to take anything from Adrogans, it did seem rather apparent that Okrannel had been ceded to the south in an attempt to split the alliance, so its loss in no way represented a lack of competence on Nefrai-kesh's part.

Even more important, Nefrai-kesh, when he was Lord Kenwick Norrington, had been from Oriosa and knew this area of the country well. Every mile further north brought Erlestoke into an area where the enemy knew it intimately, and through which the prince had ventured but once in the last five years—and that was in haste to return to Fortress Draconis. So while locals could give him information about the land, they weren't going to see it through a tactician's eyes, putting him at a severe disadvantage.

To make matters even worse, Erlestoke found himself in a curious position. His very presence was polarizing Oriosan society. Loyalists supported his father, pointing out that Scrainwood had managed to keep Oriosa safe from invasion and war for over a generation. The Aurolani had taken Sebcia and Muroso and had even struck into Alcida and Saporicia, but never Oriosa. The loyalists saw the prince as a usurper who had returned to take Oriosa because his previous realm, Fortress Draconis, had fallen. As they told it, he was really just a foreign invader who had no more love for Oriosa than Chytrine, and his fight with her would be conducted on Oriosan soil, killing Oriosans because they meant nothing to him.

The patriots, on the other hand, were united in their opposition to Chytrine, but Erlestoke recognized that this was not exactly the same as being united in support of his effort. Like Count Wightman, they would be with him as long as his crusade seemed to be in their best interests. If they could get fame and territory out of it, they would back him completely. If at any point it seemed that his effort would fail, their backing would evaporate. Erlestoke would again be reduced to an interloper using foreign troops to oust the king, and they—the true patriots—would fight him for the good of the nation.

Erlestoke would have liked to sidestep all of that by making a pledge that after Chytrine had been defeated he would just return to Fortress Draconis and never again set foot in Oriosa. He had been prepared to do that a month ago when he crossed the border, but in that time his mind had slowly changed. As he traveled through the country, he recognized places from his youth, and they brought smiles. An affection for his nation was rekindled, though that could have just been billed as nostalgia.

No, it was the people who changed his mind. The transformation started with Nay, Rounce, and especially Borell. It had begun back in Narriz. Borell had faced a *sullanciri* to save his father, but he had done so with the courage and confidence that were the hallmarks of Oriosan warriors. He reminded Erlestoke of the Oriosans who had refused to evacuate Fortress Draconis, despite being given leave to do so and knowing they were facing certain death. They'd just packed their life masks off with their loved ones and prepared to die defending a pile of rock hundreds of miles from their homes.

The Hawkriders, Count Wightman notwithstanding, had continued to change his mind. Part of the reason they wanted to parade back to their home province before heading north was to show those left behind that they were part of something greater than one of Wightman's plots. They were joining the prince to rid Oriosa of a scourge that had taken root there a generation before. They weren't concerned with political ploys and maneuvering, but with making their nation safe for their children. They were willing to put their lives on the line to do that, and Erlestoke began to feel responsible for making sure the nation would be safe after Chytrine was vanquished.

He could not abandon his homeland the way he had intended. He had to walk a slender line, allowing the fractious lords to underestimate his political acumen, while at the same time cultivating their personal loyalty. Even as he tried to read flows of power and assess the character of those who supported and opposed him, he wished he was back at Fortress Draconis. *At least there I knew the enemy easily, what they could do, what they were likely to do, and plan accordingly. Here, I just don't know.*

High in the hills, trumpets began to blare. The first of the Aurolani refugees had reached the infantry and the battle was joined. With the trumpets all the troops would begin to move down, trapping the enemy and exterminating them. Within the hour, well before dusk, the vale would be free of Aurolani.

Preyknosery landed in front of Erlestoke. His blades dripped blood and a fair amount of it had spattered his breast and wings. "There are some Aurolani moving north, but only a small group of gibberers. A handful, no more. I have highfliers watching them."

"Good, thank you." The prince nodded. "Some of the locals have suggested another nest up by the lake at Two Rocks. It will take us two days to get up there."

"We'll have it scouted." The Gyrkyme pointed back to the south. "There is a large dust cloud twenty miles back, not yet in the Midlands. It is what you would call a regiment, mixed horse and foot. More are joining them daily. They're not in a hurry."

"I'll send scouts to watch them. I doubt my father is

fielding troops against us, but I don't like having a shadow back there. I'll wait and see how they react to the nest we got at Oak Grove. That will tell us a lot."

"I agree." The winged warrior smiled. "You're doing very well, Highness. Your troops are learning. By the time we face the big battle, they will be ready."

"I hope so." Erlestoke smiled. "Thank you for saving me."

"My pleasure."

"I wish there was a way I could reward you."

"There is." Preyknosery pointed at the quadnel. "I have mastered many weapons, and would like to learn how to use this one."

"I'll teach you myself."

"You honor me, Prince Erlestoke." Preyknosery bowed his head. "I once served another prince. I saved his daughter, but was not there to save him. I shan't let harm befall you as I did him."

"Well, I hope I won't give you too many other opportunities to need to protect me." The prince sighed. "Unfortunately, given what we will face—and despite my best intentions—you will be overworked in that regard."

CHAPTER 44

Terror lent Kerrigan's feet wings and was the only thing that kept him going. Once Resolute had made the decision to head north to rescue both DragonCrown fragments, rest and respite became fond memories. He and the princess got the weak and wounded hustled away south. Pretty much everyone knew the courier mission was nothing but a blind, and those who were selected to leave weren't wholly reluctant to depart.

As the Gyrkyme flew, a hundred and twenty-five miles stood between them and the north coast of Loquellyn. The fragments remained roughly in line with their goal, but were hidden away in an area Trawyn referred to as "the Splinters." In some long-distant time a glacier from the north had stabbed down into that area, gouging up all manner of rocks. And while plants gradually recolonized the area, Oracle said it was also known in Elvish as "Stone Forest."

As they hurried north, Trawyn explained why the fragments' location should give them heart. "The Splinters are sparingly populated. Someone who knows the area can remain hidden for months and even years. There are a few buildings—hunting lodges and retreats for poets—but more than enough caves. Were Loquellyn a human nation, that region would be filthy with outlaws."

While that did seem a good sign, at least in terms of the fragments remaining out of Aurolani hands, it meant their being able to effect a rescue would be very difficult. Kerrigan took the problem a step further. Whoever had the Vorquellyn fragment had been in its possession for over a century, and no one and nothing had been aware he had it. Kerrigan found it very easy to imagine someone like Resolute hoarding the fragment. Trying to get it away from Resolute would have been difficult, and he figured it would be no less so with its current guardian.

Kerrigan wasn't certain why, but he did know the thief was male. He also got the impression that he was an elf, but the youth almost dismissed that deduction as being far too easy. He tried to limit himself to whatever impressions he could sort out from his search spell, and each evening when he cast it anew, he tinkered with it to try to get more of an impression of the person protecting the fragments.

But Kerrigan's ability to modify his spell was minimal because of the pace they set. Resolute drove them all hard. They kept moving for as much as ten hours at a time. On one day, moving through a river valley, they actually managed to make it thirty miles, if the elven waystones could be believed. Other days they didn't move any less swiftly, but didn't get as far because Aurolani activity in the area forced them to wait. They didn't want to fight as that would draw attention to their group. Once danger passed, however, they were up and off again.

In six days they covered the distance that should have taken them a week and a half. That pace brought them to the southern edge of the Splinters. While the name Stone Forest conjured up images—and the translation in Elvish, *Taltentil*, made Kerrigan smile—the Splinters really did apply. Most of the rocks had been piled up by a glacier, but hills and hollows had massive stone spikes upthrust through the earth as if they had grown there.

Kerrigan patted a massive boulder with his left hand. "Bok, looking at this, I'd almost figure there was an urZrethi mountain stronghold that was crushed. What do you think?"

The urZrethi scratched at his head. "There were many ruins after the dragons made war on us. It's possible the ice mountain smashed one. Equally possible, however, is that the glacier gouged the bottom of the Crescent Sea and scraped up the home of these *nyressanii*. Could be what you are touching was once their capital."

Kerrigan shivered despite never having seen one of the creatures. Trawyn's description of them had been enough to give him fits, especially when Resolute had urged everyone to be careful as they crossed swamps. "It's probably best there are things I don't know about."

Bok smiled. "Ignorance isn't something to be sought, but a temporary state to be corrected as soon as possible."

"Well, if I ever find myself at the bottom of the sea, in conversation with Tagothcha, I'll ask him."

That first night in the Splinters Kerrigan cast the search spell and got his results even more quickly than he expected. The fragments were still north, but seemed to have moved closer. Kerrigan sought Resolute and informed him of his impression.

The Vorquelf's face closed up. "There have been signs of activity in the area. Lots of gibberers, with a few *turekadine* to lead them. This is good in that it means our opposition is smaller. It's not good in that the heaviest troops are now headed off to fight in the east."

Resolute looked to the north. "If the courier is heading in this direction, it may be because the Aurolani landed more troops on the coast and has them moving south. Can you change your spell to give me troop dispositions?"

"I could, but if they are moving, I'd have to be casting constantly to keep track of them. I could pick up gibberers, vylaens, and frostclaws easily enough. Probably the *turekadine*, too, but the batrachians and *slurriki* would get past me."

Oracle came over to the two of them, helped by Trawyn. "Resolute, you have to go now. You have to find him. He is very close, but so are they. We all have to hurry."

Without question, Resolute stood and whistled sharply. "We're moving north, *now*." He shrugged off his pack and stuffed it behind a bush and beneath a rock. "If it is not one of us and it is moving out there, kill it. You know what we are looking for. You've never done anything but steal your whole lives, so steal this one from Chytrine."

The Grey Misters and Trawyn's companions likewise divested themselves of their packs, then drew their weapons and began to move north. Kerrigan struggled out of his pack and found Resolute helping him. "Listen to me carefully, Kerrigan."

"Yes, Resolute?"

"You and Bok are the most important people here tonight. You can find our quarry, so you must go for him and direct others to any opposition in your way. Qwc will stay with you and carry messages. Unless you're forced to, you cast no combat spells, just keep getting closer to the fragments, got it?"

He nodded.

"Good. The second thing is that you're also responsible for Oracle and Trawyn. You're in command of the search; the rest of us will handle the rescue. Once you find our target and free him, you all head north. The rest of us will come as fast as we can, but you know our mission. You wait for no one; just go."

Kerrigan's throat tightened. "But what if . . . ?"

Resolute laughed. "Something happens to me?" The Vorquelf came around in front of him and rested his hands on the mage's shoulders. "Do you honestly think I won't be there? I'm taking it as a personal affront that Chytrine didn't send her *turekadine* after me the second they were spawned. I intend she know that even they are not enough to stop me."

Kerrigan smiled, his heart beating a bit faster. "I won't wait for anyone."

"Good." Resolute's eyes narrowed for a moment. "You remember when Orla said to stay with Crow and me?"

The image of his mentor, as she lay dying in the cabin of a ship, came back. So did the lump in his throat. He nodded.

"She did that so you'd learn enough for today. If it comes down to you leading the force north alone, I know you can do it. Furthermore, I think *you* know you can do it."

Kerrigan hesitated, then closed his eyes and thought for a moment. When he first left Vilwan he couldn't have done any of what had been accomplished since before Bok had kidnapped him and begun to instruct him in the true paths of power. Even the long hard marches they had made in the past six days would have been beyond him, not only physically, but mentally and emotionally. He would have been one of the first sent back.

Now, however, Resolute's words found purchase in his heart. He still felt afraid, but he also had a need to push on. *Back when I left Vilwan, I was the center of my own world. My world was limited by what I could do and what I thought I could do. Now the world is much bigger. It challenges me and I rise to that challenge.*

Kerrigan slapped the Vorquelf on the shoulder. "North to Vorquellyn, get Will, north again, and get the Nor'witch. If you get lost, we'll leave signs of our passing."

Resolute smiled, and Kerrigan didn't find it as frightening a thing as he had in the past. "Good. Let's go kill some Aurolani and, while we're at it, push the world a little further from destruction."

* * *

Moving through the Splinters in darkness would have been impossible for him, so, despite Resolute's admonition about the use of magick, Kerrigan did resort to a spell that amplified the visible light. He could have used a stronger spell that would have rendered night as day, but that was far more easy to detect than the one he chose, and much easier to dispel. By his choosing something slightly less efficient and more complicated, a magicker would have to work to destroy the spell, and Kerrigan would have a chance to rid himself of his tormentor.

His spell showed him a world of grey and yellow. He brushed past trees and scrambled over rocks, pausing to help Oracle or Trawyn along. Bok, who had lengthened his legs and sharpened his arms, became an odd yellow stick figure striding through the night. He again bore on his back the chest in which Rym resided, but it slowed him down not at all.

From all around them came the sounds of combat, but not those of a raging battle. People did scream, but mostly there were muffled groans, or the sharp crack of a neck snapping. More than one gibberer lay on the ground, his throat slit or a hole over his heart. Part of Kerrigan wanted to cast diagnostic spells to see what had killed them, for the information would have been invaluable, but the mission kept him focused.

Half a mile into the forest, Resolute intercepted them after Qwc made a quick flyby. Wordlessly he beckoned for Kerrigan to come with him. As the mage moved through the night, he saw a number of gibberer bodies on the ground and could smell the stink of singed fur. Resolute brought him to a place between two standing stones where two gibberers and one of the Grey Misters lay dead.

The flesh had been burned from the elf's face. A few other elves stood around, but Resolute quickly deployed them to watch, then sent Qwc to bring the rest of the group in. Resolute moved toward the stones, and extended his left arm toward the space between them, but he didn't stick it in there. As his skin grew close, a couple of the tattoos on his forearm began to glow faintly.

Kerrigan nodded and cast a quick spell. In his sight, the stones lit up as if they were mirrors reflecting the noonday sun. "Wards, very powerful wards that were worked a long time ago, but not activated until now. I can feel them linked to other setups." He glanced back in the direction whence they had come. "There's more out there. We're trapped inside two rings."

They heard a couple more screams from a position about ninety degrees away from them on the inner ring, then a harsh horn. A grim expression settled over Resolute's face. "They've figured out what we've figured out. They'll attribute their dead to the ring and its maker, so they don't know we're here at the moment. Can you get through the wards?"

Kerrigan nodded. "I think so. They're elven, but complicated. Could be, however, if I get through, *all* the wards stop working. If they're closer to the hiding place, they get there first."

"I'll take care of them. Predator, get your people ready. We're going around to the east and we're hitting them hard."

The Grey Mister nodded and started gathering his charges.

Resolute smiled. "Fast, Kerrigan. Get in there but be careful."

"I will."

"Go, then." The Vorquelf shot him a little salute, then vanished in the night. Like a feral fog, the Grey Misters drifted in his wake.

As Bok brought Trawyn and Oracle up, Kerrigan pondered the wards. He cast another diagnostic spell, carefully looking for any traps or any telltale signs of modifications to the spells. Wards usually were fairly simple. They linked two or more points and had a lot of magickal energy flowing between them. When someone tried to cross between those points, the spell evaluated them as a target. If they didn't have a talisman, or the right bloodline or any of thousands of other traits that would make them harmless from the spell's point of view, they suffered the consequences.

Kerrigan could have easily gotten lost in a search for a key to the ward. Finding the right key, then crafting a spell that would make it appear as if he had the key would take a lot of time. That was the standard way of getting through a ward. It wasn't easy, and took not only a very good magick-user to do so, but also a lot of time.

Instead he picked up on a trickle of a diagnostic spell coming through the wards and smiled. It was clearly Aurolani magick. Kerrigan smiled and punched a spell back along that line that reported to the Aurolani magicker that there was a key, and that it was to appear to be an elf.

A triumphant blast on the Aurolani horn was followed by a hideous scream. Kerrigan got no sense of the magicker's death through the ward, though he did get something else. Seconds later more screams sounded, along with war cries, as Resolute's raid on the Aurolani began. The clash of steel on steel rang through the darkness.

Bok tapped him on the shoulder. "Moving quickly would be good."

"Yes, and I think I can now." He shook his head and set his shoulders. What he'd caught when the Aurolani magicker died was a momentary flicker in the wards' intensity. The mage who had created the wards had used several spells to create his trap, which made it almost impossible to dispel quickly. Most important, to avoid its detection and the slaying of things for no reason at all, he made the spell that channeled energy into the wards as something that required conscious control and recasting.

"Just as the dragonbone armor causes me trouble with spell casting, this ought to work for you."

Kerrigan quickly recalled the impressions of the *tureka-dine*, vylaens, and gibberers, then shaped each one into the equivalent of a disguise spell and cast it at the ward. The defensive spell looked at all aspects of the spell, evaluated it as a disguise, then pulsed power back to kill whatever it was hiding. Faster and faster Kerrigan sent these little spells. Bok picked up on what he was doing and began to cast as well.

The wardmaster's reaction time faded. It took him longer and longer to get the power flowing back into the spells and then, all at once, the wards collapsed. Kerrigan cast one more disguise to see if it was a ruse, then followed with his search spell. The response came so quickly that his head snapped around and he began to run. Behind him, Bok scooped the princess and Oracle up in his arms and streaked after him.

To his right, out of the darkness, a *turekadine* burst from the brush. It snarled loudly and brandished a curved longknife. Before it could advance, however, a bladestar whirred through the air and caught it in the ribs. The creature had enough time to look down, then the poison on the throwing star's point took effect.

Kerrigan leaped over the thrashing beast and plunged on into a dark cavern. He ducked his head and raised his hands, saving him a nasty knock on the skull. He quickly dropped to his hands and knees and crawled along a twisting passage that had been reshaped by magick. The tunnel wove back on itself once, then opened into a grotto.

A cadaverous figure hung in the middle of it, ensnared in long pale roots from above—roots that had been woven into a web. Kerrigan had a hard time telling where the elf's hair ended and the roots began, for his fine hair hung to his waist and spread behind him as if a cape. The elf's head lolled to the side. A thin rope of saliva and another of snot slowly dripped down. Most curious of all, his pale skin had a lavender cast to it.

Two large pouches, one on each hip, hung from his belt. Kerrigan assumed they contained the DragonCrown fragments, but it wasn't an assumption he wanted to test. The elf's skill at wards and Kerrigan's own experience enchanting a fragment kept him back.

Trawyn entered the cave next and hissed. "Stay away from him, Kerrigan. Cast no spell."

"What's the matter?"

She pointed at the figure. "His purple flesh. He is an eater of dreamwing."

"You've mentioned it before. What is it?"

She exhaled slowly. "It is a narcotic plant, which can be addictive. It soothes great pain, emotional pain, at least temporarily, and can help one cast powerful magicks. Use begets use, however. When one is as far gone as he is, he cannot tell dream fantasy from reality. He may lash out without warning, and he would hurt you badly."

"Who is he?"

Trawyn shook her head, but Oracle appeared behind her. "He would be the last adult Vorquelf in the world. He is our key to the *coriiesci* in Saslynnae."

Trawyn looked at her as if she were insane. "A dreamwing eater can't enter a *coriiesci*. He hasn't the presence of mind to open the way."

The Vorquelven soothsayer shrugged. "We will have to make him recover before we need him on Vorquellyn."

Kerrigan smiled. "Resolute will sober him up."

"Oh, I wish that were true, Kerrigan. The Aurolani have been scattered. The others will be coming in." Oracle shook her head slowly. "Unfortunately, Resolute will not be in their number."

CHAPTER 45

Princess Alexia did not let Tythsai's force escape entirely. She used her cavalry to chase, scout, and harass the Aurolani as they retreated. Once the rear guard felt sufficiently threatened by fast-moving light horse units, Tythsai would be forced to form her army up and offer the rear guard support. Alexia would keep her harassing troops in place, bring the rest of her army up, then allow the Aurolani to decline an engagement and move off again.

While the mix of chase and release might have seemed pointless, Alexia actually managed to accomplish several things at the same time. The raids against the rear guard did cost the Aurolani soldiers. More important, every time Tythsai had to stop her army and march them back west to support the rear guard, the Aurolani were being made to retrace their steps again and again. The fact that when they got there they were allowed to march off again built up resentment and began to erode morale.

The Aurolani did try to strike back. They set up ambushes on the roads and within the forests, but Alexia was able to deploy the Alcidese Mountain Rangers, Zyean Free

Swords, and Nybali Longsteps against these. Unseen in the woods a war of small units raged, with squads tangling as battalions on both sides moved through the tree-strewn gloom, hunting and killing the enemy wherever they stood.

Almost a week after the first battle, when combat had been thrice offered and declined, both forces moved to within the shadow of Fronosa. The tusklike mountains thrust up through the landscape, save for one gap where one of the teeth clearly had been knocked loose in some ancient combat. Nestled beneath the tooth to the north, the fortress of Fronosa commanded the road running around its base, then down through switchbacks to the plains of Muroso. Though the fortress itself was not large, the steep slope upon which it rested made bringing siege machinery against it all but impossible. Conversely, though the weaponry in Fronosa was small, it could do devastating amounts of damage to forces trying to work up the slope, especially from the Murosan side.

Alexia stepped up her harassment and brought her foot soldiers up quickly. The fortress could never house all the Aurolani troops, but the reach of their siege engines could supply a nice umbrella beneath which the Aurolani troops could take cover. Tythsai, though undead, was not wholly stupid. She reinforced the rear guard, then withdrew the remains of her army to Fronosa's shadow.

Alexia faced little more than a regiment of troops astride the road. At its center stood three battalions of heavy infantry made up mostly of gibberers, with a few hoargoun and *kryalniri* to stiffen them. The frost giants wielded prodigious clubs which, in most cases, were little more than uprooted trees. A few had taken to using spikes to affix bits and pieces of armor and shields, both making the weapons more deadly and showing contempt for the human warriors from whom the items had been stripped.

On each wing, slightly behind the infantry, a light cavalry battalion waited. Their job would be to attack from the edges when whatever assault Alyx sent at the heavy infantry got bogged down. The force guarding the road would be crushed—of that there was no doubt on either side. If Alyx went after them hard and fast, her cavalry would suffer losses. If she waited to mass more troops, the Aurolani army could fully shelter in Fronosa.

Alyx had her signalman blow an alert, which brought all of her cavalry forward. She massed her heavy cavalry in front, with the two battalions of the Saporician Crown Lancers getting the honor of first contact. Next up were the Alcidese Iron Horse's two battalions, then the single Mask Battalion made up of Murosan and Oriosan volunteers. Her light cavalry was arrayed on each wing, in position to counterattack the Aurolani light cavalry.

Signals to troops were drummed out from the Aurolani force and the foot soldiers set themselves for the southern charge. The formation bristled with spears that were leveled, with butts planted in the ground in hopes of impaling horses. Soldiers raised shields and hunkered down. The hoargoun began to swing their clubs in circles, moving ever more swiftly. One blow could lift a horse and rider from the ground, armor and all, and neither would fight again.

She looked at her signalman. "Blow the attack for plan two, please."

The man nodded, then raised a bugle to his lips. Staccato notes blasted out. The Saporician lancers began trotting forward. Their lances lowered, the pennants on them snapped, then they moved into a gallop. Behind them came the Alcidese Iron Horse. Hoofbeats sounded as thunder. Alyx felt the ground shaking beneath her, and the horse she sat astride snorted with impatience. She patted his neck, and whispered, "There will be more than enough war coming."

Alexia, in studying the maps created by the Gyrkyme scouts she'd sent out, had assumed Tythsai would try to stop her at this point. She'd further assumed that one possible arrangement would be the one that had been used.

Neither the princess nor any of her advisors doubted it would be very bloody when the light cavalry attacked the flanks of her cavalry.

To respond to that threat, Alyx developed a variety of attack plans. The only flaw in what Tythsai had set up was that it required the light cavalry to have a clear corridor to attack the flanks of the southern cavalry. The clear corridors existed and, with plan two, the south exploited them before the Aurolani could.

As the Saporicians neared the Aurolani infantry, they left the road to the north, cutting around that formation, and bringing their full weight to bear on the light cavalry to the rear. Hoargoun watched in amazement as men and horses encased in steel bypassed them and slammed into the frostclaws and their riders. A few of the Aurolani cavalry did manage to lower their lances and begin to advance, but that just meant their weapons splintered first on shields, and their bodies trailed blood and feathers as they were blasted back.

To the south, the Alcidese Iron Horse cut around and hit the other light cavalry. That battalion, having seen what happened to their brethren, had set themselves and started to advance, but to no avail. The heavy cavalry thrust through them, splitting their formation before the second battalion reached their target. The resulting melee had men and gibberers spilling from saddles. Frostclaws leaped and slashed, horses reared and stomped. Swords, axes, maces, and flails finished what broken lances had started.

The Aurolani infantry had no idea what to do when the light cavalry came racing in. As they had done previously, the horse archers peppered their enemy with shots. Against such a mass, arrows were bound to find targets. As gibberers fell, so did spears or shields. Hoargoun roared in pain as arrows easily stuck them. Aurolani screamed in pain and frustration, unable to get at the tormentors who rode around in circles, loosing flight after flight of arrows.

Finally, the infantry could take no more and their formation broke. Some squads charged at the archers while others just turned to run. In their minds, they were close enough to hear drums, so safety was not that far away.

Unfortunately for them, the heavy cavalry units that had shorn away their wings now waited between them and the succor Fronosa offered. That slowed their flight, and one hoargoun bellowed orders that tightened their formation. They set themselves for the heavy cavalry charge. Once they'd withstood that, they would break and run for their own lines.

About the time they were braced for that charge, the Mask Battalion hit them from their new rear. The masked warriors, many of whom knew that these very troops had despoiled their nation, plunged headlong into the Aurolani formation. Spears flew, lances bowed and cracked, swords dented helms and clove skulls. Aurolani combatants spun away, bones broken or limbs hacked away. Blood pulsed as animals screamed. Riders slashed mercilessly at those who would pull them from the saddle. Spells exploded, wreathing some riders in fire, then bloodied *kryalniri* would fall into the mud churned up with their own vital fluids.

A few of the Aurolani cavalry survived and fled across the plain to their own lines. One of the hoargoun tried to do the same thing, but the cavalry quickly made sport of a creature they had feared. Lancers thrust repeatedly at his heels, though it was one of the Iron Horse who used an ax to sever one heel tendon. The giant fell heavily, but before he could get up, more lancers thrust spears through his legs. As he reached out to drag himself along, another stabbed a spear down through his hand, pinning it to the ground. As he tore at that spear, more pierced his body and more, until his labored breathing could do nothing more than raise a cloud of dust. Blood bubbled from dozens of chest wounds and flowed freely from countless other cuts, then the hoargoun roared one last time, weakly, and died.

The signalman blew for the cavalry to regroup, which they did, well past the point of Aurolani defense. Barely a thousand yards separated Alexia's forces from those of the enemy, but the last two hundred of those yards would be within range of Fronosa's trebuchets and catapults. Regardless, Alexia rode forward, and behind her came the rest of her army.

The Aurolani took up defensive positions. A rubble field to the north had so many rocks scattered around it and so much talus over it that horses could not function there. Mounting an assault on that position would call for infantry and it would be very slow going. Tythsai stationed her two battalions of draconetteers there. They could rake the flanks of Alyx's forces, or just kill any infantry sent to root them out.

The rest of the army spread out with the remaining heavy infantry in the center, and the light deployed to each side. Tythsai kept her cavalry all the way over to the east. They anchored her flank, but had direct access to the road so they could charge as needed. Because of the way the land dropped off to the east, Alexia couldn't flank them. The cavalry had dismounted and were digging small trenches, as were all the troops, making the hill yet more difficult to take.

The only choice for the southern force was a frontal assault. A frontal assault that would take them uphill against an enemy in good defensive positions, and the whole time they would be subjected to shots from Fronosa. Alyx's assault would be suicidal, and could cripple her army. If enough damage was done, she might not be able to push into Muroso.

As if to reinforce how dangerous the assault would be, a ballista let fly from within Fronosa. A spear trailing a red banner arced high into the air, then came down and stabbed into the earth. It quivered there, a graphic demonstration of exactly how far Alexia's troops would have to march beneath its range. The wind teased the pennant and a great, defiant cry arose from the Aurolani ranks.

Alexia brought her troops along at a brisk march and

signalmen got them arrayed in the proper order. Once they were spread out over a broad front, she nodded to the signalman, and he blew a general advance. Slowly, at an easy walk, the infantry advanced: heavy in the center, light on the wings, with her own cavalry positioned to counter the Aurolani cavalry. Inside a minute the southerners reached the spear. They never even paused.

The catapults, trebuchets, and ballistae in Fronosa began to operate in earnest. The larger machines sent heavy stones, iron balls, or, in a few cases, smoking crocks containing flammable oil high into the sky. The ballistae shot either spears like the one before, or sheaves of arrows with lead weights right behind the heads. As they sped to earth, the weight would encourage the arrow's head to pierce armor.

The employment of the siege engines was a disaster. The stones fell amid troops, crushing them. A stone might smash one helmet, then bounce away, its energy only partially spent, to smash into someone else's face or leg. Spears transfixed warriors, and arrows drilled through them. When the firecrocks hit the hard ground, their cargo ignited immediately. Soldiers became living torches, screaming until they breathed in enough fire to close their throats.

Alexia watched it all and felt nothing. Not so her troops. Despite their discipline, they could not ignore what was happening. Unbidden, they raised their voice in a war cry. Not one of defiance or pity, but of amazement. Flight after flight of stones, arrows, spears, and fire arced up and fell quickly. It fell short of the advancing southern formation and instead sowed death and misery amid the Aurolani troops.

With a nod, Alyx instructed her signalman to blow a "hold advance," which he did. Up and down her line the call was repeated. Her troops stopped moving forward, while cheering all the more loudly as fire exploded among the Aurolani. Arrows cut down whole companies. The missiles from within the fortress concentrated on the heavy infantry and one heavy rock rolled down the slope, crushing those who were too slow or unlucky to get out of the way.

With another order call, Alyx's cavalry withdrew from their position threatening the road. Aurolani drums spoke and Tythsai's troops began to withdraw down the trail. She left her cavalry to screen her force, but it was never in jeopardy from anyone on her side of the battlefield. The missiles flew from Fronosa until the people inside the fortress had nothing more to shoot.

By late afternoon, the Aurolani forces had withdrawn and the lead elements could be seen on the Zamsina road. Various reports flowed in, estimating the Aurolani losses at well over two thousand—almost a third of the force Tythsai had started the campaign with. While Alexia could have pressed the attack, letting Tythsai slip away was still a part of her strategy. The Aurolani had been made to quit Saporicia and, as far as she was concerned, that was enough for one day.

As that thought occurred to her, she smiled. Actually, it wasn't enough, and would only be a minor part of her day.

Up on the battlements of Fronosa she saw Crow and decided her day had really just begun.

She lay on Crow's chest, licking sweat from his throat, with his arms strong around her. She squeezed his thighs with her calves, then kissed him. "So, lover, you enjoy it when a plan of mine works?"

Crow coughed lightly, then nodded. He followed that quickly with a smile. "Oh, you mean the taking of Fronosa. Yes, my dear."

She gave his ribs a quick slap, more noise than sting. "What else did you think I was referring to? No, don't answer that." She kissed him again as his upthrust hips settled back into the mattress. "I had hoped it would work."

"Perfectly, lover." Crow reached up and tucked a strand

of her hair behind her ear. "We harassed a number of supply trains, stealing everything we could. Then, as per your plan, we camped here on the plains so they could see us, along with our now long loot-string of wagons. A Gyrkyme landed, we brought everyone together, slew the draft animals, and made a halfhearted attempt to burn the wagons before we rode away to the east. As you expected, they sent scouts in our wake to see if we were truly gone. They waited for as long as they felt they could, then the garrison poured out and across the plain to loot our wagons.

"We'd headed east, but cut back around to the south and were in a perfect position to hit them as they were in a frenzy of looting. I used the Vilwanese warmages to ride to the fortress and make sure it remained open, but the *kryalniri* commander who was in charge was one of the first to die when we attacked the looters. Interrogation of a few survivors gave us what we needed to respond to signals when Tythsai brought her troops up, though you gave her no real time to suspect anything was amiss."

Alexia smiled. "It was a gamble to use that strategy, but it paid off."

"There would have been no taking Fronosa otherwise." Crow frowned. "We couldn't have done it as the Aurolani did—infiltrating renegades with the Murosan refugees who had been given sanctuary there."

"I am very glad it worked. Your attack utterly broke them." Alexia gave him another kiss, then rolled to her right and stretched her legs out. The sweat on her stomach quickly cooled, so she reached down with a toe and drew a blanket up over both of them. "Have you any idea how much I have missed you?"

Crow rolled onto his left side, resting his head on his hand, and traced a finger over her jaw. "Well, since it took you only ten minutes to demand a full and private debriefing from me concerning the situation here, I would guess it was a lot. Almost as much as I missed you."

"We can debate in the morning who missed whom

more, my love." Alyx turned her face and kissed his finger, then flicked her tongue at it. "There have been many cold nights . . ."

"I can toss another log on the fire."

She looked into his eyes and could see the reflection of the red coals from the small room's hearth. "It wasn't that sort of cold, Crow. It was a soul-cold. I needed and wanted you physically, yes—very much—but I also needed the sound of your voice. I needed to hear your thoughts and to share mine with you. To share everything with you."

He smiled, and it warmed her heart to see him do so quite so easily. "There is no doubt, then, that we were in similar states of need. The days of our being apart are ended, however."

"True." She reached up and took his left hand in her right. He rolled onto his back as she brought his hand down and squeezed it. "With you beside me, I have no worries."

"Nor do I." His voice came warm, rich, and deep, music to her soul as well as her ears. "Sleep well, lover."

She nodded and was fairly certain she said, "I love you, Crow," before she drifted off. She could not be sure and as sleep claimed her, she determined she would say it twice in the morning, and find a way to prove it to him.

Crow's convulsion brought her awake, snapping her eyes open. It had been forceful enough to tear his hand from hers. She tried to turn her head to look at him, but could not. Paralysis had seized her body. For a moment she thought she was dreaming and stuck the way one so often was in dreams. What she saw, however, convinced her she was very much awake.

And yet trapped in a nightmare.

Alyx didn't know where she had come from, but the *sullanciri* Myrall'mara stood at Crow's side of the bed. Her pale form glowed, almost making her seem like a ghost.

Alexia would have believed she was, and that what she was seeing was a hallucination of some sort, save that she could hear the strained whisper of the pillowcase as Chytrine's creature held the pillow down over Crow's face in a tight grip.

The *sullanciri* looked at her. "Fear not, child, you shall not be long separated from him. He will only abandon you for a little while."

Myrall'mara's cold voice coiled a viper in Alexia's guts. She struggled against the incapacity of her limbs to move. She couldn't twitch, she couldn't even feel a shiver. Something, magick or something else, held her prisoner as her enemy slowly smothered her lover. Panic rose in her, born of a feeling of impotence, but she forced it away.

Alyx turned inward and in the blink of an eye she found herself on the wheeldeck of Maroth's boat in the Communion. The Black Dragon stood there with the metal construct. "Why, Princess, this is a surprise."

"I need help, now! Myrall'mara is smothering Crow and I can do nothing." She grabbed the Black Dragon's hand. "You must help me."

"Of course, daughter." The man's tone became steel. He gripped her hand tightly in his. "Go back. Take me there. Maroth, *attend me*."

Alexia willed herself back into her body and there, at the foot of the bed, the Black Dragon appeared. He came around the end quickly, his shape shifting as he did. Myrall'mara's head turned and the *sullanciri* gasped. The Black Dragon's mailed left fist came around in a back-handed blow that caught her on the side of the face and knocked her back into the wall.

The pillow came off Crow's face. He loudly sucked in a lungful of air. The Black Dragon looked down at him, his inhuman visage gone, transformed into something Alexia found very familiar and yet a face she had never seen before. The Black Dragon looked down at Crow and at her, then smiled.

"So proud," he said, his words trailing to whispers as he faded from existence.

Snarling, Myrall'mara dove across the bed. Her clawed hands passed through where the Black Dragon had been, but his disappearance left her sprawled over their legs. She snarled, then she shifted around and straddled Crow much as Alexia had done before. She ground her hips against his in a parody of their lovemaking, then batted away his weak hands when he tried to shove her off.

The *sullanciri* smiled at Alexia, then slipped her hands around Crow's throat. "Better he dies this way, seeing me. Seeing me as I was when I delighted him."

Her fingers tightened, but only for a moment. A black metal hand closed on the back of her neck. She shrieked and clawed at it, scoring the metal with bright silver scratches. Maroth lifted her from Crow, then shook her hard. Alexia heard a loud snap, then the *sullanciri* hung from his hand limply, and the glow that had suffused her slowly died.

As it went away, control returned to Alyx's limbs. She turned and reached out, gathering Crow to her. She pressed her body to his back and kissed his shoulders and head. She could feel him breathe, even hear it. "Tell me you are all right, Crow. Say something, please."

He coughed once, heavily, then let his left arm rest on hers clumsily. His grip on her wrist lacked strength, but he was moving. He whispered hoarsely, "That wasn't a dream, was it?"

She kissed the back of his neck. "It was, in a way. It was the dream I had a long time ago in Okrannel. My nightmare."

Crow cleared his throat, then shifted in her arms to face her and enfold her in his arms. "Myrall'mara I recognize." His voice failed for a moment. "The man who stood over us . . . Do you know who that was?"

She wanted to say, "No," but she could not. She clung to

Crow and rested her head on his shoulder. "In the dream, my father saved me, saved *us*. It couldn't have been, but . . ."

Crow reached up and stroked her cheek, brushing away tears. "It looked like your father to me. How he was here, I don't know."

Alexia took a deep breath, and began to explain to Crow about the Communion of Dragons. It surprised her that she could, and part of her wondered if Maroth's presence in the real world meant that the Communion was somehow destroyed. Her prohibition against speaking about it certainly was, for the words poured out of her easily.

As she spoke, she reexamined everything in her mind. She recalled first meeting the Black Dragon and taking umbrage at his calling her "daughter." That she really was his daughter made more sense. If he was her father, he must have projected himself into the Communion in that last second before his body was destroyed at Fortress Draconis. He had lived since then in the Communion, gathering information and orchestrating plans to defeat Chytrine.

The implications of all that shook her. He had known of her through Preyknosery, and that neither of them had told her the truth felt like a betrayal. Then again, both of them were holding themselves to a higher duty than all others in the world—destroying Chytrine. For her father to have known of her, and to be denied the chance to hold her or touch her without dying, had to be agonizing. There was no doubting his love for her, though, as he made the ultimate sacrifice in coming to save her.

Crow nodded as she explained her thinking. "That would be your father. He would have carried his duty beyond the grave. And he would be very proud of you."

"I think he was proud of us both." Alexia smiled despite her tears. "In your memoirs, I can see how much you liked my father. I know he liked you. He told me I could trust you well before we grew close. He even talked to me about how I felt when I learned who you really were." Her voice dropped to a whisper. "And I think he was happy to know I was well loved."

Crow's arms tightened around her and he held her as she sobbed. She'd always hoped that her life would make her father proud. She wanted to live up to the heroic example he'd set. She never expected his approval, since he was dead. In an instant she knew she had it, and then had lost her father again. *Not lost, really, but found he was even more of a hero than anyone expected.*

She nestled in the cocoon of Crow's arms, with tears running down her face. He kissed her forehead and whispered soothingly. He clung to her tightly and never slacked his embrace until she gently pushed against his chest.

"A bit of a shock, all of this. I'm sorry."

Crow's right hand tipped her chin up and he looked her straight in the eyes. "You never have to apologize for what you feel, Alexia. All this—from a *sullanciri* trying to murder us to seeing your father and having him vanish—would have wrung emotions from Chytrine. That you feel them is proof that the goals your father set for you have been realized. You are not a killing machine, a general who will spend troops as if they were copper coins, but a thinking, feeling person who is capable of weighing every factor that impinges on a battle. Without that skill—without your feelings—you would fail. It will take time for you to come to grips with all this, and that's okay. I will be here. I will support you as you need it and want it. Your father loves you, I love you, your troops love and trust you. You are everything Chytrine is not, and you will be victorious."

Alyx sniffed, then shook her head and choked back more tears. The lump finally cleared her throat, allowing her to speak in a whisper. "I could not feel more loved than now, here in your arms. With you I can be myself. I can have my doubts and work them out. This is but one of the gifts you give me. I love you."

"I love you, too, Alexia." He kissed her again, then nodded toward Maroth. "If you don't mind telling me, what is that thing holding a dead *sullanciri*? How does it work?"

"That is Maroth, the Communion boatman." Alexia wiped away tears and sat up in bed. "Maroth, you can put her down. He follows simple commands, but I have no idea how he works."

The automaton did as he was bid by casting Myrall'mara's body aside. His arm returned to his side, then something clicked in his chest. A faint line of shifting, varicolored light grew from throat to abdomen as the metal chest plate parted. Both halves swung open and, nestled there in his chest, much in the same way Rymramoch's Truestone rested inside the puppet, was a dark, opalescent stone set in gold. The colors in it shifted the way an aurora undulates across the sky.

Alexia felt a fluttering in her stomach. "I think I now know a lot more about how he works than I ever wanted to."

Crow sat up beside her, hugging his knees to his chest. "That, I'll presume, is the missing piece of the DragonCrown."

"I think that's a safe assumption." Alexia rubbed a hand over her face. "It used to be secured in a place where Chytrine could never find it. Now it's in this world."

Crow nodded. "Not like we needed it, but now we have yet another reason to make sure Chytrine is defeated."

CHAPTER 46

Resolute did not move when he came awake. Part of him remained still so he could listen for sounds of the enemy around him. Another part wanted to assess his injuries. The pounding in his head indicated why he was just then waking up, and the fact that he was waking up suggested his wounds weren't fatal. That would have been taken as a very good sign under normal circumstances.

But things felt far from normal, and the biggest reason Resolute did not move was because he was disgusted with himself. Last he could recall, he had left Kerrigan with Trawyn, Oracle, Bok, and Rym to try to get inside the ward ring and find the DragonCrown fragments. He'd led the Grey Misters off to attack the Aurolani hunters, and it had been a savage and swift assault. A *kryalniri* they had working on the wards cast a spell and stepped forward, then instantly burst into flame. Even if that had not temporarily blinded many of the gibberers and *turekadine,* the shock of the creature's screams would have been enough to distract them.

The Grey Misters attacked fiercely and Resolute had felt utterly in his element. With Syverce in his left hand, he flicked bladestars through the night. More than one of the *turekadine* fell to those weapons. The gibberers who came at him with longknives found his slender sword more than a match for them, and his skills with it made him nearly invincible.

Resolute allowed himself a little derisive snort as that thought came to his mind. That tiny bit of motion let him feel the crust crack on his scalp, and a small trickle of blood rolled down behind his right ear. The pain in his head spiked, but tolerably so. He flexed some muscles and found himself mightily bruised, but with nothing else broken as near as he could tell. He didn't want to chance gross movements yet, but soon would find himself impatient to do so.

Anger pulsed through him. Thinking he was invincible, he'd charged off into the darkness after several of the gibberers. As he caught one by the scruff of the neck, the creature mewed piteously and just went limp. Resolute had been prepared for anything but that. The creature's legs became entangled with his own and he went down hard. He cracked his head on a tree and struggled to get up, but by then three or four terrified gibberers had surrounded him and beat on him with sticks and rocks until he passed out.

He did recall, a couple times, being carried along, and the presence of more than four pairs of hands on his body couldn't be denied. He assumed that once they'd run off, the Grey Misters had not pursued them and, without leadership, the gibberers had re-formed and were trying to figure out what to do next. One of them had to be of above average intelligence because they'd kept him alive. There was not a *sullanciri* in Chytrine's employ that wouldn't like to be able to deliver him to her feet.

If his head hadn't hurt so much, he would have shaken it. His thinking he was invincible was pure hubris. Somehow he had come to assume that, because he had fought for Vorquellyn's redemption so hard and so long, fate would let him be there to see it. It was an unwarranted assumption, and the hollowness of it battered him. His role, in many ways, had been one of mentor. He had trained Crow, both before and after his disgrace. He'd trained Will and even had a hand in training Kerrigan. His last moments with Kerrigan, telling him he'd have to take command and knowing that the boy actually could, should have been a clear signal to Resolute that his part in things was over.

He flexed his hands and found he could curl them into fists. Bringing his hands up to his shoulders, he gingerly pushed his body from the floor. His arms quivered, so he shifted to a hip and slowly sat up. A wave of vertigo washed over him, and a smaller one came in its wake. He steadied himself against the floor, then reached a hand out, found a stone wall, and inched over to it.

His arms and legs worked fine, though the stiffness in them was something he'd have to overcome before he made any attempt at escape.

That very idea brought a smile to his face, but one that tugged on a split lip. *Escape? You don't even know where you are. You're hurt, unarmed, and your friends have moved on.*

He shrugged slowly and opened his eyes. He found himself in a small room of stone. The wall opposite the door had a very small window, barred, set very high. Through it slanted enough dawnlight that he could see the door. Rough-hewn, though constructed solidly, it had a simple latch to open it and brackets that would allow it to be barred from his side. In an instant it registered in his brain that the door was most probably open, and all he had to do to escape was to walk out.

This time he did shake his head ever so slightly. Though he had a little ringing in his ears, it was not nearly enough to disguise the distant sound of snoring from the other room. It might have been four or a half-dozen gibberers who had brought him down, but more had joined them. He concentrated for a moment and estimated at least a dozen and a half lurked out there, and that was if *all* of them snored. There could have been triple that number of *turekadine* or *kryalniri* out there and he couldn't have told.

The lack of a lock and restraints on him suggested against intelligent Aurolani leadership, but to assume that was to be even more stupid than he'd been in getting trapped in the first place. He pulled his knees up to his chest and sat back against the wall. He listened hard, beyond the snores to the sounds from outside.

It had been forever since he thought about the time before the conquest, but memories came unbidden. He'd been in rooms like this before. On Vorquellyn they had such way-buildings out in the wilderness. Everyone from weary travelers to artists or poets seeking inspiration used them. Small sleeping rooms like this would open onto a large common room with a fire pit in the center, an open roof to let the smoke out, and enough furnishings to make everyone comfortable on long nights when tales could be shared.

Resolute had loved those nights—nights well before he had ever taken his exile name. He'd loved to go out hiking in the countryside, thinking up stories, remembering other tales. Writing poems.

A shiver ran down his spine. He had forgotten ever writing a poem. In the wake of the invasion, doing that had seemed so self-indulgent. Had he spent that wasted time learning how to handle a bow or a sword, he could have defended his homeland. Were he there and prepared, the Aurolani would have been turned back.

And while he knew that was nonsense, somewhere deep inside him it still felt true. He wondered if part of the trouble he'd had with Will had been that the youth fancied himself a poet, too. Resolute had abandoned that pursuit for something more important and here was the Norrington, the salvation of his nation, wasting his time with poetry and other frivolous pursuits.

Resolute cradled his head in his hands. The fingers of

his right hand found the wet blood and traced it back to a tear in his scalp. It would be nothing for anyone with healing magick, but that was nothing Resolute had ever bothered to learn. *Another bit of foolishness for which I now pay.*

He pulled in a deep breath, then slowly let it out. He had a simple problem that was without solution. At some point the gibberers would decide he had to be restrained or killed, and he could do nothing to prevent them from doing so. If he was to escape, he would have to get out of his prison and pick his way through them. Just one raising the alarm—and he had to assume at least one was awake and on watch—and he would be torn to pieces.

Either I stay here and die, or I go out there and take as many of them with me as I can.

He entertained that fantasy for a moment. Though unarmed, he could kill easily enough. Stiffened fingers driven into a throat would crush the windpipe and leave a gibberer choking out its life. Grabbing one by the muzzle was tricky, but once he had it, wrenching its head around so its chin tickled its spine wasn't hard. His kicks could shatter ribs and send them to puncture lungs, and just generally flinging a gibberer into a wall or pillar would do serious damage.

But so would their claws as they struck at him, or even flailed while dying. A gibberer bite could take a chunk out of him. If the blood loss didn't kill him fast, the blood poisoning would later. Just the mass of them out there would be enough to grab him, get him down, and even smother him—and all that was if they didn't bring weapons to bear.

How at odds that sort of ending would be with the heroic tales he used to enjoy. His cousins, Oracle and Seethe, would let him pretend to be a hero defending them from hordes. He would duel with shadows and phantoms while they laughed and cheered. Seethe was especially good at describing hideous foes that he would dispatch with élan, but usually not before taking some wound that threatened him. Oracle would then affect to heal him and he would continue the battle.

He started to think that those had been carefree times, but that made him laugh. *Everyone describes childhood that way.* It was a time before certain possibilities had been closed off. When he had been bound to Vorquellyn, his homeland would communicate its needs to him, and he would fulfill those needs. As with all young elves, he had sampled life and found the things he liked, in hopes that Vorquellyn would match him with his passion. That was supposed to be the way of it, that the homeland would direct one to occupations that made them feel most alive.

And now my passion is killing.

Resolute began to wonder what Vorquellyn would make of him now, but before that dark path could be descended, a tiny sound interrupted him. It came as a light tapping low on the door. He wasn't certain he'd actually heard it at first. Then he forced himself to focus, and it came again.

It came again, followed by wearily whispered pleas.

"Open. Now."

Resolute sprang to his feet, then dizzily went to his knees again. He crawled to the door and reached for the latch, slipping it quietly. He opened the door, looking toward the bottom, whence the tapping had come. Even as he opened it, the scent wafting in from the other room told him what he would find.

Despite being prepared, he could not choke off his gasp at what he found.

With all four hands wrapped around his spear, Qwc knelt on the stone floor. Blood had pooled around him. It stained his wings. It pasted one of his antennae to his skull. His head hung low, with his chin on his chest. The little Spritha's body heaved as he labored to breathe.

"Had to be here." His words came out tight and filled with agony. "Had to be."

Resolute's head came up and his heart sank. *Oh, Qwc, that spear stabbed far more than winterberries.*

He surveyed the common room. Gibberers, over twenty of them, lay still and silent. Some had a mask of webbing over their muzzles, or a torn mask hanging from clawed fingers. In brief flickers of firelight from the pit, the Vorquelf saw trickles of black fluid running from ears or eyes or noses. In some places wounds appeared between collarbone and neck, stabbed right down in and deep, or on others they were opened on the insides of the thighs.

The gibberers lay there, growing cold.

Without saying a word, Resolute scooped Qwc into his arms and slowly stood. He waited for his dizziness to clear, then stumbled into the common room. The Vorquelf carefully stepped over bodies and around puddles of blood. He set Qwc down on a bench near where the gibberers had piled Syverce and a pouch of bladestars, then found a bowl. He discarded the water in it, then went to the way station's cistern and filled it with fresh. He returned to the fire pit, used a longknife to scoop up a couple of cherry coals, and dropped them into the water.

Their hissing sounded preternaturally loud in the abattoir. Resolute dipped a finger into the water, found it warm enough, then tore a piece of a blanket free and wetted it. Slowly and carefully he began to wash the Spritha. He started with Qwc's head and once both antennae were clean and again erect, the Spritha revived a little.

He looked up at Resolute. "You are safe?"

"We are safe, Qwc." Resolute smiled at him carefully. "I've seen what you did here . . ."

Qwc shivered. "Had to be here. Resolute has to be free."

"I am." The Vorquelf dabbed blood from Qwc's tiny hands. "Qwc, you had no choice."

"That does not make it better."

"Nothing ever does, Qwc." Resolute smiled. "Nothing but the gratitude of a friend you have saved. Thank you, Qwc. I had been ready to die."

"Qwc watched Resolute a long time. Knew where to

stab because of you." The Spritha's voice grew distant. "You saved you, Resolute."

Another one I've trained, even without trying. He wiped down along Qwc's torso. "No more talking right now, Qwc. You took care of me. I'll take care of you. And soon, my little friend, we'll take care of the world."

CHAPTER 47

Markus Adrogans doffed his helmet and scratched at his head. With his disguise no longer needed, he had stopped shaving his head and his hair was growing back in. It itched. Scratching it did not wholly satisfy that itch, but he was content with even a modicum of relief.

The same was not true with the situation on the ground in the Ghost March.

From Logbal his force had headed east behind the shield of Caro's horsemen. It only took them three days to reach the frontier with the Aurolani domain. Queen Winalia had sent a legion of scouts with Adrogans, and they had proven most useful. While he suspected her of playing games, the people she gave him clearly had some pride and no small amount of hatred for the Aurolani. Adrogans had them watched carefully, but none of them tried to communicate with the enemy, nor did they act to provoke an attack which would engage Adrogans' forces.

The frontier had been marked rather clearly. Many trees had been hewn and shaped into crosses, with the lower two portions stuck firmly in the ground and the upper two clawing at the skies. The individuals who had been bound to them ankle and wrist had no support for their backs and heads. As they slowly suffocated, with their viscera pressing in on their lungs, their heads fell back and their shoulders ground in the sockets.

The crucified individuals marked the frontier both in length and in depth. As they rode in, not only did crucifixions stretch as far as the eye could see to the north and south, but the first three miles of Aurolani frontier likewise sprouted them on every hilltop and in every hollow. Gyrkyme scouts confirmed that more waited in the hills much further north and south. As the sun rose that next day, the first thing it silhouetted was yet more victims bound to their trees.

Adrogans had expected to feel the agony in his shoulders and hips. He'd waited for the burning of exhausted lungs to start in his chest, or the dry discomfort of a parched throat to make it hard to swallow. He imagined the sting of sweat searing into eyes or—gods be merciful— the harsh sound of a carrion bird landing, not waiting for the victim to die before slicing flesh with a razored beak and beginning the feasting.

He would have felt all of those things if this scene had been in Okrannel. Pain would have spared him none of it. He would have known the rising panic as breathing became more labored and shorter. He would have felt the burn of ropes against his wrists and ankles. *And if some carrion bird decided to help death claim me . . .*

But so far from the Zhusk homeland, the power of the *yrûn* had been blunted. Adrogans had been glad for that in part because it made it easier for him to concentrate. He did not have to devote part of his mind to dealing with the demands of his mistress. Nothing stood between him and planning the next assault.

As much as he liked having his mind clear, however, he also missed Pain's presence. She reminded him that what he was doing would make so many of his men her wards. They would fight for him, die for him, and endure endless agonies for him. Without her it was always a temptation to forget that and somehow accept that casualties and deaths were just part of war.

A day's march inside the frontier, his scouts found an ancient tower that had been repaired by the Aurolani, but not much expanded. A legion or so of creatures seemed to be occupying it. The garrison looked to be composed mostly of gibberers, but a few *kryalniri* and a couple of giant gibberers seemed to be in command. A small stable held frostclaws and, in the day they watched, a squad went out on patrol but had not returned by dusk.

The patrol's direction did seem to indicate they were looking to keep people *in* not out, but the fortress' position meant that any lumber caravans would have to pass by it. Without knowing how many patrols the fortress had out, or the locations of other towers in the area, slipping the bulk of his forces into the Aurolani domain without notice seemed impossible. Laying siege to the tower was something that could be done easily enough, but if a patrol escaped and warned those at the shipyard what was coming, the Aurolani might be able to bring enough troops in to stop his advance.

And if there is a single arcanslata *in there, alarm could be given even as we array our forces in the field to take the tower down.* The war-mages under his command said they detected no such devices, but Adrogans dismissed their assurances. Magickal communication, no matter the means, had to be assumed and, somehow, worked around.

Adrogans sent his scouts out and around the tower. They searched for signs of patrols, their circuits, and if their routes seemed regular. When reports came back that it seemed as if patrols moved from one tower to another—based on one set of tracks going out and another coming back—he set up ambushes along the routes to kill the pa-

trols. He assumed a day's delay in a patrol arriving from another post might not raise too much concern, but anything
longer than that would be trouble.

With his war-mages set up to detect use of *arcanslata*,
he then put his next phase of the plan in place. A ragged
band made up of six of Queen Winalia's scouts rode toward
the tower under a flag of truce. One of the large gibberers
asked what they wanted. The scouts told them that an
Alcidese general with a thousand horsemen was headed in
their direction and that Queen Winalia wanted them
warned.

Adrogans was willing to give them that much information, since he had to assume news of Caro's advance had already filtered over the border. The scouts were dismissed,
and they headed back west. Within an hour, two riders on
frostclaws headed east at high speed. That told Adrogans
that the Aurolani were not using magick to communicate
and, further, that other towers or way stations along the
road would provide fresh mounts for the couriers. He
would have to watch out for them.

The war-mages confirmed that no magick they could
identify had been used to communicate with the east. So
Adrogans let the two couriers move on without molesta-
tion. The gaps in the patrol schedule created when his ambushes killed the Aurolani scouts let him slip the bulk of his
forces past. He then had Caro's cavalry ride all over those
tracks, obscuring them—which would let any subsequent
scouting parties assume Caro's people had killed the patrols.

A day after Winalia's scouts had warned the Aurolani of
Caro's presence, his horde arrived at the fortress. Caro advanced under a white flag and informed the tower's commander that Queen Winalia had been deposed. He said
trade in wood and other goods would continue, but that
any incursion into his kingdom would be swiftly repulsed.
Caro and his people then rode west again.

Aurolani scouts trailed after them, but were swiftly murdered. Two more couriers headed east and were let pass with the confirmation of the earlier news about Caro. Adrogans fully expected the Aurolani commander—either a *sullanciri* at the shipyard or a local commander—would react to the news swiftly. He felt quite certain of that, for reasons he could not pinpoint, and reacted accordingly.

The road to the west wove through some hills between the tower and the nearest town, which served as a way station for couriers. Adrogans had the luxury of two days in which to prepare for the arrival of Aurolani reinforcements for the tower. During that time Caro's people regularly patrolled the frontier and skirmished with Aurolani scouts, drawing all attention to the west.

Adrogans only had twenty dragonels to use, so he set them up in four groups. He placed two batteries of two dragonels at one point along a long stretch of roadway. They pointed back along the road toward the east and had been filled with scatter-shot. Likewise another pair of batteries were set up seven hundred yards further west, though they pointed east. The east and west batteries could have hit each other at that range.

In the middle he arranged the remaining dozen dragonels along a hill on the south side of the road. There he placed the best of Agitare's crews, since they would have to reorient their weapons depending on where their shots were needed. The east and west batteries could remain fixed for the most part, and just needed to be loaded quickly.

Infantry was deployed behind the hills, but in a position to support the dragonels. The enemy trying to get at them would have to charge up a hill, and infantry would deny them their goal. He placed the Gurol Stonehearts on the hill directly across from the central battery, hoping they would be brave when the dragonels were shooting in their general direction. A lot of Aurolani would attempt to escape up that hill, so they would have plenty to do to keep them bottled up.

The ambush went off almost too easily. The reinforcements consisted of a regiment of infantry. The gibberers were being driven hard by *kryalniri* and the large gibberers, which Adrogans took to calling gibberkings in his mind. While they did have a small squad out in front to act as scouts, clearly their commanders feared no trouble until they reached the frontier. The scouts passed the well-hidden western battery and the main body of troops moved into the kill zone.

Once the last of the Aurolani had moved past the easternmost battery, it fired. All four dragonels blasted canisters of plum-sized shot into the last legion of gibberers. White plumes of smoke gave away the batteries' positions, but it mattered not at all as the closest enemy group evaporated. The iron shot came with sufficient force to blow through one gibberer and still manage to take an arm or leg off another. Bodies exploded, with blood, bone, and brains splashing far enough to paint the roadway. Horrid howls filled the hollow in the wake of the dragonel thunder.

As could be expected, half the troops in the middle turned to see what was happening behind them, while the other half began to run from the danger. The confusion and collisions further compacted the formation. Gibberkings and *kryalniri* shouted commands, but few of their troops complied. Given time, they might have been able to summon order from chaos, but that was not afforded them.

The southern battery vomited smoke and metal into the milling masses of gibberers. The shot vaporized the nearest ranks. Those behind fell as their legs were carried away, or their bellies were opened. Headless corpses tottered about for a heartbeat or two, blood geysering from ragged neck stumps, then pitched over. Those left miraculously untouched crawled from beneath their dying brethren, throwing off ropes of intestines or severed limbs, and moved away from the cloud of smoke slowly drifting down the hillside at them.

The west battery then spoke, ripping through the forward legion. Its standard wavered and fell. One gibberking scooped it up and raised it defiantly. He shouted at his troops, but could not be heard above the cacophony of screams. Dying gibberers clutched at him, forcing him to use the butt of the standard to knock them away.

The east battery let loose with another volley, then a ripple of fire came from the south battery. More gibberers died as a metal storm ripped them to bits. Survivors clawed at the hillside and raced upward, both at the batteries and away from them. In their hasty flight they never saw the soldiers waiting for them. Those who escaped hot iron met cold steel and ended up just as dead.

A third volley from each dragonel finished the grisly work. The light southerly breeze slowly cleared the smoke. Adrogans and every other soldier stared down at the road now paved with torn fur, pulverized bone, and an occasional twitching of a limb. Adrogans saw a heart beating within the shattered rib cage of a gibberking, and the matching spurt of blood from where the creature's left arm had once been. The spurt trailed into a drip and the heart's sluggish rhythm ceased altogether.

It had been one thing for him to see the destruction done by the dragonels to a building, and yet another to view the aftermath of the boombags on troops. This, however, had been something Adrogans had no way of putting into perspective. Before that ambush, slaughter on this scale would have been something only the gods could have engineered.

Adrogans shook his head. *And there are crowns who would not blanch from seeing men and women bobbing in such a death-soup.* He shivered, then looked away from the road at Captain Agitare.

"Your people are to be commended, Captain."

"Thank you, General." The young man's face had a bit of an ashen hue to it. "We'll do even better next time."

"I'm sure you will, Captain." Adrogans ran his hand back over his skull. "And the prospect of that fills me with dread."

CHAPTER 48

Erlestoke groaned inwardly as he and his command
company came around a hill and started down the
road. He glanced right and saw Count Wightman taking in the sight below. The other man's eyes widened for a
moment, then narrowed in calculation. *When next I have to
deal with him, I will see this again.*

The road descended to a narrow bridge over a small
river that flowed slowly. It was not terribly deep, but did
have steep sides and was too wide for a horse to leap. On it
waited a group of mounted warriors beneath the banner of
the Malviston family. Erlestoke looked for Baron Hallard
Malviston, but saw no one with his long white mane or his
thick beard in that group.

There was, however, a wagon behind them draped in
black. A single horse drew it. The cargo in the back rested
on a bier likewise covered in black. It contrasted with the
white pine of the casket, and Erlestoke had no trouble
imagining where the baron rested.

Beyond the bridge, on each side of the road, square
breastworks had been raised. Spiked logs decorated the

gradual slope leading to the small earthworks. The necessity of weaving in and out of the abatises meant any cavalry charge at the breastworks would fail—not that any horseman would take his mount at the earthworks, since they bristled with spears and were filled with men. Past that, at the top of the hill, more abatises blocked the road, and another line of earthworks crested the hill.

Dranae rode up between the prince and Count Wightman. "It would appear you're not to pass. Would you like me to deal with this?"

"Your offer is tempting, my friend, but I think we try talk first. Do come with me, however." The prince glanced at Borell. "Will you fix a flag of white to that lance you're carrying?"

"Yes, Highness."

The youth complied with the request, then rode out a few yards ahead of the command company. He raised the standard three times and got a white flag raised three times below. Borell looked back once, then led Erlestoke, Dranae, and Nay forward. Overhead, Preyknosery Ironwing drifted lazily, cradling Erlestoke's quadnel in his arms. With a Gyrkyme and a dragon to act as bodyguards, Erlestoke knew he should fear nothing.

But only a fool fears nothing.

They approached the bridge at a walk, which gave Erlestoke enough time to recognize the tall man with long red hair flowing from beneath his helmet. The baron had one son who lived. Sambell Malviston was someone Erlestoke had met before but not particularly liked. Sambell had seemed to loathe Erlestoke, much as he loathed King Scrainwood, but the baron had been one of Scrainwood's staunchest allies, so Sambell's hatred for him had been left to simmer in silence.

The slender man's head came up, and even at twenty yards distant the intensity of his blue stare chilled Erlestoke. At half that distance the prince saw the orphan notch cut in Sambell's mask, confirming the old baron's death. With hatred that bald and cold, and a corpse on a wagon, the death was recent. And clearly the new baron thought Erlestoke had something to do with it.

Erlestoke reined up and rested both hands on his saddle horn. "Greetings, cousin. I grieve for your loss."

Malviston spat. "Call me not cousin, murderer. My father lies there in that box, cold and dead because of you. You'll not enter our lands without paying a blood price—and a dear one."

Erlestoke lifted his chin. "If there is a blood price to be paid, I shall pay it, dear or not. The fact is you have me at a disadvantage. How is it that the price of your father's death is presented to me?"

Those in the baron's company looked at each other, but the baron kept his eyes on Erlestoke. "Don't even attempt to feign innocence, Erlestoke. You and your Bloodmasks have done much work here, much horrible work. The countryside is up in arms against you. It is not enough that you have rebelled against your father. You now lead invaders into a nation that does not want you, and you slay loyal sons of Oriosa because they will not support your usurpation of the throne."

"I see." Erlestoke crossed his arms over his chest. "I won't feign innocence, but I will plead ignorance. Tell me who the Bloodmasks are and inform me of the circumstances of your father's death."

The baron pointed back toward the command company. "There, one of the Bloodmasks rides openly with you."

Erlestoke looked back, then frowned. "Rumbellow? He's a Murosan, one of the Addermages."

"A murderer by any other name is yet so foul. They have been slinking around here in the Midlands, making sheep miscarry, souring milk, raising root weevils in the fields, stealing children, and poisoning wells. You boldly admit they are mages, but this we knew, and adder fits them well

since they wait and strike from hiding, vicious and viru-
lent."

"And one of them slew your father?"

The baron hesitated for a moment, then nodded emphatically. "My father had heard of the Hawkriders and
their treason. He exhorted his people to remain neutral and
to see to themselves. He said he would not support you in
the illegitimate usurpation of your father. For that, you had
him slain. For that I will see that neither you nor your army
takes another step into the Midlands."

Behind him the lordlings he had chosen for his entourage nodded in agreement.

Erlestoke frowned mightily. "How did your father die?"

Another rider, an older man who, by the marks on his
mask, had served the elder baron for many years, spoke.
"My lord baron was found dead in his bed, alone and cold,
with no sign of violence. He was slain with sorcery, of this
there is no doubt at all. Had honorable assassins come
upon him, they would have died with him, perhaps instead
of him. Your Bloodmasks stole into his castle and murdered him at your command."

The prince pressed a finger to his lips as he thought. He
sorted fact from speculation in an attempt to understand
fully the situation he faced. The baron had been an old man
and, even if hale, dying suddenly in his sleep could not be
discounted. Sambell supposed that because his father had
counseled against joining Erlestoke, the prince had murdered his father. Because the baron had been advocating
neutrality, killing him would have been a self-indulgent
luxury on Erlestoke's part—and a stupid one since it would
certainly create exactly the sort of hostile response he now
faced.

The existence of the Bloodmasks intrigued him, however. Having magicker agents causing trouble throughout
the Midlands could be a strategy conceived by either the
Aurolani or his father. Mayhem committed by the
Bloodmasks might be enough to turn Hallard Malviston

from neutral to actively hostile. If the man were reluctant to shift in that direction, killing him and pointing at Erlestoke as the instigator likewise benefited the enemy. King Scrainwood would have known enough of Sambell and his animosity to assume the new baron would jump to the conclusion that the prince had blood on his hands, and that would aid the enemy a great deal.

Erlestoke's hand returned to the saddle horn. "My lord, where were you when your father died?"

Sambell stiffened. "My father had bid me to come south and see what it was you were doing."

"Did you have a chance to send him a report? What did you say we were doing?"

The baron waved those questions away. "It's immaterial, though it would have been to your benefit. You were ridding the countryside of Aurolani."

"Doing what you wanted to do, but your father stopped you from doing?"

Sambell shifted his shoulders stiffly. "What passed between my father and me does not bear on his murder."

"No, it doesn't, but something else does." Erlestoke pointed to the casket. "Your father sent you south to watch what I was doing, but he never told you to order me to stop, did he?"

"No."

"So he did not believe the Bloodmasks were my agents, did he?"

"No, and he died by their hand because of his naïve belief, murderer."

Borell levered his lance in the baron's direction. "Keep a civil tongue in your mouth."

Erlestoke shook his head. "Borell, no."

"But, Highness, he has thrice said you murdered his father." The young man's eyes hardened. "Once is tolerable for his grief, a second for his rank, but a third?"

"Count it another for his grief, Borell. Return to my side." The prince waited for the youth to comply, then he looked at Sambell again. "Your father wisely preached neutrality, but he did not mind my moving into his land to destroy the enemy. That is my goal, and you know it because Meredo does not burn behind me. My father remains on the throne. All rumors of usurpation are nonsense. Your father might not have supported me, but he did not *oppose* me, and that is all I ask. Murdering him would simply have provoked the anger you feel now and spawned the opposition I see before me. If you count me wise enough to dispatch Bloodmasks and murder your father, you cannot at the same time believe me stupid enough to have lost sight of that fact."

Malviston snorted. "Perhaps you are even more clever. You use your Bloodmasks to incite people, you murder my father to focus their ire at you, then you use your trickery to seduce me to your side. With me come my people. With my people comes the middle of the nation, and with it comes the Dales and Norweshire. As goes the north, so goes the south—and your father will flee for Saporicia."

Erlestoke canted his head to the right. "Fascinating plan, and one with merit, save for one thing. All I have done is make war on the Aurolani. You know as well as I do that my attacks are only provoking the Aurolani. The troops I have slain are the vanguard of a larger group. There will be a war here. If you let me pass, it will take place in the Dales. If not, you risk its taking place in the Midlands."

"Don't threaten me."

"I don't. You're already threatened, and you know it. You saw what I was doing as vital, and you reported that to your father, didn't you?"

The baron nodded. "If he had only listened."

"Perhaps he did."

"What do you mean?"

"It is plain, I think. It is possible your father died naturally, finally able to let go because he knew his realm would at last be safe from the Aurolani. No more sacrificing his pride, your pride, to keep my father happy and the

Aurolani benign. And, if murdered, perhaps it was because someone intercepted a message he sent to you, or one from you to him. In either case, the message led the enemy to believe your father would no longer be neutral. His murder, with the blame fixed on me, would reverse the situation to the enemy's benefit."

Sambell Malviston stroked a gloved hand over his jaw. "If I did not consider your words, I would be a fool."

"If you did not consider them long and hard, I would be surprised." Erlestoke looked back at his command company and the troops arrayed beyond them. "It is late in the day. We shall make camp here, with your permission, while you think."

The baron nodded. "You'll forgive me if I do not offer you hospitality."

"Of course. But I would beg of you one indulgence."

"That being?"

"I promised you a blood price for your father. I shall keep that vow." The prince smiled slowly. "While you think, I shall harvest Bloodmasks."

CHAPTER 49

Predator, the leader of the Grey Mist, had followed Oracle into the small cave and heard her pronouncement about Resolute. Her words had made Kerrigan's stomach turn inside out, but appeared to have a different effect on the sapphire-eyed Vorquelf. He sheathed the longsword he'd been carrying, then smeared a blood spatter across his left cheek with his sleeve. His blue eyes narrowed as he looked from Kerrigan to Trawyn, and then at the old elf hanging in the web of roots.

"What's wrong with him?"

The Loquelf answered. "Dreamwing. You can tell by the tinge of his skin. He's highly unpredictable and dangerous."

Predator pointed at the belt pouches. "Those are the Crown fragments?"

Trawyn nodded. "Yes. The Lakaslin fragment, and the Vorquellyn fragment."

The Vorquelf squatted. "Okay, what we're going to do is this. We kill the elf . . ."

"No!" Kerrigan shifted himself between the elf and Predator. "You're not going to kill him."

"Be quiet, boy." Predator looked at Trawyn. "You said he is unpredictable and dangerous. I say we kill him and end that threat. We take the fragments and head back south. Keeping them away from Chytrine is our number one priority."

Trawyn nodded. "I agree, but we don't kill the Vorquelf."

Oracle nodded. "This Vorquelf is the key to the *coriiesci* on Vorquellyn. We need him to rescue the Norrington."

The princess waved that consideration away. "He may well be, but that is a secondary problem right now."

Oracle closed her eyes. "If we do not get the Norrington soon, he will be lost to us forever. He is where he needs to be to fulfill the prophecy. We must get to him or everything is for naught."

Predator laughed sharply. "Trying to get to the Norrington is a fool's errand."

Kerrigan's mouth hung open for a moment. "But you came all the way from Yslin to help Resolute."

"And he's not here now, is he?" Predator snorted. "Doesn't matter. Even Resolute would agree with the shift in priorities."

Kerrigan frowned. "No, he wouldn't. He didn't want to come after the fragments. He just wanted to go to Vorquellyn."

Predator snarled. "I told you to be quiet, boy. Your elders are talking."

The venom in his voice lashed at Kerrigan and he shrank back. His heels bumped the root web. He started to flail his arms, fearing he would fall, but he regained his balance. He blushed, supposing the elves would berate him further, but they just ignored him.

They so thoroughly dismissed him that they began speaking in Elvish. That was a grave insult. They were treating him as if he didn't even exist. As far as they were concerned, his opinions and feelings, his thoughts and insights, were valueless.

Kerrigan shivered and hugged his arms around himself. With Resolute gone, he felt alone. Yes, Bok and Rym were there, but the dragon remained in his box, and Bok squatted in the shadows, saying nothing. Even Oracle had fallen silent as Predator and Trawyn danced their way through a power-sharing agreement that would allow them to lead the group back south.

Kerrigan hung his head. *I'm sorry, Resolute, I have failed you.* A chill puckered his flesh. Orla, Will, and now Resolute—and with him Crow and Oracle, and even Alexia. He had failed them all. The living were off fighting, hoping that this expedition would manage to destroy Chytrine so they could destroy her troops. That's what he knew the group should be doing, but without Resolute there, everything was falling apart.

A thought shook him. Resolute had left *him* in charge. Kerrigan didn't know what to do, but Resolute would have. The youth frowned. *What would Resolute do?*

That thought erased the frown and replaced it with a smile, albeit a small one. He could see Resolute's eyes blazing, and his hand closing on the back of Predator's neck. He'd set Predator back, and he'd stare the princess down, and things would be going the way they were supposed to. Resolute was a force of nature, and that's what was needed to deal with the current situation.

Kerrigan's hands balled into fists as Predator said, "Then it is agreed. We will take the fragments and . . ."

"No! NO!" Kerrigan matched their Elvish easily. "Nothing is agreed until I agree to it. Resolute entrusted me with this expedition. We are going to Vorquellyn. We are going to rescue Will, then we're going to kill Chytrine."

Predator's head turned slowly and the sapphire stare met his as he fingered a dagger. "Shut your mouth or I'll open a second one for you."

What would Resolute do? Kerrigan snorted, then gestured casually. The spell hit Predator hard in the chest, knocking him back into a knot of Grey Misters. They all went down in a tangle of limbs and curses.

Kerrigan shifted his gaze to Trawyn. "With all due respect, Princess, I will do the same to you. By his reckoning and yours, I might be a child, but that's not what Resolute thought. You're not going south. We're going north to Vorquellyn."

Trawyn eyed him carefully. "You'll not stop us if we want to leave."

"No?" Kerrigan reached back and fingered the root web. "I broke the wards; I can establish them again. No one leaves."

A thrown dagger hit him in the right shoulder and bounced off the dragonbone armor. Kerrigan looked at where Predator crouched. "That didn't work. Do you know how foolish that was, or do I have to punish you?"

"I'm not following you to Vorquellyn."

"Actually, yes, you are." Kerrigan raised his right hand, then convulsed it into a fist, and the Grey Misters flinched. "You're going to follow me and help me because we're going to get your homeland back. You left Yslin because you decided it was time you did something useful. You made a grand sacrifice for a grand goal, and now you're going to stop because you found a lesser goal and the sacrifice was beginning to be inconvenient? You've got sore feet so you go home? No wonder *real* elves think of you as children."

He opened his hand again and lowered it. "Sure, fighting Chytrine is not fun, but did you think war would be? You need to think of your elders who were driven off Vorquellyn, or died there. What happened to them wasn't fun.

"If they were here they'd be just like this guy behind me, having to medicate themselves because the pain of your land is driving them mad. You want her to do that to everyone else? You want to *let* her do that to everyone else?

"Besides, how far can you run? It won't be far enough. Are some of us going to die? Yes, without a doubt, just like Resolute. Just like Will. Just like Orla and Lombo. Just like the thousands massacred in Sebcia and Muroso. Maybe you don't have any pride. Maybe you don't have any courage. Maybe you don't have any hope. Maybe you need to find a little bit of each, because if you walk away from here, you're not really walking, you're crawling. You'll be on your belly and ready to lick Chytrine's boots. And all you'll get for that is a kick in the teeth."

Kerrigan whirled on Trawyn. "As for you, maybe you're just tired. Maybe you want to be dosed with dreamwing to ease your mind. You know as well as I do that if you don't want Loquellyn to be the same as Vorquellyn, Chytrine has got to die. We're taking this elf north to Vorquellyn, getting Will, and saving Loquellyn in the process."

The Loquelf raised her chin. "I have told you he will be dangerous. You've never seen anyone withdrawing from the effects of dreamwing. I have. He could kill us all with a nightmare. If it takes us a week to get to Vorquellyn, he might be sufficiently free to open the *coriiesci*, but we'll never make it all the way there with him. If we keep him dosed, he can't be of use. How do you propose to solve that problem?"

"Oh, I don't have to solve it."

"No?" She shook her head slowly. "I'm content to stay here, because traveling with him is to die. I do think you need to solve *that* problem, Kerrigan."

"I don't have to solve it because it's already been solved." Kerrigan smiled and began to weave a spell. "Chytrine solved it. You want him isolated until he's rational, so he shall be."

The spell Kerrigan used on the Vorquelf was the same one Chytrine had used on him, with a couple of modifications. The magickal cocoon surrounding the elf absorbed any magick he cast, but didn't cut him entirely off from the source of magick. Kerrigan also wove a key into it that involved logic problems. He hoped that unless the dreamwing-eater was rational and lucid, they would be beyond his ability to solve.

The Vorquelves, feral and unmannerly though they were, respected Kerrigan's power. He actually thought they respected the dragonbone armor more, but he was willing to accept anything as long as they followed orders. Trawyn appeared to be surprised by his solution to the dreamwing-withdrawal problem, but remained true to her word and agreed to accompany him.

They cut the elf down and bundled him up in the roots and some blankets. Grey Misters created a stretcher for him and took turns carrying him. Kerrigan didn't think the elf weighed that much, but to hear them grumble, he could have been carved of granite. The Grey Misters did not like Kerrigan's constant commands to be quiet, but they complied because even they could see signs of gibberers in the area.

But mostly they complied with his orders because whenever he had a problem, he asked himself what Resolute would do, and then he did it to the best of his ability. He tried not to hurt anyone too much, but some of the Grey Misters were not open to reason. He took to boosting them skyward and having them fall back down through foliage in what became known as "tree-dancing." Only one Vorquelf needed a second dance, and while Kerrigan's obvious display of power cowed most of them, he could also feel resentment rising.

Qwc's loss made Kerrigan's job even harder. The Spritha had been able to lighten everyone's spirits no matter how difficult things had been. The trek north actually was much easier than the previous trek, as the mountains sloped down toward the sea and the lush rain forests provided a lot of shade, water, and even edible flowers or some early seeds and berries. None of this quelled the Grey Misters' grumbling, and things came to a head at the shore of the Crescent Sea.

Kerrigan had high hopes when they came down to a

cove where an Aurolani ship sheltered. A quick spell put everyone on board asleep. The Grey Misters swarmed over the single-masted vessel, dispatching the crew and pitching their bodies overboard. Kerrigan, Oracle, Bok, Rym, Trawyn, and the sleeper had remained onshore during the ship's takeover. With the assault successfully completed, they came on board. Some of the Vorquelves brought the gangway aboard while others quickly surrounded them on the rowers' deck and Predator looked down on them from the wheeldeck.

"There has been a change of plans. We are sailing south."

Kerrigan shook his head. "You know that won't happen. I won't let that happen."

"What are you going to do, Kerrigan? Are you going to hole this boat? No, of course not." Predator began to strut. "I have tolerated what you have done because heading north was in keeping with my plans. Had we turned south, we would have been in more danger. But now we have a ship and will be able to sail back to Yslin with the fragments. You can't stop us because you can't sail this ship all by yourself."

Kerrigan gaped at him. "You can't stop now, Predator." He pointed north toward Vorquellyn. "We are so close."

"We are *too* close." The Vorquelf shook his head. "When you brought the Lakaslin fragment to Loquellyn they wouldn't let you take it to Fortress Draconis because they knew there was a chance that Chytrine would take it from you there. Now you want us to take *two* fragments to an island she's owned for more than a century? The foolishness of that choice is obvious. The Loquelves wouldn't let you do it, and neither will I."

Kerrigan shook his head. "The only place this ship is sailing is to Vorquellyn. Count on that."

"Idle threat, Kerrigan." Predator folded his arms across his chest. "The only way to stop us from taking it is to kill us, and you won't do that. You're not a killer."

"He's not, but *I* am."

Predator whirled to face the speaker. "But . . . You're dead!"

"Not really; I just feel like it." Resolute, sodden from his swim to the ship and climb up the tiller, caught Predator in the side of the head with a punch. The blow knocked the smaller Vorquelf into the ship's wheel, where his arms caught and he hung limply. Resolute shook his hand out, then rubbed at it. After a moment he looked out over the knot of Grey Misters.

"We're going to Vorquellyn. Now let's get moving."

"Wait." Oracle took a step forward. "Before we go, we have to offer gifts to Tagothcha to guarantee safe passage."

Resolute nodded. "I'll toss him Predator."

"Gifts, Resolute, not something you don't want."

The silver-eyed Vorquelf shrugged. "The gibberers left me little save Syverce. I really have nothing to offer."

"I do." Kerrigan shucked his pack and rooted around in it. He withdrew a slender cloth-wrapped cylinder. He undid the ties, then peeled the cloth from a long, slender crystal with gold collars on each end. The collars had been set with various gemstones. Several of the Grey Misters gasped when they saw it, and greed lit their faces. "I'll give him this."

Resolute shook his head. "That's too valuable."

"Which makes it even more appropriate. I got this from the urZrethi to reward me for helping them do something important. That's what we want Tagothcha to do, so this is fitting."

Holding it before him, he walked to the prow. Tagothcha, the *weirun* of the Crescent Sea, had a reputation for being notoriously capricious and even malevolent. Fishermen and traders regularly offered him gifts of wine or gold before setting out on a journey in hope the sea would be kind to them. While the mages of Vilwan tended to be dismissive of the gods, even they offered gifts to appease Tagothcha before sailing.

Kerrigan smiled. "Tagothcha, this is a treasure carried from the heart of Bokagul to you. Please grant us safe passage in our journey." He pulled his hand back, then threw the wand out into the darkness and heard it splash.

After him, one by one, the Grey Misters made their own offerings. None of them had anything to equal the wand, but coins, a ring or two, several knives, and a dozen gibberer pelts all sank beneath the waves. Resolute carved Elvish words on a wooden plate he'd taken from below and sailed that out into the night.

Kerrigan looked at him with an upraised eyebrow. "What did you offer?"

"Dozens of gibberers driven into his arms."

Trawyn likewise inscribed a plate and flung it into the night. "There are wards at Rellaence Bay that bar his entry. I will have them removed."

Qwc, who had flown to the ship after Predator had been dealt with, landed on the masthead and raised his spear over his head. "Yours. Qwc is done with it." The silver spear spun out and sank beneath the waves with a tiny splash.

By far the most curious of the gifts was the one offered by Oracle. She lowered a bucket on a rope and brought it up full of water. She sank her face into it and spoke—or so Kerrigan assumed, since the water bubbled—then poured the water back into the sea. She wiped her face on a sleeve, but refused to say much about what she had offered. "A vision of the future, nothing more."

Resolute watched for a moment, then nodded. "I believe, then, we are ready to go. To the oars."

The Grey Misters moved to comply with his order. Resolute, Bok, and Kerrigan brought the anchor up while Trawyn stepped over Predator and took hold of the wheel.

Resolute pointed at a star winking above the horizon. "Steer by Plenariath and soon enough we'll be home."

CHAPTER 50

I thought I was never to see you again."

Sayce's comment, voiced in little more than a whisper, sank like a knife into Isaura's heart. The first time she'd spoken to the woman had been less than two weeks before, and Isaura had brought her food every day. They'd conversed a little and Sayce had become a bit emboldened and even feisty. It was an aspect of people Isaura had not seen before, and she had come to enjoy it.

Then, barely a half week past, her mother fell into a towering rage. Isaura didn't know what to do. Ferxigo had told her to be available to her mother constantly while the *sullanciri* headed south to deal with Aurolan's defenses. While nothing was said, Isaura felt there must have been some sort of reversal in the south. Her mother had not been nearly as upset when Okrannel had been lost, so this was clearly something that had not been expected.

Isaura had not been able to visit Sayce. Hlucri had seen to it that the Murosan got her food and had enough in the way of blankets to keep her warm, but for the last six days,

Sayce's shackles had not been loosed, nor had she been allowed to leave her cell, even fettered.

Isaura slipped an arm around Sayce's shoulders and could feel the woman shivering beneath the drearbeast cloak. "I wanted to come, but my mother needed me."

Sayce, walking along beside Isaura through the castle corridors, kept her voice small. "Something happened, didn't it?"

Isaura nodded. She had pieced things together from her mother's mutterings, of which she heard far too much. Her mother spent most of her time in the highest reaches of the palace working at spells, or deep in the bowels of the earth visiting the Oromise. Isaura had accompanied her on one trip down there, and spent hours listening to her mother in her *arcanorium*.

Neither experience made her feel good, and both made her wonder after her mother's sanity.

Isaura knew she should not tell Sayce anything about the war, and especially nothing that would suggest difficulty with the Aurolani effort. It would be cruel to give the woman false hope. A momentary setback would not stop her mother's march to victory. Isaura did not doubt the final outcome of the war, but she also could not bring herself to crush Sayce's spirit, especially when the woman already felt abandoned and alone.

Much as I do these days.

Isaura kept her voice low, though she knew Hlucri could hear her despite his remaining at a discreet distance behind them. "One of my mother's *sullanciri* died. About the same time another *sullanciri* had her army mauled in Saporicia. That army has fallen back and will join with Nefrai-kesh's forces in Muroso."

Sayce stiffened at the mention of her home.

"I'm sorry."

"Actually you are not, Isaura, but I know that. I don't mind." The smaller woman turned her head, offering

Isaura half a smile from within a furred hood. "I would tell you that I'm sorry your mother lost a *sullanciri*, but I am not. Was that Dark Lancer a friend of yours?"

What was she to me? Myrall'mara had always kept herself apart, even more than the other *sullanciri*, save perhaps for the dead ones. They offered nothing in the way of conversation or intellectual engagement at all. But Myrall'mara had always been melancholy around her and avoided her as much as possible. Isaura had returned the favor, and while she would have thought that would have been something the *sullanciri* wanted, Isaura's withdrawal seemed to cause Myrall'mara more pain, not less.

"Myrall'mara was someone I had known, but not well. None of my mother's *sullanciri*, except Hlucri, were exactly what you would call friendly. Though Nefrai-kesh is always nice to me and brings me things." Isaura slipped a glove off her hand and showed the sapphire ring he'd brought from Oriosa. "He gave me this. He said the Oriosan Queen wanted me to have it."

Sayce shivered again. "You know he murdered her, don't you?"

"I don't . . ."

"Twisted her head off and put it in the hands of her son, Scrainwood." The Murosan nodded toward the ring. "He must have taken that from her corpse and presented it to you. Must have cleaned it first, though."

Isaura looked closely at the ring, seeking any tiny fleck of blood. She knew it was impossible that there would be any, but still she could almost feel blood flowing from beneath the stone and washing over her hand in a warm, sticky coat. *He couldn't have, could he?*

"You must be mistaken. He was quite clear about her intent."

Sayce sighed. "You surprise me."

"How so?"

"You are Chytrine's heir. You command many people here, and yet you are so naive. Why would she offer you the ring when no one knew you existed? Had anyone known Chytrine had an heir, and that gifts offered might curry favor, there would be miles of caravans waiting to enrich you beyond all knowing. And why, if she did offer you the ring, would he murder her?"

"How do you know he did?"

"There are witnesses and he is a *sullanciri*. Either explanation suffices."

The dull finality in Sayce's reply sent a shiver crawling down Isaura's spine. She peered at the ring even more closely and thought about using a spell to see if there were impressions left on the ring by the queen's death. She could have cast it and learned, once and for all, if Sayce told the truth, but she already knew what the outcome of that casting would be.

She quickly pried the tainted ring off her finger and tossed it to Hlucri.

The *sullanciri* caught it, sniffed, then let it hang from a talon.

"When we get outside, throw it as far away as you can."

Hlucri nodded silently.

"We're going outside?"

"Yes. You can't outrun Hlucri." Isaura turned left and made quickly for a doorway that led into the ice garden. When Neskartu still instructed students from the south in the ways of Aurolani magick, they used to come to the garden and practice spells that would grow marvelous things from a seed of enchanted ice. Neskartu was dead, and most of his students were as well—with most of the survivors in the south already fighting. The garden would have fallen to ruin save for Isaura's work and Drolda's careful tending.

Sayce gasped as she saw the garden. Plants, complete with flowers, and creatures of incredible delicacy, had been grown from ice. Glassine trees had leaves that swayed in unfelt breezes, and birds had individually rendered feathers fletching them. Timid rabbits peered out from the base of ice bushes, and flowers pointed their crystal faces toward the sun—never having to move much in so northern a clime.

"Isaura, this is so beautiful." Sayce reached a gloved hand toward a flower, but held back from touching it. "I don't want to ruin anything."

Isaura grasped the flower for which she reached and snapped it off, then handed it to her. "You see, there *is* beauty in my nation."

Sayce took the proffered flower and slowly nodded her head. "I never thought there wasn't."

"You hate Aurolan."

"No, I don't. I hate what Aurolan is doing to my nation. I know your mother is making those things happen. I can understand people following her. That doesn't mean I don't think there is beauty here." Sayce raised the flower to her nose and sniffed. "You have shown me the beauty of Aurolan."

Isaura frowned. "This is but one part of it."

The Murosan shook her head. "Not this, not the countryside, but the true beauty of it. Isaura, you could have left me to starve in the dungeons. You didn't have to bring me food. You didn't have to befriend me. You did that because of something inside you. Chytrine may be your mother in one way or another, but you don't have her heart. You have a loving heart, a *good* heart. You would be cherished anywhere, respected anywhere, accepted anywhere, and loved anywhere."

The redheaded woman's face came up. "Have you ever been in love?"

Isaura shook her head quickly. "No."

"Oh, Isaura." Sayce lowered the flower and began to walk deeper into the garden. "I have. It is beautiful. I loved—I *love*—Will Norrington."

"Why?"

"Why?" Sayce laughed lightly. "Hard to say, really. He

wasn't what I expected him to be. You grow up hearing the Norrington Prophecy and you expect him to be this huge man with bulging muscles who could break a hoargoun over his knee. That's what I thought I would find when I met him but . . . Well, you saw him when you healed him."

"He was nothing as you described him."

"No, he wasn't. I think that is how he got to me. Here he was, this little thief, but someone who could be kind and gentle. He made me laugh. He reminded me that kings and princes and lords and ladies were just people, too, and not always very good. In him I found a nobility—a little tarnished, but nobility nonetheless—that born nobles seldom possess."

Sayce's eyes lit up. "You should have seen him with the Freemen, Isaura. These men of Oriosa came to pledge their fealty to him. They offered to spend their lives in his defense, and to further his cause. He accepted them and realized that he was responsible for them. He rewarded them for good acts and encouraged them. He made every one of them feel as if their lives were even more valuable than his, and that they were part and parcel of the Norrington Prophecy."

Isaura heard Sayce's words, but listened more closely to her tone. Will Norrington was dead, yet in speaking of him Sayce was happy. The memory made her proud. Just as Will Norrington had given of himself to the Freemen, he clearly had given to Sayce. Her love for him gave her strength despite his death.

That emotion was utterly foreign to her. She'd felt other emotions of similar intensity, but fear was the one she most commonly recalled. Fear of her mother's wrath. Fear of the Oromise. Both of them were very intense, and she had nothing positive to balance against them.

Even the affection Nefrai-kesh had shown her evaporated from her mind as Hlucri arced the ring out into the distance. It vanished from sight, and with it went Isaura's feeling of complacency. Aurolan used to feel right to her, but that was because it was the only place she had known. It was familiar, but it no longer fit as well in her life as it once had. She had been to the south. She had seen horrible things done in her mother's name. She once would have thought she could appeal to her mother to change things, but her mother groveled before the Oromise so obsequiously that Isaura wondered if her mother had ever been acting on her own or had always been a thrall to the creatures buried beneath the earth.

Isaura took Sayce by the shoulders and turned the smaller woman to face her. "I have to ask you something. Don't lie to me."

"I would never."

"Yes, you would. You see it as your duty. You want to escape for yourself and your child."

Sayce nodded. "I would lie, but not now, not to you right now."

"Is love why people in the south laugh?"

The Murosan smiled and raised a hand to caress Isaura's cheek. "Oh, love can make you laugh, and it can make you cry and be angry and overjoyed and quiet and loud, serious and gay. It can make you do almost anything."

"Does everyone in the south know love?"

"No, Isaura, they don't." Sayce's voice softened. "But love is something to which everyone aspires. We write songs and poems and plays and stories about it. We work out great strategies to attract the notice of someone we favor. We arrange parties and celebrations and holidays as an excuse to spend time with those we love. Most importantly, though, when we find that special person, we make a life with him. We make a future and fill it with babies and even more love."

Isaura pressed her lips together. A tear formed in her left eye and seared a track down her cheek.

"Oh, Isaura, what is it?"

Chytrine's daughter swallowed hard. "I love my mother. I love Aurolan. No one loves me."

"Someone will, Isaura, I know it."

"I know it, too." Isaura set her shoulders and exhaled slowly. "And that someone, I am certain, lives in the south. It is time, Sayce, that you and I go find him."

CHAPTER 51

In the dawn's growing light, the battlefield looked different than it had in the twilight. The day before, as night fell, soldiers still stood and banners waved fiercely. There had been the clash of swords, the thunder of drums, and the endless keening of people in pain. Those sounds continued as night swallowed the bloody field, and the fighting drifted back toward the town of Merysval, but Alexia had not seen what had been left behind until dawn.

The battle itself had gone almost too easily. It paralleled very closely what she had related in her dreams to her aunt. Tythsai had retreated into Muroso and taken up a position around the village, then advanced into fallow fields to make a stand. The Aurolani had positioned themselves on an upslope, but they had been reduced to just under four thousand, with only nine hundred cavalry. The fields around Merysval were meant for cavalry, and once the Aurolani frostclaws had been eliminated, the rest of the army would be picked apart.

The sides met in a straightforward battle where infantry crashed into infantry and cavalry swept the edges, trying to turn a line. The Alcidese Iron Horse did manage to turn the Aurolani right wing, so Tythsai called a withdrawal toward the village. Alexia's entire army pivoted to the left and center forward, and, while she could not envelop the Aurolani before they reached the village, she did manage to surround it. Nothing would be leaving that hamlet.

Nothing had, save for a legion of cavalry surrounding Tythsai. Less than half of them broke through the cavalry ring and sped northeast along the Zamsina road. Alexia would have preferred for the *sullanciri* to have died right there, but her departure meant that much quicker of a collapse for her forces.

Not that their destruction was ever in question.

The fighting in the town had taken place by the light of burning buildings. Alexia's forces had not fired the first of them, and when the larger buildings went up, the twinned scents of oil and burning flesh combined in a black fog that drifted through the streets. Alexia could not hear people in the burning buildings crying out for help, but some soldiers did. Alexia hoped they were mistaken.

The Aurolani hid wherever they could in the town, forcing Alexia's people to go house to house. She relied on the Yslin Guards and Jeranese Palace Guards to fight in such close quarters. As they cleared sections of Merysval, lighter infantry came in to hold the territory.

Arimtara fought along with the Yslin Guards and had been incredible. She smelled out ambushes and managed to destroy the attackers before they had a chance to do much damage. She would plunge into a building armed with nothing more than her taloned hands and emerge shortly after, bathed in gore and ready to move on to the next site.

The draconetteers hurt the southern forces the worst. They chose buildings that had good commands of wide streets and shot at soldiers trying to approach. Because they waited until the last moment, their fusillades would cut down a half-dozen, then they sniped at anyone trying to help fallen comrades. A dozen of them could pin down a whole legion.

Unfortunately for them, once their locations had been isolated, Perrine or another of the Gyrkyme could hit the place with a firecock. Just like the flaming munitions used at Fronosa against the Aurolani, these oil-filled pieces of pottery exploded in a shower of flaming fluid when the Gyrkyme dropped them. Once a draconetteer nest had started burning, the soldiers outside waited for their enemies to run, or let them roast.

It had taken almost until dawn to clear the town. Alexia's eyes burned from fatigue and smoke. She rode back from Merysval toward her camp, slowly passing weary and bloodstained soldiers heading in the same direction. Beyond them lay the battlefield. As much as she wanted to look away from it, she could not, because she knew that the field would be a testament to how she had handled the battle.

That there were far more Aurolani dead than southern troops was a good sign, of that she had no doubt. Out there, across the plain, in little hollows and on little hills, bodies had been mounded. A small heap surrounded an Aurolani standard that leaned crookedly against bodies. She could imagine how gibberers had tried to raise it again, and how her people went after it in a back-and-forth battle that left the dead piled around what was now just a broken stick.

The white-furred *kryalñiri* corpses were easy to pick out. Most of them had been slain at close range by arrows, with a few others dead by magick or more mundane and close-up methods. *All* of the corpses had been beheaded, however. The *kryalniri* had been very difficult to kill in the past, and within the army a story started that suggested they could not truly die, so men systematically decapitated them. The heads would be buried at a crossroads and the bodies would be burned.

Most of the rest of the Aurolani would be left for carrion birds and packs of feral dogs. Vultures had already congregated on a hoargoun's nose, picking at his eyes and lips. She watched, both fascinated and revolted, then wondered if, on her way back to Saporicia, she would find the hoargoun's bones picked clean and bleached by the sun, still where they lay.

Soldiers moved throughout the battlefield, looking for comrades, bringing water to the wounded, or dispatching the wounded enemy. There was no passion in killing the Aurolani, just efficiency. It was less mercy than expedience, and a desire to stop their cries. Everyone knew they would have given no mercy to the southerners, so none was shown to them.

Other men and women moved across the battlefield, picking over the corpses for any valuables. They were not the folk of Merysval, but camp followers who had come out from Bacirro. Soldiers shooed them away from their own comrades, but many of the mercenary companies had no such sense of loyalty. For their part, the camp followers pointed out the living in hopes of a reward.

Crow came riding up from Merysval and reined in beside her. Smoke had smudged his face and blood had spattered one cheek. His silverwood bow rode in its saddle scabbard, but his quiver was empty. His sword, Hand, had seen limited action in the darkness.

"It looks as if your initial suspicions were accurate," he said. "There were many people trapped in the buildings that were fired. Out to the northeast, in a gully they used for dumping their refuse, there are a lot more bodies."

Alexia nodded slowly. "Any indication if the people were alive when the fires were lit?"

He shook his head. "Apparently not. Out in the midden the bones showed signs of having been gnawed. In a couple of the larger houses, the kitchens had big soup pots boiling and ovens with meat roasting. There's little question what happened to the people of Merysval."

"All along the roads we've found the remains of

refugees in a similar state. Why would the people of Merysval be any different?"

"We had to hope, didn't we?"

"That's all we have." Alexia's stomach tightened. The Aurolani had been living off the land. She had no idea if they ate manflesh by preference, or just considered it when horse, cow, sheep, goat, and pig were all consumed. Cat, too, for that matter. They didn't seem to like dogs, though she supposed the gibberers viewed themselves as closer to dogs than they did humans.

There had been no keeping the news of the consumption of human flesh a secret from the troops, and their reactions had been odd. The Alcidese soldiers, because of their tradition of ancestor worship, did all they could to make sure their dead were removed from the battlefield as fast as possible and buried well enough that the scavengers wouldn't get them. Others, including some of the Nybali mercenaries, would roast themselves a gibberer or vylaen in recompense. They freely offered the meat around, but few partook. Many others did butcher fallen frostclaws and consume them, but the most common action was to make sure the remains of those who had been eaten were burned in the hopes the fires would clean their remains of any Aurolani taint.

Just thinking about being devoured made Alexia shiver. There was a large difference between being bitten in combat and actually consumed. Biting in a fight she understood. It was desperate and yet brave at the same time, a savage and intimate attack. Consumption, however, was yet more intimate and, at the same time, irreverent. While she had heard Nybali shamans talk about how they were drawing the essence of the enemy into them, she rejected the idea. She felt it was just the ultimate insult: once you'd killed the enemy, you chewed him up and, in the end, reduced him to a stinking pile of excrement.

Riding up to her tent, Alexia dismounted and tossed the reins to a squire. The man likewise took the reins to Crow's horse and led the two of them away. Warriors at the flap of her tent snapped to attention. She acknowledged them with a brief salute, then entered.

The flap fell behind Crow, and it took a moment for Alexia's eyes to adjust to the darkness. She started, for over in the far left corner, Maroth seemed to materialize out of shadows. He stood there, unmoving and decidedly inanimate.

Crow rested hands on her shoulders. "I don't think I'll ever get used to his doing that."

"No, but I'm not inclined to complain." Alexia frowned. Maroth had not actually traveled with them from Fronosa. When last she saw him, he'd been standing in the corner of the room where he had appeared at her father's bidding. His chest had closed again and the scratches made on him by Myrall'mara had vanished. She'd left guards on the room and told them no one was to be admitted there without her express permission.

But that night, when her tent had been erected on the road, Maroth was there in his corner. So it had been on the road, and when she'd entered Merysval during the fighting, he lurked in shadows. Maroth had killed one *kryalniri* before it could cast a spell at her, and had taken one draconette blast in the chest. She wasn't sure how many other Aurolani creatures he'd killed, but the predilection of assassins to go sneaking about in shadows definitely put them at a disadvantage when he was around.

Alexia turned around and gathered Crow into a fierce hug, then stepped back and unbuckled her sword belt. "Was that battle too easy?"

"The glib answer would be not if you are the Aurolani. They lost over three regiments." Crow removed his sword belt, then pulled daggers from the tops of his boots. "You're thinking that Chytrine orchestrated this battle, this loss, much as she did the loss of Okrannel. She wants us overconfident and she wants you believing things will go as they have in your dreams."

"Right, the dreams I *didn't* have."

"That may be what she intended, but your dream didn't involve fighting in the town, did it?"

Alexia shook her head, then doffed her coat of mail and let it rustle into a puddle at her feet. "No, in my dream we freed the town and the townsfolk were happy. This is more the sort of ending that Adrogans reported about Svoin."

"I was thinking the same thing. It makes me wonder if Nefrai-kesh is now in command of the defending forces, and if he wanted to send us a signal. If he wanted to let us know that, no matter how bad it's been before, it will get worse?"

Alexia considered that for a moment, then frowned. "He's a curious one. Your memoir makes it quite clear Lord Norrington was a very good tactician. Throwing away three regiments is not a wise thing."

"I agree, which means he must have more troops coming in. That would coincide with your assumption that Chytrine is using your dreams against you and will ambush you down the line."

She raised an eyebrow. "But if we follow that line of logic, then he should not have sent the message that suggests he has more troops, and he should not have deviated from the dream, because now I have to be aware that things are not going to happen as planned. I will be on guard."

Crow nodded. "But Nefrai-kesh would know that you'd read his message correctly, so he must be doing something else."

Alyx laughed, sat on a chest, and pulled her boots off. "I don't care what he does, just as long as a shadow falls across him when we finally meet. Maroth can finish him."

Crow's face closed. "No. Nefrai-kesh is mine."

"Beloved, you don't need to make any demonstration for me."

"It's not a show of bravado. I just owe it to the man he was before. I won't be stupid about it, but I just know it will happen. It has to happen this way. I didn't kill him when he asked me to, so now I will when it is what he least wants."

Alexia nodded solemnly. "I won't gainsay you that opportunity. When do you think he will face us?"

Crow frowned. "The next battle he will let Tythsai die. The one after that."

"That's the last battle of my dreams."

"That would be it, then." Crow rested his left hand on his sword's hilt. "Within the month, this could all be over."

CHAPTER 52

Resolute ducked his head as he entered the Aurolani galley's cabin. He found he couldn't straighten up all the way, and the stench of the place quickly overrode the salt and wet-leather scent of his clothes. There didn't seem to be enough room in the small cabin to hide a putrefying gibberer, but Resolute's nose was telling him one had been chopped up and concealed in all the nooks and crannies.

Kerrigan looked up from the foot of the berth. He had the small chest there filled with clean cloth, and had fashioned a small bed for Qwc. The Spritha had stretched out and lay beneath a scarf.

"How is he, Kerrigan?"

The youth shook his head. "I used some spells to see if he was hurt. I don't know Spritha physiology too well, but I think he is okay. He didn't say anything, though, not a word. What happened?"

Resolute held on to a crossbeam. "The Aurolani had captured me. Qwc rescued me."

"He led you to safety?"

"No, he actually rescued me." Resolute nodded toward

the sleeping Spritha. "He put his spear to great use. Tagothcha should treasure it."

Kerrigan blinked. "Qwc killed someone?"

"Many someones. All of them."

The young mage glanced down at Qwc, then drew the scarf up a bit further and tucked it in. "Don't worry, Qwc. You'll be okay."

Resolute watched the tenderness with which Kerrigan acted, and felt a smile growing on his face. He'd done his best to care for Qwc on their journey in the others' wake, but they had been moving fast. Qwc might have wanted to talk about his experience, and that might have been helpful, but silence had been the rule. So the Spritha had taken to sleeping more and more, and Resolute had fashioned a sling bed for him and had carried him as a child might carry a doll.

Kerrigan stood, then frowned. "Why don't you sit down? That's a nasty wound on your head."

"It's nothing."

"Resolute, it's open and oozing. I'll handle it. Please?"

The Vorquelf nodded and took Kerrigan's seat. He jerked his head toward the figure in the bed. "Who's this?"

Kerrigan shrugged as he probed the wound with his fingertips. "He's the person who took the fragments. Oracle said he's the last adult Vorquelf in the world. Trawyn said he was a dreamwing-eater. She said he was likely to be dangerous until he had been free of dreamwing for a while, so I hit him with the spell Chytrine used on me. I modified it a bit, of course. He can come out of it when he's sane."

"That was a good precaution." Resolute winced as a crusted scab broke. "Predator on the wheeldeck . . . That wasn't the first time he tried to go back, was it?"

"No."

"You dealt with it?"

"I had to." Resolute couldn't read the expression on Kerrigan's face in the backlight of the spell the youth cast. Heat seared into the wound with a golden light flashing. It felt as if all the itching the wound had done and would ever do had been combined. It kept building and building. Resolute longed to scratch away at it, but instead he grabbed the edge of the stool between his legs and held on.

Then the light faded, and slowly the itch began to subside. The Vorquelf nodded, but still didn't release the stool. "Thank you. Want to tell me about Predator?"

"Not much to tell. You put me in charge. He didn't like it." Kerrigan shrugged again. "I just asked myself what you would have done, and I did it."

"Hardly. He's still alive."

"You didn't kill him either."

"He can still pull an oar."

"He could still carry a stretcher." Kerrigan gave Resolute a lopsided grin. "I pretty much asked myself what you would do whenever I had to make a decision—well, except I didn't do any killing. It worked—until we got here, that is. I'm glad you showed up because I don't know what I would have done if you hadn't."

"You'd have thought of something. You made good time coming north."

Kerrigan's grin grew. "I told them you'd have marched them further and faster, and that I *could* if they forced me to."

"Clever." The itching having vanished, Resolute stood. "If they keep pulling strongly, we should make Saslynnae inside a day and a half."

"We'll put into the main port? Isn't that dangerous?"

"What part of going to Vorquellyn isn't?" Resolute sighed. "We go directly in, make straight for the *coriiesci,* and hope our sleeping friend can get us in. We get Will and go."

Kerrigan sighed heavily. "Does that sound as impossible to you as it does to me?"

Resolute started to give him a sharp answer, but hesitated. The youth had actually risen above himself and taken charge of the expedition at a point when it could have fallen apart. Resolute firmly believed Will was the key to destroying Chytrine and redeeming Vorquellyn. Kerrigan's efforts made certain they'd be able to rescue Will. For that, if nothing else, he deserved more than sarcasm.

"Yes, it does sound impossible, doesn't it?" Resolute smiled slowly. "But if Will's going to come back from the dead, our task is nothing by comparison."

"Good point, Resolute. I'm glad you're back."

"As am I. Take care of our two charges here, will you? Let me know if anything changes."

"I will."

Resolute returned to the wheeldeck and breathed deeply of the fresh air. Below, the Grey Misters pulled on the oars. Spray splashed against the prow where Oracle stood looking north. Resolute had no doubt that, despite her being blind, she'd see Vorquellyn well before the island appeared on the horizon.

Trawyn looked back at him. "You should know that anyone standing here can listen in on conversations in the main cabin."

"Thank you. Did you hear something interesting?"

She nodded slowly. "Predator was not alone in wanting to turn back. I was ready to go along with him to keep the fragments out of Chytrine's clutches. I think it's wrong for us to be taking them to Vorquellyn."

Resolute slowly smiled. "Kerrigan faced you down as well?"

Her good eye narrowed. "He did."

"Really? And when we visited Rellaence before, it was Will who made you Loquelves back away from your prejudice against the Gyrkyme."

"It was."

"That's rather remarkable."

"Yes? How so?"

"You, a princess of Loquellyn, and human children give you fits?"

She barked a sharp laugh. "Vorquelf children are giving me more fits."

"The Grey Misters are no problem for you, so you mean Oracle."

Trawyn looked north, toward the ship's bow. "Yes, I must admit, her quiet adamancy about the prophecy and how things should go is an annoyance. It was only logical and right for us to return to the south. You were gone, we had two fragments and a very dangerous person to deal with. But she said he was the key to the *coriiesci*. There was never any doubt on her part that we would get to Vorquellyn and find Will."

"That's just how she sees things."

"Oh, I understand that. I respect her gift." The Loquelf shifted her shoulders. "That gift is rare in children, but not unknown. Still, no one has ever been wholly right. What if she is wrong?"

Resolute shook his head. "There are more ways for her to be wrong than there are stars in the sky. I decided long ago to believe she is right and not to worry about it. All the signs point to it."

"But what would you know, Resolute? You are a child. You carry a Syverce, but you are not bound to a homeland. You cannot know the sort of duty that weapon confers on you." She turned and pointed back to Loquellyn. "I am bound to my home, and it tells me what I must do."

He arched a snowy eyebrow. "And are you being told that what you are doing is wrong?"

She faltered. "No."

Resolute rested his left hand on the sword's hilt. "You know that were I not meant to bear this sword, I could not touch it without pain."

"And I know enough of you to know you'd not show pain if you felt it."

"That may be true, but I don't feel pain. Oracle said I would have a sword from the hand of the Norrington. Will gave me this blade. That was just one more sign that we are right. Will is the Norrington, and the Norrington is the redemption of Vorquellyn."

The sea breeze tugged at her short locks. "You have such faith in that prophecy, Resolute, that I almost want to believe it, too."

"Why don't you? There is something here I don't understand."

She shook her head once, then fixed him with a one-eyed stare. "Haven't you ever wondered why we never took Vorquellyn back from the Aurolani?"

"Of course. I assumed it was because you felt no urgency. What are years and centuries to immortals?"

"It wasn't that. Our passenger down there, he looks peaceful in sleep, but wait until he awakes. You will see pure agony in his eyes." She rubbed a hand over her forehead. "You were perhaps too young to understand. I remember. We isolated the children because we feared what would happen. You didn't see it. When they took Vorquellyn your adults were hurt and heartsick, much as I am now. But when Chytrine desecrated Vorquellyn, the pain in their eyes, the way they shrieked . . . They were a people driven mad by a land that was dying.

"Don't you see, Resolute? We never took Vorquellyn back because it is *dead*. There is no redeeming it. There can't be."

Her words shot through his middle like a crossbow quarrel. He thought back. Had he seen the pity he now read in her eyes in others? Had he been beguiled by the patronizing attitudes of most elves? Had he somehow missed how they ached to be wrong, but how they knew they were not? How they ached because the lost children of Vorquellyn could never be redeemed?

Resolute's hands curled into fists and his lips pressed into a thin, grim line. Fury built in him, sharply and quickly, but just as quickly he forced his hands open. He let his anger drain away.

"I understand what you have just told me, Princess. Thank you."

"How can you thank me for that? I've just told you that you're on a fool's mission."

"Yes, you have. You've also just told me why you never acted to free my homeland. It makes sense, which means I can release all the energy I've used up resenting Loquelves, Croquelves, and Harquelves. That you are wrong doesn't matter."

"Wrong? Do you think we came to this conclusion without thinking about it? I was privy to councils. Our greatest minds—military, political, and magickal—say Vorquellyn cannot be redeemed. Even Adrogans saw that in Svoin, and burned the city to the ground. There is no relieving a place from the Aurolani taint."

Resolute's silver eyes became slits. "Just because you don't know how to do it doesn't mean it can't be done. If Chytrine spoiled it, there must be a way to change the taint."

"And if there isn't, what do you do then?"

"Doesn't matter, does it? At least the idea you hold in your head will be proven right or wrong. If you're right, I'm no better off, but the world is because Chytrine is dead. If you're wrong, then I will have a home and a future. Fool's quest or not, that's worth the effort."

"I don't know, Resolute, if you are just a child or a fool or both."

"Probably both, but when Vorquellyn is redeemed, I'll be neither." He gave her a half smile. "Keep the ship steady north and we'll be all the sooner learning the truth."

CHAPTER 53

Markus Adrogans had not quite been prepared for the Aurolani reaction to his destruction of their regiment. He had expected one of three possibilities. The first was a major push into the border area where the regiment had disappeared, and perhaps further, into Winalia's domain. The second was a general reinforcement of border stations. The third, and the very least he expected, was an increase of patrols within the Aurolani holdings.

He got none of these. It was easy for him to suppose the regiment had been an independent command that was expected to operate on its own based on orders, but the lack of mentions of it in even the most cursory reports back from the border should have been cause for alarm. Had he been in the Aurolani commander's position, he would have sent orders for border forces to find the regiment and report back on its status.

The lack of reaction surprised him, but he found a reason for it: the wood kept flowing. His scouts reported seeing wagonload after wagonload of wood being brought into the domain, and in less than a week his forces had located the shipyards. While he accepted the veracity of the initial reports, he and Phfas went forward with scouts to spy things out.

The shipbuilding operation was far more massive than he could have imagined. The old maps of Noriva called the city that had once been there Alcytlin. When Noriva had been an independent nation, that city had been a major trading port, and many said it was the finest deep-water port in the world. With the Boreal mountains as a backdrop, and white cliffs on either side of the harbor entrance, the naturally beautiful location would have screamed haven to any sailor.

Adrogans studied the shipyards from a hilltop to the north, and the hills upon which the old city had been built did shield much of the ruins from view. It reminded him of what Svarskya probably would look like after decades of weathering. All immediate signs of violence had been erased, and the crumbled edges of once-proud buildings had softened. The whole city looked as if it had eroded, and aside from the port area, it showed few signs of life.

The shipyards were another thing entirely. That area had been rebuilt on a massive scale. To the north were the foundries, mills, and curing houses for the wood. Beyond them were lumberyards, with small ships moving back and forth with loads. In the center and along to the south of the crescent bay, four shipyards were in full production, and the ships they were working on dwarfed anything Adrogans had seen before. Two of the ships would be ready to launch inside a week where, if the half-dozen behemoths already bobbing in the bay were any indication, they would be finished and made seaworthy. Based on reports he'd had of the pirate attack on Vilwan, he assumed these big ships would carry dragonels.

In addition to the big ships, the shipyards also were working on a bunch of smaller galleys. The little boats would be fast and would keep southern ships away from the big transport craft. They would clear the way, and the big ships would shoot dragonels at ports while the small ships took battalions off and landed them onshore.

Further from the sea stood barracks. Because of the landscape, Adrogans could only see a couple and parts of a couple more, but he could guess that there were ten in all, and each would be capable of housing a full regiment. Unseen but also implied were warehouses bulging with food and supplies for these troops, as well as small shops for making barrels, sails, oars, and anything else they would need.

Adrogans made some quick mental calculations. He chose to estimate that each ship could carry a regiment. If three of them were to hit Lakaslin, three Yslin, and the others to raid selected ports, they would do serious damage to the war effort. The alliance would be shattered as nations fell or rushed to defend their homes.

The only logical plan would be for him to bring all of his troops up and stage an immediate attack. If the barracks were full already, his troops would be outnumbered two to one, and would be attacking an enemy already behind fortifications. The enemy would be able to bring dragonels to bear, and likely more than he could. He had visions of two or more of the ships—each of which looked as if it carried at least as many dragonels as his entire force—blasting his troops as they came in. The ambush in the road would be a raindrop to a flood when compared to that slaughter.

But to wait was to risk many other things. For all he knew, a half-dozen ships were already seaworthy, loaded, and out on trials. If they returned, there would be even *more* troops and dragonels to deal with. Waiting might also mean that if the barracks were not already full now, they would be later, and he would miss his only chance to destroy the fleet.

He snarled. "I need more information."

Phfas shrugged. "For a decision like this, is there ever enough?"

"No. At least we know now why the Aurolani commander isn't worried about a cavalry regiment on the border. It's not disrupting her supply of wood, and it is no threat here."

The Zhusk shaman looked at him oddly. " '*Her* supply'?"

Adrogans frowned. No one had made any mention of the gender of the Aurolani commander, but in making his comment, he knew he had the right information. He searched his mind for how he had come to that conclusion, then slowly turned inward, seeking something.

In the past, that inward journey would have brought him to Pain. He would have felt her raking claws over his flesh and gnawing on nerve endings. Since leaving Okrannel, however, the touch of the *yrûn* had faded. As he looked inside himself, he expected to find nothing.

There was something there, however.

It came to him dimly and faintly. At first he thought it might be his connection with Pain returning, for the presence definitely was female, but quickly he realized it was not his mistress. The new presence did have claws and fangs, but felt far more feline. Her blatant sense of sexuality surprised him, for Pain had always been intimate, but had never excited carnal interest—merely the perversion of same by substituting pain for pleasure. Not so what he felt now. And, if he cared to draw a further conclusion, he would have said that the being he sensed was either currently involved in sating base desires or lingered in the afterglow of satiation.

Adrogans' eyes focused again. "Uncle, when we met *sullanciri* before, did you have a sense of them through the *vrûn*?"

The old man shook his head slightly. "No. They had no connection to the old spirits."

"Then there is something different about the one down there, assuming it is a *sullanciri*."

"Safe to assume."

"I agree." Adrogans rubbed a hand back through his

short hair. "This one has a bit of Pain in her. I can feel her, read some things. She seems very open. She has concerns, but none at the moment is military."

"You read her thoughts?"

"No, not yet, not in any organized sense. I get emotions and desires. It's as if, in listening to someone talk in his sleep, you tried to figure out what he was dreaming."

"This could be good." Phfas nodded. "And dangerous."

"I agree. I have to assume it will be possible for her to read the same from me. I will be careful."

"Good. Do not try to get into her mind."

"I wouldn't know how."

Phfas chuckled. "That would not stop you if you needed to. That mind will be the lair of nightmares."

"How fitting." Adrogans looked back at the city. "She exists in a lair of nightmares. I need more information, and I'm going to have to get it. Some of our people will have to take a load of wood in there and get back out with samples from the buildings."

"Choose volunteers."

"I will."

"Make sure they are orphans."

"Yes, Uncle, I shall." Adrogans raised an eyebrow. "Anything else?"

"Her goal and your goal are not the same." The little man smiled slowly. "Use her goal against her, and the road to yours will be much better."

CHAPTER 54

The three days spent hunting Bloodmasks were very harrowing. Erlestoke halted his army and engaged, daily, in conversations with Sambell Malviston. The two of them made quite a show of it, even having serious shouting matches. Erlestoke wished their interchanges had been sham discussions, but they were not. Even though Malviston had come to accept that Erlestoke had not murdered his father, the old Midlands resentment against Meredo still poisoned their relationship.

Erlestoke remembered Sambell from his youth, but only barely. After all, he was just a lordling from the Mids. The prince realized that when Malviston provoked him enough, he still thought of him dismissively in those terms. To his credit, he never voiced his outrage at the upland noble's berating him. *If I do that, everything comes apart.*

Malviston did have a great deal of anger to deal with concerning Erlestoke. The Midlands, and most of the country for that part, had hated having pockets of Aurolani forces in Oriosa. All the nobles labored under the same burden his father did: fearing Nefrai-kesh or another *sullanciri* coming to twist their heads off. They resented their fear and wanted to show their courage by opposing Chytrine, but to do anything overt would invite her wrath *and* that of King Scrainwood.

Where Erlestoke was seen by many as having gone wrong was in abandoning Oriosa in favor of Fortress Draconis. There was a time when his service had made the nation proud, but that had all been twisted after Chytrine had smashed the stronghold. Erlestoke's return and his rift with his father, especially with an Aurolani army so close by, seemed designed to provoke the Aurolani to attack. From the point of view of people like Malviston, Erlestoke wanted to strike at Chytrine, and would sacrifice his nation to do it.

Malviston likewise berated him for not knowing his own people. "How they have suffered under your father has to be obvious. Could you not hear our laments in Fortress Draconis?" He reminded Erlestoke that even if he hated his father, he still had a duty to the people of Oriosa.

And Erlestoke had to allow that Malviston had a point: he had abandoned his people. The prince told himself he had done so for two very good reasons. The first was that he was needed at Fortress Draconis, and that Fortress Draconis performed a vital function in keeping Chytrine bottled up in the north. The second was that for him to return and oppose his father, directly or indirectly, would be to spawn a civil war in the nation—*or get me murdered.*

Both of those reasons were true. Both of them were good. Still, the prince understood that neither absolved him of the duty incumbent upon him because of his blood. His father did have to be balanced and even opposed, and no one else in the whole world had the legitimate right or position to be able to lead that opposition. As much as he did not want to take a blood-drenched throne, better the throne should run with the blood of his father than the countryside with the blood of the citizenry.

Erlestoke resolved to deal with his father's control of

Oriosa once he'd completed the war against Chytrine. *If I survive it.* He couldn't tell Malviston his decision, since that would be open treason, and sharing the idea would be an invitation to have Malviston join him. That would be delicate politically, for while Malviston could join him in opposing the Aurolani with no internal political difficulties, to join a rebellion would make him a target for all manner of grasping lordlings throughout the nation.

So while the two of them argued and rumors flew through both armies, Dranae, Nay, Borell, and the Addermages conducted their search for the Bloodmasks. Nay and Borell knew how to talk with crofters and herders, and even knew some of them from market days in Valsina. From them they learned how the Bloodmasks operated. The Addermages used spells both to repair some of the damage done and to gain impressions of the Bloodmasks.

Rumbellow reported their findings to Erlestoke in the early evening before they mounted their final hunting expedition. "The impression we have is of two groups of people. Some are soldiers, a company or so, and a similar number of mages. I'm sure they're Vilwanese, which, among other things, means they are wearing masks under false pretenses."

Despite his having been away from Oriosa for so long, that comment flared Erlestoke's nostrils. Muroso, Alosa, and Oriosa had long ago revolted from the Estine Empire, and those who led the revolution had worn masks to conceal their identities. Their descendants had the right to wear masks to honor the sacrifices their ancestors had made to free their nations. For someone who had no right to a mask to wear anything but a courtesy mask was enough to sour the stomach of any true son of Oriosa.

The fact that their using masks had to have been sanctioned by his father made Erlestoke feel even more ill.

"They have tried to be crafty in how they work, but we have plotted their appearances." Rumbellow spread a map of the Midlands out on a table and used candlesticks to hold the corners down. "While they struck in a vast arc, making it look as if they were sweeping down from the north and around to the west, all of the strikes are a day's hard ride from this place here."

Erlestoke nodded. "Nyresina."

Rumbellow looked up. "You know it?"

"Yes. It was my mother's dowry. Before she died we would summer there, away from Meredo." Erlestoke's hands convulsed into fists. "We're within striking distance, yes?"

"A day's ride. They know we're here, and they'd know we're coming." The Addermage shook his head. "I would guess they will leave soon, if they have not already gone. Don't worry, we'll find a way to track them."

"I don't want them tracked. I want them *dead*." Erlestoke knelt by the chest in his tent and flipped the lid back. He pulled out his quadnel, pouch of shot, and powder horn. "We go tonight."

Rumbellow shook his head. "I and my fellow mages are good, but even we can't get us there that fast."

"I know." Erlestoke slung his sword belt over his right shoulder. "You can't, but Dranae can. Get your ten best combat mages. They'll be watching the roads for us, which means when we come in, they won't know what hit them."

Never having seen the estate at Nyresina from the air, it took Erlestoke a moment or two to recognize it. He spotted the oxbow in the river as it reflected silver moonlight. The trees had been thinned, and it looked as if the vineyards to the north had been expanded, but the estate building itself had run to ruin. The original tower at the northeast corner had partially collapsed and the old coach house's roof sagged. Other than that, however, the boxy main house appeared to be habitable.

Dranae dove fast, then flared his wings, touching down softly in the courtyard on the west side of the main house, between it and a small lake where Erlestoke and his brother had sailed as boys. Since the road came in from the east and reached the house on the other side, they assumed any watchers would be most alert there. In reality, the sentries were stationed much further down the road with *arcanslata,* so they offered no warning at all to those in the house.

In an eyeblink Dranae shifted from dragon to manform. Erlestoke tossed him his draconette and a swath of cloth that the man fashioned into a kilt. The Addermages spread out before them, running for the house. None of them were willing to imagine that a dragon could land without notice, and they knew that magickal alarms need not make any sound. If they did have surprise on their side, so much the better.

Rumbellow smacked the door with an iron-shod baton and the weathered wood exploded inward. The Addermages poured into the building. Erlestoke followed with Dranae at his heels. The doorway admitted them to the kitchen, then a cut to the left brought them into the hallway that led to the Grand Hall.

By the time they got there, a thaumaturgical battle had begun to rage. Lurid red bats and glowing green eagles wheeled and dove, twisted and flapped within the room's vaults. Gouts of golden flame lit the room, and smashed impotently on magickal shields. A mage's hand opened, releasing a shower of sparks that transformed into blue arrows. The flight curved in at a Bloodmask mage who raised a shield that stopped all but two. They hit, spinning him and dumping him to the floor with smoking holes breast and back.

Erlestoke brought the quadnel to his shoulder, cocked, and shot. The weapon's thunder echoed loudly, but the splash of flame was nothing compared to the magick. The lead ball caught one of the Bloodmasks over her breastbone, knocking her back before she could complete the casting of a spell. The energy that had been gathering in green tendrils around her clawed hands now consumed them, filling the air with greasy smoke.

Dranae shot as well, shattering a Bloodmask's leg. The shield he'd raised against a fiery torrent collapsed. The golden flame jet hit him solidly and burned away everything between hips and collarbones.

The prince shot again, then drew Crown. He parried a sword thrust by one of the Bloodmask soldiers, then slashed back again, opening the man's belly. The wounded man reeled back, clutching his midsection, and knocked another soldier askew. Erlestoke lunged, skewering the second soldier. Dranae shot again, snapping the head back on a third soldier, and those spattered with her brains turned and ran.

Erlestoke's third shot killed one more of the Bloodmask mages, but his contribution to the battle was almost unnecessary. Murosan sorcerers took great pride in their combat abilities, and their Vilwanese brethren were no match for them. As they went through the estate, room by room, they quickly killed those mages who offered resistance, and found several already dead by poison. They'd clearly killed themselves after sending out a message via *arcanslata*.

Rumbellow hefted one of the devices. "I can try to learn who was getting the messages, but if the person at the other end smashes his *arcanslata*, I've got no way of figuring that out."

"It doesn't matter. I know where the messages eventually ended up." Erlestoke toed the mage's dead body. "And I know what message I want him to get. Dranae, if you wouldn't mind helping me, I think we can deliver it pretty quickly."

In the Oriosan Throne Room, Erlestoke and Dranae took a step back and viewed their handiwork. They had beheaded every one of the Bloodmasks and, using tools at the estate, nailed every mask to its owner's face. Then they gathered them all up in a sack, and Dranae flew to Meredo. Using passages he knew about, Erlestoke entered the palace unseen.

Once in the throne room they placed the heads on the throne and around it in a circle. In the mouth of each head they placed a gold coin. On each of the coins, King Scrainwood's profile had been defiled by having the eye gouged out.

The dragonman looked at the prince. "How do you think he will react to this?"

"He'll be angry and terrified. Nefrai-kesh beheaded my grandmother and left my father holding her head. He'll relive that moment for each and every one of these. He'll know we know, and he'll know we got in here and out again without being seen. It will give him pause."

"You know Vilwan is involved."

"I do. First things first, however. Chytrine, then my father, then Vilwan."

Dranae smiled as they started back to the passage that would take them out of the castle. "You humans are interesting. You use such a barbaric way to send a message that, while direct, is also subtle."

"This, *subtle*?" Erlestoke frowned. "How would a dragon have sent this message?"

"Your father's head would have been the centerpiece."

"Okay, I see it. Yes, by dragon standards, this would be subtle. Let's head back to the Midlands, and I'll work on not being so subtle." Erlestoke clapped his friend on the back. "After all, we don't want Chytrine to have difficulty understanding our message to her."

CHAPTER 55

Kerrigan woke with a start as Resolute and Trawyn entered the cabin arguing in Elvish. It took him a moment or two to realize what they were speaking and to start translating. It didn't help that Trawyn's Loquelven tended to be rather highborn and Resolute's Elvish deliberately swam through the gutters.

Before Kerrigan could figure out what they were fighting about, Resolute switched to the common tongue and pointed at the comatose elf. "Wake him up now."

Trawyn held a hand out. "Do nothing of the kind, Kerrigan." Her eye flashed at Resolute. "Look at him. He still has that purplish cast to his skin. His system has not been purged of the dreamwing. He's as likely to kill us as anything else."

"Nonsense. If he were that helpless, he'd have been caught and killed by the Aurolani long ago." The silver-eyed Vorquelf looked at Kerrigan. "Have you seen any sign that he is out of control?"

"No, none. He's not even been casting magick, as near as I can tell. He's just been sleeping soundly."

"Remove your spell and wake him up."

"Resolute, consider what you are doing."

"I am, Highness." The Vorquelf pointed north. "In two hours we'll be coming into Saslynnae. I want to be able to move fast, get to the *coriiesci*, get Will, and get out. I've waited too long to wake him up. I need him able to get us in quickly, and if he's addled, I need to know now."

"He is addicted to dreamwing, Resolute. He might be lucid one moment and utterly insane the next. Suicidal at the worst, useless at best."

"Better we learn now, Highness. Kerrigan, do it."

The young mage stood and pulled his sleeves up. He looked down at the elf, then reached his right hand out. He let energy gather, then a golden spark drifted from his palm as lightly as a lint flower seedpod. It danced in an unseen breeze, then sank and touched the invisible shell of the spell he'd cast. The instant the spark touched the spell, it shot off in skitter-jagging golden lines all over and around the elf. For a heartbeat he vanished from sight, then reappeared but did not move.

Resolute frowned. "What's wrong?"

"I don't know." Kerrigan prepared and cast a simple diagnostic spell. It started at the elf's feet and worked up, cataloging his well-being. Nothing overmuch seemed wrong, save for traces of something Kerrigan assumed to be dreamwing in his system and some foreign object encysted near a rib. *Feels like a stone, maybe an arrowhead.* The spell crept up his body uneventfully until it reached the level of his icy blue eyes.

They snapped open, and Kerrigan jolted back. The top of the chest housing Qwc snapped shut. The youth sat abruptly, vaguely aware that in his former state he would have crushed the chest and the Spritha. He grabbed at the foot of the bed to steady himself, then felt another pulse of power and fury slam into him.

Who dares?

The words came without sound, but had an essence to

them that Kerrigan quickly dissected. That the interrogator was the elf came as no surprise, but his venerability belied his appearance. He was millennia old—older by far than anyone Kerrigan had ever dealt with. The DragonCrown fragment from Vorquellyn had tainted him. Fury and profound sadness perfused him. The dreamwing did dull him, but his presence sharpened with each heartbeat, and once he attained clarity, he'd be able to reduce Kerrigan's brain to mush.

Unbidden, the dragonbone armor rose through Kerrigan's flesh. Bone plates covered him from head to toe, shredding his shirt at shoulders and popping buttons. The laces on one boot snapped and his belt buckle screamed under the pressure. Talons grew on his fingers, gouging wood as he held on tighter.

Kirûn?

The elf's assault faltered for a moment and Kerrigan took the chance to push back. He drove his consciousness into the Elf's brain and, despite finding himself dwarfed by what he found there, announced himself loudly. *Not Kirûn, but one of those who would keep his legacy from Chytrine.*

Kerrigan realized he was taking a calculated risk there. This elf had known Kirûn—otherwise he'd not have recognized the look of the armor. Since he had secured two fragments of the DragonCrown and fought Aurolani forces, the youth assumed he was Chytrine's enemy.

The elf's presence grew quiet and the pressure against Kerrigan relented. Then, as if being inside the elf's mind were not strange enough, something truly odd happened. The elf's mind turned away and began to have a conversation with another presence. Kerrigan could not decipher anything that was going on between them, but he recognized some sense of what was happening.

He's conversing with the dragon in the Vorquellyn fragment! Kerrigan had similarly conversed with the dragon associated with the ruby fragment. Kerrigan had not realized who it was he'd spoken with at the time, and the experience had not been wholly pleasant. *Imagine having a dragon as your only companion for over a century.*

It was not so unpleasant. Her capacity for enduring my torment is infinite. The elf's mind redirected attention to him. *Leave me.*

Another push rocked Kerrigan back and the bed's footboard broke. Kerrigan fell off the chest and onto his back, clutching a piece of wood. The armor did not cushion his impact with the deck, for it had faded, leaving him on the floor with splinters under his fingernails.

Trawyn helped him up, then opened the chest. Qwc still slept, and it worried Kerrigan that he had been doing so much of that. As he knelt and cast a diagnostic spell, the old elf sat up and Resolute pressed the point of Syverce to his throat.

The elf glanced at Resolute and spoke in even tones, though condescension dripped from his words. "Remove the blade, child, or we shall be forced to take it from you."

"In common. Make it easy for us."

The old Vorquelf considered for a moment, then nodded. He repeated his warning. "Did you understand us this time?"

Resolute lowered the blade, but did not resheathe it. "I'm sure you have a very interesting story to tell, but I need to know one thing and one thing only. Can you get us into the *coriiesci* at Saslynnae?"

He looked past Resolute to Trawyn. "You are a Loquelf. Why are you in the company of feral children?"

She sighed heavily. "You would do best to answer Resolute's question."

"Resolute?" The old one looked at him again. "That was not your birth name."

"Understand something, Grandfather, we haven't much time here."

Kerrigan rose from his place by the chest and rested a hand on Resolute's shoulder. "Resolute, give him a chance."

The young mage looked at the old elf. "I'm Kerrigan Reese, late of Vilwan. That is Princess Trawyn. You know she's a Loquelf. In the chest over there is Qwc. He's a Spritha."

"We know, boy. We've been in the world since before the Spritha existed." He threw back the thin blanket they'd used to cover him. "We are known as Magarric."

He looked up at Resolute and Kerrigan, then at Trawyn. "They are children. Certainly you know our name."

She frowned for a moment, then her eye widened and she sank to a knee. "My lord, forgive me."

Resolute snarled. "I don't care who you are. Can you get us into the *coriiesci* at Saslynnae?"

"We can."

The Vorquelf frowned. "Princess Trawyn seems to think your dreamwing addiction makes you unstable and possibly dangerous."

"We know. That's the only explanation for the spell this human put on us." Magarric bowed his head in Kerrigan's direction. "A dreamwing addict would be dangerous, but we have used the herb enough to make accommodations to it. We knew what we were doing when we bred the plant."

"Your claiming to have created that blossom does nothing to make me confident of your sanity."

"That's a risk you will have to endure if you wish to enter the *coriiesci*, isn't it?" The elder elf shrugged. "We will get you in."

"Are you sure you can?"

"Of course, child, we are very certain." Magarric smiled as he swung his feet onto the deck. "You see, I created it."

Kerrigan felt the jolt running through Resolute. The Vorquelf dropped to both knees, then pulled Kerrigan down beside him. Resolute reached out and laid Syverce at Magarric's feet. "I beg you forgive my rudeness."

"You are a child, albeit a large one. We wondered how you would fare. Kerrigan tells us you are Chytrine's enemies."

"Yes, my lord." Kerrigan found himself joining Trawyn and Resolute in replying. It was as if there was something about Magarric that prompted a response.

"Why do you wish to enter the *coriiesci*?"

Resolute's head came up. "My lord, it has been told to us that the one who would destroy Chytrine is waiting for us within the *coriiesci*."

Kerrigan glanced at Resolute. "He might like more information than that."

Magarric smiled for a moment, then his eyes unfocused. His body shook once, then he blinked. "Doubtless we do wish the whole of the story. How long have we until we reach Saslynnae?"

"Less than two hours."

"Very good. Leave us. We must prepare." He looked down at Syverce. "You wield that blade from Sylquellyn without pain?"

Resolute nodded, then took it up again. "It was given to me by the one we seek."

"Indeed." The old Vorquelf smiled again, then his face contorted and his back bowed as if he'd been stabbed. He gasped for air and Kerrigan prepared a spell, but Magarric held a hand up. "No, do not bother. Your magicks cannot cure this pain, Kerrigan. We are linked to Vorquellyn. Its pain is our pain. The closer we get, the more we shall hurt."

Kerrigan raised his eyebrows. "And stepping on the island?"

"Excruciating, we are certain. It matters not, however." Magarric sighed slowly. "Even at this distance, we have a sense of the one you seek. To meet him, we would endure anything."

Kerrigan pulled Qwc's chest with him as they left the cabin. Trawyn and Resolute both remained even more quiet than usual. As they came up into the wheeldeck, he set Qwc down by the railing, then looked at the two elves. "Who is he?"

Trawyn leaned heavily back against the rail as Resolute paced beyond the wheel and back. The wind tugged at her hair and chilled Kerrigan through the rents in his shirt. She seemed lost in thought, then she nodded.

"Kerrigan, you know there are four elven homelands now, including Vorquellyn. You know because of the presence of Resolute's sword, which is from a homeland that no longer exists, that there have been others. At one time there was only one homeland. The coming of men and other creatures created pressure, and instead of going to war the nine princes of the then king decided to split the homeland into smaller realms. They took centuries to determine how to do this and they established that to do it, they would create *coriiesci*. They laid out the boundaries of their realms, created magicks to define them, then invested great power in the *coriiesci*. They created the homelands and bound themselves to the *coriiesci*."

Resolute folded his arms over his chest. "When an elf is bound to his homeland, he enters the *coriiesci* and is greeted by its keeper. The keeper is bound to it. As long as he lives, it will remain. I had assumed that whoever the keeper of the *coriiesci* at Saslynnae was, he had left the world with others, but yet lived."

"Were all the keepers those original princes?"

Trawyn shook her head. "No. There are rituals that allow others to assume that mantle. The names are not known outside the adult population, and not mentioned to those who are not yet adults. I know of Magarric's name only because I know the history of the creation of the homelands."

Kerrigan frowned. "How do you know he's *that* Magarric?"

Both of the elves pressed a hand to their breastbones. Resolute's reply came in a whisper. "I just know."

Oracle came up onto the wheeldeck. "Magarric is awake then?"

The human mage's jaw opened. "You knew?"

She laughed. "I *see* many things, Kerrigan. *Knowing* is different. I have his name because I happened to be up here when he introduced himself."

Resolute rested a hand on Oracle's shoulder. "Yes, cousin, he is awake. He car get us into the *coriiesci*. He says Will is there waiting."

Oracle smiled. "Now there are other things I know."

Kerrigan gathered Qwc up, wrapped him in cloth, and tucked him inside his shirt. "What do you know?"

"Many futures narrow to a point here. Few pass through to blossom fully beyond." She turned to face north. "Within the day the Norrington Prophecy will be proved true, or its falsity will kill us all."

Kerrigan happily took his position in the ship's bow as the Vorquelves pulled hard for Saslynnae. The ship came around a headland, then plunged in toward the port. He recalled having sailed into Rellaence, Loquellyn's capital. Even with the melancholy that had seized him at that time, he had been astounded by its beauty. His heart had been lifted despite his mentor's lying dead in the ship's cabin.

He felt no such lift from his first vision of Saslynnae. The hillsides around the city were overgrown with some low black growth that looked to Kerrigan to be mildew. Red vines like blood vessels twisted over the landscape, wrapping around the dark, leafless carcasses of trees. Ugly little bushes the color of dried blood, thick with thorns, sprang up in tufts here and there.

What once had been magnificent buildings, shaped of wood and almost appearing to have been grown in place, now served only as foundations for the mildew and vines. Fungi, varicolored and gigantic, clung to buildings, most of which had crumbled to some extent or other. In fact, aside from the docks and a few poorly constructed warehouses, only one building had resisted corruption.

Banausic pointed. "That is the *coriiesci*. The courtyard before it is overgrown, but Chytrine had it cleared when she wanted to use it."

Kerrigan nodded and measured the distance from the docks to the *coriiesci*. He figured it was five hundred yards, but they were all uphill, along a road that meandered across the face of the hill. Buildings lined it, and while none of them looked inhabited, gibberers could be hiding anywhere. Moving to the *coriiesci*, they would be very exposed. A volley of arrows or draconette shots would kill them all.

Except me. Kerrigan shivered as he imagined the rattle of draconette balls bouncing off his armor while his friends died around him. He'd seen close-up the wounds the weapons could create, and had no desire to see his friends thrashing and bleeding.

He turned and waved Resolute forward. "No one is waiting for us."

Resolute shaded his eyes with a hand. "Two hours until sunset. Most of the Aurolani are sleeping. Those keeping watch will see one of their ships coming in."

"I could put them to sleep, too."

"If we need to." Resolute patted him on the shoulder. "We just want to move fast. We get Will, we get out."

"But if things go badly, I can cast spells as I see fit?"

"Yes, Kerrigan, I trust you."

The Grey Mister piloting the ship brought it toward a dock and the word was passed to ship oars. The Vorquelves hauled them in, then began to gird themselves for battle. Trawyn and her handful of survivors had full coats of mail and, as the ship scraped along the dock, they went over the side with cables to secure the ship. Aside from a dozen Vorquelves designated to remain with the ship and Oracle, the rest of the company ran down the dock and to the shore.

Kerrigan, with Qwc in a converted wineskin strapped to

his body, ran toward the head of the pack, behind Resolute, Banausic, and Trawyn's people. Magarric ran beside him, and Bok behind the both of them. He'd left Rymramoch's box back on the ship, warded with enough spells to deal with legions of Aurolani. Behind came the Grey Misters.

He could feel eyes on him, watching him. All of the buildings, though wrapped in the scarlet weed and furred with the black growth, did not seem abandoned. The space behind doors and windows might be dark, but he just knew Aurolani lurked there.

"Resolute, they are waiting for us."

"I know."

"How?"

"Logic. Scrainwood was present when Oracle said Will was waiting for us in the *coriiesci*. Chytrine's tried to get in, but couldn't."

"It was the dreamwing." Magarric winced and hissed his words. "They sought me, but dreamwing changed my essence enough to elude them. Had they killed me, it would have fallen."

Kerrigan ran a bit faster to come abreast of Resolute. "If you knew they were waiting, that this was a trap, why did you let us fall into it?"

"Kerrigan, think for a moment."

"Yes?"

"You once lifted a ship out of the sea and smashed it."

"I remember."

"So, how difficult will it be for you to reach out and crush a tower full of gibberers?"

The youth hesitated for a moment. As rotten as they were, the effort would be as nothing. *To kill that easily . . .* He shivered. *But if it saves my friends . . .*

"You could have told me that was your plan."

Resolute laughed as they rounded the last corner in the road. "Had I thought you needed preparation, I would have."

The company moved into the courtyard before the *cori-*

iesci. Some of the thornbushes had grown up from between cobbles and red vines wrapped themselves around the bases of columns. The mildew clung to stones, but thinned as it neared the building. The Aurolani plants stopped ten yards from the *coriiesci,* and as Magarric walked forward through the Loquelves, the very building glowed as if a ray of light had burst through the clouds to illuminate it.

The building itself looked akin to a bit of tree root that had grown up out of the ground. A thin bark covered it save at the round portal door. The edges had thickened as if the tree were growing around a lopped limb, and the wood within the circle alternated rings of pale and dark wood.

Magarric paused in front of the doorway and closed his eyes. His chest rose and fell as he took deep breaths, and a sweet scent entered the air. The door itself appeared to be sweating, or covered with dew. The droplets began to run down the wood, which slowly evaporated.

The Vorquelf entered the portal, then turned slowly and spread his arms. "Welcome, all of you, to the *coriiesci* of Vorquellyn. He you seek awaits within." Magarric turned and waved them after him as he passed into the elven hall.

His jaw slack, Kerrigan entered the *coriiesci.* Beyond the door was a broad, crescent-shaped landing that led to a score of stairs. They descended to the floor of a long hall. The columns supporting the roof were all thick oaks, growing there inside the building as if they were outdoors. The roof rested upon their canopy of leaves, all of which displayed brilliant autumnal colors.

Magarric all but skipped down the stairs. When his foot touched the main floor, the two nearest trees began to change. Their leaves flooded with green, beginning at a light spring color, then deepening to a dark color rich with life. The ancient elf moved with no signs of pain at all, and almost seemed to regain his youth as he moved deeper into the *coriiesci.*

Kerrigan started after him. Halfway down through the

columns, he spotted one tree that had not recovered its
lively colors. It remained red and gold, and fallen leaves
surrounded it. In their midst he also spotted something
black and anomalous, but until he was almost on top of it
he couldn't tell what it was.

A stone forearm had thrust itself up through the floor's
woody flesh. Thick fingers clawed at the air. The hand was
far too huge to be Will's, but Kerrigan knew Will was in
there nonetheless.

"Resolute, what do I do?"

"Get him out."

"I know that. How?"

A rippling crack of thunder came from the landing,
snapping Kerrigan's head around. A dozen draconetteers—
turekadine, it was easy to tell by their size—had shot into
the last of the Grey Misters heading down the stairs. The
shots that did not hit Vorquelves gouged splinters from
stairs, walls, and floor. Magarric cried out and dropped to
his knees, but Kerrigan didn't turn to look at him. He knew
none of the draconettes could have hit him at that range
and, besides, they had a greater problem than Aurolani
sharpshooters.

The front row of *turekadine* parted and withdrew to re-
load. Up through their ranks came a tall, slender elf with
flowing golden hair, bearing an emerald staff. Pale, as
Trawyn had once been, the elf would have been beautiful
save for her empty eye sockets. Kerrigan could still feel a
cold gaze sweep over him.

"That's a *sullanciri.*"

Resolute nodded. "Quiarsca."

She descended a step as another rank of draconetteers
came up behind her. Around them came the frog creatures
Trawyn had called *nyressanii.* They bore axes and leaped
down the stairs. They brandished their weapons at the
swiftly retreating Grey Misters, then hacked at the dead and
dying on the stairs. When the axes bit through bodies, or

missed altogether and just hit wood, Magarric jerked and cried out.

The *sullanciri* opened her arms. "Fret not over how you will free the Norrington. We will do that. Thank you for opening the way to us."

"Resolute, what do I do?"

"Get him out."

"We've gone around this once already. *How?*"

"I don't know. Just do it while I go kill a *sullanciri*." Resolute drew Syverce, then motioned the Grey Misters aside. "I am going to kill you, Quiarsca."

She laughed almost melodically as he began to trot toward her. "Ah, Resolute. Always so determined. You might want to kill me, but I won't let you get that close." Quiarsca pointed at him. "Shoot."

Draconettes came to shoulder and hammers were cocked back. The *turekadine* took aim, tracking Resolute as he came. They waited as each one of his long strides ate up the distance. Already he'd gotten within their range. Every step brought him closer to them, closer to her, and closer to death.

Not right now! Kerrigan gestured, using the very spell to which Resolute had alluded before. It was the telekinesis spell he'd learned long ago, which allowed him to lift a ship, or would allow him to crush a tower. He could have just swept them all out of the *coriiesci*, and likely that would have been a more effective way of using the spell, but something in Resolute's words resonated inside him.

I could crush towers. Kerrigan smiled, and made his goal much more modest, but equally devastating.

One of the *turekadine* growled an order and fingers tightened on triggers. Hammers fell, touching the burning embers of match cord to the fine firedirt that primed the weapons. A thin jet of white smoke marked successful ignition. From the pan the fire raced into the barrel, where it started other firedirt burning. The powder combusted swiftly and the hot gas it created expanded quickly. The lead ball and cloth patch clogging the barrel began to move forward, racing faster, as the fire and gas pushed it along. In the blink of an eye it would go from standing still to blasting through Resolute's chest.

Or would have save for Kerrigan's efforts.

Instead of crushing towers, he'd just pinched the draconette barrels shut. The shot hit the closed end of the weapon and, in two cases where Kerrigan's effort had cracked the metal, the barrels exploded and sprayed Quiarsca and some *nyressanii* with hot metal fragments. With all the other draconettes, the pressure in the barrel continued to build and sought the easiest route out. That turned out to be the joint between the fire chamber and the barrel. The draconettes exploded, driving the fire chambers or lock mechanisms back into the faces of the *turekadine.*

Trawyn screamed a war cry in ancient Elvish and sailed forward at the head of her group. Grey Misters rallied and flew after them. More *turekadine* with conventional weapons appeared at the head of the stairs, and the *nyressanii* leaped into the battle. Calmly, as if she were out for a stroll, Quiarsca descended, then stopped and drove the pointed base of her staff into a step.

Magarric howled as if he'd been stabbed.

Kerrigan whirled and saw the elf writhing on the floor. His hands and face were covered with little cuts. Small dottings of blood spotted his shirt. *He created the* coriiesci. *He is linked to it, and it to him. Kill him and it dies, but damage it and you damage him.* Kerrigan looked down at the stone hand clawing its way up through the floor. *Of course.*

Kerrigan deliberately faced away from the battle and knelt beside Magarric. He grabbed the old elf by the shoulders, spun him around, and dragged him into a hug from behind. Magarric thrashed as more draconettes shot and the echo of Quiarsca stabbing the floor again filled the building. Kerrigan hung on tightly and forced the cacophony of screams and explosions from his mind.

He opened himself to the flow of magick and quickly sought a current full of power and purity. He reached out and captured it, then directed it into a healing spell. He cast it on Magarric but, try though he might, he could not escape being dragged into the vortex of pain that filled the old elf.

For Kerrigan it was all but unimaginable. Magarric had been alive before Spritha and Men entered the world. He had lost kin and friends; he had loved many times and known heartbreak many more. The creation of Vorquellyn had been joyous, but the knowledge that something greater was being destroyed to give it birth tore at him. He had seen so much, had lived so many lifetimes, then had his realm taken from him, despoiled, and left to fester in corruption.

The human fell into the elf's life and felt his attention being dragged in all directions. Kerrigan fought to keep himself together, but he felt like oil poured on an infinite sea. He might calm the water, but he was being pulled to the point of transparency.

He focused on healing Magarric's wounds. The cuts from the axes, the pinpricks from the draconette balls, and the vicious stabs that Quiarsca continued to inflict, all drained life from Magarric. She drove the staff into his flesh—*into our flesh*—and twisted it. Tendrils of pain flooded through them—*us*—and the part that was yet Kerrigan struggled to repair the damage. He sought out every other anomaly and malady. He pushed the encysted stone from his chest, found even more ancient scars, and repaired them.

Kerrigan plunged through the center of Magarric's being and into the *coriiesci* itself. He could see all that was happening from every angle, all at once. The Loquelves had driven into the *turekadine,* but had been surrounded. Some of the Aurolani creatures raced past them and engaged Grey Misters. One of the *turekadine* broke free and sprinted, with a bloody sword upraised, toward Kerrigan's back. The youth knew the sword would just bounce off the armor, so wasn't concerned.

Resolute, dueling with a *turekadine,* and Bok, blasting *nyressanii* with spells, never saw the *turekadine* get loose, though Quiarsca did. She laughed triumphantly, driving her staff deep enough to crack an entire step.

That stab shook Magarric. Kerrigan could feel the damage penetrating to the elf's heart. One more strike and she would kill him. She knew that; he could read it on her face and in the slow, deliberate way she pulled the staff free and raised it for one final thrust. No one was near enough to her to stop her.

Except me.

Kerrigan sought inside himself quickly and pushed a spell out through Magarric and into the *coriiesci.* Quiarsca's staff came down. The glittering, needle-sharp point sped toward the crack in the wood. The wound already wept with golden sap. The staff would gouge deeper than before, through to the heartwood. It would kill Magarric, kill the *coriiesci,* and complete the subjugation of Vorquellyn with one swift stroke.

Only the staff came apart in Quiarsca's grasp. Fashioned from a single emerald crystal, the staff shattered as dragonbone armor rose to shield the wound. Sharp slivers of green crystal pierced her hands, face, torso, and thighs. By reflex she raised her hands to her face, further shredding her flesh. She screamed, blood flowing from the empty eyes.

Magarric's consciousness flooded through Kerrigan. *What have you done? You gave your armor to us. You are defenseless.*

Kerrigan closed his eyes and waited for the *turekadine* sword to split him crown to waist. *You* must *live.*

Distantly, as if from a thousand leagues away, he heard Resolute scream his name. Closer he heard the *turekadine's* labored breath. He could feel the thunder of the footfalls. He braced for the hiss of sword through air and that initial crack, as the sword shattered his skull. He half wondered if he'd hear the pops of parting vertebrae. With his last conscious thought, he shoved Magarric away so the blow would not kill him, too.

The blow seemed to take forever to land. Kerrigan half wondered if that was because the legends were true: that in the moment of death your life flashed before your eyes. With so long a wait he'd have enough time, he thought, to watch Magarric's life, too. *Hurry, now, be done with it!*

He expected a hiss and a crack.

He got a squeal and a gurgle.

Kerrigan spun and rolled onto his back as the sword that would have cloven him in two dropped to the ground with a clatter. There, a good twelve feet in the air, the *turekadine* struggled. Its legs thrashed. Its eyes bulged. Its tongue protruded from its mouth, rapidly turning purple. It clawed at the hand wrapped around its throat, but those efforts weakened quickly, then its hands went limp.

Standing there, facing away from Kerrigan, was a man-shaped thing of stone. It was the same obsidian of the hand that had been sticking out of the floor. *That was the rock I pushed out of Magarric.* The figure had to be at least eight feet tall, and far broader than Will had ever been. *Broader even than Dranae.*

Kerrigan scrambled to his feet and slapped the figure on the back. "Don't worry, Will, we'll get you out of here. There has to be a way. Thank you."

The creature turned its head toward him. It had no ears, no nose, no mouth. It had no eyes per se, though two spots on its face glowed red-gold, as had the lava that had consumed Will. It regarded him for a moment, then its head swiveled back and faced the battle, with the dead *turekadine* still dangling from its upheld hand.

Kerrigan looked toward the entrance just in time to see Quiarsca scrambling up the bloodied steps. She was trying to escape, blindly clawing her way along on hands and knees. She did her best to move swiftly, but the very wood seemed to impede her. Her hands rose with difficulty, and her robe stuck to the steps.

Magarric chuckled. "That which does not kill us makes us very testy. She is going nowhere."

Resolute slashed his way past the last *turekadine*, then bounded up the stairs to where the *sullanciri* struggled. She turned to look at him, and her left hand came up as if in supplication. She rolled onto her back, her hair caught in the sap that had risen at Magarric's bidding.

With a simple thrust, Resolute drove Syverce through her heart. She stiffened at once and, though her muscles then slackened, her body hung there on the steps, trapped. More sap flowed, welling up around her, slowly encapsulating her corpse.

Elsewhere Bok burned the life from the last of the *nyressanii*. Trawyn knelt beside one of her company and closed his eyes. Wounded Grey Misters looted the bodies of the *turekadine*, several of them brandishing draconettes. Resolute, at the top of the stairs, pointed toward the doorway.

"You've closed us in."

"I've closed them out." Magarric strode forward. "Let those who are wounded smear their hurts with the sap from the stairs. It will speed healing. For the dead I can do nothing but offer my tears."

Kerrigan ran after him and caught him by the shoulder. "What about Will? What can you do about him?"

Magarric turned. "Who is Will?"

Kerrigan pointed at the stone figure still holding up the dead *turekadine*. "That is Will. Will is in there. We have to get him out."

Trawyn, Bok, and Resolute reached Kerrigan and Magarric as the ancient elf shook his head. "You did not come for Will. You came for the *Norrington*. There he is."

Kerrigan's stomach collapsed in on itself. He stumbled back and would have sat down hard, but Resolute's hands steadied him. "What?"

"Oh, Kerrigan, we didn't listen."

"What do you mean? I don't understand!"

Resolute's voice tightened. "Oracle said the Norrington was waiting for us. She never said *Will*. Will died on Vael, but *the Norrington* survived."

Tears began to blur Kerrigan's vision. "How?" He began to sob. "How can that be? I didn't save him then, and I wanted to save him now. How . . ."

Resolute shifted and hugged Kerrigan tight. "I don't know, Kerrigan, but I can guess. Will wasn't really Will, you know."

"I know. His name was Wilburforce. He told me."

"Well, maybe Will was just part of the Norrington. The part of him that had to get to a point where he could change. And somehow he knew it. Just like his father and grandfather had changed, so would he. We lost Will on Vael, but here we find the Norrington."

Something fluttered against Kerrigan's stomach. Qwc struggled free of the cloth-and-leather cocoon, then flew straight toward the obsidian figure. Qwc circled him once, then landed on his right shoulder. The Spritha cupped all four hands to its mouth and whispered where an ear should have been.

The *turekadine* fell with a thump as the hand opened, then the left arm lowered and the figure started forward. For a creature made of stone, the Norrington moved lightly. The *turekadine*'s heavy tread had been much easier to feel. As the Norrington drew closer it became obvious that the right shoulder had developed a depression in it that fit Qwc snugly.

The Spritha patted the Norrington on the shoulder. "Go. Go. Will wants to go."

Resolute gave Kerrigan another squeeze. "Qwc, that's not Will."

"Look closer. Qwc sees."

Kerrigan's head came up. He couldn't see anything, could he? Was there a flash in the eyes? Was there something about the movement of a hand? The thing did move as lightly as Will had. Was that what Qwc saw, or did the Spritha manage to see beyond the shell to what lurked within?

Resolute released Kerrigan and moved in the direction of the door. "Qwc's right. We have to get going. There's probably a horde of them out there."

Magarric shook his head. "The warrens are all but empty, and we have a few tricks to keep them occupied while you leave."

The silver-eyed Vorquelf frowned. "You say that as if you are staying here."

"We are. We will keep the fragments here."

Trawyn shook her head. "Is that wise? Their presence in a *coriiesci* will be . . ."

Magarric looked at her. "Distracting enough to drive us insane?"

"Forgive me, my lord."

"Easily done, child." The Vorquelf smiled. "The fragments will be safe here with us until you succeed. If you don't, we'll wander again with them."

Trawyn adjusted the patch over her eye. "You said there were warrens. This is where Chytrine bred troops?"

"Some of them. The ones you see here, the *kryalniri*—which are not nearly as nasty as the originals, and the lesser ones, too."

"And you say the warrens are empty?"

"All but a few. Many went to Loquellyn, and we would imagine others went east."

Kerrigan frowned. "To Sebcia and Muroso. The princess will be running into a trap."

Resolute nodded. "All the more reason for us to head north fast. All of you, grab some of these *turekadine*. Bring them with you."

Predator wiped a smear of blood from his face. "Easier to scalp them right here, Resolute."

"True, Predator, but scalps don't row." Resolute tapped one of the tattoos on his arm. "Unless you want to be pulling an oar all the way to the Ghost March, bring a volunteer. As long as we're going to visit Chytrine in one of her ships, she might as well provide us the power to get there."

CHAPTER 56

I saura had never seen her mother in such a state. She'd
long known her mother could change shape. As a child
she had delighted in this ability and still thrilled when
her mother assumed the form of a dragon to soar over her
realm. Isaura was aware that to change took discipline on
her mother's part—both to effect the change and to maintain it.

Standing in the doorway of her mother's tower-top *arcanorium,* Isaura barely recognized Chytrine. She had expected something was wrong when her mother had not
summoned her for days. Isaura assumed this was because
of the deaths of two *sullanciri:* Myrall'mara and Quiarsca.
Her mother had never shown much affection for them, but
their deaths had to be a concern.

So grief could have accounted for the way she found
Chytrine. The woman's gown, soiled and ill-fitting, hung
from hunched shoulders. Her long hair, which usually was
lustrous and golden, had become more brittle and shot
through with white. Her features had sharpened and she'd

acquired a muzzle. More important were the ivory scales that covered her flesh. They were not as thick or large as they were when her mother assumed dragon form, but flashed akin to the scales of a fish.

"You sent for me, Mother?"

Chytrine's head turned as casually as a drearbeast's when it deigns to take notice of potential prey. "I did, Isaura." She smiled, revealing fangs. "I have been working diligently on the spell which discovered me in Narriz. The shape I have now is one of the precautions I am taking against its working again. I have other wards in place that will blunt detection or misdirect it."

Isaura's right hand rested on the cool stone of the doorway. "That is good, Mother. I knew you could do that."

"Oh, and I did, easily, but then I began working with the spell. The man who invented it is quite talented for one so young." Chytrine breathed into the air and within the vapor an image of Kerrigan appeared.

Isaura gasped. "He is the one who slew Neskartu."

"Hardly a surprise. He is a curious mix of Vilwanese, Murosan, and other magicks. He has been instructed by dragons and my father, of course. What is fascinating is that the magick he used to find me was innovative. I have reshaped it to search for fragments of the DragonCrown. It has been successful in searching them out.

"Two I have here, and one is on Vael. The Ruby is in Oriosa. Scrainwood has hidden it, but I know where it is. Once Anarus destroys the army there, I will send him for it." Chytrine rubbed scaled hands together. "I have had some reports of two other fragments—the Sapphire and Vorquellyn's lost Diamond. Given the direction they were moving and their having vanished, along with Quiarsca's death, I shall assume they are on Vorquellyn and in the *coriiesci*. You, my sweet one, will be vital to opening that place so we may complete the Crown."

"Of course, Mother, I will be happy to do anything."

Isaura hoped she managed to keep her voice light. "What of the seventh fragment?"

"Ah, this is the most important thing. As with the Vorquellyn fragment, it was well warded against conventional searching spells. Now, however, I am able to locate it—at least intermittently. I am casting the spell south hourly, and there are times I find it and times I do not. The simple fact, however, is that it is now available to me."

Her mother's gleeful cackle made Isaura shiver.

"The very best part of it all, daughter, is that it appears to be traveling with Princess Alexia and coming directly into our trap. Once I have it, and secure the other pieces, the dragons will give me the Truestone they hold at Vael. Then I will complete the Crown and my Masters' will shall again be the law of the lands."

"That is wonderful, Mother. Shall you send me to Vorquellyn now?"

The empress's forked tongue flicked out for a moment, then she shook her head. "No, I cannot. The searching takes my time and I need you here."

"Do you wish to teach me the spell? I could search for you."

Her mother slowly shuffled around the center of the dark tower room, then turned quickly to face her, giving her a start. "Perhaps that would be a good idea, yes. Come here."

Isaura drifted forward obediently, stopping before her mother. Chytrine reached up and pressed her right palm to Isaura's forehead, sinking her talons into her daughter's hair. The flesh felt dry, yet warm against her skin. The talons bit into her scalp ever so slightly, and she became certain her mother could crush her skull with an absent-minded twitch.

Chytrine closed her eyes and heat built against Isaura's forehead. She resisted her mother's presence for a moment, then the spell burst into her consciousness. In an instant the young woman grasped it and its elegance. All the disparate elements of it had been woven together brilliantly. All one had to do was define parameters for the search and fix the information transfer point for the heralds, and the spell would work, as well as insulate the user from detection. She especially liked how the sorcerer had shielded the searching spells in such a way that the shields themselves could mislead anyone trying to locate the source of the spell.

Isaura took a step back, then raked fingers through her white hair. "Oh, yes, Mother, I understand it. As you need, I shall help you."

"I know you will, Isaura-sweet." The empress again flashed fangs as she smiled. "I regret having been so hasty as to have killed the creator of this spell. Had I been able to make him over into one of my *sullanciri* he would have been a fitting replacement for Neskartu—exceeding him by leaps and bounds."

"Yes, Mother, that is a shame." Isaura hesitated, then spoke. "You said two fragments are on Vorquellyn. Does that mean they have gone there and freed the Norrington?"

Chytrine nodded as she turned and walked back to a workbench covered with books, scrolls, alembics, vials, and a small chest of drawers full of things ancient and rare. "I assume they have. It is as I have intended."

"How can that be? He is the one fated to destroy you."

"Oh he is, yes, but it becomes a question of *when*, my darling." The empress turned back and wove her fingers together. "You must understand something vital. A prophecy carries with it a great deal of potential. Because of it all possibilities narrow, as if its fulfillment is the eye of a needle and all that can possibly happen needs to fit through or be excluded from the future. The Norrington Prophecy could cover any Norrington. That is why I have collected them. During this era, the prophecy is further energized because a rash youth, Tarrant Hawkins, made a pledge that

Vorquellyn would be liberated in his lifetime. I was hoping to free some of that energy when he was slain, but that was not to be. Yet. So as the Norrington gets closer to fulfilling the prophecy and possibilities squeeze down, more power gathers, and that is the power I need."

Isaura slowly nodded. "To free the Oromise?"

"Yes."

"But what if the Norrington kills you?"

"I have taken precautions. If he does, other forces will swing into play and the Oromise will yet be freed. If I stop him, if I make him hesitate, then I will be in a position to tap that power and release my Masters. The coming together of the DragonCrown similarly gathers power, though much less. I will need less, however, as the Crown will allow me to turn the dragons on themselves and destroy them. Once they are gone, the power needed to free my Masters will be much less."

"What if the Norrington never makes it here?"

"I have his child. It will do."

Isaura forced herself to smile. "Oh, Mother, I am so happy. I have been worried for you. Now I know nothing will go wrong."

Chytrine's face brightened. "Very good, my daughter, I am glad you are no longer worried. Now, I must to work. I wanted you to know the end is nigh. I will call you to me when I need help. Farewell."

"And you, Mother." Isaura turned and fled from the tower, raising the hem of her skirts so she could race down the curved steps. All her mother had said sped her along. Her mother was insane; of that she had no doubt. What might have once been a true desire to prevent the south from subjugating Aurolan had long since been warped by the Oromise. Her brief experience with the Oromise, and her knowledge and respect of dragons, led Isaura to the conclusion that she did not want the former again controlling the world.

At the base of the tower she found Hlucri lurking in a

shadow. "There you are. Pull together all the things we have been hiding away for our escape."

The *sullanciri* nodded. "And Sayce?"

"I will get her." Isaura exhaled sharply. "We need to head south and quickly. If we don't, my mother's plans will bear fruit, and the world will become something we never wanted to know."

Ferxigo shifted her shape to make herself as small as possible before she knelt at her mistress' feet. "It is as you said, Mistress. Isaura has taken the prisoner and headed south."

"Hlucri is with them?"

"Yes, Mistress."

"Very good." Chytrine smiled, her teeth now all dragonish pegs. "Of course she had to be the one to betray me. It's in her blood. She will always help the Norringtons. And she failed to understand me when I told her of potential. One Norrington coming against me constitutes power. Two, for Sayce will not stay behind, merely amplifies it. She seeks to stop me, and all she does is empower me."

Ferxigo risked an upward glance. "She will be able to find them?"

"Oh, yes, with the spell I've given her, she will find them. You will give her a two-day head start, then you will head south. You will bring me Sayce and the Norrington. You will slay all the others."

"What about your daughter?"

"I have no daughter."

"I understand, Mistress." Ferxigo pressed her forehead to the ground. "Shall I station troops at the pass?"

Chytrine paused, then nodded. "Alexia will not get past Nefrai-kesh, but might he come at me, too, you wonder?"

"No, Mistress, he would not betray you."

"No, but if he did, to have three Norringtons converging . . ." Chytrine's smile grew. "Then perhaps even the Oromise would bow to me as you do."

"As well they should, Mistress."

"Indeed, pet, as well they should." The Aurolani Empress nodded slowly. "Go and prepare your troops. Be swift in your mission. The sooner you succeed, the sooner our future will become reality."

CHAPTER 57

Alexia listened to the Murosan refugee again explain what it was she'd seen as she fled south. The woman claimed, and markings on her mask confirmed, that she was from Caledo. She had fled the capital when it fell to the Aurolani. With her family they had swung south and then west. They remained in the countryside, holed up in a cave, until the thaw came, when they decided to move west to see if Zamsina had fallen.

"It had been destroyed, just melted down to nothing by dragonfire." Her voice took on the monotone of someone both weary and numb. "Everything had been burned down to the foundations. Looking at the city from a hill was like looking at a hedge maze from a tower. Southwest of there, though, that's what we saw that we had to tell you."

Alexia gave her a smile. "Please, I know you have told your story many times, but I want to hear it." As she spoke she moved to the maps others had provided, based on the woman's testimony and that of her family, all of whom had been separated and interrogated. Their stories matched, and once she had told it again they would be gathered together and housed in one of the outlying estates near the town of Notirri.

If what she says is true, just over twenty miles from here, Nefrai-kesh has gathered an army that will destroy me. Part of her wanted to scoff at that idea, since the dream she'd allegedly had posited a final battle in Sebcia. Had things shifted such that Chytrine was abandoning the artifice of following the dreams, or was Nefrai-kesh not following his mistress' plan? Or was her plan just to get Alyx thinking she knew the dreams would be played out, and subsequently she would underestimate the enemy?

"I am not good with numbers, but my son counted banners. He said there were almost a hundred of the little banners and six of the big standards. That's what my husband said you called the big ones. He fought Chytrine back in the old days. My son said there were eighty of the small ones, but I couldn't count them."

Alexia glanced at Crow, who frowned. Eighty small banners would amount to eighty legions, or eight thousand of the enemy. The larger standards would represent regiments, and six of them tallied close with the legion banners. The extra legions were just reinforcing legions. Though Alexia commanded nearly half again as many troops, other factors would make the Aurolani seem superior.

"We couldn't move during the night, but we did see a lot of fires. They were in the hills southwest of Zamsina, making battlements and building a fort. They might have been using slaves from the area. We didn't see any hunting parties, but my son said he could see men working with them. Men would have to be slaves, wouldn't they? They wouldn't work for her unless captive, would they?"

Alexia shook her head, but kept looking at a rough map of the fortifications drawn by the son. Nefrai-kesh had laid out a square structure where the southwest corner was higher than those of the southeast or northwest. The lowest corner could only be reached through a narrow valley between two lines of hills, which were steep enough to stop anyone riding up and out of an ambush. And if there ever was a place for an ambush, that was it. Getting siege machinery through the valley would be nigh impossible, and then it would be all but useless since there weren't any walls to pound down, just revetments and ditches.

What disturbed Alexia about the fort is that Nefrai-kesh was putting himself in the position she had described her own forces occupying as an Aurolani force came against her. It beat itself to death through repeated assaults, and even though breaching that low northeast corner had let the Aurolani into the fortress, a solid counterattack had driven them back in defeat. Her forces sallied through the breach and slashed at the Aurolani rear by racing out through the valley and around to the southwest, where they overwhelmed the flank and rolled up the Aurolani forces.

In her supposed dream, the eleven thousand troops she had inside could have easily managed that. They'd been facing twenty thousand Aurolani and there was her current problem. Fortifications such as those described would be sufficient to let an army hold off one twice its size, perhaps even three times its size. And if the Aurolani had dragonels, they might well be invincible.

"I know you want to know if they had dragonels. I saw them at Caledo and heard them. I thought my ears were going to bleed. I didn't see any. I didn't see any digging of the type my son says they would have to have done to use them. I don't know."

"That's fine." Alexia did turn this time. "We will be able to figure that out before we get there."

Arimtara approached the woman and squatted. She breathed out a white vapor, within which appeared the image of a dracomorph. "Did you see anything that looked like this?"

The woman shrank back at first, then her eyes narrowed and she peered at it. "No, nor anything like you, but there were so many people there I could not tell. There weren't any Gyrkyme there, either."

Peri smiled. "Any *araftii*?"

"I saw nothing flying there. And after seeing dragons, I was looking."

"I'm certain you were." Alexia came over and helped the woman from her chair. "Outside you will find a lieutenant who will take you to your family. Thank you for your help."

The woman nodded, then smiled. "You will free our nation, won't you?"

"Of course we will."

"And rescue Her Highness?"

"Without a doubt."

The woman seized Alexia's hands and smothered them with kisses. "May the gods bless you in all things."

"Thank you for your help."

Arimtara guided the woman along to the door being held open by General Pandiculia. The Salnian warrior closed it behind her. "Gratitude just for a promise. How interesting."

Alyx shrugged. "Hope is all she has now. That, and her family. I gave her more hope. What she gave us, on the other hand, isn't very hopeful."

"Hopeful, no. But helpful, yes." Crow walked over to the map of the fort. "Her son and husband agree on the nature of the fort. The son's lame, so he never could join the army, but has a keen interest in history. He was specific about many of the regimental standards, and very specific about seeing new types of soldiers in the ranks."

"I know. They sound like the things Resolute saw in Loquellyn." Alexia shivered. The information about Loquellyn had been sent via *arcanslata* and was sketchy at best, but mentioned *turekadine* and *nyressanii* as being two new creatures Chytrine had sent into the field.

Peri looked at the map. "There is one thing I don't understand. The fort is strong, and with the numbers described, we would have a hard time defeating it. But there is a flaw in the fortress. There is no source of water. Even if they were to dig wells, they could never get enough to sustain their army. Why would you have dreamed of putting *your* army in such a place?"

The princess smiled. "I did it by accident. When I had described things to my cousin, I told him of a couple battles and said there were more. The Crown Circle pressed me for details on all of them. I started to recall ancient battles and give details. This situation is really a battle in Valician history during which a Jeranese army managed to trap some Valicians in a fortress and wait them out. I'd always thought the Valician commander was a fool, and had been mulling over how he could have won. In my haste, I put myself in his position, and offered a possible solution. In reality, the northeast corner fell when thirsty soldiers could not defend it."

"So, that is what we do, then? We surround it, lay siege, and wait?" Crow stroked his beard. "It *is* one solution."

"Yes, but only if Nefrai-kesh is an idiot, and we both know he isn't." Alexia tapped the map with a finger. "If we surround the place and he has more troops in reserve, he falls on us and we're done."

Crow nodded. "Agreed, but if we go hard and fast at the fortress, we are going to lose a lot of people."

"I know that is a problem, too. All he has to do is wear us down, draw us out. Erlestoke has reported that an army is coming to Oriosa. If it stops and backtracks as we chase Nefrai-kesh to Caledo or Sebcia, we are caught between two armies and crushed."

General Pandiculia frowned. "We could use my army as a screening force to the east, but I doubt we would hold them off for long. Still, the warning you'd get would be useful."

Alexia nodded. "In whatever we do, your army is going to be crucial."

Peri gave a small cry of annoyance. "We can't ignore Nefrai-kesh's army because then it would just pour down into Saporicia. We have to attack him there, on a ground of his own choosing."

"Exactly. To us it may look like a poor choice. To him it's what he wants." Alexia sighed, then narrowed her eyes. "I try to guess what he knows, he tries to guess what I know, and so it goes."

"And the killer will be what neither of you knows." Crow shook his head. "It's pretty clear we're never going to know enough, so we just have to stumble on ahead in ignorance."

"Yes, my love, exactly." The princess hugged her arms around her belly. "And hope that what we don't know won't hurt us too badly."

CHAPTER 58

After enchanting the *turekadine* to row, Resolute had re-tired to the ship's cabin for rest. His sleep came easy—easier than it had in over a century. While his homeland had been nothing as he remembered, just setting foot on it and having slain the enemy there had given him some peace. Not enough for him to abandon his quest, but sufficient that he could imagine his struggle might some-day see an end.

The sun was dawning by the time he awakened and headed up to the wheeldeck. Down on the oardeck, where the undead *turekadine* pulled at the oars with a tirelessness that no living creature could match, the Norrington stood unmoving. Qwc slept on his right shoulder. The stone crea-ture seemed not to notice anything around him, yet Resolute had the distinct feeling that had one of the *tureka-dine* done something unexpected, it would not get past him.

Up near the prow, Kerrigan stood with Oracle. Resolute looked over at Trawyn, who was taking a turn at the wheel. "Has Kerrigan slept?"

"No."

"Have you?"

She turned and looked at him. "No. I couldn't sleep with our crew rowing."

Resolute frowned. "They will be no problem. They'll get us to the Ghost March."

"And then what?"

"I don't know. I've never had one survive long enough to wonder. If they are still vital, I'll have them jump into the sea. I owe that much to Tagothcha."

The Loquelf princess turned and looked forward again. "I never approved of what some of your Vorquelves did in getting yourselves enchanted in that way."

"It wasn't your choice. We decided we had to do it, and there were still Vorquelves around who could perform those rituals."

Her voice remained low. "Few of the tattoos on your flesh are Vorquelven in nature."

"True. I spent a certain amount of time learning my trade. There were those who wanted things and I provided them. There was a time when gibberkin gall was thought to be an aphrodisiac, and a fan of frostclaw feathers once was highly sought after in Alcidese society. They got what they wanted, and so did I."

Trawyn looked at him again, and the intensity of her stare surprised him. "Was doing what you have done to yourself worth it?"

"What do you mean, what I have done to myself?"

"Look at you! You're nothing like an elf. You have abandoned your birth name. Do you even remember it?"

His nostrils flared. "Immaterial to your point, Princess, so get to it."

"My point is that, in an effort to redeem your homeland, you became something that never could live there." She shook her head. "Don't take me wrong. I actually have admiration for what you have done."

"Even though you think Vorquellyn can never be redeemed?"

"Yes. You didn't give up hope or become a parasite like Predator and the rest. And you don't play at being an adult the way Amends and his people do." Her brow furrowed and her voice caught. "If you do succeed, you know you will win your home back for them, don't you? They may hail you as a hero, but they will never make you feel at home."

"It doesn't matter, Princess." Resolute gave her a slow smile. "Once Vorquellyn is redeemed, Vorquellyn will make me feel at home. Once I have my homeland, once I am bound to it, it will tell me my place. Until that time, yes, I am what I have made myself. I am elven, and perhaps more, or just different. But it's what I needed to be. Do you understand that?"

Trawyn slowly nodded. "I do."

The Vorquelf looked out over the wheeldeck at the Norrington. "The redemption requires sacrifice, but until the prophecy, we did not have a direction. When Crow and I found Will, I took his name as an omen. Will: a word such as we took for our names. And he was very willful. Sometimes, almost too much."

"I can see how his name would be seen as a good sign." Trawyn nodded. "Now Will seems inappropriate, and *the Norrington* too forbidding."

"I agree." Resolute closed his eyes for a moment, then half smiled. "Will was actually a name he adopted. As Kerrigan reminded me, his true name was Wilburforce."

"He adopted an aspect of his name for an aspect of his life."

"So it seems. Perhaps now he's just Force." As the Vorquelf said it, the stone creature half turned his head as if he'd overheard. Resolute resisted the urge to ask him if that was his true name, the way someone might question a pet. "Force you shall be."

Trawyn shook her head. "His sacrifices continue. His life, now his name."

Resolute hesitated for a moment, then softened the

tone he had intended for his words. "You're afraid, aren't you, of what losing your homeland would do to you? What you would have to sacrifice."

"I am wondering if I could do to myself what you have to win it back."

Resolute shrugged. "Let us hope you never have to learn what you would do for your homeland." He looked toward the prow and saw the hint of clouds on the horizon. "We'll make landfall by noon?"

"I believe so, yes."

"Good. I'll spell you here so you can sleep. First, however, I want to talk with Kerrigan."

"He needs to sleep, too."

"I know." Resolute descended the ladder to the oardeck, worked his way around Force and climbed up to the foredeck. "Kerrigan, you need to sleep."

The youth wore a haunted expression. "I can't sleep. I keep thinking about Will."

Oracle rested a hand on Resolute's forearm. "I have apologized for the errors. I knew only that the Norrington was waiting for us. I did not know his shape or his nature."

Resolute patted her hand, but his mind returned to the cavern in Gyrvirgul where Oracle had spent her time creating a vast mural that depicted some of her visions. In one section an image of Will had been painted on a bit of rock that was emerging from the wall. *Was that conscious on her part, or just a piece of her gift?*

Kerrigan looked up. "I don't blame you, Oracle. You said what came to you, and I asked no questions. I just assumed."

"As did I, Kerrigan, and I thought we'd crack that shell and find Will, too."

"I know, Resolute." Kerrigan's hands closed into fists. "What I keep wrestling with is the prophecy and Will's part in it. You said that maybe Will was just part of the Norrington, and that he had to go through a transformation. Maybe his father and grandfather, at one time, could have had that mantle, but events just conspired to settle it on Will. If he fails, if we fail, does that fall to Sayce's child, or one of Will's half brothers? Did Will get someone else pregnant and is her child the newest Norrington?"

Oracle pressed her hands together. "Those possibilities are present, but only as *potential*. The Norrington Prophecy is a reality that will see itself fulfilled by one means or another."

The youth's brow furrowed. "I guess it goes deeper than worrying about the prophecy. I've been told that I was bred by Vilwan to fight Chytrine. Defeating her is the only purpose for which I was created. Will, it seems, was born to fulfill the prophecy. Alexia, while born free, was trained to be Chytrine's enemy. Did any of us have a choice? Could we have been other than we are?"

Resolute glanced back to where Trawyn stood at the wheel, feeling odd echoes of their conversation reverberating. "You could ask if any of us have any choices. Perhaps there are prophecies out there that foretell all of this, from the fall of Vorquellyn and even earlier. Could it be that there are no free choices? Perhaps our ending just determines how our life runs, as if time flowed backward and we were propelled from our deaths on a course to our births."

Kerrigan nodded. "Yes, exactly."

Oracle brushed a droplet of spray from her cheek. "If you allow that, then Kerrigan, you, Princess Alexia, and Will are no different than anyone. The note of self-pity in your question is thereby invalidated, for everyone's life is determined before they live it. You three just have more obvious and grand ends toward which you are heading."

The youth stared at her for a moment, then slumped back against the wale. "This philosophical question is new to me, but you've had a *long* time to think about it, right?"

"I have, Kerrigan. Moreover, I have been forced to think about it." Oracle sighed. "I have a gift of seeing. I see futures. I have had to wonder if what I see determines the outcome, or if things can be changed."

"What have you concluded?"

"It seems there are points where outcomes can be changed, and actions that cast futures into flux. Other forces—like the prophecy, or Crow's vow to see Vorquellyn redeemed in his lifetime—serve as levees to channel the possibilities. Futures are contracting right now. I cannot choose which among them will win out, for there is a point beyond which I have no vision. Because I do not know which will be true, to tell you of them would be useless."

Resolute nodded. "And the very act of our learning it might make us do something that changes it."

Kerrigan sighed heavily. "So it sounds to me as if I have a choice: to decide that everything has been determined and what's going to happen is what is going to happen and I have no choice or say in the matter; or to decide that free will and choices are the way of the world, and I've got to make the best choices I can."

Oracle smiled. "I think you have the problem well defined."

"Which leaves me with only one choice, the latter one." Kerrigan smiled wearily. "If things are predetermined, and I am meant to make the best choices, I will. Since I believe I have free will, I am determined to make the best choices."

Resolute patted him on the shoulder. "I agree with your choice."

"Because it makes the most sense."

"Pretty much. I also figure it annoys the gods."

"I didn't think you believed in the gods."

The Vorquelf smiled. "I don't, but why should that stop me from angering them?"

Kerrigan held his hands up. "Okay, you're beginning to make sense, which means I seriously need sleep. Wake me when we arrive."

The ship sailed up a small estuary into a swamp with the Grey Misters at the oars for the last leg. True to his promise to Tagothcha, Resolute sent the *turekadine* over the side before they left the sea. The ship finally ran aground on a sandbar, so they made it fast with ropes and headed inland. Resolute was fairly certain that they'd never return to use it, but he didn't want it just floating back down to the sea. While they'd seen no patrol craft along the coast, he didn't feel like taking chances.

The battle at Saslynnae had taken its toll on his company. Of the fifty that made it to Vorquellyn, only thirty-five remained and many of them had wounds from which they were still recovering despite the sap from the *coriiesci*. Trawyn's people again spearheaded their force, with Resolute, Oracle, Force, Kerrigan, and Bok coming next. Qwc had roused himself enough to come along, but rode on Force's shoulder and did not fly about at all. The Grey Misters formed the rest of the company. Predator, Banausic, and a knot of a half-dozen made up the rear guard.

Resolute kept his voice low as he replied to Kerrigan's question. "Yes, I've been in the Ghost March before, but not for a while. Men still live here, paying tribute to Chytrine, and some do serve her. I have to assume there are Aurolani forces here, too, but most closer to the Boreal Pass. Where we've come in there is another, little-known pass, so we might get in with less trouble."

Trawyn's Loquelves had gotten ahead on the narrow trail that ran over hummocks and around hills. Resolute had just lost sight of them when a rustling in the brush alerted him to the ambush. Men of every stripe—universally filthy and wearing ragtag clothes—emerged from cover and leveled crossbows or arrows at them.

"Don't move and you don't have to die."

Resolute surveyed the situation quickly and dispassionately. He had bladestars in a pouch on his belt and was certain he could kill the tall man who had spoken and two others. But, by then, crossbow bolts would rip through him and everyone else. The rest of the group might kill a few, but they would die, too, and rather swiftly.

Resolute's heart sank. *To be so close.* He glanced around at the others, then slowly held his hands up. "We'll think of something later," he reassured Kerrigan and Oracle.

Kerrigan took a step forward and Resolute realized that to make a grab for him would be to trigger an attack. The mage got an odd look on his face as he studied the soldiers. "Don't I know you?"

The group's leader frowned. "Be quiet."

"I *do* know you. You're with the Jeranese Crown Guards. Your wife was wet-nursing a child, one of the twins the baker's wife had had. You're Fossius."

The tall man blinked. "That's . . . How did you know that?"

"I read that letter to you. I'm Kerrigan."

The man snorted. "You're not the Kerrigan I remember."

"I've missed a few meals, Fossius. That's Resolute. You might remember him." The mage smiled. "And if you don't, General Adrogans will. In fact, I think he'll want to see us immediately."

CHAPTER 59

Though his tent had been erected in the shade of several trees, Marcus Adrogans found the day's heat had built to an oppressive degree. He'd stripped off his tunic and boots, wearing only free-flowing trousers styled after those favored by the Alcidese in his command. Uniforms had become a thing of the past anyway, and at least the cloth did not cling to his body. Sweat coursed down his chest, but no longer stung the piercings from which hung little talismans of the *yrûn* to which he had bound himself.

The intelligence reports coming in from his scouts had been exacting, but did little to reassure him that he could affect the situation facing him. He picked up one of the wood samples—a core as long as his finger with writing on it that carefully noted when and where it was taken—and absently twirled it between his fingers.

The unseasonable heat had a good side to it. As disagreeable as he found it, the Aurolani suffered even more. The scouts he had in the actual city of Alcytlin had noted that gibberers and even the gibberkings were sluggish—though the *kryalniri* seemed not to mind it overmuch. That would stand them in good stead when it came to fighting, for it was always a hot and tiring business.

The bad part of the heat, aside from being as easily able to exhaust his men as it was the enemy, was that it tended to keep the Aurolani in their barracks and did not promote them lighting fires at night to keep warm. Their remaining undercover meant he had a difficult time assessing how many of them there were. Without that knowledge, to strike at them would be foolhardy.

But if I don't attack . . .

A man appeared at the flap of his tent. "Begging the general's pardon, but the coast patrol from yesterday is back. They have some captives."

Adrogans frowned and barely glanced in his direction. "You know procedure. Have the interrogators find out what they know and bring me a report."

"I'd have done that, sir, but I think you'll want to see them."

Adrogans turned, his grey eyes tightening. He recognized the man: Fossius, with the Jeranese Crown Guards. "Deciding who I want to see, Sergeant, is not usually a decision made at your rank."

"I know that, sir, but I really think you'll want to see them without delay."

Before Adrogans could reply, the tent's other flap got flung aside and Phfas entered. His left hand was in the grasp of an enormous stone creature that ducked its head to enter the tent. As it straightened up, its head strained the roof canvas. On its right shoulder rode a Spritha, and behind it came a slender young man of passing familiarity, and a tall Vorquelf the general recognized easily.

He glanced at Fossius. "You were correct, Sergeant. Thank you."

Phfas clapped his hands like a child. "You see, nephew, your prayers are answered."

"Really." Adrogans nodded a salute to Resolute. "A

fighter of your prowess I welcome. And you clearly didn't come alone."

The Vorquelf shook his head. "I have about thirty other fighters—Vorquelves and some Loquelves. That includes Princess Trawyn. She's talking to the Blackfeathers now. Loquellyn was overrun, but still survives."

"And the Spritha would be Qwc?"

Qwc nodded, but did not get up from his perch and fly around. He seemed subdued, but Adrogans didn't know enough about the wee ones to know if that was normal or not. "And your companions?"

The young man raised a hand in a brief wave. "We've met before. I'm Kerrigan Reese."

"Of course. You've changed, but your voice remains the same." He looked at the stone creature's featureless face. The glowing spots that served it for eyes gave no indication where—*or even* if—the creature was looking somewhere. "Who might this be?"

"It's Will." Kerrigan's reply came fast. "You might have to look close, but he's in there."

Resolute squeezed Kerrigan's shoulder. "More correctly, this is the Norrington. Will died on Vael to save the life of a dragon. The Norrington is a lot harder to kill, and has returned to fulfill the prophecy. We have, some of us, taken to calling him Force. He's come with us to destroy Chytrine."

"You're bound north, then?"

Resolute nodded. "That's our intent."

Adrogans folded his arms across his chest. "I will help you in any way I can. You may draw supplies from our stores. Getting from here to the pass is not going to be easy because of the shipyards at Alcytlin. There might be as many as ten thousand Aurolani troops there waiting to sail south to attack Yslin, or just reinforce the army going to attack Alexia."

Resolute smiled. "That reminds me, I once was carrying orders to tell you to remain in Svarskya."

"Noted."

"And we're not using the Boreal Pass. I know of another way north, usually more dangerous, but with the hot spring, the more treacherous parts should be free of ice."

The Jeranese general nodded. "If you wouldn't mind, I'd like to send some of my scouts with you. If we can't get past the shipyards, or if we are mauled in doing so, slipping a small force into Aurolan through your pass might just work."

The Vorquelf hooked his thumbs in his sword belt. "You've twice voiced doubts about the shipyards. I do not remember you being anything but confident in the past. Why does this daunt you so? Is it the sea?"

"My fear of the sea? No, there are ample land routes for getting there." Adrogans drew in a deep breath, then rather quickly, sketched out the difficulties facing his army. While he did have dragonels—and discovering that Resolute knew of them somehow did not surprise him—the potential mismatch in forces, with the possibility of Aurolani ships turning their dragonels on his troops, left him with too many variables to try to control.

"I know we have to attack soon. My sources have informed me of Alexia's victories, and the impending battle near Zamsina. The fleet will launch after her battle, either to strike at Yslin, Lakaslin, and Narriz, or to pour new troops into Muroso through the coastal ports. The ships are loading supplies and some already have a full complement of dragonels. If I assume I am facing less than eight regiments, I'm a fool."

Kerrigan's brow furrowed. "You said most of the Aurolani stay inside during the day, right?"

"Yes."

"So, if they never come out to fight, you don't have to deal with them, right?"

"True, but casting a spell to lock all the windows and doors won't keep them in, my friend. The buildings shelter them, but are hardly so stout that they couldn't carve a new door through a wall."

"I know that." Kerrigan raised a hand and gestured. The wooden core Adrogans had been playing with flew from his grasp to that of the young mage. "You said you have a lot of these?"

"We've got them from every piece of wood we were able to find."

"Good. I'm willing to bet that not all of the wood went into ships. There's probably a bunch in those buildings. With a little work, I can figure out which cores are part of main beams or pillars, and that means I can bring their flimsy houses down on top of them. Would that help even your odds?"

Adrogans grinned and rubbed a hand over his jaw. "I think it just might. We'll draw up a plan of attack, get our people positioned, and go to war. If you can take the barracks down, or keep the ships away, we only have one thing to worry about."

"The *sullanciri* that commands the fleet?"

Adrogans nodded.

The Vorquelf was clearly about to speak, but just then a grinding sound and an intense burst of heat came from Force. He raised his right hand and tightened it into a fist. The purple-black stone began to glow, then cracks appeared in it. Molten stone flowed out, then shaped itself into a double-bitted axe blade with serrated edges.

Adrogans glanced at Resolute. "He doesn't speak, but he does manage to communicate."

"Indeed he does, General."

CHAPTER 60

Erlestoke had hoped for two things. The first was that his army would be able to make it into the Dales before they had to face the Aurolani army. But Anarus, the Aurolani commander, had decided to deny him that wish, pushing his army forward into Oriosa. The *sullanciri* used the Bokagul mountains to secure his western flank, and chose his battleground carefully. He picked a shallow valley with a fordable river running through it, and positioned his troops on the northern slope.

The second thing the prince had hoped for was that his army would be bigger than the Aurolani force. This wish he got, but only by luck and by a margin that didn't make much difference. After the Bloodmasks had been hunted down and the throne in Meredo had been redecorated, the force that had been shadowing his army came forward. It was made up of just under two thousand fighters from the East Country, led by Count Storton. He added six hundred heavy cavalry and a regiment of light infantry to the army. Likewise Malviston had brought his troops over, with nine hundred light cavalry and a regiment of light infantry. As they moved forward, another thousand volunteers joined the army, though Erlestoke put no great store by them.

Borell begged to differ. "Highness, they wear masks."

The youth's quiet confidence did buoy Erlestoke's spirits for as long as it took to find Anarus' army. Just by reading the standards in the Aurolani force, Erlestoke calculated that his force had nearly two thousand more soldiers than the north, and that did not include the irregulars. That gave him a thirty percent edge in personnel, but the presence of dragonels or draconetteers could shave away that advantage. The Aurolani also appeared to have more magick-users, if all the white specks were *kryalniri*. His Addermages were formidable, but unless they could counteract everything the Aurolani cast, the damage would be serious.

With the coming of dawn, bugles roused the troops, though Erlestoke had long been awake. He watched the sunlight catch the tips of the mountains and slowly crawl down as the sun rose. The battlefield went from dark to dim, then color seeped into it. Across the way the Aurolani were organizing themselves. Around his camp his troops gathered, with the heavy infantry in the middle, the light on the wings, and the cavalry massed and deployed behind the wings. The irregulars—two battalions of light cavalry and three of light infantry—were held in reserve to the rear.

Sheathed in mail, with Crown at his left hip, Erlestoke came upon Nay strapping on bits and pieces of borrowed armor. "You don't need to fight. You've done your duty, Nay."

"Still my nation. Killed Aurolani while Moonmasked and still remember how." He straightened up and brandished a maul. "Figured to stiffen the boys."

The prince nodded. The irregulars had earned the sobriquet "the boys" because of their youth and cavalier attitudes. Though all of them were past Moonmasks, most had only few markings on their life masks. They'd come, some in search of adventure, others out of patriotism, but none of them with much training or much more in the way of weaponry than Nay.

"That would be good, Nay." The prince swiped a hand over his forehead and it came away wet. "It's not going to be an easy day. We will need them."

"Yes, Highness. Mind you, cut quick and good with that sword, and you might not."

"I'll do that." The prince left him and continued to walk toward where his bodyguard waited.

Preyknosery landed near him and caught up with him quickly. "It is as you suspected, Highness. They have been here several days and have dug warrens. I do not know if they have more troops hidden in them, but there are trenches and revetments from which they can fight. Either they will withdraw as we advance, letting us tire ourselves out, or will retreat if we break through. Behind their current line, it is a tangle. Horsemen cannot go there, and the fighting in the tunnels will be horrible."

"Thank you, Ironwing." Erlestoke felt a weight descend on him as if a dragon had fallen from the sky. The only reason attacking was in the least viable was because of his numerical advantage. If more troops were hidden away, or they all withdrew into the earth so he could not root them out, his march to join Alexia was over. *As it is, she'll only get the ragged remnants of my force.*

Generals Percurs and Quantusa waited for him, but before they could report the readiness of their troops, cries and moans from the southern soldiers snapped Erlestoke's head around. A dragon with golden scales appeared with wings spread. The scales over its left haunch were broken or missing, and that leg appeared to be a bit stiff as it advanced, but there was no infirmity in the fury lighting its red-black eyes.

Dranae smiled as he reached the prince's side. "That is Adachoel. He was at Vilwan."

"You weren't the one who gave him that bite on the hip, were you?" Erlestoke still recalled how Dranae, in his true form, had nearly bitten a dragon about Adachoel's size in half.

"No, that was a friend. You needn't worry about Adachoel. I shall deal with him." Dranae handed Preyknosery his draconette, then moved to a large open area between the prince's tent and the troops. The man pulled his arms in around himself and almost seemed to be grabbing the flesh at his waist as if it were a tunic. He started to pull up and out, and in an eyeblink he transformed into a massive green dragon whose claws effortlessly gouged grave-deep furrows in the greensward.

Erlestoke had to smile. The cries of terror from his army quickly shifted to cheers of triumph as the men realized their dragon was bigger than the enemy's beast. Men began beating swords against shields, raising a horrible din.

On the other side a lone figure stepped from the dragon's shadow and suddenly the Aurolani had two dragons. The second one had purple scales tinged with gold. The human force began to grow quiet as the thunder of Aurolani drums built.

Dravothrak shook his head slowly, the dawnlight glinting from gold flecks in his scales. "They are nothing, my friend. Pups only. Procimre was chased from Navval, as I will chase him from here."

Erlestoke saluted him. "Signalman, bring all troops to arms."

The bugler began to play, but his song tailed off as a third dragon, this one larger than either of the other two, made his presence known. He was green like Dravothrak, save for gold stripes over his rear haunches and tail. And he reared up and walked forward on his hind legs. Spreading his wings, he battered the other two aside, then roared a challenge to Dravothrak.

Dravothrak raised his muzzle to the sky and replied with a shriek that chilled Erlestoke to the bone. Toward the rear came the sounds of men screaming and running.

Those would be the irregulars. Erlestoke flicked a hand out, smacking the bugler in the shoulder. "To arms, *now!*"

Dravothrak looked at Erlestoke. "I will keep them off you for as long as I can. Any two I could kill, but Sidrachuil . . ."

"What about him?"

"If you ever have a hatchling who hates you, never let him live long enough to steal a name." Dravothrak lowered his body, then his wings unfurled as he sprang into the air. The powerful downbeat flattened the bugler and blew apart Erlestoke's tent.

The prince, having braced for it, was only driven to a knee. He looked up, quickly remembering the fluid ease with which Dravothrak's muscles worked when they'd flown to Meredo. He recalled the dragon's having slain a copper dragon in Sarengul. "You *can* do it, Dranae; you can."

Sidrachuil took to the air first, but with a twist of his tail and the furling of one wing, slid to the side to let the other, smaller dragons make for Dravothrak first. As they drove in directly, flapping their wings hard, the striped dragon curved around to the east. For a heartbeat Erlestoke feared the dragon would lace the southern lines with fire before soaring up to engage his father. Fortunately, he was content to drift over the lines, letting men scream, faint, and run, then he began his drive up toward Dravothrak's back.

The younger dragons must have thought Dravothrak ancient enough to be senile, or hoped he would be distracted by their larger companion, for they sped toward him. Dravothrak waited, then thrust his head forward and vomited out a great gout of fire. Erlestoke felt the heat and watched it engulf the gold dragon. Adachoel's wings folded in and he fell from the sky, trailing smoke. It did not seem as if he were on fire, but as if the force of the attack had stunned him. He slammed hard into a hillside, flattening bushes and leaving a ten-foot-deep indentation, then bounced once and rolled.

Procimre twisted in midair, then looped over onto his back. His tail flicked by slowly, tantalizingly. Dravothrak lunged at it, snapping his teeth on empty air, then started to dive toward the point at which the purple would come out of his loop. As he did so, his tail came up and left his belly open to Sidrachuil's attack.

The striped dragon blasted out flames. Almost impossibly for a dragon of his size, Dravothrak rolled and twisted his tail past the fiery jet. His tail continued around as his body twisted, then flicked out, smashing Sidrachuil in the shoulder. Scales shattered and fell to the Bokagul foothills.

Sidrachuil, clearly surprised, spun away, then looped and climbed. Beneath him, Procimre came out of his lazy loop and craned his neck around to find Dravothrak. He looked back over his own right shoulder, but the green's roll had taken him further to the left. Procimre's head twisted around even more, his body beginning to roll to relieve the pressure, when Dravothrak's mouth snapped shut over the purple's head. Scales parted with the thunder of a distant avalanche, then the purple's headless corpse began an awkward tumble from the sky.

Dravothrak spat Procimre's head out, bouncing it through one of the Aurolani light cavalry units. He then folded his left wing, slewing his body around to the right. Sidrachuil's dive carried him just to the left, narrowly missing the green. The gold-striped tail did hit, however: a flailing blow that crushed scales over Dravothrak's spine. Dravothrak's left hind leg spasmed, extending and clawing at air.

At that moment Adachoel hit him from below and tore at his belly. The gold's slashing claws ripped away lighter green scales. Black blood began to well up in the wound. Droplets rained down and smoked, and spring grasses withered where they landed.

Despite the wounding, Dravothrak twisted in the air swiftly. With a flick of his right forepaw, he snapped Adachoel's right wing. The gold dragon flapped hard, but uselessly, the broken wing fluttering raggedly. Adachoel screamed, then smashed into the ground again, this time on his left flank. Something snapped with a report crisper than a draconette shot. Adachoel clawed at the ground, struggling to regain his feet, but sagged back onto one rear haunch.

With the speed of a stooping hawk, Sidrachuil slammed into Dravothrak's left side. Claws tore at scales, but that was just insult added to injury, for the impact had already crushed scales and bones beneath. Dravothrak fell from the sky.

If a last-second flapping of his wings did soften Dravothrak's landing, Erlestoke could not tell. When the dragon hit, the ground shook beneath the prince's feet. Horses reared and plunged, soldiers were knocked to the ground. Over on the Aurolani side, the drums stopped and a half-dozen draconettes shot. Dravothrak did land on his feet, but his belly hit hard as well. Flames shot from his mouth and nostrils as the impact knocked his breath from him.

Sidrachuil took no chances, but cruised past and hit Dravothrak with a pillar of fire. The flames laced the fallen dragon's left flank, and where scales had been broken, flesh sizzled. Dravothrak roared and rolled to the left, smothering most of the flames. His head came up and his return blast of fire caught Sidrachuil beneath the tail. The striped dragon's cloaca bubbled and blistered. But the wound, while painful, was not life-threatening.

At the base of the hill where he had landed, Dravothrak regained his feet and curled his tail around to protect his belly. He kept his body low and watched warily as Sidrachuil circled. He hissed something in dragontongue that Erlestoke could not recognize, but the tone dripped with contempt. There he was, bleeding, black wounds smoking, his armor broken and his belly leaking, defying his offspring to come down and fight.

To Erlestoke it seemed obvious that the only way

Dravothrak stood a chance of defeating Sidrachuil would be for the younger dragon to descend. *And for him to oblige would be foolish, but pride can promote so much foolishness.*

Sidrachuil made another pass and wreathed Dravothrak with fire again. From within that conflagration a fiery lance rose, but missed the striped dragon's tail. Dravothrak beat his wings and extinguished the fire, but had trouble furling them again. Raising his head, he snarled defiantly at the flying dragon and spat flame at him.

That attack never even came close to hitting Sidrachuil.

The striped dragon rolled in the air, then furled his wings and landed solidly on the hilltop. His claws digging deep, he shrieked at Dravothrak. Again the words needed no translation, for the venom in the tone told all. Erlestoke could have imagined his using that tone with his father and wondered what Dravothrak had done to make Sidrachuil hate him so.

Sidrachuil roared, then leaped onto his father. Claws scored some scales and ripped others away cleanly. Sidrachuil's head darted down, biting Dravothrak at the base of the neck. Fire appeared around his mouth and Dravothrak shrieked. The larger dragon rolled onto his back and kicked out with his hind legs.

That attack boosted Sidrachuil into the air and back up the hill. He landed on his rump, with his tail flicking up between his legs. The scales over his breast and belly had been grooved and gouged, and some were gone altogether. Had the blow to Dravothrak's spine not damaged one of his legs, the attack could have easily eviscerated the younger dragon. Sidrachuil glanced down at his own ruined middle and howled, but even that painful cry ended victoriously.

Below him, at the hill's base, Dravothrak struggled to rise, but he could not. The bite at the base of his neck ran black with blood and burned in several places. His left rear leg dragged and his right foreleg was not working. Though Erlestoke could not see much of his belly, black blood ran from beneath him in an oily sheet that withered grasses.

His every motion became weaker until his last attempt to raise his head did nothing more than shift his muzzle a couple of feet.

Dravothrak's chest rose and fell once more, then the green dragon lay still.

Sidrachuil raised his head to the sky and roared loudly. Fire shot high and Adachoel, crippled though he was, joined him in celebrating. To the north, the Aurolani drums began again, pounding out with ceaseless regularity.

Preyknosery screamed angrily and launched himself skyward. The Gyrkyme's call rang with agony and resonated deep in Erlestoke's chest. Dranae, though inhuman, had been incredibly human. Erlestoke realized he had become friends with the dragon, and that their friendship had transcended their different natures. Seeing Dranae in his dragon form, and not seeing his manform dead, gave Erlestoke a moment of detachment, then the full impact of the loss slammed into him.

Fury and despair warred in his chest. Erlestoke, hearing the enemy drums throbbing powerfully, threw himself into that fury. Despair would just suck the life from him, and that he could not afford. Anger hurt less and, even better, fueled his desire to make Dranae's killers pay.

The prince grabbed the bugle from the signalman and raised it to his own lips. He tried to blow an alert, but all he got was a weak squeak. Disgusted, he tossed the horn back to the signalman. "To arms, for the third time. Do it!"

The bugler nodded and blew the alert perfectly. Up and down the southern line other bugles echoed the call. The southern formation stiffened as men moved back into line. They checked their armor, checked their weapons, and prepared for whatever their leader would demand.

Erlestoke marveled at their devotion. He supposed it could have been that each and every one of them assumed that the dragons from the other side would just hunt them down if they ran. But then he decided his warriors finally understood that if they did not oppose Chytrine here, there would be no escape. A line had been drawn, and the Aurolani could not be allowed to cross it. For if they did, all of Oriosa and all of the world would fall. In that light, it didn't matter if they were going to die; their task was to take as many of the enemy as possible with them.

Sidrachuil roared one more time, his throaty rumble mocking the southerners. Erlestoke drew Crown and wondered how it would fare against a beast that size. A thrust through an eye might work, or perhaps there was enough of a gap on his chest for the blade to reach his heart. Erlestoke wasn't thinking he'd survive too well being bathed in dragon blood, but avenging his friend might well be worth the experience.

Suddenly that roar switched to a squeak, then a squeal. Erlestoke looked up from his sword and saw the hill around Sidrachuil boiling, almost the way sand jumps on the head of a drum. Brown and red, yellow and black, humanoid creatures emerged from the earth and swarmed over the dragon's haunches and tail. Some had reached a wing and others were climbing up his flanks.

UrZrethi! The prince's heart started to pound faster. *The Bokagul have joined us!*

The urZrethi went after Sidrachuil as if they had been created for the sole purpose of killing dragons. Though tiny by dragon standards, they were incredibly strong. They had all shifted the shape of one arm into a wedge that could be driven beneath a scale, and the other a hook. Their toes had spikes, allowing them to pull themselves beneath the dragon's own armor. Though Sidrachuil clawed at them and beat on his own flesh, smearing some of them over his scales, blood began to flow from countless other places. More and more urZrethi seeped from the earth and swarmed over Adachoel, too, dragging him down.

Even more urZrethi appeared in the foothills—legions of them. All of them had changed themselves for battle. Their skins had thickened into spiked armor. Their arms ended in hooks and blades and spikes. As they gathered,

Sidrachuil tried to leap into the air, only to fall to the ground and roll helplessly toward his father's corpse. The Aurolani drums faltered.

"Blow an advance, *now*!" Erlestoke leaped into the saddle and reined his horse around. The bugler complied with his order, but it was hardly necessary. Already the human lines had begun to surge forward. The cavalry on the right wing hooked toward the east. The heavy infantry moved forward, solidly packed, and forded the river without breaking formation. The lighter infantry had a bit more trouble, but the Aurolani did not hit them before they could re-form, thereby losing their only real chance at disrupting the southern force.

On Erlestoke's troops came, not hurrying, waiting until they could get into range for their charge. The prince realized that he could issue orders, but they would not matter. Every warrior in his force had gone from hope to despair, then the certainty of death. There was not one of them that did not think three dragons opposing one was somehow unfair, and Dranae's willingness to fight for them was a sacrifice they could not dishonor. This was their land, these were invaders, and by all the gods and then some they were going to rid their land of Aurolani vermin once and for all.

The Aurolani plan had doubtlessly been to retreat to their defenses, so the shift of drumming to an advance seemed to catch some of their troops by surprise. They started forward, then the drums ordered a charge. It made sense, given they were uphill and would have momentum. Howling and screaming, the Aurolani poured down in a rush.

General Percurs snapped an order, and the Alcidese Throne Guards set themselves for the Aurolani charge. Shields came to the fore; spears were leveled at the enemy. Soldiers prepared themselves for the shock of impact, but even the strongest were driven back as gibberers crashed into their shields.

Many of the Aurolani were wounded by spears, and often impaled, but more got past their stuck brethren and hammered at the Alcidese shield wall. Behind them came hoargoun. Their clubs battered men aside, sending their limp bodies wheeling through the air. Crushed helmets and dented shields arced, and spears flew in the opposite direction. Pierced hoargouns faltered, then fell, only to be hacked to pieces as men moved forward.

Blood slicked the grasses. Bodies twitched and writhed on the ground. The two armies struggled along a line, with blood splashing those at the meeting point. The wounded fell back and fresh soldiers took their places. Out on the flank, cavalry turned and drove, slashing their counterparts and having their horses disemboweled by frostclaws. A man leaped from a dying horse's saddle, stooped to raise his legion's standard, then fell as a gibberer rode past and decapitated him with a heavy stroke.

Erlestoke watched the battle unfold. The urZrethi legions stalked forward, pressing the Aurolani eastward. They began to roll up the flank, which thinned the ranks on his own left wing, allowing them to move forward and accelerate the process. Calling to him the cavalry that had been backing the left wing, Erlestoke rode out and around to the east. There his right wing's cavalry was holding the flank, so his bodyguards poured behind them and slashed straight toward the enemy command and reserves.

Drums pounded and a reserve battalion of Aurolani cavalry swept out from around the command pavilions toward his formation. The Oriosans who had come with him from Saporicia had formed themselves into the Prince's Guards, and they stiffened their formation around him. With them came lighter cavalry from Hawkride and Midlands. Though the southerners outnumbered the Aurolani, the frostclaw riders did not swerve or shrink from their duty. On they came as southern lances swung in their direction.

Some frostclaws leaped high and forward before the cavalry smashed into each other. They sailed into the midst of the guards, slashing with claws, their riders laying about with flails or swords. Those at the point of the charge were knocked back or pierced. Screaming and thrashing they went down, to be trampled into a pulp.

Ranks of the guards were peeled away by the assault, but the core bored on, reaching the outer ring of Aurolani command pavilions. Horsemen rode through, slashing at tents and ropes. They laughed happily, chopping down fleeing gibberers. Erlestoke rode in their midst, looking for Anarus, knowing only he and Borell had weapons that could slay a *sullanciri*.

Distantly he heard a sound. It came from the north, back from where Preyknosery had reported the maze of trenches and tunnels. Erlestoke had heard the noise before. It took him a moment to recognize it, and as he began to shout at men to turn back, a force blew him from the saddle.

What he had heard was the sound of a skycaster launching a thunderball. The short, squat dragonel launched an iron ball full of firedirt and other debris that, if all were timed right, would explode in the air. In setting up the command pavilions, which they fully expected to be overrun, the Aurolani had plenty of time to calculate the precise charges and fuse lengths that would make the thunderballs spray their deadly cargo right on target.

Erlestoke landed hard and his helmet bounced back toward the lines. He came up on one knee. All around him men and horses were down and bleeding. He became aware of a dozen cuts over his flank and back, but he'd clearly been at the outer edge of the blast. Other thunderballs exploded elsewhere, but the cavalry had already begun to withdraw. More important, to the west, urZrethi were advancing quickly into the trenches. Their advance had come swiftly and had cut off the Aurolani line of retreat. *And if the urZrethi are not suited to fighting in tunnels, no one is.*

"Highness, are you all right?" Borell came crawling over toward him, sword in hand, dragging his left leg.

"Yes, Borell, better off than you."

"Look out!" The boy pushed the prince away as a sword plowed into the ground between them.

Erlestoke rolled, then came to his feet. Crown lay a dozen feet to his left; but the hulking, lupine *sullanciri* followed his eyes, then slowly shook his head. The prince raised an eyebrow. "Afraid to do me the honor of a fair fight?"

Anarus snickered. "Pride might have lured Sidrachuil into foolishness, but not me."

"Afraid I'll just twist your head off?" Erlestoke straightened up and brushed dust from his mail. "The battle is done here. You've lost. Let's end this like honorable men."

"You are a fool, Prince Erlestoke. Pity, for my mistress might have had a use for you were you wiser."

"Ah, yes, I had forgotten. There is no honor within the *sullanciri,* no sense of fair play."

The wolf-man spat. "There is nothing fair in life, Erlestoke."

The prince nodded. "I think we all get the message." He lowered his head and started to run straight at Anarus.

The *sullanciri,* who clearly had expected anything but that, stood his ground and shifted his sword to impale the man.

And in that way he made it very easy for Borell, who had never lost his grip on Eye, to thrust it up into the *sullanciri*'s torso. The tip of the blade passed above his hip and beneath his ribs, ripping through intestines, stomach, and liver before puncturing a lung. Anarus turned toward the pain, tearing the blade from the youth's grasp. He raised his sword to cleave Borell in twain.

Erlestoke hit the *sullanciri* with his shoulder and knocked him to the ground. Anarus caught Erlestoke in the side of the head with an elbow, spinning him off. Stars sizzled before Erlestoke's eyes as he rolled across the ground. The prince tried to get back up, but stumbled and landed on his hands and knees. He looked up and saw the *sullanciri* coming toward him, one hand over the hole in his side, Eye lying on the ground in a pool of steaming blood.

Anarus' big, black blade spun with twitches of his hand. "I will heal. You will not."

Then a draconette spoke and the left side of Anarus' head crumpled. The *sullanciri* fell to the right and landed on a knee. Before he could rise, Preyknosery descended and slammed the draconette's butt end into the wolf-man's head. A second blow smashed teeth in his muzzle. A fountain of black blood bubbled from his mouth as Anarus crashed to the ground.

A dozen other Gyrkyme armed with spears and bows descended. The elder Gyrkyme helped Erlestoke to his feet and brandished Dranae's draconette. "Even with one shot these are useful."

"It slowed him down, but we have to kill him." Erlestoke trotted over to where Crown lay. He recovered his sword, then returned to Anarus. Light still burned in the *sullanciri*'s eyes and he had no doubt that, given sufficient time, Chytrine's creature would recover.

The prince shook his head. "You're right. Nothing is fair." He pressed the point of Crown to the *sullanciri*'s throat and thrust. Anarus' body jolted, then life fled from it and it melted into the earth.

Erlestoke backed away, covering his mouth with his hands. The Gyrkyme surrounded him and the cavalry soon returned. The urZrethi had overrun the trenches, silencing the skycasters. Below, the southern force—with its Boka allies—had surrounded the Aurolani. No quarter was asked, and none given. The slaughter would continue until noon, and the river would run red for days.

Erlestoke looked beyond the flank of his army. Bodies littered the ground, each twisted in an awkward pose it never would have known in life. *Never* could *have known in life.* Aurolani, urZrethi, and southerners, masked and unmasked, lay there together, all anonymous from that distance.

Then his gaze drifted to Dravothrak. There was no mistaking him there. Sidrachuil had died leaning against him, but somehow Dravothrak's forepaw rested on the striped dragon's throat. The prince thought of Dranae's smiling face, his booming laugh, the way he had taken delight in simple things. *There are some men who never live life as well as a dragon did in manform. And he gave his life to give them the chance to do whatever they wanted with their lives.*

Erlestoke walked over to Borell. "I can't thank Dranae for saving us, but I can thank you for saving me."

The youth looked up as he knotted off a bandage around his leg. "You saved both of us. I was just following orders."

The prince glanced back at Dravothrak. "There's some things that can't be ordered, they just get done. And those who do them are heroes, just like you."

CHAPTER 61

Y ou're leaving?" Kerrigan looked up from where he was working with wood samples. "You're going without me? What did I do wrong?"

Resolute entered the tent and slowly shook his head. "You've done nothing wrong, Kerrigan. I would love to have you come with us."

"Then wait. It's not going to take that long to help Adrogans destroy the shipyard. You can even help fight. Think of all the gibberers you'll get." The young mage stood and pointed at the map on the table. "There are thousands in those barracks, I'm sure of it."

"I know, Kerrigan, I do." Resolute pointed off north. "There are a couple of tactical reasons why we have to go now. You mentioned, last evening, feeling your search spell being used, and you thought Chytrine was the one who figured it out. You said it made sense, since she'd had it used on her."

He nodded. "She's looking for DragonCrown fragments."

"But she could just as easily shift it to search for you."

"I'm pretty sure I can shield myself."

"But better she find you someplace far away than with us. Moreover, if you cast your search spell looking for her, you'll make her think we're still searching." Resolute ticked a second reason off on his fingers. "You're going to be the key to Adrogans' success here. Third, and the thing that decided it, Oracle says we have to go on without her."

"What?"

Resolute nodded. "She's staying here. So is Rym. Force, Qwc, Trawyn, Bok, and I will head north with a squad of Adrogans' scouts. When you hit the shipyards, Chytrine will have to react. She'll garrison the Boreal Pass, assuming Adrogans will be coming up through there to go after her. If you're still casting those search spells, that will reinforce that idea in her mind, allowing the five of us to get through and to her domain."

Kerrigan sat down again, his shoulders slumped. He glanced up. "You're not doing this because you think I'd be killed up there, right?"

"No, not at all." Resolute gave him a grin. "I figure if we can't stop her, you'll be there in the vanguard of Alexia's army when it does."

"Thanks for saying that, but you don't have to."

Resolute's expression sharpened. "Think, Kerrigan. When have I *ever* said anything to make someone feel good?"

The youth opened his mouth, then shut it. The Vilwanese had created him to be able to fight Chytrine, then they came to fear him. Somehow he had translated that into their being afraid he would fail to be able to deal with her—that in some way he was flawed. Despite all he had done, that thought had become intertwined with his inability to save his friends, leaving him certain that he would fail. Resolute's decision to leave hit on that same note, but his comment ran completely counter to it.

"You really think I could defeat her?"

The Vorquelf thought for a moment, then nodded.

"You have the ability, the skill, and the intelligence. You lack a little experience. Your difficulty is that you don't kill."

The mage took one of the wood samples and rolled it between his hands. "I've killed before."

"Yes, but only when you've been forced to it." Resolute came and sat on the edge of the table. "I won't tell you that is wrong, because killing isn't something that should come easy. Never. There comes a time, though, when you have to remember that those we are fighting won't stop. They don't have your qualms. They have killed, and they will continue to kill. And the only effective way we have to stop them is to kill them, too."

"But how do you know who has to die?"

"There is the crux of the problem." Resolute shrugged. "For me, deciding who dies has been simple. The Aurolani took my homeland and slew my people. They die."

"But they have wives and children."

The Vorquelf held his hands up. "I know, but I can't afford to think about that. You're considering who they are, and I am looking at what they are doing. I don't care what they think or feel; all I care about is how they put those thoughts into action. When what they *do* is harmful, I have to stop them."

Kerrigan nodded. "You take a lot on yourself when you do that."

"Not really. They make the choice by acting. The real question that stops many people is this: do I have a right to judge whether or not someone should live or die?" Resolute rested his hands on his thighs. "Making that decision is accepting a responsibility many people don't want to accept. The burden of being wrong is too much. The allure of killing without considering each case is terrifying. I was willing to accept that responsibility. Crow was as well. I think you can accept it."

"Me?"

The Vorquelf slowly nodded. "Your instinct in crushing that ship was good. What you did in destroying Vionna's fleet on Wruona, what you did in igniting the firedirt that killed all those gibberers as we sought to escape, what you did in killing Neskartu—all of those things were right. Have you used other spells to put creatures to sleep when you could have slain them? Yes, and that is not wrong, but even you would admit that the *turekadine,* when awakened, would not repudiate their actions, nor regret them, nor re-form them."

"That's true." Kerrigan sighed. "Still, can't it be that there is another solution besides killing?"

"Where evil is concerned, no." Resolute opened his hands. "Evil is selfish. It wants to put itself first. There is no safety from it."

"But in killing evil creatures, am I not being selfish and evil, too?"

"No, because you act to keep yourself free and to protect others. That makes all the difference." Resolute smiled slowly. "You're never going to be a killing machine, Kerrigan, because you think too much about it. That's no vice. You just have to acknowledge that sometimes, no matter how much you want to avoid it, the price of liberty is exacted in blood. Better it's taken from evil than innocence."

Kerrigan let his words sink in. The whole time he'd been trained, no one had ever asked him to look to the consequences of what he would be doing. Because he was so powerful, he'd been taught combat spells, but never really trained to use them, out of fear he would hurt opponents. At the same time, he was highly praised for mastering healing spells that humans had not used for centuries. This left him with the idea that healing and preservation of life was to be cherished, while combat was to be avoided.

He realized that what Resolute was saying wasn't what he himself believed, but it added a new dimension to it. In an ideal world, killing was absolutely wrong, but this was not an ideal world. Chytrine and her troops were out to master it, and kill all those who opposed them. The rest would be enslaved, which was just like being killed but would take a lot longer. Given those choices, the only effective way he could resist was to fight the enemy, and that meant slaying them. Perhaps not each and every one of them, but enough so they would retreat and peace would again rule.

He looked up. "You really think I can handle that sort of responsibility?"

"If I didn't, I wouldn't leave you here. You are, without a doubt, the most powerful mage living. If I didn't think you were responsible, I would have to see to it, however I could, that you were not a threat." The Vorquelf shrugged. "That's not a problem."

Kerrigan straightened up and shifted his shoulders. "I think I've been ducking this responsibility. I failed to save friends, so I guess I was afraid of what I would do if I . . ."

"I know. That you are concerned is good. When you stop being concerned, that's when the rest of us will get worried." Resolute stood, then clapped him on the shoulders. "You'll do very well, and I *am* counting on you to come avenge us if things go wrong."

"I will." Kerrigan stood and followed him from the tent. Outside, a squad of scouts waited by two other horses. Trawyn had already mounted up. Bok, with his legs lengthened, stood beside her. Force waited unmoving, but Qwc leaped from his shoulder and buzzed around Kerrigan excitedly.

"Bye for now, Kerrigan." The Spritha landed on his right shoulder and hugged his head with all four arms. "Be back soon."

Kerrigan laughed, as did the others. The mage offered Bok his hand. "You're going to be okay going after your daughter?"

"Chytrine was always her own person. She tried to slay me at Narriz, and likely would have tried before had I let her know I was alive. She has to be stopped, so we will stop her."

"Good luck." Kerrigan nodded to Resolute as he went

by, then patted Trawyn on the knee. "I really wish I could have saved your eye."

She shrugged. "When I come back, you'll find a way to fashion me a new one."

"I'll do that. Good hunting."

Leaving her behind, he moved to Force. The stone giant didn't offer a hand or even look down. Qwc leaped up and took his seat. Kerrigan studied Force's face for a moment and thought he noted a change. What had been featureless before had shifted, with the eyes sinking a little, and perhaps the hint of a nose emerging. It could have been a trick of the twilight, but Kerrigan didn't think so.

He patted Force in the chest with his right hand. "I don't know if I call you Will or Force, and I'm pretty sure it doesn't matter. You and I are alike in one thing: we have changed. We were created to destroy Chytrine, and we are still being created. I trust that both of us will continue, and that our creation will be enough to do the job."

The giant's head rotated a bit, and the eyes glowed more brightly for a heartbeat. Then Force looked back up and the eyes returned to their dull red-gold state.

Kerrigan took a step back and found himself between Adrogans and Rymramoch. "Good luck, all of you."

Resolute nodded. "Just create a big diversion, will you? Anytime in the next week will do."

Kerrigan nodded. "We will. It will be huge. No matter where you are, even if you're in Chytrine's sitting room having tea, you'll see it."

Adrogans turned and looked at him. "You must have something very special in mind, Adept Reese."

"I do, General, I do."

CHAPTER 62

News of activity at the Aurolani fortress brought Alexia and her army out quickly from Notirri. The scouts had reported that the Aurolani were preparing to march. A push south would make sense, and any of the places en route to Notirri would make for excellent battlegrounds. Neither side would have an advantage, and since she had the larger army, she would have done well.

As her cavalry rode forward, scouts continued to stream along the Zamsina road, bathed in sweat and their horses lathered, all but bursting with news. First she learned that the Aurolani had left their fortress and were heading north toward the road. The next report had them forming up on the road, and another that they were actually marching northeast, toward Zamsina.

Alexia listened with a rising sense of joy. She turned to Crow, who rode beside her. "Abandoning that fort doesn't really make sense, does it?"

"It depends. We know, from *arcanslata* messages, that Erlestoke won a victory in Oriosa. If he could bring his army along quickly enough, they could cut the Zamsina road, and Nefrai-kesh would have had no supplies. With poor water in that spot, he had no reason to stay. He's shortening his supply lines while we stretch ours."

"I'm aware of that, and also aware he does nothing without a reason." Alexia frowned, closed her eyes, and almost tried to project herself into the Communion, but she held back. She wanted to consult with the Black Dragon, but she knew he'd not be there. She'd not tried to access the Communion since his death, and wasn't certain she ever would try again.

A shiver ran down her spine. She had so many questions she would have liked to ask her father, and now would never get the chance. She thought she understood why he had not told her who he was; his presence there would have distracted her from her task.

But in many ways it didn't matter who the Black Dragon had been. He had offered good counsel and would be sorely missed. And while she did miss him, she clearly had the sense that he loved her, and that slowly worked to fill the void that had always existed in her heart.

A void Crow possesses in his heart, and will never have filled. Crow's memoir had made apparent the agony of having his father reject him. In many ways she did not wonder if Crow's initial drive in fighting Chytrine had not been to prove his father wrong, or to destroy himself. She felt he no longer had self-destructive tendencies, but to forever be unable to satisfy himself that his father would have forgiven him still ate at him.

They continued their ride northeast, and the scouts led them to the hills overlooking the fortress. From there they could see the structure, putting reality to what before had only been crude sketches. Tall revetments and wide trenches would have made assaulting the fortress difficult. While Alexia still thought the tactical plan she'd worked up would have been effective, the cost would have been far higher than she was comfortable with. Just as Erlestoke's force had been mauled, so hers would have been, which would have left in question any ability to continue the fight.

Off in the distance Alexia could see the rear guard of the Aurolani column. They'd left the fortress by the northeast corner, and had even trailed out through the narrow valley that was the only avenue of attack open to them. She had planned to use General Pandiculia's force to swing wide to the northeast, then attack, effectively wiping out any ambushing force. But Pandiculia's troops were still a day from their staging area, and Alexia would issue orders for them to move northeast and shadow Nefrai-kesh's column.

From the rear guard came a brilliant flash that moved into the air. In the distance she could not see what it was, but as the light diminished and the object drew closer, it resolved itself into a horse with fiery dragonwings. She'd seen it before in Narriz, when Chytrine had escaped.

"He knows we are here."

Crow nodded and, leaning back, pulled a strip of white cloth from a saddlebag. He drew Alarien and tied it to the tip, then spurred his horse forward. "He'll want to talk. He did to Adrogans. He'll want to talk with you, too."

Alexia followed Crow down the hillside and along to one of the flatter, grassy spots to the southwest of the fortress. She had to look up at it from there, as her troops would have done when mounting an assault. She revised her estimates of casualties upward.

Nefrai-kesh, who bore a spear with a white flag on it, circled the fortress once, then landed opposite them. His horse's wings vanished and, for all intents and purposes, the creature appeared to be normal. It even cropped some grass, though the tender bits it nibbled did smoke.

Nefrai-kesh nodded, his Panqui cowl and cloak supple enough to remind Alexia of Lombo. "I do apologize, Princess, for withdrawing from this place. I had longed to meet you here. The battle would have been glorious, but you would have won."

He pointed back to the northeast. "I have my scouts

watching your other army, you see. General Adrogans used that tactic successfully at Svoin, and I am one to learn from others' mistakes. It pleases me that you chose to learn from Adrogans. Perhaps you could learn more from him."

Alexia raised an eyebrow. "And what could I learn?"

"He is off establishing his own empire. You could do the same. You have the troops and the skills. You would eventually meet him and, I believe, defeat him. You know you wish to see who is the greater commander. I can read it in your eyes."

She shrugged. "I don't care who is greater, just as long as both of us have defeated you."

The *sullanciri* laughed. "Very good. You have spirit. You'll need it." He drove the butt of his spear into the ground. "Before we continue, I wish to apologize for Myrall'mara's attempt at murder. I was against that, and am glad she failed."

Alyx gave him a hard stare. "Wanted the privilege for yourself?"

"If that is an answer you accept, yes. I detested the underhanded nature of it." The ears in his cowl twitched. "I prefer clean battles. My mistress felt that you would be beguiled by your dreams into believing you could defeat me here, but I recognized the historical battle upon which you drew your dream. She thought you a fool, and you thought her a fool, but I am glad I did not have to test the idea that you are stupid. I do not believe you are."

Nefrai-kesh leaned forward with his hands on the saddle horn. "In this fortress, I give you a *new* Norrington Prophecy. When you inspect it, you will get a vision of our final meeting in Sebcia. I am preparing a battlefield for you. Unlike Adrogans, who fought well but merely won more swiftly what I would have given him in time, you will not be played with softly. Our battle will decide the fate of the world, and you will lose."

Crow laughed lightly. "So far we have not."

"True, Hawkins, so far you have done well. But then you

have been fighting a general whose brain has shrunk to the size of a walnut, and you have yet been unable to kill her. I would have expected more from you, but then, I have learned to expect nothing from you, haven't I?"

Crow's chin came up. "You asked me to kill you once before. I will oblige you yet."

"I'm sure that will be your intent." Nefrai-kesh slowly smiled, his white teeth shining from within a black and shadowed face. "So, tell me, Hawkins, do you continue in your betrayal of me, or do you betray the princess here?"

Alexia frowned. "What are you riddling at?"

"Have you told her my secret, or do you conceal it from her? She would not doubt you because of it, I am certain. As you have just said, it would not stay your hand this time, would it?"

She glanced at her lover and saw pain wash over his face. "Crow, what is it?"

He shook his head. "Not now."

The *sullanciri* laughed aloud. "It had best be now, Tarrant, lest it be never. Never, which is exactly when you will get around to killing me."

Nefrai-kesh bowed his head to Alexia. "You will make a most remarkable foe, I am certain, Alexia. I will slay you, of course, but preserve enough of you to let you serve my mistress."

"It will only be as one dead that I do that."

"That will be more than enough." Nefrai-kesh's smile broadened. "I will see you on the throne of Okrannel yet."

He sat back in the saddle and his horse's wings suddenly appeared in full flame. "Fare thee well. The next time we meet, no pleasantries will be exchanged." With a touch of spur, his horse leaped into the sky. The *sullanciri* circled once more, then flew to the northeast after his troops.

Alexia said nothing until he had become a star in the sky, then she looked at Crow. "You don't have to tell me his secret. I trust you."

"Can you, Alexia?" Crow shook his head slowly. "When

you hear it, you could wonder how I did not share it with you before."

"I'm sure you had your reasons."

"I do, but he has rendered them as nothing." Crow exhaled slowly. "He did this to scourge me, and perhaps I deserve it. I would not tell you this. I would tell no one this, but he has said I will stay my hand and not slay him."

She reached out and squeezed his forearm. "I know you will kill him, Crow. I need know nothing else." She tried to put into those words all she felt. Her love for him allowed no doubt. That he had kept a secret from her was a bit of a surprise, but she was aware she didn't know *everything* about him. What she did know was enough to make her love him, and that was all that was important.

"The reason I did not kill him before is the reason I must now." Crow's brows arrowed down. "I was barely a man when he asked me to kill him. I admired him and loved him, as my father had. From my father I had learned to love him, respect him, and obey him. I thought it was because that was the way one did things with one's liege lord. Always a Hawkins has served a Norrington, without question."

"I know that. You make that clear in your memoir." Alexia gave him a smile in the hopes he would reciprocate. "Something stayed your hand then. It had to have been a good reason."

"To kill him would have killed my father."

"Of course, your father loved him well and truly. That *is* the way a vassal deals with his master."

"Alexia, that was not it." Crow's lips pressed together for a moment. "My father loved him like a son."

"Of course, he'd trained him, he'd helped raise him."

"You don't understand." Crow's voice came in a choked whisper. "The Norringtons were a long and venerable line. Kenwick's father had been unable to father children. He asked of my father a great duty. I don't think he ever told my mother what had happened, and I doubt she would have seen anything wrong with it. He was a young man, he knew his duty. Kenwick was born and took for his wife a cousin, bringing the Norrington blood back into the family. Leigh truly was a Norrington."

Alexia blinked in shock. "What exactly are you saying?"

"I could not kill Lord Norrington because he is my *brother*." Crow shook his head. "Kenwick Norrington's father asked my father to get an heir on his wife. My father could not refuse that command. Leigh was my nephew."

She hugged her arms around herself. "You never knew?"

"Any hint of it would have been a betrayal of my father's duty, so there were no clues to be had." Crow swallowed hard. "In Oriosa one is given his life mask by his father, or his oldest male relative available. I was in Yslin and had it from Lord Norrington's hand. Maybe I should have guessed then why I was so honored.

"When we were in Boragul and Lord Norrington lay dying, I was determined to save him. When he removed his mask, I saw my father's face. He told me who he was, and I knew then I could not kill him. I had to save him, and I failed to do so."

Alexia gathered her arms around herself. "I can only guess as to what you thought at the time, what you felt. You were young."

"I had taken a life mask. With that came adult responsibilities."

"Yes, they did, but you forget something." She pointed off to the northeast. "*He* had taken a life mask, too. He had adult responsibilities. Asking you to kill him was abrogating those responsibilities. What he did was unfair. Accepting the bargain from Chytrine that you refused was abrogating those responsibilities. He might have been in pain, he might have known he was dying and been afraid of that, but those were things *he* needed to deal with, not you. They were not your responsibilities. And even now, by making you feel guilty, he continues the crime against you he committed ages ago."

Crow shook his head. "You don't understand."

"Oh, Crow, my love, I do. I understand many things. I understand you are a man of honor who has harbored that secret for a quarter century to protect your family, to protect others." She shook her head. "When I said Will had been a son to you, and you said, 'No, a nephew,' you were trying to tell me your secret. You knew then, as well as I do now, that being saddled with that secret was unfair."

His strained whisper barely reached her. "When my father took my mask, it was not for striking Scrainwood. It was for letting his son become a monster. In doing that I gave him a second son who was a monster. He disowned me so I could not betray any of my other brothers."

"But, Crow, he was *wrong*."

Crow's head came up and a hand swiped at tears. "He hated me."

"No, he was deeply hurt, that's all." Alexia reached out and brushed a tear from his cheek. "When we see your brother again, ask him if news of your supposed death hurt your father or not. I'm sure it did. I'm sure he knew he'd been wrong. His pride might not have let him admit it to your family, but I think he would have to you. He'd have asked your forgiveness."

Crow caught her hand and kissed it. "How is it that one so young is so wise?"

"I learn from the wise around me." Alyx smiled, reversed her grip, and squeezed his hand. "I think, my love, we'd best head back up the hill lest the scouts be offering all manner of odd reports to those we have left behind."

"Shouldn't we check the fort?"

"In due time." She leaned in and kissed him lightly. "Come with me, Crow. We're bringing our army to destroy the Aurolani host. When we have done that, Nefrai-kesh is yours. Once he is dead, the honor of the Norringtons and the Hawkinses will again be restored."

CHAPTER 63

How often have you been through here?"

Resolute turned in the saddle and looked at Trawyn. She had spoken to him in Elvish, which was unusual since, beyond some simple courtesies, they had spoken in the common tongue so Adrogans' scouts would not feel left out. Neither they nor anyone else was particularly close in the column as it narrowed to enter the Boreal mountains, so he answered her in kind.

"Not often, but more than once."

"How far north have you gotten?"

He shrugged. "Not as far as we are going, but I have ranged over Aurolan. Mostly alone, but more recently with Crow."

The princess nodded slowly. She rode on his right so she could see him. "It surprises me, your affection for Crow. Even you should have seen the danger of rescuing one who had been completely repudiated by his people."

Resolute's eyes narrowed. "Do you say that because you value humans so little, or you do not think a child is capable of recognizing injustice and seeking to right it?"

Her single eye widened. "Your sword is clearly not all that is sharp. I value humans."

"But not before meeting Will Norrington and seeing how strong they can be emotionally?"

Trawyn hesitated, then nodded. "It is true that I have not much been exposed to them. You have spent lots of time among them. You know them far better than I."

"I know them far better than I know most elves." Resolute faced forward, scanning the pathway as it wound up through foothill valleys toward the mountains. "In many ways I find them more honest than elves—at least emotionally. We are so long-lived that we tend to be laconic as far as our emotions are concerned. We hold them too tightly."

"That's not true. We have great passions, Resolute."

"Perhaps, but we do not show them, not to the world."

She frowned. "How can you look at the *coriiesci* or the gardens of Rellaence and say that?"

"You make my point, Highness." He let his gaze travel up the mountains where, at their tips, clouds whipped and curled down. "The *coriiesci* is clearly Magarric's passion, and the gardens were cared for lovingly, but over time. It may be true that a trickle of water will wear stone more effectively than a flood, but a flood is more cleansing."

"And more destructive."

"But not all human emotion is destructive." He smiled at her. "I first met Crow in Atval. He and his companions faced hundreds of gibberers. The chances of their surviving were nil, but still they fought. Crow, in particular, faced four of them. They had longknives and he had a dagger. He stood there, defiant, promising the first of them to reach him would die, and did not quail when they all came for him at once. I intervened, saving him, then taught him how to fight, and he did. He fought very hard, doing all I told him and more. And, later, when he learned about Vorquellyn, he vowed on his honor and life he would see my home liberated in his lifetime."

"And you saw merit in what was the rash declaration of a child?"

"I heard a declaration that could only have been made by an adult. He assumed full responsibility for what he said. After the decision was made to go north, but not to liberate Vorquellyn, I chose not to go with the expedition. That decision hurt him, and he tried to convince me to go. But he accepted my explanation and vowed that, after it was done, the two of us would go liberate Vorquellyn. I agreed that we would."

Resolute reined his horse up a small hillock. "A Spritha came to me, dragged me to the Ghost March and through this pass. At the end of our journey I again found Crow beset by gibberers, but still fighting. I brought him out, and that is when his people betrayed him."

"But, Resolute, even then you should have known that to befriend him would alienate the same human leaders you needed to see your homeland free."

"I knew that, yes, but they had sent me off on an expedition, supposedly to verify what he had told them. They really wanted all support removed from him. In isolation they broke him, and they used my absence as part of that process. I knew then that he was worth more than any of them. A few, like Augustus, have proven themselves true, but it was not until Chytrine came again that the others chose to face reality."

As his horse came down the hillock and rejoined the trail, he rode knee to knee with her. "So you wonder at my affection for Crow when he was the only person in the world who would not be dissuaded from the necessity of destroying Chytrine and liberating my home? He is more true to my cause than even I was."

Trawyn remained silent for a time, then glanced at him. "Do you find yourself hating elves because we have not helped you more?"

He shrugged, swallowing the words he wanted to say. "You told me you felt Vorquellyn could never be liberated and restored. If that was your belief, why would you commit people to certain death in a futile effort?"

"Because it was the right thing to do?"

Resolute laughed. "To Chytrine, conquering the world is the right thing to do. You know, Highness, I may have spent my entire life killing things, but that does not mean I don't understand how precious life can be. Crow is not my first friend. I have lost others in this war, and I mourn. Seethe, like Oracle, was a cousin of mine. I have seen others die—through war, through their own hands, or through foolishness. I feel those losses. I cannot fault you for not wanting to lose friends and kin."

She reached up and adjusted the patch over her right eye. "You may be right, Resolute."

"I undoubtedly am, but on which point are you seeing how wise I have become?"

"There is something to be said for human passion. I think, as we bind ourselves to our homeland, our passion becomes entwined with it. I think that is why those bound to Vorquellyn had to leave. It was painful for them, yes, but it also left them emotionally barren. They could not feel at all. You, because you are not bound, have your emotions intact. You have great passions, almost human passions, and they have kept you alive and thriving. I don't have that, and I envy you." She smiled at his reaction. "Don't look so surprised. Days pass slowly for me, and I am not anxious about their passing because I know they will continue. There are times, however, when the anticipation of waiting for a flower to open loses its edge because I have seen thousands of flowers open, and I know I shall see thousands more. What a human may regard as a once-in-a-lifetime experience, I can relive countless times."

Resolute frowned. "I would find that incredibly boring."

"I sense that about you, which makes me wonder something else." Her voice shrank. "Something terrible."

"What's that?"

She pointed toward the mountains. "In a week or two

we will have slain Chytrine, or will have been slain by her. If we are successful, what will you do? If Vorquellyn is redeemed and you are bound to it, will you find that existence boring? Have you made yourself into something that is a means for achieving for others what will never satisfy you?"

Her questions slammed home and caused him to bow his head as he considered them. His life had been about combat. The child he had once been—the innocent lad who reveled in stories and wished to be a hero—had been caked in so many layers of blood that a million floods might never uncover him again. *Could I go back to being that child?*

In an instant he knew he could not. A small trickle of fear seeped into his guts. What if the world post-Chytrine was one without a place for him? He could, he had no doubt, continue to hunt down gibberers and frostclaws and other remnants of her evil for centuries, but what then? Could the world become a place that did not need someone whose skill was killing?

And what role would Vorquellyn demand of him? His thoughts ran to his father, who kept bees. Resolute had loved helping out, learning all there was to the apiarian arts, but could he be content doing what his father had done?

It became clear in asking himself that question that part of him did not want to surrender who he had become. He had worked so very hard to develop his skills, and he had done things to win the magicks that aided him. He had slain more creatures more ways than most could imagine, and he was very good at what he did. Granted, his goal was a world where no one like him would be needed, and he did not repudiate that end at all. That it would make him obsolete was something he thought of as good in a general sense. *But, for me, it will be a world that smothers me and views me as a relic!*

He smiled. Perhaps he would be like Temmer, the terrible sword that had lain hidden for centuries until needed again. That thought pleased him until he recalled the sword's being shattered. Even if another evil rose in the world, it might be a challenge that was beyond him. *How driven will I be to succeed if the cause for which I fight is no more?*

That was the key, he decided. Ever since Vorquellyn had fallen he had had a purpose for his life: its liberation. Once that had been accomplished, he would need a new purpose. But would the purpose given to him through the linking to Vorquellyn satisfy him? Would it require him to give over a piece of himself and become less than he was now? *Being Resolute is not a costume I can remove.*

His left hand drifted to the hilt of Syverce. That the blade did not sting him gave him heart. At least something elven understood him and his value in the world. He had to hope the same would be true of Vorquellyn. *Perhaps the task I will be given is not just what Vorquellyn requires of me, but what I require of Vorquellyn.*

Finally, he glanced at Trawyn, noticing, for the first time, how the sunlight softened her features and reminded him of more peaceful times. "What you ask could be true, Highness. It could be that I am something not suited to the world that will come. I shall hope, however, that because I have had a hand in the world's shaping, there will be room for me in it."

She canted her head for a moment, then nodded. "I shall hope that, too, Resolute. A world that cannot accommodate you will be a sad one, and likely one not worth the price paid to attain it."

CHAPTER 64

A small part of Marcus Adrogans found it curious that he, and not Phfas, felt impatient with Kerrigan Reese and whatever Rymramoch was. Phfas had never had much patience for anything, save perhaps the ways of the *yrûn*. He'd also been quite contemptuous of most magicians, but Kerrigan Reese fascinated him, and the diminutive Zhusk shaman had been positively enchanted by the scarlet-robed Rymramoch.

Adrogans had spent the days while Reese and Rymramoch worked on the wood samples preparing his troops for their fight. He'd slowly infiltrated troops into Alcytlin. The Loquelven Blackfeathers had all but demanded the honor of being the first in, and he granted it. He understood well what the rape of Loquellyn meant to them. While elves generally seemed quite reserved, what emotions they did possess had come boiling toward the surface when Princess Trawyn had briefed them about things back home.

Along with them he sent in the Nalisk Mountain Rangers and two battalions of the Jeranese Mountain

Guards. That gave him almost a regiment of heavy and elite foot soldiers in the ruins. When Kerrigan's plan went into effect, he expected a flood of Aurolani to flee into the city. Rooting them out of the ruins would take a long time, so having troops in place to slay them before they could hide would make the job much easier.

Most of his cavalry he was holding back, instead preparing to deploy his infantry in the waterfront area. The only exception to that rule was to have the Alcidese Wolves, the Alcidese Horse Guards, and the Jeranese Horse Guards ready to race through to what they took to be a firedirt factory. Adrogans wanted that taken and held. The Savarese Knights had demanded a target of similar importance, so they were given the job of holding what Adrogans believed was an armory. He was hoping he might capture draconettes or more dragonels—though whether or not he'd be able to make use of them in the future was a serious question.

He cleared his throat. "I am well aware we wanted this operation to begin at noon. All will be ready?"

Rymramoch turned his masked face toward Adrogans, and the general could have sworn he heard a slight squeak. "It shall, General."

Kerrigan looked up from his work area. A huge table had been created and a map of the city nailed onto its surface. Each wooden sample had been painstakingly tested, using some manner of searching spell that located correspondences between the samples and the products the wood had been put into or come out of. Much of the wood coming from the west remained in the lumberyard, but some had been incorporated into a few ships, some boats, and other little things. Adrogans' scouts had been very skillful at obtaining samples and shavings from almost everything else, including all of the barracks buildings. There were a couple of ships that had no sampled wood in them, and most of those that did were still in the shipyards.

"Okay, we're ready." He looked to Rymramoch. "Aren't we?"

"Indeed, we are."

Between the two of them had been set a tripod of iron rods, and snugly fitted within the uprights was an iron pot. Coals had been poured into it and Adrogans could feel the heat coming off it—heat that was hardly welcome on what proved by noon to be a blistering day. Rymramoch had worked some sort of magick over it. Kerrigan picked up one of the wood samples, snapped it in half, and tossed it almost casually into the pot.

Adrogans walked up the hill to where he could see over the crest and looked down at the quiet city. In the harsh noon light he saw a supply hoy moving out toward the fleet's flagship. That displeased him, but nothing could be done about it now. The flagship had been one of those with no sampled wood in it, so if it weighed anchor and sailed, a *sullanciri* and an Aurolani regiment, along with many dragonels, would be free.

He turned inward for a moment and sought the *sullanciri*. He found her easily and smiled. She lay asleep, unsuspecting that anything was about to happen. It had been her own carelessness that left her in that particular state, since she had done little to make sure the surrounding countryside was safe. Because he had done nothing, so far, to disrupt the creation of her fleet, she'd been content. By focusing on the future, she lost sight of the present and that would cost her dearly.

He came back into himself as, down on the waterfront, one of the warehouses began to burn. Yellow-gold flames licked at the edges of the roof, and watchmen on some of the ships began ringing bells in alarm.

Down on the wooden waterfront, city people began to stir. Figures ran through the day, and though they were far distant, it was easy to see they were *kryalniri* and vylaens. Kerrigan had explained that magickers would be called to fight the fires first. Their casting spells to combat the fires would pull them out of position to fight invading troops and would exhaust them. Rymramoch had hinted at some darker things, and Phfas had chuckled.

Below him, Kerrigan picked up one of the samples that corresponded to a barracks where the wood played a key structural role. As the sky began to darken with smoke, the youthful mage let the wooden dowel rest on his open left palm. His eyes closed, then golden energy rose through his hand. It shrouded the sample and tightened. Adrogans heard a small crack from below, which, moments later, echoed more loudly from the city.

The barracks in question shook. The roof sagged in the middle, then the whole building shifted to the left. Planking splintered, and whole sections of boards sprang free and whirled through the air. Wooden shingles fell like feathers from a stricken bird, then the whole structure collapsed. A corner of it smashed into another barracks, holing it.

Kerrigan tossed the splinters into the pot and the fallen building ignited with a *whump!* Beyond it, *kryalniri* and vylaens at the original fire spun and began running. They gestured, magick sprang from their hands and staves, but the fire continued burning.

Rymramoch laughed. "Oh, they think they are just fighting fire. *Natural* fire." He waved a hand at the pot and fire flared there. "It's time they learn their error."

In Alcytlin the flames roared and leaped skyward, carrying with them burning bits of debris. The fiery rain fell on other buildings, starting their roofs smoldering. More alarm bells rang. Creatures shouted and began running. From within, Adrogans felt the *sullanciri* waken, slowly and groggily. He felt her shock as she looked out from the cabin on her ship and saw part of her shipyard burning.

Then the shock redoubled.

There could be only one reason for that.

Adrogans spun, raising his hands to his mouth.

"Kerrigan, there's a hoy bearing on the flagship. It's carry-ing firedirt. Burn them all!"

Without hesitation, Kerrigan scooped up a double handful of the samples representing the small ships and tossed them into the pot. Down below, a dozen fires sprang up, some at the docks, a couple on the decks of the larger ships as their longboats ignited, and one that had been hid-den in a warehouse by an enterprising thief.

Adrogans watched the firedirt hoy intently. He saw noth-ing, no light, no smoke, and cursed. "Come on, come on!"

Then in the blink of an eye, he saw a single tongue of flame geyser up in the middle of the craft. The tillerman immediately leaped into the water, and the oarsmen did their best to follow. Several just rolled over the side, but one—*who probably likes the water as little as I do*—hesi-tated on the wale. Adrogans saw him as a silhouette, but for a heartbeat only.

The hoy exploded, opening a hole in the water from which another sun was born. The force of the blast struck Adrogans like a hammer, driving him back a step or two. The thunder drowned out all other noises and set his ears ringing. The noise echoed back off the surrounding hills. Adrogans smiled. *There, Resolute, you have your diversion.*

The general climbed back up the hill and swung his head left and right so he could see around the black ghost of the fireball. It had died, though the rippling rings in the water showed where the hoy had been. Debris, much of it flaming, floated on the water, but other bits had landed on nearby ships.

The hoy, while heading for the flagship, had actually been closer to one of the leviathans. The blast had utterly savaged the aft portion of that ship. The rudder and chunks of the stern had been vaporized. Adrogans could see into the ship's interior, both because the back of the ship had been blown in, and many of the hull fragments were burn-ing. Crewmen fought the fire, but the ship was already list-ing badly at the stern and would never leave the harbor.

The flagship was already a hive of activity. Buckets were being lowered to gather water to fight fires. Other crew members were already bringing the anchors up, and some of the galley's oars were digging at the water. The crew even raised the triangular sail, allowing the ship to move out to deeper water.

Adrogans surveyed the city again. The blast had been sufficient to knock down the smoldering warehouse, which started other small buildings burning. There were barracks to the north that still stood. Once they were down, the remaining Aurolani would be channeled into the areas where Adrogans had wanted to fight.

"North one and two, please, Kerrigan."

"Yes, sir."

Those barracks shook with a staccato series of cracks, then sagged together, blocking a main route into the ruins. One of them started burning, then the other. A few of the gibberers who had escaped through north-side doors and windows fled into the ruins, but at least one of them fell as an elven arrow burst his heart.

Adrogans pointed to a signalman. "All advance please."

The bugler relayed the order loudly. Adrogans could not be certain if any of the Aurolani heard the call, but he could see no reactions to suggest they had. The sharp crackling sound of another barracks collapsing and the roar of another warehouse going up in flames certainly provided them enough distractions. Perhaps they thought the horn was another alarm.

It didn't matter—not to him—nor to them. Down below, his troops poured into the city. The cavalry entered from the east and reached their targets quickly. The fires had all been to the west and, not surprisingly, those individuals in the firedirt factory had fled as fast as they could. The troops designated to take it wore leather armor and had fashioned leather boots to cover their horses' hooves, so no chance sparks would be struck. The Savarese Knights, on the other hand, charged for the armory in full battle gear, and rode through a fleeing knot of refugees before occupying the building.

The infantry fed into the city through several gates the Zhusk scouts opened from within. They'd slipped over the walls the moment the alarms had gone off, so by the time the Aurolani were running for their lives, the gates had been opened and his troops were marching in. Though the troops started into Alcytlin in good order, things began to break down pretty quickly.

Adrogans had anticipated that happening, so he had briefed the leader of each legion. Each one was given a specific target to reach, and then a goal from there. Adrogans had expected the work to be little more than butchery, but as long as his people slaughtered the Aurolani and not each other, the job would be accomplished.

Moving with the legions were the Vilwanese war-mages he'd been given. They sought and engaged the *kryalniri* and other Aurolani magickers. From his vantage point the Jeranese general saw no mage duels, but neither did he see legions retreating from some Aurolani sorcerer's magickal attacks. He took that as a good sign.

Phfas climbed up the hill and stood beside him. "She is escaping."

Adrogans watched the Aurolani flagship clear the headland and make for the open sea. "Not many naval commanders are comfortable with a land war."

"The opposite is also true, nephew."

Adrogans looked down at Phfas. "What are you suggesting, Uncle?"

"What you have been thinking." Phfas flicked one small talisman tied to the *yrûn* of water that dangled from his own left breast. "She is gone. You should hunt her."

"That would be a fool's errand. I don't know where she is going, and she has a lead I cannot hope to match."

"And you will not travel by sea."

Adrogans waved that idea away. "My army can best serve if we march to the Boreal Pass and invade Aurolan."

"To be trapped there when Nefrai-kesh marches home with Svarskya's head."

"That won't happen." He thought for a moment and knew his comment had not been convincing. He greatly respected Princess Alexia as a military commander, but she would be facing a force of untold strength. Resolute had said that the force that had taken Loquellyn had been infiltrated into Muroso. While it was true that the flagship, with its regiment of infantry, could be heading anywhere, the only goal that made sense would be Muroso.

He had over four regiments under his command. If he delivered them to Sebcia, they would be a big surprise. *I deploy a decoy force to reconnoiter the Boreal Pass and that freezes Chytrine's troops there. I show up in Sebcia and land behind Aurolani lines. I could hit them from the rear while Alexia engages them from the south. I have dragonels. We could break them.*

Adrogans looked out over the harbor at the six ships bobbing there and the unforgiving ocean beyond. "I could do it, Uncle, but would it be enough?"

"Enough? Maybe." Phfas shrugged. "It would be *more.* And there are times when that is all that is needed."

CHAPTER 65

At the head of the column Erlestoke rode up a hill and looked northwest. On his last journey from Meredo to Fortress Draconis, he had traveled via Caledo. He remembered very well the tall white towers of the city in the plains. It had been a proud place, and he had seen it as something of an eternal city. He remembered thinking that if it were the capital of Oriosa, he would not mind inheriting the throne.

What had once been the white city of the plains had been laid to waste. Parts of it still stood, but the towers had been broken and the walls melted. What had once been pristine now had the pockmarks of a city under siege, with fire scars striping buildings and burned rafters clawing the sky. Carrion birds circled here and there and fires burned, leaking black smoke into the sky.

The prince smiled as his brother rode up beside him. "Have you been here before?"

Linchmere shook his head. "I always sailed to Fortress Draconis when I visited. It must have been beautiful."

"It will be again."

"Easier for it than me."

Erlestoke looked at his brother for a moment and marveled at how many changes there had been in him. Even listening to his voice, the changes could be detected. His brother had left Meredo with the Freemen: a group of Oriosans who pledged themselves to the service of Will Norrington. They had come to Muroso originally to help defend it, then had traveled to Sarengul. There they had fought fiercely to drive the Aurolani from the urZrethi domains of Sarengul. The Freemen, a group of Oriosan *meckanshii*, and a full regiment of Sarengul infantry had emerged from Sarengul and joined Erlestoke's army as it left Tolsin and entered Muroso.

The fighting in the tunnels of Sarengul had not been kind to his brother. Linchmere's head had been shaved because half his hair had been singed off, and fire scars still puckered flesh on the right side of his head. That ear had wilted as well. His brother had also lost his left arm from just below the elbow. When he walked, it was with a limp, but Erlestoke noted that was just from a cut that would heal soon enough.

When Erlestoke had asked what happened to his arm, Linchmere had shrugged. "He took my shield, I skewered his heart. Fair enough trade."

The fatalism in that comment, and the one concerning how easy it would be to rebuild him, squeezed Erlestoke's heart. All his life he'd trained to be a warrior. He had seen friends killed at Fortress Draconis and in the race from it. He'd seen Will Norrington die. All of those deaths hurt him, but he thought himself somehow prepared for them by his training.

His brother had none of that training and, had he been asked to predict Linchmere's reaction to war and such injuries, Erlestoke would have said he'd end up in a mewing ball. But Linchmere had remained detached from the world after their mother's death. Even Erlestoke had thought it was good that Linchmere had someone between him and the throne of Oriosa, for he would be a poor leader, easily led by others, with little of a spine to stand up for himself.

But that had not proven true. Linchmere, who was known as Lindenmere within the Freemen, had not risen to lead them, but he'd clearly earned their respect. He'd become stronger and leaner, looking much more like Erlestoke's brother than ever before. More than one of the Freemen, including their leader, Wheatly, had informed him that Linchmere had lost his arm fighting off an ambush, and that without his effort, many would have died.

The prince marveled again at the changes wrought in the crucible of war. War was, without a doubt, the most horrific of human experiences, and it put everything into sharp relief. All choices were life and death. Friendships were formed strongly, and their sundering hurt terribly. War crushed some people, and others—his brother being one—emerged from it as new people. Erlestoke found himself proud to have his brother riding beside him.

"We will have your arm replaced through *meckanshii* magick. As for the scars, your hair will grow back and cover most of them. When this war is done, scars such as yours will be a thing of beauty."

Linchmere regarded his brother with brown eyes which, up to their previous meeting, Erlestoke would have described as bovine. "Those are the external changes. What about the ones wrought in my heart? I have seen terrible things. I have done them."

"Those are all things with which you will wrestle." Erlestoke started his horse down the hill and Linchmere followed. "Those are the things of war. The world that will follow her defeat will be content to leave them in the past. You've accepted responsibility, and that is the most important change."

Linchmere smiled. "There was a time when you would have suggested I was irresponsible, and I would have had a tantrum or sulked. Now I just wonder why you didn't tell me that more often?"

"Because until you were of a mind to accept responsibility, it wouldn't have mattered what I said." Erlestoke turned and looked at him. "How much are you ready to accept?"

"What do you mean?"

Erlestoke pointed to Caledo. "You remember what General Pandiculia told us when we linked up with her forces?"

"Yes, that Princess Alexia is waiting for us in Caledo."

"Precisely." Erlestoke recalled Pandiculia looking haggard and harried. She seemed anxious to reach Caledo, and was a bit surprised when he introduced his brother to her. *She had expected the fop, not a veteran.* "So, the question becomes this: do I introduce you to Princess Alexia as Prince Linchmere of Oriosa and give you a command, or do you remain Lindenmere of the Freemen?"

His brother's pinched expression hid nothing of his discomfort. "Part of me wants to return to who I was, but you would have to give me a command, wouldn't you? I left Meredo because our father laughed at my request to lead our troops to this very place and attack the Aurolani host. I know now that I was utterly unsuited to being a leader. While having one more prince might hearten some, I think Lindenmere Halfarm in the Freemen ranks will do more good in the long run." Linchmere raised his stump. "You should give Wheatly more of a command. He was a militia officer before leading the Freemen, and he is very smart. He is worthy of elevation."

Erlestoke smiled. "I expected you to say the first. The second, however, marks how much you have grown. I already know you have committed selfless acts, as your wounding proclaims, but now you honor another when you had no reason to."

"Oh, but I have ample reason. Wheatly does deserve elevation. His skills will save lives and win battles. He inspires troops. If you do not use him, you cheat yourself and needlessly jeopardize people."

"Noted. And thank you."

Linchmere nodded. "So, how will you introduce me?"

"I don't know yet." Erlestoke smiled. "I respect your wishes, but if I need a prince more than I need a sword on the line, I will put you to the best use possible. A half-armed fighter will inspire a few, but a half-armed prince will inspire many. They are here because they have to be, but you don't. Your presence will confer greater honor on them."

"I see that, but you know that I *do* need to be here."

"I do. We both do."

"Erlestoke, is the rumor I've heard true? That you decorated our father's throne with heads?"

The prince nodded slowly. "It had to be done."

"Do you hate him?"

Hate him? He's unworthy of so strong an emotion. "I try not to think that much about him."

"I do." Linchmere focused distantly. "Hate him. Not because of what he did to me or Mother or you, but for what he did to Oriosa. Mark me, when this war is over . . . if you fall, I will see Oriosa free."

"And if I don't?"

"A *meckanshii* prince will serve in Fortress Draconis, wed as his king wishes, and wish you a fecund consort who will place many heirs between him and the throne."

Erlestoke reined back and, as his brother drew abreast, slapped him on the shoulder. "It's been a long time since I recognized my brother in you. Welcome back, Linchmere. Come with me. It's time we show Chytrine that one generation's weakness has not been conferred on the next."

CHAPTER 66

Kerrigan Reese waited on the dock as Banausic helped Oracle into the small barge that would take them to the fleet's new flagship. Once the city had been subdued, it had taken half a week to inventory the supplies available in Alcytlin. The inventory determined that Adrogans' army would be able to travel to Sebcia on the ships easily. The journey was projected to take no more than four days.

Working out the logistics had not been that difficult, though there were several concerns that had to be addressed. The first was the crewing of the ships. Few enough of Adrogans' people had any experience, and a number shared the general's loathing of the sea. The Grey Misters did have some expertise, and Queen Winalia sent some crews to help out. As for rowers, they had ample supplies in captured gibberers, who were quickly converted into galley slaves.

Of the six ships in the harbor, only one had been outfitted with dragonels. That doubled the number Adrogans' people could use. The only difficulty with the ones on the ship was that their truck was suited to shipboard use, but would make them impossible to take on the road. That ship, which Adrogans had named the *Svarskya,* served as the flagship and would defend the convoy against any Aurolani shipping.

Once it had been determined that they were going to head out to sea, the main focus of the operation settled on getting the ships provisioned. The Alcidese Wolves set to work in the firedirt factory packaging up as much firedirt as it was possible to create. The Savarese Knights did uncover six hundred draconettes, so they and the Jeranese Queen's Guard light cavalry practiced with the weapons and became an interesting mounted draconetteer force.

The Jeranese Queen's Guard was exempted from traveling to Sebcia. To them went the job of heading east in the Ghost March to scout out and harass any Aurolani troops coming to relieve Alcytlin. As Adrogans explained it, being confronted by draconetteers was bound to slow down any Aurolani force. That would buy him more time to get his people situated in Sebcia without the main Aurolani army being aware they were there.

Aside from the *Svarskya,* the fleet consisted of the *Highlander,* the *Zhusk,* the *Noriva,* the *Alcytlin,* and the *Jerana.* The ships' names had been hastily painted on their afts and bows. The figureheads had once been shaped in the likeness of Chytrine, but talented carvers had remade them into other images, including Queen Carus of Jerana and Princess Alexia. While fitting troops and supplies onto each ship did result in crowding, the soldiers seemed resigned to accept it since the voyage would be short.

Kerrigan had watched with interest as the soldiers had boarded the ships to which they had been assigned. As each mounted the gangway, he or she pitched an offering to Tagothcha into the waters of Alcytlin Bay. Some tried to bribe him with food and others gold coins. Soldiers tended to be superstitious individuals, and many took the opportunity to rid themselves of dice and other ill-omened items. Once Oracle had taken her place in the barge, Phfas stepped forward and removed an *yrûn* talisman related to water. He kissed it, then tossed it into the water, where it sank with a small splash and a flash of gold.

Adrogans, standing beside Kerrigan, shook his head. "A waste, Uncle."

Phfas shrugged. "She is at home."

Kerrigan frowned. "Why is it a waste?"

The Jeranese general focused on the distant ship for a moment, then gave Kerrigan a sidelong glance. "When I was a child, I was sent on a fishing vessel. It was thought I might find a trade there, or at least learn enough about the sea that I could join my family's maritime trading business later. I was very young, but I listened to the fishermen. Half the tales they told were lies, the rest were pure fancy, but they made offerings to Tagothcha whenever they sailed. I did as they did, even giving up a gold coin my father had pressed into my hand when he sent me off to the sea."

Adrogans' brows slanted inward. "That first voyage a horrible storm came and the boat I was on sank without much of a trace. As we began to go down, a fisherman tossed me into the water, told me to swim for a bobbing cask. I did what he said and held on as the boat went down. I clung there as waves crashed over me. I coughed and sputtered and called out for friends. No one answered me.

"I was alone throughout that night. I called on Tagothcha. I begged him to save me. I got nothing. I pleaded and got nothing. I cursed him with every curse I had heard or could imagine. I got nothing. But I survived.

"When the storm ended and the sea calmed, I pulled together more debris and stayed alive until another boat found me. They deposited me onshore, claiming I was bad luck and that Tagothcha hated me for some reason or other. They even suggested I'd not made an offering to him, but I had, so I decided he was capricious and not worth the time to appease."

Kerrigan frowned. "Seems to me I failed to make any offering when we sailed from Vilwan, and that ended in disaster. On the trip from Loquellyn, though, I gave him an urZrethi wand and we made the trip just fine. And the trip here to the Ghost March went without incident."

Adrogans clapped him on the shoulder. "I'm glad he took notice of your gift. I hope that will be enough for all of us, for I'll offer him nothing. He owes me a safe journey, and this will be when I collect."

Once Adrogans and Kerrigan entered the barge, Norivese crewmen rowed out to the *Svarskya*. Kerrigan let Adrogans mount the ladder first, then used his magick to lift Oracle to the wheeldeck. He chose to climb the ladder himself, and joined her and Banausic on the wheeldeck as soldiers turned the capstan and raised the anchor. As a crew master pounded out a rhythm on drums, the gibberers began to row in unison, and the half-dozen ships cruised from the bay.

Kerrigan made his way toward the bow. The *Svarskya*, being far more immense than the small ship they'd taken to the Ghost March, created far more of a bow wave, but little of the blue water splashed up to reach either him or Adrogans. The wind of the passage tugged at Adrogans' cloak and Kerrigan's tunic.

"Do you think the Aurolani will be fooled?"

Adrogans shrugged. "It would be nice, but I am not counting on it. All that is important is that we deliver our troops to Sebcia and get a chance to kill Aurolani. But surprise would allow us to kill more, and make it likely we'll lose fewer. That would please me."

Kerrigan nodded and had opened his mouth to make a reply when suddenly the sea around the convoy began to boil. Before the mage could even ask what was going on, a hole opened in the Crescent Sea and swallowed Adrogans' fleet whole.

CHAPTER 67

The journey south had not been so much harrowing as it had been hard. Isaura, with Hlucri's help, had gathered together ample supplies and had outfitted a sled to be drawn by two drearbeasts. With the massive ursinoid creatures pulling tirelessly, the trio made swift time. They passed over endless ice fields, always bearing south, toward the mountains and the direction indicated whenever Isaura used magick to locate the Norrington.

She had met Will in Meredo and had healed him, so she knew his essence. The spell she cast did bring back positive confirmation that he was heading toward her, but there was something odd about how he felt. Isaura rationalized it away by noting to herself that Will had not really been himself when she met him, full of venom as he was—but she knew that was not the whole of the situation either.

She gave no voice to her doubts about Will to Sayce. The Murosan had welcomed the escape and become very composed. She did as much as she could around their various campsites, but her nervousness betrayed her in how she played with the amulet around her neck.

Barely half a week south, the weather turned warmer and the drearbeasts became irritable. Hlucri slew and slaughtered them, providing fresh meat—most of which he consumed. For a day more he drew the sled himself, but another twenty miles south the glaciers gave way to plains crisscrossed with streams running from the mountains.

From that point forward they had walked and made rather poor time. Neither Isaura nor Sayce was practiced in walking long distances. The brooding *sullanciri* would range ahead of them, topping a rise of hills, or trotting out to find game, easily covering triple the distance they did.

The rivulets did provide fresh water, which kept them going, though the rising heat assaulted them. Sayce went so far as to tear the lower half of her skirts away, baring her legs to the sun. Isaura did the same, and both women's flesh quickly burned, though magick and a mud-and-grass poultice of Hlucri's devising did help.

Finally, fourteen days after setting out, Hlucri galloped back after a scouting mission and quickly guided them to an outcropping of rock on the northern side of a hill. The stones had burst up through the earth at an angle, with many dolmen standing, but a few had cracked and fallen. The two women huddled there in the shadow of a stone and Hlucri lurked behind another as two elves topped the rise, and an urZrethi followed them.

Isaura had never seen any of them before and they looked as much a sight as did she and Sayce, ragged and mud-spattered as they were. The male elf had silver eyes and a stripe of white hair cresting his head. She knew him for a Vorquelf, for she had seen them before on Vorquellyn, when she was bound to the island. The other elf, a female, was smaller in stature and build, tending toward willowy. She had lost her right eye, which surprised Isaura.

The only surprising thing about the urZrethi was that he was male. His malachite flesh complemented the spring green of the grasses so well she could almost have imagined him to be a *weirun* of the plains. His dark eyes flitted side to side and clearly he was not mad, as all males outside of urZrethi homelands were supposed to be.

Sayce immediately jumped up and started to run at the trio. "Resolute! Bok!"

The male elf's head snapped around and a hand dropped to the hilt of his sword. He moved to eclipse the female, and she dropped back a step before drawing her sword. Resolute's wary expression softened just a bit. "Princess Sayce?"

"Yes, it's me. We escaped. We've come south to find you and Will. Where is he?"

Resolute held a hand up. "We, Princess?"

Sayce, now halfway between the elves and Isaura, stopped. "Yes, I am not alone. Isaura is with me. She is Will's Lady Snowflake. And Hlucri. He's a *sullanciri*, but he used to be Lombo. He's helped us."

Hlucri moved from his hiding place and crept midway along a fallen stone before sitting. The sunlight sparked in the jade armor of his flesh. His claws remained extended, but his hands rested with their backs pressed to the stone, palms up and open.

Before Isaura could stand, she heard a buzzing. A Spritha appeared before her and settled on the stone. "Qwc knows you." He sprang up again, circled her once, then flew to Resolute's shoulder and whispered in his ear.

The silver-eyed Vorquelf looked toward her. "You may come out. No harm will befall you, Lady Snowflake. We are in your debt."

Isaura stood, straightened her dress, and moved from the shadows. "I am Isaura, daughter of Empress Chytrine."

Resolute canted his head for a moment, then shook it slightly. "Not by blood."

"No, not by birth. I've brought you Sayce. I have to tell you that you cannot bring the Norrington north. That is what my mother wants. Every league nearer brings her grand plan that much closer to fruition."

The female elf laughed. "If your mother wants the Norrington, she is a fool."

Isaura slowly shook her head. "My mother may not be capable of rational thought, but she is not a fool."

"I will grant your mother is clever." Resolute raised a hand to shade his eyes and looked north. "There are two reasons she would have sent you south with Sayce."

"We *escaped*!"

Resolute gave her such a harsh stare that she blushed. *He is right! We were let go.* The implications of how her mother had used her shook her. Isaura's stomach tightened and sour bile rose in her throat.

"The first reason is that you might be successful in convincing us to get Sayce south to safety, thus removing a threat to your mother. The other is that you were tracked."

Isaura looked to the north and high in the sky saw a dozen specks, which grew larger as they descended. All but one had the squat bodies of carrion birds, but with flat dugs on their bare breasts. Their black wings had an oily sheen that matched the greasy appearance of the lank locks on their hag's heads. The *araftii* called harshly and circled, then landed. A half-dozen formed a semicircle to the south. Two landed on a dolmen, while the remaining trio arrayed themselves to block the way north.

The last creature was as elegant as the *araftii* were ugly. Yellow in color, with black tracing each feather and painting each talon, the huge bird made one low swoop before turning on a wing tip and landing as light as a drifting leaf. She stretched her wings, raising the tips to the sky, then they shrank down into arms. The transformation went slowly, and was mesmerizing in its majesty, as the urZrethi *sullanciri* Ferxigo reshaped her body. The expression on her face went from pure ecstasy to one of mild frustration.

As Qwc sprang into the air, Resolute shrugged off his pack and drew his sword. "Sayce, come here."

Letting her right forearm shift into a long slender blade the equal of his, Ferxigo shook her head. "No, Resolute, she

will be going with us. As will the Norrington. Produce him
and you will be allowed to live."

The Vorquelf arched an eyebrow. "Your mistress is not
known for keeping her deals."

The *sullanciri*'s clawed feet tore at the turf. "She is not
this generous, but I am. The Norrington for your life."

Resolute shook his head. "Not in your lifetime."

Without warning, Ferxigo launched herself into an attack. Her initial leap closed the gap between them and
ended in a lunge that slashed through his leather jerkin. He
hissed and her hand drew back bloodied. The Vorquelf batted her blade aside, then spun, giving her a brief glimpse of
his back before he came around and slashed at her eyes.

The cut should have carved her skull down to the
bridge of her nose or at least blinded her, but it missed.
Ferxigo shifted her shape, flattening the dome of her skull
and broadening her face. Her eyes moved to either end of a
bar as the blade passed above them, then her head returned
to something approximating a normal shape. Her left fist
came around, smashing Resolute in the ribs and driving
him back several steps.

On she came, fast and hard, thrusting at him. Resolute
leaped and dodged. Her blade scored turf, slashed jerkin
and boots, but never quite managed to spit him. When he
would parry, little puffs of sulfurous smoke would rise, but
Ferxigo gave no sign of any discomfort. She forced him
back, further and further, until she trapped him against a
dolmen.

The *sullanciri* lunged. The Vorquelf dodged right as her
blade cracked stone and, for a heartbeat, became lodged.
Resolute slashed at her left arm, but it went from being
solid to boneless. It shifted into a tentacle and his blade just
missed scoring its thick coils.

She whipped her left arm at him and caught him across
the thighs with a mighty blow. Resolute smashed into the
stone. His right elbow hit hard and his sword was jarred
from his fist. Ferxigo pounced, her clawed feet digging into

the rock. She pinned him to it with her own body, her back suddenly armoring. A loop of her left arm closed around his neck and tightened while her right hand rose and shifted into twin tines set as wide apart as his eyes.

Sayce dashed at Ferxigo and leaped onto her tortoise-shell back. Isaura wondered what she thought she could do bare-handed against a *sullanciri*. She thought Sayce was smarter than that. *Even dead she could serve my mother's purpose.* Her heart rose to her mouth, afraid for her friend yet proud of her courage.

But the Murosan Princess was not unarmed. Silver flashed in her hand. She had torn the amulet from her neck and driven it into the creature's armpit. Black blood spurted and the *sullanciri* convulsed, flinging Sayce off.

Sayce flew a dozen feet and landed hard on her upper back. She bounced once and rolled to the female elf's feet. The *sullanciri* sprang from the rock and tried to whip Resolute away. Had the Vorquelf not had a grip on her tentacle, the motion would have snapped his neck. As it was, he hung on, throwing her off-balance. To save herself, she released him, though she left him far away from his weapon.

Again shifting her hand, Ferxigo dug in her armpit and pulled the amulet Sayce had worn from her flesh. "Powerful, yes, but far too short to do the job." She looked around at her allies. "Save for the human girl, slay them all."

The *araftii* sprang into the air or danced forward, wings spread. The two on the dolmen behind her squawked horribly, sending a shiver up her spine, but Isaura did not turn to look at them. Death closed from every side and Isaura sought a spell that could stop her mother's creatures from attacking.

She never got a chance to cast any magick. With a furious roar, Hlucri streaked along the stone and leaped, arms upraised and claws glinting. His descending form eclipsed Ferxigo, but Isaura caught a flash of pure astonishment on her face. Hlucri's arms crisscrossed in slashing motions, releasing a bloody black mist into the air. Ferxigo's tentacle writhed on the ground, but Hlucri did not pause. Instead, he landed on two of the *araftii* from the southern group and they disintegrated into a wet cloud of feathers.

The Spritha wheeled and twisted through the air, then turned and spat a gob of webbing that collapsed an *araftii*'s wing. That creature crashed heavily to the earth while the female elf cut another in half with a quick sword slash. Two others diving at her screamed as Resolute hurled metal stars that spitted them. Hlucri killed a third with a back-handed swat, and two others fled for the sky, flapping their wings hard.

That only leaves two.

Isaura spun and saw the last of the two *araftii* on the dolmen sinking into its shoulders. Molten eyes burned in an almost featureless face. As she looked up into those red-gold spots, flames actually flared, the way they had in Nefrai-laysh's eyes.

She held a hand out, slowly, tentatively. "You are the Norrington?"

The stone creature lifted his chin and two dark spots appeared on his throat where the horrid wounds had been when she healed him.

Isaura looked back over her shoulder and saw Sayce was still facedown, with the Spritha and female elf hovering over her. She crossed to her, knelt, and cast a diagnostic spell.

The elf grabbed her shoulder. "What are you doing to her?"

"Checking to see if she or the baby is hurt." Isaura recognized the concern in the elf's voice, as the spell she used manifested with the red glow of Aurolani magick as she cast it. Isaura looked up and smiled. "She will be sore, but the child is fine."

Isaura shivered as she caught the Norrington out of the corner of her eye. *Oh, Sayce, this is not at all what you expected. Physically you will recover, but will your heart be broken anew?*

Off to Isaura's left Resolute had gotten his sword back and stood looking at Hlucri. "Which are you? Hlucri or Lombo?"

The *sullanciri* shrugged. "Guardian. Lady Snowflake."

Isaura rose from Sayce's side and approached them. "Nefrai-kesh made him a *sullanciri*. He charged him with watching out for me."

Resolute frowned deeply. "A *sullanciri* creates a *sullanciri* who is capable of destroying other *sullanciri*? Curious."

"How so?"

The Vorquelf shifted his shoulders uneasily. "I knew Kenwick Norrington. I always found it hard to believe he would become one of Chytrine's creatures. Was he able to hold a part of himself back so he could be her undoing? Did he make that sacrifice so this generation could do what he could not? He gave Adrogans Okrannel and firedirt. It makes sense for him to give you Hlucri to keep you safe, but did he intend it as more?"

"What do you mean, more?"

Resolute gave her a frank gaze, which softened slightly. "Hlucri attacked because an order was given that would have had you killed."

"I understand that."

"Where do you think that order came from?"

The answer hit her with the force of one of Hlucri's blows. She stumbled back a step, then found her body cushioned and supported. She looked up and saw the Norrington looking down at her. His eyes flared for a moment, then the glow withdrew ever so slightly, as if sockets were beginning to form.

Hlucri trotted over slowly, then sniffed and sat, licking blood from his claws.

"My mother was willing to have me killed?"

Resolute nodded. "I can't think of any other answer."

Isaura pointed north, in the direction the two surviving *araftii* were flying. "She'll know we're coming."

"She's always known we'd be coming. She knows what we will do when we get there." Resolute shrugged and slid his sword back into its scabbard. "I don't see any reason to keep her waiting."

CHAPTER 68

A lexia leaned forward, placing her hands on a portion of Caledo's wall. The dragonfire had left it smooth, as if centuries of river water had worn it away. That cool soft erosion contrasted sharply with the crumbled edges of buildings that had been shattered by dragonel balls in the city behind her.

Facing her and drawn up in ranks were the troops Prince Erlestoke had brought with him from Oriosa. She knew what he'd gone out with from Saporicia, and those troops had been roughly used. The Alcidese Throne Guards had lost a quarter of their strength, and the Oriosan Volunteers had been all but wiped out. Soldiers from the East Country, Hawkride, and the Midlands had supplemented his force, but a third of his strength was made up of troops who, generously, would be classed as militia and had seen nothing of war.

That was, however, not true of the urZrethi troops who had joined the Oriosan host. The Boka Dragonkillers and the Saren Guards each mustered a full regiment. Just having the Dragonkillers—who had been known as the Coal

Seam Guards prior to their work in Oriosa—had been a boost to morale. Alexia's mind was fairly bursting with ways to employ them.

She turned and nodded to Erlestoke and, past him, to his brother. "These troops are a wonderful addition to our force."

Alexia turned to face the troops and raised her voice. "I have been told all you have done to get here, and I cannot express my amazement, respect, and gratitude for your having joined us. You all have left your homes and your loved ones to fight in a war that could tear your nation apart as it has sundered so many others. Some of you have fought off invasions; others seek to prevent them from happening. *All* of you will help restore many people to their homes—people who now have nothing but memories.

"All of you have lost comrades, but all of you have seen bravery played out in countless ways. I deeply regret the news that Dranae was slain, but his courage must be something to which we all look in the coming days. When faced with overwhelming odds, he did not shrink, but thrust himself into battle as the situation demanded. No, he was not like us—he was a dragon—but that makes his sacrifice that much greater. He could have chosen to sit this war out, as many have, but he did not."

She nodded to them all. "You, too, have answered the call that will shield the unprepared from evil's touch. The lives we have all left—the lives to which we shall return—are not easily secured. What we will do in the coming days is to win them for a generation, and another and another. We will fight and bleed and some of us die, so our children, and their children, may never again have to face the decision to go to war. For this, no price is too great. Welcome all of you, and thank you."

A cheer rose through the ranks, loudest from the irregular formations. Alexia saluted the troops, then the Oriosan Princes. Then the three royals descended from the wall as officers started shouting orders and dispersing the troops.

Erlestoke descended directly behind her. "I've taken time to go over the maps the Gyrkyme scouts are making. Nefrai-kesh is setting up a vicious fortification."

She nodded, her own stomach fluttering at the strained tone in Erlestoke's voice. "You're right. It's even more hideous when you look at the model we've got. Come with me."

Alexia led them through a couple of twists of streets, and then down into the subterranean levels of Caledo. She'd located her command center underground, just in case the dragon Nefrai-kesh had working on the fortifications was sent south. In reality, the dragon could destroy her army pretty easily, since there was no way to house all of them in the ruins, and the ruins would have offered little or no protection anyway. And while Arimtara would give as good as she got, having her die the way Dranae did would have been utterly demoralizing.

They entered a dim room thick with the scent of candles and oil lamps. Perrine and her father stood near the three-dimensional map, pointing out new features to the engineer. Across from them, Crow was in deep conversation with a pair of *meckanshii*—his brother Sallitt and his wife, Jancis Ironside. Crow smiled at her as she approached, but stayed with his brother as she led the Oriosan Princes to the south end of the table.

"This is what we will be facing."

The Aurolani position had once been a trio of three hills, with the one in the middle slightly south of the other two. The hills had been flattened and dropped in elevation several hundred feet, or so she had been told. The earth had been used to fill in the gaps between them, presenting an undulating wall of earth with a fairly steep pitch. From the plains to the top was about a hundred yards, and every inch of it—as well as the approaches to it—would be studded with dragonels.

From the northern hills, trenching had been dug that went east and west respectively for a thousand yards. The eastern trench had a leg that went off north at an angle, and both of them ended with a small hill that likewise had been flattened and fitted into a dragonel battery. The only way up to the hills was a serpentine road to the north, which had several switchbacks and could be raked easily by dragonels.

Along the southern edge of the hills lay a dry riverbed. The Aurolani had succeeded in damming the river just to the east of their position, making a huge lake. Not only did the top of the dam provide a place where troops could be stationed, but if the dam was destroyed, it would flood the battlefield and sweep away any troops moving to the assault.

As if the possibility of drowning were not bad enough, the model showed each of the dragonel batteries. The three large hills had four of them, each of which had been dug out and reinforced with logs. Dragonels could be moved easily within them, so they could be massed to shoot at any concentration of troops. Logs even formed a roof over the batteries so the chances of the skycasters Erlestoke had captured in Okrannel damaging the dragonels were severely limited.

Erlestoke stroked his chin with his left hand. "Even though the site is only four miles inland from the coast, we can't ship troops around through Porjal and come in from behind. The approach up that road will be just as deadly as any frontal assault."

Alexia nodded. "If we lay a conventional siege, I don't know how long he can hold out, but the amount of spare earth spread around there makes me believe the hills are honeycombed with supply bunkers and lots of surprises—if the fortification near Zamsina was truly prophetic in its creation. Nefrai-kesh will anticipate our having urZrethi allies, so the potential for a war beneath the earth will not have been discounted."

Linchmere pointed with his stub. "Any idea how many troops he has there, as well as their composition?"

"We can guess, but nothing solid." Alexia shrugged. "With what you've brought in, we have nearly twenty-two thousand. Three-quarters of the force I would consider reliable, and a full third the best in the world. A third of it is also cavalry, which is going to be less than useful here."

The elder Oriosan Prince shook his head. "There's going to be no easy way to do this, is there?"

"No." Alexia pointed at the straight line of the western trench. "This protects the slope of the northwest hill. It is, by far, the easiest approach, but to get a force over there would take so long, it would give the Aurolani ample time to reorient their dragonels to sweep the area. Moreover, if they've hidden troops in the forest to the west, past this clear area, our backs will be vulnerable when we attack that trench. This is going to be bloody, but that isn't the thing that scares me the most."

"Then what is?"

Alexia snarled. "I have to assume these hills are a hive, and that when we attack, Aurolani are going to come pouring forth to man the trenches and the dragonels. But what if they aren't? What if he's got another army staging elsewhere? While we prepare our assault, he just hooks east and marches fast to Narriz or Yslin or Meredo? Do I devote some of my forces to range out there and see? What do I do if I find an army out there?"

Erlestoke nodded. "Worse, what if that army waits until we're engaged here and marches at our rear?"

"Exactly." Alexia sighed. "That's our situation. The fate of the world hangs in the balance, and we have no way of knowing if what we're going to do will tip it in our favor or throw it so far out that it will never be right again."

CHAPTER 69

Resolute found himself surprised by Princess Sayce's reaction to Force. She'd been taken to Aurolan long before Oracle had mentioned that the Norrington was waiting on Vorquellyn. And he was thankful for that. If she had believed she would see Will again, then found a stone creature in his place, that would have been cruel beyond words.

Instead, when she'd been revived and reassured her child was safe, she'd been told what Force was. The news did come as a blow to her. It summoned tears, but not many and not for long. She spoke to Force, but the stone creature showed no real understanding of what she was saying. His eyes glowed and even flamed at one point, but Force did not reach out for her.

Qwc, on the other hand, spent a great deal of time with her, riding on her shoulder as he had on Force's.

Resolute had spoken to her after Sayce had conversed with Force. "He has dealt with you no better or no worse than any of the rest of us."

Sayce nodded. "I understand. To die and to come back

as something no longer flesh and blood . . . You've explained that Force is not Will, that he is just another aspect of the Norrington. I actually understand that very well."

"How so, Princess?"

She smiled carefully. "Just that title, for example. Am I a princess, or has the slaughter of my family made me into the queen? Will the powers liberating Muroso decide that it should be parceled out to Saporicia or Oriosa, or combined with Sebcia, or turned into a nation that is the equivalent of Fortress Draconis? You know what the crowns did to Crow. They could do that to me and my nation. Through acts far less traumatic than dying, I could be elevated or discarded."

The Vorquelf watched her carefully as they marched back north. "That is far more philosophical than I would have expected."

"Don't mistake me, Resolute, or think me callous. Will's death hurt very much, but I have learned to deal with it. I have learned to accept that my child will have no father. Force may be part of the Norrington, but Will was the father of my child. This baby is no more Force's responsibility than Force is capable of assuming that responsibility."

"You're a wise woman." He frowned. "You've traveled with Isaura for a while, and spoken with her before. Has she told you who her parents were?"

The Murosan stiffened for a moment. "I know she isn't truly Chytrine's child, but I have no idea who her parents were. Why are you asking?"

Resolute glanced over to where Isaura walked in silence next to Force. "It's not truly important. I was just curious."

"Resolute, I've not known you long, but I don't believe your curiosity has ever been idle."

Trawyn joined them. "It hasn't; this I would vouchsafe. The secret of her identity should not be difficult to ascertain. She's clearly a *desariel*."

Sayce shifted the straps on her pack. "I don't know that word."

Resolute's voice tightened slightly. "It's Elvish. It means

a child of mixed parentage. It's most commonly used to denigrate the Gyrkyme."

"You seek to scourge me with it, Resolute, but I have met Gyrkyme and I repudiate their condemnation." Trawyn laid a hand on Sayce's shoulder. "It is possible for an elf and another race to bear children. The elf blood in her is obvious, as is the human. I would assume she was the child of one of the *sullanciri*, wouldn't you, Resolute?"

"Is there a purpose for your speculation, Highness?"

Trawyn laughed. "Only the same as yours. I have heard the prophecy in the original. I know the nuances."

Sayce glanced at one elf and then the other. "You might as well have this whole conversation in Elvish because I'm not understanding anything other than that who her parents were might have a bearing on the prophecy."

Resolute lowered his voice. "The prophecy has many nuances, dealing with the number of companions for the Norrington, and it hints at identities. A Hawkins seems always to accompany a Norrington when the latter succeeds at something. It would be greatly significant if her mother were Seethe and her father were Tarrant Hawkins."

"Crow?" Sayce's eyes grew wide. She looked over at Isaura, then closed her eyes. "Around the eyes a little. The ears throw it off, but those are from her mother, clearly. And the white hair is there."

Trawyn smiled. "You *could* ask, Resolute."

He gave her a withering glance. "I don't believe she knows. Chytrine would never have told her if Crow was her father. Besides, I'm sure of it." *I knew it the moment I heard her speak.* "We have a Hawkins to help our Norrington. The strands of fate are getting bound up tight."

Hlucri and Resolute did most of the scouting for the expedition. For the most part they were able to move fairly quickly. They saw no more signs of *araftii*, though Hlucri had to slay a drearbeast that had slipped from its den and started looking for food. But that was the only threat they faced from the natural fauna in the area.

Resolute did come upon one curious spot. The easiest path for them to take through some hills led them near a series of depressions that, given the rising grasses, remained hidden. A company of soldiers could have been lurking in one of the grassy bowls to ambush them. So Resolute scouted each one, and in the third found something.

A company of Aurolani gibberers, or so he imagined, had indeed been waiting there. It was difficult for him to tell if they had been slain in the day or at night precisely because of how they died. It seemed readily apparent that a lot of fire, very *hot* fire, had filled that bowl. If they had tents, blankets, or even clothing, it had been burned away instantly. The bodies had been well roasted, and all of the corpses showed signs of various animals having feasted on them.

Resolute squatted at the edge of the bowl. A dragon had clearly been responsible for their deaths. What one was doing traveling ahead of them, he had no clue. If it was an ally, it could simply have flown them to Chytrine's fortress and been done with it. *If it is not . . .*

Resolute stood and spat into the bowl. "Dragons' games. They were the start of this, and they'll be played past the end. No matter. As long as they play around us and not with us, we'll fulfill the prophecy and leave them to their contests."

CHAPTER 70

For Princess Alexia of Okrannel, the day should have been a glorious one. The month of Toil had given way to Green, and the premature heat had abated slightly, so that the long march to Sebcia—barely sixty miles northeast—would not be too brutal or tiring for her troops. Her army had come to mass over twenty-five thousand troops, which made it the largest force assembled in the world for centuries.

General Pandiculia's army had departed two days earlier. Alexia had met with the woman for several hours and had confidence that Pandiculia would be able to handle her assignment well. The Salnian general had given her a frank stare after she outlined the mission. "You're not just asking us to do this because, so far, we've been unblooded?"

"No, not at all." Alexia had rested her hands on the woman's shoulders. "You've taken a sloppy force and brought it to the point where I know you'll be able to hold off any Aurolani troops. Moreover, I am counting on you to be my reserve. I'm not going to put troops I don't trust in that position."

"I didn't think you would, but I had to ask. If we can get through the rest of this war with nothing bloodier than blisters, I won't mind, but we are ready for more than that."

"I know, which is why I am trusting you to do this job."

Pandiculia's army was tasked with acting as a screening force on the road first, then moving to block the Murosan city of Porjal. Porjal had fallen to the Aurolani early in the war and had been used as a resupply point for things being shipped down from the north. Scouting reports indicated that the city had a very light garrison, but Alexia did not want to take the time to conquer it. It didn't matter how many troops Nefrai-kesh had hidden away there. As long as they remained bottled up in the city, they were of no consequence. If her own forces ran into serious trouble, she could call on Pandiculia's troops as relief, which gave her a means of retreat and avoiding annihilation.

Now she stood alone in her command center and looked around. The maps and the models they had created had all been modified to suggest she had far more in the way of troops than she did. She expected Aurolani spies to pour over the place once she'd gone. She doubted Nefrai-kesh would believe any of the information gleaned from the place, but if it even caused him a moment's hesitation, she would be happy.

Alyx stared down at the model. She had been trained her entire life to be able to solve the most difficult military puzzles. She knew every battle from history and fable. Looking at the situation she was facing, were she to be dispassionate and detached, she could figure the odds of success and the casualty rates for the battle. She refrained from doing that because even the most optimistic estimate was too hideous to contemplate.

The problem of Nefrai-kesh's fortress was a new one. A host of factors complicated it, and the dragonels were the most obvious. They allowed him to project mass death at hundreds of feet. The grapeshot would blow through more than one soldier, scything down whole ranks. They could even splinter mantlets, so her troops could have no protection. About the only thing that could save them would be to move quickly, but in armor that was impossible.

And that's before he uses firedirt to destroy his dam and let the lake flood back through the riverbed, drowning all those he's not already shot to pieces.

Draconettes then became another factor, for a volley from them would cut down the leading ranks of attackers. Even before her people came into range, she would have lost ten percent of them or more. After that, the makeup of Nefrai-kesh's troops complicated things. Gibberers and vylaens were one thing, but what if his ranks were stiffened by *turekadine* and *kryalniri*? What if there were other Aurolani creations that had been saved for this battle? And how many troops did he have in those hills? How deep did the warrens run and where were there other outlets? Though her scouts had found no signs of armies waiting elsewhere in hiding, she could not be certain they didn't exist.

For her to have even a ghost of a chance of winning, she estimated that she needed at least three times the number of troops on the Aurolani side. If Nefrai-kesh produced a dragon . . . Well, she had Arimtara on her side, but she was mindful of Dranae's death. One dragon might not be enough.

She heard a noise behind her and spun. Maroth stood there in a shadow. Alyx shifted her hand away from her breastbone and began to breathe again. "Yes, Maroth, I am aware you are here, too, and I have no doubt you have talents I would find useful." She resisted the urge to tell him to "go forth and conquer," because she wasn't certain what he would do. Moreover, if the thing in his chest *was* the lost piece of the DragonCrown, sending him against the Aurolani would be handing victory to Chytrine.

But, if there is no other choice . . . Alyx shook her head. "There is always another choice." As she had discussed with her commanders, it could be that they would have to break the army apart, retreat, and force Nefrai-kesh to leave his stronghold. The summer would wear on his troops, and if he were forced into attacking a fortified position, he would be hurt. But it was a weak strategy and she knew it, for without a decisive victory, the war could drag on for years.

Her thoughts turned fleetingly to Resolute, Kerrigan, and the others. The last message she'd had from them told of the fall of Loquellyn and their determination to push on to Vorquellyn. They certainly had to have been through there. And, if they had Will with them, they were pressing north. Her victory or defeat could be rendered moot by the success or failure of their mission. Alexia didn't like the idea of facing Resolute as the new king of the *sullanciri*, but she would if she had to.

And if Nefrai-kesh wins and they fail, the world we know is gone forever.

Taking one last look around, she exited the room and was not surprised to see that Maroth had long since vanished. As she came up the last flight of stairs, she met Crow waiting for her. She gave him a smile, then slipped into his arms and hugged him tightly.

He grunted. "What's that for?"

Alyx smiled and kissed him. "You've never once asked if I think I can do this. You've never once questioned my judgment in how we are approaching this assault."

Crow pulled his head back. "Why would I?"

She slackened her embrace and stepped back. "Crow, I am very young, especially when my age is measured against those who are under my command. Yes, I was trained to be the best military mind I could, but all the wisdom in the world doesn't mean every puzzle has a solution. At least not an elegant one. And this puzzle appears to be one we will solve with a lot of blood. Is my lack of experience consigning my soldiers to pain and death?"

He frowned. "I think you're forgetting two things. The first is that while you're right not to underestimate Nefrai-kesh, you can't also make him invincible. It's true that he gave away Okrannel but, even so, he made tactical errors.

Adrogans has said—and you and I have discussed the fact—that Nefrai-kesh could have inflicted a lot more damage than he did at Svarskya. While he has had no compunction about slaying people like Queen Lanivette, he didn't kill Sayce when he could have."

"What are you saying?"

"I've been thinking about the *sullanciri*. The original ones were all corrupted individuals who went to Chytrine willingly. This current crop were different. They were dead or dying and certainly desperate. They may have been unable to resist her—at the time, anyway."

Her violet eyes narrowed. "You think he might truly want to see his mistress defeated?"

"Is there a slave who doesn't hate his master?"

"Your point is well-taken, but I can't act on it."

Crow reached out and caressed her cheek. "I know that. I'm just trying to say that Nefrai-kesh may have his own problems. This style of warfare is as new to him as it is to you, but you've had a chance to study how to fight against it. He's only had to try to make it work better. The closest we've seen to this fight is the battle for Fortress Draconis."

She nodded. "Yes, but Chytrine's forces had dragonels there, and we don't. I see your point, however. You're telling me he could make mistakes."

"Exactly." He smiled. "The second thing you are forgetting is this: our troops are fighting for their nations, their families, and their future. For them, losing is not an option. They know how far we've pushed the Aurolani. We've pushed them from Saporicia and Muroso. We've pushed them from Bokagul, Sarengul, and Oriosa. We've pushed them from Okrannel. This is one more push—a mighty one, but they will give way. That's the knowledge in the heart of every man and woman out there."

Alexia nodded solemnly, then pulled Crow back into her embrace and kissed him again. Then she broke the kiss and hugged him ferociously. As his arms encircled her and tightened, she whispered in his ear, "I fight for our future, too, Crow. For the peace neither of us has known."

He nodded and kissed her ear. "We both fight for that, beloved. It's one more edge we have over Nefrai-kesh. We have something to fight for, and a future to look forward to. He has nothing. We know *why* we continue to fight, but neither he nor his troops have that."

Alexia pulled back and took his hands in hers. "Well, then, Crow, let us ride north, leading the army of the future. Half a week hence, we will face the Aurolani host and drive them back into the frozen wastes where they can languish forever."

CHAPTER 71

Isaura discovered that, for the others, reaching the glacier brought discomfort, but not the same sort of discomfort as it did for her. For them, living on the ice and snow was hard because of the cold. The way the night's winds blew fiercely sapped them of strength. Hlucri built ice shelters as he had on the trip down, but the lack of firewood meant cold camps, which left everyone irritable and cross.

Isaura could further tell Trawyn neither liked nor trusted her. The Loquelf's home had been overrun by her mother's troops, and her resentment at that slopped over onto Isaura. She could not blame the princess, but the fact that Isaura was accompanying them north again to attack her mother provided her no protection from Trawyn's ire. Save for invoking Hlucri's wrath, Isaura thought Trawyn would have been content to leave her behind.

Sayce, who had been her friend, had her own burdens. While she had dealt with Will's transformation well, the bravery with which she had handled his death had eroded. Isaura, though never having known love or lovers, still could imagine how it felt to have Force around as a constant reminder of Will, yet to get no satisfaction or even recognition from him. The image of Will that Sayce carried in her heart had to be slowly merging with Force, forever stealing away her lover.

So while the cold did not bother Isaura, their march north made her feel more and more uneasy. On one level she loved Chytrine. Save for the role she'd been given, there would have been no place for Isaura in Aurolani society. She did not have the avaricious edge of the recruits Neskartu had instructed in his Conservatory. Barring Chytrine's acceptance, she'd likely have been left to die on some hillside or fed to frostclaws.

Were she still a child, that simple gratitude would have been enough to make her revolt against what they were going to do. It would have led to thinking that there was a way to make Chytrine see sense. Just as the Norrington was going to redeem Vorquellyn, so her mother could be redeemed.

But the last chance of that died when Ferxigo had ordered her death. It would have not been difficult for Isaura to believe that order had been given in error, but Hlucri had reacted to the reality of it. He'd immediately slain his fellow *sullanciri*, confirming for Isaura that the order had been genuine. And, as Resolute suggested, that it came from her mother.

It saddened her that Chytrine had been twisted and warped enough by the Oromise to be willing to spurn Isaura's love. Chytrine saw her as nothing but a means to an end. The searching spell she'd been given had not been entrusted to her for any reason other than to search out the Norrington and lead Ferxigo south. Her mother had used her, and once she had accomplished her task was willing to discard her.

Isaura wondered for how long she had known, in her heart of hearts, that her mother saw her as an object. Consciously Isaura had not known it until now, but it now occurred to her that the whims of magick might not have led her to the Norrington in Meredo. Instead, she might have been drawn to him by other forces, which were aided and abetted by what she knew of her mother. *Did I find him because I knew that if she were not destroyed, she would kill me?*

That question, viewed from a myriad of positions, occupied her mind for much of the journey up the glacier and across it. She replayed every scene of her life, reading new meaning into her interactions with her mother. She caught nuances she'd not seen before, and suddenly realized that not only had her mother seen her as a tool but had shaped her to be one. Isaura was clearly meant to be drawn to the Norrington. It explained the affection shown her by Nefrai-kesh and even the attention of his son.

Her thoughts sank her deeper and deeper into a grim mood that matched those of most of her companions. Only Qwc did not get angry; he just slept a lot on Force's shoulder or nestled against Sayce's bosom. And Force gave no sign of his emotions, just trudging on tirelessly. The rest grumbled, growled, and glared.

The advent of a swirling ice column two days before they reached the capital valley broke her mood. She smiled as the ice cone collapsed, then re-formed itself as Drolda. "Yes, I am happy to see you, too."

Hlucri showed no alarm at Drolda's appearance, but Resolute drew his sword and approached. "What is this?"

Drolda turned to Resolute and bowed, shifting his shape a bit. As Isaura said, "This is my friend, Drolda," recognition blossomed on the Vorquelf's face.

"Drolda, of course." Resolute's silver eyes became crescent slits. "Drugi Oldach. He was the one member of Lord Norrington's expedition who went missing. He was never found, never made into a *sullanciri*, but what is he now?"

Drolda immediately signed to Isaura and she translated, rather amazed at what he was saying. "Drolda says you are right, that Drolda was all I could understand of his name when I was a child. He did wander off and escaped the *grichothka* chasing him. He died in the snow and left his body behind, taking his form and substance from the ice and snow. In the early days he'd been unable to take this shape, but he still helped. He created the storm that hid Hawkins from pursuit and guided the fevered young man to the place where you found him."

Resolute slowly nodded. "Then you remained in Aurolan, because you still had a duty to your comrade, Hawkins."

Drolda nodded solemnly.

Isaura looked at the Vorquelf. "What are you talking about?"

"Do you know who your parents were?"

She shook. "No. My mother said I was a foundling. She said there was no knowledge of my father."

"And you have no guess at the identity of she who gave you birth?" Resolute's voice became tight. "You know she gave birth on Vorquellyn. That is the only way you could have been bound to the island."

"I guess I knew that, yes. But as for my mother's identity . . ." Isaura stopped, raising a hand to her mouth. "The one who wanted nothing to do with me. Myrall'mara."

"She was probably afraid that since Chytrine had claimed you, you would be destroyed were she to befriend you." Resolute looked at Drolda. "You weren't on Vorquellyn, but you must have seen Seethe with child."

Again the ice creature nodded.

"And you befriended me because my father had been your friend?"

Linking his thumbs, Drolda shaped his hands into a bird and flapped fingers as wings. His face melted into an expression of extreme sympathy.

Isaura looked down and suddenly found herself sitting hard in the snow. "I am the daughter of Tarrant Hawkins?"

Resolute squatted next to her. "You find that more distasteful than to be sprung from the loins of a *sullanciri*?"

"You don't understand. My mother would speak of

Hawkins only in horrible terms. He would be the one to come steal me away if I were to disobey. He was the slaughterer of innocents. He had betrayed all of the *sullanciri*. He had been a coward and he had been rude enough to refuse my mother's offer to set him above even Nefrai-kesh. She offered him the chance to become her consort and he spurned her. Why? Because he was so arrogant and evil that he went south to collect an army to take from her what she had willingly offered him in the name of peace between their realms."

She glanced at Drolda. "Now I know why you don't like my mother."

The ice man nodded.

The Vorquelf rested his arms across his knees. "If you have any question whether or not your mother's stories are lies, just think how a friend of his clung to existence here, as a creature of wind, snow, and ice, to protect you, his daughter. Drugi Oldach did not know Hawkins that long, but he came to know him well enough to accept and acquit that duty to him."

Isaura slowly nodded. "So she knew that I would join with the Norrington. She just had to watch me to see if it were true. She sent me to Meredo to prove it to herself. Once she knew that, she knew she would be warned when he approached and—if she was speaking truly about the nature of potential, and the power being gathered as the prophecy neared a point of fulfillment—then she wanted me close to make sure that would happen."

Sayce knelt by her right side and hugged her. "That's a lot to learn about how your family saw you. Are you okay?"

Isaura swallowed hard against the lump rising in her throat. "Yes, thank you. I think I will be fine." She glanced at Resolute. "After all, I've known all along I was not Chytrine's daughter. Now I see I was her tool, but I've also discovered something more. I am a Hawkins. A Hawkins wouldn't let this stop her, would she?"

Resolute actually smiled, then stood and helped her to her feet. "No Hawkins I know."

"Good, then I won't break the pattern." She pulled her cloak more tightly around her and started to march north. Drolda sped ahead of them, returning to warn them of dangers and to find good places to rest. Once they passed a perfect place for an ambush, but the dozen gibberers who had been waiting were frozen solid.

Finally, at dawn—at the end of the first week of the month of Green—they crested the mountains surrounding the capital valley. There, still sheathed in shadow, lay the black eminence of her mother's fortress. Everyone paused in the rocks of the pass, staring at the journey's end.

Isaura remembered the last time she'd looked upon that black castle. She'd been riding Procimre, returning from the siege of Navval. *I'd been very happy to be home.*

She thought for a moment and realized she was happy once more, but it was a different kind of happiness. Gone was the childlike delight at returning to a sanctuary. This was a happiness drawn from the knowledge that great things were about to happen, that evil would be stopped, and that the poison her mother bled into the world would cease.

"We're here. This was once my home; now it is the lair of my enemy." Isaura rose from a crouch and looked at Force. "I do believe, Force Norrington, that you and I have a prophecy to fulfill."

CHAPTER 72

E rlestoke's day began well before dawn as he reviewed the latest information and orders being sent by Alexia, then relayed the same to his commanders. His troops had been given the honor of holding the right wing of the army. Alexia's force held the center and left, with Pandiculia's army acting as a reserve force that still watched for intervention from the rear. Seventeen thousand troops spread out over the hills facing the Aurolani position, ready to cross through the riverbed and march up the hills into dragonel and draconette shots, Aurolani magick, and, finally, into combat with the enemy.

The army set up camp a half mile from the Aurolani fortress, with forward positions overlooking the valley to give warning of any sudden attacks. The Army of the South occupied the whole of a valley, with his people taking the easternmost reaches. That meant they got the freshest water from the stream running through the valley. His men also liked the willingness of the urZrethi to dig trenching, and happily traded food for the digging. Under normal circumstances Erlestoke would have forbidden that sort of laziness, but the experience allowed the two groups to bond, and his own men did not complain when he had them take guard watches while the urZrethi slept.

Erlestoke reorganized his staff, making Colonels Sallitt Hawkins and his wife, Jancis, his direct subcommanders. Jullagh-tse Seegg, an urZrethi who had been with Erlestoke at Fortress Draconis, had survived both the escape run from the Fortress and the battling in Sarengul. She became his liaison with the urZrethi forces in his command. Counts Storton and Wightman, as well as Baron Malviston, commanded their own troops, while Wheatly, the leader of the Oriosan Freemen, took charge of the irregulars. No one expected much out of them; but Wheatly seemed able to inspire them to work hard, so much of the support work that needed doing fell to them.

Linchmere had abandoned his identity as Lindenmere, but still spent most of his time with the Freemen working on getting the irregulars to function. Erlestoke had learned that his brother had been a good organizer within the Freemen, and his skill supplemented Wheatly's leadership to get supplies delivered and things prepared for the final assault. Kenleigh Norrington, Will's half brother, remained anonymous, but his natural abilities had the name North on everyone's lips. Linchmere had confided Kenleigh's identity to his brother, but Erlestoke had agreed not to call any attention to him.

With his staff gathered in a large tent, Erlestoke went over the map. "Our responsibility is the eastern end of the battlefield. We have this odd jog of the trenching. It leaves about a hundred-yard gap between it and the dam that's holding that lake. The top of the dam does not have enough space for dragonels, but putting a battalion of dra-conetteers up there would hurt anyone moving between the dam and the trench. Taking the dam won't help, since we assume they have tunnels that will let them explode the dam, much as we were able to explode the exterior batteries at Fortress Draconis."

Jullagh-tse tapped the map right at the point he was talking about. "I have assembled a legion of fast diggers. If we can get close, we can get down there and perhaps cut those tunnels."

"Noted. Thank you."

Sambell Malviston crossed his arms over his skinny chest. "Clearly you are aware of this, but I must make certain. If we enter that dry riverbed, they can open the dam at any time and just sweep us all out to sea."

The prince nodded. "Very true. Alexia assumes that would be a tactic of last resort since the waters would run fast and high enough to flood the trenches. If Nefrai-kesh has very few people and we press hard, that's when we can expect to get wet. If the battle is even, there is no reason for him to flood the place."

Sallitt Hawkins traced a metal finger along the northern bank of the river. "The bank rises about five feet here. We will have trouble scrambling over it."

Linchmere smiled. "I have three hundred ramps to put in place, and Jullagh-tse has two other legions of diggers who will collapse the bank. Even cavalry should be able to make that ride."

The *meckanshii* officer looked at the urZrethi. "Do you have people prepared to tunnel into the hills through the bank?"

"I do, and will assign teams to do that, but asking them to go at least a hundred yards, perhaps more, before they might reach the warrens on the other side is tough. The tunnels would not be big enough to allow a lot of troops to head in fast. I would expect, if we were successful, Nefrai-kesh would just destroy the dam and flood everything."

Sallitt nodded, then looked at the other commanders. "You're going to have to make sure your officers do not let their men huddle beneath the bank here. If they do, they leave the men behind them exposed to the dragonels. The only way we succeed is to move fast and move up."

Count Storton, who was by far the shortest of the warriors, wore only leather armor. "I agree. I have two battalions of my infantry stripped down to leather armor, spears, and longknives. I expect us to move fast and hit the junction between the east hill and the trenching. If we can get into their trench, I think we can get into the warrens."

"You've told me your plan, my lord, and I have relayed it to Princess Alexia." Erlestoke sighed. "I've given it my highest recommendation and I believe she will approve it. When the timing is right, I want you to go in behind a screening force and see if you can succeed."

"We shall, my prince. We shall."

Erlestoke raised a hand to his mask and settled it. "I know—and Princess Alexia knows—that we are facing a fierce enemy and we are at a disadvantage. We are going to ask you and your people for everything you have, and even that might not be enough. We just have to keep going until we win the day.

"Now, get to your people and let them know that by the time the sun sets, we will know victory, and their days of fear will be at an end."

He shook hands with each of his commanders, then embraced Jullagh-tse and his brother. "I will see you after the battle and we will rejoice."

"As always, Prince Erlestoke." The urZrethi bowed, then slipped from the tent.

Linchmere beamed. "We *are* going to win, you know. You wait and see."

"I know." He gave his brother a light cuff, then followed him from the tent. Erlestoke accepted his quadnel, a pouch of shot, and a horn of firedirt from a *meckanshii* and nodded a salute. "Thank you, Verum."

"A pleasure to serve you again, sir. Took the liberty of giving my old quad to that Gyrkyme who liked yours so much."

"Good thinking." Shouldering the draconette, he walked to his horse, then slid the weapon in the saddle scabbard. He mounted up, then nudged his horse into a canter up the far side of the valley. Trailing discreetly came his bodyguard. Borell Carver rode with them, smiling broadly, and weathering the jests of the other soldiers.

Erlestoke dismounted at the crest of the hill and again studied Nefrai-kesh's fortress. As much as the models and maps had prepared him, the sight of it curdled his stomach. The mounds of earth marking the trenches had been fixed with wooden spikes, providing one more obstacle for Storton's sprinters. Activity was apparent in the dragonel batteries, and he estimated as many as fifteen per station. That put ninety of the weapons facing the line, with a half-dozen more from each trench cap.

The forest west of the fortress had surrendered a hundred yards of trees for its building, but looked dark and brooding beyond. That hundred yards appeared to be a tempting gap, but shifting out past the trench and back in would give the other side plenty of time to move the dragonels around. Moreover, any army driven into the woods would simply disintegrate, as the trees and land forced them to separate. *And the gods alone know what he has hidden in there.*

A shiver ran through Erlestoke. If Nefrai-kesh had hidden more dragonels in there, any force making that loop would be blown to pieces. The woods would make a counterattack all but impossible. Every one of the tree stumps would have a dead or dying man huddled behind it.

Behind him the army came up. From his position high on the hill he had the chance to thrill at their advance. Cavalrymen in shining silver armor rode forth, carrying lances with bright pennants. Warriors marched in orderly ranks, with drums beating out cadence and trumpets blaring orders and unit identifiers. Small knots of war-mages strode forward, staves in hand, and his own Bloodadders rode up with enthusiasm.

At the head of the Army of the South came Princess Alexia. The dawning sun made her golden mail gleam. She rode without a helmet, so her long braid was easy to see.

Tall in the saddle, with her shoulders squarely set, there was no questioning that she was about grim business.

And every one of us will follow her into the fire and flood to come.

As the army crested the hill and flowed halfway down, activity began to the north. Drums boomed, and on the southern hill three figures appeared. One was obviously Nefrai-kesh. The other two were female, one crouching cat-like for a moment before bounding off to the west hill. The other made her way to the east hill in a slow gait, then passed over the edge, descending behind the line of the trench. Troops filed from within the hills to fill the trenches on both sides, and some sprinted to the top of the dam. All of them looked to be draconetteers and spearmen, so taking the trenches would be very costly.

Then something else happened. The *sullanciri* on the east hill did something and her right arm changed, flashing brightly in the sunlight as it did so. She raised it to her mouth and apparently blew, for a clarion call sounded loudly, even piercingly. Dogs that had trotted along with their masters howled and a few ran from the sound.

At her call, troops began to pour from the hills and assemble behind the crooked trenching. Legion upon legion—mostly of gibberers, but with enough *turekadine* and *kryalniri* to make Erlestoke grimace. Legions grouped into battalions and then regiments. On the hills more troops appeared, again in thick ranks. Erlestoke started counting regimental standards, then stopped when he reached twenty.

Sallitt Hawkins rode up beside him. "Their numbers and ours are almost equal."

"That they are." The prince pointed toward the dam. "They can bring the troops assembled behind that trench over or around it, then just hit us from the flank and drive us into the woods, blasting us every step of the way."

The *meckanshii* nodded. "And if we send anyone down

to plug that gap and stop them? They won't last long enough for someone to blow retreat."

"Agreed. This is bad, very bad." Erlestoke shook his head. "In fact, I can't see how it could get any worse."

And as those words left his mouth, the dragonels hidden in the woods spat fire and metal.

CHAPTER 73

Whipping himself into a column of storm, Drolda lifted the party, one at a time, down to the basin. Only Hlucri eschewed his service and leaped from the cliffside. His flesh flashed jet and green as he descended. He landed in a huge puff of snow, which slowly settled again as the *sullanciri* dashed forward. For a heartbeat Resolute thought this might be the final betrayal, that the *sullanciri* would rally Aurolani forces to trap them.

But Hlucri's ploy soon made itself apparent as gibberers began to emerge from both the caverns and the fortress itself. *Kryalniri* and some humans also poured from the Conservatory edifice—though their distance from where Drolda had deposited the group eliminated them as an immediate threat. The gibberers focused on Hlucri, but there were enough of them that the party would be bottled up in their drive toward the fortress, and the magickers would then be able to move into range and destroy them.

Nine against an empire. Resolute shivered, recalling a long-ago conversation he'd had with Kerrigan. Then, it was only supposed to be eight against an empire. *If you were here, Kerrigan, I'd pay those magickers no mind at all.* The Vorquelf drew Syverce and tossed a salute off toward the south. *Best of luck to you.*

Sayce landed and drew the twin longknives they'd taken from dead gibberers in the field. She'd long since donned the winter clothing she and Isaura had discarded on their trip south and since recovered, supplementing it with bits and pieces of armor and mail from dead gibberers. "We have to move fast, Resolute."

"I know." *Nine against an empire, and only two of them are critical.* "Trawyn, Sayce, you guard Isaura. Isaura, any spells you have that will help, we need them now. Bok, the *kryalniri* . . ."

The urZrethi nodded and began to move in that direction, but Drolda swirled around him, nudged him back, and sailed off. As he moved closer to the Conservatory, he grew into an icy cyclone of towering proportions. Shocked shouts drifted past the howl of the wind that formed his core.

"Bok, keep your eye on them. Let's move. Force . . ."

Resolute stopped, for Force had already begun to trudge in Hlucri's wake. Each step left yard-deep holes in the snow—which was packed hard enough that the rest of them ran over the top of it with ease. Ahead, Hlucri had already torn into the front ranks of a gibberer legion; bodies or their bleeding parts were flying high in the air.

A hoargoun emerged from the fortress at the head of some gibberkings. He wielded a huge ax with a blade large enough to split a bullock in one stroke. The frost giant, with his flesh tinged blue and his hair and beard snow-white, shifted his course to head directly for Force. But if Force noticed him, he gave no sign.

With Qwc flying before him and Bok coming up on his right side, Resolute sprinted into battle. Anomalous thoughts coursed through his mind. The sound of the snow crunching beneath his feet and the burning of the cold air in his lungs, the contrast of Bok's green flesh with the stark white of the snow, the distant scream of Drolda's storm and the piercing screams of the gibberers Hlucri was flensing alive; all of those things came to him and he cataloged them. *As I would have when I was a child.*

For the blink of an eye he wondered if this was the first step in his reviewing his life before he died. He thought about that for just a moment longer, then laughed aloud in a cloud of steam. "No, I'm nowhere near dead."

And with that his war cry, Resolute leaped into battle. Syverce became less a sword than a scythe. The blade parted flesh as if it were smoke. He hacked no bones, but with a twist and flip, Syverce negotiated joints—be they hip, knee, or elbow—severing ligaments and removing the appendages from the bodies.

The gibberkings he battled did their best against him, and slashes did score his armor. Rings popped and twisted. The leather jerkin beneath it opened, as did his flesh, but only in tiny cuts. He gave far better than he got, and Bok did likewise. The urZrethi's right fist had become a mace, crushing bone as if it were eggshell. Gibberking swords rang off Bok's carapace, but never cracked it.

Behind them Sayce and Trawyn fought furiously. Sayce positioned herself to Trawyn's right, defending her blind side with her longknives. More than one *turekadine* closed swiftly, thinking she could be overwhelmed, only to find one blade turning his slash, and the other licking out to open his belly or an artery. Trawyn, with her speed and reach, got past guards and stabbed deeply, often before her foes realized she was within range.

Ahead of them, however, the main battle had been set. Hlucri had left a trail of pulsing flesh, pumping steaming crimson jets over the snow. The gibberers had swarmed him, making it impossible for others to get their knives and spears into him. Hlucri, well armed with claws and teeth, ripped and tore, pulping his foes.

The hoargoun and Force squared off. Force showed far more agility than Resolute would have thought possible, as he dodged a chop that buried the ax deep in the permafrost. With his right fist tightened into a stone ball, Force smashed the frost giant in the foot, crushing bone The hoargoun howled and twisted back, yanking his ax free. He set his foot down gingerly, then flicked out his hand and slapped Force aside.

The stone creature tumbled sideways, then fell into the hole the ax had created. Force lay there for a moment, on his back, as if in a grave. He curled forward, reaching for the edges to pull himself free, but by then the ax had come up and descended again. With a thunderous clang it smashed into Force's left shoulder and took the arm off in a spray of molten blood that sizzled into the snow.

Qwc arrowed in at the hoargoun's face and spat webbing that covered his left eye. The frost giant swiped at it with his right hand, still guffawing over the fate of the stone man that had opposed him. He cleared the webbing from his face, then swatted at Qwc. He missed, but Qwc's next attack just splashed webbing across his cheek. As he wiped that webbing away, he looked down, and his pale eyes widened, just for a moment.

The only thing in the hole was Force's arm.

Force stood half as tall as the hoargoun, so this time his right fist slammed into the taller creature's kneecap. The blow utterly shattered it, fragments of bone tearing the hoargoun's flesh. The frost giant roared, but that became a squeal as Force's next blow caught him over the left hip and fractured the pelvis.

The hoargoun crashed down hard, cracking the snow crust and disappearing in a cloud of powder. As the crystals drifted down, Force leaped onto his right shoulder. The balled fist swung down again, crushing the base of the hoargoun's skull. The huge creature grunted and thrashed, flinging his ax far enough to bisect a *turekadine*.

The hoargoun's fall and the way a bloody Hlucri dove into the midst of the remaining *turekadine* formation scattered the Aurolani troops. Resolute dashed forward to the hoargoun and stared at Force. "Are you hurt?"

The stone creature just looked down at him blankly, but his face had taken on enough detail that Resolute *could* identify it as a blank look. The left shoulder still radiated heat, but the wound had crusted over as a lava flow might in such cold weather. His right hand redefined itself with fingers and pointed back at the hole. Force opened and closed his fist twice, then Bok dragged the stone limb over.

The Vorquelf looked at the urZrethi. "Can you fix him?"

Bok raised an eyebrow. "I don't even know what he is, Resolute. But I can try."

Isaura laid a hand on Bok's shoulder. "Let me. It's my duty as a Hawkins and . . ." She dropped to one knee and pressed her left hand to the severed shoulder. A light appeared in her palm. "Tythsai has an arm that imitates the *meckanshii*. It is fluid. I created the spell that controls the most recent one and keeps it together. Force, come down here."

The stone creature knelt. Isaura touched his body at the shoulder and invoked a spell. Force seemed to waver for a moment. Then Bok lifted the arm and touched it to the body, and it, too, became momentarily indistinct. Heat rolled off Force as the two pieces of him fused together again and mineral blood flowed around the edges. Other little fragments flew from the snow to rejoin him and melted into the glowing seam.

He rose and cracked both hands together. His shoulder once again produced the depression in which the Spritha sat. Force raised a hand and pointed toward the fortress.

Resolute nodded. "Agreed." He looked off toward the Conservatory and no longer saw Drolda. What he did see were magickers coming after them, but far fewer than there had been before. Of more minor concern was the appearance of an Aurolani formation high on the cliff face. Whether they were a patrol returning or troops that had been recalled after Ferxigo died, Resolute had no clue. *We'll have to deal with them after we've handled Chytrine. If we survive.*

"Isaura, where will your mother be?"

"The Grand Hall. Or below."

"We'll sweep the Grand Hall, then we'll ferret her out below if we must."

They set off again with Hlucri and Force in the lead. The *turekadine* had fled toward the fortress, some trailing blood. The black stone structure stabbed into the sky, and on an upper balcony Resolute caught a flash of gold. He glanced at Isaura, but she just shrugged.

As they neared the fortress, draconettes barked from the shadowed doorway. Balls flattened against Force's broad chest. One ricocheted, tearing off the lower of Qwc's left arms and shattering a wing before spilling him from his perch. Hlucri grunted as shots hit him. Sayce somersaulted backward, landing on her shoulders and head in the snow, while Bok spun to the ground. Resolute heard one shot whine past him, but he had already moved to the left and flicked bladestars into that opening. He heard some clang, and then a scream; at least one had found its mark.

Force eclipsed his view of the doorway. Resolute glanced back for a second. Trawyn was helping Sayce to her feet. Isaura stood over Bok's body, but even Resolute could see the urZrethi's skull was missing a huge chunk. "Hlucri, get Isaura now. There's nothing she can do for Bok."

The *sullanciri* grunted and galloped toward her. Resolute rushed up the fortress' steps and had to stop short inside the doorway lest he crash headlong into Force. The half-dozen draconetteers that had been there were dead. Two had fallen to his bladestars and the rest looked as if they had been kneaded together into a mass of flesh and fur.

"Forward, Force. We have to find Chytrine, and you have to kill her."

The Norrington stomped forward. Hlucri set Isaura down inside the doorway, then handed Qwc to her. Trawyn got Sayce within the fortress and the Murosan smiled bravely. "It hit a bit of plate. Knocked my wind out. I'll be okay. *We'll* be okay."

Trawyn nodded. "Bok is . . ."

"Dead, I know. The urZrethi would leave him where he fell. Let's go."

Deeper they went into the fortress. A few *turekadine* and gibberers did show themselves, but fled before Hlucri and Force. The party continued straight in until they reached the Grand Hall.

Chytrine waited for them at the far end. The hall should have dwarfed her, but she had grown in size to match the Norrington. Her hair had a golden luster to it, and her pale flesh likewise glittered. As she nodded a greeting, the delicate scales that covered her became apparent. Her body's coloration matched the ivory-and-gold gown she wore, rendering her far more elegant than Resolute could have ever imagined. Sharpened ears rose through her hair, and her hands pressed against each other casually, revealing thick talons of gold.

"Myrall'mara said it would be you, Resolute, who came here in the end. I see you've brought the Norrington. Thank you."

Resolute shook his head. "This will be the fulfillment of the prophecy, Chytrine. You die, my homeland is redeemed, and your evil is at an end forever."

The empress laughed. "I would find your little pronouncement quite tedious were it not so predictably charming. You see, Resolute, you and all the world believe in one prophecy, but there are many. A prophecy will be fulfilled here today, but it shall not be the one to which you refer."

Chytrine opened her arms. "For the short time you will be here, I welcome you. All of you, in fact—save for the one who has betrayed me."

She flicked a finger out and magic sizzled hot and red. The scintillating sphere smashed Hlucri in the chest and bled into his flesh. The *sullanciri* jerked, his arms flung wide and his head retracted as his spine bowed. The magick flowed over him, then away, stripping him of the skin Nefrai-kesh had given him. As the magic vanished, Hlucri fell to the floor with a wet thump, bare muscles twitching, blood leaking from him.

Isaura's hand fell from her mouth and she strode forward. "Mother, you can't do that."

"I am not your mother." The Aurolani Empress again flicked a finger. Isaura flew back, smashing against Force. She fell to the ground, still breathing but limp. Force dropped to one knee and carefully slid her body behind him.

"Of course, as a Norrington must, you protect your vassal. But you are a mix, a mongrel—part Norrington, part Hawkins, and part brothel-whore." Chytrine's blue-green eyes blazed. "And I am the Aurolani Empress. No prophecy can empower you to destroy me!"

Force rose and sprinted toward Chytrine. His heavy footfalls shook the floor. Stone on stone, relentless and pounding, they filled the room with thunder. Force's hands shifted into stone blades, poised to cut Chytrine in half.

The empress did not retreat, but instead thrust her face forward and opened her mouth so wide her jaw must have unhinged. A searingly brilliant gout of flame poured forth, golden white at the core. The heat struck Resolute about the same time the light half blinded him. The fire silhouetted Force in stark black. Resolute turned his face away and tried to watch, but the heat drove him back. Hlucri's body began to roast. Trawyn and Sayce dragged Isaura back. And, with her, Qwc.

The five of them retreated as a thick vapor filled the room. Resolute coughed at the bitter smoke, not wanting to think about inhaling Force. Trawyn sneezed violently and Sayce gagged. The Vorquelf shifted to shield the others as best he could, catching the acrid scent of singed hair—his, mostly—on the air.

As quickly as it had come, the light and heat abated.

Resolute turned, brandishing Syverce. "Force? Show me you're alive."

He caught movement in the smoke and his heart rose for a moment, then sank again swiftly. The grey cloud slowly drifted down, revealing Chytrine as a dragon, her ivory scales stained with ash. *Ash that had been Force.*

The empress' chest heaved as she breathed. "Your savior is no more." The smoke swirled around her muzzle much in the same way the colors swirled in her eyes. "Your prophecy is done. The fulfillment of the one I serve will now commence."

CHAPTER 74

K errigan awoke and struggled against the weight on his
chest. A blanket had been laid over him and he went to
fling it off, only his limbs felt heavy and sluggish. Then
he opened his eyes and saw the blurry blanket peeling off
him as if it were curling through water.

Which is exactly what it is doing. That realization shook
him and his body rebelled. He coughed, trying to rid his
lungs of water. Kerrigan had suffered far more near-miss
drownings than he wanted to think about, but his cough
produced no bubbles and expelled little in the way of fluid.
Rather, it expelled some, but he breathed it back in again.

For Kerrigan, one thing was abundantly clear: he'd been
breathing water for a long time and he was still alive. This
meant either he was enchanted, or the water was. *Or I'm
dead and a* sullanciri. He quickly cast a spell that told him
magick hadn't been worked on him. The water, on the
other hand, appeared to be different. Somehow it was
breathable.

Kerrigan rolled out of the bed he was on and surveyed
his surroundings. The room wasn't very big and had no

window. In fact, the only opening was where, in a normal room, one would find a skylight. The room itself had been grown of variously colored coral, striping and dotting the walls in an abstract but pleasing pattern. Passing a hand over his eyes, Kerrigan invoked a spell that gave him clear sight beneath the water, and smiled as the coral pattern sharpened beautifully.

He wasn't certain what was going on, because the last thing he remembered was a huge wave smashing him in the chest and knocking him overboard. By all rights he should have been dead, but he wasn't. That left him one logical conclusion, which was that Tagothcha had preserved his life, but exactly why he'd do that, Kerrigan could not be certain. *The wand was a great treasure, yes, but . . .*

The young magicker crouched, then pushed off the floor and reached for the edges of the doorway. He grabbed hold and propelled himself through easily. He emerged into a circular corridor, likewise grown of coral, with other openings along its length. Curiously, he felt one current hitting his upper back and another on his legs flowing the other way. He dove forward into the upper stream and, kicking his feet occasionally, propelled himself along the corridor.

Around him others poked their heads out of holes. He didn't recognize many until he found Oracle. He stopped himself and helped her into the stream. Others began to flow past, all heading in the direction Kerrigan had chosen. None of them did more than nod, but he assumed they couldn't see much of anything since they didn't have his magick.

Then again, underwater, we can't speak, can we?

He tried saying something to Oracle, but it made no sense at all. Despite that, she gripped his arm firmly and smiled. Together they floated off, in the middle of the pack of sailors and soldiers from Adrogans' fleet. Kerrigan didn't see any indication that the people were any the worse for

wear, but the anxiety of being in Tagothcha's realm clearly
was taxing them all.

The long corridor turned up and soon merged with
others. The flow brought everyone into a large chimney,
with the current nearest the edges propelling them upward.
Kerrigan squeezed Oracle's arm as they ascended. He
wanted to tell her that everything would be fine, but he
found her expression so serene that he drew confidence
from it instead.

They floated up into a huge domed chamber large
enough to have housed Fortress Draconis. The structure
most closely resembled a head of garlic in shape, though
here coral had given way to mother-of-pearl. The walls had
to be incredibly thin because they glowed with light from
above. The way the light shifted, Kerrigan assumed it was
sunlight filtering down through the water, but he had no
idea how deep they were.

Ahead, perhaps a hundred yards in front of them,
Tagothcha waited on a throne of pearl. It had not been created of many pearls cemented together, but grown in one
giant pearl with a hollow indentation suitable for someone
of his size to sit. Beside it, at its right hand, a black pearl
throne of human dimensions had likewise been created,
and a woman occupied it.

Tagothcha would have been smaller than a hoargoun,
but not by much. His long white hair floated on the water
and his beard, which had been divided into three braids,
moved lazily, like tentacles. He wore only a girdle of shells
and gold coins interwoven, a gold ring, and a crown of
coral that had grown up around gemstones. Having seen
the world's royalty festooned in their own finery for the
New Year's celebration, Kerrigan thought the *weirun*'s
crown more majestic. The way the coral had grown up
around the gems reminded him of the magick dragons
used to shape Vael, and that pleased him.

The woman who sat beside him had an unearthly beauty.
Her pale skin had a translucent quality that rendered her

ageless. She wore her long hair unbound and it had the silvery sheen of fish scales to it, save where a thread of blue or red might flash. Delicately featured and clean of limb, she was clearly human. She wore a gown of white silk that clung to her lithe body, and it had been belted with gold. A circlet of gold on her brow and a gold ring served as her only jewelry.

Tagothcha gestured and Kerrigan found himself drifting forward, along with Oracle, Adrogans, Phfas, and Rymramoch. As they came toward Tagothcha, a bit of magick flowed out from the *weirun*. Kerrigan didn't have time to analyze it before the water itself tightened around him. He expelled most of the water in his lungs, then a secondary wave hit him and he found himself in an air-filled bubble.

Tagothcha's voice boomed as water drained from Kerrigan's ears. "You are invaders of my realm, but I have chosen not to kill you."

Adrogans, off to Kerrigan's right, dropped to a knee and coughed heavily, gushing water from his lungs. He waited a moment, then stood and lifted his chin. "I expect that is an oversight you will remedy quickly."

The *weirun*'s cerulean gaze played over Adrogans. "Many hate me, but few with such vehemence. You are far from home, and would do well to keep a civil tongue in your head."

"Civil did not help me years ago. Nor did pleading." Adrogans gripped the cuff of a sleeve and wrung water from it. "I survived by cursing, and I failed to give you an offering before we sailed. I suppose that is why you took us. You prove your capricious nature by dooming six ships for the folly of one man. Take me; let them go."

Tagothcha frowned, then a smile blossomed on his face. He began to laugh with the force of waves smashing against a breakwater. "Now I remember you. Markus, the fishbait boy."

Adrogans nodded. "The one who survived your best attempts to drown him."

The *weirun* snorted, then gestured. A column of water poured down from the top of the bubble, smashing Adrogans to the floor. Adrogans fought against it, holding himself up on his hands and knees, but sputtered in spite of himself when the *weirun* stopped the flow.

"*That*, Markus Fishbait, is not even a fraction of my best effort to drown you. If I had meant to kill you when you were a child, you would have died. You clung to a cask. You gathered debris for a raft. Who do you think pushed those scraps close to you? Who do you think pushed you toward a ship that could save you?"

Adrogans stood and wiped the water from his face. "You expect me to believe you had mercy on me? You destroyed that boat and killed all on board."

Tagothcha's fingers flowed together into an intricate weave. "I did. You gave me an offering, a true offering. The others did not. The captain of that vessel would collect offerings, put them in a sack, then throw another sack overboard with fish heads and rusty nails in it. The others knew, for he had bragged on it when deep in his cups, then bought them all drinks to assuage them. They grew bold and foolish. They had to die, but you did not. You needed to tell the tale of their destruction."

"You should have just swept the captain overboard."

The *weirun* shrugged. "Kill a man, it's his bad luck. Destroy a ship, and it is a demonstration of why I should be appeased. It was effective, and had the added benefit of getting you off the sea. Your destiny was not on water."

"No, but clearly my fate has been."

Tagothcha smiled. "I shall enjoy spending time with you here."

Kerrigan cleared his throat. "We can't remain here. We have to get to Sebcia."

"That is not possible."

The magicker squared his shoulders. "I would have

thought the gift I gave you would have been special enough to earn us some consideration."

The sea spirit smiled slyly. "Your company offered many things, and the wand from your hand was indeed unique." He raised his hand and thumbed the ring he wore. "I, however, have *many* unique things. You gave me a wand. A generation ago I was given a consort. Your gift does not please me as well."

Oracle squeezed Kerrigan's arm, silencing him. "I would beg leave, great Tagothcha, for you to consider the gift I gave you."

"Whisperings, nothing more. Worth less than nothing."

Oracle turned her blind eyes toward the woman in the black pearl throne. "I am not certain your consort would agree. I gave you those whisperings for her."

The woman turned serenely to Tagothcha. "Why did you not tell me, beloved?"

The *weirun* hesitated, shifting in his throne. "They were ravings, my sweetness. They meant nothing."

"Highness, they meant merely to warn you." Oracle bowed in the woman's direction. "I wished to save you heartache."

The woman's eyes flashed darkly at Tagothcha. "I'm certain you wished to preserve me from anxiety as well, my lord. What were these words?"

"Inconsequential nonsense, beloved; evanescent persiflage." Tagothcha twisted in his throne and waved an idle hand in Oracle's direction. "Repeat your ravings if you must."

"As my lord Tagothcha commands." Oracle composed her face gravely. "I informed him that in Sebcia your sons would die. The first you would know of it would be when their blood is washed from the Eirsena River into the sea."

The woman reached out and took Tagothcha's wrist in her hand. "Is this true? What news from Eirsena?"

Tagothcha's expression darkened. "No news from Eirsena."

"But your sister is never silent at this time. What has happened? What else have you kept from me?"

Tagothcha's nostrils flared. "The others burble in floods, but from my favorite I have nothing. She is silent."

Kerrigan frowned. "You're talking about rivers as if they are people."

Adrogans shot him a hot glance. "Remember where you are, Kerrigan. The river *weirun* are kin to Tagothcha."

"Oh, right." The youth scratched at the back of his neck. "I guess they must have dammed the river."

Adrogans smiled. "Yes, of course they did. So hot and early a spring, everything is flooding save the Eirsena. How could it be aught but a dam? The Aurolani did it, for they possess Sebcia. They have kidnapped your sister."

The *weirun* flowed to his feet and smashed his fists up through the bubble's ceiling. "Chytrine will be made to pay for that!"

"But how?" Adrogans raised his chin. "You can smash her ships, but she has no more; she doesn't need them. And if she stays away from you, you can't get at her. And even if you make her pay, how can you ease the pain your sister is feeling? It is not just Chytrine who must pay, but it is your sister who must be freed."

He turned and pointed at the sailors and soldiers floating like lost souls outside the bubble. "Send us. We will free your sister. We will save your sons. Let us go to Sebcia and we will make things right."

"No, you cannot. My brothers and sisters have told me what has crossed river and stream to reach the battlefield."

The woman looked up at Tagothcha. "Have they told you of my sons? What of them? What have you not told me?"

Oracle held up a hand. "Highness, be calmed. Your sons are alive and well. They are warriors, well loved and well respected. They have escaped their heritage, for no taint of their father lingers on them. They are brave, which is why they now are in danger's path. If we are allowed to go to Sebcia, chances are good they will live."

The woman's eyes widened. "Good? I would like better than that."

"There can be no guarantees."

She stood and caressed Tagothcha's knee. "Beloved, I have asked so little of you . . ."

"Do not ask this."

"Would you refuse me?"

Tagothcha lowered his arms, then sat. "I cannot refuse you."

"Then grant them what they need. You have been given treasures beyond measure by men. Choose this way to remind them how great you are. You need not destroy a ship when you can save the world."

Tagothcha's expression eased and, as it did, the *weirun* changed. His body shrank to human proportions, or very nearly so. His beard and hair became shorter and the stern antiquity on his face vanished. As he looked at his consort, youth flooded him. "When your husband gave you to me, he surrendered that which could have made him great." Tagothcha gazed into her eyes for several more moments, then turned and regarded Adrogans. "You have made a bold claim that you will free my sister. You are also correct in suggesting that I cannot effect her rescue. I will have to trust you to do it, but I do not have to trust your means."

"You'll find my troops are the best in the world."

"Perhaps, but I can make certain they are better." He raised both arms and a thick column of water descended to engulf him. In a heartbeat he became almost transparent, discernible only as a flickering outline within the water. He threw his head back, and while Kerrigan only heard a muffled squeak, the troops still outside the bubble quickly pressed their hands to their ears.

The column ascended again and Tagothcha solidified his shape. "A generation ago the champions of the world tricked me, then made amends. From them I obtained my consort. One of them had his favorite horse driven into the ocean for me. That steed was magnificent, and his offspring have been incredible."

Bursting into the bubble came a wonderful horse that shook his head, splashing water everywhere. A white star decorated the forehead of the otherwise black horse. Kerrigan did not know much about horses, but this one looked like the type Resolute would choose to ride. The expression of amazement on Adrogans' face further confirmed his opinion that this horse was very special.

"I saw a painting of this horse in Yslin. It is Cursus. It was King Augustus that gave you this horse."

"So it was." Tagothcha smiled. "Cursus has a thousand children and they shall leave the sea with you at Sebcia."

Adrogans approached and patted the horse on the neck. "Living here, they will be much stronger than horses from the surface. They'll have more endurance. If I put my heavy cavalry on them, they will be unstoppable."

"Good. Then my sister shall be freed."

The woman stood and gestured to her right. "And, my lord, since my sons will benefit, I, too, will contribute to this effort."

Kerrigan looked to the bubble wall as dozens of mages in kilts of blue hovered outside. Two entered: a man with a blond beard and a woman. They looked frighteningly familiar, but he could not place them. They studied him for a moment, then the male smiled. "Adept Reese, how is it that you are so young?"

Kerrigan shook his head. "Do I know you?"

The blond shook his head. "I am Therian Cole. I was an apprentice and on the boat you took from Vilwan when the pirates attacked."

A shiver shot down Kerrigan's spine. He dimly recalled the face, but only as much younger. A year ago when they had shipped from Vilwan, this apprentice had barely entered his teens. *Now he has a beard.*

Tagothcha waved a hand casually. "In my realm, time is fluid. Some places it moves quickly, and others not at all.

Perhaps there are places where one could even return to youth were one to linger. Those who were lost with you, Adept Reese, were gathered here by my wife. They have learned much of the magick in my realm, and will be of great use to you."

Kerrigan turned to the *weirun*'s consort. "Your kindness in saving those I could not is much appreciated. I will do everything I can to see to the safety of your sons. If I might inquire . . ."

Oracle squeezed his arm again. "Do you not recognize Queen Morandus, late of Oriosa? You know her sons."

"Erlestoke and Linchmere?" Kerrigan smiled as all manner of stories locked into place in his mind. "I know them, Highness. If they die, it will only be because I will be dead first."

Tagothcha stared hard at him. "And my sister? What of her?"

Kerrigan nodded solemnly. "As we flow from here to Sebcia, so your sister shall soon flow back to you."

Tagothcha was able to bring Kerrigan and the flotilla to the coast of Sebcia, very close to the mouth of the Eirsena. The Nalisk Mountain Rangers and the Loquelven Blackfeathers plunged inland into the forests to scout as the half-dozen ships rose from the depths and bobbed in the small bay. The sailors and soldiers who had traveled beneath the sea on them quickly set about off-loading cargo, which, by dint of Tagothcha's power, was as dry as the day it had been loaded.

And true to his word, Tagothcha produced a thousand of the most beautiful horses Kerrigan had ever seen. Tall and strong, with long, flowing manes and horseshoes of silver, the horses exuded power. The cavalrymen who were given them seemed pleased, and no one commented on the unusual color schemes, stripes, spots, and patches that decorated the horses' coats and manes.

Tagothcha stood knee deep in the water and looked at Adrogans. "I saved you once, but that was in exchange for the gold you gave me. Release my sister, and I shall be deeply in your debt."

"I'll find a way to collect."

The *weirun* laughed, then bent to bring his face to Phfas' level. "We have a kinship, for you are bound to the stuff that gives me life. You think that your removal from your home has weakened that connection. Is Zhusk water different from any other? The air? The earth?"

The diminutive shaman smiled slyly. "Sweeter; much sweeter."

"But it is the same." Tagothcha opened his arms. "What you seek is here, too. You long for your home, but your only distance from it, from the *yrûn*, is in your longing. Open yourself and you will find them here. You are of the world, not just the Zhusk. Believe that and you will find you are not alone."

Phfas' face contorted in all manner of interesting expressions, then ended with widened eyes. "Thank you."

The sea spirit turned to Kerrigan and raised his left hand. Flowing up through it came the wand Kerrigan had offered when they left Loquellyn. "You may find this useful."

"Probably, but I gave it to you." Kerrigan bowed his head respectfully. "I knew the consequences of throwing it away."

"Yes, but my wife bids I give it back to you. To help you save her sons."

Kerrigan accepted it. "I'll do that."

The *weirun* took a step back. "Know that if your bodies are washed into me, you shall be venerated. All speed to you, and all death to your enemies." He opened his arms, then his body simply flowed down into the water.

Kerrigan smiled and tucked the wand into his belt. "We're here."

Adrogans shook his head. "I would have settled for a

long sailing. Sun's got two hours before it goes down. We have to move inland and bring our dragonels with us. We'll find the enemy, get set up, and get ready to kill."

The young mage looked at the *Svarskya*. "Too bad we can't float it up the river and use its dragonels."

"If we could, we'd not be here, since then his sister would be free. I'll leave a skeleton crew on it to fend off Aurolani ships that come to investigate."

Phfas ran a hand over his chin. "The *weirun* was right. The *yrûn* are here. The Aurolani have a fortress, very close. Svarskya is also close."

Adrogans hesitated for a moment, then nodded. "The *sullanciri* from the Ghost March is here, too. Not very distant. Let's move."

The army moved inland slowly. The scouts reported contact with Aurolani troops consisting mostly of light infantry and several dragonel batteries. Orders were issued for the wholesale slaughter of the troops. And Kerrigan and the sea mages were able to magickally silence and send to sleep enough of the enemy troops that the batteries in the woods west of the Aurolani position fell without alarm. The Alcidese Wolves moved into the Aurolani positions, added their own dragonels, and two hours before dawn had forty dragonels ready to shoot.

Kerrigan stood with Adrogans at the edge of the forest as dawn came. "General, don't you want to get word to Princess Alexia about your position?"

"Do you have a manner that can guarantee it won't be intercepted? We're very vulnerable here. I know how we'll signal her, but it won't be in advance. It can't be."

Kerrigan nodded. Up on the hills overlooking the southern bank of the dry Eirsena, the southern army began to assemble itself. Ranks upon ranks of warriors, including a number of urZrethi, arrayed themselves across the face of the hill. Cavalry with horses in shimmering armor and warriors fleshed in metal took their places in the grand formation. Alexia's army was larger than any host he'd seen assembled, and the sheer majesty of it awed him.

In the Aurolani fortress, drums began to pound. A trio of *sullanciri* appeared on the tallest hill, then the Aurolani troops poured from their hill forts and filled the trench extending west. Behind Kerrigan came the creaks of dragonel carriages being shifted as the weapons were sighted. The acrid stink of burning match cord reached his nostrils.

Adrogans raised a hand. "Time to let Alexia know we're here."

"But how . . ."

The Jeranese general smiled. "When these dragonels speak, she'll get the message."

His hand dropped, and all along the line match cord plunged into touchholes. Fire and smoke jetted and hissed, then the main charges detonated thunderously. Tongues of flame roared from the muzzles, and their cargo of metal sped forth. All the dragonels, save the eight southernmost, had been trained on the trench. Their firing line ran at an oblique angle to it, but their fire raked it with grapeshot. Troops packed tightly in the trench simply evaporated as the metal balls blew into them.

Those at the southernmost end of the position had been aimed at the dragonel battery capping the trench. Three swept the hilltop with grapeshot, killing the crews. The other five had been loaded with eighteen-pound iron balls that smashed carriages and dented dragonels.

Though his ears rang with the thunder of the shots, Kerrigan could still hear bugles blowing on the southern side of the line and drums thundering opposite them. Agitare shouted orders for the dragonels to be reloaded as southern troops began to pour down the hillside. Aurolani dragonels shot prematurely but still skipped balls through formations, killing a few. Southern cavalry swept toward the west to exploit the gap, but a lot of Aurolani troops appeared to the east, at the base of the dam holding the Eirsena back.

Adrogans nodded solemnly. "A fine start to the day. Now we'll finish it."

Kerrigan smiled and looked up at him, intending to agree, but a wave of nausea passed over him. Before he could say a word, his knees went weak, and darkness stole his sight.

CHAPTER 75

The eruption of dragonels from the western woods shocked Alexia. The possibility that something had been hidden there had haunted her. The scouts she had sent out had run into Aurolani screening forces, all but confirming some trap lay in that direction. After all, she would have had something nasty hidden there were she in Nefrai-kesh's position, but the sheer ferocity of the attack, the number of dragonels employed, and the surprising premature commencement of it dropped her jaw.

Then she saw where the shots hit and further surprise shook her. In one quick strike, dragonels had shredded the defenders on the western edge of the fortress.

All of a sudden the play of the battle unfolded. Nefrai-kesh would have to push the troops on the east around. If he could threaten her flank, she couldn't drive troops around to the west to exploit his weakness. To prevent him from doing that, she had to plug the gap between the dam and the eastern trench. *Which leaves those troops in a position to be shot by the draconetteers on the dam and in the trench.*

But she had no choice. She glanced at Peri. "Go to Prince Erlestoke. Tell him his troops are to hold that gap. Immediately."

"Yes, sister."

Perrine took wing and landed beside the prince. He listened, then turned to a signalman. The bugler to whom he gave orders blew loudly. On Alyx's right flank, the prince's people surged forward even as Aurolani drums pounded out the orders for Tythsai's people. The draconetteers on the dam prepared to fight, and Aurolani troops filed through that gap to intercept Erlestoke's troops.

Alexia caught a black shadow out of the corner of her eye. She pointed to the dam. "Maroth, clear that dam." In an eyeblink the metal dragon vanished, but she did not see him reappear at the dam. *He'll come through. He must.*

She reined her horse to the left, then ordered a signalman to blow orders. She commanded the cavalry and heavy infantry on the left to head into that gap even as more Aurolani moved into the trench. As her troops moved, she had another bugler call on the troops in the center to shift west, which opened a gap in her line between the center and Erlestoke's formation.

That sort of opening would be fatal to her if exploited, but unless Nefrai-kesh's troops could battle past Erlestoke's army, they'd never get to it. If they did . . . *If they can do that, the battle is long since lost.*

Crow rode over, armored in dull grey mail with a green Oriosan tabard over it. "Things have changed. What's the new plan?"

Alyx's violet eyes half shut. "We shift to the west, and when Nefrai-kesh turns his dragonels to the action on the east and the west, we smash right up the center."

Crow stood in the stirrups and took another look at the battlefield. "That will take hard riding and a lot of luck."

"But it will be a surprise."

"So it will." He smiled. "When it's time to go, promise me one thing?"

"And that is?"

"In the race to kill Nefrai-kesh, you won't lag too far be-hind."

Something else moved in the smoke through which Chytrine advanced. The fleshless Panqui leaped at her, splashing her scales with his blood. He grabbed her lower jaw and pulled himself onto her muzzle, holding on tight. She shook her head, spattering the rest of them with his blood. The Panqui's claws scored a scale, then tore it away.

It clattered on the ground, and Chytrine howled. She jerked her head more violently, upward this time, which the Panqui had not expected. The bleeding creature lost his grip and flew up, then Chytrine snapped him out of the air and devoured him in a gulp.

"Lombo, no!" Sayce reached a hand out, then drew it back and sat down hard. Tears glistened on her cheeks and cut trails through the soot.

Chytrine looked down at them and started to speak, but Resolute's right hand flicked forward. The poisoned bladestar hit the corpse-white flesh beneath where the scale had been torn off. She shrieked sharply, shook her head once, then delicately raised a paw to pluck the tiny weapon free.

"I have seen these many times before. Alas, your poison has no effect on me." The dragon shook her head. "What did you think you would do when you got here? Did you think I would let you kill me? I have lived for centuries—far more time than you have known combined—and I have learned so much more than you. I am so much more pow-erful than you, too. Do you have magick there you want to employ against me, Resolute? Please, do your best."

The Vorquelf shook his head and raised Syverce. "None of us are fools."

"No? You're here. In my lair, about to die. That is fool-ishness by any reckoning."

"We believed a prophecy would come true."

"It didn't." Chytrine raised her head, stretching her long throat, and snorted flames into the Grand Hall's vaults. Then she brought her head back down, and looked along her serpentine snout at him. "Your champion is dead. To the south your army will be shattered. I will go from here to Vorquellyn, get those pieces of the Crown, collect the others, then the dragons will give me what they possess. It is over, though you did well."

Trawyn crouched beside Sayce, resting her hands on the woman's shoulders. "So you reward us by making us *sullanciri*?"

"Some of you, perhaps. Resolute will be magnificent. To have the fruit of Sayce's womb born of a *sullanciri*, that will also be spectacular. The rest of you will die."

Resolute felt his flesh crawling and pulled the point of his sword around to hover over Sayce's heart. "I can guarantee you won't get your wish."

"Silly elf, you can guarantee nothing." Chytrine raised her right paw and curled the claws through the air.

A jolt shook Resolute. All of the tattoos on his body began to glow an angry shade of red, which was something he'd not seen before. *Aurolani magick is red.* He tried to move, but found himself paralyzed. Then, much to his amazement, his right arm swung the blade away from Sayce and pressed it beneath Isaura's right breast.

"That's right, Resolute. All the magick, all the lore that went into giving you those tattoos and that power, whence do you think it came?" The dragon laughed almost warmly. "I expected you and your people for decades, and I found a way to guarantee you would not hurt me. You have been mine for ages and did not know it. Now, I think, it is time you do my bidding directly."

The instant he heard Alexia's orders, Erlestoke knew his day was likely to end shortly, although it would seem as if it had taken forever to do so. He snapped orders to his signalman, who translated them into bugle calls. Ahead of him the infantry began to move. Tightly packed and heavily armored, they clanked forward, their voices rising in song. Standards flew high and swords glittered in the morning light as men marched toward death. Beyond them, on the enemy line, draconetteers and dragonel crews busied themselves.

Erlestoke turned in his saddle. "Count Storton, I want your sprinters going straight up that eastern hill. Jullaghtse, the same goes for your people. You just have to get up there fast. They're going to be shooting at us as we come in, and they're not going to have time to shift aim. Your people are literally running for their lives."

Both of them acknowledged the orders and sped off to their troops. Erlestoke signaled the cavalry around to the east and saw that Wheatly was already bringing the irregulars up to plunge into battle after the infantry. The prince gave him a salute, then started the cavalry trotting forward. Drawing Crown, he raised it on high, then snapped it down.

Digging his heels into his horse's flanks, he started a headlong charge down the slope. Behind him came just over two regiments of horsemen almost evenly split between light and heavy troops. As they galloped forward, some of his guardsmen moved to the fore, closing ranks around him, and leveled their lances at the massed Aurolani infantry in the gap. The Aurolani clearly would have preferred to stay in place to take the charge, but the pressure from behind kept pushing them forward.

Erlestoke recognized how their precarious position benefited his troops. *At least, in theory.* Infantry that is not set in position, bristling with spears, is fodder for a cavalry charge. His people should be into and through that first battalion as if it were nothing more menacing than grass stalks.

But there were many other things to take into account, such as the dragonels that were already shooting up the middle. On his left, as his horse crested the far bank of the Eirsena, he watched a dragonel crew lever their weapon around so it could bear on his troops. Part of him wanted to protest how poorly they were working, but he held his tongue.

On the right, on the top of the dam, Aurolani sharpshooters triggered their draconettes. A horse fell, spilling his rider. Other warriors spun from the saddle, or just sagged forward. The draconetteers were not so powerful a force that they could break up his charge, but they could certainly chew on his troops.

But before he could give them any more thought, the cavalry hit the Aurolani line. He watched wide-eyed gibberers get launched high in the air, only to tumble back and flatten other comrades. His horse slammed into a *turekadine,* spinning him about like a toy, then another rider spitted him. Crown whipped down and around, slashing.

Draconettes from the trench spoke. Warriors and horses all around Erlestoke fell, peeling away his unit's left flank. Nothing and no one shielded Erlestoke from the Aurolani trench. For the barest of moments he entertained the fantasy of charging the trench and clearing his way to the base of the hill where Tythsai waited. *I can die battling the consort of the* sullanciri *that died in Oriosa.*

But that fantasy died as reality spoke in another ripple of shots from the dam. Before he had time to turn and study that situation, an unearthly shriek sounded. Up over the Aurolani trench, leaping ten and fifteen feet in the air, came an Aurolani cavalry unit. The frostclaws easily cleared the trench and drove straight at Erlestoke's troops. His horsemen wheeled to face this new threat, but none of the Aurolani wanted to engage the prince.

He wondered after that for a moment, then a grand temeryx sailed over the line. Heavier than its white cousins, the colorful temeryx carried Tythsai. She leveled her right arm at him. What appeared to be a limb of quicksilver shifted, beginning at the wrist. It thinned and lengthened, becoming almost a whipcord. The hand folded into a fist, then sprouted spikes.

Erlestoke raised his sword in a salute. He watched a crimson droplet of blood drip over the silver blade, then he flicked it away as he brought his sword down. "Come to me, Tythsai. Let me reacquaint you with death and free you from the burden it has given you."

The dragonbone armor had not erupted up through his flesh, but that did not make Kerrigan feel any better. His vision cleared, but only with the sensation of thorns being raked across his eyes. As he focused, he found himself on the *Svarskya*'s wheeldeck beside a terrified crewman. At the wheel stood a huge metal dragon.

Even before Kerrigan could decide which was more important—learning *how* he'd gotten there or *who* the dragon was—reality shifted again and it felt as if his skull had been opened with an ax. Something was doing its best to scramble his mind, but it gave up after a moment or two.

Kerrigan focused again as the ship dropped a dozen feet with a great splash. It took him a second or two to realize it, but off the starboard side he saw the battlefield. Across the hills, the dragonels in the woods spoke again with devastating effect. The southern cavalry already was reaching the riverbed on the western flank and starting the move around past the woods. Further north Adrogans' cavalry was moving out. In the middle of Alexia's line a gap had opened.

And, closer at hand . . . The *Svarskya*'s landing in the lake behind the dam had one immediately beneficial effect. The ship displaced a lot of water, which rose in a wave and swept over the dam. All the draconetteers who had been up there shooting tumbled down and into the formations of men who had been their targets.

Kerrigan hauled himself to his feet and pointed. "We can use the dragonels to shoot the Aurolani."

The metal helmsman remained silent and impassive. Below, on the dragonel deck, the crewmen Adrogans had left behind were down and twitching. *They liked traveling this way even less than I did.* Kerrigan shrugged, drew his wand, and invoked a spell.

Ten blue sparks flew from the wand's tip and hit the dragonels' touchholes in a tidy succession. The ship rolled as each weapon detonated, blasting iron balls deep into the masses of Aurolani troops. The hot metal killed some, crushed others, and maimed yet more. Up on the hill, one battery blasted back, smashing timbers and spilling one dragonel off its truck.

"At least they're not shooting my friends!" Kerrigan nodded, then looked at the helmsman. "You want to bring her about, or shall I? We've got the other side to fight, and there will be no better time than now to do it."

Chytrine's claw twitched and Syverce slid forward a hair. The tip punctured Isaura's thick coat. Another twitch and it went further, enlarging the hole. The tip had not yet met fleshy resistance, but Resolute knew it would not be long before it did. When the blade slid into Isaura it would seek her heart, penetrating her inch by inch until her life spilled out.

Resolute snarled, and the next time Chytrine flicked a talon, the blade did not move. The red heat of his tattoos slackened for a heartbeat and he was able to withdraw the blade a bit. He set himself to resist her, but when the redness flared again, it brought with it all the pain he had known when decorating his body.

"Ah, you fight me. Good, very good. I like that in a *sullanciri*. You *are* mine, Resolute, now and forever." The dragon nodded and moved her claw a bit more deliberately. Resolute's arm responded despite his best effort to hold it back. It reentered the hole and reached Isaura's flesh.

Resolute wanted to shake his head, but he couldn't do even that. Vorquelves, in adopting new names and getting themselves enchanted, had played a dangerous game. *In having this done to me, I gave her information she needed to control me.*

His arm inched forward and the blade pierced Isaura's side. The woman groaned, but even the pain was not enough to rouse her. Resolute stared at his arm as if it were not part of him, and if he could have cut it off he would have. He fought Chytrine again and gained respite, but then she gestured even more strongly and his blade cut Isaura again.

The idea that his arm was acting as if it belonged to someone else reminded him of the conversation he'd had with Kerrigan after they had discovered the Norrington. *Will was part of the Norrington, but the Norrington was more. My arm is part of me, but I am more. And I've not always been Resolute. Resolute is just part of me.*

The Vorquelf's silver eyes became slits and his lips peeled back from teeth in a snarl. He fought Chytrine as hard as he could physically, but his mind was focused in another way. *I was not always Resolute. Who was I?*

His eyes opened wide. "My name is Dunardel."

The tattoos on his flesh went dark. He whipped the sword from Isaura, then placed himself between her and Chytrine. "I am Dunardel of Vorquellyn. I am not your creature."

Chytrine snorted. "Very well. Die, Dunardel of Vorquellyn. I will resurrect Resolute and you shall reign over Vorquellyn for me."

She drew in a deep breath and Resolute brought Syverce into a guard. He knew the blade would not turn the fire, but that was how he chose to die.

Her head came forward and jaws opened, but instead of fire, all she produced was a half-choked hiss. The dragon coughed with enough force to knock Resolute down, then raised her head again. She stretched her throat and

Resolute would have gotten up to plunge his sword as deep as he could into her breast, but what he saw stopped him.

All over her ivory-and-gold scales, the ash moved. Splotches and dots, stripes and blobs, it flowed over her. The ash on his skin likewise crawled forward. The floor all but writhed as ash converged. Clumps formed and rolled across the floor to splash over her feet and belly. It covered her scales for a moment, then crept like shadow underneath them.

Resolute coughed up dark phlegm and spat it toward the dragon. *Just imagine how much ash she's inhaled.*

Chytrine's head came back down. She shook it side to side, then coughed again. "No!" Her comment came as a harsh croak. "This cannot happen." She rolled on her side and began to claw at herself, tearing the scales on her breast and belly.

Resolute stood. "Of course it can. It's been prophesied."

Skycasters that had meant to explode thunderballs over the killing ground between hill and wood had been aimed again. Their muffled *whumps* were all but lost in the cacophony of cavalry charging around through the gap, and the thunder of dragonels attempting to stem the tide of men, horses, and metal. The thunderballs overshot the steel-skinned warriors and burst among the trees. The explosions rained down hot iron shrapnel and jagged wooden splinters on the dragonel crews and those standing nearby.

Something burned in Adrogans' left arm, and the pain spiked as he spun to the ground. A shriek rose from his throat as his *yrûn* mistress used the wound as a portal. She flooded into him and with her came other awarenesses.

The sullanciri!

Adrogans struggled to his feet and found a foot-long piece of wood as thick around as his thumb poking through his left biceps and brushing against the mail on his chest. The wood firmly filled the wound so that very little blood dripped from it, but the arm no longer worked.

Adrogans snorted and thrust Pain away. "Release the cavalry. I want them up the back of that hill *now*! Captain Agitare, elevate and blast that hilltop."

Pain tore at him again as more thunderballs exploded in the trees above, but the assaults were distant—the agony inflicted on others, not on him. His awareness of the *sullanciri* grew. And there, coming down the hillside, he caught sight of the feline form. It moved like a grand black tiger, its prodigious leaps carrying it above the lances. As it landed, it batted aside spears and swords, snapping the former and bending the latter, then leaped again. With each bound it came closer, directly toward him.

Adrogans drew his sword and moved forward. Thunderballs burst overhead, scattering leaves, branches, and screaming soldiers, but Adrogans never took his eyes off the approaching *sullanciri*. She only paused once, flicking a paw out to snap the spine of a warrior whose horse she'd crushed, then she came at him in a rush. She even voiced a low, throaty growl that rose in pitch as she leaped again.

In midair her shape shifted from that of a big cat to a feline humanoid with sharp claws and a tufted tail that whipped about as she flew. Adrogans cut right, pulling himself from her line of flight, then slashed at her. His cut didn't miss, catching her below the ribs and above her right hip, but she rolled away and came up unharmed.

She snarled furiously, then leaped again, her arms outstretched. Once more Adrogans dodged and slashed, this time catching her full in the belly. He felt the impact and watched her body fold around the blade. He twisted it and yanked it free, but she landed on all fours, then spun in a crouch.

The delight on her face could not be denied. Moreover, Adrogans had felt no pain in her—and given his connection *through* Pain, he should have felt her wounds as if they were his own. He began to panic, and though he fought it down, his left arm throbbed.

Pain's laughter kissed his ears like sparks burning flesh.

She's enjoying this. We are both her creatures, and here we fight each other. She wins and wins. Then Adrogans shook his head. *I've played her games before, and I've won.*

As the feline *sullanciri* drove at him again, Adrogans shifted away from the line of her attack, but not fast enough. She caught him with a swipe of a claw on his right thigh that ripped away mail, leather trousers, and flesh beneath. The blow had enough force that Adrogans whirled away, then smashed into a small tree. He rebounded and fell to his back.

The *sullanciri* crouched again, her tail twitching as she shook her paw to rid it of the mail, then licked at the blood on her claws. Her delicate pink tongue took special care to clean her fingers, curling about each, then flicking right beneath the claws. The link they shared through Pain let Adrogans once again feel her carnal nature, and his fingers tingled as if she were licking him.

But her antics gave him a moment to clear his head. As she began to suck on a finger, confident that he could not hurt her, Adrogans struck. Using the link he pumped the agony of his wounds right back into her. As he did so, she shrieked and blood began to drip from her left arm and right thigh.

Adrogans laughed. "That's right. We are linked—and as long as we are linked, what happens to me happens to you." He looked up, hoping against hope that a thunderball might, even at that moment, be falling from the sky to land on him before it exploded.

The only thing descending toward him, however, was the bleeding *sullanciri*. She sprang from her crouch and rose high in the air. The claws on her rear paws extended. Her toes reached for him. She'd land on his chest, sinking claws into his midsection, then her forepaws would slash through his body. She doubtlessly imagined that if he were dead, the link would be broken.

Could be she's right.

The *sullanciri* came down, tail snaking through the air, eyes blazing. Then she stopped. She just *stopped*. She hung there, a dozen feet above him, unmoving and barely breathing, her attempted snarl reduced to a squeaked mew.

"Finish her, nephew." Phfas stood off to the right, his trembling hand extended. Bound to air, he had used his *yrûn* to catch and hold her. As the perspiration pouring down his body made apparent, he couldn't hold her forever. "Do it *now*."

Adrogans closed his eyes and sank into himself. He found his mistress and grabbed her by the hair, forcing her down onto hands and knees. He mounted her like a horse and she shifted her shape to accommodate him. Kicking her in the ribs, yanking her mane left and right, he directed her out into the battlefield. Together they rode over it and through it, experiencing pain as song, then passing it back through into the *sullanciri*.

Horses torn in half, with both parts thrashing, established the melody of his deathsong. Men shrieking as life pumped in spurts through severed limbs added the high notes, while disemboweled gibberers clutching cooling entrails provided more somber base tones. The quick, sharp pain of shrapnel piercing victims provided tempo, while the snap of limbs and crushing blows of sword and mace gave the music its percussive quality.

Discordant and hideous, full of sharps and flats, shifting key and beat, with no overture and no true rhythm, the deathsong Adrogans wove and forced into the *sullanciri* did not lack for power. It moved through him like a diet of thistle, bramble, and iron scrap, then flowed into his suspended enemy. Even the notes of agony he caught in her mews he fed back into her. Only when she grew silent and he could no longer feel her did he open his eyes.

He almost wished he had not.

Had he not known what she had been, he never could have identified her. Blood matted the sleek black pelt, which now hung in ribbons from her body. He could see many of her bones, for most poked through her flesh. All had been broken, some sharply, and some twisted around until the bone had fragmented. Various organs dangled and intestines descended in a white, ropy curtain.

Phfas released her and she puddled to the ground, splashing Adrogans with noxious fluid that itched and burned.

The general pulled himself away, then gingerly rose to his feet. He leaned heavily on the tree he'd slammed into previously, and found his grip not quite as strong as he would have liked.

Phfas crossed to him and began to wrap the wound in his leg. "This is more than a scratch."

"I've noticed." Adrogans smiled. "Thank you for saving me, Uncle."

"You saved me. It was fair."

"I did? How so?"

Phfas smiled. "I made her angry. If you hadn't killed her, she would have killed us."

"So we are even?"

The little man cackled and Adrogans accepted that answer on all its various levels.

Chytrine coughed again and an ebon fluid began to ooze from her mouth. It looked like black saliva and Resolute expected it to drip to the floor. One tendril of it did reach toward the ground for about a foot, then retracted. All of it flowed back into her mouth and she gurgled. Her chest contracted and she tried to cough, but only produced a thick, wet sound that was a prelude to rales as she inhaled.

Her body jerked again, her stomach tightening as if she were attempting to vomit. But nothing came out, and as her chest contracted again, Resolute noticed that something spiky seemed to be pushing against her skin. The projection appeared at the base of her breastbone, and Resolute could not shake the impression that it was shaped like a foot.

The colors in the dragon's eyes swirled faster and faster, though the blues and greens no longer appeared in distinct patterns, but melded and merged. One hue would predominate for a moment, then the other, as if thin clouds were cloaking the sky. Chytrine still tore at her stomach and chest with her claws. Then there was a distinct snapping sound, and her whole body shook. A twitch of her tail pulverized a chunk of the floor.

Another snap sounded and another—a bit muffled, but growing more distinct. The dragon thrashed more, then a scale on her chest popped out. Another protuberance forced more scales loose. Then, with the loudest crack of all, the curve of her breastbone took on a distinctly angular shape.

Scales flew and her pale flesh parted around a milk-white gemstone the size of a melon, shaped very much like an egg. A small hand—grey but distinct, with five fingers detailed down to the nails—shoved it from her breast. The opening widened as another hand tore at it, then in a gush of blackened mucus a small, nimble figure emerged in a somersault and stood dripping.

"Will!"

Sayce's shout fell deafly on stone ears. The Norrington spun and held the stone up for Chytrine's inspection. Her eyes widened and the flow of colors slowed as his fingers grew up and around the stone like ivy on a tree trunk. The Norrington held the stone higher and Chytrine screamed. Popping and snapping sounds presaged the appearance of cracks, then the Norrington tightened his grip, and Chytrine's Truestone exploded into a spray of scintillating fragments.

* * *

Erlestoke reached across his saddle and drew the quadnel with his left hand as Tythsai began to whirl her flail. She looked at him with blank eyes, as if to invite a shot, but he shook his head. His heels dug into his horse's flanks and it leaped forward, charging toward the *sullanciri's* mount. He set up to pass her to the left but, at the last second, swerved his horse directly into her path.

As grand as the temeryx she rode was, compared to a horse in armor it was a minor obstacle. Erlestoke's mount smashed it with a shoulder. Bones cracked and the impact knocked the temeryx sideways. Tythsai's flail whipped around, but passed above Erlestoke's head as she fell back in the saddle.

It didn't pass above his raised quadnel, however. The flail's leash wrapped tight around the weapon and Tythsai yanked at it. Whether to free her hand or tear the weapon from his grasp, Erlestoke didn't know, nor did he care. Her efforts merely brought the draconette in line with her body and when the muzzle was aimed at her chest, he pulled the trigger.

As with Anarus, the ball of metal wasn't enough to kill a *sullanciri*, but it did blast Tythsai from the saddle. Erlestoke retained his grip on the quadnel, then brought Crown around and down. The enchanted blade severed the quicksilver leash. The piece encircling the quadnel started to drip to the ground and flow toward the *sullanciri.* Given a minute or so, it would return to Tythsai and she would be rearmed.

Erlestoke didn't give her that time. He turned his horse and slashed, catching the *sullanciri* on the back, beneath her right shoulder blade. Crown ripped through her, spinning her around. Tythsai bounced off another horse but didn't go down.

With a snap of his wrist, Erlestoke slashed once more and harvested her head. The stitching keeping it in place parted and it popped into the air, spinning swiftly. As it did so, the flesh tightened and aged, splitting over the bones, then flying away as wispy fragments, like burned parchment. The skull smashed to the ground, staining the earth with ivory powder.

Dragonels blasted to the west and east. As the Saporician Crown Lancers raced around the western trench and thunderballs exploded in the woods, Alexia watched a new cavalry force enter the field. At that distance it took her a moment or two to recognize the crest. "Crow, those are the Alcidese Horse Guards. That's Caro leading them."

Crow smiled. "So that's Adrogans down there. Not only does he have dragonels, but his people can shoot them. But look at their horses."

She nodded. Even as the feline *sullanciri* bounded down toward the forest, the Alcidese Horse Guards pounded forward on huge steeds that flew faster than any she'd seen before. Behind them came the Jeranese Horse Guards, the Valician White Mane, and the Savarese Knights. They moved with alacrity and made for the northern side of the fortress. Even though a dragonel battery there could cover their approach, they came with such speed that Alexia doubted the Aurolani could get off more than one volley before the cavalry was among them.

On the left and right wings, the infantry poured forward. The ship that had appeared on the lake cut loose with a second volley that smashed into the masses of Aurolani troops. Already to the rear of that formation, some units began to pull back.

A figure near Nefrai-kesh stepped away from him. In a shimmer of golden light, that person vanished and a dragon appeared. Black with green wing membranes and belly scales, he raised his head, shrieked, then took to the air. He looped north and around to the east. A quick blast of fire turned some of the Aurolani troops and prompted others to push forward. The dragon pumped his wings and made one pass over the ship, dipping a wing lazily to come back around.

Before Alexia could issue an order, Arimtara sprinted along the hilltop and leaped from the steepest point. As she flung her arms wide, they became wings. Her body grew in an eyeblink. She swooped low over Erlestoke's army, then came up swiftly. Only as she closed with the Aurolani dragon did it become apparent how small the enemy dragon truly was.

Arimtara let loose a blast of red-gold fire that caught the black dragon right between the wings. That blasted him sideways through the air until his wingtip began to drag. He tried to right himself, but his tail struck the water. Unable to pull up, he landed with a big splash and she circled overhead, chattering in a sibilant tongue that conveyed more in tone alone than many human orators could muster with an overabundance of words.

Alexia looked at Crow. "Now, beloved. Now is the time." She signaled a bugler and the center of her army pushed forward. Gyrkyme made runs at the central dragonel batteries. They hurled firecocks, which, for the most part, exploded harmlessly before or on top of the roofs over the batteries. One did swoop low and come in on a level flight. He pulled up at the last moment, releasing the firecock in a flat trajectory that exploded on the edge of the battery. As he came up, a half-dozen arrows brought him down, but a second, far more violent explosion shook the battery. The expanding fireball touched off several other explosions— shredding the roof, blowing gibberers high into the air, and sending one flaming dragonel careening down the slope toward Alexia's oncoming troops.

Her infantry came on as quickly as they could, but Alexia, Crow, and the Alcidese Iron Horse used the gap to swing around them. Reaching a full gallop, they sped through the riverbed and up the slope. They drifted toward the west, using the fire and smoke to screen them from the intact battery, then rode through the gap the explosion had torn in the Aurolani defenses.

The heavy cavalry burst through the lines. The explosion had stunned many, terrified others, and left no one in their fixed positions. With Heart, Alexia slashed and chopped her way through a milling throng of gibberers. The *turekadine* were doing their best to organize defenses, but too much was happening at once. To the east and west the *sullanciri* in command had left their posts. The cavalry coming in from the north had demanded attention and a diversion of troops, all of whom had been caught on the hilltop when the battery blew up. Though the *turekadine* shouted orders, Alexia doubted many of those who had been close to the explosion could hear them, much less have the presence of mind to follow the commands.

The scattered Aurolani infantry fell swiftly. It occurred to her that bards might suggest they were ripe wheat before scythes, but that analogy was simply too pristine. Wheat stalks did not scream when an arm hung by a ligament. They did not bleed or whimper and they certainly couldn't leap at a warrior, drag him down, and bite his throat out. That would ever be the way of it, though—that bards would sanely describe the utter insanity of war.

At the center of the plain, in a circle oddly devoid of bodies, Nefrai-kesh waited with sword drawn. Burning fragments of the dragonel battery surrounded him like the votive candles in an Alcidese ancestor shrine. Neither their guttering flames nor the day's light could penetrate the shadow of his mask nor, oddly enough, did he cast a shadow.

Alexia saw riders directing their mounts at him. Lances were leveled, spurs drew blood, but for twenty feet around the *sullanciri*, nothing could pass. Horses, foam-flecked and wide-eyed, shied away. Gibberers, even those fleeing mindlessly, skirted him. Men who had lost their mounts would reach the perimeter of his domain, then double over, as if stuck in the guts with the black sword he rested his weight on.

She reined her horse around and drove at the invisible barrier. As she drew close, something curdled in her stomach and her hands began to shake. Her horse fought her and tried to shy. Alyx dug her heels into the beast's flanks, trying to urge it on, but a sour taste rose in her mouth. The *sullanciri's* image grew huge, dark and terrible, oozing corruption. She jerked the reins to the right, moving out of the way, catching a flash of Crow as he bore on.

Nefrai-kesh's head came up, his eyes white in a black face. Crow rode within the circle and sprang from the saddle. His mount leaped away as if off hot coals. Alexia's lover raised Alarien in a salute, then brought it down. "What you asked before, I do today."

"Pity your hand was stayed then. Had you struck, neither you nor they would have died here today."

Crow shook his head. "You know that's not true. The guilt for what happened here, and in Okrannel, and everywhere else, is not mine. It belongs to you and your mistress."

The *sullanciri* nodded, then brought his sword up in a salute. "Pity our sword master is not here to watch us."

"Did you think so little of him that you would wish upon him the pain of watching us kill one another?"

Nefrai-kesh hesitated. "The man I once was understands that question. The creature I am now is beyond that."

The two men closed and Alexia saw similarities in how they moved. She could have ascribed it to them having been trained by the same swordsman, but she knew it was more. The jawline, the eyes, the length of their limbs—they were not identical by any means, but close enough that blood kinship was inescapable. Each moved with the same grim economy and the energy gathered for decades in preparation for this encounter.

Swords flashed. The silver of Alarien countered the

black of the *sullanciri*'s blade with a ringing crash. Crow caught and turned a cut at his head, then lunged. Nefrai-kesh pulled his left shoulder out of line, avoiding Alarien's point, then snapped his wrist and brought his blade down in a low slash.

Crow leaped above the slash, then kicked out with his right foot. He smashed Nefrai-kesh in the chest, driving the *sullanciri* back two steps. The shadow on his chest devoured the dusty boot print. Crow landed, dropping into a crouch to let another slash pass over his head, then came up and lunged again. Nefrai-kesh parried that lunge wide, then slammed his blade's pommel against Crow's forehead.

Crow spun away, bleeding from a cut over his left eye. He raised his left hand, probed the wound, and smeared the blood down over his cheek. Then readjusting his helmet, he came in again at his brother. The two of them struck, parried, riposted, and parted so quickly Alexia could only read their bodies, not follow their blurred blades. Crow moved strongly and deliberately, coiling then striking. Nefrai-kesh held back more, flowing as if he were shadow, letting the attacks come, shifting so they narrowly missed, then launching his own attacks. Those Crow beat back strongly, buying himself time to riposte, but the *sullanciri* always managed to evade him.

Then Alexia saw it. Nefrai-kesh lunged and Crow leaned away from the blow. With both hands wrapped around Alarien's hilt, he brought the silver sword around and down, catching the *sullanciri* across the right forearm. He carved away a piece of the cloak and split the sleeve. It should have amputated the limb cleanly, but somehow Nefrai-kesh kept his grip on his sword, and his arm connected to the wrist.

His left hand came up and around in an open-handed slap that caught Crow over the ear, spinning him one way and launching his helmet another. Crow went to one knee, then turned fast in a cloud of dust, knocking a level slash high. His return cut snapped his blade through the *sullanciri*'s right hip. A portion of Nefrai-kesh's belt flew free, his scabbard dropping clear of the other hip, but Chytrine's creature showed no sign of injury as he backed away, kicking the sword belt from beneath his feet.

Crow stood and swiped at more blood. "It's not possible."

The king of the *sullanciri* laughed low and coldly. "No? Temmer destroyed her other Dark Lancers. Why would she not proof us against it?"

"But if she could do that, why not proof you against *all* magickal weapons?"

Nefrai-kesh shrugged. "She is powerful, not omnipotent. The gifts she gives are the gifts we desire. Certain invulnerability was what I desired, and what I have. I regret this means I will be your death."

Crow spat. "You regret nothing of the kind."

"So true."

Nefrai-kesh flew at him, slashing high and low, lunging swiftly, his cloak a swirl of shadow. The *sullanciri* attacked without fear of injury and Crow was hard-pressed to turn the attacks. He blocked and parried, but could do nothing beyond that. Even if he were able to disarm the *sullanciri,* what then? His sword could not kill him. Might Nefrai-kesh's blade do the job?

Crow fought with the valor of a thousand heroes. He parried cuts low, driving Nefrai-kesh's black blade into the ground, then kicking out to knock him back. The very fact that Crow could touch him and affect him gave Alexia hope, but she knew the elbows and kicks with which Crow hit the *sullanciri* were doing no serious damage. The *sullanciri* as a lot had been incredibly resilient, so chances were that even if the blows did hurt, he healed quickly from them.

Her mind raced. If Nefrai-kesh could not be hurt by magickal weapons, perhaps the opposite was true, that mundane weapons might affect him. But while the physical attacks Crow made against him with hand, elbow, and foot would seem to support that idea, she rejected it. Being vulnerable to normal things would have made Nefrai-kesh useless, not to mention *dead* long ago. It had to be something else that allowed Crow to hurt him. But what? Their blood, or something else?

Nefrai-kesh backhanded a slash at Crow's head. The white-haired man half ducked, half spun away from the blow. The black blade carved through the mail on his shoulder, taking away slices of jerkin, flesh, and muscle. It traveled on, twisting, and slapped almost sideways into the right side of Crow's head. It clipped the top of his ear off and opened his scalp with enough force to lift him from his feet.

He completed his spin and smashed down hard on his back. Crow shook his head to clear it, spraying blood from the scalp wound, then started back up at his brother. Nefrai-kesh loomed over him, his sword poised to plunge down through Crow's chest.

The *sullanciri* slowly shook his head. "I thought you, of all people, knew me well enough to slay me."

"I do." Crow's left hand tightened around a burning bit of debris. "I remember. A Phoenix Knight has to be burned."

Lunging up, he thrust the jagged piece of wood into Nefrai-kesh's stomach. The *sullanciri* jerked back, flinging the sword away. He looked down at the fiery stick in his guts. For a heartbeat the flames illuminated the surprise on his face, then his expression shifted. It became serene.

His eyes closed and Nefrai-kesh became an inferno.

Crow rolled away, then whatever had maintained the perimeter around them collapsed. Alexia spurred her horse forward, reached down, and, taking Crow's arm, swung him into the saddle behind her. Her horse leaped away from the burning figure a heartbeat before it exploded.

The Alcidese Iron Horse rallied around them, but the Aurolani were already fleeing. General Caro and Adrogans' cavalry had swept up the hill from the north, slaughtering the resistance there, and had already turned their attention to the eastern hilltop. Beyond it, Aurolani troops had begun to flee north, past the pyres that the dragon had made of earlier deserters.

Crow clung to Alexia from behind. "I think it is over, beloved."

"If not yet, Crow, then soon. Very soon." Alexia raised Heart and pointed it east. "With me, armies of the south. We have more work to do."

The Norrington stood in a circle of gemstone shards. He lowered his hands to his sides stiffly, as he had done when he was larger. His eyes remained glowing spots in his face, but at least he had a face. When he looked up, he smiled. Not fully, the way Will had done, but he smiled nonetheless.

Sayce ran to him and hugged him tightly. The Norrington's expression betrayed no surprise, but his arms were slow to come up and enfold her. Resolute actually read no reluctance to do so in his action, but just a fear of hurting so delicate a creature as a human. His arms and hands became as smooth as river stone as he rubbed her back.

Sayce pulled away, tears staining her face and his chest. "I know you're not the Will I love, but I want you to know that our child will never want for love or peace or wonder what sort of man her father was. You will come with us, live in Muroso, be with us."

Resolute stepped up and rested his hands on her shoulders. "Princess, I believe you are thinking much too far ahead."

She looked up at him. "What are you talking about? Do you think I care what people will say about whom I choose to be my consort?"

The Vorquelf shook his head. "No, Highness, I do not. It's just that we're in Chytrine's stronghold, and we've just killed her. In about as much time as it will take for us to walk back to the entrance, the magickers from the Conservatory will be there—unless they chose to wait for the troops we saw on the edge of the valley. And there is no telling how many other creatures lurk here that aren't going to be pleasantly disposed toward us."

Isaura nodded as she sat up. "Resolute is right. She once told me that even if she were to die, she had forces in place to make sure her goals were accomplished."

Trawyn frowned. "Let's hope Alexia has been able to deal with them."

"I don't think it was her armies to which she referred."

Resolute held his hands up. "Debating her meaning comes later. We need to leave. How do we do that, Isaura?"

She shook her head. "Through the caves, perhaps, but they are home to the gibberers. That, or back the way we came."

Trawyn turned toward the Grand Hall's entrance. "We have visitors."

Resolute sighed. "We have to get out of here. Lead us."

Isaura nodded and stood, then directed them to the room's back corner. She touched a piece of stonework and a small passage opened. They entered and started up a set of stairs that curved around and around. They kept going up until she opened another passage, then entered a large hall that, at the far end, had windows and doors that overlooked the valley.

She touched two other stones beside the door. One closed it. "This other stone activates wards that will keep us safe for a while." She marched across the room and led them to the doors, which she threw open, waving them out onto the balcony.

Resolute came first and his heart sank. A dark line of gibberers snaked across the white snowfields. "A couple of regiments. Your mother must have recalled them from the pass when Ferxigo died."

Trawyn stepped up beside him and looked down at the

throng. "As good as you are, Resolute, you're not going to be able to carve us free of this place."

"I know." He half smiled. "Despite your predilections, I bet you would enjoy seeing a wing of Gyrkyme in the skies right now, coming to carry us away."

Sayce snorted. "Doesn't have to be Gyrkyme. I'd settle for eagles."

"I'd settle for crows." Trawyn smiled, but it died quickly. "How do you think the war in the south is going?"

"Well enough, I hope." Resolute broadened his smile. "Now, were Crow here, we *could* fight our way free."

"I'm sure that's true." Sayce rubbed her hands over her belly. "They'll know in the south that we succeeded, won't they?"

"I think so." The Vorquelf looked at Isaura. "Do you know where your mother kept her fragments of the DragonCrown?"

"In this room. I can get them."

He shook his head. "Just work some nasty spells on the hiding place so your mother's subjects don't make away with them."

"I will."

Before Isaura could move, a dark shape swept past the fortress' top. Broad wings spread and a black dragon sailed down. His head thrust toward the ground, then a golden light silhouetted him. As his right wing dipped and he came back around toward the fortress, a column of steam rose from a boiling lake in which gibberers floated in black lumps. All around it gibberers broke and ran.

The dragon landed on a small tower and furled his wings. "You are Resolute. You were at Vael with this little Spritha." His voice came higher and tighter than Resolute remembered, but the dragon had spoken his own tongue on Vael, with translation accomplished through magick.

"And you are Vriisuroel. You destroyed Aurolani waiting to ambush us on the way here."

The dragon's eyes half lidded. "Even I can get bored as events unfold."

"What prevents you from being bored right now?"

Vriisuroel's lower jaw gaped for a moment. Spittle flowed and burned down the tower's black stone. "I wish to see if you will strike a bargain. The fragments here for your safe conduct south."

Trawyn frowned. "If you know the fragments are here, why not just take the tower down and sift the debris?"

"Would Trawyn of Loquellyn wish reconsideration of my part of the bargain?"

Resolute laid a hand on her shoulder. "We'll accept, with one caveat. You will take us south to Princess Alexia and her army, and you will aid me in one other task."

"And that would be?"

Resolute shook his head. "Wondering about it will prevent you from being bored."

Vriisuroel raised his head and snorted, sending twin jets of flame into the frigid air. "Very well. Provide the Truestones, make a riding harness, and away south will you go."

EPILOGUE

ORIOSA

King Scrainwood peered out the window of his throne room and watched the people dancing in the streets. Torches and lanterns burned brightly in the night, and bonfires blazed at crossroads despite the early summer's heat. Gyrkyme had brought the news of Chytrine's defeat within a day of its happening, and the celebrations had continued for the half week since.

Scrainwood had known instantly when she died. She had made him one of her *sullanciri*, but he had not known what power she'd given him. Upon her death it manifested. Thoughts and images, rushes of power, filled him so swiftly that he literally fainted and had spent two days in bed. He had even raved feverishly, but those attending him put it down to his fear of Erlestoke's return rather than any fundamental transformation on his part.

While he lay in the throes of these changes, Scrainwood did what he did best: he schemed. Part of the knowledge he'd been given was of Chytrine's life—literally, her life flashed before his eyes as she died. He did his best to ignore all the forces that shaped her, for he found those boring. But the Oromise fascinated him, and he expected them to reach him somehow. He even contemplated a trip north to finish what Chytrine had started, but not quite yet.

She, it seemed, had failed in her quest because of her failure to recognize when she was at her best. Her disguise as Tatyana of Okrannel had been brilliant and did more to sow discord and chaos in the south than any military action she undertook. Had she remained in the shadows, she could have sundered the south and conquered them at her leisure.

He would not repeat her mistake, and had an advantage in that he already dwelt in the shadows. No one knew he was a *sullanciri*, so they would not fear him on those grounds. In fact, given that his nation had proved itself in defeating Chytrine, he would be courted by many. While Erlestoke might be a bother, Scrainwood knew he did not really want to govern Oriosa. *If I give my support to others, they will support my suggestion that Erlestoke become the new Draconis baron.*

Scrainwood smiled. The moment he'd recovered from his transformation, he'd used *arcanslata* to propose that the crowns who had so recently met at Narriz come to Meredo for another conference that would decide the fate of the world after Chytrine. He pointed out that the problem of the DragonCrown would have to be solved once and for all, as well as the political situations in Sebcia, Noriva, and Muroso. Either those nations would be rebuilt or partitioned, and meeting to divide the spoils was something no one would avoid.

And once I have them here... He idly twisted the ring he wore and sensed no hostility toward him beyond a few malcontents somewhere in the city. With the powers Chytrine had given him, he could have reached out and found them easily. Depending on their strength of will and the distance, he could even have influenced their thoughts to the point of having them kill themselves.

That, however, was too trivial a use for his power. Once he had the crowns together, then he could manipulate them into hating each other. Little wars would blossom all through the land. Played correctly one against another, the nations would be weakened to the point where he could establish an empire. *Once I do that, the decision to release the Oromise will be mine. They will find I bargain far harder than Chytrine ever did.*

He turned from the window and caught a flash of motion from the shadows across the room. Something whirred through the air, then the bladestar hit him square in the chest. One of the blades cracked his breastbone and drove into his heart. The metal tore tissue and the poison on the weapon began to spread throughout his body. He could feel it burning through his arteries. They weakened, and blood began to leak through them.

Scrainwood absently calculated that if he were mortal he would have been dead before he could pull the weapon free. Even as he tugged at it, his lip curled in a snarl at the figure emerging from the shadows. "You know this can't hurt me."

Resolute shrugged. "It wasn't meant to. It was meant to get your attention. Now that I have it, I'll kill you."

Scrainwood snorted. "You're bluffing. You want something. The red fragment, is that it?"

The Vorquelf drew his sword. "No, that I can find, thanks to Kerrigan, and I have a dragon to fly me there as he did here. Likewise, thanks to Kerrigan, you think I'm bluffing because that ring isn't telling you I'm hostile."

Scrainwood glanced at the ring as he yanked the weapon from his chest. Blood spurted, splashing over the ring, then the wound began to close. "This isn't possible."

"It is. The Vilwanese fixed the ring so it wouldn't recognize me." He lunged and Syverce stabbed through the bloodstained rent in Scrainwood's jerkin. The king backed away, trying to slide off the blade, but Resolute stayed with him and kept the blade buried as Scrainwood fell to the ground.

Resolute loomed over him. "It's not just murder. Chytrine told her daughter that things were in place to continue her reign after her death. You were the best choice." He shrugged and twisted the sword's blade. "Not that I wouldn't have killed you anyway, but now I won't feel bad about enjoying it."

Scrainwood opened his mouth, but blood instead of words poured forth.

The Vorquelf shook his head. "I'll choose to assume your last words concerned not yourself but your heir. I'll not leave your body here to be discovered. You'll just vanish. Only you and I will know what happened. If you think your people are happy now, just imagine how joyously they will greet King Erlestoke."

VILWAN

Kerrigan Reese's arrival at Vilwan on the back of Vriisuroel seemed to surprise everyone save for the Grand Magister. By the time he and Rymramoch had dismounted in the courtyard before the Grand Magister's alabaster tower, two purple-robed Adepts Kerrigan had never seen before arrived and conducted the pair into the tower. They offered refreshment and bid them wait in an antechamber to the Council of Magisters.

As the two of them departed, Kerrigan smiled and glanced at his dragon mentor. "What would Resolute do?"

Rymramoch laughed and flicked a gloved hand toward the chamber's massive bronze doors. They rippled and snapped like diaphanous drapes in a gale, then froze in that position, all twisted and wrapped halfway around the chamber columns nearest the door.

Kerrigan strode into the room and glanced around at

the men and women gathered there. The circular chamber's domed ceiling was upheld by twelve columns—one for each of the twelve divisions of the floor. Each of the eight magickal disciplines had its own section of the floor, from Combat to Conjuration, with two for the Grand Magister himself, and one each for the Magisters of Personnel and Suppression. None of them looked pleased to see him, though neither the Magister of Combat nor the Grand Magister let their discomfort register on their faces for more than a heartbeat.

The wizened old man who was the Grand Magister raised his open hands above his stooped shoulders. "We welcome your return to Vilwan, Adept Reese. Your efforts on our behalf have been noted and praised. We are inordinately proud of you."

Kerrigan raked fingers back through his hair. "I'd ask you to forgive me for what I'm about to say, but I really don't care if you do or not. I've come from Oriosa. I did some investigating. I know about the Bloodmasks."

The Magister of Suppression, a corpulent woman with grey hair, cleared her throat. "The Bloodmasks were not authorized by anyone here. That was Magister Tadurienne's doing entirely. Once we learned of what she had done, she was returned here, tried, and sanctioned. She is dead."

"Slain for her failure, no doubt, not her effort." Kerrigan shook his head. "When I left here I might have been naive enough to believe you, but now I know better. A company of warmages doesn't just wander off and commit murder and mayhem without someone here knowing about it. And the crowns, as they gather in Meredo, will hear about it. They will know Vilwan has dabbled in politics and allied itself with one of Chytrine's *sullanciri*."

Suppression raised her hand. "Do not be hasty, Adept Reese. We have dealt with this matter. There is no need for you to share your insights with the crowns."

Kerrigan shook his head. "You're not listening to me. I don't have to share it. Erlestoke already knows. The

Addermages figured it out for themselves. They know and the crowns will know."

The Grand Magister chuckled lightly. "But we will explain to them what they know, Kerrigan. Unbeknownst to us, Tadurienne had become a servant of Chytrine. She had a history with Heslin."

"Neskartu." The young mage nodded. "A mage you put in service to the Norringtons because you knew they were special even before the prophecy, yes? Someone saw something and you acted to control the Norrington bloodline?"

"We sought to safeguard it."

Kerrigan's eyes narrowed as a couple of facts connected themselves in his mind. "No, 'control' is the right word. I've talked with Crow. I know the truth of Kenwick Norrington's bloodline. You prevented his father from being able to produce children, didn't you? You sterilized him. And why? Because you saw far enough in advance to know that, if there was a Norrington, this day would come."

The Magister of Clairvoyance shook his head. "And what day is that?"

"The day that changes Vilwan forever."

The Magister of Conjuration snarled. "I told you twenty years ago that breeding our own hero to make the Norrington superfluous would not stave off disaster."

"Disaster for whom?" Kerrigan pointed to the east. "You are fools, all of you. Centuries ago, after Kirûn's reign of terror made you fear for Vilwan's future, you agreed to hobble yourselves so you could continue your monopoly on power. Through the centuries, however, you resented what you had done. You have no idea what you have lost, and when the time came that you needed it again, you didn't seek to educate everyone; you took people and fashioned us into weapons. Why? Because we would be easy to control, whereas knowledge is not.

"I am not a puppet. You do not control me, nor do you control your own fate."

The Grand Magister's face darkened. "No? Who does? You?"

"If you force me to it, yes."

Suppression laughed. "To what end would you control Vilwan, Reese? Do you believe that as Grand Magister you will be given a voice at Meredo? Do you think the crowns will let you pull together all the pieces of the DragonCrown so you can unmake it?"

"Yes, that's one thing. They will let me do that."

She shook her head slowly. "I tell you this with no animus, but they will never agree to it. None of them will trust you because, no matter how much they owe you for Chytrine's defeat, they fear, Kerrigan Reese. They *fear* what will happen in the moment you don that Crown so you can take it apart again. You are the most powerful mage in the world, perhaps the equal of Kirûn. They cannot chance that with the Crown in your power you will not control all dragons and lay waste to the world."

Kerrigan's green eyes narrowed. "And do you know why that is?"

Suppression shrugged. "You'll tell me."

"It's because you hold all the power. You set yourselves up to be the equal of the crowns, so they see you—us, *me*—as their rivals, not their partners and helpers. I hope, for the sake of the world, your prediction will not come true."

Clairvoyance smiled. "It will."

"Then I have even more work to do here. Vilwan is going to change, from top to bottom. We will teach everyone all we can. We will teach them all disciplines and *styles* of magick."

Combat, bare-chested, with his hands clasped at the small of his back, raised an eyebrow. "Styles?"

"We will incorporate bits of various traditions. Elven, urZrethi, Murosan, Zhusk, and even hydromancy."

"Hydromancy?"

"Yes, Grand Magister. We have a cadre of wizards who

have been trained in Tagothcha's realm. We will even explore the methods Neskartu used in his Conservatory."

The Grand Magister shook his head. "No, none of that is possible. The crowns would not allow it, though they matter not. You will be stopped, here and now, for you will destroy magick."

Kerrigan snorted. "I will destroy your grip on power. You can't stop me."

The Grand Magister laughed harshly and his eyes burned with an arcane purple light. "Neither you nor this puppet behind you has enough power to defy us."

Kerrigan glanced again at Rymramoch. "You were right. Stopping at Vael en route was a good idea. In this situation, what would Resolute do?"

Rymramoch nodded once, then his body expanded. He grew to ten feet in height, with spikes bristling up through his robe. Claws shredded his gloves and his mask fell away to reveal a scarlet-scaled face with glowing eyes. Smoke drifted from his slit nostrils, and ivory fangs flashed as he spoke. "I believe, Kerrigan Reese, he would proceed with a graphic demonstration of where they have overestimated their power."

"Right." Kerrigan curled his hands down into fists and felt power gather in them. "Minimize the damage to the real estate. It, unlike the people here, may be useful in the future."

VORQUELLYN

Alexia, Queen of Okrannel, stood proudly among her peers. The blue gown she had donned had been trimmed hem, cuff, and neckline with black ribbon in mourning for her grandfather. He'd passed away in his sleep the very day she had defeated the Aurolani forces. Crow, Perrine, and Preyknosery knew she also wore the ribbon for her father, to honor the man who should have had the throne she now claimed.

The day could not have been more beautiful, with the summer sun shining brightly in a cloudless sky. Rumors had abounded that vast sums had been given to Tagothcha to keep the ocean calm and the day bright, but she knew the truth of it. She'd seen King Erlestoke wade into the Saslynnae bay and speak with his mother, asking her to make sure the day would be perfect.

For her part, Alexia could not have been happier, both to be on Vorquellyn and well away from Meredo. The crowns—in person or later through envoys—had discussed and argued for two months over topics trivial and substantial. There seemed to be little differentiation between the two classes of items, since both were argued with equal passion and length. For the most part the trivial decisions were made with minimal pain, but not so the substantial ones.

The first and key battle had concerned the fate of Muroso and the other nations that had been overrun by the Aurolani forces. After Nefrai-kesh's defeat, Markus Adrogans had taken command of the army, freeing the crowns to head south to Meredo. He had cleared the Aurolani from Sebcia and chased them north to Aurolan. He stationed a force at the gap, then returned to the ruins of Fortress Draconis and established it as his new headquarters.

Muroso lay in ruins and a number of nations wanted to make it and Sebcia into an international zone, akin to Fortress Draconis, so if another force in the north arose, they would all be prepared to defeat it. That was the pretense, in any event, under which discussions began. In truth—and everyone knew it—the various nations wanted to colonize the two nations and reap the economic benefits of trade.

Erlestoke engineered a solution that preserved Murosan independence. He married his younger brother to Queen Sayce and pledged his nation's army to defend his sister nation to the north. Moreover, it was made known that he had influence with Tagothcha, and that any shipping going into or out of colonies would not make it home. The crowns, therefore, applauded the rebirth of Muroso.

Alexia glanced further down the reviewing stand, where Sayce and Linchmere stood together. They certainly made an odd couple, but a perfect one for what Muroso needed. Sayce had the fiery nature that made people see her as a leader. The story of her capture, escape from Aurolan, and return with the Norrington to kill Chytrine had already spawned several cycles of songs that guaranteed her immortality. And Linchmere had grown in confidence, especially since his arm had been replaced. With the Freemen, he had displayed a talent for resource acquisition and distribution that was vital for rebuilding a nation. He retained Rounce Playfair as an economic advisor, putting the merchant's considerable trade experience and resources at his service.

Sebcia would likewise be rebuilt. Among the refugees there had been found someone distantly related to the old royal family, so that person was established as the ruler. Veterans of the war were given land grants in Sebcia to repay them for their service and many moved their families there. General Pandiculia of Salnia remembered her king having exiled her for defying him, so she chose to move to Sebcia. She became Regent for the ruler and the rebuilding of Sebcia began—starting with the destruction of the dam that kept the Eirsena captive.

Items that might have seemed more trivial were also argued at length. The nature of Nefrai-kesh's involvement with Chytrine's downfall became a point of interest because it was suggested that he truly was the Norrington who was Chytrine's undoing. The loss of Okrannel, the less than effective campaign defending Muroso and, ultimately, his inability to kill a Hawkins were all pointed to as reasons to assume he had slipped his leash and was working against his mistress. This concept comforted some of those whose countrymen and -women had become *sullanciri*.

Alexia found herself unable to make a decision on the point. She knew his being *the Norrington* was nonsense because of his really being a Hawkins. That didn't help much because his action could be seen as actively aiding a Norrington in his quest to destroy Chytrine. After all, at his request, Sayce had not been slain and she'd proved important on the quest to kill the Nor'witch. On the other hand, Nefrai-kesh had not turned the Aurolani army on Chytrine, nor had he surrendered it. Were it not for Adrogans' intervention, the south would have been badly hurt. As far as Alyx was concerned, that point could be debated without end.

Only two things in the Meredo meetings came as a surprise. Alexia favored the first, but still recalled the pain in Queen Carus' voice when she proposed Markus Adrogans should become the new Draconis Baron. She pointed out that he already possessed the fortress and that he also possessed the secret of firedirt. She read a message from Adrogans in which he said he intended to surrender neither, so the crowns were presented with a fait accompli, which they approved with much hollow speechmaking.

The surprise that disappointed her concerned the DragonCrown. Many impassioned speeches were made advocating its destruction, with Rymramoch speaking for dragons and offering the three fragments they had would the rest of the world agree to it. Kerrigan Reese, the new Grand Magister of Vilwan, explained what would be done, and even noted the various safeguards that he would put in place to make sure he did not become another Kirûn, but that was all for naught.

Some of the crowns found his rise to power too ruthless for them to believe what he was saying. Alexia had spoken in his defense, but that mattered not. Too many of them still could not trust him. Moreover, as long as the DragonCrown could still be available, some crowns dreamed it might become theirs. That was reason enough for them to bar its destruction forever.

The example they make of Scrainwood is not someone who was wrong, but someone who failed in his attempts to take power.

In the end the dragons retained their three fragments and were said to have hidden them away in inaccessible places. Of the other four, two returned to Fortress Draconis and one was given to Tagothcha for safekeeping. The piece in Maroth returned to the Communion, with only Alexia, Crow, and Kerrigan being aware of its existence. While Rymramoch was able to identify the dragons who had their Truestones incorporated into the Crown, no one could tell the source of the Truestone in the centerpiece. Until that could be done and someone could figure out what effect it might have on someone wearing it, Alexia felt certain the DragonCrown would never be reconstructed and destroyed.

As if he was aware of how her thoughts were running, Crow reached over and took her left hand in his right and squeezed it gently. His long hair had been gathered at the nape of his neck with a leather tie fashioned from the ends of the cord binding his mask to him. King Erlestoke had revoked all edicts concerning Tarrant Hawkins, and a new coin had been struck with the Norrington and Hawkins crests on one side and the king's profile on the other. Coins with Scrainwood's face on them were quickly and happily exchanged for the new one, and Oriosa's minters were working all hours to meet demand.

Crow looked at her, and the mask he wore could not hide the joy on his face. "Soon, beloved, everything Resolute has waited and fought for will come true."

"I know, Crow, I know." She smiled at him and squeezed his hand back. "A century of effort is rewarded."

The reviewing stand on which they stood faced the courtyard before the *coriiesci*. It had all been cleared of brambles and debris from the Aurolani occupancy. Gaily colored banners, bunting, and ribbons had been hung from nearby buildings, pillars, and trees to dance on the breeze. It made for strange foliage, but matched the wonderful costumes the Vorquelves wore.

Down in the front ranks Alexia saw Banausic and Predator looking very proper in soft silks of green, blue, and silver. Amends had come all the way from Yslin and, after some fierce discussion, was allowed to be in the first group of forty to be bound to Vorquellyn. He had dressed very well and Alexia was pleased to see his split lip was nearly healed.

Closest to her she spotted Oracle and Resolute. The seer wore a gown of pale yellow, with copper ribbons decorating it at the sleeves and hem. Slightly wider ribbons of the same hue twined around her waist, then up over her body, hugging the bodice tightly to her. She wore her white hair unbound, but small white flowers had been tucked into it at her temples. The whole of her attire made her seem little more than a child, and the huge smile she wore only added to that impression.

Resolute, by contrast, seemed an incarnation of Kedyn, the god of war to whom Crow had long ago pledged himself. Resolute wore black hunting leathers from boots to shoulders. The jerkin had no sleeves, but the hooded cloak of gibberer skin—trimmed now with white pelt strips from *kryalniri* at the hem and hood—hid his arms. Unlike anyone else, he wore his sword and, she had no doubt, had a pouch of bladestars on his belt. The hood effectively hid his expression and reminded her, just for a chilling moment, of the way Nefrai-kesh's face had been veiled in Sebcia.

The doorway to the *coriiesci* melted away. Magarric emerged, followed by Isaura, Kerrigan Reese, and a huge stone behemoth that was the Norrington. Alexia had been told that at the time he killed Chytrine, the Norrington had appeared to be very much the embodiment of Will. Chytrine's breath had vaporized him, but Isaura had cast a spell on him previously that allowed his body parts to merge back together if sundered. When Chytrine had breathed in the vapor, his form had coalesced inside her, allowing him to claw his way free and kill her. Over the months since then, more and more of the dust that had made him up had come back to him, returning him to the shape he had been when pulled from the *coriiesci*. Even so, his body had taken on some definition and, without much effort, Alexia could recognize Will in the creature's face.

Magarric wore a rainbow robe with dozens of small ribbons hanging from it. Isaura followed in a gown white enough to match her hair. Kerrigan had adopted a Vilwanese robe of black, but circled his waist with a red rope. The Norrington came last, unadorned, though his eyes did contain flames that flared up to lick at his forehead.

The ancient elf paused at the edge of the courtyard, opened and raised his hands. "We welcome you all, friends, children, and very special guests. Today we will see the fulfillment of a portion of the Norrington Prophecy. This day Vorquellyn will be redeemed. For over a century Chytrine's creatures have held sway here. They desecrated our land. Those bound to it feel the pain of its rape, but we also know healing can happen. For while others have been of a different opinion, we know this to be true."

Alexia saw Trawyn off to her right slowly smile and Qwc, who was seated on the elf's shoulder, playfully tugged at a braided sidelock. Trawyn's presence was a break with certain orthodox elven groups that had maintained any effort to redeem Vorquellyn would be doomed to failure. She'd left Loquellyn and its reconstruction effort over those differences. She had surrendered her title and all claim to her mother's throne because of the disagreement. When she had spoken to Alexia of it, Trawyn had been surprised that her homeland did not indicate its feelings one way or another concerning her decision.

Magarric turned and drew the Norrington forward. The behemoth knelt easily, then sank back on his haunches. His right hand narrowed to a point and his left hand lay across his lap.

Kerrigan moved behind him, then held out his right hand and accepted Isaura's left. They exchanged glances for a moment—Alexia did not know what to make of that—then began to chant in unison. Their words came in a tongue Alyx did not recognize, though its sibilant tones and the very antiquity of the sounds would have had her betting on dragon. The words themselves had substance and seemed to thrum in her chest. As they chanted—as the words picked up speed—power gathered.

Isaura's white hair and gown began to glow with purple highlights. Alyx glanced at Crow and saw his beard and hair picking up the same highlights. Energy poured into Isaura, turning her into a noontime sun, then crept along her arm to spread to Kerrigan. The slender young man shook for a moment, then his voice strengthened and became louder.

The words beat at Alyx as if they were fat raindrops. Even more curiously, she felt the ground react as if they were. It seemed as if whenever a droplet struck the earth, an invisible puddle accepted it. The silent, ethereal rainstorm continued and even increased its pace as Isaura and Kerrigan chanted faster and faster. Alyx found herself mouthing the same syllables, and power tingled through her, too.

More swiftly came the words, harder and heavier came the power. The ground fairly rippled with impacts. They'd gone from blood-red to the pink of a newborn child's cheek, with the same soft texture. And, Alexia could have sworn, the same clean scent.

Kerrigan brought his left hand to Force's left shoulder and Isaura touched the stone creature on the right. The aura of power that had linked the two of them now spread down to Force, but it did not engulf him. The light entered him at his shoulders. The fire in his eyes flared, then went from red-yellow to pure white, and disappeared altogether, with only the wavering images of Isaura and Kerrigan to mark where the invisible flames burned.

Force punched the point of his right hand into his left wrist. Molten blood began to drip, running down his thighs and hitting the ground. It pooled there for a moment, then a tendril found a crack between stones and Force's blood sank into it. The Norrington contracted his left hand into a fist, pumping more blood out.

Alyx shivered as Force bled. Kerrigan had described to her in great detail what they would be doing to redeem Vorquellyn. As with most of his explanations of things thaumaturgical, she caught very little, but what she had recalled was vital. Isaura, having being born on and bound to Vorquellyn, was schooled in the Aurolani magicks that had destroyed the island. As she worked to break those spells, Kerrigan—who, likewise, had been born on Vorquellyn and therefore also had a link to it—would work spells to purge the island of the poisons instilled in it during the Aurolani occupation. Force, who had been reborn on and *of* Vorquellyn, was fated to revitalize the island. His body, cleansed by dragonfire, had a vital essence that could quicken the island and bring it back to life.

A trembling that communicated itself through the ground began. The air seemed to hum and the stands squeaked as the wood shifted slightly. Outside the courtyard one of the blackened trees trembled. Its bark split, peeling away in dark curls as verdant growth thickened the branches and extended them. Deadwood fell with a clatter, then buds appeared. Most blossomed into leaves that unfurled with a silver hue. Blue flowers with yellow splashes exploded, filling each tree with color that rivaled the ribbons now hidden in argent splendor.

As those leaves shimmered the vibration grew. The stands groaned again but Alexia feared no collapse. The very wood that made them up wanted to grow again. Joints fused, locking more solidly than their peg construction had ever allowed, and branches sprouted here and there. The people in the stands laughed delightedly and, down below, even Resolute managed a smile.

Magarric turned away from the trio and raised his hands. "As our land is healed, so its people must be healed. Answer these questions from your hearts, and you will be joined to Vorquellyn forever and all evers."

His eyes sharpened and his voice rose. "Do you acknowledge Vorquellyn as the place of your birth?"

The forty Vorquelves answered as one. "Yes and yes."

"Is it your desire to serve your homeland with all you are?"

Again they replied in unison. "Yes and yes."

With their second answer, the brilliant energy wreathing Isaura and Kerrigan began to seep upward through the ground. The stones of the courtyard began to glow brightly enough to swallow boots and hems. The glow spread outward from the courtyard like a low fog and flowed beneath the stands, hiding the ground completely.

Magarric's voice reached a high pitch.

"Do you acknowledge yourself, always and in all ways, a creature of Vorquellyn, its will to be your will, its joy your joy, its pain your pain, its life your life?"

"Yes and yes."

The incandescent glow rose to the Vorquelves' knees, then flashed up and out, blindingly brilliant. It encompassed everyone in the courtyard and those watching, linking them in an instant, fusing their futures and further binding their destinies. In that moment Alexia knew what it was to be Oracle, to see so many possibilities blaze past. The potential for the future of Vorquellyn seemed infinite.

At the same time Alexia felt something stir in her belly. Her grip on Crow's hand tightened. Life burned within her. *Lives.* Two lives; her sons. She knew it in an instant and caught sight of them, clean-limbed and strong, riding outside Svarskya with their father on a trip north.

She looked at Crow as the glow began to fade. She tried to speak, but a lump caught in her throat.

He said nothing, but pulled her to him and hugged her tightly. He kissed her cheek, then whispered to her, "I know, Alexia, I know. Two sons. I saw them, and our daughters, too."

Down below, in the courtyard, the Vorquelves all blinked. Amends and Predator, as unlikely a pair as could be thought possible, laughed and hugged each other. Banausic stared down at his hands. Even Oracle looked around, the dot in her copper eyes black instead of white. The way her eyes darted, Alexia felt certain she could see again, and smiled for her.

The smile died as Oracle's gaze fell upon Resolute. His hood had fallen back. He met her stare openly—with pure silver eyes. His expression combined dismay with disbelief and just a touch of fury. Of those present, he alone had not been changed. By the same token, he had not been destroyed as had the *kryalniri* Chytrine had tried to bind to Vorquellyn.

Hand in hand, Alexia and Crow descended to the courtyard and found Resolute. Trawyn and Qwc joined them and, for a moment, no one said anything. Then Crow reached out with both hands and settled them on his friend's shoulders. "We'll figure this out, Resolute. You *will* be bound to Vorquellyn."

Resolute shook his head. "You don't understand, my friend. When called upon to answer from my heart, I did. This is my place of birth. I wish to serve. I would be Vorquellyn's creature for eternity. I could perform this ritual a thousand times. My answers to those questions would be the same. The results would be the same, too."

"No, that's not right." Crow's nostrils flared. "After all you have done for Vorquellyn, you cannot be refused."

"I would beg to differ, Kedyn's Crow." Magarric cut through the milling crowd of Vorquelves and their well-wishers. "There is one reason why Resolute was refused. It is not, as Trawyn is thinking, that he has become a creature for which Vorquellyn has no use."

Trawyn blushed, then looked down. "That's not what I think of you, Resolute."

The Vorquelf turned and stroked the cheek beneath her eye patch. "Of this I am aware, Trawyn."

Magarric smiled briefly. "Resolute, have you seen images from the time before the homelands were created?"

He shook his head. "I was barely aware there was a time before. I do know stories of heroes like Raisasel. They would have been from that time."

"They would indeed. Do you know what his name means?"

Resolute thought for a moment. " 'Eyes of ebony' I believe."

Vorquellyn's founder nodded. "Exactly. You see, in the days before the homelands, all of our eyes were as yours are, one color. What elves now decry as the eyes of children were once the eyes of ancients. You have ancient eyes, Resolute. The ritual of the binding has become an acceptance of adult roles. In the time before the homelands, it was experience that made us adults. You have passed into adulthood and need no binding."

Resolute frowned. "But that is hardly a reason for Vorquellyn to reject me."

"It rejected you because your destiny is one that reaches beyond Vorquellyn. You became an adult fighting to redeem Vorquellyn. That is your nature, and your task in life is to fulfill that nature."

"I don't understand."

Magarric reached out and flipped Resolute's cloak back from his right hip. "You wear the Syverce of Sylquellyn."

"Yes."

"You have redeemed one homeland." Magarric smiled. "It is time for you reestablish another. Your task is to go into the world, create a *coriiesci*, and bring a homeland to life."

"What? That's not possible." Resolute slipped the clasp

of his cloak and let it slide from him. "I have no magick that heals or creates."

"I know, Resolute. All your spells destroy. Reverse them." Magarric held a hand up. "Do not tell me it is not possible, for I know it is. You can't do it alone. Choose your help and your place well. It is your destiny, and the final victory over the witch from the north."

OKRANNEL

To my beloved sons,

It may strike you as odd that I would be writing to you barely an hour after your birth, but I cannot bear to be apart from you and your mother, I love you all so well. Here I sit, then, in the same room in Svarskya as you and your mother slumber. I pray the scratch of quill on paper will not awaken you.

Kirill, you are firstborn and are named for your mother's father. As you will hear down through the years, he was a brave man, and wise. He was a hero who saved my life more than once. He did the same for your mother, sacrificing himself for us both. There is no greater sign of love for someone than to put their lives before your own. It is a lesson few learn and even fewer embrace. Only the great can do that.

Dunardel, you bear an elven name, also that of a hero. He saved my life more times than I can count. You will have the opportunity to meet him, for he lives in Sylquellyn, the elven homeland he founded on the site of the city of Svoin. In six months he has managed to reverse the poisoning done by the Aurolani. The Gyrkyme have joined with him to create this homeland and, with his consort, Trawyn, they are creating a paradise in the south of our nation.

You will, the both of you, hear many tales of the

times before your birth. It was a grand age of heroes and villains, wizards, dragons, monsters, and hideous weapons. With luck and wisdom, the world's leaders like your mother will ensure that such an age does not return. In time—a time that knows only peace—it might be that the horrors are forgotten and the scars are healed. I pray you never have to know the crucible of war that shaped the world you will inherit.

I do not think you will. Aside from your mother and other leaders who value peace, there is another who will guarantee it. By the time you are the age we found him, he will probably be little more than a rumor—a report from trappers venturing far north. You will hear tales of a massive stone man who wanders Aurolan, rooting out the remnants of Chytrine's evil; alone, ever alert, ever vigilant, that her evil does not return.

The DragonCrown War, which birthed your world, was terrible. Many people died—your grandfather one among many heroes—to bring peace. I will tell you many tales of those days, though perhaps not all of them. The grandest, however, will be the story of the Norrington. The Norrington you will know will seem a myth. He was flesh and blood, but became more, and he does yet wander the north. Someday we will go north; we will disturb his solitude so you may meet him.

Peace does not come without sacrifice. The Norrington is that sacrifice. People may forget the price at which their freedom was won, but we will not. He is our reminder, so I shall take you to him, and you will take your sons, and they will take theirs, forever and ever, so war never has to come again to the land.

Your loving father,
Tarrant Hawkins.

ABOUT THE AUTHOR

Michael A. Stackpole is an award-winning game and computer designer who now is also an award-winning author. (His novel *Ghost War* was chosen the Best Long-form Fiction by the Academy of Gaming Arts and Design for 2002.) By the time you're reading this, he'll be fully recovered from the rotator cuff injury that slowed his work on this book. (Yes, it was indoor soccer. Just because I'd knocked the guy down earlier in the game was no reason he should have taken me into a wall later. He was having a bad day and, shucks, just decided to share.)

Also by the time you're reading this, he'll have finished *The Secret Atlas*, the first in a new trilogy of fantasy novels. (He'll have finished, or Anne Groell will be tearing her hair out yet again.) Mike spends way too much time on airplanes, playing with his iPod, playing indoor soccer, reading, and trying to figure out why he alternates between first and third person in biographies like this.

If you loved the DragonCrown War Cycle,
be sure not to miss the first book
in the next exciting trilogy

from

Michael A. Stackpole

A SECRET ATLAS

Book One of the Age of Discovery Trilogy

On sale March 2005

Here's a special preview:

A SECRET ATLAS

On sale March 1, 2005

Moraven Tolo reached the crest of the hill a few steps before his traveling companions. The half-blind old man who wheezed up behind him gasped involuntarily. He looked back as his grandson and great-grandson joined him, and gestured at the city in the distance. "There it is. Moriande, the grandest city in the world.'

The swordsman nodded slowly in agreement. The road ran down the forested hillside, and glimpses of it could be seen twisting through the Gold River valley to the city. It had been years since he'd seen Nalenyr's capital, and it had grown but was still easily recognizable. Wentokikun, the tallest of the city's nine towers, dominated its eastern quarter, and using that as a landmark made fixing other places easier.

The old man, his wispy beard and hair dancing in the light breeze, nodded toward Moriande. "The biggest tower, there to the east, is the Imperial Palace. I may not see well now, but I see it clear. It makes me remember when I last saw it."

Moraven remained silent, though the sight of the capital filled him with much the same awe as it did the rest of the pilgrims. Many times over the last week Moraven had heard about how the old man had come to Moriande eighty-one years previously, for the first grand festival celebrating the Dseane Dynasty. It had survived nine cycles of nine years then, and double that now. With this being the ninth year of the current Imperial Prince's Court, people knew the festival was a double blessing.

The city remained two days' walk from where they stood yet was so huge that it seemed far closer. The Gold River split the white sprawl down the middle, with a broad oxbow curving to the north. Six of the city's nine towers stood in the northern half; the other three, including the Prince's Dragon Tower, Wentokikun, lay on the southern side of the river. Equally magnificent, though harder to see at that distance, were the nine soaring bridges arching over the sparkling river. Their height allowed even the grandest ship to pass beneath them with ease, and their width made the Imperial Road look like a game path.

Matut, the old man, tousled his great-grandson's hair with an arthritically twisted hand. "I was ten when I came to the festival. You are but nine, as old as the court and a tenth my age. I'm sure the gods will make something of that. Ours will be a grand time in the city, for the week's festival will be as none other."

His grandson, the boy's father, tapped a belt pouch that rang with the muffled sound of coins. "We will do this right, make our offerings to the gods, then enjoy the festival."

"Of course, Alait, of course." The old man chuckled himself into a wheeze. "There will be pleasures a young man like yourself and our friend here can enjoy. I was too young last time, and am too old this time."

Moraven smiled and smoothed his long black hair at the back of his neck. "You are of a blessed age, grandfather. There will be many who will seek your touch for fortune's sake."

"May they all be as comely and soft as the Lady of Jet

and Jade." The old man looked at him with rheumy brown eyes and flexed a stiff hand. "It might be I don't see so well anymore, but I *can* feel."

Alait laughed and Moraven joined him. Dunos, the boy, looked puzzled, and a richly robed merchantman's wife sniffed. She had often done this when conversations had revolved around Matut's stories of the festival and all the carnal pleasures he'd seen before. She, they had been informed, was going to the capital at the invitation of "people" who, they were also told, would get her husband an imperial appointment—though she had always remained vague on what it was and why he wasn't with her.

The rest of the traveling folk were a fair mix of people from within and without Nalenyr. Four were entertainers coming up from Erumvirine, while the rest were from Nalenyr itself. They'd all agreed that traveling in a company of eighteen was a very good omen, and numerous offerings had been made in the shrines scattered along the roadway to ensure the favor of the gods on their party. Each made offerings according to his means, with the peasants clad in brown or grey homespun being a bit more quiet and circumspect in their devotions than the more extravagantly dressed.

The merchantman's wife had, in Matut's words, been "Loud in prayer, but offerings spare."

Moraven Tolo fell into the middle of the two groups, being neither rich nor poor. Black woolen trousers were tucked into leather boots and his shirt had been made of undyed linen. Only his quilted sleeveless overshirt of white silk, with the wide starched shoulders and the black tigers embroidered on breast and back, hinted at any prosperity. It wrapped closed and was belted with a black sash, and into that had been slipped his sword. He alone in the company bore one, though two of the farmers had flails that they carried over their shoulders.

Matut's eyes half-lidded and the old man shook. "It was here it happened on that first trip. I remember it now."

Dunos clutched at his left hand. "The bandits?"

The merchantman's wife hissed, "Be quiet, child. Don't give the gods ideas."

Moraven glanced further down the road as three figures, two male, one female, slipped from the woods to the center of the road. "The mind of gods was not the womb of this idea."

The female bandit, wearing black beneath an overshirt of scarlet and gold, drew her sword and led her two companions lazily toward the pilgrims. To her left the smaller one, wearing a motley collection of greens and browns, carried a recurve bow and fitted an arrow to it. He hung back slightly and moved further to the side, giving himself a clear line to shoot.

The third figure wore a ragged brown robe that might have come to mid-shin on most men but barely covered the tops of his thighs. A long tangle of unkempt hair matched the giant's scraggy beard. Dirt caked every inch of his exposed flesh and drew black lines beneath his fingernails. As imposing as he was, however, the long-hafted mallet he carried made more of an impression. With a head as big around as a melon and irregular darkness staining its face, it gave the appearance of a tool well versed in crushing skulls.

The bandit woman tried to smile, but a scar on her left cheek curdled the expression. "We welcome you pilgrims to the Imperial Road. We are your servants, who keep it open and free of banditry. Surely you will want to show your appreciation to us."

Conoursai, the merchantman's wife, waved them aside with a courtly gesture full of arrogance. "This is the Prince's highway. His troops keep it clear."

The highwaywoman shook her head. "Clearly, then, they are negligent in their duty, *grandmother*." She offered the honorific to shock Conoursai, and was rewarded with an offended hiss. "But as we are not the Prince's troops, we must be highwaymen. Will you pay tribute and be honored or suffer as victims?"

Matut moaned. "This is how it began last time."

Moraven patted him on the shoulder. "This has long been known as a place where people stop in awe to look at the city. Bandits sneak up unawares."

The little boy stooped down and picked up a rock. "I'll fight them."

"No need, brave one." Moraven Tolo moved again to the fore, slipping effortlessly past Conoursai. He motioned to the two farmers to stay back. Taking a position in the center of the road, he bowed toward the bandits.

"I am *xidantzu*. I wish harm to come to none. These people are under *my* protection. It will cost you nothing to walk away."

"*Xidantzu*." The woman spat contemptuously and plucked at her overshirt. "The last wandering meddler coming through here gave me this, and those he protected gave us their gold."

Moraven's head came up. The scarlet overshirt had bats on the wing woven into it. He knew the man to whom it belonged. "Did you steal it or was Jayt Macyl slain?"

She gestured with her sword to the west, then swung the blade in a short arc. "There are pieces of him all along here. He was *zaserrdin*. I am Pavynti Syolsar, and I am *lirserrdin*."

He considered for a moment. Jayt Macyl had indeed been a swordsman of the sixth rank. Her defeating him might well make her seventh rank, or just someone who had gotten lucky. He was tempted, given her relative youth, to believe it was the latter case, but he also knew appearances could be deceiving.

"I am Moraven Tolo. Name your terms."

Pavynti's brown eyes narrowed. "To the death, of course."

He nodded. "Draw the circle."

That stopped her and brought gasps from his traveling companions and a joyous shout from Dunos. His father cut that shout off by clapping a hand over the boy's mouth as he dragged his son back. The rest of the company likewise retreated, putting the crest of the hill between themselves and the combatants.

"A c-circle?"

Moraven nodded again and slid his sword, yet in its wooden scabbard, from his belt. "It would be best."

Shaken, she began to toe a line in the roadway's dirt. Her companions, understanding the import of his request and possessing the faint honor of bandits, acted. The archer loosed an arrow as the giant bellowed and began to charge up the hill. By the time the giant had passed Pavynti, the archer's second and third missiles were also in the air.

Moraven Tolo twisted his right shoulder back, letting the first shaft pass harmlessly wide. The second tugged at his overshirt's sleeve, passing through it but cleanly missing flesh. He slid forward a half step, letting the third arrow pass behind him, then ran at the giant, clutching his sword mid-scabbard in his left hand.

The giant's mallet rose above his head, and his mouth gaped in a horrid display of misaligned, yellowed teeth. Black eyes shrank, veins throbbed forehead and neck, and his incoherent war cry took on the bass tones of a water-buffalo's challenge. The mallet, its haft bending beneath the incredible power of the stroke, arced up and smashed down at Moraven.

Ducking low, Moraven had already moved inside the mallethead's arc. He plunged the hilt of his sword into the giant's middle. Then, planting his right hand on the lower part of the scabbard, he pivoted the blunted blade into the man's groin. As the bellow rose into a squeak, Moraven lifted and twisted, flipping the giant over his shoulder. The man smashed down on his back and bounced once. Another spin let Moraven crack the giant in the head with his scabbard as a fourth arrow flew past harmlessly.

Completing the spin, Moraven let the sword shoot forward until the hilt filled his right hand. He tightened his grip, letting momentum bare the blade. The scabbard flew off flatly and smacked the archer's left hand, crushing fingers against the bow. The man screamed, dropping his weapon, and turned away with his broken hand nestled beneath his right armpit.

Moraven Tolo's sword came up, the silver blade pointing straight at Pavynti's throat. "Have you finished that circle yet?"

She threw her sword aside and dropped to her knees, then fell to her belly and kept her face in the dirt.

"Jaecaiserr, forgive this wretched one for her arrogance."

"Which arrogance was that, Pavynti? Claiming ranks you do not have? Believing those who travel to the capital are your prey?" Moraven let his voice get cold and deeper. "Or the dishonorable arrogance of letting your friends attack me before we could engage in our duel?"

"All of them, master."

"Up. Remove that overshirt. Take up your sword."

Disbelief widening her eyes, the woman rose, dusted the overshirt off, then removed it. Hesitantly she picked up her sword. "Do I continue drawing the circle?"

He shook his head. "Scorpion form, the first."

Pavynti blinked, then moved into that stance. Her sword, held high in the right hand, pointed in the same direction as her nose and left hand. She spread her feet apart and got into a low crouch. She faced her left palm out, then curled the last two fingers in to her palm.

He nodded, then called another form, and another. She flowed through them quickly enough, doing best with Crane and Eagle, least well with Wolf and Dog. He kept her at it, changing things faster and faster for a full nine minutes, which was all the time it took for his traveling companions to crest the hill again. The two farmers positioned themselves to thump the giant soundly if he regained consciousness.

When she was dripping with sweat, he called a halt, and she dropped to one knee. He could tell she was tempted to stab her sword into the ground and hang on to the hilt, but she knew better than to show that level of disrespect to her weapon before him. Breathing heavily, she glanced up. "What else would you have of me, master?"

"The answer to a question."

"Yes?"

"You have Jayt's overshirt, but not his sword. What became of it?"

The flesh around her eyes tightened. "I am a bandit, master, but not a barbarian. The blade was sent on to his family, for their shrine."

Moraven said nothing, but crossed to where the archer cowered and kicked the bow into a tangle of thornbushes. Resheathing his sword, he slid it back into his overshirt's sash and waved the archer further from his weapon. By the time he turned around again, Conoursai had advanced and raised her quirt to lash the bandit.

"Don't do that."

The merchantman's wife sputtered indignantly. "She is a bandit. She was going to kill us all. She should be punished. You should kill her."

Moraven slowly shook his head. "A life broken can be mended. A life taken cannot."

"Then break her." The woman gestured imperiously, though not quite as confidently as before. "Have the farmers thrash the giant and the archer."

"They struck at me, not you. Their fate is in my hands." He turned and eyed the archer. "How much have you stolen from the festival pilgrims?"

"Not a prince's ransom. Not even his petty spending."

"It is too much. You and your giant will take all you have stolen and go to the festival. You will give alms to the beggars until you have nothing, then you will leave for the west and will no longer be bandits."

"But there are Viruk and Soth there, and wildmen. The chances of our survival . . ."

". . . Are better there than here." Moraven smiled. "Chances are excellent I shall never see you again if you go west."

The archer thought for a moment. "It is very crowded here. West, then."

Conoursai snorted with outrage, but Moraven ignored

her. He turned to Pavynti. "And now your fate must be decided."

"My lord's will be done."

Moraven crossed his arms over his chest and furrowed his brows. He did so less to make the bandit writhe in fear than to annoy Conoursai, but accomplished both quickly. "You will go to the town of Derros. You will present yourself at the Serrian of *Dicaiserr* Istor Derael. You will tell him I have sent you to join his school. He will see to your training and when he releases you, you will have nine years of wandering the road meddling in the affairs of other bandits."

"Yes, master." Again she put her belly to the road in a deep bow.

"Care for your companions tonight, then go tomorrow. This is my will."

The farmers, between the two of them, lifted the mallet and broke the haft. The others in the group started forward again, following the farmers and allowing Conoursai to flow with them, complaining as she went. Moraven moved past the bandits, but did so slowly, waiting for the old man and his kin, who were bringing up the rear.

Matut reached out with a hand and rested it on Moraven's shoulder. "A moment of your time, Serrcai."

The swordsman nodded and the two younger men moved on. "What is it, grandfather?"

The old man kept his voice low. "In this place, when the bandits stopped us nines of nine years ago, a young man of our company challenged them. He told them to draw a circle, and they did."

"And what happened?"

"He slew them all. An autumn breeze works harder stirring leaves than he did slaughtering them. He did not wear your name, but he did bear the crest of the black tiger hunting."

"That would be something hard to forget."

"I never have." The old man sighed. "If my eyes were

good, I could see that you are the same man, untouched by time. Why didn't you kill them this time?"

"As you agreed, grandfather, that was something hard to forget." Moraven's blue eyes gazed again toward Moriande. "I haven't forgotten, and I *have* learned."